THE WORLD OVER

THE
WORLD OVER

W.
SOMERSET
MAUGHAM

The Collected Stories

VOLUME ONE

THE REPRINT SOCIETY LONDON

FIRST PUBLISHED 1951
THIS EDITION PUBLISHED BY THE REPRINT SOCIETY
BY ARRANGEMENT WITH WM HEINEMANN LTD
1954

PRINTED IN GREAT BRITAIN BY RICHARD CLAY AND COMPANY, LTD.,
BUNGAY, SUFFOLK

Contents

VOLUME ONE

Preface to this Edition

THESE two volumes contain all the short stories that I have wished to reprint. One of the most difficult things an author has to deal with when he wants to gather together a quantity of stories in volume form is to decide in what order to place them. It is satisfaction to an author if he can so arrange his material that the book he finally offers to his readers has a pattern. The pattern of a novel is of course plain, it has a beginning, a middle and an end; and it is fairly simple to arrange a number of stories in a pattern if they are of about the same length and are placed in the same locale. But some of my stories are very short, some are long. I have sojourned in most parts of the world, and while I was writing stories I could seldom stay anywhere for a length of time without getting material for one or more. I have written tragic stories and I have written humorous ones. It has been an arduous task to get some kind of symmetry and at least the semblance of a pattern into a collection of a large number of stories of such different lengths, placed in so many different countries and of such different character; and at the same time to make it as easy as possible for the reader to read them.

Though to be read is not the motive which impels the author to write, his motive is other; once he has written, his desire is to be read, and in order to achieve that he must do his best to make what he writes readable. With this intention, so that the reader should not be required to leap suddenly from China to Peru and back again, I have grouped, as well as I conveniently could, stories of which the scene is set in a particular country. In that way I hoped to give the reader a chance to take his bearings in whatever distant land I chose to lead him to. After a batch of long stories I have placed two or three short ones so as to give the reader a rest; but in one batch I have not been able to do this. These are stories dealing with the adventures of an agent in the Intelligence Department during the First World War. I gave him the name of Ashenden. Since they are connected by this character of my invention I have thought it better, notwithstanding their great length, to put them together. They are founded on experiences of my own during that war, but I should like to impress upon the reader that they are not what the French call *reportage*, but works of fiction. Fact is a poor story-teller. It starts a story at haphazard, generally long before the beginning, rambles on inconsequently and tails off, leaving loose ends hanging about, without a conclusion. The work of an agent in the Intelligence Department is on the whole monotonous. A lot of it is uncommonly useless. The material it offers for stories is scrappy and pointless; and the author has himself to make it coherent, dramatic and probable. That is what I have tried to do in this particular series.

The reader will notice that many of my stories are written in the first person singular. That is a literary convention which is as old as the hills. The object is of course to achieve credibility, for when someone tells you what he states happened to himself you are more likely to believe that he is telling you the facts as they occurred than when he tells you what happened to somebody else. It has besides the merit from the story-teller's point of view that he need only tell you what he knows and can leave to your imagination what he doesn't or couldn't know. Some of the older novelists who wrote in the first person were in this respect very careless. They would narrate long conversations that they couldn't possibly have heard and incidents which in the nature of things they couldn't possibly have witnessed. Thus they lost the great advantage of verisimilitude which writing in the first person singular offers. But the *I* who writes is just as much a character in the story as the other persons with whom it is concerned. He may be the hero or he may be an onlooker or a confidant. But he is a character. The writer who uses this device is writing fiction and if he makes the *I* of his story a little quicker on the uptake, a little more level-headed, a little shrewder, a little braver, a little more ingenious, a little wittier, a little wiser than he, the writer, really is, the reader must show indulgence. He must remember that the author is not drawing a faithful portrait of himself, but creating a character for the particular purposes of his story.

The scene of many of the stories in these two volumes is set in Malaya. They were written long before the Second World War and I should tell the reader that the sort of life with which they deal no longer exists. When I first visited those countries the lives the white men and their wives led differed but little from what they had been twenty-five years before. They got home-leave once in five years. They had besides a few weeks' leave every year. If they lived where the climate was exhausting they sought the fresh air of some hill-station not too far away; if, like some of the government servants, they lived where they might not see another white man for weeks on end, they went to Singapore so that they might consort for a time with their kind. *The Times* when it arrived at a station up-country, in

Borneo for instance, was six weeks old and they were lucky if they received the Singapore paper in a fortnight.

Aviation has changed all that. Even before the war people who could afford it were able to spend even their short leave at home. Papers, illustrated weeklies, magazines reached them fresh from the press. In the old days Sarawak, say, or Selangor were where they expected to spend their lives till it was time for them to retire on a pension; England was very far away and when at long intervals they went back was increasingly strange to them; their real home, their intimate friends, were in the land in which the better part of their lives was spent. But with the rapidity of communication it remained an alien land, a temporary, rather than a permanent, habitation, which circumstances obliged them for a spell to occupy; it was a longish halt in a life that had its roots in the Sussex downs or on the moors of Yorkshire. Their ties with the homeland, which before had insensibly loosened and sometimes broken asunder, remained fast. England, so to speak, was round the corner. They no longer felt cut off. It changed their whole outlook.

The countries of which I wrote were then at peace. It may be that some of those peoples, Malays, Dyaks, Chinese, were restive under the British rule, but there was no outward sign of it. The British gave them justice, provided them with hospitals and schools, and encouraged their industries. There was no more crime than anywhere else. An unarmed man could wander through the length of the Federated Malay States in safety. The only real trouble was the low price of rubber.

There is one more point I want to make. Most of these stories are on the tragic side. But the reader must not suppose that the incidents I have narrated were of common occurrence. The vast majority of these people, government servants, planters and traders, who spent their working lives in Malaya were ordinary people ordinarily satisfied with their station in life. They did the jobs they were paid to do more or less competently. They were as happy with their wives as are most married couples. They led humdrum lives and did very much the same things every day. Sometimes by way of a change they got a little shooting; but as a rule, after they had done their day's work, they played tennis if there were people to play with, went to the club at sundown if there was a club in the vicinity, drank in moderation and played bridge. They had their little tiffs, their little jealousies, their little flirtations, their little celebrations. They were good, decent, normal people.

I respected, and even admired them, but they were not the sort of people I could write stories about. The stories I wrote were about

people who had some singularity of character which suggested to me
that they might be capable of behaving in such a way as to give me
an idea that I could make use of, or about people who by some
accident or another, accident of temperament, accident of environment, had been involved in unusual contingencies. But, I repeat,
they were the exceptions.

Rain

IT was nearly bed-time and when they awoke next morning land would be in sight. Dr. Macphail lit his pipe and, leaning over the rail, searched the heavens for the Southern Cross. After two years at the front and a wound that had taken longer to heal than it should, he was glad to settle down quietly at Apia for twelve months at least, and he felt already better for the journey. Since some of the passengers were leaving the ship next day at Pago-Pago they had had a little dance that evening and in his ears hammered still the harsh notes of the mechanical piano. But the deck was quiet at last. A little way off he saw his wife in a long chair talking with the Davidsons, and he strolled over to her. When he sat down under the light and took off his hat you saw that he had very red hair, with a bald patch on the crown, and the red, freckled skin which accompanies red hair; he was a man of forty, thin, with a pinched face, precise and rather pedantic; and he spoke with a Scots accent in a very low, quiet voice.

Between the Macphails and the Davidsons, who were missionaries, there had arisen the intimacy of shipboard, which is due to propinquity rather than to any community of taste. Their chief tie was the disapproval they shared of the men who spent their days and nights in the smoking-room playing poker or bridge and drinking. Mrs. Macphail was not a little flattered to think that she and her husband were the only people on board with whom the Davidsons were willing to associate, and even the doctor, shy but no fool, half unconsciously acknowledged the compliment. It was only because he was of an argumentative mind that in their cabin at night he permitted himself to carp.

"Mrs. Davidson was saying she didn't know how they'd have got through the journey if it hadn't been for us," said Mrs. Macphail, as she neatly brushed out her transformation. "She said we were really the only people on the ship they cared to know."

"I shouldn't have thought a missionary was such a big bug that he could afford to put on frills."

"It's not frills. I quite understand what she means. It wouldn't have been very nice for the Davidsons to have to mix with all that rough lot in the smoking-room."

"The founder of their religion wasn't so exclusive," said Dr. Macphail with a chuckle.

"I've asked you over and over again not to joke about religion," answered his wife. "I shouldn't like to have a nature like yours, Alec. You never look for the best in people."

He gave her a sidelong glance with his pale, blue eyes, but did not reply. After many years of married life he had learned that it was more conducive to peace to leave his wife with the last word. He was undressed before she was, and climbing into the upper bunk he settled down to read himself to sleep.

When he came on deck next morning they were close to land. He looked at it with greedy eyes. There was a thin strip of silver beach rising quickly to hills covered to the top with luxuriant vegetation. The coconut trees, thick and green, came nearly to the water's edge, and among them you saw the grass houses of the Samoans; and here and there, gleaming white, a little church. Mrs. Davidson came and stood beside him. She was dressed in black and wore round her neck a gold chain, from which dangled a small cross. She was a little woman, with brown, dull hair very elaborately arranged, and she had prominent blue eyes behind invisible pince-nez. Her face was long, like a sheep's, but she gave no impression of foolishness, rather of extreme alertness; she had the quick movements of a bird. The most remarkable thing about her was her voice, high, metallic, and without inflection; it fell on the ear with a hard monotony, irritating to the nerves like the pitiless clamour of the pneumatic drill.

"This must seem like home to you," said Dr. Macphail, with his thin, difficult smile.

"Ours are low islands, you know, not like these. Coral. These are volcanic. We've got another ten days' journey to reach them."

"In these parts that's almost like being in the next street at home," said Dr. Macphail facetiously.

"Well, that's rather an exaggerated way of putting it, but one does look at distances differently in the South Seas. So far you're right."

Dr. Macphail sighed faintly.

"I'm glad we're not stationed here," she went on. "They say this is a terribly difficult place to work in. The steamers' touching makes the people unsettled; and then there's the naval station; that's bad for the natives. In our district we don't have difficulties like that to contend with. There are one or two traders, of course, but we take care to make them behave, and if they don't we make the place so hot for them they're glad to go."

Fixing the glasses on her nose she looked at the green island with a ruthless stare.

"It's almost a hopeless task for the missionaries here. I can never be sufficiently thankful to God that we are at least spared that."

Davidson's district consisted of a group of islands to the north of Samoa; they were widely separated and he had frequently to go long distances by canoe. At these times his wife remained at their headquarters and managed the mission. Dr. Macphail felt his heart sink when he considered the efficiency with which she certainly managed it. She spoke of the depravity of the natives in a voice which nothing could hush, but with a vehemently unctuous horror. Her sense of delicacy was singular. Early in their acquaintance she had said to him:

"You know, their marriage customs when we first settled in the islands were so shocking that I couldn't possibly describe them to you. But I'll tell Mrs. Macphail and she'll tell you."

Then he had seen his wife and Mrs. Davidson, their deck-chairs close together, in earnest conversation for about two hours. As he walked past them backwards and forwards for the sake of exercise, he had heard Mrs. Davidson's agitated whisper, like the distant flow of a mountain torrent, and he saw by his wife's open mouth and pale face that she was enjoying an alarming experience. At night in their cabin she repeated to him with bated breath all she had heard.

"Well, what did I say to you?" cried Mrs. Davidson, exultant next morning. "Did you ever hear anything more dreadful? You don't wonder that I couldn't tell you myself, do you? Even though you are a doctor."

Mrs. Davidson scanned his face. She had a dramatic eagerness to see that she had achieved the desired effect.

"Can you wonder that when we first went there our hearts sank? You'll hardly believe me when I tell you it was impossible to find a single good girl in any of the villages."

She used the word *good* in a severely technical manner.

"Mr. Davidson and I talked it over, and we made up our minds the first thing to do was to put down the dancing. The natives were crazy about dancing."

"I was not averse to it myself when I was a young man," said Dr. Macphail.

"I guessed as much when I heard you ask Mrs. Macphail to have a turn with you last night. I don't think there's any real harm if a man dances with his wife, but I was relieved that she wouldn't. Under the circumstances I thought it better that we should keep ourselves to ourselves."

"Under what circumstances?"

Mrs. Davidson gave him a quick look through her pince-nez, but did not answer his question.

"But among white people it's not quite the same," she went on, "though I must say I agree with Mr. Davidson, who says he can't understand how a husband can stand by and see his wife in another man's arms, and as far as I'm concerned I've never danced a step since I married. But the native dancing is quite another matter. It's not only immoral in itself, but it distinctly leads to immorality. However, I'm thankful to God that we stamped it out, and I don't think I'm wrong in saying that no one has danced in our district for eight years."

But now they came to the mouth of the harbour and Mrs. Macphail joined them. The ship turned sharply and steamed slowly in. It was a great land-locked harbour big enough to hold a fleet of battleships; and all around it rose, high and steep, the green hills. Near the entrance, getting such breeze as blew from the sea, stood the governor's house in a garden. The Stars and Stripes dangled languidly from a flagstaff. They passed two or three trim bungalows, and a tennis court, and then they came to the quay with its warehouses. Mrs. Davidson pointed out the schooner, moored two or three hundred yards from the side, which was to take them to Apia. There was a crowd of eager, noisy, and good-humoured natives come from all parts of the island, some from curiosity, others to barter with the travellers on their way to Sydney; and they brought pineapples and huge bunches of bananas, tapa cloths, necklaces of shells or sharks' teeth, kava-bowls, and models of war canoes. American sailors, neat and trim, clean-shaven and frank of face, sauntered among them, and there was a little group of officials. While their luggage was being landed the Macphails and Mrs. Davidson watched the crowd. Dr. Macphail looked at the yaws from which most of the children and young boys seemed to suffer, disfiguring sores like torpid ulcers, and his professional eyes glistened when he saw for the first time in his experience cases of elephantiasis, men going about with a huge, heavy arm or dragging along a grossly disfigured leg. Men and women wore the lava-lava.

"It's a very indecent costume," said Mrs. Davidson. "Mr. Davidson thinks it should be prohibited by law. How can you expect people to be moral when they wear nothing but a strip of red cotton round their loins?"

"It's suitable enough to the climate," said the doctor, wiping the sweat off his head.

Now that they were on land the heat, though it was so early in the morning, was already oppressive. Closed in by its hills, not a breath of air came in to Pago-Pago.

"In our islands," Mrs. Davidson went on in her high-pitched tones, "we've practically eradicated the lava-lava. A few old men still continue to wear it, but that's all. The women have all taken to the Mother Hubbard, and the men wear trousers and singlets. At the beginning of our stay Mr. Davidson said in one of his reports: the inhabitants of these islands will never be thoroughly Christianised till every boy of more than ten years is made to wear a pair of trousers."

But Mrs. Davidson had given two or three of her birdlike glances at heavy grey clouds that came floating over the mouth of the harbour. A few drops began to fall.

"We'd better take shelter," she said.

They made their way with all the crowd to a great shed of corrugated iron, and the rain began to fall in torrents. They stood there for some time and then were joined by Mr. Davidson. He had been polite enough to the Macphails during the journey, but he had not his wife's sociability, and had spent much of his time reading. He was a silent, rather sullen man, and you felt that his affability was a duty that he imposed upon himself Christianly; he was by nature reserved and even morose. His appearance was singular. He was very tall and thin, with long limbs loosely jointed; hollow cheeks and curiously high cheek-bones; he had so cadaverous an air that it surprised you to notice how full and sensual were his lips. He wore his hair very long. His dark eyes, set deep in their sockets, were large and tragic; and his hands, with their big, long fingers, were finely shaped; they gave him a look of great strength. But the most striking thing about him was the feeling he gave you of suppressed fire. It was impressive and vaguely troubling. He was not a man with whom any intimacy was possible.

He brought now unwelcome news. There was an epidemic of measles, a serious and often fatal disease among the Kanakas, on the island, and a case had developed among the crew of the schooner which was to take them on their journey. The sick man had been brought ashore and put in hospital on the quarantine station, but telegraphic instructions had been sent from Apia to say that the schooner would not be allowed to enter the harbour till it was certain no other member of the crew was affected.

"It means we shall have to stay here for ten days at least."

"But I'm urgently needed at Apia," said Dr. Macphail.

"That can't be helped. If no more cases develop on board, the schooner will be allowed to sail with white passengers, but all native traffic is prohibited for three months."

"Is there a hotel here?" asked Mrs. Macphail.

Davidson gave a low chuckle.

"There's not."

"What shall we do then?"

"I've been talking to the governor. There's a trader along the front who has rooms that he rents, and my proposition is that as soon as the rain lets up we should go along there and see what we can do. Don't expect comfort. You've just got to be thankful if we get a bed to sleep on and a roof over our heads."

But the rain showed no signs of stopping, and at length with umbrellas and waterproofs they set out. There was no town, but merely a group of official buildings, a store or two, and at the back, among the coconut trees and plantains, a few native dwellings. The house they sought was about five minutes' walk from the wharf. It was a frame house of two storeys, with broad verandahs on both floors and a roof of corrugated iron. The owner was a half-caste named Horn, with a native wife surrounded by little brown children, and on the ground-floor he had a store where he sold canned goods and cottons. The rooms he showed them were almost bare of furniture. In the Macphails' there was nothing but a poor, worn bed with a ragged mosquito net, a rickety chair, and a washstand. They looked round with dismay. The rain poured down without ceasing.

"I'm not going to unpack more than we actually need," said Mrs. Macphail.

Mrs. Davidson came into the room as she was unlocking a portmanteau. She was very brisk and alert. The cheerless surroundings had no effect on her.

"If you'll take my advice you'll get a needle and cotton and start right in to mend the mosquito net," she said, "or you'll not be able to get a wink of sleep to-night."

"Will they be very bad?" asked Dr. Macphail.

"This is the season for them. When you're asked to a party at Government House at Apia you'll notice that all the ladies are given a pillowslip to put their—their lower extremities in."

"I wish the rain would stop for a moment," said Mrs. Macphail. "I could try to make the place comfortable with more heart if the sun were shining."

"Oh, if you wait for that, you'll wait a long time. Pago-Pago is about the rainiest place in the Pacific. You see, the hills, and that bay, they attract the water, and one expects rain at this time of year anyway."

She looked from Macphail to his wife, standing helplessly in different parts of the room, like lost souls, and she pursed her lips. She saw that she must take them in hand. Feckless people like that made her impatient, but her hands itched to put everything in the order which came so naturally to her.

"Here, you give me a needle and cotton and I'll mend that net of yours, while you go on with your unpacking. Dinner's at one. Dr. Macphail, you'd better go down to the wharf and see that your heavy luggage has been put in a dry place. You know what these natives are, they're quite capable of storing it where the rain will beat in on it all the time."

The doctor put on his waterproof again and went downstairs. At the door Mr. Horn was standing in conversation with the quartermaster of the ship they had just arrived in and a second-class passenger whom Dr. Macphail had seen several times on board. The quartermaster, a little, shrivelled man, extremely dirty, nodded to him as he passed.

"This is a bad job about the measles, doc," he said. "I see you've fixed yourself up already."

Dr. Macphail thought he was rather familiar, but he was a timid man and he did not take offence easily.

"Yes, we've got a room upstairs."

"Miss Thompson was sailing with you to Apia, so I've brought her along here."

The quartermaster pointed with his thumb to the woman standing by his side. She was twenty-seven perhaps, plump, and in a coarse fashion pretty. She wore a white dress and a large white hat. Her fat calves in white cotton stockings bulged over the tops of long white boots in glacé kid. She gave Macphail an ingratiating smile.

"The feller's tryin' to soak me a dollar and a half a day for the meanest-sized room," she said in a hoarse voice.

"I tell you she's a friend of mine, Jo," said the quartermaster. "She can't pay more than a dollar, and you've sure got to take her for that."

The trader was fat and smooth and quietly smiling.

"Well, if you put it like that, Mr. Swan, I'll see what I can do about it. I'll talk to Mrs. Horn and if we think we can make a reduction we will."

"Don't try to pull that stuff with me," said Miss Thompson. "We'll settle this right now. You get a dollar a day for the room and not one bean more."

Dr. Macphail smiled. He admired the effrontery with which she bargained. He was the sort of man who always paid what he was asked. He preferred to be over-charged than to haggle. The trader sighed.

"Well, to oblige Mr. Swan I'll take it."

"That's the goods," said Miss Thompson. "Come right in and have a shot of hooch. I've got some real good rye in that grip if you'll bring it along, Mr. Swan. You come along too, doctor."

"Oh, I don't think I will, thank you," he answered. "I'm just going down to see that our luggage is all right."

He stepped out into the rain. It swept in from the opening of the harbour in sheets and the opposite shore was all blurred. He passed two or three natives clad in nothing but the lava-lava, with huge umbrellas over them. They walked finely, with leisurely movements, very upright; and they smiled and greeted him in a strange tongue as they went by.

It was nearly dinner-time when he got back, and their meal was laid in the trader's parlour. It was a room designed not to live in but for purposes of prestige, and it had a musty, melancholy air. A suite of stamped plush was arranged neatly round the walls, and from the middle of the ceiling, protected from the flies by yellow tissue-paper, hung a gilt chandelier. Davidson did not come.

"I know he went to call on the governor," said Mrs. Davidson, "and I guess he's kept him to dinner."

A little native girl brought them a dish of Hamburger steak, and after a while the trader came up to see that they had everything they wanted.

"I see we have a fellow lodger, Mr. Horn," said Dr. Macphail.

"She's taken a room, that's all," answered the trader. "She's getting her own board."

He looked at the two ladies with an obsequious air.

"I put her downstairs so she shouldn't be in the way. She won't be any trouble to you."

"Is it someone who was on the boat?" asked Mrs. Macphail.

"Yes, ma'am, she was in the second cabin. She was going to Apia. She has a position as cashier waiting for her."

"Oh!"

When the trader was gone Macphail said:

"I shouldn't think she'd find it exactly cheerful having her meals in her room."

"If she was in the second cabin I guess she'd rather," answered Mrs. Davidson. "I don't exactly know who it can be."

"I happened to be there when the quartermaster brought her along. Her name's Thompson."

"It's not the woman who was dancing with the quartermaster last night?" asked Mrs. Davidson.

"That's who it must be," said Mrs. Macphail. "I wondered at the time what she was. She looked rather fast to me."

"Not good style at all," said Mrs. Davidson.

They began to talk of other things, and after dinner, tired with their early rise, they separated and slept. When they awoke, though the sky was still grey and the clouds hung low, it was not raining and they went for a walk on the high road which the Americans had built along the bay.

On their return they found that Davidson had just come in.

"We may be here for a fortnight," he said irritably. "I've argued it out with the governor, but he says there is nothing to be done."

"Mr. Davidson's just longing to get back to his work," said his wife, with an anxious glance at him.

"We've been away for a year," he said, walking up and down the verandah. "The mission has been in charge of native missionaries and I'm terribly nervous that they've let things slide. They're good men, I'm not saying a word against them, God-fearing, devout, and truly Christian men—their Christianity would put many so-called Christians at home to the blush—but they're pitifully lacking in energy. They can make a stand once, they can make a stand twice, but they can't make a stand all the time. If you leave a mission in charge of a native missionary, no matter how trustworthy he seems, in course of time you'll find he's let abuses creep in."

Mr. Davidson stood still. With his tall, spare form, and his great eyes flashing out of his pale face, he was an impressive figure. His sincerity was obvious in the fire of his gestures and in his deep, ringing voice.

"I expect to have my work cut out for me. I shall act and I shall act promptly. If the tree is rotten it shall be cut down and cast into the flames."

And in the evening after the high-tea which was their last meal, while they sat in the stiff parlour, the ladies working and Dr. Macphail smoking his pipe, the missionary told them of his work in the islands.

"When we went there they had no sense of sin at all," he said. "They broke the commandments one after the other and never knew they were doing wrong. And I think that was the most difficult part of my work, to instil into the natives the sense of sin."

The Macphails knew already that Davidson had worked in the Solomons for five years before he met his wife. She had been a missionary in China, and they had become acquainted in Boston, where they were both spending part of their leave to attend a missionary congress. On their marriage they had been appointed to the islands in which they had laboured ever since.

In the course of all the conversations they had had with Mr. Davidson one thing had shone out clearly and that was the man's unflinching courage. He was a medical missionary, and he was liable to be called at any time to one or other of the islands in the group. Even the whaleboat is not so very safe a conveyance in the stormy Pacific of the wet season, but often he would be sent for in a canoe, and then the danger was great. In cases of illness or accident he never hesitated. A dozen times he had spent the whole night baling for his life, and more than once Mrs. Davidson had given him up for lost.

"I'd beg him not to go sometimes," she said, "or at least to wait till the weather was more settled, but he'd never listen. He's obstinate, and when he's once made up his mind, nothing can move him."

"How can I ask the natives to put their trust in the Lord if I am afraid to do so myself?" cried Davidson. "And I'm not, I'm not. They know that if they send for me in their trouble I'll come if it's humanly possible. And do you think the Lord is going to abandon me when I am on his business? The wind blows at his bidding and the waves toss and rage at his word."

Dr. Macphail was a timid man. He had never been able to get used to the hurtling of the shells over the trenches, and when he was operating in an advanced dressing-station the sweat poured from his brow and dimmed his spectacles in the effort he made to control his unsteady hand. He shuddered a little as he looked at the missionary.

"I wish I could say that I've never been afraid," he said.

"I wish you could say that you believed in God," retorted the other.

But for some reason, that evening the missionary's thoughts travelled back to the early days he and his wife had spent on the islands.

"Sometimes Mrs. Davidson and I would look at one another and the tears would stream down our cheeks. We worked without ceasing, day and night, and we seemed to make no progress. I don't know what I should have done without her then. When I felt my heart sink, when I was very near despair, she gave me courage and hope."

Mrs. Davidson looked down at her work, and a slight colour rose to her thin cheeks. Her hands trembled a little. She did not trust herself to speak.

"We had no one to help us. We were alone, thousands of miles from any of our own people, surrounded by darkness. When I was broken and weary she would put her work aside and take the Bible and read to me till peace came and settled upon me like sleep upon the eyelids of a child, and when at last she closed the book she'd say: 'We'll save them in spite of themselves.' And I felt strong again in the Lord, and I answered: 'Yes, with God's help I'll save them. I must save them.' "

He came over to the table and stood in front of it as though it were a lectern.

"You see, they were so naturally depraved that they couldn't be brought to see their wickedness. We had to make sins out of what they thought were natural actions. We had to make it a sin, not only to commit adultery and to lie and thieve, but to expose their bodies, and to dance and not to come to church. I made it a sin for a girl to show her bosom and a sin for a man not to wear trousers."

"How?" asked Dr. Macphail, not without surprise.

"I instituted fines. Obviously the only way to make people realise that an action is sinful is to punish them if they commit it. I fined them if they didn't come to church, and I fined them if they danced. I fined them if they were improperly dressed. I had a tariff, and every sin had to be paid for either in money or work. And at last I made them understand."

"But did they never refuse to pay?"

"How could they?" asked the missionary.

"It would be a brave man who tried to stand up against Mr. Davidson," said his wife, tightening her lips.

Dr. Macphail looked at Davidson with troubled eyes. What he heard shocked him, but he hesitated to express his disapproval.

"You must remember that in the last resort I could expel them from their church membership."

"Did they mind that?"

Davidson smiled a little and gently rubbed his hands.

"They couldn't sell their copra. When the men fished they got no share of the catch. It meant something very like starvation. Yes, they minded quite a lot."

"Tell him about Fred Ohlson," said Mrs. Davidson.

The missionary fixed his fiery eyes on Dr. Macphail.

"Fred Ohlson was a Danish trader who had been in the islands a good many years. He was a pretty rich man as traders go and he wasn't very pleased when we came. You see, he'd had things very much his own way. He paid the natives what he liked for their copra, and he paid in goods and whisky. He had a native wife, but he was flagrantly unfaithful to her. He was a drunkard. I gave him a chance to mend his ways, but he wouldn't take it. He laughed at me."

Davidson's voice fell to a deep bass as he said the last words, and he was silent for a minute or two. The silence was heavy with menace.

"In two years he was a ruined man. He'd lost everything he'd saved in a quarter of a century. I broke him, and at last he was forced to come to me like a beggar and beseech me to give him a passage back to Sydney."

"I wish you could have seen him when he came to see Mr. Davidson," said the missionary's wife. "He had been a fine, powerful man, with a lot of fat on him, and he had a great big voice, but now he was half the size, and he was shaking all over. He'd suddenly become an old man."

With abstracted gaze Davidson looked out into the night. The rain was falling again.

Suddenly from below came a sound, and Davidson turned and looked questioningly at his wife. It was the sound of a gramophone, harsh and loud, wheezing out a syncopated tune.

"What's that?" he asked.

Mrs. Davidson fixed her pince-nez more firmly on her nose.

"One of the second-class passengers has a room in the house. I guess it comes from there."

They listened in silence, and presently they heard the sound of dancing. Then the music stopped, and they heard the popping of corks and voices raised in animated conversation.

"I daresay she's giving a farewell party to her friends on board," said Dr. Macphail. "The ship sails at twelve, doesn't it?"

Davidson made no remark, but he looked at his watch.

"Are you ready?" he asked his wife.

She got up and folded her work.

"Yes, I guess I am," she answered.

"It's early to go to bed yet, isn't it?" said the doctor.

"We have a good deal of reading to do," explained Mrs. Davidson. "Wherever we are, we read a chapter of the Bible before retiring for the night and we study it with the commentaries, you know, and discuss it thoroughly. It's a wonderful training for the mind."

The two couples bade one another good-night. Dr. and Mrs. Macphail were left alone. For two or three minutes they did not speak.

"I think I'll go and fetch the cards," the doctor said at last.

Mrs. Macphail looked at him doubtfully. Her conversation with the Davidsons had left her a little uneasy, but she did not like to say that she thought they had better not play cards when the Davidsons might come in at any moment. Dr. Macphail brought them and she watched him, though with a vague sense of guilt, while he laid out his patience. Below the sound of revelry continued.

It was fine enough next day, and the Macphails, condemned to spend a fortnight of idleness at Pago-Pago, set about making the best of things. They went down to the quay and got out of their boxes a number of books. The doctor called on the chief surgeon of the naval hospital and went round the beds with him. They left cards on the governor. They passed Miss Thompson on the road. The doctor took off his hat, and she gave him a "Good-morning, doc," in a loud, cheerful voice. She was dressed as on the day before, in a white frock, and her shiny white boots with their high heels, her fat legs bulging over the tops of them, were strange things on that exotic scene.

"I don't think she's very suitably dressed, I must say," said Mrs. Macphail. "She looks extremely common to me."

When they got back to their house, she was on the verandah playing with one of the trader's dark children.

"Say a word to her," Dr. Macphail whispered to his wife. "She's all alone here, and it seems rather unkind to ignore her."

Mrs. Macphail was shy, but she was in the habit of doing what her husband bade her.

"I think we're fellow lodgers here," she said, rather foolishly.

"Terrible, ain't it, bein' cooped up in a one-horse burg like this?" answered Miss Thompson. "And they tell me I'm lucky to have gotten a room. I don't see myself livin' in a native house, and that's what some have to do. I don't know why they don't have a hotel."

They exchanged a few more words. Miss Thompson, loud-voiced and garrulous, was evidently quite willing to gossip, but Mrs. Macphail had a poor stock of small talk and presently she said:

"Well, I think we must go upstairs."

In the evening when they sat down to their high-tea Davidson on coming in said:

"I see that woman downstairs has a couple of sailors sitting there. I wonder how she's gotten acquainted with them."

"She can't be very particular," said Mrs. Davidson.

They were all rather tired after the idle, aimless day.

"If there's going to be a fortnight of this I don't know what we shall feel like at the end of it," said Dr. Macphail.

"The only thing to do is to portion out the day to different activities," answered the missionary. "I shall set aside a certain number of hours to study and a certain number to exercise, rain or fine—in the wet season you can't afford to pay any attention to the rain—and a certain number to recreation."

Dr. Macphail looked at his companion with misgiving. Davidson's programme oppressed him. They were eating Hamburger steak again. It seemed the only dish the cook knew how to make. Then below the gramophone began. Davidson started nervously when he heard it, but said nothing. Men's voices floated up. Miss Thompson's guests were joining in a well-known song and presently they heard her voice too, hoarse and loud. There was a good deal of shouting and laughing. The four people upstairs, trying to make conversation, listened despite themselves to the clink of glasses and the scrape of chairs. More people had evidently come. Miss Thompson was giving a party.

"I wonder how she gets them all in," said Mrs. Macphail suddenly breaking into a medical conversation between the missionary and her husband.

It showed whither her thoughts were wandering. The twitch of Davidson's face proved that, though he spoke of scientific things, his mind was busy in the same direction. Suddenly, while the doctor was giving some experience of practice on the Flanders front, rather prosily, he sprang to his feet with a cry.

"What's the matter, Alfred?" asked Mrs. Davidson.

"Of course! It never occurred to me. She's out of Iwelei."

"She can't be."

"She came on board at Honolulu. It's obvious. And she's carrying on her trade here. Here."

He uttered the last word with a passion of indignation.

"What's Iwelei?" asked Mrs. Macphail.

He turned his gloomy eyes on her and his voice trembled with horror.

"The plague spot of Honolulu. The Red Light district. It was a blot on our civilisation."

Iwelei was on the edge of the city. You went down side streets by the harbour, in the darkness, across a rickety bridge, till you came to a deserted road, all ruts and holes, and then suddenly you came out into the light. There was parking room for motors on each side of the road, and there were saloons, tawdry and bright, each one noisy with its mechanical piano, and there were barbers' shops and tobacconists. There was a stir in the air and a sense of expectant gaiety. You turned down a narrow alley, either to the right or to the left, for the road divided Iwelei into two parts, and you found yourself in the district. There were rows of little bungalows, trim and neatly painted in green, and the pathway between them was broad and straight. It was laid out like a garden-city. In its respectable regularity, its order and spruceness, it gave an impression of sardonic horror; for never can the search for love have been so systematised and ordered. The pathways were lit by a rare lamp, but they would have been dark except for the lights that came from the open windows of the bungalows. Men wandered about, looking at the women who sat at their windows, reading or sewing, for the most part taking no notice of the passers-by; and like the women they were of all nationalities. There were Americans, sailors from the ships in port, enlisted men off the gunboats, sombrely drunk, and soldiers from the regiments, white and black, quartered on the island; there were Japanese, walking in twos and threes; Hawaiians, Chinese in long robes, and Filipinos in preposterous hats. They were silent and as it were oppressed. Desire is sad.

"It was the most crying scandal of the Pacific," exclaimed Davidson vehemently. "The missionaries had been agitating against it for years, and at last the local press took it up. The police refused to stir. You know their argument. They say that vice is inevitable and consequently the best thing is to localise and control it. The truth is, they were paid. Paid. They were paid by the saloon-keepers, paid by the bullies, paid by the women themselves. At last they were forced to move."

"I read about it in the papers that came on board in Honolulu," said Dr. Macphail.

"Iwelei, with its sin and shame, ceased to exist on the very day we arrived. The whole population was brought before the justices. I don't know why I didn't understand at once what that woman was."

"Now you come to speak of it," said Mrs. Macphail, "I remember seeing her come on board only a few minutes before the boat sailed. I remember thinking at the time she was cutting it rather fine."

"How dare she come here!" cried Davidson indignantly. "I'm not going to allow it."

He strode towards the door.

"What are you going to do?" asked Macphail.

"What do you expect me to do? I'm going to stop it. I'm not going to have this house turned into—into . . ."

He sought for a word that should not offend the ladies' ears. His eyes were flashing and his pale face was paler still in his emotion.

"It sounds as though there were three or four men down there," said the doctor. "Don't you think it's rather rash to go in just now?"

The missionary gave him a contemptuous look and without a word flung out of the room.

"You know Mr. Davidson very little if you think the fear of personal danger can stop him in the performance of his duty," said his wife.

She sat with her hands nervously clasped, a spot of colour on her high cheek-bones, listening to what was about to happen below. They all listened. They heard him clatter down the wooden stairs and throw open the door. The singing stopped suddenly, but the gramophone continued to bray out its vulgar tune. They heard Davidson's voice and then the noise of something heavy falling. The music stopped. He had hurled the gramophone on the floor. Then again they heard Davidson's voice, they could not make out the words, then Miss Thompson's, loud and shrill, then a confused clamour as though several people were shouting together at the top of their lungs. Mrs. Davidson gave a little gasp, and she clenched her hands more tightly. Dr. Macphail looked uncertainly from her to his wife. He did not want to go down, but he wondered if they expected him to. Then there was something that sounded like a scuffle. The noise now was more distinct. It might be that Davidson was being thrown out of the room. The door was slammed. There was a moment's silence and they heard Davidson come up the stairs again. He went to his room.

"I think I'll go to him," said Mrs. Davidson.

She got up and went out.

"If you want me, just call," said Mrs. Macphail, and then when the other was gone: "I hope he isn't hurt."

"Why couldn't he mind his own business?" said Dr. Macphail.

They sat in silence for a minute or two and then they both started, for the gramophone began to play once more, defiantly, and mocking voices shouted hoarsely the words of an obscene song.

Next day Mrs. Davidson was pale and tired. She complained of headache, and she looked old and wizened. She told Mrs. Macphail that the missionary had not slept at all; he had passed the night in a state of frightful agitation and at five had got up and gone out. A glass of beer had been thrown over him and his clothes were stained and stinking. But a sombre fire glowed in Mrs. Davidson's eyes when she spoke of Miss Thompson.

"She'll bitterly rue the day when she flouted Mr. Davidson," she said. "Mr. Davidson has a wonderful heart and no one who is in trouble has ever gone to him without being comforted, but he has no mercy for sin, and when his righteous wrath is excited he's terrible."

"Why, what will he do?" asked Mrs. Macphail.

"I don't know, but I wouldn't stand in that creature's shoes for anything in the world."

Mrs. Macphail shuddered. There was something positively alarming in the triumphant assurance of the little woman's manner. They were going out together that morning, and they went down the stairs side by side. Miss Thompson's door was open, and they saw her in a bedraggled dressing-gown, cooking something in a chafing-dish.

"Good-morning," she called. "Is Mr. Davidson better this morning?"

They passed her in silence, with their noses in the air, as if she did not exist. They flushed, however, when she burst into a shout of derisive laughter. Mrs. Davidson turned on her suddenly.

"Don't you dare to speak to me," she screamed. "If you insult me I shall have you turned out of here."

"Say, did I ask Mr. Davidson to visit with me?"

"Don't answer her," whispered Mrs. Macphail hurriedly.

They walked on till they were out of earshot.

"She's brazen, brazen," burst from Mrs. Davidson.

Her anger almost suffocated her.

And on their way home they met her strolling towards the quay. She had all her finery on. Her great white hat with its vulgar, showy flowers was an affront. She called out cheerily to them as she went by, and a couple of American sailors who were standing there grinned as the ladies set their faces to an icy state. They got in just before the rain began to fall again.

"I guess she'll get her fine clothes spoilt," said Mrs. Davidson with a bitter sneer.

Davidson did not come in till they were half-way through dinner. He was wet through, but he would not change. He sat, morose and silent, refusing to eat more than a mouthful, and he stared at the slanting rain. When Mrs. Davidson told him of their two encounters with Miss Thompson he did not answer. His deepening frown alone showed that he had heard.

"Don't you think we ought to make Mr. Horn turn her out of here?" asked Mrs. Davidson. "We can't allow her to insult us."

"There doesn't seem to be any other place for her to go," said Macphail.

"She can live with one of the natives."

"In weather like this a native hut must be a rather uncomfortable place to live in."

"I lived in one for years," said the missionary.

When the little native girl brought in the fried bananas which formed the sweet they had every day, Davidson turned to her.

"Ask Miss Thompson when it would be convenient for me to see her," he said.

The girl nodded shyly and went out.

"What do you want to see her for, Alfred?" asked his wife.

"It's my duty to see her. I won't act till I've given her every chance."

"You don't know what she is. She'll insult you."

"Let her insult me. Let her spit on me. She has an immortal soul, and I must do all that is in my power to save it."

Mrs. Davidson's ears rang still with the harlot's mocking laughter.

"She's gone too far."

"Too far for the mercy of God?" His eyes lit up suddenly and his voice grew mellow and soft. "Never. The sinner may be deeper in sin than the depth of hell itself, but the love of the Lord Jesus can reach him still."

The girl came back with the message.

"Miss Thompson's compliments and as long as Rev. Davidson don't come in business hours she'll be glad to see him any time."

The party received it in stony silence, and Dr. Macphail quickly effaced from his lips the smile which had come upon them. He knew his wife would be vexed with him if he found Miss Thompson's effrontery amusing.

They finished the meal in silence. When it was over the two ladies got up and took their work, Mrs. Macphail was making another of the innumerable comforters which she had turned out since the beginning of the war, and the doctor lit his pipe. But Davidson remained in his chair and with abstracted eyes stared at the table. At last he got up and without a word went out of the room. They heard him go down and they heard Miss Thompson's defiant "Come in" when he knocked at the door. He remained with her for an hour. And Dr. Macphail watched the rain. It was beginning to get on his nerves. It was not like our soft English rain that drops gently on the earth; it was unmerciful and somehow terrible; you felt in it the malignancy of the primitive powers of nature. It did not pour, it flowed. It was like a deluge from heaven, and it rattled on the roof of corrugated iron with a steady persistence that was maddening. It seemed to have a fury of its own. And sometimes you felt that you must scream if it did not stop, and then suddenly you felt powerless, as though your bones had suddenly become soft; and you were miserable and hopeless.

Macphail turned his head when the missionary came back. The two women looked up.

"I've given her every chance. I have exhorted her to repent. She is an evil woman."

He paused, and Dr. Macphail saw his eyes darken and his pale face grow hard and stern.

"Now I shall take the whips with which the Lord Jesus drove the usurers and the money-changers out of the Temple of the Most High."

He walked up and down the room. His mouth was close set, and his black brows were frowning.

"If she fled to the uttermost parts of the earth I should pursue her."

With a sudden movement he turned round and strode out of the room. They heard him go downstairs again.

"What is he going to do?" asked Mrs. Macphail.

"I don't know." Mrs. Davidson took off her pince-nez and wiped them. "When he is on the Lord's work I never ask him questions." She sighed a little.

"What is the matter?"

"He'll wear himself out. He doesn't know what it is to spare himself."

Dr. Macphail learnt the first results of the missionary's activity from the half-caste trader in whose house they lodged. He stopped the doctor when he passed the store and came out to speak to him on the stoop. His fat face was worried.

"The Rev. Davidson has been at me for letting Miss Thompson have a room here," he said, "but I didn't know what she was when I rented it to her. When people come and ask if I can rent them a room all I want to know is if they've the money to pay for it. And she paid me for hers a week in advance."

Dr. Macphail did not want to commit himself.

"When all's said and done it's your house. We're very much obliged to you for taking us in at all."

Horn looked at him doubtfully. He was not certain yet how definitely Macphail stood on the missionary's side.

"The missionaries are in with one another," he said, hesitatingly. "If they get it in for a trader he may just as well shut up his store and quit."

"Did he want you to turn her out?"

"No, he said so long as she behaved herself he couldn't ask me to do that. He said he wanted to be just to me. I promised she shouldn't have no more visitors. I've just been and told her."

"How did she take it?"

"She gave me Hell."

The trader squirmed in his old ducks. He had found Miss Thompson a rough customer.

"Oh, well, I daresay she'll get out. I don't suppose she wants to stay here if she can't have anyone in."

"There's nowhere she can go, only a native house, and no native'll take her now, not now that the missionaries have got their knife in her."

Dr. Macphail looked at the falling rain.

"Well, I don't suppose it's any good waiting for it to clear up."

In the evening when they sat in the parlour Davidson talked to them of his early days at college. He had had no means and had worked his way through by doing odd jobs during the vacations. There was silence downstairs. Miss Thompson was sitting in her little room alone. But suddenly the gramophone began to play. She had set it on in defiance, to cheat her loneliness, but there was no one to sing, and it had a melancholy note. It was like a cry for help. Davidson took no notice. He was in the middle of a long anecdote and without change of expression went on. The gramophone continued. Miss Thompson put on one reel after another. It looked as though the silence of the night were getting on her nerves. It was breathless and sultry. When the Macphails went to bed they could not sleep. They lay side by side with their eyes wide open, listening to the cruel singing of the mosquitoes outside their curtain.

"What's that?" whispered Mrs. Macphail at last.

They heard a voice, Davidson's voice, through the wooden partition. It went on with a monotonous, earnest insistence. He was praying aloud. He was praying for the soul of Miss Thompson.

Two or three days went by. Now when they passed Miss Thompson on the road she did not greet them with ironic cordiality or smile; she passed with her nose in the air, a sulky look on her painted face, frowning, as though she did not see them. The trader told Macphail that she had tried to get lodging elsewhere, but had failed. In the evening she played through the various reels of her gramophone, but the pretence of mirth was obvious now. The ragtime had a cracked, heart-broken rhythm as though it were a one-step of despair. When she began to play on Sunday Davidson sent Horn to beg her to stop at once since it was the Lord's day. The reel was taken off and the house was silent except for the steady pattering of the rain on the iron roof.

"I think she's getting a bit worked up," said the trader next day to Macphail. "She don't know what Mr. Davidson's up to and it makes her scared."

Macphail had caught a glimpse of her that morning and it struck him that her arrogant expression had changed. There was in her face a hunted look. The half-caste gave him a sidelong glance.

"I suppose you don't know what Mr. Davidson is doing about it?" he hazarded.

"No, I don't."

It was singular that Horn should ask him that question, for he also had the idea that the missionary was mysteriously at work. He had an impression that he was weaving a net around the woman, carefully, systematically, and suddenly, when everything was ready, would pull the strings tight.

"He told me to tell her," said the trader, "that if at any time she wanted him she only had to send and he'd come."

"What did she say when you told her that?"

"She didn't say nothing. I didn't stop. I just said what he said I was to and then I beat it. I thought she might be going to start weepin'."

"I have no doubt the loneliness is getting on her nerves," said the doctor. "And the rain—that's enough to make anyone jumpy," he continued irritably. "Doesn't it ever stop in this confounded place?"

"It goes on pretty steady in the rainy season. We have three hundred inches in the year. You see, it's the shape of the bay. It seems to attract the rain from all over the Pacific."

"Damn the shape of the bay," said the doctor.

He scratched his mosquito bites. He felt very short-tempered. When the rain stopped and the sun shone, it was like a hot-house, seething, humid, sultry, breathless, and you had a strange feeling that everything was growing with a savage violence. The natives, blithe and childlike by reputation, seemed then, with their tattooing and their dyed hair, to have something sinister in their appearance; and when they pattered along at your heels with their naked feet you looked back instinctively. You felt they might at any moment come behind you swiftly and thrust a long knife between your shoulder-blades. You could not tell what dark thoughts lurked behind their wide-set eyes. They had a little the look of ancient Egyptians painted on a temple wall, and there was about them the terror of what is immeasurably old.

The missionary came and went. He was busy, but the Macphails did not know what he was doing. Horn told the doctor that he saw the governor every day, and once Davidson mentioned him.

"He looks as if he had plenty of determination," he said, "but when you come down to brass tacks he has no backbone."

"I suppose that means he won't do exactly what you want," suggested the doctor facetiously.

The missionary did not smile.

"I want him to do what's right. It shouldn't be necessary to persuade a man to do that."

"But there may be differences of opinion about what is right."

"If a man had a gangrenous foot would you have patience with anyone who hesitated to amputate it?"

"Gangrene is a matter of fact."

"And Evil?"

What Davidson had done soon appeared. The four of them had just finished their mid-day meal, and they had not yet separated for the siesta which the heat imposed on the ladies and on the doctor. Davidson had little patience with the slothful habit. The door was suddenly flung open and Miss Thompson came in. She looked round the room and then went up to Davidson.

"You low-down skunk, what have you been saying about me to the governor?"

She was spluttering with rage. There was a moment's pause. Then the missionary drew forward a chair.

"Won't you be seated, Miss Thompson? I've been hoping to have another talk with you."

"You poor low-life bastard."

She burst into a torrent of insult, foul and insolent. Davidson kept his grave eyes on her.

"I'm indifferent to the abuse you think fit to heap on me, Miss Thompson," he said, "but I must beg you to remember that ladies are present."

Tears by now were struggling with her anger. Her face was red and swollen as though she were choking.

"What has happened?" asked Dr. Macphail.

"A feller's just been in here and he says I gotter beat it on the next boat."

Was there a gleam in the missionary's eyes? His face remained impassive.

"You could hardly expect the governor to let you stay here under the circumstances."

"You done it," she shrieked. "You can't kid me. You done it."

"I don't want to deceive you. I urged the governor to take the only possible step consistent with his obligations."

"Why couldn't you leave me be? I wasn't doin' you no harm."

"You may be sure that if you had I should be the last man to resent it."

"Do you think I want to stay on in this poor imitation of a burg? I don't look no busher, do I?"

"In that case I don't see what cause of complaint you have," he answered.

She gave an inarticulate cry of rage and flung out of the room. There was a short silence.

"It's a relief to know that the governor has acted at last," said Davidson finally. "He's a weak man and he shilly-shallied. He said she was only here for a fortnight anyway, and if she went on to Apia, that was under British jurisdiction and had nothing to do with him."

The missionary sprang to his feet and strode across the room.

"It's terrible the way the men who are in authority seek to evade their responsibility. They speak as though evil that was out of sight ceased to be evil. The very existence of that woman is a scandal and it does not help matters to shift it to another of the islands. In the end I had to speak straight from the shoulder."

Davidson's brow lowered, and he protruded his firm chin. He looked fierce and determined.

"What do you mean by that?"

"Our mission is not entirely without influence at Washington. I pointed out to the governor that it wouldn't do him any good if there was a complaint about the way he managed things here."

"When has she got to go?" asked the doctor, after a pause.

"The San Francisco boat is due here from Sydney next Tuesday. She's to sail on that."

That was in five days' time. It was next day, when he was coming back from the hospital where for want of something better to do Macphail spent most of his mornings, that the half-caste stopped him as he was going upstairs.

"Excuse me, Dr. Macphail, Miss Thompson's sick. Will you have a look at her?"

"Certainly."

Horn led him to her room. She was sitting in a chair idly, neither reading nor sewing, staring in front of her. She wore her white dress and the large hat with the flowers on it. Macphail noticed that her skin was yellow and muddy under her powder, and her eyes were heavy.

"I'm sorry to hear you're not well," he said.

"Oh, I ain't sick really. I just said that, because I just had to see you. I've got to clear on a boat that's going to 'Frisco."

She looked at him and he saw that her eyes were suddenly startled. She opened and clenched her hands spasmodically. The trader stood at the door, listening.

"So I understand," said the doctor.

B

She gave a little gulp.

"I guess it ain't very convenient for me to go to 'Frisco just now. I went to see the governor yesterday afternoon, but I couldn't get to him. I saw the secretary, and he told me I'd got to take that boat and that was all there was to it. I just had to see the governor, so I waited outside his house this morning, and when he come out I spoke to him. He didn't want to speak to me, I'll say, but I wouldn't let him shake me off, and at last he said he hadn't no objection to my staying here till the next boat to Sydney if the Rev. Davidson will stand for it."

She stopped and looked at Dr. Macphail anxiously.

"I don't know exactly what I can do," he said.

"Well, I thought maybe you wouldn't mind asking him. I swear to God I won't start anything here if he'll just only let me stay. I won't go out of the house if that'll suit him. It's no more'n a fortnight."

"I'll ask him."

"He won't stand for it," said Horn. "He'll have you out on Tuesday, so you may as well make up your mind to it."

"Tell him I can get work in Sydney, straight stuff, I mean. 'Tain't asking very much."

"I'll do what I can."

"And come and tell me right away, will you? I can't set down to a thing till I get the dope one way or the other."

It was not an errand that much pleased the doctor, and, characteristically perhaps, he went about it indirectly. He told his wife what Miss Thompson had said to him and asked her to speak to Mrs. Davidson. The missionary's attitude seemed rather arbitrary and it could do no harm if the girl were allowed to stay in Pago-Pago another fortnight. But he was not prepared for the result of his diplomacy. The missionary came to him straightway.

"Mrs. Davidson tells me that Thompson has been speaking to you."

Dr. Macphail, thus directly tackled, had the shy man's resentment at being forced out into the open. He felt his temper rising, and he flushed.

"I don't see that it can make any difference if she goes to Sydney rather than to San Francisco, and so long as she promises to behave while she's here it's dashed hard to persecute her."

The missionary fixed him with his stern eyes.

"Why is she unwilling to go back to San Francisco?"

"I didn't enquire," answered the doctor with some asperity. "And I think one does better to mind one's own business."

Perhaps it was not a very tactful answer.

"The governor has ordered her to be deported by the first boat that leaves the island. He's only done his duty and I will not interfere. Her presence is a peril here."

"I think you're very harsh and tyrannical."

The two ladies looked up at the doctor with some alarm, but they need not have feared a quarrel, for the missionary smiled gently.

"I'm terribly sorry you should think that of me, Dr. Macphail. Believe me, my heart bleeds for that unfortunate woman, but I'm only trying to do my duty."

The doctor made no answer. He looked out of the window sullenly. For once it was not raining and across the bay you saw nestling among the trees the huts of a native village.

"I think I'll take advantage of the rain stopping to go out," he said.

"Please don't bear me malice because I can't accede to your wish," said Davidson, with a melancholy smile. "I respect you very much, doctor, and I should be sorry if you thought ill of me."

"I have no doubt you have a sufficiently good opinion of yourself to bear mine with equanimity," he retorted.

"That's one on me," chuckled Davidson.

When Dr. Macphail, vexed with himself because he had been uncivil to no purpose, went downstairs, Miss Thompson was waiting for him with her door ajar.

"Well," she said, "have you spoken to him?"

"Yes, I'm sorry, he won't do anything," he answered, not looking at her in his embarrassment.

But then he gave her a quick glance, for a sob broke from her. He saw that her face was white with fear. It gave him a shock of dismay. And suddenly he had an idea.

"But don't give up hope yet. I think it's a shame the way they're treating you and I'm going to see the governor myself."

"Now?"

He nodded. Her face brightened.

"Say, that's real good of you. I'm sure he'll let me stay if you speak for me. I just won't do a thing I didn't ought all the time I'm here."

Dr. Macphail hardly knew why he had made up his mind to appeal to the governor. He was perfectly indifferent to Miss Thompson's affairs, but the missionary had irritated him, and with him temper was a smouldering thing. He found the governor at home. He was a large, handsome man, a sailor, with a grey toothbrush moustache; and he wore a spotless uniform of white drill.

"I've come to see you about a woman who's lodging in the same house as we are," he said. "Her name's Thompson."

"I guess I've heard nearly enough about her, Dr. Macphail," said the governor, smiling. "I've given her the order to get out next Tuesday and that's all I can do."

"I wanted to ask you if you couldn't stretch a point and let her stay here till the boat comes in from San Francisco so that she can go to Sydney. I will guarantee her good behaviour."

The governor continued to smile, but his eyes grew small and serious.

"I'd be very glad to oblige you, Dr. Macphail, but I've given the order and it must stand."

The doctor put the case as reasonably as he could, but now the governor ceased to smile at all. He listened sullenly, with averted gaze. Macphail saw that he was making no impression.

"I'm sorry to cause any lady inconvenience, but she'll have to sail on Tuesday and that's all there is to it."

"But what difference can it make?"

"Pardon me, doctor, but I don't feel called upon to explain my official actions except to the proper authorities."

Macphail looked at him shrewdly. He remembered Davidson's hint that he had used threats, and in the governor's attitude he read a singular embarrassment.

"Davidson's a damned busybody," he said hotly.

"Between ourselves, Dr. Macphail, I don't say that I have formed a very favourable opinion of Mr. Davidson, but I am bound to confess that he was within his rights in pointing out to me the danger that the presence of a woman of Miss Thompson's character was to a place like this where a number of enlisted men are stationed among a native population."

He got up and Dr. Macphail was obliged to do so too.

"I must ask you to excuse me. I have an engagement. Please give my respects to Mrs. Macphail."

The doctor left him crestfallen. He knew that Miss Thompson would be waiting for him, and unwilling to tell her himself that he had failed, he went into the house by the back door and sneaked up the stairs as though he had something to hide.

At supper he was silent and ill-at-ease, but the missionary was jovial and animated. Dr. Macphail thought his eyes rested on him now and then with triumphant good-humour. It struck him suddenly that Davidson knew of his visit to the governor and of its ill success. But how on earth could he have heard of it? There was something sinister about the power of that man. After supper he saw Horn on the verandah and, as though to have a casual word with him, went out.

"She wants to know if you've seen the governor," the trader whispered.

"Yes. He wouldn't do anything. I'm awfully sorry, I can't do anything more."

"I knew he wouldn't. They daren't go against the missionaries."

"What are you talking about?" said Davidson affably, coming out to join them.

"I was just saying there was no chance of your getting over to Apia for at least another week," said the trader glibly.

He left them, and the two men returned into the parlour. Mr. Davidson devoted one hour after each meal to recreation. Presently a timid knock was heard at the door.

"Come in," said Mrs. Davidson, in her sharp voice.

The door was not opened. She got up and opened it. They saw Miss Thompson standing at the threshold. But the change in her appearance was extraordinary. This was no longer the flaunting hussy who had jeered at them in the road, but a broken, frightened woman. Her hair, as a rule so elaborately arranged, was tumbling untidily over her neck. She wore bedroom slippers and a skirt and blouse. They were unfresh and bedraggled. She stood at the door with the tears streaming down her face and did not dare to enter.

"What do you want?" said Mrs. Davidson harshly.

"May I speak to Mr. Davidson?" she said in a choking voice.

The missionary rose and went towards her.

"Come right in, Miss Thompson," he said in cordial tones. "What can I do for you?"

She entered the room.

"Say, I'm sorry for what I said to you the other day an' for—for everythin' else. I guess I was a bit lit up. I beg pardon."

"Oh, it was nothing. I guess my back's broad enough to bear a few hard words."

She stepped towards him with a movement that was horribly cringing.

"You've got me beat. I'm all in. You won't make me go back to 'Frisco?"

His genial manner vanished and his voice grew on a sudden hard and stern.

"Why don't you want to go back there?"

She cowered before him.

"I guess my people live there. I don't want them to see me like this. I'll go anywhere else you say."

"Why don't you want to go back to San Francisco?"

"I've told you."

He leaned forward, staring at her, and his great, shining eyes seemed to try to bore into her soul. He gave a sudden gasp.

"The penitentiary."

She screamed, and then she fell at his feet, clasping his legs.

"Don't send me back there. I swear to you before God I'll be a good woman. I'll give all this up."

She burst into a torrent of confused supplication and the tears coursed down her painted cheeks. He leaned over her and, lifting her face, forced her to look at him.

"Is that it, the penitentiary?"

"I beat it before they could get me," she gasped. "If the bulls grab me it's three years for mine."

He let go his hold of her and she fell in a heap on the floor, sobbing bitterly. Dr. Macphail stood up.

"This alters the whole thing," he said. "You can't make her go back when you know this. Give her another chance. She wants to turn over a new leaf."

"I'm going to give her the finest chance she's ever had. If she repents let her accept her punishment."

She misunderstood the words and looked up. There was a gleam of hope in her heavy eyes.

"You'll let me go?"

"No. You shall sail for San Francisco on Tuesday."

She gave a groan of horror and then burst into low, hoarse shrieks which sounded hardly human, and she beat her head passionately on the ground. Dr. Macphail sprang to her and lifted her up.

"Come on, you mustn't do that. You'd better go to your room and lie down. I'll get you something."

He raised her to her feet and partly dragging her, partly carrying her, got her downstairs. He was furious with Mrs. Davidson and with his wife because they made no effort to help. The half-caste was standing on the landing and with his assistance he managed to get her on the bed. She was moaning and crying. She was almost insensible. He gave her a hypodermic injection. He was hot and exhausted when he went upstairs again.

"I've got her to lie down."

The two women and Davidson were in the same positions as when he had left them. They could not have moved or spoken since he went.

"I was waiting for you," said Davidson, in a strange, distant voice. "I want you all to pray with me for the soul of our erring sister."

He took the Bible off a shelf, and sat down at the table at which they had supped. It had not been cleared, and he pushed the tea-pot out of the way. In a powerful voice, resonant and deep, he read to them the chapter in which is narrated the meeting of Jesus Christ with the woman taken in adultery.

"Now kneel with me and let us pray for the soul of our dear sister, Sadie Thompson."

He burst into a long, passionate prayer in which he implored God to have mercy on the sinful woman. Mrs. Macphail and Mrs. Davidson knelt with covered eyes. The doctor, taken by surprise, awkward and sheepish, knelt too. The missionary's prayer had a savage eloquence. He was extraordinarily moved, and as he spoke the tears ran down his cheeks. Outside, the pitiless rain fell, fell steadily, with a fierce malignity that was all too human.

At last he stopped. He paused for a moment and said:

"We will now repeat the Lord's prayer."

They said it and then, following him, they rose from their knees. Mrs. Davidson's face was pale and restful. She was comforted and at peace, but the Macphails felt suddenly bashful. They did not know which way to look.

"I'll just go down and see how she is now," said Dr. Macphail.

When he knocked at her door it was opened for him by Horn. Miss Thompson was in a rocking-chair, sobbing quietly.

"What are you doing there?" exclaimed Macphail. "I told you to lie down."

"I can't lie down. I want to see Mr. Davidson."

"My poor child, what do you think is the good of it? You'll never move him."

"He said he'd come if I sent for him."

Macphail motioned to the trader.

"Go and fetch him."

He waited with her in silence while the trader went upstairs. Davidson came in.

"Excuse me for asking you to come here," she said, looking at him sombrely.

"I was expecting you to send for me. I knew the Lord would answer my prayer."

They stared at one another for a moment and then she looked away. She kept her eyes averted when she spoke.

"I've been a bad woman. I want to repent."

"Thank God! thank God! He has heard our prayers."

He turned to the two men.

"Leave me alone with her. Tell Mrs. Davidson that our prayers have been answered."

They went out and closed the door behind them.

"Gee whizz," said the trader.

That night Dr. Macphail could not get to sleep till late, and when he heard the missionary come upstairs he looked at his watch. It was two o'clock. But even then he did not go to bed at once, for through the wooden partition that separated their rooms he heard him praying aloud, till he himself, exhausted, fell asleep.

When he saw him next morning he was surprised at his appearance. He was paler than ever, tired, but his eyes shone with inhuman fire. It looked as though he were filled with an overwhelming joy.

"I want you to go down presently and see Sadie," he said. "I can't hope that her body is better, but her soul—her soul is transformed."

The doctor was feeling wan and nervous.

"You were with her very late last night," he said.

"Yes, she couldn't bear to have me leave her."

"You look as pleased as Punch," the doctor said irritably.

Davidson's eyes shone with ecstasy.

"A great mercy has been vouchsafed me. Last night I was privileged to bring a lost soul to the loving arms of Jesus."

Miss Thompson was again in the rocking-chair. The bed had not been made. The room was in disorder. She had not troubled to dress herself, but wore a dirty dressing-gown, and her hair was tied in a sluttish knot. She had given her face a dab with a wet towel, but it was all swollen and creased with crying. She looked a drab.

She raised her eyes dully when the doctor came in. She was cowed and broken.

"Where's Mr. Davidson?" she asked.

"He'll come presently if you want him," answered Macphail acidly. "I came here to see how you were."

"Oh, I guess I'm O.K. You needn't worry about that."

"Have you had anything to eat?"

"Horn brought me some coffee."

She looked anxiously at the door.

"D'you think he'll come down soon? I feel as if it wasn't so terrible when he's with me."

"Are you still going on Tuesday?"

"Yes, he says I've got to go. Please tell him to come right along. You can't do me any good. He's the only one as can help me now."

"Very well," said Dr. Macphail.

During the next three days the missionary spent almost all his time with Sadie Thompson. He joined the others only to have his meals. Dr. Macphail noticed that he hardly ate.

"He's wearing himself out," said Mrs. Davidson pitifully. "He'll have a breakdown if he doesn't take care, but he won't spare himself."

She herself was white and pale. She told Mrs. Macphail that she had no sleep. When the missionary came upstairs from Miss Thompson he prayed till he was exhausted, but even then he did not sleep for long. After an hour or two he got up and dressed himself, and went for a tramp along the bay. He had strange dreams.

"This morning he told me that he'd been dreaming about the mountains of Nebraska," said Mrs. Davidson.

"That's curious," said Dr. Macphail.

He remembered seeing them from the windows of the train when he crossed America. They were like huge mole-hills, rounded and smooth, and they rose from the plain abruptly. Dr. Macphail remembered how it struck him that they were like a woman's breasts.

Davidson's restlessness was intolerable even to himself. But he was buoyed up by a wonderful exhilaration. He was tearing out by the roots the last vestiges of sin that lurked in the hidden corners of that poor woman's heart. He read with her and prayed with her.

"It's wonderful," he said to them one day at supper. "It's a true rebirth. Her soul, which was black as night, is now pure and white like the new-fallen snow. I am humble and afraid. Her remorse for all her sins is beautiful. I am not worthy to touch the hem of her garment."

"Have you the heart to send her back to San Francisco?" said the doctor. "Three years in an American prison. I should have thought you might have saved her from that."

"Ah, but don't you see? It's necessary. Do you think my heart doesn't bleed for her? I love her as I love my wife and my sister. All the time that she is in prison I shall suffer all the pain that she suffers."

"Bunkum," cried the doctor impatiently.

"You don't understand because you're blind. She's sinned, and she must suffer. I know what she'll endure. She'll be starved and tortured and humiliated. I want her to accept the punishment of man as a sacrifice to God. I want her to accept it joyfully. She has an opportunity which is offered to very few of us. God is very good and very merciful."

Davidson's voice trembled with excitement. He could hardly articulate the words that tumbled passionately from his lips.

"All day I pray with her and when I leave her I pray again, I pray with all my might and main, so that Jesus may grant her this great mercy. I want to put in her heart the passionate desire to be punished so that at the end, even if I offered to let her go, she would refuse. I want her to feel that the bitter punishment of prison is the thank-offering that she places at the feet of our Blessed Lord, who gave his life for her."

The days passed slowly. The whole household, intent on the wretched, tortured woman downstairs, lived in a state of unnatural excitement. She was like a victim that was being prepared for the savage rites of a bloody idolatry. Her terror numbed her. She could not bear to let Davidson out of her sight; it was only when he was with her that she had courage, and she hung upon him with a slavish dependence. She cried a great deal, and she read the Bible, and prayed. Sometimes she was exhausted and apathetic. Then she did indeed look forward to her ordeal, for it seemed to offer an escape, direct and concrete, from the anguish she was enduring. She could not bear much longer the vague terrors which now assailed her. With her sins she had put aside all personal vanity, and she slopped about her room, unkempt and dishevelled, in her tawdry dressing-gown. She had not taken off her night-dress for four days, nor put on stockings. Her room was littered and untidy. Meanwhile the rain fell with a cruel persistence. You felt that the heavens must at last be empty of water, but still it poured down, straight and heavy, with a maddening iteration, on the iron roof. Everything was damp and clammy. There was mildew on the walls and on the boots that stood on the floor. Through the sleepless nights the mosquitoes droned their angry chant.

"If it would only stop raining for a single day it wouldn't be so bad," said Dr. Macphail.

They all looked forward to the Tuesday when the boat for San Francisco was to arrive from Sydney. The strain was intolerable. So far as Dr. Macphail was concerned, his pity and his resentment were alike extinguished by his desire to be rid of the unfortunate woman. The inevitable must be accepted. He felt he would breathe more freely when the ship had sailed. Sadie Thompson was to be escorted on board by a clerk in the governor's office. This person called on the Monday evening and told Miss Thompson to be prepared at eleven in the morning. Davidson was with her.

"I'll see that everything is ready. I mean to come on board with her myself."

Miss Thompson did not speak.

When Dr. Macphail blew out his candle and crawled cautiously under his mosquito curtains, he gave a sigh of relief.

"Well, thank God that's over. By this time to-morrow she'll be gone."

"Mrs. Davidson will be glad too. She says he's wearing himself to a shadow," said Mrs. Macphail. "She's a different woman."

"Who?"

"Sadie. I should never have thought it possible. It makes one humble."

Dr. Macphail did not answer, and presently he fell asleep. He was tired out, and he slept more soundly than usual.

He was awakened in the morning by a hand placed on his arm, and, starting up, saw Horn by the side of his bed. The trader put his finger on his mouth to prevent any exclamation from Dr. Macphail and beckoned to him to come. As a rule he wore shabby ducks, but now he was barefoot and wore only the lava-lava of the natives. He looked suddenly savage, and Dr. Macphail, getting out of bed, saw that he was heavily tattooed. Horn made him a sign to come on to the verandah. Dr. Macphail got out of bed and followed the trader out.

"Don't make a noise," he whispered. "You're wanted. Put on a coat and some shoes. Quick."

Dr. Macphail's first thought was that something had happened to Miss Thompson.

"What is it? Shall I bring my instruments?"

"Hurry, please, hurry."

Dr. Macphail crept back into the bedroom, put on a waterproof over his pyjamas, and a pair of rubber-soled shoes. He rejoined the trader, and together they tiptoed down the stairs. The door leading out to the road was open and at it were standing half a dozen natives.

"What is it?" repeated the doctor.

"Come along with me," said Horn.

He walked out and the doctor followed him. The natives came after them in a little bunch. They crossed the road and came on to the beach. The doctor saw a group of natives standing round some object at the water's edge. They hurried along, a couple of dozen yards perhaps, and the natives opened out as the doctor came up. The trader pushed him forwards. Then he saw, lying half in the water and half out, a dreadful object, the body of Davidson. Dr. Macphail bent down—he was not a man to lose his head in an emergency—and turned the body over. The throat was cut from ear to ear, and in the right hand was still the razor with which the deed was done.

"He's quite cold," said the doctor. "He must have been dead some time."

"One of the boys saw him lying there on his way to work just now and came and told me. Do you think he did it himself?"

"Yes. Someone ought to go for the police."

Horn said something in the native tongue, and two youths started off.

"We must leave him here till they come," said the doctor.

"They mustn't take him into my house. I won't have him in my house."

"You'll do what the authorities say," replied the doctor sharply. "In point of fact I expect they'll take him to the mortuary."

They stood waiting where they were. The trader took a cigarette from a fold in his lava-lava and gave one to Dr. Macphail. They smoked while they stared at the corpse. Dr. Macphail could not understand.

"Why do you think he did it?" asked Horn.

The doctor shrugged his shoulders. In a little while native police came along, under the charge of a marine, with a stretcher, and immediately afterwards a couple of naval officers and a naval doctor. They managed everything in a businesslike manner.

"What about the wife?" said one of the officers.

"Now that you've come I'll go back to the house and get some things on. I'll see that it's broken to her. She'd better not see him till he's been fixed up a little."

"I guess that's right," said the naval doctor.

When Dr. Macphail went back he found his wife nearly dressed.

"Mrs. Davidson's in a dreadful state about her husband," she said to him as soon as he appeared. "He hasn't been to bed all night. She heard him leave Miss Thompson's room at two, but he went out. If he's been walking about since then he'll be absolutely dead."

Dr. Macphail told her what had happened and asked her to break the news to Mrs. Davidson.

"But why did he do it?" she asked, horror-stricken.

"I don't know."

"But I can't. I can't."

"You must."

She gave him a frightened look and went out. He heard her go into Mrs. Davidson's room. He waited a minute to gather himself together and then began to shave and wash. When he was dressed he sat down on the bed and waited for his wife. At last she came.

"She wants to see him," she said.

"They've taken him to the mortuary. We'd better go down with her. How did she take it?"

"I think she's stunned. She didn't cry. But she's trembling like a leaf."

"We'd better go at once."

When they knocked at her door Mrs. Davidson came out. She was very pale, but dry-eyed. To the doctor she seemed unnaturally composed. No word was exchanged, and they set out in silence down the road. When they arrived at the mortuary Mrs. Davidson spoke.

"Let me go in and see him alone."

They stood aside. A native opened a door for her and closed it behind her. They sat down and waited. One or two white men came and talked to them in undertones. Dr. Macphail told them again what he knew of the tragedy. At last the door was quietly opened and Mrs. Davidson came out. Silence fell upon them.

"I'm ready to go back now," she said.

Her voice was hard and steady. Dr. Macphail could not understand the look in her eyes. Her pale face was very stern. They walked back slowly, never saying a word, and at last they came round the bend on the other side of which stood their house. Mrs. Davidson gave a gasp, and for a moment they stopped still. An incredible sound assaulted their ears. The gramophone which had been silent for so long was playing, playing ragtime loud and harsh.

"What's that?" cried Mrs. Macphail with horror.

"Let's go on," said Mrs. Davidson.

They walked up the steps and entered the hall. Miss Thompson was standing at her door, chatting with a sailor. A sudden change had taken place in her. She was no longer the cowed drudge of the last days. She was dressed in all her finery, in her white dress, with the high shiny boots over which her fat legs bulged in their cotton stockings; her hair was elaborately arranged; and she wore that enormous hat covered with gaudy flowers. Her face was painted, her eyebrows were boldly black, and her lips were scarlet. She held herself erect. She was the flaunting queen that they had known at first. As they came in she broke into a loud, jeering laugh; and then, when Mrs. Davidson involuntarily stopped, she collected the spittle in her mouth and spat. Mrs. Davidson cowered back, and two red spots rose suddenly to her cheeks. Then, covering her face with her hands, she broke away and ran quickly up the stairs. Dr. Macphail was outraged. He pushed past the woman into her room.

"What the devil are you doing?" he cried. "Stop that damned machine."

He went up to it and tore the record off. She turned on him.

"Say, doc, you can that stuff with me. What the hell are you doin' in my room?"

"What do you mean?" he cried. "What d'you mean?"

She gathered herself together. No one could describe the scorn of her expression or the contemptuous hatred she put into her answer.

"You men! You filthy, dirty pigs! You're all the same, all of you. Pigs! Pigs!"

Dr. Macphail gasped. He understood.

The Fall of Edward Barnard

BATEMAN HUNTER slept badly. For a fortnight on the boat that brought him from Tahiti to San Francisco he had been thinking of the story he had to tell, and for three days on the train he had repeated to himself the words in which he meant to tell it. But in a few hours now he would be in Chicago, and doubts assailed him. His conscience, always very sensitive, was not at ease. He was uncertain that he had done all that was possible, it was on his honour to do much more than the possible, and the thought was disturbing that, in a matter which so nearly touched his own interest, he had allowed his interest to prevail over his quixotry. Self-sacrifice appealed so keenly to his imagination that the inability to exercise it gave him a sense of disillusion. He was like the philanthropist who with altruistic motives builds model dwellings for the poor and finds that he has made a lucrative investment. He cannot prevent the satisfaction he feels in the ten per cent which rewards the bread he had cast upon the waters, but he has an awkward feeling that it detracts somewhat from the savour of his virtue. Bateman Hunter knew that his heart was pure, but he was not quite sure how steadfastly, when he told her his story, he would endure the scrutiny of Isabel Longstaffe's cool grey eyes. They were far-seeing and wise. She measured the standards of others by her own meticulous uprightness and there could be no greater censure than the cold silence with which she expressed her disapproval of a conduct that did not satisfy her exacting code. There was no appeal from her judgment, for, having made up her mind, she never changed it. But Bateman would not have had her different. He loved not only the beauty of her person, slim and straight, with the proud carriage of her head, but still more the beauty of her soul. With her truthfulness, her rigid sense of honour, her fearless outlook, she seemed to him to collect in herself all that was most admirable in his countrywomen. But he saw in her something more than the perfect type of the American girl, he felt that her exquisiteness was peculiar in a way to her environment, and he was assured that no city in the world could have produced her but Chicago. A pang seized him when he remembered that he must deal so bitter a blow to her pride, and anger flamed up in his heart when he thought of Edward Barnard.

But at last the train steamed in to Chicago and he exulted when he saw the long streets of grey houses. He could hardly bear his impatience at the thought of State and Wabash with their crowded pavements, their hustling traffic, and their noise. He was at home. And he was glad that he had been born in the most important city in the United States. San Francisco was provincial, New York was effete; the future of America lay in the development of its economic possibilities, and Chicago, by its position and by the energy of its citizens, was destined to become the real capital of the country.

"I guess I shall live long enough to see it the biggest city in the world," Bateman said to himself as he stepped down to the platform.

His father had come to meet him, and after a hearty handshake, the pair of them, tall, slender, and well-made, with the same fine, ascetic features and thin lips, walked out of the station. Mr. Hunter's automobile was waiting for them and they got in. Mr. Hunter caught his son's proud and happy glance as he looked at the street.

"Glad to be back, son?" he asked.

"I should just think I was," said Bateman.

His eyes devoured the restless scene.

"I guess there's a bit more traffic here than in your South Sea island," laughed Mr. Hunter. "Did you like it there?"

"Give me Chicago, dad," answered Bateman.

"You haven't brought Edward Barnard back with you."

"No."

"How was he?"

Bateman was silent for a moment, and his handsome, sensitive face darkened.

"I'd sooner not speak about him, dad," he said at last.

"That's all right, my son. I guess your mother will be a happy woman to-day."

They passed out of the crowded streets in the Loop and drove along the lake till they came to the imposing house, an exact copy of a château on the Loire, which Mr. Hunter had built himself some years before. As soon as Bateman was alone in his room he asked for a number on the telephone. His heart leaped when he heard the voice that answered him.

"Good-morning, Isabel," he said gaily.

"Good-morning, Bateman."

"How did you recognise my voice?"

"It is not so long since I heard it last. Besides, I was expecting you."

"When may I see you?"

"Unless you have anything better to do perhaps you'll dine with us to-night."

"You know very well that I couldn't possibly have anything better to do."

"I suppose that you're full of news?"

He thought he detected in her voice a note of apprehension.

"Yes," he answered.

"Well, you must tell me to-night. Good-bye."

She rang off. It was characteristic of her that she should be able to wait so many unnecessary hours to know what so immensely concerned her. To Bateman there was an admirable fortitude in her restraint.

At dinner, at which beside himself and Isabel no one was present but her father and mother, he watched her guide the conversation into the channels of an urbane small-talk, and it occurred to him that in just such a manner would a marquise under the shadow of the guillotine toy with the affairs of a day that would know no morrow. Her delicate features, the aristocratic shortness of her upper lip, and her wealth of fair hair suggested the marquise again, and it must have been obvious, even if it were not notorious, that in her veins flowed the best blood in Chicago. The dining-room was a fitting frame to her fragile beauty, for Isabel had caused the house, a replica of a palace on the Grand Canal at Venice, to be furnished by an English expert in the style of Louis XV; and the graceful decoration linked with the name of that amorous monarch enhanced her loveliness and at the same time acquired from it a more profound significance. For Isabel's mind was richly stored, and her conversation, however light, was never flippant. She spoke now of the Musicale to which she and her mother had been in the afternoon, of the lectures which an English poet was giving at the Auditorium, of the political situation, and of the Old Master which her father had recently bought for fifty thousand dollars in New York. It comforted Bateman to hear her. He felt that he was once more in the civilised world, at the centre of culture and distinction; and certain voices, troubling and yet against his will refusing to still their clamour, were at last silent in his heart.

"Gee, but it's good to be back in Chicago," he said.

At last dinner was over, and when they went out of the dining-room Isabel said to her mother:

"I'm going to take Bateman along to my den. We have various things to talk about."

"Very well, my dear," said Mrs. Longstaffe. "You'll find your father and me in the Madame du Barry room when you're through."

Isabel led the young man upstairs and showed him into the room of which he had so many charming memories. Though he knew it so well he could not repress the exclamation of delight which it always wrung from him. She looked round with a smile.

"I think it's a success," she said. "The main thing is that it's right. There's not even an ash-tray that isn't of the period."

"I suppose that's what makes it so wonderful. Like all you do it's so superlatively right."

They sat down in front of a log fire and Isabel looked at him with calm grave eyes.

"Now what have you to say to me?" she asked.

"I hardly know how to begin."

"Is Edward Barnard coming back?"

"No."

There was a long silence before Bateman spoke again, and with each of them it was filled with many thoughts. It was a difficult story he had to tell, for there were things in it which were so offensive to her sensitive ears that he could not bear to tell them, and yet in justice to her, no less than in justice to himself, he must tell her the whole truth.

It had all begun long ago when he and Edward Barnard, still at college, had met Isabel Longstaffe at the tea-party given to introduce her to society. They had both known her when she was a child and they long-legged boys, but for two years she had been in Europe to finish her education and it was with a surprised delight that they renewed acquaintance with the lovely girl who returned. Both of them fell desperately in love with her, but Bateman saw quickly that she had eyes only for Edward, and, devoted to his friend, he resigned himself to the rôle of confidant. He passed bitter moments, but he could not deny that Edward was worthy of his good fortune, and, anxious that nothing should impair the friendship he so greatly valued, he took care never by a hint to disclose his own feelings. In six months the young couple were engaged. But they were very young and Isabel's father decided that they should not marry at least till Edward graduated. They had to wait a year. Bateman remembered the winter at the end of which Isabel and Edward were to be married, a winter of dances and theatre-parties and of informal gaieties at which he, the constant third, was always present. He loved her no less because she would shortly be his friend's wife; her smile, a gay word she flung him, the confidence of her affection, never ceased to delight him; and he congratulated himself, somewhat complacently, because he did not envy them their happiness. Then an accident happened. A great bank failed, there was a panic on the exchange, and Edward Barnard's father found himself a ruined man. He came home one night, told his wife that he was penniless, and after dinner, going into his study, shot himself.

A week later, Edward Barnard, with a tired, white face, went to Isabel and asked her to release him. Her only answer was to throw her arms round his neck and burst into tears.

"Don't make it harder for me, sweet," he said.

"Do you think I can let you go now? I love you."

"How can I ask you to marry me? The whole thing's hopeless. Your father would never let you. I haven't a cent."

"What do I care? I love you."

He told her his plans. He had to earn money at once, and George Braunschmidt, an old friend of his family, had offered to take him into his own business. He was a South Sea merchant, and he had agencies in many of the islands of the Pacific. He had suggested that Edward should go to Tahiti for a year or two, where under the best of his managers he could learn the details of that varied trade, and at the end of that time he promised the young man a position in Chicago. It was a wonderful opportunity, and when he had finished his explanations Isabel was once more all smiles.

"You foolish boy, why have you been trying to make me miserable?"

His face lit up at her words and his eyes flashed.

"Isabel, you don't mean to say you'll wait for me?"

"Don't you think you're worth it?" she smiled.

"Ah, don't laugh at me now. I beseech you to be serious. It may be for two years."

"Have no fear. I love you, Edward. When you come back I will marry you."

Edward's employer was a man who did not like delay and he had told him that if he took the post he offered he must sail that day week from San Francisco. Edward spent his last evening with Isabel. It was after dinner that Mr. Longstaffe, saying he wanted a word with Edward, took him into the smoking-room. Mr. Longstaffe had accepted good-naturedly the arrangement which his daughter had told him of and Edward could not imagine what mysterious communication he had now to make. He was not a little perplexed to see that his host was embarrassed. He faltered. He talked of trivial things. At last he blurted it out.

"I guess you've heard of Arnold Jackson," he said, looking at Edward with a frown.

Edward hesitated. His natural truthfulness obliged him to admit a knowledge he would gladly have been able to deny.

"Yes, I have. But it's a long time ago. I guess I didn't pay very much attention."

"There are not many people in Chicago who haven't heard of Arnold Jackson," said Mr. Longstaffe bitterly, "and if there are they'll have no difficulty in finding someone who'll be glad to tell them. Did you know he was Mrs. Longstaffe's brother?"

"Yes, I knew that."

"Of course we've had no communication with him for many years. He left the country as soon as he was able to, and I guess the country wasn't sorry to see the last of him. We understand he lives in Tahiti. My advice to you is to give him a wide berth, but if you do hear anything about him Mrs. Longstaffe and I would be very glad if you'd let us know."

"Sure."

"That was all I wanted to say to you. Now I daresay you'd like to join the ladies."

There are few families that have not among their members one whom, if their neighbours permitted, they would willingly forget, and they are fortunate when the lapse of a generation or two has invested his vagaries with a romantic glamour. But when he is actually alive, if his peculiarities are not of the kind that can be condoned by the phrase, "he is nobody's enemy but his own", a safe one when the culprit has no worse to answer for than alcoholism or wandering affections, the only possible course is silence. And it was this which the Longstaffes had adopted towards Arnold Jackson. They never talked of him. They would not even pass through the street in which he had lived. Too kind to make his wife and children suffer for his misdeeds, they had supported them for years, but on the understanding that they should live in Europe. They did everything they could to blot out all recollection of Arnold Jackson and yet were conscious that the story was as fresh in the public mind as when first the scandal burst upon a gaping world. Arnold Jackson was as black a sheep as any family could suffer from. A wealthy banker, prominent in his church, a philanthropist, a man respected by all, not only for his connections (in his veins ran the blue blood of Chicago), but also for his upright character, he was arrested one day on a charge of fraud; and the dishonesty which the trial brought to light was not of the sort which could be explained by a sudden temptation; it was deliberate and systematic. Arnold Jackson was a rogue. When he was sent to the penitentiary for seven years there were few who did not think he had escaped lightly.

When at the end of this last evening the lovers separated it was with many protestations of devotion. Isabel, all tears, was consoled a little by her certainty of Edward's passionate love. It was a strange feeling that she had. It made her wretched to part from him and yet she was happy because he adored her.

This was more than two years ago.

He had written to her by every mail since then, twenty-four letters in all, for the mail went but once a month, and his letters had been all that a lover's letters should be. They were intimate and charming, humorous sometimes, especially of late, and tender. At first they suggested that he was homesick, they were full of his desire to get back to Chicago and Isabel; and, a little anxiously, she wrote begging him to persevere. She was afraid that he might throw up his opportunity and come racing back. She did not want her lover to lack endurance and she quoted to him the lines:

> "*I could not love thee, dear, so much,*
> *Loved I not honour more.*"

But presently he seemed to settle down and it made Isabel very happy to observe his growing enthusiasm to introduce American methods into that forgotten corner of the world. But she knew him, and at the end of the year, which was the shortest time he could possibly stay in Tahiti, she expected to have to use all her influence to dissuade him from coming home. It was much better that he should learn the business thoroughly, and if they had been able to wait a year there seemed no reason why they should not wait another. She talked it over with Bateman Hunter, always the most generous of friends (during those first few days after Edward went she did not know what she would have done without him), and they decided that Edward's future must stand before everything. It was with relief that she found as the time passed that he made no suggestion of returning.

"He's splendid, isn't he?" she exclaimed to Bateman.

"He's white, through and through."

"Reading between the lines of his letter I know he hates it over there, but he's sticking it out because . . ."

She blushed a little and Bateman, with the grave smile which was so attractive in him, finished the sentence for her.

"Because he loves you."

"It makes me feel so humble," she said.

"You're wonderful, Isabel, you're perfectly wonderful."

But the second year passed and every month Isabel continued to receive a letter from Edward, and presently it began to seem a little strange that he did not speak of coming back. He wrote as though he were settled definitely in Tahiti, and what was more, comfortably settled. She was surprised. Then she read his letters again, all of them, several times; and now, reading between the lines indeed, she was puzzled to notice a change which had escaped her. The later letters were as tender and as delightful as the first, but the tone was different. She was vaguely suspicious of their humour, she had the instinctive mistrust of her sex for that unaccountable quality, and she discerned in them now a flippancy which perplexed her. She was not quite certain that the Edward who wrote to her now was the same Edward that she had known. One afternoon, the day after a mail had arrived from Tahiti, when she was driving with Bateman he said to her:

"Did Edward tell you when he was sailing?"

"No, he didn't mention it. I thought he might have said something to you about it."

"Not a word."

"You know what Edward is," she laughed in reply, "he has no sense of time. If it occurs to you next time you write you might ask him when he's thinking of coming."

Her manner was so unconcerned that only Bateman's acute sensitiveness could have discerned in her request a very urgent desire. He laughed lightly.

"Yes. I'll ask him. I can't imagine what he's thinking about."

A few days later, meeting him again, she noticed that something troubled him. They had been much together since Edward left Chicago; they were both devoted to him and each in his desire to talk of the absent one found a willing listener; the consequence was that Isabel knew every expression of Bateman's face, and his denials now were useless against her keen instinct. Something told her that his harassed look had to do with Edward and she did not rest till she had made him confess.

"The fact is," he said at last, "I heard in a roundabout way that Edward was no longer working for Braunschmidt and Co., and yesterday I took the opportunity to ask Mr. Braunschmidt himself."

"Well?"

"Edward left his employment with them nearly a year ago."

"How strange he should have said nothing about it!"

Bateman hesitated, but he had gone so far now that he was obliged to tell the rest. It made him feel dreadfully embarrassed.

"He was fired."

"In heaven's name what for?"

"It appears they warned him once or twice, and at last they told him to get out. They say he was lazy and incompetent."

"Edward?"

They were silent for a while, and then he saw that Isabel was crying. Instinctively he seized her hand.

"Oh, my dear, don't, don't," he said. "I can't bear to see it."

She was so unstrung that she let her hand rest in his. He tried to console her.

"It's incomprehensible, isn't it? It's so unlike Edward. I can't help feeling there must be some mistake."

She did not say anything for a while, and when she spoke it was hesitatingly.

"Has it struck you that there was anything queer in his letters lately?" she asked, looking away, her eyes all bright with tears.

He did not quite know how to answer.

"I have noticed a change in them," he admitted. "He seems to have lost that high seriousness which I admired so much in him. One would almost think that the things that matter—well, don't matter."

Isabel did not reply. She was vaguely uneasy.

"Perhaps in his answer to your letter he'll say when he's coming home. All we can do is to wait for that."

Another letter came from Edward for each of them, and still he made no mention of his return; but when he wrote he could not have received Bateman's enquiry. The next mail would bring them an answer to that. The next mail came, and Bateman brought Isabel the letter he had just received; but the first glance at his face was enough to tell her that he was disconcerted. She read it through carefully and then, with slightly tightened lips, read it again.

"It's a very strange letter," she said. "I don't quite understand it."

"One might almost think that he was joshing me," said Bateman, flushing.

"It reads like that, but it must be unintentional. That's so unlike Edward."

"He says nothing about coming back."

"If I weren't so confident of his love I should think . . . I hardly know what I should think."

It was then that Bateman had broached the scheme which during the afternoon had formed itself in his brain. The firm, founded by his father, in which he was now a partner, a firm which manufactured all manner of motor vehicles, was about to establish agencies in Honolulu, Sydney, and Wellington; and Bateman proposed that himself should go instead of the manager, who had been suggested. He could return by Tahiti; in fact, travelling from Wellington, it was inevitable to do so; and he could see Edward.

"There's some mystery and I'm going to clear it up. That's the only way to do it."

"Oh, Bateman, how can you be so good and kind?" she exclaimed.

"You know there's nothing in the world I want more than your happiness, Isabel."

She looked at him and she gave him her hands.

"You're wonderful, Bateman. I didn't know there was anyone in the world like you. How can I ever thank you?"

"I don't want your thanks. I only want to be allowed to help you."

She dropped her eyes and flushed a little. She was so used to him that she had forgotten how handsome he was. He was as tall as Edward and as well made, but he was dark and pale of face, while Edward was ruddy. Of course she knew he loved her. It touched her. She felt very tenderly towards him.

It was from this journey that Bateman Hunter was now returned.

The business part of it took him somewhat longer than he expected and he had much time to think of his two friends. He had come to the conclusion that it could be nothing serious that prevented Edward from coming home, a pride, perhaps, which made him determined to make good before he claimed the bride he adored; but it was a pride that must be reasoned with. Isabel was unhappy. Edward must come back to Chicago with him and marry her at once. A position could be found for him in the works of the Hunter Motor Traction and Automobile Company. Bateman, with a bleeding heart, exulted at the prospect of giving happiness to the two persons he loved best in the world at the cost of his own. He would never marry. He would be godfather to the children of Edward and Isabel, and many years later when they were both dead he would tell Isabel's daughter how long, long ago he had loved her mother. Bateman's eyes were veiled with tears when he pictured this scene to himself.

Meaning to take Edward by surprise he had not cabled to announce his arrival, and when at last he landed at Tahiti he allowed a youth, who said he was the son of the house, to lead him to the Hotel de la Fleur. He chuckled when he thought of his friend's amazement on seeing him, the most unexpected of visitors, walk into his office.

"By the way," he asked, as they went along, "can you tell me where I shall find Mr. Edward Barnard?"

"Barnard?" said the youth. "I seem to know the name."

"He's an American. A tall fellow with light brown hair and blue eyes. He's been here over two years."

"Of course. Now I know who you mean. You mean Mr. Jackson's nephew."

"Whose nephew?"

"Mr. Arnold Jackson."

"I don't think we're speaking of the same person," answered Bateman, frigidly.

He was startled. It was queer that Arnold Jackson, known apparently to all and sundry, should live here under the disgraceful name in which he had been convicted. But Bateman could not imagine whom it was that he passed off as his nephew. Mrs. Longstaffe was his only sister and he had never had a brother. The young man by his side talked volubly in an English that had something in it of the intonation of a foreign tongue, and Bateman, with a sidelong glance, saw, what he had not noticed before, that there was in him a good deal of native blood. A touch of hauteur involuntarily entered into his manner. They reached the hotel. When he had arranged about his room Bateman asked to be directed to the premises of Braunschmidt & Co. They were on the front, facing the lagoon, and, glad to feel the solid earth under his feet after eight days at sea, he sauntered down the sunny road to the water's edge. Having found the place he sought, Bateman sent in his card to the manager and was led through a lofty barn-like room, half store and half warehouse, to an office in which sat a stout, spectacled, bald-headed man.

"Can you tell me where I shall find Mr. Edward Barnard? I understand he was in this office for some time."

"That is so. I don't know just where he is."

"But I thought he came here with a particular recommendation from Mr. Braunschmidt. I know Mr. Braunschmidt very well."

The fat man looked at Bateman with shrewd, suspicious eyes. He called to one of the boys in the warehouse.

"Say, Henry, where's Barnard now, d'you know?"

"He's working at Cameron's, I think," came the answer from someone who did not trouble to move.

The fat man nodded.

"If you turn to your left when you get out of here you'll come to Cameron's in about three minutes."

Bateman hesitated.

"I think I should tell you that Edward Barnard is my greatest friend. I was very much surprised when I heard he'd left Braunschmidt & Co."

The fat man's eyes contracted till they seemed like pin-points, and their scrutiny made Bateman so uncomfortable that he felt himself blushing.

"I guess Braunschmidt & Co. and Edward Barnard didn't see eye to eye on certain matters," he replied.

Bateman did not quite like the fellow's manner, so he got up, not without dignity, and with an apology for troubling him bade him good-day. He left the place with a singular feeling that the man he had just interviewed had much to tell him, but no intention of telling it. He walked in the direction indicated and soon found himself at Cameron's. It was a trader's store, such as he had passed half a dozen of on his way, and when he entered the first person he saw, in his shirt-sleeves, measuring out a length of trade cotton, was Edward. It gave him a start to see him engaged in so humble an occupation. But he had scarcely appeared when Edward, looking up, caught sight of him, and gave a joyful cry of surprise.

"Bateman! Who ever thought of seeing you here?"

He stretched his arm across the counter and wrung Bateman's hand. There was no self-consciousness in his manner and the embarrassment was all on Bateman's side.

"Just wait till I've wrapped this package."

With perfect assurance he ran his scissors across the stuff, folded it, made it into a parcel, and handed it to the dark-skinned customer.

"Pay at the desk, please."

Then, smiling, with bright eyes, he turned to Bateman.

"How did you show up here? Gee, I am delighted to see you. Sit down, old man. Make yourself at home."

"We can't talk here. Come along to my hotel. I suppose you can get away?"

This he added with some apprehension.

"Of course I can get away. We're not so business-like as all that in Tahiti." He called out to a Chinese who was standing behind the opposite counter. "Ah-Ling, when the boss comes tell him a friend of mine's just arrived from America and I've gone out to have a drain with him."

"All-light," said the Chinese, with a grin.

Edward slipped on a coat and, putting on his hat, accompanied Bateman out of the store. Bateman attempted to put the matter facetiously.

"I didn't expect to find you selling three and a half yards of rotten cotton to a greasy nigger," he laughed.

"Braunschmidt fired me, you know, and I thought that would do as well as anything else."

Edward's candour seemed to Bateman very surprising, but he thought it indiscreet to pursue the subject.

"I guess you won't make a fortune where you are," he answered, somewhat dryly.

"I guess not. But I earn enough to keep body and soul together, and I'm quite satisfied with that."

"You wouldn't have been two years ago."

"We grow wiser as we grow older," retorted Edward, gaily.

Bateman took a glance at him. Edward was dressed in a suit of shabby white ducks, none too clean, and a large straw hat of native make. He was thinner than he had been, deeply burned by the sun, and he was certainly better-looking than ever. But there was something in his appearance that disconcerted Bateman. He walked with a new jauntiness; there was a carelessness in his demeanour, a gaiety about nothing in particular, which Bateman could not precisely blame, but which exceedingly puzzled him.

"I'm blest if I can see what he's got to be so darned cheerful about," he said to himself.

They arrived at the hotel and sat on the terrace. A Chinese boy brought them cocktails. Edward was most anxious to hear all the news of Chicago and bombarded his friend with eager questions. His interest was natural and sincere. But the odd thing was that it seemed equally divided among a multitude of subjects. He was as eager to know how Bateman's father was as what Isabel was doing. He talked of her without a shade of embarrassment, but she might just as well have been his sister as his promised wife; and before Bateman had done analysing the exact meaning of Edward's remarks he found that the conversation had drifted to his own work and the buildings his father had lately erected. He was determined to bring the conversation back to Isabel and was looking for the occasion when he saw Edward wave his hand cordially. A man was advancing towards them on the terrace, but Bateman's back was turned to him and he could not see him.

"Come and sit down," said Edward gaily.

The new-comer approached. He was a very tall, thin man, in white ducks, with a fine head of curly white hair. His face was thin too, long, with a large, hooked nose and a beautiful, expressive mouth.

"This is my old friend Bateman Hunter. I've told you about him," said Edward, his constant smile breaking on his lips.

"I'm pleased to meet you, Mr. Hunter. I used to know your father."

The stranger held out his hand and took the young man's in a strong, friendly grasp. It was not till then that Edward mentioned the other's name.

"Mr. Arnold Jackson."

Bateman turned white and he felt his hands grow cold. This was

the forger, the convict, this was Isabel's uncle. He did not know
what to say. He tried to conceal his confusion. Arnold Jackson
looked at him with twinkling eyes.

"I daresay my name is familiar to you."

Bateman did not know whether to say yes or no, and what made
it more awkward was that both Jackson and Edward seemed to be
amused. It was bad enough to have forced on him the acquaintance
of the one man on the island he would rather have avoided, but
worse to discern that he was being made a fool of. Perhaps, however,
he had reached this conclusion too quickly, for Jackson, without a
pause, added:

"I understand you're very friendly with the Longstaffes. Mary
Longstaffe is my sister."

Now Bateman asked himself if Arnold Jackson could think him
ignorant of the most terrible scandal that Chicago had ever known.
But Jackson put his hand on Edward's shoulder.

"I can't sit down, Teddie," he said. "I'm busy. But you two boys
had better come up and dine to-night."

"That'll be fine," said Edward.

"It's very kind of you, Mr. Jackson," said Bateman, frigidly, "but
I'm here for so short a time; my boat sails to-morrow, you know;
I think if you'll forgive me, I won't come."

"Oh, nonsense. I'll give you a native dinner. My wife's a wonderful cook. Teddie will show you the way. Come early so as to see the
sunset. I can give you both a shake-down if you like."

"Of course we'll come," said Edward. "There's always the devil
of a row in the hotel on the night a boat arrives and we can have a
good yarn up at the bungalow."

"I can't let you off, Mr. Hunter," Jackson continued with the utmost cordiality. "I want to hear all about Chicago and Mary."

He nodded and walked away before Bateman could say another
word.

"We don't take refusals in Tahiti," laughed Edward. "Besides,
you'll get the best dinner on the island."

"What did he mean by saying his wife was a good cook? I happen
to know his wife's in Geneva."

"That's a long way off for a wife, isn't it?" said Edward. "And
it's a long time since he saw her. I guess it's another wife he's talking
about."

For some time Bateman was silent. His face was set in grave lines.
But looking up he caught the amused look in Edward's eyes, and he
flushed darkly.

"Arnold Jackson is a despicable rogue," he said.

"I greatly fear he is," answered Edward, smiling.

"I don't see how any decent man can have anything to do with him."

"Perhaps I'm not a decent man."

"Do you see much of him, Edward?"

"Yes, quite a lot. He's adopted me as his nephew."

Bateman leaned forward and fixed Edward with his searching eyes.

"Do you like him?"

"Very much."

"But don't you know, doesn't everyone here know, that he's a forger and that he's been a convict? He ought to be hounded out of civilised society."

Edward watched a ring of smoke that floated from his cigar into the still, scented air.

"I suppose he is a pretty unmitigated rascal," he said at last. "And I can't flatter myself that any repentance for his misdeeds offers one an excuse for condoning them. He was a swindler and a hypocrite. You can't get away from it. I never met a more agreeable companion. He's taught me everything I know."

"What has he taught you?" cried Bateman in amazement.

"How to live."

Bateman broke into ironical laughter.

"A fine master. Is it owing to his lessons that you lost the chance of making a fortune and earn your living now by serving behind a counter in a ten-cent store?"

"He has a wonderful personality," said Edward, smiling good-naturedly. "Perhaps you'll see what I mean to-night."

"I'm not going to dine with him if that's what you mean. Nothing would induce me to set foot within that man's house."

"Come to oblige me, Bateman. We've been friends for so many years, you won't refuse me a favour when I ask it."

Edward's tone had in it a quality new to Bateman. Its gentleness was singularly persuasive.

"If you put it like that, Edward, I'm bound to come," he smiled.

Bateman reflected, moreover, that it would be as well to learn what he could about Arnold Jackson. It was plain that he had a great ascendancy over Edward, and if it was to be combated it was necessary to discover in what exactly it consisted. The more he talked with Edward the more conscious he became that a change had taken place in him. He had an instinct that it behoved him to walk warily, and he made up his mind not to broach the real purport of his visit till he saw his way more clearly. He began to talk of one thing and another, of his journey and what he had achieved by it, of politics in Chicago, of this common friend and that, of their days together at college.

At last Edward said he must get back to his work and proposed that he should fetch Bateman at five so that they could drive out together to Arnold Jackson's house.

"By the way, I rather thought you'd be living at this hotel," said Bateman, as he strolled out of the garden with Edward. "I understand it's the only decent one here."

"Not I," laughed Edward. "It's a deal too grand for me. I rent a room just outside the town. It's cheap and clean."

"If I remember right those weren't the points that seemed most important to you when you lived in Chicago."

"Chicago!"

"I don't know what you mean by that, Edward. It's the greatest city in the world."

"I know," said Edward.

Bateman glanced at him quickly, but his face was inscrutable.

"When are you coming back to it?"

"I often wonder," smiled Edward.

This answer, and the manner of it, staggered Bateman, but before he could ask for an explanation Edward waved to a half-caste who was driving a passing motor.

"Give us a ride down, Charlie," he said.

He nodded to Bateman, and ran after the machine that had pulled up a few yards in front. Bateman was left to piece together a mass of perplexing impressions.

Edward called for him in a rickety trap drawn by an old mare, and they drove along a road that ran by the sea. On each side of it were plantations, coconut and vanilla; and now and then they saw a great mango, its fruit yellow and red and purple among the massy green of the leaves, now and then they had a glimpse of the lagoon, smooth and blue, with here and there a tiny islet graceful with tall palms. Arnold Jackson's house stood on a little hill and only a path led to it, so they unharnessed the mare and tied her to a tree, leaving the trap by the side of the road. To Bateman it seemed a happy-go-lucky way of doing things. But when they went up to the house they were met by a tall, handsome native woman, no longer young, with whom Edward cordially shook hands. He introduced Bateman to her.

"This is my friend Mr. Hunter. We're going to dine with you, Lavina."

"All right," she said, with a quick smile. "Arnold ain't back yet."

"We'll go down and bathe. Let us have a couple of pareos."

The woman nodded and went into the house.

"Who is that?" asked Bateman.

"Oh, that's Lavina. She's Arnold's wife."

Bateman tightened his lips, but said nothing. In a moment the woman returned with a bundle, which she gave to Edward; and the two men, scrambling down a steep path, made their way to a grove of coconut trees on the beach. They undressed and Edward showed his friend how to make the strip of red trade cotton which is called a pareo into a very neat pair of bathing-drawers. Soon they were splashing in the warm, shallow water. Edward was in great spirits. He laughed and shouted and sang. He might have been fifteen. Bateman had never seen him so gay, and afterwards when they lay on the beach, smoking cigarettes, in the limpid air, there was such an irresistible light-heartedness in him that Bateman was taken aback.

"You seem to find life mighty pleasant," said he.

"I do."

They heard a soft movement and looking round saw that Arnold Jackson was coming towards them.

"I thought I'd come down and fetch you two boys back," he said. "Did you enjoy your bathe, Mr. Hunter?"

"Very much," said Bateman.

Arnold Jackson, no longer in spruce ducks, wore nothing but a pareo round his loins and walked barefoot. His body was deeply browned by the sun. With his long, curling white hair and his ascetic face he made a fantastic figure in the native dress, but he bore himself without a trace of self-consciousness.

"If you're ready we'll go right up," said Jackson.

"I'll just put on my clothes," said Bateman.

"Why, Teddie, didn't you bring a pareo for your friend?"

"I guess he'd rather wear clothes," smiled Edward.

"I certainly would," answered Bateman, grimly, as he saw Edward gird himself in the loincloth and stand ready to start before he himself had got his shirt on.

"Won't you find it rough walking without your shoes?" he asked Edward. "It struck me the path was a trifle rocky."

"Oh, I'm used to it."

"It's a comfort to get into a pareo when one gets back from town," said Jackson. "If you were going to stay here I should strongly recommend you to adopt it. It's one of the most sensible costumes I have ever come across. It's cool, convenient, and inexpensive."

They walked up to the house, and Jackson took them into a large room with white-washed walls and an open ceiling in which a table was laid for dinner. Bateman noticed that it was set for five.

"Eva, come and show yourself to Teddie's friend, and then shake us a cocktail," called Jackson.

Then he led Bateman to a long low window.

"Look at that," he said, with a dramatic gesture. "Look well."

Below them coconut trees tumbled down steeply to the lagoon, and the lagoon in the evening light had the colour, tender and varied, of a dove's breast. On a creek, at a little distance, were the clustered huts of a native village, and towards the reef was a canoe, sharply silhouetted, in which were a couple of natives fishing. Then, beyond, you saw the vast calmness of the Pacific and twenty miles away, airy and unsubstantial like the fabric of a poet's fancy, the unimaginable beauty of the island which is called Murea. It was all so lovely that Bateman stood abashed.

"I've never seen anything like it," he said at last.

Arnold Jackson stood staring in front of him, and in his eyes was a dreamy softness. His thin, thoughtful face was very grave. Bateman, glancing at it, was once more conscious of its intense spirituality.

"Beauty," murmured Arnold Jackson. "You seldom see beauty face to face. Look at it well, Mr. Hunter, for what you see now you will never see again, since the moment is transitory, but it will be an imperishable memory in your heart. You touch eternity."

His voice was deep and resonant. He seemed to breathe forth the purest idealism, and Bateman had to urge himself to remember that the man who spoke was a criminal and a cruel cheat. But Edward, as though he heard a sound, turned round quickly.

"Here is my daughter, Mr. Hunter."

Bateman shook hands with her. She had dark, splendid eyes and a red mouth tremulous with laughter; but her skin was brown, and her curling hair, rippling down her shoulders, was coal-black. She wore but one garment, a Mother Hubbard of pink cotton, her feet were bare, and she was crowned with a wreath of white scented flowers. She was a lovely creature. She was like a goddess of the Polynesian spring.

She was a little shy, but not more shy than Bateman, to whom the whole situation was highly embarrassing, and it did not put him at his ease to see this sylph-like thing take a shaker and with a practised hand mix three cocktails.

"Let us have a kick in them, child," said Jackson.

She poured them out and smiling delightfully handed one to each of the men. Bateman flattered himself on his skill in the subtle art of shaking cocktails and he was not a little astonished, on tasting this one, to find that it was excellent. Jackson laughed proudly when he saw his guest's involuntary look of appreciation.

"Not bad, is it? I taught the child myself, and in the old days in Chicago I considered that there wasn't a bar-tender in the city that could hold a candle to me. When I had nothing better to do in the penitentiary I used to amuse myself by thinking out new cocktails, but when you come down to brass-tacks there's nothing to beat a dry Martini."

Bateman felt as though someone had given him a violent blow on the funny-bone and he was conscious that he turned red and then white. But before he could think of anything to say a native boy brought in a great bowl of soup and the whole party sat down to dinner. Arnold Jackson's remark seemed to have aroused in him a train of recollections, for he began to talk of his prison days. He talked quite naturally, without malice, as though he were relating his experiences at a foreign university. He addressed himself to Bateman, and Bateman was confused and then confounded. He saw Edward's eyes fixed on him and there was in them a flicker of amusement. He blushed scarlet, for it struck him that Jackson was making a fool of him, and then because he felt absurd—and knew there was no reason why he should—he grew angry. Arnold Jackson was impudent—there was no other word for it—and his callousness, whether assumed or not, was outrageous. The dinner proceeded. Bateman was asked to eat sundry messes, raw fish and he knew not what, which only his civility induced him to swallow, but which he was amazed to find very good eating. Then an incident happened which to Bateman was the most mortifying experience of the evening. There was a little circlet of flowers in front of him, and for the sake of conversation he hazarded a remark about it.

"It's a wreath that Eva made for you," said Jackson, "but I guess she was too shy to give it you."

Bateman took it up in his hand and made a polite little speech of thanks to the girl.

"You must put it on," she said, with a smile and a blush.

"I? I don't think I'll do that."

"It's the charming custom of the country," said Arnold Jackson.

There was one in front of him and he placed it on his hair. Edward did the same.

"I guess I'm not dressed for the part," said Bateman, uneasily.

"Would you like a pareo?" said Eva quickly. "I'll get you one in a minute."

"No, thank you. I'm quite comfortable as I am."

C

"Show him how to put it on, Eva," said Edward.

At that moment Bateman hated his greatest friend. Eva got up from the table and with much laughter placed the wreath on his black hair.

"It suits you very well," said Mrs. Jackson. "Don't it suit him, Arnold?"

"Of course it does."

Bateman sweated at every pore.

"Isn't it a pity it's dark?" said Eva. "We could photograph you all three together."

Bateman thanked his stars it was. He felt that he must look prodigiously foolish in his blue serge suit and high collar—very neat and gentlemanly—with that ridiculous wreath of flowers on his head. He was seething with indignation, and he had never in his life exercised more self-control than now when he presented an affable exterior. He was furious with that old man, sitting at the head of the table, half-naked, with his saintly face and the flowers on his handsome white locks. The whole position was monstrous.

Then dinner came to an end, and Eva and her mother remained to clear away while the three men sat on the verandah. It was very warm and the air was scented with the white flowers of the night. The full moon, sailing across an unclouded sky, made a pathway on the broad sea that led to the boundless realms of Forever. Arnold Jackson began to talk. His voice was rich and musical. He talked now of the natives and of the old legends of the country. He told strange stories of the past, stories of hazardous expeditions into the unknown, of love and death, of hatred and revenge. He told of the adventurers who had discovered those distant islands, of the sailors who, settling in them, had married the daughters of great chieftains, and of the beach-combers who had led their varied lives on those silvery shores. Bateman, mortified and exasperated, at first listened sullenly, but presently some magic in the words possessed him and he sat entranced. The mirage of romance obscured the light of common day. Had he forgotten that Arnold Jackson had a tongue of silver, a tongue by which he had charmed vast sums out of the credulous public, a tongue which very nearly enabled him to escape the penalty of his crimes? No one had a sweeter eloquence, and no one had a more acute sense of climax. Suddenly he rose.

"Well, you two boys haven't seen one another for a long time. I shall leave you to have a yarn. Teddie will show you your quarters when you want to go to bed."

"Oh, but I wasn't thinking of spending the night, Mr. Jackson," said Bateman.

"You'll find it more comfortable. We'll see that you're called in good time."

Then with a courteous shake of the hand, stately as though he were a bishop in canonicals, Arnold Jackson took leave of his guest.

"Of course I'll drive you back to Papeete if you like," said Edward, "but I advise you to stay. It's bully driving in the early morning."

For a few minutes neither of them spoke. Bateman wondered how he should begin on the conversation which all the events of the day made him think more urgent.

"When are you coming back to Chicago?" he asked, suddenly.

For a moment Edward did not answer. Then he turned rather lazily to look at his friend and smiled.

"I don't know. Perhaps never."

"What in heaven's name do you mean?" cried Bateman.

"I'm very happy here. Wouldn't it be folly to make a change?"

"Man alive, you can't live here all your life. This is no life for a man. It's a living death. Oh, Edward, come away at once, before it's too late. I've felt that something was wrong. You're infatuated with the place, you've succumbed to evil influences, but it only requires a wrench, and when you're free from these surroundings you'll thank all the gods there be. You'll be like a dope-fiend when he's broken from his drug. You'll see then that for two years you've been breathing poisoned air. You can't imagine what a relief it will be when you fill your lungs once more with the fresh, pure air of your native country."

He spoke quickly, the words tumbling over one another in his excitement, and there was in his voice sincere and affectionate emotion. Edward was touched.

"It is good of you to care so much, old friend."

"Come with me to-morrow, Edward. It was a mistake that you ever came to this place. This is no life for you."

"You talk of this sort of life and that. How do you think a man gets the best out of life?"

"Why, I should have thought there could be no two answers to that. By doing his duty, by hard work, by meeting all the obligations of his state and station."

"And what is his reward?"

"His reward is the consciousness of having achieved what he set out to do."

"It all sounds a little portentous to me," said Edward, and in the lightness of the night Bateman could see that he was smiling. "I'm afraid you'll think I've degenerated sadly. There are several things

I think now which I daresay would have seemed outrageous to me three years ago."

"Have you learnt them from Arnold Jackson?" asked Bateman, scornfully.

"You don't like him? Perhaps you couldn't be expected to. I didn't when I first came. I had just the same prejudice as you. He's a very extraordinary man. You saw for yourself that he makes no secret of the fact that he was in a penitentiary. I do not know that he regrets it or the crimes that led him there. The only complaint he ever made in my hearing was that when he came out his health was impaired. I think he does not know what remorse is. He is completely unmoral. He accepts everything and he accepts himself as well. He's generous and kind."

"He always was," interrupted Bateman, "on other people's money."

"I've found him a very good friend. Is it unnatural that I should take a man as I find him?"

"The result is that you lose the distinction between right and wrong."

"No, they remain just as clearly divided in my mind as before, but what has become a little confused in me is the distinction between the bad man and the good one. Is Arnold Jackson a bad man who does good things or a good man who does bad things? It's a difficult question to answer. Perhaps we make too much of the difference between one man and another. Perhaps even the best of us are sinners and the worst of us are saints. Who knows?"

"You will never persuade me that white is black and that black is white," said Bateman.

"I'm sure I shan't, Bateman."

Bateman could not understand why the flicker of a smile crossed Edward's lips when he thus agreed with him. Edward was silent for a minute.

"When I saw you this morning, Bateman," he said then, "I seemed to see myself as I was two years ago. The same collar, and the same shoes, the same blue suit, the same energy. The same determination. By God, I was energetic. The sleepy methods of this place made my blood tingle. I went about and everywhere I saw possibilities for development and enterprise. There were fortunes to be made here. It seemed to me absurd that the copra should be taken away from here in sacks and the oil extracted in America. It would be far more economical to do all that on the spot, with cheap labour, and save freight, and I saw already the vast factories springing up on the island. Then the way they extracted it from the coconut seemed to me hopelessly inadequate, and I invented a machine which divided the nut and scooped out the meat at the rate of two hundred and forty an hour. The harbour was not large enough. I made plans to enlarge it, then to form a syndicate to buy land, put up two or three large hotels, and bungalows for occasional residents; I had a scheme for improving the steamer service in order to attract visitors from California. In twenty years, instead of this half-French, lazy little town of Papeete I saw a great American city with ten-storey buildings and street-cars, a theatre and an opera house, a stock exchange and a mayor."

"But go ahead, Edward," cried Bateman, springing up from the chair in excitement. "You've got the ideas and the capacity. Why, you'll become the richest man between Australia and the States."

Edward chuckled softly.

"But I don't want to," he said.

"Do you mean to say you don't want money, big money, money running into millions? Do you know what you can do with it? Do you know the power it brings? And if you don't care about it for yourself think what you can do, opening new channels for human enterprise, giving occupation to thousands. My brain reels at the visions your words have conjured up."

"Sit down, then, my dear Bateman," laughed Edward. "My machine for cutting the coconuts will always remain unused, and so far as I'm concerned street-cars shall never run in the idle streets of Papeete."

Bateman sank heavily into his chair.

"I don't understand you," he said.

"It came upon me little by little. I came to like the life here, with its ease and its leisure, and the people, with their good-nature and their happy smiling faces. I began to think. I'd never had time to do that before. I began to read."

"You always read."

"I read for examinations. I read in order to be able to hold my own in conversation. I read for instruction. Here I learned to read for pleasure. I learned to talk. Do you know that conversation is one of the greatest pleasures in life? But it wants leisure. I'd always been too busy before. And gradually all the life that had seemed so important to me began to seem rather trivial and vulgar. What is the use of all this hustle and this constant striving? I think of Chicago now and I see a dark, grey city, all stone—it is like a prison —and a ceaseless turmoil. And what does all that activity amount to? Does one get there the best out of life? Is that what we come into the world for, to hurry to an office, and work hour after hour till night, then hurry home and dine and go to a theatre? Is that how I must spend my youth? Youth lasts so short a time, Bateman. And when I am old, what have I to look forward to? To hurry from my home in the morning to my office and work hour after hour till night, and then hurry home again, and dine and go to a theatre? That may be worth while if you make a fortune; I don't know, it depends on your nature; but if you don't, is it worth while then? I want to make more out of my life than that, Bateman."

"What do you value in life then?"

"I'm afraid you'll laugh at me. Beauty, truth, and goodness."

"Don't you think you can have those in Chicago?"

"Some men can, perhaps, but not I." Edward sprang up now. "I tell you when I think of the life I led in the old days I am filled with horror," he cried violently. "I tremble with fear when I think of the danger I have escaped. I never knew I had a soul till I found it here. If I had remained a rich man I might have lost it for good and all."

"I don't know how you can say that," cried Bateman indignantly. "We often used to have discussions about it."

"Yes, I know. They were about as effectual as the discussions of deaf mutes about harmony. I shall never come back to Chicago, Bateman."

"And what about Isabel?"

Edward walked to the edge of the verandah and leaning over looked intently at the blue magic of the night. There was a slight smile on his face when he turned back to Bateman.

"Isabel is infinitely too good for me. I admire her more than any woman I have ever known. She has a wonderful brain and she's as good as she's beautiful. I respect her energy and her ambition. She was born to make a success of life. I am entirely unworthy of her."

"She doesn't think so."

"But you must tell her so, Bateman."

"I?" cried Bateman. "I'm the last person who could ever do that."

Edward had his back to the vivid light of the moon and his face could not be seen. Is it possible that he smiled again?

"It's no good your trying to conceal anything from her, Bateman. With her quick intelligence she'll turn you inside out in five minutes. You'd better make a clean breast of it right away."

"I don't know what you mean. Of course I shall tell her I've seen you." Bateman spoke in some agitation. "Honestly I don't know what to say to her."

"Tell her that I haven't made good. Tell her that I'm not only poor, but that I'm content to be poor. Tell her I was fired from my job because I was idle and inattentive. Tell her all you've seen to-night and all I've told you."

The idea which on a sudden flashed through Bateman's brain brought him to his feet and in uncontrollable perturbation he faced Edward.

"Man alive, don't you want to marry her?"

Edward looked at him gravely.

"I can never ask her to release me. If she wishes to hold me to my word I will do my best to make her a good and loving husband."

"Do you wish me to give her that message, Edward? Oh, I can't. It's terrible. It's never dawned on her for a moment that you don't want to marry her. She loves you. How can I inflict such a mortification on her?"

Edward smiled again.

"Why don't you marry her yourself, Bateman? You've been in love with her for ages. You're perfectly suited to one another. You'll make her very happy."

"Don't talk to me like that. I can't bear it."

"I resign in your favour, Bateman. You are the better man."

There was something in Edward's tone that made Bateman look up quickly, but Edward's eyes were grave and unsmiling. Bateman did not know what to say. He was disconcerted. He wondered whether Edward could possibly suspect that he had come to Tahiti on a special errand. And though he knew it was horrible he could not prevent the exultation in his heart.

"What will you do if Isabel writes and puts an end to her engagement with you?" he said, slowly.

"Survive," said Edward.

Bateman was so agitated that he did not hear the answer.

"I wish you had ordinary clothes on," he said, somewhat irritably. "It's such a tremendously serious decision you're taking. That fantastic costume of yours makes it seem terribly casual."

"I assure you, I can be just as solemn in a pareo and a wreath of roses, as in a high hat and a cut-away coat."

Then another thought struck Bateman.

"Edward, it's not for my sake you're doing this? I don't know, but perhaps this is going to make a tremendous difference to my future. You're not sacrificing yourself for me? I couldn't stand for that, you know."

"No, Bateman, I have learnt not to be silly and sentimental here. I should like you and Isabel to be happy, but I have not the least wish to be unhappy myself."

The answer somewhat chilled Bateman. It seemed to him a little cynical. He would not have been sorry to act a noble part.

"Do you mean to say you're content to waste your life here? It's nothing less than suicide. When I think of the great hopes you had when we left college it seems terrible that you should be content to be no more than a salesman in a cheap-John store."

"Oh, I'm only doing that for the present, and I'm gaining a great deal of valuable experience. I have another plan in my head. Arnold Jackson has a small island in the Paumotas, about a thousand miles from here, a ring of land round a lagoon. He's planted coconut there. He's offered to give it me."

"Why should he do that?" asked Bateman.

"Because if Isabel releases me I shall marry his daughter."

"You?" Bateman was thunderstruck. "You can't marry a half-caste. You wouldn't be so crazy as that."

"She's a good girl, and she has a sweet and gentle nature. I think she would make me very happy."

"Are you in love with her?"

"I don't know," answered Edward reflectively. "I'm not in love with her as I was in love with Isabel. I worshipped Isabel. I thought she was the most wonderful creature I had ever seen. I was not half good enough for her. I don't feel like that with Eva. She's like a beautiful exotic flower that must be sheltered from bitter winds. I want to protect her. No one ever thought of protecting Isabel. I think she loves me for myself and not for what I may become. Whatever happens to me I shall never disappoint her. She suits me."

Bateman was silent.

"We must turn out early in the morning," said Edward at last. "It's really about time we went to bed."

Then Bateman spoke and his voice had in it a genuine distress.

"I'm so bewildered, I don't know what to say. I came here because I thought something was wrong. I thought you hadn't succeeded in what you set out to do and were ashamed to come back when you'd failed. I never guessed I should be faced with this. I'm so desperately sorry, Edward. I'm so disappointed. I hoped you would do great things. It's almost more than I can bear to think of you wasting your talents and your youth and your chance in this lamentable way."

"Don't be grieved, old friend," said Edward. "I haven't failed. I've succeeded. You can't think with what zest I look forward to life, how full it seems to me and how significant. Sometimes, when you are married to Isabel, you will think of me. I shall build myself a house on my coral island and I shall live there, looking after my trees—getting the fruit out of the nuts in the same old way that they have done for unnumbered years—I shall grow all sorts of things in my garden, and I shall fish. There will be enough work to keep me busy and not enough to make me dull. I shall have my books and Eva, children, I hope, and above all, the infinite variety of the sea and the sky, the freshness of the dawn and the beauty of the sunset, and the rich magnificence of the night. I shall make a garden out of what so short a while ago was a wilderness. I shall have created something. The years will pass insensibly, and when I am an old man I hope that I shall be able to look back on a happy, simple, peaceful life. In my small way I too shall have lived in beauty. Do you think it is so little to have enjoyed contentment? We know that it will profit a man little if he gain the whole world and lose his soul. I think I have won mine."

Edward led him to a room in which there were two beds and he threw himself on one of them. In ten minutes Bateman knew by his regular breathing, peaceful as a child's, that Edward was asleep. But for his part he had no rest, he was disturbed in mind, and it was not till the dawn crept into the room, ghostlike and silent, that he fell asleep.

Bateman finished telling Isabel his long story. He had hidden nothing from her except what he thought would wound her or what made himself ridiculous. He did not tell her that he had been forced to sit at dinner with a wreath of flowers round his head and he did not tell her that Edward was prepared to marry her uncle's half-caste daughter the moment she set him free. But perhaps Isabel had keener intuitions than he knew, for as he went on with his tale her eyes grew colder and her lips closed upon one another more tightly. Now and then she looked at him closely, and if he had been less intent on his narrative he might have wondered at her expression.

"What was this girl like?" she asked when he finished. "Uncle Arnold's daughter. Would you say there was any resemblance between her and me?"

Bateman was surprised at the question.

"It never struck me. You know I've never had eyes for anyone but you and I could never think that anyone was like you. Who could resemble you?"

"Was she pretty?" said Isabel, smiling slightly at his words.

"I suppose so. I daresay some men would say she was very beautiful."

"Well, it's of no consequence. I don't think we need give her any more of our attention."

What are you going to do, Isabel?" he asked then.

Isabel looked down at the hand which still bore the ring Edward had given her on their betrothal.

"I wouldn't let Edward break our engagement because I thought it would be an incentive to him. I wanted to be an inspiration to him. I thought if anything could enable him to achieve success it was the thought that I loved him. I have done all I could. It's hopeless. It would only be weakness on my part not to recognise the facts. Poor Edward, he's nobody's enemy but his own. He was a dear, nice fellow, but there was something lacking in him, I suppose it was backbone. I hope he'll be happy."

She slipped the ring off her finger and placed it on the table. Bateman watched her with a heart beating so rapidly that he could hardly breathe.

"You're wonderful, Isabel, you're simply wonderful."

She smiled, and, standing up, held out her hand to him.

"How can I ever thank you for what you've done for me?" she said. "You have done me a great service. I knew I could trust you."

He took her hand and held it. She had never looked more beautiful.

"Oh, Isabel, I would do so much more for you than that. You know that I only ask to be allowed to love and serve you."

"You're so strong, Bateman," she sighed. "It gives me such a delicious feeling of confidence."

"Isabel, I adore you."

He hardly knew how the inspiration had come to him, but suddenly he clasped her in his arms; she, all unresisting, smiled into his eyes.

"Isabel, you know I wanted to marry you the very first day I saw you," he cried passionately.

"Then why on earth didn't you ask me?" she replied.

She loved him. He could hardly believe it was true. She gave him her lovely lips to kiss. And as he held her in his arms he had a vision of the works of the Hunter Motor Traction and Automobile Company growing in size and importance till they covered a hundred acres, and of the millions of motors they would turn out, and of the great collection of pictures he would form which should beat anything they had in New York. He would wear horn spectacles. And she, with the delicious pressure of his arms about her, sighed with happiness, for she thought of the exquisite house she would have, full of antique furniture, and of the concerts she would give, and of the *thés dansants*, and the dinners to which only the most cultured people would come.

"Poor Edward," she sighed.

Honolulu

THE wise traveller travels only in imagination. An old Frenchman (he was really a Savoyard) once wrote a book called *Voyage autour de ma Chambre*. I have not read it and do not even know what it is about, but the title stimulates my fancy. In such a journey I could circumnavigate the globe. An eikon by the chimney-piece can take me to Russia with its great forests of birch and its white, domed churches. The Volga is wide, and at the end of a straggling village, in the wine-shop, bearded men in rough sheepskin coats sit drinking. I stand on the little hill from which Napoleon first saw Moscow and I look upon the vastness of the city. I will go down and see the people whom I know more intimately than so many of my friends, Alyosha, and Vronsky, and a dozen more. But my eyes fall on a piece of porcelain and I smell the acrid odours of China. I am borne in a chair along a narrow causeway between the padi fields, or else I skirt a tree-clad mountain. My bearers chat gaily as they trudge along in the bright morning and every now and then, distant and mysterious, I hear the deep sound of a monastery bell. In the streets of Peking there is a motley crowd and it scatters to allow passage to a string of camels, stepping delicately, that bring skins and strange drugs from the stony deserts of Mongolia. In England, in London, there are certain afternoons in winter when the clouds hang heavy and low and the light is so bleak that your heart sinks, but then you can look out of your window, and you see the coconut trees crowded upon the beach of a coral island. The strand is silvery and when you walk along in the sunshine it is so dazzling that you can hardly bear to look at it. Overhead the mynah birds are making a great to-do, and the surf beats ceaselessly against the reef. Those are the best journeys, the journeys that you take at your own fireside, for then you lose none of your illusions.

But there are people who take salt in their coffee. They say it gives it a tang, a savour, which is peculiar and fascinating. In the same way there are certain places, surrounded by a halo of romance, to which the inevitable disillusionment which you must experience on seeing them gives a singular spice. You had expected something wholly beautiful and you get an impression which is infinitely more complicated than any that beauty can give you. It is like the weakness in the character of a great man which may make him less admirable but certainly makes him more interesting.

Nothing had prepared me for Honolulu. It is so far away from Europe, it is reached after so long a journey from San Francisco, so strange and so charming associations are attached to the name, that at first I could hardly believe my eyes. I do not know that I had formed in my mind any very exact picture of what I expected, but what I found caused me a great surprise. It is a typical western city. Shacks are cheek by jowl with stone mansions: dilapidated frame houses stand next door to smart stores with plate-glass windows; electric cars rumble noisily along the streets; and motors, Fords, Buicks, Packards, line the pavement. The shops are filled with all the necessities of American civilisation. Every third house is a bank and every fifth the agency of a steamship company.

Along the streets crowd an unimaginable assortment of people. The Americans, ignoring the climate, wear black coats and high, starched collars, straw hats, soft hats, and bowlers. The Kanakas, pale brown, with crisp hair, have nothing on but a shirt and a pair of trousers; but the half-breeds are very smart with flaring ties and patent-leather boots. The Japanese, with their obsequious smile, are neat and trim in white duck, while their women walk a step or two behind them, in native dress, with a baby on their backs. The Japanese children, in bright coloured frocks, their little heads shaven, look like quaint dolls. Then there are the Chinese. The men, fat and prosperous, wear their American clothes oddly, but the women are enchanting with their tightly-dressed black hair, so neat that you feel it can never be disarranged, and they are very clean in their tunics and trousers, white, or powder-blue, or black. Lastly there are the Filipinos, the men in huge straw hats, the women in bright yellow muslin with great puffed sleeves.

It is the meeting-place of East and West. The very new rubs shoulders with the immeasurably old. And if you have not found the romance you expected you have come upon something singularly intriguing. All these strange people live close to each other, with different languages and different thoughts; they believe in different gods and they have different values; two passions alone they share, love and hunger. And somehow as you watch them you have an impression of extraordinary vitality. Though the air is so soft and the sky so blue, you have, I know not why, a feeling of something hotly passionate that beats like a throbbing pulse through the crowd. Though the native policeman at the corner, standing on a platform, with a white club to direct the traffic, gives the scene an air of respectability, you cannot but feel that it is a respectability only of the surface; a little below there is darkness and mystery. It gives you just that thrill, with a little catch at the heart, that you have when at night in the forest the silence trembles on a sudden with the low, insistent beating of a drum. You are all expectant of I know not what.

If I have dwelt on the incongruity of Honolulu, it is because just this, to my mind, gives its point to the story I want to tell. It is a story of primitive superstition, and it startles me that anything of the sort should survive in a civilisation which, if not very distinguished, is certainly very elaborate. I cannot get over the fact that such incredible things should happen, or at least be thought to happen, right in the middle, so to speak, of telephones, tram-cars, and daily papers. And the friend who showed me Honolulu had the same incongruity which I felt from the beginning was its most striking characteristic.

He was an American named Winter and I had brought a letter of introduction to him from an acquaintance in New York. He was a man between forty and fifty, with scanty black hair, grey at the temples, and a sharp-featured, thin face. His eyes had a twinkle in them and his large horn spectacles gave him a demureness which was not a little diverting. He was tall rather than otherwise and very spare. He was born in Honolulu and his father had a large store which sold hosiery and all such goods, from tennis racquets to tarpaulins, as a man of fashion could require. It was a prosperous business and I could well understand the indignation of Winter *père* when his son, refusing to go into it, had announced his determination to be an actor. My friend spent twenty years on the stage, sometimes in New York, but more often on the road, for his gifts were small; but at last, being no fool, he came to the conclusion that it was better to sell sock-suspenders in Honolulu than to play small parts in Cleveland, Ohio. He left the stage and went into the business. I think after the hazardous existence he had lived so long, he thoroughly enjoyed the luxury of driving a large car and living in a beautiful house near the golf-course, and I am quite sure, since he was a man of parts, he managed the business competently. But he could not bring himself entirely to break his connection with the arts and since he might no longer act he began to paint. He took me to his studio and showed me his work. It was not at all bad, but not what I should have expected from him. He painted nothing but still life, very small pictures, perhaps eight by ten; and he painted very delicately, with the utmost finish. He had evidently a passion for detail. His fruit pieces reminded you of the fruit in a picture by Ghirlandajo. While you marvelled a little at his patience, you could not help being impressed by his dexterity. I imagine that he failed as an actor because his effects, carefully studied, were neither bold nor broad enough to get across the footlights.

I was entertained by the proprietary, yet ironical air with which he showed me the city. He thought in his heart that there was none in the United States to equal it, but he saw quite clearly that his attitude was comic. He drove me round to the various buildings and swelled with satisfaction when I expressed a proper admiration for their architecture. He showed me the houses of rich men.

"That's the Stubbs' house," he said. "It cost a hundred thousand dollars to build. The Stubbses are one of our best families. Old man Stubbs came here as a missionary more than seventy years ago."

He hesitated a little and looked at me with twinkling eyes through his big round spectacles.

"All our best families are missionary families," he said. "You're not very much in Honolulu unless your father or your grandfather converted the heathen."

"Is that so?"

"Do you know your Bible?"

"Fairly," I answered.

"There is a text which says: The fathers have eaten sour grapes and the children's teeth are set on edge. I guess it runs differently in Honolulu. The fathers brought Christianity to the Kanaka and the children jumped his land."

"Heaven helps those who help themselves," I murmured.

"It surely does. By the time the natives of this island had embraced Christianity they had nothing else they could afford to embrace. The kings gave the missionaries land as a mark of esteem, and the missionaries bought land by way of laying up treasure in heaven. It surely was a good investment. One missionary left the business—I think one may call it a business without offence—and became a land agent, but that is an exception. Mostly it was their sons who looked after the commercial side of the concern. Oh, it's a fine thing to have a father who came here fifty years ago to spread the faith."

But he looked at his watch.

"Gee, it's stopped. That means it's time to have a cocktail."

We sped along an excellent road, bordered with red hibiscus, and came back into the town.

"Have you been to the Union Saloon?"

"Not yet."

"We'll go there."

I knew it was the most famous spot in Honolulu and I entered it with a lively curiosity. You get to it by a narrow passage from King Street, and in the passage are offices, so that thirsty souls may be supposed bound for one of these just as well as for the saloon. It is a large square room, with three entrances, and opposite the bar, which runs the length of it, two corners have been partitioned off into little cubicles. Legend states that they were built so that King Kalakaua might drink there without being seen by his subjects, and it is pleasant to think that in one or other of these he may have sat over his bottle, a coal-black potentate, with Robert Louis Stevenson. There is a portrait of him, in oils, in a rich gold frame; but there are also two prints of Queen Victoria. On the walls, besides, are old line engravings of the eighteenth century, one of which, and heaven knows how it got there, is after a theatrical picture by De Wilde; and there are oleographs from the Christmas supplements of the *Graphic* and the *Illustrated London News* of twenty years ago. Then there are advertisements of whisky, gin, champagne, and beer; and photographs of baseball teams and of native orchestras.

The place seemed to belong not to the modern, hustling world that I had left in the bright street outside, but to one that was dying. It had the savour of the day before yesterday. Dingy and dimly lit, it had a vaguely mysterious air and you could imagine that it would be a fit scene for shady transactions. It suggested a more lurid time, when ruthless men carried their lives in their hands, and violent deeds diapered the monotony of life.

When I went in, the saloon was fairly full. A group of business men stood together at the bar, discussing affairs, and in a corner two Kanakas were drinking. Two or three men who might have been store-keepers were shaking dice. The rest of the company plainly followed the sea; they were captains of tramps, first mates, and engineers. Behind the bar, busily making the Honolulu cocktail for which the place was famous, served two large half-castes, in white, fat, clean-shaven and dark-skinned, with thick, curly hair and large bright eyes.

Winter seemed to know more than half the company, and when we made our way to the bar a little fat man in spectacles, who was standing by himself, offered him a drink.

"No, you have one with me, Captain," said Winter.

He turned to me.

"I want you to know Captain Butler."

The little man shook hands with me. We began to talk, but, my attention distracted by my surroundings, I took small notice of him, and after we had each ordered a cocktail we separated. When we had got into the motor again and were driving away, Winter said to me:

"I'm glad we ran up against Butler. I wanted you to meet him. What did you think of him?"

"I don't know that I thought very much of him at all," I answered.

"Do you believe in the supernatural?"

"I don't exactly know that I do," I smiled.

"A very queer thing happened to him a year or two ago. You ought to have him tell you about it."

"What sort of thing?"

Winter did not answer my question.

"I have no explanation of it myself," he said. "But there's no doubt about the facts. Are you interested in things like that?"

"Things like what?"

"Spells and magic and all that."

"I've never met anyone who wasn't."

Winter paused for a moment.

"I guess I won't tell you myself. You ought to hear it from his own lips so that you can judge. How are you fixed up for to-night?"

"I've got nothing on at all."

"Well, I'll get hold of him between now and then and see if we can't go down to his ship."

Winter told me something about him. Captain Butler had spent all his life on the Pacific. He had been in much better circumstances than he was now, for he had been first officer and then captain of a passenger-boat plying along the coast of California, but he had lost his ship and a number of passengers had been drowned.

"Drink, I guess," said Winter.

Of course there had been an enquiry, which had cost him his certificate, and then he drifted further afield. For some years he had knocked about the South Seas, but he was now in command of a small schooner which sailed between Honolulu and the various islands of the group. It belonged to a Chinese to whom the fact that his skipper had no certificate meant only that he could be had for lower wages, and to have a white man in charge was always an advantage.

And now that I had heard this about him I took the trouble to remember more exactly what he was like. I recalled his round spectacles and the round blue eyes behind them, and so gradually reconstructed him before my mind. He was a little man, without angles, plump, with a round face like the full moon and a little fat round nose. He had fair short hair, and he was red-faced and clean-shaven. He had plump hands, dimpled on the knuckles, and short fat legs. He was a jolly soul, and the tragic experience he had gone through seemed to have left him unscarred. Though he must have been thirty-four or thirty-five he looked much younger. But after all I had given him but a superficial attention, and now that I knew of this catastrophe, which had obviously ruined his life, I promised myself that when I saw him again I would take more careful note of him. It is very curious to observe the differences of emotional response that you find in different people. Some can go through terrible battles, the fear of imminent death and unimaginable horrors, and preserve their soul unscathed, while with others the trembling of the moon on a solitary sea or the song of a bird in a thicket will cause a convulsion great enough to transform their entire being. Is it due to strength or weakness, want of imagination or instability of character? I do not know. When I called up in my fancy that scene of shipwreck, with the shrieks of the drowning and the terror, and then later, the ordeal of the enquiry, the bitter grief of those who sorrowed for the lost, and the harsh things he must have read of himself in the papers, the shame and the disgrace, it came to me with a shock to remember that Captain Butler had talked with the frank obscenity of a schoolboy of the Hawaiian girls and of Iwelei, the Red Light district, and of his successful adventures. He laughed readily, and one would have thought he could never laugh again. I remembered his shining, white teeth; they were his best feature. He began to interest me, and thinking of him and of his gay insouciance I forgot the particular story, to hear which I was to see him again. I wanted to see him rather to find out if I could a little more what sort of man he was.

Winter made the necessary arrangements and after dinner we went down to the water front. The ship's boat was waiting for us and we rowed out. The schooner was anchored some way across the harbour, not far from the breakwater. We came alongside, and I heard the sound of a ukalele. We clambered up the ladder.

"I guess he's in the cabin," said Winter, leading the way.

It was a small cabin, bedraggled and dirty, with a table against one side and a broad bench all round upon which slept, I supposed, such passengers as were ill-advised enough to travel in such a ship. A petroleum lamp gave a dim light. The ukalele was being played by a native girl and Butler was lolling on the seat, half lying, with his head on her shoulder and an arm round her waist.

"Don't let us disturb you, Captain," said Winter, facetiously.

"Come right in," said Butler, getting up and shaking hands with us. "What'll you have?"

It was a warm night, and through the open door you saw countless stars in a heaven that was still almost blue. Captain Butler wore a sleeveless undershirt, showing his fat white arms, and a pair of incredibly dirty trousers. His feet were bare, but on his curly head he wore a very old, a very shapeless felt hat.

"Let me introduce you to my girl. Ain't she a peach?"

We shook hands with a very pretty person. She was a good deal taller than the captain, and even the Mother Hubbard, which the missionaries of a past generation had, in the interests of decency, forced on the unwilling natives, could not conceal the beauty of her form. One could not but suspect that age would burden her with a certain corpulence, but now she was graceful and alert. Her brown skin had an exquisite translucency and her eyes were magnificent. Her black hair, very thick and rich, was coiled round her head in a massive plait. When she smiled in a greeting that was charmingly natural, she showed teeth that were small, even, and white. She was certainly a most attractive creature. It was easy to see that the captain was madly in love with her. He could not take his eyes off her; he wanted to touch her all the time. That was very easy to understand; but what seemed to me stranger was that the girl was apparently in love with him. There was a light in her eyes that was unmistakable, and her lips were slightly parted as though in a sigh of desire. It was thrilling. It was even a little moving, and I could not help feeling somewhat in the way. What had a stranger to do with this lovesick pair? I wished that Winter had not brought me. And it seemed to me that the dingy cabin was transfigured and now it seemed a fit and proper scene for such an extremity of passion. I thought I should never forget that schooner in the harbour of Honolulu, crowded with shipping, and yet, under the immensity of the starry sky, remote from all the world. I liked to think of those lovers sailing off together in the night over the empty spaces of the Pacific from one green, hilly island to another. A faint breeze of romance softly fanned my cheek.

And yet Butler was the last man in the world with whom you would have associated romance, and it was hard to see what there was in him to arouse love. In the clothes he wore now he looked podgier than ever, and his round spectacles gave his round face the look of a prim cherub. He suggested rather a curate who had gone to the dogs. His conversation was peppered with the quaintest Americanisms, and it is because I despair of reproducing these that, at whatever loss of vividness, I mean to narrate the story he told me a little later in my own words. Moreover he was unable to frame a sentence without an oath, though a good-natured one, and his speech, albeit offensive only to prudish ears, in print would seem coarse. He was a mirth-loving man, and perhaps that accounted not a little for his successful amours; since women, for the most part frivolous creatures, are excessively bored by the seriousness with which men treat them, and they can seldom resist the buffoon who makes them laugh. Their sense of humour is crude. Diana of Ephesus is always prepared to fling prudence to the winds for the red-nosed comedian who sits on his hat. I realised that Captain Butler had charm. If I had not known the tragic story of the shipwreck I should have thought he had never had a care in his life.

Our host had rung the bell on our entrance and now a Chinese cook came in with more glasses and several bottles of soda. The whisky and the captain's empty glass stood already on the table. But when I saw the Chinese I positively started, for he was certainly the ugliest man I had ever seen. He was very short, but thick-set, and he had a bad limp. He wore a singlet and a pair of trousers that had been white, but were now filthy, and, perched on a shock of bristly, grey hair, an old tweed deer-stalker. It would have been grotesque on any Chinese, but on him it was outrageous. His broad, square face was very flat as though it had been bashed in by a mighty fist, and it was deeply pitted with smallpox; but the most revolting thing in him was a very pronounced harelip which had never been operated on, so that his upper lip, cleft, went up in an angle to his nose, and in the opening was a huge yellow fang. It was horrible. He came in with the end of a cigarette at the corner of his mouth and this, I do not know why, gave him a devilish expression.

He poured out the whisky and opened a bottle of soda.

"Don't drown it, John," said the captain.

He said nothing, but handed a glass to each of us. Then he went out.

"I saw you lookin' at my Chink," said Butler, with a grin on his fat, shining face.

"I should hate to meet him on a dark night," I said.

"He sure is homely," said the captain, and for some reason he seemed to say it with a peculiar satisfaction. "But he's fine for one thing, I'll tell the world; you just have to have a drink every time you look at him."

But my eyes fell on a calabash that hung against the wall over the table, and I got up to look at it. I had been hunting for an old one and this was better than any I had seen outside the museum.

"It was given me by a chief over on one of the islands," said the captain, watching me. "I done him a good turn and he wanted to give me something good."

"He certainly did," I answered.

I was wondering whether I could discreetly make Captain Butler an offer for it, I could not imagine that he set any store on such an article, when, as though he read my thoughts, he said:

"I wouldn't sell that for ten thousand dollars."

"I guess not," said Winter. "It would be a crime to sell it."

"Why?" I asked.

"That comes into the story," returned Winter. "Doesn't it, Captain?"

"It surely does."

"Let's hear it then."

"The night's young yet," he answered.

The night distinctly lost its youth before he satisfied my curiosity, and meanwhile we drank a great deal too much whisky while Captain Butler narrated his experiences of San Francisco in the old days and of the South Seas. At last the girl fell asleep. She lay curled up on the seat, with her face on her brown arm, and her bosom rose and fell gently with her breathing. In sleep she looked sullen, but darkly beautiful.

He had found her on one of the islands in the group among which, whenever there was cargo to be got, he wandered with his crazy old schooner. The Kanakas have little love for work, and the laborious Chinese, the cunning Japs, have taken the trade out of their hands. Her father had a strip of land on which he grew taro and bananas and he had a boat in which he went fishing. He was vaguely related to the mate of the schooner, and it was he who took Captain Butler up to the shabby little frame house to spend an idle evening. They took a bottle of whisky with them and the ukalele. The captain was not a shy man and when he saw a pretty girl he made love to her. He could speak the native language fluently and it was not long before he had overcome the girl's timidity. They spent the evening singing and dancing, and by the end of it she was sitting by his side and he had his arm round her waist. It happened that they were delayed on the island for several days and the captain, at no time a man to hurry, made no effort to shorten his stay. He was very comfortable in the snug little harbour and life was long. He had a swim round his ship in the morning and another in the evening. There was a chandler's shop on the water front where sailormen could get a drink of whisky, and he spent the best part of the day there, playing cribbage with the half-caste who owned it. At night the mate and he went up to the house where the pretty girl lived and they sang a song or two and told stories. It was the girl's father who suggested that he should take her away with him. They discussed the matter in a friendly fashion, while the girl, nestling against the captain, urged him by the pressure of her hands and her soft smiling glances. He had taken a fancy to her and he was a domestic man. He was a little dull sometimes at sea and it would be very pleasant to have a pretty little creature like that about the old ship. He was of a practical turn too, and he recognised that it would be useful to have someone around to darn his socks and look after his linen. He was tired of having his things washed by a Chink who tore everything to pieces; the natives washed much better, and now and then when the captain went ashore at Honolulu he liked to cut a dash in a smart duck suit. It was only a matter of arranging a price. The father wanted two hundred and fifty dollars, and the captain, never a thrifty man, could not put his hand on such a sum. But he was a generous one, and with the girl's soft face against his, he was not inclined to haggle. He offered to give a hundred and fifty dollars there and then and another hundred in three months. There was a good deal of argument and the parties could not come to any agreement that night, but the idea had fired the captain, and he could not sleep as well as usual. He kept dreaming of the lovely girl and each time he awoke it was with the pressure of her soft, sensual lips on his. He cursed himself in the morning because a bad night at poker the last time he was at Honolulu had left him so short of ready money. And if the night before he had been in love with the girl, this morning he was crazy about her.

"See here, Bananas," he said to the mate, "I've got to have that girl. You go and tell the old man I'll bring the dough up to-night and she can get fixed up. I figure we'll be ready to sail at dawn."

I have no idea why the mate was known by that eccentric name. He was called Wheeler, but though he had that English surname there was not a drop of white blood in him. He was a tall man, and well-made though inclined to stoutness, but much darker than is usual in Hawaii. He was no longer young, and his crisply curling, thick hair was grey. His upper front teeth were cased in gold. He was very proud of them. He had a marked squint and this gave him a saturnine expression. The captain, who was fond of a joke, found in it a constant source of humour and hesitated the less to rally him on the defect because he realised that the mate was sensitive about it. Bananas, unlike most of the natives, was a taciturn fellow and Captain Butler would have disliked him if it had been possible for a man of his good nature to dislike anyone. He liked to be at sea with someone he could talk to, he was a chatty, sociable creature, and it was enough to drive a missionary to drink to live there day after day with a chap who never opened his mouth. He did his best to wake the mate up, that is to say, he chaffed him without mercy, but it was poor fun to laugh by oneself, and he came to the conclusion that, drunk or sober, Bananas was no fit companion for a white man. But he was a good seaman and the captain was shrewd enough to know the value of a mate he could trust. It was not rare for him to come aboard, when they were sailing, fit for nothing but to fall into his bunk, and it was worth something to know that he could stay there till he had slept his liquor off, since Bananas could be relied on. But he was an unsociable devil, and it would be a treat to have someone he could talk to. That girl would be fine. Besides, he wouldn't be so likely to get drunk when he went ashore if he knew there was a little girl waiting for him when he came on board again.

He went to his friend the chandler and over a peg of gin asked him for a loan. There were one or two useful things a ship's captain could do for a ship's chandler, and after a quarter of an hour's conversation in low tones (there is no object in letting all and sundry know your business), the captain crammed a wad of notes in his hip-pocket, and that night, when he went back to his ship, the girl went with him.

What Captain Butler, seeking for reasons to do what he had already made up his mind to, had anticipated, actually came to pass. He did not give up drinking, but he ceased to drink to excess. An evening with the boys, when he had been away from town two or three weeks, was pleasant enough, but it was pleasant too to get back to his little girl; he thought of her, sleeping so softly, and how, when he got into his cabin and leaned over her, she would open her eyes lazily and stretch out her arms for him: it was as good as a full hand. He found he was saving money, and since he was a generous man he did the right thing by the little girl: he gave her some silver-backed brushes for her long hair, and a gold chain, and a reconstructed ruby for her finger. Gee, but it was good to be alive.

A year went by, a whole year, and he was not tired of her yet. He was not a man who analysed his feelings, but this was so surprising that it forced itself upon his attention. There must be something very wonderful about that girl. He couldn't help seeing that he was more wrapped up in her than ever, and sometimes the thought entered his mind that it might not be a bad thing if he married her.

Then, one day the mate did not come in to dinner or to tea. Butler did not bother himself about his absence at the first meal, but at the second he asked the Chinese cook:

"Where's the mate? He no come tea?"

"No wantchee," said the Chink.

"He ain't sick?"

"No savvy."

Next day Bananas turned up again, but he was more sullen than ever, and after dinner the captain asked the girl what was the matter with him. She smiled and shrugged her pretty shoulders.

She told the captain that Bananas had taken a fancy to her and he was sore because she had told him off. The captain was a good-humoured man and he was not of a jealous nature; it struck him as exceeding funny that Bananas should be in love. A man who had a squint like that had a precious poor chance. When tea came round he chaffed him gaily. He pretended to speak in the air, so that the mate should not be certain that he knew anything, but he dealt him some pretty shrewd blows. The girl did not think him as funny as he thought himself, and afterwards she begged him to say nothing more. He was surprised at her seriousness. She told him he did not know her people. When their passion was aroused they were capable of anything. She was a little frightened. This was so absurd to him that he laughed heartily.

"If he comes bothering round you, you just threaten to tell me. That'll fix him."

"Better fire him, I think."

"Not on your sweet life. I know a good sailor when I see one. But if he don't leave you alone I'll give him the worst licking he's ever had."

Perhaps the girl had a wisdom unusual in her sex. She knew that it was useless to argue with a man when his mind was made up, for it only increased his stubbornness, and she held her peace. And now on the shabby schooner, threading her way across the silent sea, among those lovely islands, was enacted a dark, tense drama of which the fat little captain remained entirely ignorant. The girl's resistance fired Bananas so that he ceased to be a man, but was simply blind desire. He did not make love to her gently or gaily, but with a black and savage ferocity. Her contempt now was changed to hatred and when he besought her she answered him with bitter, angry taunts. But the struggle went on silently, and when the captain asked her after a little while whether Bananas was bothering her, she lied.

But one night, when they were in Honolulu, he came on board only just in time. They were sailing at dawn. Bananas had been ashore, drinking some native spirit, and he was drunk. The captain, rowing up, heard sounds that surprised him. He scrambled up the ladder. He saw Bananas, beside himself, trying to wrench open the cabin door. He was shouting at the girl. He swore he would kill her if she did not let him in.

"What in hell are you up to?" cried Butler.

The mate let go the handle, gave the captain a look of savage hate, and without a word turned away.

"Stop here. What are you doing with that door?"

The mate still did not answer. He looked at him with sullen, bootless rage.

"I'll teach you not to pull any of your queer stuff with me, you dirty, cross-eyed nigger," said the captain.

He was a good foot shorter than the mate and no match for him, but he was used to dealing with native crews, and he had his knuckleduster handy. Perhaps it was not an instrument that a gentleman would use, but then Captain Butler was not a gentleman. Nor was he in the habit of dealing with gentlemen. Before Bananas knew what the captain was at, his right arm had shot out and his fist, with its ring of steel, caught him fair and square on the jaw. He fell like a bull under the pole-axe.

"That'll learn him," said the captain.

Bananas did not stir. The girl unlocked the cabin door and came out.

"Is he dead?"

"He ain't."

He called a couple of men and told them to carry the mate to his bunk. He rubbed his hands with satisfaction and his round blue eyes gleamed behind his spectacles. But the girl was strangely silent. She put her arms round him as though to protect him from invisible harm.

It was two or three days before Bananas was on his feet again, and when he came out of his cabin his face was torn and swollen. Through the darkness of his skin you saw the livid bruise. Butler saw him slinking along the deck and called him. The mate went to him without a word.

"See here, Bananas," he said to him, fixing his spectacles on his slippery nose, for it was very hot. "I ain't going to fire you for this, but you know now that when I hit, I hit hard. Don't forget it and don't let me have any more funny business."

Then he held out his hand and gave the mate that good-humoured, flashing smile of his which was his greatest charm. The mate took the outstretched hand and twitched his swollen lips into a devilish grin. The incident in the captain's mind was so completely finished that when the three of them sat at dinner he chaffed Bananas on his appearance. He was eating with difficulty and, his swollen face still more distorted by pain, he looked truly a repulsive object.

That evening, when he was sitting on the upper deck, smoking his pipe, a shiver passed through the captain.

"I don't know what I should be shiverin' for on a night like this," he grumbled. "Maybe I've gotten a dose of fever. I've been feelin' a bit queer all day."

When he went to bed he took some quinine, and next morning he felt better, but a little washed out, as though he were recovering from a debauch.

"I guess my liver's out of order," he said, and he took a pill.

He had not much appetite that day and towards evening he began to feel very unwell. He tried the next remedy he knew, which was to drink two or three hot whiskies, but that did not seem to help him much, and when in the morning he surveyed himself in the glass he thought he was not looking quite the thing.

"If I ain't right by the time we get back to Honolulu I'll just give Dr. Denby a call. He'll sure fix me up."

He could not eat. He felt a great lassitude in all his limbs. He slept soundly enough, but he awoke with no sense of refreshment; on the contrary he felt a peculiar exhaustion. And the energetic little man, who could not bear the thought of lying in bed, had to make an effort to force himself out of his bunk. After a few days he found it impossible to resist the languor that oppressed him, and he made up his mind not to get up.

"Bananas can look after the ship," he said. "He has before now."

He laughed a little to himself as he thought how often he had lain speechless in his bunk after a night with the boys. That was before he had his girl. He smiled at her and pressed her hand. She was puzzled and anxious. He saw that she was concerned about him and tried to reassure her. He had never had a day's illness in his life and in a week at the outside he would be as right as rain.

"I wish you'd fired Bananas," she said. "I've got a feeling that he's at the bottom of this."

"Damned good thing I didn't, or there'd be no one to sail the ship. I know a good sailor when I see one." His blue eyes, rather pale now, with the whites all yellow, twinkled. "You don't think he's trying to poison me, little girl?"

She did not answer, but she had one or two talks with the Chinese cook, and she took great care with the captain's food. But he ate little enough now, and it was only with the greatest difficulty that she persuaded him to drink a cup of soup two or three times a day. It was clear that he was very ill, he was losing weight quickly, and his chubby face was pale and drawn. He suffered no pain, but merely grew every day weaker and more languid. He was wasting away. The round trip on this occasion lasted about four weeks and by the time they came to Honolulu the captain was a little anxious about himself. He had not been out of his bed for more than a fortnight and really he felt too weak to get up and go to the doctor. He sent a message asking him to come on board. The doctor examined him, but could find nothing to account for his condition. His temperature was normal.

"See here, Captain," he said, "I'll be perfectly frank with you. I don't know what's the matter with you, and just seeing you like this don't give me a chance. You come into the hospital so that we can keep you under observation. There's nothing organically wrong with you, I know that, and my impression is that a few weeks in hospital ought to put you to rights."

"I ain't going to leave my ship."

Chinese owners were queer customers, he said; if he left his ship because he was sick, his owner might fire him, and he couldn't afford to lose his job. So long as he stayed where he was his contract safeguarded him, and he had a first-rate mate. Besides, he couldn't leave his girl. No man could want a better nurse; if anyone could pull him through she would. Every man had to die once and he only wished to be left in peace. He would not listen to the doctor's expostulations, and finally the doctor gave in.

"I'll write you a prescription," he said doubtfully, "and see if it does you any good. You'd better stay in bed for a while."

"There ain't much fear of my getting up, doc," answered the captain. "I feel as weak as a cat."

But he believed in the doctor's prescription as little as did the doctor himself, and when he was alone amused himself by lighting his cigar with it. He had to get amusement out of something, for his cigar tasted like nothing on earth, and he smoked only to persuade himself that he was not too ill to. That evening a couple of friends of his, masters of tramp steamers, hearing he was sick came to see him. They discussed his case over a bottle of whisky and a box of Philippine cigars. One of them remembered how a mate of his had been taken queer just like that and not a doctor in the United States had been able to cure him. He had seen in the paper an advertisement of a patent medicine, and thought there'd be no harm in trying it. That man was as strong as ever he'd been in his life after two bottles. But his illness had given Captain Butler a lucidity which was new and strange, and while they talked he seemed to read their minds. They thought he was dying. And when they left him he was afraid.

The girl saw his weakness. This was her opportunity. She had been urging him to let a native doctor see him, and he had stoutly refused; but now she entreated him. He listened with harassed eyes. He wavered. It was very funny that the American doctor could not tell what was the matter with him. But he did not want her to think that he was scared. If he let a damned nigger come along and look at him, it was to comfort *her*. He told her to do what she liked.

The native doctor came the next night. The captain was lying
alone, half awake, and the cabin was dimly lit by an oil lamp. The
door was softly opened and the girl came in on tip-toe. She held the
door open and someone slipped in silently behind her. The captain
smiled at this mystery, but he was so weak now, the smile was no
more than a glimmer in his eyes. The doctor was a little, old man,
very thin and very wrinkled, with a completely bald head, and the
face of a monkey. He was bowed and gnarled like an old tree. He
looked hardly human, but his eyes were very bright, and in the half
darkness they seemed to glow with a reddish light. He was dressed
filthily in a pair of ragged dungarees, and the upper part of his body
was naked. He sat down on his haunches and for ten minutes looked
at the captain. Then he felt the palms of his hands and the soles of
his feet. The girl watched him with frightened eyes. No word was
spoken. Then he asked for something that the captain had worn.
The girl gave him the old felt hat which the captain used constantly
and taking it he sat down again on the floor, clasping it firmly with
both hands; and rocking backwards and forwards slowly he muttered
some gibberish in a very low tone.

At last he gave a little sigh and dropped the hat. He took an old
pipe out of his trouser pocket and lit it. The girl went over to him
and sat by his side. He whispered something to her, and she started
violently. For a few minutes they talked in hurried undertones, and
then they stood up. She gave him money and opened the door for
him. He slid out as silently as he had come in. Then she went over
to the captain and leaned over him so that she could speak into his
ear.

"It's an enemy praying you to death."

"Don't talk fool stuff, girlie," he said impatiently.

"It's truth. It's God's truth. That's why the American doctor
couldn't do anything. Our people can do that. I've seen it done. I
thought you were safe because you were a white man."

"I haven't an enemy."

"Bananas."

"What's he want to pray me to death for?"

"You ought to have fired him before he had a chance."

"I guess if I ain't got nothing more the matter with me than
Bananas' hoodoo I shall be sitting up and taking nourishment in a
very few days."

She was silent for a while and she looked at him intently.

"Don't you know you're dying?" she said to him at last.

That was what the two skippers had thought, but they hadn't
said it. A shiver passed across the captain's wan face.

"The doctor says there ain't nothing really the matter with me. I've only to lie quiet for a bit and I shall be all right."

She put her lips to his ear as if she were afraid that the air itself might hear.

"You're dying, dying, dying. You'll pass out with the old moon."

"That's something to know."

"You'll pass out with the old moon unless Bananas dies before."

He was not a timid man and he had recovered already from the shock her words, and still more her vehement, silent manner, had given him. Once more a smile flickered in his eyes.

"I guess I'll take my chance, girlie."

"There's twelve days before the new moon."

There was something in her tone that gave him an idea.

"See here, my girl, this is all bunk. I don't believe a word of it. But I don't want you to try any of your monkey tricks with Bananas. He ain't a beauty, but he's a first-rate mate."

He would have said a good deal more, but he was tired out. He suddenly felt very weak and faint. It was always at that hour that he felt worse. He closed his eyes. The girl watched him for a minute and then slipped out of the cabin. The moon, nearly full, made a silver pathway over the dark sea. It shone from an unclouded sky. She looked at it with terror, for she knew that with its death the man she loved would die. His life was in her hands. She could save him, she alone could save him, but the enemy was cunning, and she must be cunning too. She felt that someone was looking at her, and without turning, by the sudden fear that seized her, knew that from the shadow the burning eyes of the mate were fixed upon her. She did not know what he could do; if he could read her thoughts she was defeated already, and with a desperate effort she emptied her mind of all content. His death alone could save her lover, and she could bring his death about. She knew that if he could be brought to look into a calabash in which was water so that a reflection of him was made, and the reflection were broken by hurtling the water, he would die as though he had been struck by lightning; for the reflection was his soul. But none knew better than he the danger, and he could be made to look only by a guile which had lulled his least suspicion. He must never think that he had an enemy who was on the watch to cause his destruction. She knew what she had to do. But the time was short, the time was terribly short. Presently she realised that the mate had gone. She breathed more freely.

Two days later they sailed, and there were ten now before the new moon. Captain Butler was terrible to see. He was nothing but skin and bone, and he could not move without help. He could hardly speak. But she dared do nothing yet. She knew that she must be patient. The mate was cunning, cunning. They went to one of the smaller islands of the group and discharged cargo, and now there were only seven days more. The moment had come to start. She brought some things out of the cabin she shared with the captain and made them into a bundle. She put the bundle in the deck cabin where she and Bananas ate their meals, and at dinner time, when she went in, he turned quickly and she saw that he had been looking at it. Neither of them spoke, but she knew what he suspected. She was making her preparations to leave the ship. He looked at her mockingly. Gradually, as though to prevent the captain from knowing what she was about, she brought everything she owned into the cabin, and some of the captain's clothes, and made them all into bundles. At last Bananas could keep silence no longer. He pointed to a suit of ducks.

"What are you going to do with that?" he asked.

She shrugged her shoulders.

"I'm going back to my island."

He gave a laugh that distorted his grim face. The captain was dying and she meant to get away with all she could lay hands on.

"What'll you do if I say you can't take those things? They're the captain's."

"They're no use to you," she said.

There was a calabash hanging on the wall. It was the very calabash I had seen when I came into the cabin and which we had talked about. She took it down. It was all dusty, so she poured water into it from the water-bottle, and rinsed it with her fingers.

"What are you doing with that?"

"I can sell it for fifty dollars," she said.

"If you want to take it you'll have to pay me."

"What d'you want?"

"You know what I want."

She allowed a fleeting smile to play on her lips. She flashed a quick look at him and quickly turned away. He gave a gasp of desire. She raised her shoulders in a little shrug. With a savage bound he sprang upon her and seized her in his arms. Then she laughed. She put her arms, her soft, round arms, about his neck, and surrendered herself to him voluptuously.

When the morning came she roused him out of a deep sleep. The early rays of the sun slanted into the cabin. He pressed her to his heart. Then he told her that the captain could not last more than a day or two, and the owner wouldn't so easily find another white man to command the ship. If Bananas offered to take less money he would get the job and the girl could stay with him. He looked at her with love-sick eyes. She nestled up against him. She kissed his lips, in the foreign way, in the way the captain had taught her to kiss. And she promised to stay. Bananas was drunk with happiness.

It was now or never.

She got up and went to the table to arrange her hair. There was no mirror and she looked into the calabash, seeking for her reflection. She tidied her beautiful hair. Then she beckoned to Bananas to come to her. She pointed to the calabash.

"There's something in the bottom of it," she said.

Instinctively, without suspecting anything, Bananas looked full into the water. His face was reflected in it. In a flash she beat upon it violently, with both her hands, so that they pounded on the bottom and the water splashed up. The reflection was broken in pieces. Bananas started back with a sudden hoarse cry and he looked at the girl. She was standing there with a look of triumphant hatred on her face. A horror came into his eyes. His heavy features were twisted in agony, and with a thud, as though he had taken a violent poison, he crumpled up on the ground. A great shudder passed through his body and he was still. She leaned over him callously. She put her hand on his heart and then she pulled down his lower eye-lid. He was quite dead.

She went into the cabin in which lay Captain Butler. There was a faint colour in his cheeks and he looked at her in a startled way.

"What's happened?" he whispered.

They were the first words he had spoken for forty-eight hours.

"Nothing's happened," she said.

"I feel all funny."

Then his eyes closed and he fell asleep. He slept for a day and a night, and when he awoke he asked for food. In a fortnight he was well.

It was past midnight when Winter and I rowed back to shore and we had drunk innumerable whiskies and sodas.

"What do you think of it all?" asked Winter.

"What a question! If you mean, have I any explanation to suggest, I haven't."

"The captain believes every word of it."

"That's obvious; but, you know, that's not the part that interests me most: whether it's true or not, and what it all means; the part that interests me is that such things should happen to such people. I wonder what there is in that common-place little man to arouse such a passion in that lovely creature. As I watched her, asleep there, while he was telling the story I had some fantastic idea about the power of love being able to work miracles."

"But that's not the girl," said Winter.

"What on earth do you mean?"

"Didn't you notice the cook?"

"Of course I did. He's the ugliest man I ever saw."

"That's why Butler took him. The girl ran away with the Chinese cook last year. This is a new one. He's only had her there about two months."

"Well, I'm hanged."

"He thinks this cook is safe. But I wouldn't be too sure in his place. There's something about a Chink, when he lays himself out to please a woman she can't resist him."

The Luncheon

I CAUGHT sight of her at the play and in answer to her beckoning I went over during the interval and sat down beside her. It was long since I had last seen her and if someone had not mentioned her name I hardly think I would have recognised her. She addressed me brightly.

"Well, it's many years since we first met. How time does fly! We're none of us getting any younger. Do you remember the first time I saw you? You asked me to luncheon."

Did I remember?

It was twenty years ago and I was living in Paris. I had a tiny apartment in the Latin Quarter overlooking a cemetery and I was earning barely enough money to keep body and soul together. She had read a book of mine and had written to me about it. I answered, thanking her, and presently I received from her another letter saying that she was passing through Paris and would like to have a chat with me; but her time was limited and the only free moment she had was on the following Thursday; she was spending the morning at the Luxembourg and would I give her a little luncheon at Foyot's afterwards? Foyot's is a restaurant at which the French senators eat and it was so far beyond my means that I had never even thought of going there. But I was flattered and I was too young to have learned to say no to a woman. (Few men, I may add, learn this until they are too old to make it of any consequence to a woman what they say.) I had eighty francs (gold francs) to last me the rest of the month and a modest luncheon should not cost more than fifteen. If I cut out coffee for the next two weeks I could manage well enough.

I answered that I would meet my friend—by correspondence—at Foyot's on Thursday at half-past twelve. She was not so young as I expected and in appearance imposing rather than attractive. She was in fact a woman of forty (a charming age, but not one that excites a sudden and devastating passion at first sight), and she gave me the impression of having more teeth, white and large and even, than were necessary for any practical purpose. She was talkative, but since she seemed inclined to talk about me I was prepared to be an attentive listener.

I was startled when the bill of fare was brought, for the prices were a great deal higher than I had anticipated. But she reassured me.

"I never eat anything for luncheon," she said.

"Oh, don't say that!" I answered generously.

"I never eat more than one thing. I think people eat far too much nowadays. A little fish, perhaps. I wonder if they have any salmon."

Well, it was early in the year for salmon and it was not on the bill of fare, but I asked the waiter if there was any. Yes, a beautiful salmon had just come in, it was the first they had had. I ordered it for my guest. The waiter asked her if she would have something while it was being cooked.

"No," she answered, "I never eat more than one thing. Unless you had a little caviare. I never mind caviare."

My heart sank a little. I knew I could not afford caviare, but I could not very well tell her that. I told the waiter by all means to bring caviare. For myself I chose the cheapest dish on the menu and that was a mutton chop.

"I think you're unwise to eat meat," she said. "I don't know how you can expect to work after eating heavy things like chops. I don't believe in overloading my stomach."

Then came the question of drink.

"I never drink anything for luncheon," she said.

"Neither do I," I answered promptly.

"Except white wine," she proceeded as though I had not spoken. "These French white wines are so light. They're wonderful for the digestion."

"What would you like?" I asked, hospitable still, but not exactly effusive.

She gave me a bright and amicable flash of her white teeth.

"My doctor won't let me drink anything but champagne."

I fancy I turned a trifle pale. I ordered half a bottle. I mentioned casually that my doctor had absolutely forbidden me to drink champagne.

"What are you going to drink, then?"

"Water."

She ate the caviare and she ate the salmon. She talked gaily of art and literature and music. But I wondered what the bill would come to. When my mutton chop arrived she took me quite seriously to task.

"I see that you're in the habit of eating a heavy luncheon. I'm sure it's a mistake. Why don't you follow my example and just eat one thing? I'm sure you'd feel ever so much better for it."

"I *am* only going to eat one thing," I said, as the waiter came again with the bill of fare.

She waved him aside with an airy gesture.

"No, no, I never eat anything for luncheon. Just a bite, I never

D

want more than that, and I eat that more as an excuse for conversation than anything else. I couldn't possibly eat anything more—unless they had some of those giant asparagus. I should be sorry to leave Paris without having some of them."

My heart sank. I had seen them in the shops and I knew that they were horribly expensive. My mouth had often watered at the sight of them.

"Madame wants to know if you have any of those giant asparagus," I asked the waiter.

I tried with all my might to will him to say no. A happy smile spread over his broad, priest-like face, and he assured me that they had some so large, so splendid, so tender, that it was a marvel.

"I'm not in the least hungry," my guest sighed, "but if you insist I don't mind having some asparagus."

I ordered them.

"Aren't you going to have any?"

"No, I never eat asparagus."

"I know there are people who don't like them. The fact is, you ruin your palate by all the meat you eat."

We waited for the asparagus to be cooked. Panic seized me. It was not a question now how much money I should have left over for the rest of the month, but whether I had enough to pay the bill. It would be mortifying to find myself ten francs short and be obliged to borrow from my guest. I could not bring myself to do that. I knew exactly how much I had and if the bill came to more I made up my mind that I would put my hand in my pocket and with a dramatic cry start up and say it had been picked. Of course it would be awkward if she had not money enough either to pay the bill. Then the only thing would be to leave my watch and say I would come back and pay later.

The asparagus appeared. They were enormous, succulent and appetising. The smell of the melted butter tickled my nostrils as the nostrils of Jehovah were tickled by the burned offerings of the virtuous Semites. I watched the abandoned woman thrust them down her throat in large voluptuous mouthfuls and in my polite way I discoursed on the condition of the drama in the Balkans. At last she finished.

"Coffee?" I said.

"Yes, just an ice-cream and coffee," she answered.

I was past caring now, so I ordered coffee for myself and an ice-cream and coffee for her.

"You know, there's one thing I thoroughly believe in," she said, as she ate the ice-cream. "One should always get up from a meal feeling one could eat a little more."

"Are you still hungry?" I asked faintly.

"Oh, no, I'm not hungry; you see, I don't eat luncheon. I have a cup of coffee in the morning and then dinner, but I never eat more than one thing for luncheon. I was speaking for you."

"Oh, I see!"

Then a terrible thing happened. While we were waiting for the coffee, the head waiter, with an ingratiating smile on his false face, came up to us bearing a large basket full of huge peaches. They had the blush of an innocent girl; they had the rich tone of an Italian landscape. But surely peaches were not in season then? Lord knew what they cost. I knew too—a little later, for my guest, going on with her conversation, absentmindedly took one.

"You see, you've filled your stomach with a lot of meat"—my one miserable little chop—"and you can't eat any more. But I've just had a snack and I shall enjoy a peach."

The bill came and when I paid it I found that I had only enough for a quite inadequate tip. Her eyes rested for an instant on the three francs I left for the waiter and I knew that she thought me mean. But when I walked out of the restaurant I had the whole month before me and not a penny in my pocket.

"Follow my example," she said as we shook hands, "and never eat more than one thing for luncheon."

"I'll do better than that," I retorted. "I'll eat nothing for dinner to-night."

"Humorist!" she cried gaily, jumping into a cab. "You're quite a humorist!"

But I have had my revenge at last. I do not believe that I am a vindictive man, but when the immortal gods take a hand in the matter it is pardonable to observe the result with complacency. To-day she weighs twenty-one stone.

The Ant and the Grasshopper

WHEN I was a very small boy I was made to learn by heart certain of the fables of La Fontaine, and the moral of each was carefully explained to me. Among those I learnt was *The Ant and the Grasshopper*, which is devised to bring home to the young the useful lesson that in an imperfect world industry is rewarded and giddiness punished. In this admirable fable (I apologise for telling something which everyone is politely, but inexactly, supposed to know) the ant spends a laborious summer gathering its winter store, while the grasshopper sits on a blade of grass singing to the sun. Winter comes and the ant is comfortably provided for, but the grasshopper has an empty larder: he goes to the ant and begs for a little food. Then the ant gives him her classic answer:

"What were you doing in the summer time?"

"Saving your presence, I sang, I sang all day, all night."

"You sang. Why, then go and dance."

I do not ascribe it to perversity on my part, but rather to the inconsequence of childhood, which is deficient in moral sense, that I could never quite reconcile myself to the lesson. My sympathies were with the grasshopper and for some time I never saw an ant without putting my foot on it. In this summary (and as I have discovered since, entirely human) fashion I sought to express my disapproval of prudence and commonsense.

I could not help thinking of this fable when the other day I saw George Ramsay lunching by himself in a restaurant. I never saw anyone wear an expression of such deep gloom. He was staring into space. He looked as though the burden of the whole world sat on his shoulders. I was sorry for him: I suspected at once that his unfortunate brother had been causing trouble again. I went up to him and held out my hand.

"How are you?" I asked.

"I'm not in hilarious spirits," he answered.

"Is it Tom again?"

He sighed.

"Yes, it's Tom again."

"Why don't you chuck him? You've done everything in the world for him. You must know by now that he's quite hopeless."

I suppose every family has a black sheep. Tom had been a sore trial to his for twenty years. He had begun life decently enough: he went into business, married and had two children. The Ramsays were perfectly respectable people and there was every reason to suppose that Tom Ramsay would have a useful and honourable career. But one day, without warning, he announced that he didn't like work and that he wasn't suited for marriage. He wanted to enjoy himself. He would listen to no expostulations. He left his wife and his office. He had a little money and he spent two happy years in the various capitals of Europe. Rumours of his doings reached his relations from time to time and they were profoundly shocked. He certainly had a very good time. They shook their heads and asked what would happen when his money was spent. They soon found out: he borrowed. He was charming and unscrupulous. I have never met anyone to whom it was more difficult to refuse a loan. He made a steady income from his friends and he made friends easily. But he always said that the money you spent on necessities was boring; the money that was amusing to spend was the money you spent on luxuries. For this he depended on his brother George. He did not waste his charm on him. George was a serious man and insensible to such enticements. George was respectable. Once or twice he fell to Tom's promises of amendment and gave him considerable sums in order that he might make a fresh start. On these Tom bought a motor-car and some very nice jewellery. But when circumstances forced George to realise that his brother would never settle down and he washed his hands of him, Tom, without a qualm, began to blackmail him. It was not very nice for a respectable lawyer to find his brother shaking cocktails behind the bar of his favourite restaurant or to see him waiting on the box-seat of a taxi outside his club. Tom said that to serve in a bar or to drive a taxi was a perfectly decent occupation, but if George could oblige him with a couple of hundred pounds he didn't mind for the honour of the family giving it up. George paid.

Once Tom nearly went to prison. George was terribly upset. He went into the whole discreditable affair. Really Tom had gone too far. He had been wild, thoughtless, and selfish, but he had never before done anything dishonest, by which George meant illegal; and if he were prosecuted he would assuredly be convicted. But you cannot allow your only brother to go to gaol. The man Tom had cheated, a man called Cronshaw, was vindictive. He was determined to take the matter into court; he said Tom was a scoundrel and should be punished. It cost George an infinite deal of trouble and five hundred pounds to settle the affair. I have never seen him in such a rage as when he heard that Tom and Cronshaw had gone off together to

Monte Carlo the moment they cashed the cheque. They spent a
happy month there.

For twenty years Tom raced and gambled, philandered with the
prettiest girls, danced, ate in the most expensive restaurants, and
dressed beautifully. He always looked as if he had just stepped out
of a bandbox. Though he was forty-six you would never have taken
him for more than thirty-five. He was a most amusing companion
and though you knew he was perfectly worthless you could not but
enjoy his society. He had high spirits, an unfailing gaiety and incredible charm. I never grudged the contributions he regularly
levied on me for the necessities of his existence. I never lent him
fifty pounds without feeling that I was in his debt. Tom Ramsay
knew everyone and everyone knew Tom Ramsay. You could not
approve of him, but you could not help liking him.

Poor George, only a year older than his scapegrace brother,
looked sixty. He had never taken more than a fortnight's holiday
in the year for a quarter of a century. He was in his office every
morning at nine-thirty and never left it till six. He was honest, industrious and worthy. He had a good wife, to whom he had never
been unfaithful even in thought, and four daughters, to whom he
was the best of fathers. He made a point of saving a third of his
income and his plan was to retire at fifty-five to a little house in the
country where he proposed to cultivate his garden and play golf. His
life was blameless. He was glad that he was growing old because
Tom was growing old too. He rubbed his hands and said:

"It was all very well when Tom was young and good-looking, but
he's only a year younger than I am. In four years he'll be fifty. He
won't find life so easy then. I shall have thirty thousand pounds by
the time I'm fifty. For twenty-five years I've said that Tom would
end in the gutter. And we shall see how he likes that. We shall see if
it really pays best to work or be idle."

Poor George! I sympathised with him. I wondered now as I sat
down beside him what infamous thing Tom had done. George was
evidently very much upset.

"Do you know what's happened now?" he asked me.

I was prepared for the worst. I wondered if Tom had got into
the hands of the police at last. George could hardly bring himself
to speak.

"You're not going to deny that all my life I've been hard-working,
decent, respectable, and straightforward. After a life of industry and
thrift I can look forward to retiring on a small income in gilt-edged
securities. I've always done my duty in that state of life in which it
has pleased Providence to place me."

"True."

"And you can't deny that Tom has been an idle, worthless, dissolute, and dishonourable rogue. If there were any justice he'd be in the workhouse."

"True."

George grew red in the face.

"A few weeks ago he became engaged to a woman old enough to be his mother. And now she's died and left him everything she had. Half a million pounds, a yacht, a house in London and a house in the country."

George Ramsay beat his clenched fist on the table.

"It's not fair, I tell you, it's not fair. Damn it, it's not fair."

I could not help it. I burst into a shout of laughter as I looked at George's wrathful face, I rolled in my chair, I very nearly fell on the floor. George never forgave me. But Tom often asks me to excellent dinners in his charming house in Mayfair, and if he occasionally borrows a trifle from me, that is merely from force of habit. It is never more than a sovereign.

Home

THE farm lay in a hollow among the Somersetshire hills, an old-fashioned stone house surrounded by barns and pens and out-houses. Over the doorway the date when it was built had been carved in the elegant figures of the period, 1673, and the house, grey and weather-beaten, looked as much a part of the landscape as the trees that sheltered it. An avenue of splendid elms that would have been the pride of many a squire's mansion led from the road to the trim garden. The people who lived here were as stolid, sturdy and unpretentious as the house; their only boast was that ever since it was built from father to son in one unbroken line they had been born and died in it. For three hundred years they had farmed the surrounding land. George Meadows was now a man of fifty, and his wife was a year or two younger. They were both fine, upstanding people in the prime of life; and their children, two sons and three girls, were handsome and strong. They had no new-fangled notions about being gentlemen and ladies; they knew their place and were proud of it. I have never seen a more united household. They were merry, industrious and kindly. Their life was patriarchal. It had a completeness that gave it a beauty as definite as that of a symphony by Beethoven or a picture by Titian. They were happy and they deserved their happiness. But the master of the house was not George Meadows (not by a long chalk, they said in the village); it was his mother. She was twice the man her son was, they said. She was a woman of seventy, tall, upright and dignified, with grey hair, and though her face was much wrinkled, her eyes were bright and shrewd. Her word was law in the house and on the farm; but she had humour, and if her rule was despotic it was also kindly. People laughed at her jokes and repeated them. She was a good business woman and you had to get up very early in the morning to best her in a bargain. She was a character. She combined in a rare degree good will with an alert sense of the ridiculous.

One day Mrs. George stopped me on my way home. She was all in a flutter. (Her mother-in-law was the only Mrs. Meadows we knew; George's wife was only known as Mrs. George.)

"Whoever do you think is coming here to-day?" she asked me. "Uncle George Meadows. You know, him as was in China."

"Why, I thought he was dead."

"We all thought he was dead."

94

I had heard the story of Uncle George Meadows a dozen times, and it had amused me because it had the savour of an old ballad: it was oddly touching to come across it in real life. For Uncle George Meadows and Tom, his younger brother, had both courted Mrs. Meadows when she was Emily Green, fifty years and more ago, and when she married Tom, George had gone away to sea.

They heard of him on the China coast. For twenty years now and then he sent them presents; then there was no more news of him; when Tom Meadows died his widow wrote and told him, but received no answer; and at last they came to the conclusion that he must be dead. But two or three days ago to their astonishment they had received a letter from the matron of the sailors' home at Portsmouth. It appeared that for the last ten years George Meadows, crippled with rheumatism, had been an inmate and now, feeling that he had not much longer to live, wanted to see once more the house in which he was born. Albert Meadows, his great-nephew, had gone over to Portsmouth in the Ford to fetch him and he was to arrive that afternoon.

"Just fancy," said Mrs. George, "he's not been here for more than fifty years. He's never even seen my George, who's fifty-one next birthday."

"And what does Mrs. Meadows think of it?" I asked.

"Well, you know what she is. She sits there and smiles to herself. All she says is, 'He was a good-looking young fellow when he left, but not so steady as his brother.' That's why she chose my George's father. 'But he's probably quietened down by now,' she says."

Mrs. George asked me to look in and see him. With the simplicity of a country woman who had never been further from her home than London, she thought that because we had both been in China we must have something in common. Of course I accepted. I found the whole family assembled when I arrived; they were sitting in the great old kitchen, with its stone floor, Mrs. Meadows in her usual chair by the fire, very upright, and I was amused to see that she had put on her best silk dress, while her son and his wife sat at the table with their children. On the other side of the fireplace sat an old man, bunched up in a chair. He was very thin and his skin hung on his bones like an old suit much too large for him; his face was wrinkled and yellow and he had lost nearly all his teeth.

I shook hands with him.

"Well, I'm glad to see you've got here safely, Mr. Meadows," I said.

"Captain," he corrected.

"He walked here," Albert, his great-nephew, told me. "When he

got to the gate he made me stop the car and said he wanted to
walk."

"And mind you, I've not been out of my bed for two years. They
carried me down and put me in the car. I thought I'd never walk
again, but when I see them elm trees, I remember my father set a lot
of store by them elm trees, I felt I could walk. I walked down that
drive fifty-two years ago when I went away and now I've walked
back again."

"Silly, I call it," said Mrs. Meadows.

"It's done me good. I feel better and stronger than I have for ten
years. I'll see you out yet, Emily."

"Don't you be too sure," she answered.

I suppose no one had called Mrs. Meadows by her first name for a
generation. It gave me a little shock, as though the old man were
taking a liberty with her. She looked at him with a shrewd smile in
her eyes and he, talking to her, grinned with his toothless gums. It
was strange to look at them, these two old people who had not seen
one another for half a century, and to think that all that long time
ago he had loved her and she had loved another. I wondered if they
remembered what they had felt then and what they had said to one
another. I wondered if it seemed to him strange now that for that
old woman he had left the home of his fathers, his lawful inheritance,
and lived an exile's life.

"Have you ever been married, Captain Meadows?" I asked.

"Not me," he said, in his quavering voice, with a grin. "I know
too much about women for that."

"That's what you say," retorted Mrs. Meadows. "If the truth
was known I shouldn't be surprised to hear as how you'd had half
a dozen black wives in your day."

"They're not black in China, Emily, you ought to know better
than that, they're yellow."

"Perhaps that's why you've got so yellow yourself. When I saw
you, I said to myself, why, he's got jaundice."

"I said I'd never marry anyone but you, Emily, and I never have."

He said this not with pathos or resentment, but as a mere statement of fact, as a man might say, "I said I'd walk twenty miles and
I've done it." There was a trace of satisfaction in the speech.

"Well, you might have regretted it if you had," she answered.

I talked a little with the old man about China.

"There's not a port in China that I don't know better than you
know your coat pocket. Where a ship can go I've been. I could keep
you sitting here all day long for six months and not tell you half the
things I've seen in my day."

"Well, one thing you've not done, George, as far as I can see," said Mrs. Meadows, the mocking but not unkindly smile still in her eyes, "and that's to make a fortune."

"I'm not one to save money. Make it and spend it; that's my motto. But one thing I can say for myself: if I had the chance of going through my life again I'd take it. And there's not many as'll say that."

"No, indeed," I said.

I looked at him with admiration and respect. He was a toothless, crippled, penniless old man, but he had made a success of life, for he had enjoyed it. When I left him he asked me to come and see him again next day. If I was interested in China he would tell me all the stories I wanted to hear.

Next morning I thought I would go and ask if the old man would like to see me. I strolled down the magnificent avenue of elm trees and when I came to the garden saw Mrs. Meadows picking flowers. I bade her good-morning and she raised herself. She had a huge armful of white flowers. I glanced at the house and I saw that the blinds were drawn: I was surprised, for Mrs. Meadows liked the sunshine.

"Time enough to live in the dark when you're buried," she always said.

"How's Captain Meadows?" I asked her.

"He always was a harum-scarum fellow," she answered. "When Lizzie took him a cup of tea this morning she found he was dead."

"Dead?"

"Yes. Died in his sleep. I was just picking these flowers to put in the room. Well, I'm glad he died in that old house. It always means a lot to them Meadows to do that."

They had had a good deal of difficulty in persuading him to go to bed. He had talked to them of all the things that had happened to him in his long life. He was happy to be back in his old home. He was proud that he had walked up the drive without assistance, and he boasted that he would live for another twenty years. But fate had been kind: death had written the full-stop in the right place.

Mrs. Meadows smelt the white flowers that she held in her arms.

"Well, I'm glad he came back," she said. "After I married Tom Meadows and George went away, the fact is I was never quite sure that I'd married the right one."

The Pool

WHEN I was introduced to Lawson by Chaplin, the owner of the Hotel Metropole at Apia, I paid no particular attention to him. We were sitting in the lounge over an early cocktail and I was listening with amusement to the gossip of the island.

Chaplin entertained me. He was by profession a mining engineer and perhaps it was characteristic of him that he had settled in a place where his professional attainments were of no possible value. It was, however, generally reported that he was an extremely clever mining engineer. He was a small man, neither fat nor thin, with black hair, scanty on the crown, turning grey, and a small, untidy moustache; his face, partly from the sun and partly from liquor, was very red. He was but a figurehead, for the hotel, though so grandly named but a frame building of two storeys, was managed by his wife, a tall, gaunt Australian of five and forty, with an imposing presence and a determined air. The little man, excitable and often tipsy, was terrified of her, and the stranger soon heard of domestic quarrels in which she used her fist and her foot in order to keep him in subjection. She had been known after a night of drunkenness to confine him for twenty-four hours to his own room, and then he could be seen, afraid to leave his prison, talking somewhat pathetically from his verandah to people in the street below.

He was a character, and his reminiscences of a varied life, whether true or not, made him worth listening to, so that when Lawson strolled in I was inclined to resent the interruption. Although not mid-day, it was clear that he had had enough to drink, and it was without enthusiasm that I yielded to his persistence and accepted his offer of another cocktail. I knew already that Chaplin's head was weak. The next round which in common politeness I should be forced to order would be enough to make him lively, and then Mrs. Chaplin would give me black looks.

Nor was there anything attractive in Lawson's appearance. He was a little thin man, with a long, sallow face and a narrow, weak chin, a prominent nose, large and bony, and great shaggy black eyebrows. They gave him a peculiar look. His eyes, very large and very dark, were magnificent. He was jolly, but his jollity did not seem to me sincere; it was on the surface, a mask which he wore to deceive the world, and I suspected that it concealed a mean nature. He was plainly anxious to be thought a "good sport" and he was hail-fellow-well-met; but, I do not know why, I felt that he was cunning and shifty. He talked a great deal in a raucous voice, and he and Chaplin capped one another's stories of beanos which had become legendary, stories of "wet" nights at the English Club, of shooting expeditions where an incredible amount of whisky had been consumed, and of jaunts to Sydney of which their pride was that they could remember nothing from the time they landed till the time they sailed. A pair of drunken swine. But even in their intoxication, for by now, after four cocktails each, neither was sober, there was a great difference between Chaplin, rough and vulgar, and Lawson: Lawson might be drunk, but he was certainly a gentleman.

At last he got out of his chair, a little unsteadily.

"Well, I'll be getting along home," he said. "See you before dinner."

"Missus all right?" said Chaplin.

"Yes."

He went out. There was a peculiar note in the monosyllable of his answer which made me look up.

"Good chap," said Chaplin flatly, as Lawson went out of the door into the sunshine. "One of the best. Pity he drinks."

This from Chaplin was an observation not without humour.

"And when he's drunk he wants to fight people."

"Is he often drunk?"

"Dead drunk, three or four days a week. It's the island done it, and Ethel."

"Who's Ethel?"

"Ethel's his wife. Married a half-caste. Old Brevald's daughter. Took her away from here. Only thing to do. But she couldn't stand it, and now they're back again. He'll hang himself one of these days, if he don't drink himself to death before. Good chap. Nasty when he's drunk."

Chaplin belched loudly.

"I'll go and put my head under the shower. I oughtn't to have had that last cocktail. It's always the last one that does you in."

He looked uncertainly at the staircase as he made up his mind to go to the cubby hole in which was the shower, and then with unnatural seriousness got up.

"Pay you to cultivate Lawson," he said. "A well-read chap. You'd be surprised when he's sober. Clever too. Worth talking to."

Chaplin had told me the whole story in these few speeches.

When I came in towards evening from a ride along the seashore Lawson was again in the hotel. He was heavily sunk in one of the cane chairs in the lounge and he looked at me with glassy eyes. It was plain that he had been drinking all the afternoon. He was torpid, and the look on his face was sullen and vindictive. His glance rested on me for a moment, but I could see that he did not recognise me. Two or three other men were sitting there, shaking dice, and they took no notice of him. His condition was evidently too usual to attract attention. I sat down and began to play.

"You're a damned sociable lot," said Lawson suddenly.

He got out of his chair and waddled with bent knees towards the door. I do not know whether the spectacle was more ridiculous than revolting. When he had gone one of the men sniggered.

"Lawson's fairly soused to-day," he said.

"If I couldn't carry my liquor better than that," said another, "I'd climb on the waggon and stay there."

Who would have thought that this wretched object was in his way a romantic figure or that his life had in it those elements of pity and terror which the theorist tells us are necessary to achieve the effect of tragedy?

I did not see him again for two or three days.

I was sitting one evening on the first floor of the hotel on a verandah that overlooked the street when Lawson came up and sank into a chair beside me. He was quite sober. He made a casual remark and then, when I had replied somewhat indifferently, added with a laugh which had in it an apologetic tone:

"I was devilish soused the other day."

I did not answer. There was really nothing to say. I pulled away at my pipe in the vain hope of keeping the mosquitoes away, and looked at the natives going home from their work. They walked with long steps, slowly, with care and dignity, and the soft patter of their naked feet was strange to hear. Their dark hair, curling or straight, was often white with lime, and then they had a look of extraordinary distinction. They were tall and finely built. Then a gang of Solomon Islanders, indentured labourers, passed by, singing; they were shorter and slighter than the Samoans, coal-black, with great heads of fuzzy hair dyed red. Now and then a white man drove past in his buggy or rode into the hotel yard. In the lagoon two or three schooners reflected their grace in the tranquil water.

"I don't know what there is to do in a place like this except to get soused," said Lawson at last.

"Don't you like Samoa?" I asked casually, for something to say.

"It's pretty, isn't it?"

The word he chose seemed so inadequate to describe the unimaginable beauty of the island that I smiled, and smiling I turned to look at him. I was startled by the expression in those fine sombre eyes of his, an expression of intolerable anguish; they betrayed a tragic depth of emotion of which I should never have thought him capable. But the expression passed away and he smiled. His smile was simple and a little naïve. It changed his face so that I wavered in my first feeling of aversion from him.

"I was all over the place when I first came out," he said.

He was silent for a moment.

"I went away for good about three years ago, but I came back." He hesitated. "My wife wanted to come back. She was born here, you know."

"Oh yes."

He was silent again, and then hazarded a remark about Robert Louis Stevenson. He asked me if I had been up to Vailima. For some reason he was making an effort to be agreeable to me. He began to talk of Stevenson's books, and presently the conversation drifted to London.

"I suppose Covent Garden's still going strong," he said. "I think I miss the opera as much as anything here. Here you seen *Tristan and Isolde?*"

He asked me the question as though the answer were really important to him, and when I said, a little casually I daresay, that I had, he seemed pleased. He began to speak of Wagner, not as a musician, but as the plain man who received from him an emotional satisfaction that he could not analyse.

"I suppose Bayreuth was the place to go really," he said. "I never had the money, worse luck. But of course one might do worse than Covent Garden, all the lights and the women dressed up to the nines, and the music. The first act of the *Walküre's* all right, isn't it? And the end of *Tristan.* Golly!"

His eyes were flashing now and his face was lit up so that he hardly seemed the same man. There was a flush on his sallow, thin cheeks, and I forgot that his voice was harsh and unpleasant. There was even a certain charm about him.

"By George, I'd like to be in London to-night. Do you know the Pall Mall restaurant? I used to go there a lot. Piccadilly Circus with the shops all lit up, and the crowd. I think it's stunning to stand there and watch the buses and taxis streaming along as though they'd never stop. And I like the Strand too. What are those lines about God and Charing Cross?"

I was taken aback.

"Thompson's, d'you mean?" I asked.

I quoted them.

> *"And when so sad, thou canst not sadder,*
> *Cry, and upon thy so sore loss*
> *Shall shine the traffic of Jacob's ladder*
> *Pitched between Heaven and Charing Cross."*

He gave a faint sigh.

"I've read *The Hound of Heaven*. It's a bit of all right."

"It's generally thought so," I murmured.

"You don't meet anybody here who's read anything. They think it's swank."

There was a wistful look on his face, and I thought I divined the feeling that made him come to me. I was a link with the world he regretted and a life that he would know no more. Because not so very long before I had been in the London which he loved, he looked upon me with awe and envy. He had not spoken for five minutes perhaps when he broke out with words that startled me by their intensity.

"I'm fed up," he said. "I'm fed up."

"Then why don't you clear out?" I asked.

His face grew sullen.

"My lungs are a bit dicky. I couldn't stand an English winter now."

At that moment another man joined us on the verandah and Lawson sank into a moody silence.

"It's about time for a drain," said the newcomer. "Who'll have a drop of Scotch with me? Lawson?"

Lawson seemed to arise from a distant world. He got up.

"Let's go down to the bar," he said.

When he left me I remained with a more kindly feeling towards him than I should have expected. He puzzled and interested me. And a few days later I met his wife. I knew they had been married for five or six years, and I was surprised to see that she was still extremely young. When he married her she could not have been more than sixteen. She was adorably pretty. She was no darker than a Spaniard, small and very beautifully made, with tiny hands and feet, and a slight, lithe figure. Her features were lovely; but I think what struck me most was the delicacy of her appearance; the half-caste as a rule have a certain coarseness, they seem a little roughly formed, but she had an exquisite daintiness which took your breath away. There was something extremely civilised about her, so that it surprised you to see her in those surroundings, and you thought of those famous beauties who had set all the world talking at the Court of the Emperor Napoleon III. Though she wore but a muslin frock and a straw hat she wore them with an elegance that suggested the woman of fashion. She must have been ravishing when Lawson first saw her.

He had but lately come out from England to manage the local branch of an English bank, and, reaching Samoa at the beginning of the dry season, he had taken a room at the hotel. He quickly made the acquaintance of all and sundry. The life of the island is pleasant and easy. He enjoyed the long idle talks in the lounge of the hotel and the gay evenings at the English Club when a group of fellows would play pool. He liked Apia straggling along the edge of the lagoon, with its stores and bungalows, and its native village. Then there were week-ends when he would ride over to the house of one planter or another and spend a couple of nights on the hills. He had never before known freedom or leisure. And he was intoxicated by the sunshine. When he rode through the bush his head reeled a little at the beauty that surrounded him. The country was indescribably fertile. In parts the forest was still virgin, a tangle of strange trees, luxuriant undergrowth, and vine; it gave an impression that was mysterious and troubling.

But the spot that entranced him was a pool a mile or two away from Apia to which in the evenings he often went to bathe. There was a little river that bubbled over the rocks in a swift stream, and then, after forming the deep pool, ran on, shallow and crystalline, past a ford made by great stones where the natives came sometimes to bathe or to wash their clothes. The coconut trees, with their frivolous elegance, grew thickly on the banks, all clad with trailing plants, and they were reflected in the green water. It was just such a scene as you might see in Devonshire among the hills and yet with a difference, for it had a tropical richness, a passion, a scented languor which seemed to melt the heart. The water was fresh, but not cold; and it was delicious after the heat of the day. To bathe there refreshed not only the body but the soul.

At the hour when Lawson went, there was not a soul and he lingered for a long time, now floating idly in the water, now drying himself in the evening sun, enjoying the solitude and the friendly silence. He did not regret London then, nor the life that he had abandoned, for life as it was seemed complete and exquisite.

It was here that he first saw Ethel.

Occupied till late by letters which had to be finished for the monthly sailing of the boat next day, he rode down one evening to the pool when the light was almost failing. He tied up his horse and sauntered to the bank. A girl was sitting there. She glanced round as he came and noiselessly slid into the water. She vanished like a naiad startled by the approach of a mortal. He was surprised and amused. He wondered where she had hidden herself. He swam downstream and presently saw her sitting on a rock. She looked at him with uncurious eyes. He called out a greeting in Samoan.

"*Talofa.*"

She answered him, suddenly smiling, and then let herself into the water again. She swam easily and her hair spread out behind her. He watched her cross the pool and climb out on the bank. Like all the natives she bathed in a Mother Hubbard, and the water had made it cling to her slight body. She wrung out her hair, and as she stood there, unconcerned, she looked more than ever like a wild creature of the water or the woods. He saw now that she was half-caste. He swam towards her and, getting out, addressed her in English.

"You're having a late swim."

She shook back her hair and then let it spread over her shoulders in luxuriant curls.

"I like it when I'm alone," she said.

"So do I."

She laughed with the childlike frankness of the native. She slipped a dry Mother Hubbard over her head and, letting down the wet one, stepped out of it. She wrung it out and was ready to go. She paused a moment irresolutely and then sauntered off. The night fell suddenly.

Lawson went back to the hotel and, describing her to the men who were in the lounge shaking dice for drinks, soon discovered who she was. Her father was a Norwegian called Brevald who was often to be seen in the bar of the Hotel Metropole drinking rum and water. He was a little old man, knotted and gnarled like an ancient tree, who had come out to the islands forty years before as mate of a sailing vessel. He had been a blacksmith, a trader, a planter, and at one time fairly well-to-do; but, ruined by the great hurricane of the nineties, he had now nothing to live on but a small plantation of coconut trees. He had had four native wives and, as he told you with a cracked chuckle, more children than he could count. But some had died and some had gone out into the world, so that now the only one left at home was Ethel.

"She's a peach," said Nelson, the supercargo of the *Moana*. "I've given her the glad eye once or twice, but I guess there's nothing doing."

"Old Brevald's not that sort of a fool, sonny," put in another, a man called Miller. "He wants a son-in-law who's prepared to keep him in comfort for the rest of his life."

It was distasteful to Lawson that they should speak of the girl in that fashion. He made a remark about the departing mail and so distracted their attention. But next evening he went again to the pool. Ethel was there; and the mystery of the sunset, the deep silence of the water, the lithe grace of the coconut trees, added to her beauty, giving it a profundity, a magic, which stirred the heart to unknown emotions. For some reason that time he had the whim not to speak to her. She took no notice of him. She did not even glance in his direction. She swam about the green pool. She dived, she rested on the bank, as though she were quite alone: he had a queer feeling that he was invisible. Scraps of poetry, half forgotten, floated across his memory, and vague recollections of the Greece he had negligently studied in his school days. When she had changed her wet clothes for dry ones and sauntered away he found a scarlet hibiscus where she had been. It was a flower that she had worn in her hair when she came to bathe and, having taken it out on getting into the water, had forgotten or not cared to put in again. He took it in his hands and looked at it with a singular emotion. He had an instinct to keep it, but his sentimentality irritated him, and he flung it away. It gave him quite a little pang to see it float down the stream.

He wondered what strangeness it was in her nature that urged her to go down to this hidden pool when there was no likelihood that anyone should be there. The natives of the islands are devoted to the water. They bathe, somewhere or other, every day, once always, and often twice; but they bathe in bands, laughing and joyous, a whole family together; and you often saw a group of girls, dappled by the sun shining through the trees, with the half-castes among them, splashing about the shallows of the stream. It looked as though there were in this pool some secret which attracted Ethel against her will.

Now the night had fallen, mysterious and silent, and he let himself down in the water softly, in order to make no sound, and swam lazily in the warm darkness. The water seemed fragrant still from her slender body. He rode back to the town under the starry sky. He felt at peace with the world.

Now he went every evening to the pool and every evening he saw Ethel. Presently he overcame her timidity. She became playful and friendly. They sat together on the rocks above the pool, where the water ran fast, and they lay side by side on the ledge that overlooked it, watching the gathering dusk envelop it with mystery. It was inevitable that their meetings should become known—in the South Seas everyone seems to know everyone's business—and he was subjected to much rude chaff by the men at the hotel. He smiled and let them talk. It was not even worth while to deny their coarse suggestions. His feelings were absolutely pure. He loved Ethel as a poet might love the moon. He thought of her not as a woman but as something not of this earth. She was the spirit of the pool.

One day at the hotel, passing through the bar, he saw that old Brevald, as ever in his shabby blue overalls, was standing there. Because he was Ethel's father he had a desire to speak to him, so he went in, nodded and, ordering his own drink, casually turned and invited the old man to have one with him. They chatted for a few minutes of local affairs, and Lawson was uneasily conscious that the Norwegian was scrutinising him with sly blue eyes. His manner was not agreeable. It was sycophantic, and yet behind the cringing air of an old man who had been worsted in his struggle with fate was a shadow of old truculence. Lawson remembered that he had once been captain of a schooner engaged in the slave trade, a blackbirder they call it in the Pacific, and he had a large hernia in the chest which was the result of a wound received in a scrap with Solomon Islanders. The bell rang for luncheon.

"Well, I must be off," said Lawson.

"Why don't you come along to my place one time?" said Brevald, in his wheezy voice. "It's not very grand, but you'll be welcome. You know Ethel."

"I'll come with pleasure."

"Sunday afternoon's the best time."

Brevald's bungalow, shabby and bedraggled, stood among the coconut trees of the plantation, a little away from the main road that ran up to Vailima. Immediately around it grew huge plantains. With their tattered leaves they had the tragic beauty of a lovely woman in rags. Everything was slovenly and neglected. Little black pigs, thin and high-backed, rooted about, and chickens clucked noisily as they picked at the refuse scattered here and there. Three or four natives were lounging about the verandah. When Lawson asked for Brevald the old man's cracked voice called out to him, and he found him in the sitting-room smoking an old briar pipe.

"Sit down and make yerself at home," he said. "Ethel's just titivating."

She came in. She wore a blouse and skirt and her hair was done in the European fashion. Although she had not the wild, timid grace of the girl who came down every evening to the pool, she seemed now more usual and consequently more approachable. She shook hands with Lawson. It was the first time he had touched her hand.

"I hope you'll have a cup of tea with us," she said.

He knew she had been at a mission school, and he was amused, and at the same time touched, by the company manners she was putting on for his benefit. Tea was already set out on the table and in a minute old Brevald's fourth wife brought in the tea-pot. She was a handsome native, no longer very young, and she spoke but a few words of English. She smiled and smiled. Tea was rather a solemn meal, with a great deal of bread and butter and a variety of very sweet cakes, and the conversation was formal. Then a wrinkled old woman came in softly.

"That's Ethel's granny," said old Brevald, noisily spitting on the floor.

She sat on the edge of a chair, uncomfortably, so that you saw it was unusual for her and she would have been more at ease on the ground, and remained silently staring at Lawson with fixed, shining eyes. In the kitchen behind the bungalow someone began to play the concertina and two or three voices were raised in a hymn. But they sang for the pleasure of the sounds rather than from piety.

When Lawson walked back to the hotel he was strangely happy. He was touched by the higgledy-piggledy way in which those people lived; and in the smiling good-nature of Mrs. Brevald, in the little Norwegian's fantastic career, and in the shining mysterious eyes of the old grandmother he found something unusual and fascinating. It was a more natural life than any he had known, it was nearer to the friendly, fertile earth; civilisation repelled him at that moment, and by mere contact with these creatures of a more primitive nature he felt a greater freedom.

He saw himself rid of the hotel which already was beginning to irk him, settled in a little bungalow of his own, trim and white, in front of the sea so that he had before his eyes always the multi-coloured variety of the lagoon. He loved the beautiful island. London and England meant nothing to him any more, he was content to spend the rest of his days in that forgotten spot, rich in the best of the world's goods, love and happiness. He made up his mind that whatever the obstacles nothing should prevent him from marrying Ethel.

But there were no obstacles. He was always welcome at the Brevalds' house. The old man was ingratiating and Mrs. Brevald smiled without ceasing. He had brief glimpses of natives who seemed somehow to belong to the establishment, and once he found a tall youth in a lava-lava, his body tattooed, his hair white with lime, sitting with Brevald, and was told he was Mrs. Brevald's brother's son; but for the most part they kept out of his way. Ethel was delightful with him. The light in her eyes when she saw him filled him with ecstasy. She was charming and naïve. He listened enraptured when she told him of the mission school at which she was educated, and of the sisters. He went with her to the cinema which was given once a fortnight and danced with her at the dance which followed it. They came from all parts of the island for this, since gaieties are few in Upolu; and you saw there all the society of the place, the white ladies keeping a good deal to themselves, the half-castes very elegant in American clothes, the natives, strings of dark girls in white Mother Hubbards and young men in unaccustomed ducks and white shoes. It was all very smart and gay. Ethel was pleased to show her friends the white admirer who did not leave her side. The rumour was soon spread that he meant to marry her and her friends looked at her with envy. It was a great thing for a half-caste to get a white man to marry her, even the less regular relation was better than nothing, but one could never tell what it would lead to; and Lawson's position as manager of the bank made him one of the catches of the island. If he had not been so absorbed in Ethel he would have noticed that many eyes were fixed on him curiously, and he would have seen the glances of the white ladies and noticed how they put their heads together and gossiped.

Afterwards, when the men who lived at the hotel were having a whisky before turning in, Nelson burst out with:

"Say, they say Lawson's going to marry that girl."

"He's a damned fool then," said Miller.

Miller was a German–American who had changed his name from Müller, a big man, fat and bald-headed, with a round, clean-shaven face. He wore large gold-rimmed spectacles, which gave him a benign look, and his ducks were always clean and white. He was a heavy drinker, invariably ready to stay up all night with the "boys", but he never got drunk; he was jolly and affable, but very shrewd. Nothing interfered with his business; he represented a firm in San Francisco, jobbers of the goods sold in the islands, calico, machinery and what not; and his good-fellowship was part of his stock-in-trade.

"He don't know what he's up against," said Nelson. "Someone ought to put him wise."

"If you'll take my advice you won't interfere in what don't concern you," said Miller. "When a man's made up his mind to make a fool of himself, there's nothing like letting him."

"I'm all for having a good time with the girls out here, but when it comes to marrying them—this child ain't taking any, I'll tell the world."

Chaplin was there, and now he had his say.

"I've seen a lot of fellows do it, and it's no good."

"You ought to have a talk with him, Chaplin," said Nelson. "You know him better than anyone else does."

"My advice to Chaplin is to leave it alone," said Miller.

Even in those days Lawson was not popular and really no one took enough interest in him to bother. Mrs. Chaplin talked it over with two or three of the white ladies, but they contented themselves with saying that it was a pity; and when he told her definitely that he was going to be married it seemed too late to do anything.

For a year Lawson was happy. He took a bungalow at the point of the bay round which Apia is built, on the borders of a native village. It nestled charmingly among the coconut trees and faced the passionate blue of the Pacific. Ethel was lovely as she went about the little house, lithe and graceful like some young animal of the woods, and she was gay. They laughed a great deal. They talked nonsense. Sometimes one or two of the men at the hotel would come over and spend the evening, and often on a Sunday they would go for a day to some planter who had married a native; now and then one or other of the half-caste traders who had a store in Apia would give a party and they went to it. The half-castes treated Lawson quite differently now. His marriage had made him one of themselves and they called him Bertie. They put their arms through his and smacked him on the back. He liked to see Ethel at these gatherings. Her eyes shone and she laughed. It did him good to see her radiant happiness. Sometimes Ethel's relations would come to the bungalow, old Brevald of course, and her mother, but cousins too, vague native women in Mother Hubbards and men and boys in lava-lavas, with their hair dyed red and their bodies elaborately tattooed. He would find them sitting there when he got back from the bank. He laughed indulgently.

"Don't let them eat us out of hearth and home," he said.

"They're my own family. I can't help doing something for them when they ask me."

He knew that when a white man marries a native or a half-caste he must expect her relations to look upon him as a gold mine. He took Ethel's face in his hands and kissed her red lips. Perhaps he could not expect her to understand that the salary which had amply sufficed for a bachelor must be managed with some care when it had to support a wife and a house. Then Ethel was delivered of a son.

It was when Lawson first held the child in his arms that a sudden pang shot through his heart. He had not expected it to be so dark. After all it had but a fourth part of native blood, and there was no reason really why it should not look just like an English baby; but, huddled together in his arms, sallow, its head covered already with black hair, with huge black eyes, it might have been a native child. Since his marriage he had been ignored by the white ladies of the colony. When he came across men in whose houses he had been accustomed to dine as a bachelor, they were a little self-conscious with him; and they sought to cover their embarrassment by an exaggerated cordiality.

"Mrs. Lawson well?" they would say. "You're a lucky fellow. Damned pretty girl."

But if they were with their wives and met him and Ethel they would feel it awkward when their wives gave Ethel a patronising nod. Lawson had laughed.

"They're as dull as ditchwater, the whole gang of them," he said. "It's not going to disturb my night's rest if they don't ask me to their dirty parties."

But now it irked him a little.

The little dark baby screwed up its face. That was his son. He thought of the half-caste children in Apia. They had an unhealthy look, sallow and pale, and they were odiously precocious. He had seen them on the boat going to school in New Zealand, and a school had to be chosen which took children with native blood in them; they were huddled together, brazen and yet timid, with traits which set them apart strangely from white people. They spoke the native language among themselves. And when they grew up the men accepted smaller salaries because of their native blood; girls might marry a white man, but boys had no chance; they must marry a half-caste like themselves or a native. Lawson made up his mind passionately that he would take his son away from the humiliation of such a life. At whatever cost he must get back to Europe. And when he went in to see Ethel, frail and lovely in her bed, surrounded by native women, his determination was strengthened. If he took her away among his own people she would belong more completely to him. He loved her so passionately he wanted her to be one soul and one body with him; and he was conscious that here, with those deep roots attaching her to the native life, she would always keep something from him.

He went to work quietly, urged by an obscure instinct of secrecy, and wrote to a cousin who was partner in a shipping firm in Aberdeen, saying that his health (on account of which like so many more he had come out to the islands) was so much better, there seemed no reason why he should not return to Europe. He asked him to use what influence he could to get him a job, no matter how poorly paid, on Deeside, where the climate was particularly suitable to such as suffered from diseases of the lungs. It takes five or six weeks for letters to get from Aberdeen to Samoa, and several had to be exchanged. He had plenty of time to prepare Ethel. She was as delighted as a child. He was amused to see how she boasted to her friends that she was going to England; it was a step up for her; she would be quite English there; and she was excited at the interest the approaching departure gave her. When at length a cable came offering him a post in a bank in Kincardineshire she was beside herself with joy.

When, their long journey over, they were settled in the little Scots town with its granite houses Lawson realised how much it meant to him to live once more among his own people. He looked back on the three years he had spent in Apia as exile, and returned to the life that seemed the only normal one with a sigh of relief. It was good to play golf once more, and to fish—to fish properly, that was poor fun in the Pacific when you just threw in your line and pulled out one big sluggish fish after another from the crowded sea—and it was good to see a paper every day with that day's news, and to meet men and women of your own sort, people you could talk to; and it was good to eat meat that was not frozen and to drink milk that was not canned. They were thrown upon their own resources much more than in the Pacific, and he was glad to have Ethel exclusively to himself. After two years of marriage he loved her more devotedly than ever, he could hardly bear her out of his sight, and the need in him grew urgent for a more intimate communion between them. But it was strange that after the first excitement of arrival she seemed to take less interest in the new life than he had expected. She did not accustom herself to her surroundings. She was a little lethargic. As the fine autumn darkened into winter she complained of the cold. She lay half the morning in bed and the rest of the day on a sofa, reading novels sometimes, but more often doing nothing. She looked pinched.

"Never mind, darling," he said. "You'll get used to it very soon. And wait till the summer comes. It can be almost as hot as in Apia."

He felt better and stronger than he had done for years.

The carelessness with which she managed her house had not mattered in Samoa, but here it was out of place. When anyone came he did not want the place to look untidy; and, laughing, chaffing Ethel a little, he set about putting things in order. Ethel watched him indolently. She spent long hours playing with her son. She talked to him in the baby language of her own country. To distract her, Lawson bestirred himself to make friends among the neighbours, and now and then they went to little parties where the ladies sang drawing-room ballads and the men beamed in silent good nature.

Ethel was shy. She seemed to sit apart. Sometimes Lawson, seized with a sudden anxiety, would ask her if she was happy.

"Yes, I'm quite happy," she answered.

But her eyes were veiled by some thought he could not guess. She seemed to withdraw into herself so that he was conscious that he knew no more of her than when he had first seen her bathing in the pool. He had an uneasy feeling that she was concealing something from him, and because he adored her it tortured him.

"You don't regret Apia, do you?" he asked her once.

"Oh, no—I think it's very nice here."

An obscure misgiving drove him to make disparaging remarks about the island and the people there. She smiled and did not answer. Very rarely she received a bundle of letters from Samoa and then she went about for a day or two with a set, pale face.

"Nothing would induce me ever to go back there," he said once. "It's no place for a white man."

But he grew conscious that sometimes, when he was away, Ethel cried. In Apia she had been talkative, chatting volubly about all the little details of their common life, the gossip of the place; but now she gradually became silent, and, though he increased his efforts to amuse her, she remained listless. It seemed to him that her recollections of the old life were drawing her away from him, and he was madly jealous of the island and of the sea, of Brevald, and all the dark-skinned people whom he remembered now with horror. When she spoke of Samoa he was bitter and satirical. One evening late in the spring when the birch trees were bursting into leaf, coming home from a round of golf, he found her not as usual lying on the sofa, but at the window, standing. She had evidently been waiting for his return. She addressed him the moment he came into the room. To his amazement she spoke in Samoan.

"I can't stand it. I can't live here any more. I hate it. I hate it."

"For God's sake speak in a civilised language," he said irritably.

She went up to him and clasped her arms around his body awkwardly, with a gesture that had in it something barbaric.

"Let's go away from here. Let's go back to Samoa. If you make me stay here I shall die. I want to go home."

Her passion broke suddenly and she burst into tears. His anger vanished and he drew her down on his knees. He explained to her that it was impossible for him to throw up his job, which after all meant his bread and butter. His place in Apia was long since filled. He had nothing to go back to there. He tried to put it to her reasonably, the inconveniences of life there, the humiliation to which they must be exposed, and the bitterness it must cause their son.

"Scotland's wonderful for education and that sort of thing. Schools are good and cheap, and he can go to the University at Aberdeen. I'll make a real Scot of him."

They had called him Andrew. Lawson wanted him to become a doctor. He would marry a white woman.

"I'm not ashamed of being half native," Ethel said sullenly.

"Of course not, darling. There's nothing to be ashamed of."

With her soft cheek against his he felt incredibly weak.

"You don't know how much I love you," he said. "I'd give anything in the world to be able to tell you what I've got in my heart."

He sought her lips.

The summer came. The highland valley was green and fragrant and the hills were gay with the heather. One sunny day followed another in that sheltered spot, and the shade of the birch trees was grateful after the glare of the high road. Ethel spoke no more of Samoa and Lawson grew less nervous. He thought that she was resigned to her surroundings, and he felt that his love for her was so passionate that it could leave no room in her heart for any longing. One day the local doctor stopped him in the street.

"I say, Lawson, your missus ought to be careful how she bathes in our highland streams. It's not like the Pacific, you know."

Lawson was surprised, and had not the presence of mind to conceal the fact.

"I didn't know she was bathing."

The doctor laughed.

"A good many people have seen her. It makes them talk a bit, you know, because it seems a rum place to choose, the pool up above the bridge, and bathing isn't allowed there, but there's no harm in that. I don't know how she can stand the water."

Lawson knew the pool the doctor spoke of, and suddenly it occurred to him that in a way it was just like that pool at Upolu where Ethel had been in the habit of bathing every evening. A clear highland stream ran down a sinuous course, rocky, splashing gaily, and then formed a deep, smooth pool, with a little sandy beach. Trees overshadowed it thickly, not coconut trees, but beeches, and the sun played fitfully through the leaves on the sparkling water. It gave him a shock. With his imagination he saw Ethel go there every day and undress on the bank and slip into the water, cold, colder than that of the pool she loved at home, and for a moment regain the feeling of the past. He saw her once more as the strange, wild spirit of the stream, and it seemed to him fantastically that the running water called her. That afternoon he went along to the river. He made his way cautiously among the trees and the grassy path deadened the sound of his steps. Presently he came to a spot from which he could see the pool. Ethel was sitting on the bank, looking down at the water. She sat quite still. It seemed as though the water drew her irresistibly. He wondered what strange thoughts wandered through her head. At last she got up, and for a minute or two she was hidden from his gaze; then he saw her again, wearing a Mother Hubbard, and with her little bare feet she stepped delicately over the mossy bank. She came to the water's edge, and softly, without a splash, let herself down. She swam about quietly, and there was something not quite of a human being in the way she swam. He did not know why it affected him so queerly. He waited till she clambered out. She stood for a moment with the wet folds of her dress clinging to her body, so that its shape was outlined, and then, passing her hands slowly over her breasts, gave a little sigh of delight. Then she disappeared. Lawson turned away and walked back to the village. He had a bitter pain in his heart, for he knew that she was still a stranger to him and his hungry love was destined ever to remain unsatisfied.

He did not make any mention of what he had seen. He ignored the incident completely, but he looked at her curiously, trying to divine what was in her mind. He redoubled the tenderness with which he used her. He sought to make her forget the deep longing of her soul by the passion of his love.

Then one day, when he came home, he was astonished to find her not in the house.

"Where's Mrs. Lawson?" he asked the maid.

"She went into Aberdeen, Sir, with the baby," the maid answered, a little surprised at the question. "She said she would not be back till the last train."

"Oh, all right."

He was vexed that Ethel had said nothing to him about the excursion, but he was not disturbed, since of late she had been in now and again to Aberdeen, and he was glad that she should look at the shops and perhaps visit a cinema. He went to meet the last train, but when she did not come he grew suddenly frightened. He went up to the bedroom and saw at once that her toilet things were no longer in their place. He opened the wardrobe and the drawers. They were half empty. She had bolted.

He was seized with a passion of anger. It was too late that night to telephone to Aberdeen and make enquiries, but he knew already all that his enquiries might have taught him. With fiendish cunning she had chosen a time when they were making up their periodical accounts at the bank and there was no chance that he could follow her. He was imprisoned by his work. He took up a paper and saw that there was a boat sailing for Australia next morning. She must be now well on the way to London. He could not prevent the sobs that were wrung painfully from him.

"I've done everything in the world for her," he cried, "and she had the heart to treat me like this. How cruel, how monstrously cruel!"

After two days of misery he received a letter from her. It was written in her school-girl hand. She had always written with difficulty:

Dear Bertie,
 I couldn't stand it any more. I'm going back home. Good-bye.
              Ethel.

She did not say a single word of regret. She did not even ask him to come too. Lawson was prostrated. He found out where the ship made its first stop and, though he knew very well she would not come, sent a cable beseeching her to return. He waited with pitiful anxiety. He wanted her to send him just one word of love; she did not even answer. He passed through one violent phase after another. At one moment he told himself that he was well rid of her, and at the next that he would force her to return by withholding money. He was lonely and wretched. He wanted his boy and he wanted her. He knew that, whatever he pretended to himself, there was only one thing to do and that was to follow her. He could never live without her now. All his plans for the future were like a house of cards and he scattered them with angry impatience. He did not care whether he threw away his chances for the future, for nothing in the world mattered but that he should get Ethel back again. As soon as he could he went into Aberdeen and told the manager of his bank that he meant to leave at once. The manager remonstrated. The short notice was inconvenient. Lawson would not listen to reason. He was determined to be free before the next boat sailed; and it was not until he was on board of her, having sold everything he possessed, that in some measure he regained his calm. Till then to those who had come in contact with him he seemed hardly sane. His last action in England was to cable to Ethel at Apia that he was joining her.

He sent another cable from Sydney, and when at last with the dawn his boat crossed the bar at Apia and he saw once more the white houses straggling along the bay he felt an immense relief. The doctor came on board and the agent. They were both old acquaintances and he felt kindly towards their familiar faces. He had a drink or two with them for old times' sake, and also because he was desperately nervous. He was not sure if Ethel would be glad to see him. When he got into the launch and approached the wharf he scanned anxiously the little crowd that waited. She was not there and his heart sank, but then he saw Brevald, in his old blue clothes, and his heart warmed towards him.

"Where's Ethel?" he said, as he jumped on shore.

"She's down at the bungalow. She's living with us."

Lawson was dismayed, but he put on a jovial air.

"Well, have you got room for me? I daresay it'll take a week or two to fix ourselves up."

"Oh, yes, I guess we can make room for you."

After passing through the customs-house they went to the hotel and there Lawson was greeted by several of his old friends. There were a good many rounds of drinks before it seemed possible to get away and when they did go out at last to Brevald's house they were both rather gay. He clasped Ethel in his arms. He had forgotten all his bitter thoughts in the joy of beholding her once more. His mother-in-law was pleased to see him, and so was the old, wrinkled beldame, her mother; natives and half-castes came in, and they all sat round, beaming on him. Brevald had a bottle of whisky and everyone who came was given a nip. Lawson sat with his little dark-skinned boy on his knees, they had taken his English clothes off him and he was stark, with Ethel by his side in a Mother Hubbard. He felt like a returning prodigal. In the afternoon he went down to the hotel again and when he got back he was more than gay, he was drunk. Ethel and her mother knew that white men got drunk now and then, it was what you expected of them, and they laughed good-naturedly as they helped him to bed.

But in a day or two he set about looking for a job. He knew that he could not hope for such a position as that which he had thrown away to go to England; but with his training he could not fail to be useful to one of the trading firms, and perhaps in the end he would not lose by the change.

"After all, you can't make money in a bank," he said. "Trade's the thing."

He had hopes that he would soon make himself so indispensable that he would get someone to take him into partnership, and there was no reason why in a few years he should not be a rich man.

"As soon as I'm fixed up we'll find ourselves a shack," he told Ethel. "We can't go on living here."

Brevald's bungalow was so small that they were all piled on one another, and there was no chance of ever being alone. There was neither peace nor privacy.

"Well, there's no hurry. We shall be all right here till we find just what we want."

It took him a week to get settled and then he entered the firm of a man called Bain. But when he talked to Ethel about moving she said she wanted to stay where she was till her baby was born, for she was expecting another child. Lawson tried to argue with her.

"If you don't like it," she said, "go and live at the hotel."

He grew suddenly pale.

"Ethel, how can you suggest that!"

She shrugged her shoulders.

"What's the good of having a house of our own when we can live here."

He yielded.

When Lawson, after his work, went back to the bungalow he found it crowded with natives. They lay about smoking, sleeping, drinking kava; and they talked incessantly. The place was grubby and untidy. His child crawled about, playing with native children, and it heard nothing spoken but Samoan. He fell into the habit of dropping into the hotel on his way home to have a few cocktails, for he could only face the evening and the crowd of friendly natives when he was fortified with liquor. And all the time, though he loved her more passionately than ever, he felt that Ethel was slipping away from him. When the baby was born he suggested that they should get into a house of their own, but Ethel refused. Her stay in Scotland seemed to have thrown her back on her own people, now that she was once more among them, with a passionate zest, and she turned to her native ways with abandon. Lawson began to drink more. Every Saturday night he went to the English Club and got blind drunk.

He had the peculiarity that as he grew drunk he grew quarrelsome and once he had a violent dispute with Bain, his employer. Bain dismissed him, and he had to look out for another job. He was idle for two or three weeks, and during these, sooner than sit in the bungalow, he lounged about in the hotel or at the English Club, and drank. It was more out of pity than anything else that Miller, the German–American, took him into his office; but he was a business man, and though Lawson's financial skill made him valuable, the circumstances were such that he could hardly refuse a smaller salary than he had had before, and Miller did not hesitate to offer it to him. Ethel and Brevald blamed him for taking it, since Pedersen, the half-caste, offered him more. But he resented bitterly the thought of being under the orders of a half-caste. When Ethel nagged him he burst out furiously:

"I'll see myself dead before I work for a nigger."

"You may have to," she said.

And in six months he found himself forced to this final humiliation. The passion for liquor had been gaining on him, he was often heavy with drink, and he did his work badly. Miller warned him once or twice and Lawson was not the man to accept remonstrance easily. One day in the midst of an altercation he put on his hat and walked out. But by now his reputation was well known and he could find no one to engage him. For a while he idled, and then he had an attack of delirium tremens. When he recovered, shameful and weak, he could no longer resist the constant pressure and he went to Pedersen and asked him for a job. Pedersen was glad to have a white man in his store and Lawson's skill at figures made him useful.

From that time his degeneration was rapid. The white people gave him the cold shoulder. They were only prevented from cutting him completely by disdainful pity and by a certain dread of his angry violence when he was drunk. He became extremely susceptible and was always on the lookout for affront.

He lived entirely among the natives and half-castes, but he had no longer the prestige of the white man. They felt his loathing for them and they resented his attitude of superiority. He was one of themselves now and they did not see why he should put on airs. Brevald, who had been ingratiating and obsequious, now treated him with contempt. Ethel had made a bad bargain. There were disgraceful scenes and once or twice the two men came to blows. When there was a quarrel Ethel took the part of her family. They found he was better drunk than sober, for when he was drunk he would lie on the bed or on the floor, sleeping heavily.

Then he became aware that something was being hidden from him.

When he got back to the bungalow for the wretched, half-native supper which was his evening meal, often Ethel was not in. If he asked where she was Brevald told him she had gone to spend the evening with one or other of her friends. Once he followed her to the house Brevald had mentioned and found she was not there. On her return he asked her where she had been and she told him her father had made a mistake; she had been to so-and-so's. But he knew that she was lying. She was in her best clothes; her eyes were shining and she looked lovely.

"Don't try any monkey tricks on me, my girl," he said, "or I'll break every bone in your body."

"You drunken beast," she said, scornfully.

He fancied that Mrs. Brevald and the old grandmother looked at him maliciously and he ascribed Brevald's good-humour with him, so unusual those days, to his satisfaction at having something up his sleeve against his son-in-law. And then, his suspicions aroused, he imagined that the white men gave him curious glances. When he came into the lounge of the hotel the sudden silence which fell upon the company convinced him that he had been the subject of the conversation. Something was going on and everyone knew it but himself. He was seized with furious jealousy. He believed that Ethel was carrying on with one of the white men, and he looked at one after the other with scrutinising eyes; but there was nothing to give him even a hint. He was helpless. Because he could find no one on whom definitely to fix his suspicions, he went about like a raving maniac, looking for someone on whom to vent his wrath. Chance caused him in the end to hit upon the man who of all others least deserved to suffer from his violence. One afternoon, when he was sitting in the hotel by himself, moodily, Chaplin came in and sat down beside him. Perhaps Chaplin was the only man on the island who had any sympathy for him. They ordered drinks and chatted a few minutes about the races that were shortly to be run. Then Chaplin said:

"I guess we shall all have to fork out money for new dresses."

Lawson sniggered. Since Mrs. Chaplin held the purse-strings, if she wanted a new frock for the occasion she would certainly not ask her husband for the money.

"How is your missus?" asked Chaplin, desiring to be friendly.

"What the hell's that got to do with you?" said Lawson, knitting his dark brows.

"I was only asking a civil question."

"Well, keep your civil questions to yourself."

Chaplin was not a patient man; his long residence in the tropics, the whisky bottle, and his domestic affairs had given him a temper hardly more under control than Lawson's.

"Look here, my boy, when you're in my hotel you behave like a gentleman or you'll find yourself in the street before you can say knife."

Lawson's lowering face grew dark and red.

"Let me just tell you once for all and you can pass it on to the others," he said, panting with rage. "If any of you fellows come messing round with my wife he'd better look out."

"Who do you think wants to mess around with your wife?"

"I'm not such a fool as you think. I can see a stone wall in front

E

of me as well as most men, and I warn you straight, that's all. I'm not going to put up with any hanky-panky, not on your life."

"Look here, you'd better clear out of here, and come back when you're sober."

"I shall clear out when I choose and not a minute before," said Lawson.

It was an unfortunate boast, for Chaplin in the course of his experience as a hotel-keeper had acquired a peculiar skill in dealing with gentlemen whose room he preferred to their company, and the words were hardly out of Lawson's mouth before he found himself caught by the collar and arm and hustled not without force into the street. He stumbled down the steps into the blinding glare of the sun.

It was in consequence of this that he had his first violent scene with Ethel. Smarting with humiliation and unwilling to go back to the hotel, he went home that afternoon earlier than usual. He found Ethel dressing to go out. As a rule she lay about in a Mother Hubbard, barefoot, with a flower in her dark hair; but now, in white silk stockings and high-heeled shoes, she was doing up a pink muslin dress which was the newest she had.

"You're making yourself very smart," he said. "Where are you going?"

"I'm going to the Crossleys."

"I'll come with you."

"Why?" she asked coolly.

"I don't want you to gad about by yourself all the time."

"You're not asked."

"I don't care a damn about that. You're not going without me."

"You'd better lie down till I'm ready."

She thought he was drunk and if he once settled himself on the bed would quickly drop off to sleep. He sat down on a chair and began to smoke a cigarette. She watched him with increasing irritation. When she was ready he got up. It happened by an unusual chance that there was no one in the bungalow. Brevald was working on the plantation and his wife had gone into Apia. Ethel faced him.

"I'm not going with you. You're drunk."

"That's a lie. You're not going without me."

She shrugged her shoulders and tried to pass him, but he caught her by the arm and held her.

"Let me go, you devil," she said, breaking into Samoan.

"Why do you want to go without me? Haven't I told you I'm not going to put up with any monkey tricks?"

She clenched her fist and hit him in the face. He lost all control of himself. All his love, all his hatred, welled up in him and he was beside himself.

"I'll teach you," he shouted. "I'll teach you."

He seized a riding-whip which happened to be under his hand, and struck her with it. She screamed, and the scream maddened him so that he went on striking her, again and again. Her shrieks rang through the bungalow and he cursed her as he hit. Then he flung her on the bed. She lay there sobbing with pain and terror. He threw the whip away from him and rushed out of the room. Ethel heard him go and she stopped crying. She looked round cautiously, then she raised herself. She was sore, but she had not been badly hurt, and she looked at her dress to see if it was damaged. The native women are not unused to blows. What he had done did not outrage her. When she looked at herself in the glass and arranged her hair, her eyes were shining. There was a strange look in them. Perhaps then she was nearer loving him than she had ever been before.

But Lawson, driven forth blindly, stumbled through the plantation and suddenly exhausted, weak as a child, flung himself on the ground at the foot of a tree. He was miserable and ashamed. He thought of Ethel, and in the yielding tenderness of his love all his bones seemed to grow soft within him. He thought of the past, and of his hopes, and he was aghast at what he had done. He wanted her more than ever. He wanted to take her in his arms. He must go to her at once. He got up. He was so weak that he staggered as he walked. He went into the house and she was sitting in their cramped bedroom in front of her looking-glass.

"Oh, Ethel, forgive me. I'm so awfully ashamed of myself. I didn't know what I was doing."

He fell on his knees before her and timidly stroked the skirt of her dress.

"I can't bear to think of what I did. It's awful. I think I was mad. There's no one in the world I love as I love you. I'd do anything to save you from pain and I've hurt you. I can never forgive myself, but for God's sake say you forgive me."

He heard her shrieks still. It was unendurable. She looked at him silently. He tried to take her hands and the tears streamed from his eyes. In his humiliation he hid his face in her lap and his frail body shook with sobs. An expression of utter contempt came over her face. She had the native woman's disdain of a man who abased himself before a woman. A weak creature! And for a moment she had been on the point of thinking there was something in him. He grovelled at her feet like a cur. She gave him a little scornful kick.

"Get out," she said. "I hate you."

He tried to hold her, but she pushed him aside. She stood up. She began to take off her dress. She kicked off her shoes and slid the stockings off her feet, then she slipped on her old Mother Hubbard.

"Where are you going?"

"What's that got to do with you? I'm going down to the pool."

"Let me come too," he said.

He asked as though he were a child.

"Can't you even leave me that?"

He hid his face in his hands, crying miserably, while she, her eyes hard and cold, stepped past him and went out.

From that time she entirely despised him; and though, herded together in the small bungalow, Lawson and Ethel with her two children, Brevald, his wife and her mother, and the vague relations and hangers-on who were always in and about, they had to live cheek by jowl, Lawson, ceasing to be of any account, was hardly noticed. He left in the morning after breakfast, and came back only to have supper. He gave up the struggle, and when for want of money he could not go to the English Club he spent the evening playing hearts with old Brevald and the natives. Except when he was drunk he was cowed and listless. Ethel treated him like a dog. She submitted at times to his fits of wild passion, and she was frightened by the gusts of hatred with which they were followed: but when, afterwards, he was cringing and lachrymose she had such a contempt for him that she could have spat in his face. Sometimes he was violent, but now she was prepared for him, and when he hit her she kicked and scratched and bit. They had horrible battles in which he had not always the best of it. Very soon it was known all over Apia that they got on badly. There was little sympathy for Lawson, and at the hotel the general surprise was that old Brevald did not kick him out of the place.

"Brevald's a pretty ugly customer," said one of the men. "I shouldn't be surprised if he put a bullet into Lawson's carcass one of these days."

Ethel still went in the evenings to bathe in the silent pool. It seemed to have an attraction for her that was not quite human, just that attraction you might imagine that a mermaid who had won a soul would have for the cool salt waves of the sea; and sometimes Lawson went also. I do not know what urged him to go, for Ethel was obviously irritated by his presence; perhaps it was because in that spot he hoped to regain the clean rapture which had filled his heart when he first saw her; perhaps only, with the madness of those who love them that love them not, from the feeling that his obstinacy could force love. One day he strolled down there with a feeling that was rare with him now. He felt suddenly at peace with the world. The evening was drawing in and the dusk seemed to cling to the leaves of the coconut trees like a little thin cloud. A faint breeze stirred them noiselessly. A crescent moon hung just over their tops. He made his way to the bank. He saw Ethel in the water floating on her back. Her hair streamed out all round her, and she was holding in her hand a large hibiscus. He stopped a moment to admire her; she was like Ophelia.

"Hulloa, Ethel," he cried joyfully.

She made a sudden movement and dropped the red flower. It floated idly away. She swam a stroke or two till she knew there was ground within her depth and then stood up.

"Go away," she said. "Go away."

He laughed.

"Don't be selfish. There's plenty of room for both of us."

"Why can't you leave me alone? I want to be by myself."

"Hang it all, I want to bathe," he answered, good-humouredly.

"Go down to the bridge. I don't want you here."

"I'm sorry for that," he said, smiling still.

He was not in the least angry, and he hardly noticed that she was in a passion. He began to take off his coat.

"Go away," she shrieked. "I won't have you here. Can't you even leave me this? Go away."

"Don't be silly, darling."

She bent down and picked up a sharp stone and flung it quickly at him. He had no time to duck. It hit him on the temple. With a cry he put his hand to his head and when he took it away it was wet with blood. Ethel stood still, panting with rage. He turned very pale, and without a word, taking up his coat, went away. Ethel let herself fall back into the water and the stream carried her slowly down to the ford.

The stone had made a jagged wound and for some days Lawson went about with a bandaged head. He had invented a likely story to account for the accident when the fellows at the club asked him about it, but he had no occasion to use it. No one referred to the matter. He saw them cast surreptitious glances at his head, but not a word was said. The silence could only mean that they knew how he came by his wound. He was certain now that Ethel had a lover and they all knew who it was. But there was not the smallest indication to guide him. He never saw Ethel with anyone; no one showed a wish to be with her, or treated him in a manner that seemed strange. Wild rage seized him, and having no one to vent it on he drank more and more heavily. A little while before I came to the island he had had another attack of delirium tremens.

I met Ethel at the house of a man called Caster, who lived two or three miles from Apia with a native wife. I had been playing tennis with him and when we were tired he suggested a cup of tea. We went into the house and in the untidy living-room found Ethel chatting with Mrs. Caster.

"Hulloa, Ethel," he said, "I didn't know you were here."

I could not help looking at her with curiosity. I tried to see what there was in her to have excited in Lawson such a devastating passion. But who can explain these things? It was true that she was lovely; she reminded one of the red hibiscus, the common flower of the hedgerow in Samoa, with its grace and its languor and its passion; but what surprised me most, taking into consideration the story I knew even then a good deal of, was her freshness and simplicity. She was quiet and a little shy. There was nothing coarse or loud about her; she had not the exuberance common to the half-caste; and it was almost impossible to believe that she could be the virago that the horrible scenes between husband and wife, which were now common knowledge, indicated. In her pretty pink frock and high-heeled shoes she looked quite European. You could hardly have guessed at that dark background of native life in which she felt herself so much more at home. I did not imagine that she was at all intelligent, and I should not have been surprised if a man, after living with her for some time, had found the passion which had drawn him to her sink into boredom. It suggested itself to me that in her elusiveness, like a thought that presents itself to consciousness and vanishes before it can be captured by words, lay her peculiar charm; but perhaps that was merely fancy, and if I had known nothing about her I should have seen in her only a pretty little half-caste like another.

She talked to me of the various things which they talk of to the stranger in Samoa, of the journey, and whether I had slid down the water rock at Papaseea, and if I meant to stay in a native village. She talked to me of Scotland, and perhaps I noticed in her a tendency to enlarge on the sumptuousness of her establishment there. She asked me naïvely if I knew Mrs. This and Mrs. That, with whom she had been acquainted when she lived in the north.

Then Miller, the fat German–American, came in. He shook hands all round very cordially and sat down, asking in his loud, cheerful voice for a whisky and soda. He was very fat and he sweated profusely. He took off his gold-rimmed spectacles and wiped them; you saw then that his little eyes, benevolent behind the large round glasses, were shrewd and cunning; the party had been somewhat dull till he came, but he was a good story-teller and a jovial fellow. Soon he had the two women, Ethel and my friend's wife, laughing delightedly at his sallies. He had a reputation on the island of a lady's man, and you could see how this fat, gross fellow, old and ugly, had yet the possibility of fascination. His humour was on a level with the understanding of his company, an affair of vitality and assurance, and his Western accent gave a peculiar point to what he said. At last he turned to me:

"Well, if we want to get back for dinner we'd better be getting. I'll take you along in my machine if you like."

I thanked him and got up. He shook hands with the others, went out of the room, massive and strong in his walk, and climbed into his car.

"Pretty little thing, Lawson's wife," I said, as we drove along.

"Too bad the way he treats her. Knocks her about. Gets my dander up when I hear of a man hitting a woman."

We went on a little. Then he said:

"He was a darned fool to marry her. I said so at the time. If he hadn't, he'd have had the whip hand over her. He's yaller, that's what he is, yaller."

The year was drawing to its end and the time approached when I was to leave Samoa. My boat was scheduled to sail for Sydney on the fourth of January. Christmas Day had been celebrated at the hotel with suitable ceremonies, but it was looked upon as no more than a rehearsal for New Year, and the men who were accustomed to foregather in the lounge determined on New Year's Eve to make a night of it. There was an uproarious dinner, after which the party sauntered down to the English Club, a simple little frame house, to play pool. There was a great deal of talking, laughing, and betting, but some very poor play, except on the part of Miller, who had drunk as much as any of them, all far younger than he, but had kept unimpaired the keenness of his eye and the sureness of his hand. He pocketed the young men's money with humour and urbanity. After an hour of this I grew tired and went out. I crossed the road and came on to the beach. Three coconut trees grew there, like three moon maidens waiting for their lovers to ride out of the sea, and I sat at the foot of one of them, watching the lagoon and the nightly assemblage of the stars.

I do not know where Lawson had been during the evening, but

between ten and eleven he came along to the club. He shambled down the dusty, empty road, feeling dull and bored, and when he reached the club, before going into the billiard-room, went into the bar to have a drink by himself. He had a shyness now about joining the company of white men when there were a lot of them together and needed a stiff dose of whisky to give him confidence. He was standing with the glass in his hand when Miller came in to him. He was in his shirt-sleeves and still held his cue. He gave the bar-tender a glance.

"Get out, Jack," he said.

The bar-tender, a native in a white jacket and a red lava-lava, without a word slid out of the small room.

"Look here, I've been wanting to have a few words with you, Lawson," said the big American.

"Well, that's one of the few things you can have free, gratis, and for nothing on this damned island."

Miller fixed his gold spectacles more firmly on his nose and held Lawson with his cold determined eyes.

"See here, young fellow, I understand you've been knocking Mrs. Lawson about again. I'm not going to stand for that. If you don't stop it right now I'll break every bone of your dirty little body."

Then Lawson knew what he had been trying to find out so long. It was Miller. The appearance of the man, fat, bald-headed, with his round bare face and double chin and the gold spectacles, his age, his benign, shrewd look, like that of a renegade priest, and the thought of Ethel, so slim and virginal, filled him with a sudden horror. Whatever his faults Lawson was no coward, and without a word he hit out violently at Miller. Miller quickly warded the blow with the hand that held the cue, and then with a great swing of his right arm brought his fist down on Lawson's ear. Lawson was four inches shorter than the American and he was slightly built, frail and weakened not only by illness and the enervating tropics, but by drink. He fell like a log and lay half dazed at the foot of the bar. Miller took off his spectacles and wiped them with his handkerchief.

"I guess you know what to expect now. You've had your warning and you'd better take it."

He took up his cue and went back into the billiard-room. There was so much noise there that no one knew what had happened. Lawson picked himself up. He put his hand to his ear, which was singing still. Then he slunk out of the club.

I saw a man cross the road, a patch of white against the darkness of the night, but did not know who it was. He came down to the beach, passed me sitting at the foot of the tree, and looked down.

I saw then that it was Lawson, but since he was doubtless drunk, did not speak. He went on, walked irresolutely two or three steps, and turned back. He came up to me and bending down stared in my face.

"I thought it was you," he said.

He sat down and took out his pipe.

"It was hot and noisy in the club," I volunteered.

"Why are you sitting here?"

"I was waiting about for the midnight mass at the Cathedral."

"If you like I'll come with you."

Lawson was quite sober. We sat for a while smoking in silence. Now and then in the lagoon was the splash of some big fish, and a little way out towards the opening in the reef was the light of a schooner.

"You're sailing next week, aren't you?" he said.

"Yes."

"It would be jolly to go home once more. But I could never stand it now. The cold, you know."

"It's odd to think that in England now they're shivering round the fire," I said.

There was not even a breath of wind. The balminess of the night was like a spell. I wore nothing but a thin shirt and a suit of ducks. I enjoyed the exquisite languor of the night, and stretched my limbs voluptuously.

"This isn't the sort of New Year's Eve that persuades one to make good resolutions for the future," I smiled.

He made no answer, but I do not know what train of thought my casual remark had suggested in him, for presently he began to speak. He spoke in a low voice, without any expression, but his accents were educated, and it was a relief to hear him after the twang and the vulgar intonations which for some time had wounded my ears.

"I've made an awful hash of things. That's obvious, isn't it? I'm right down at the bottom of the pit and there's no getting out for me. '*Black as the pit from pole to pole.*'" I felt him smile as he made the quotation. "And the strange thing is that I don't see how I went wrong."

I held my breath, for to me there is nothing more awe-inspiring than when a man discovers to you the nakedness of his soul. Then you see that no one is so trivial or debased but that in him is a spark of something to excite compassion.

"It wouldn't be so rotten if I could see that it was all my own fault. It's true I drink, but I shouldn't have taken to that if things had gone differently. I wasn't really fond of liquor. I suppose I ought not to have married Ethel. If I'd kept her it would be all right. But I did love her so."

His voice faltered.

"She's not a bad lot, you know, not really. It's just rotten luck. We might have been as happy as lords. When she bolted I suppose I ought to have let her go, but I couldn't do that—I was dead stuck on her then; and there was the kid."

"Are you fond of the kid?" I asked.

"I was. There are two, you know. But they don't mean so much to me now. You'd take them for natives anywhere. I have to talk to them in Samoan."

"Is it too late for you to start fresh? Couldn't you make a dash for it and leave the place?"

"I haven't the strength. I'm done for."

"Are you still in love with your wife?"

"Not now. Not now." He repeated the two words with a kind of horror in his voice. "I haven't even got that now. I'm down and out."

The bells of the Cathedral were ringing.

"If you really want to come to the midnight mass we'd better go along," I said.

"Come on."

We got up and walked along the road. The Cathedral, all white, stood facing the sea not without impressiveness, and beside it the Protestant chapels had the look of meeting-houses. In the road were two or three cars, and a great number of traps, and traps were put up against the walls at the side. People had come from all parts of the island for the service, and through the great open doors we saw that the place was crowded. The high altar was all ablaze with light. There were a few whites and a good many half-castes, but the great majority were natives. All the men wore trousers, for the Church has decided that the lava-lava is indecent. We found chairs at the back, near the open door, and sat down. Presently, following Lawson's eyes, I saw Ethel come in with a party of half-castes. They were all very much dressed up, the men in high, stiff collars and shiny boots, the women in large, gay hats. Ethel nodded and smiled to her friends as she passed up the aisle. The service began.

When it was over Lawson and I stood on one side for a while to watch the crowd stream out, then he held out his hand.

"Good-night," he said. "I hope you'll have a pleasant journey home."

"Oh, but I shall see you before I go."

He sniggered.

"The question is if you'll see me drunk or sober."

He turned and left me. I had a recollection of those very large black eyes, shining wildly under the shaggy brows. I paused irresolutely. I did not feel sleepy and I thought I would at all events go along to the club for an hour before turning in. When I got there I found the billiard-room empty, but half-a-dozen men were sitting round a table in the lounge, playing poker. Miller looked up as I came in.

"Sit down and take a hand," he said.

"All right."

I bought some chips and began to play. Of course it is the most fascinating game in the world and my hour lengthened out to two, and then to three. The native bar-tender, cheery and wide-awake notwithstanding the time, was at our elbow to supply us with drinks and from somewhere or other he produced a ham and a loaf of bread. We played on. Most of the party had drunk more than was good for them and the play was high and reckless. I played modestly, neither wishing to win nor anxious to lose, but I watched Miller with a fascinated interest. He drank glass for glass with the rest of the company, but remained cool and level-headed. His pile of chips increased in size and he had a neat little paper in front of him on which he had marked various sums lent to players in distress. He beamed amiably at the young men whose money he was taking. He kept up interminably his stream of jest and anecdote, but he never missed a draw, he never let an expression of the face pass him. At last the dawn crept into the windows, gently, with a sort of deprecating shyness, as though it had no business there, and then it was day.

"Well," said Miller, "I reckon we've seen the old year out in style. Now let's have a round of jackpots and me for my mosquito net. I'm fifty, remember, I can't keep these late hours."

The morning was beautiful and fresh when we stood on the verandah, and the lagoon was like a sheet of multicoloured glass. Someone suggested a dip before going to bed, but none cared to bathe in the lagoon, sticky and treacherous to the feet. Miller had his car at the door and he offered to take us down to the pool. We jumped in and drove along the deserted road. When we reached the pool it seemed as though the day had hardly risen there yet. Under the trees the water was all in shadow and the night had the effect of lurking still. We were in great spirits. We had no towels or any costume and in my prudence I wondered how we were going to dry ourselves. None of us had much on and it did not take us long to snatch off our clothes. Nelson, the little supercargo, was stripped first.

"I'm going down to the bottom," he said.

He dived and in a moment another man dived too, but shallow, and was out of the water before him. Then Nelson came up and scrambled to the side.

"I say, get me out," he said.

"What's up?"

Something was evidently the matter. His face was terrified. Two fellows gave him their hands and he slithered up.

"I say, there's a man down there."

"Don't be a fool. You're drunk."

"Well, if there isn't I'm in for D.T.s. But I tell you there's a man down there. It just scared me out of my wits."

Miller looked at him for a moment. The little man was all white. He was actually trembling.

"Come on, Caster," said Miller to the big Australian, "we'd better go down and see."

"He was standing up," said Nelson, "all dressed. I saw him. He tried to catch hold of me."

"Hold your row," said Miller. "Are you ready?"

They dived in. We waited on the bank, silent. It really seemed as though they were under water longer than any men could breathe. Then Caster came up, and immediately after him, red in the face as though he were going to have a fit, Miller. They were pulling something behind them. Another man jumped in to help them, and the three together dragged their burden to the side. They shoved it up. Then we saw that it was Lawson, with a great stone tied up in his coat and bound to his feet.

"He was set on making a good job of it," said Miller, as he wiped the water from his short-sighted eyes.

Mackintosh

HE splashed about for a few minutes in the sea; it was too shallow to swim in and for fear of sharks he could not go out of his depth; then he got out and went into the bath-house for a shower. The coldness of the fresh water was grateful after the heavy stickiness of the salt Pacific, so warm, though it was only just after seven, that to bathe in it did not brace you but rather increased your languor; and when he had dried himself, slipping into a bath-gown, he called out to the Chinese cook that he would be ready for breakfast in five minutes. He walked barefoot across the patch of coarse grass which Walker, the administrator, proudly thought was a lawn, to his own quarters and dressed. This did not take long, for he put on nothing but a shirt and a pair of duck trousers and then went over to his chief's house on the other side of the compound. The two men had their meals together, but the Chinese cook told him that Walker had set out on horseback at five and would not be back for another hour.

Mackintosh had slept badly and he looked with distaste at the paw-paw and the eggs and bacon which were set before him. The mosquitoes had been maddening that night; they flew about the net under which he slept in such numbers that their humming, pitiless and menacing, had the effect of a note, infinitely drawn out, played on a distant organ, and whenever he dozed off he awoke with a start in the belief that one had found its way inside his curtains. It was so hot that he lay naked. He turned from side to side. And gradually the dull roar of the breakers on the reef, so unceasing and so regular that generally you did not hear it, grew distinct on his consciousness, its rhythm hammered on his tired nerves and he held himself with clenched hands in the effort to bear it. The thought that nothing could stop that sound, for it would continue to all eternity, was almost impossible to bear, and, as though his strength were a match for the ruthless forces of nature, he had an insane impulse to do some violent thing. He felt he must cling to his self-control or he would go mad. And now, looking out of the window at the lagoon and the strip of foam which marked the reef, he shuddered with hatred of the brilliant scene. The cloudless sky was like an inverted bowl that hemmed it in. He lit his pipe and turned over the pile of Auckland papers that had come over from Apia a few days before. The newest of them was three weeks old. They gave an impression of incredible dullness.

Then he went into the office. It was a large, bare room with two desks in it and a bench along one side. A number of natives were seated on this, and a couple of women. They gossiped while they waited for the administrator, and when Mackintosh came in they greeted him.

"*Talofa-li.*"

He returned their greeting and sat down at his desk. He began to write, working on a report which the governor of Samoa had been clamouring for and which Walker, with his usual dilatoriness, had neglected to prepare. Mackintosh as he made his notes reflected vindictively that Walker was late with his report because he was so illiterate that he had an invincible distaste for anything to do with pens and paper; and now when it was at last ready, concise and neatly official, he would accept his subordinate's work without a word of appreciation, with a sneer rather or a gibe, and send it on to his own superior as though it were his own composition. He could not have written a word of it. Mackintosh thought with rage that if his chief pencilled in some insertion it would be childish in expression and faulty in language. If he remonstrated or sought to put his meaning into an intelligible phrase, Walker would fly into a passion and cry:

"What the hell do I care about grammar? That's what I want to say and that's how I want to say it."

At last Walker came in. The natives surrounded him as he entered, trying to get his immediate attention, but he turned on them roughly and told them to sit down and hold their tongues. He threatened that if they were not quiet he would have them all turned out and see none of them that day. He nodded to Mackintosh.

"Hulloa, Mac; up at last? I don't know how you can waste the best part of the day in bed. You ought to have been up before dawn like me. Lazy beggar."

He threw himself heavily into his chair and wiped his face with a large bandana.

"By heaven, I've got a thirst."

He turned to the policeman who stood at the door, a picturesque figure in his white jacket and lava-lava, the loincloth of the Samoan, and told him to bring kava. The kava bowl stood on the floor in the corner of the room, and the policeman filled a half coconut shell and brought it to Walker. He poured a few drops on the ground, murmured the customary words to the company, and drank with relish. Then he told the policeman to serve the waiting natives, and the shell was handed to each one in order of birth or importance and emptied with the same ceremonies.

Then he set about the day's work. He was a little man, considerably less than of middle height, and enormously stout; he had a large, fleshy face, clean-shaven, with the cheeks hanging on each side in great dew-laps, and three vast chins; his small features were all dissolved in fat; and, but for a crescent of white hair at the back of his head, he was completely bald. He reminded you of Mr. Pickwick. He was grotesque, a figure of fun, and yet, strangely enough, not without dignity. His blue eyes, behind large gold-rimmed spectacles, were shrewd and vivacious, and there was a great deal of determination in his face. He was sixty, but his native vitality triumphed over advancing years. Notwithstanding his corpulence his movements were quick, and he walked with a heavy, resolute tread as though he sought to impress his weight upon the earth. He spoke in a loud, gruff voice.

It was two years now since Mackintosh had been appointed Walker's assistant. Walker, who had been for a quarter of a century administrator of Talua, one of the larger islands in the Samoan group, was a man known in person or by report through the length and breadth of the South Seas; and it was with lively curiosity that Mackintosh looked forward to his first meeting with him. For one reason or another he stayed a couple of weeks at Apia before he took up his post and both at Chaplin's hotel and at the English Club he heard innumerable stories about the administrator. He thought now with irony of his interest in them. Since then he had heard them a hundred times from Walker himself. Walker knew that he was a character, and, proud of his reputation, deliberately acted up to it. He was jealous of his "legend" and anxious that you should know the exact details of any of the celebrated stories that were told of him. He was ludicrously angry with anyone who had told them to the stranger incorrectly.

There was a rough cordiality about Walker which Mackintosh at first found not unattractive, and Walker, glad to have a listener to whom all he said was fresh, gave of his best. He was good-humoured, hearty, and considerate. To Mackintosh, who had lived the sheltered life of a government official in London till at the age of thirty-four an attack of pneumonia, leaving him with the threat of tuberculosis, had forced him to seek a post in the Pacific, Walker's existence seemed extraordinarily romantic. The adventure with which he started on his conquest of circumstance was typical of the man. He ran away to sea when he was fifteen and for over a year was employed in shovelling coal on a collier. He was an undersized boy and both men and mates were kind to him, but the captain for some reason conceived a savage dislike of him. He used the lad cruelly so that, beaten and kicked, he often could not sleep for the pain that racked his limbs. He loathed the captain with all his soul. Then he was given a tip for some race and managed to borrow twenty-five pounds from a friend he had picked up in Belfast. He put it on the horse, an outsider, at long odds. He had no means of repaying the money if he lost, but it never occurred to him that he could lose. He felt himself in luck. The horse won and he found himself with something over a thousand pounds in hard cash. Now his chance had come. He found out who was the best solicitor in the town—the collier lay then somewhere on the Irish coast—went to him, and, telling him that he heard the ship was for sale, asked him to arrange the purchase for him. The solicitor was amused at his small client, he was only sixteen and did not look so old, and, moved by sympathy, promised not only to arrange the matter for him but to see that he made a good bargain. After a little while Walker found himself the owner of the ship. He went back to her and had what he described as the most glorious moment of his life when he gave the skipper notice and told him that he must get off *his* ship in half an hour. He made the mate captain and sailed on the collier for another nine months, at the end of which he sold her at a profit.

He came out to the islands at the age of twenty-six as a planter. He was one of the few white men settled in Talua at the time of the German occupation and had then already some influence with the natives. The Germans made him administrator, a position which he occupied for twenty years, and when the island was seized by the British he was confirmed in his post. He ruled the island despotically, but with complete success. The prestige of this success was another reason for the interest that Mackintosh took in him.

But the two men were not made to get on. Mackintosh was an ugly man, with ungainly gestures, a tall thin fellow, with a narrow chest and bowed shoulders. He had sallow, sunken cheeks, and his eyes were large and sombre. He was a great reader, and when his books arrived and were unpacked Walker came over to his quarters and looked at them. Then he turned to Mackintosh with a coarse laugh.

"What in Hell have you brought all this muck for?" he asked.

Mackintosh flushed darkly.

"I'm sorry you think it muck. I brought my books because I want to read them."

"When you said you'd got a lot of books coming I thought there'd be something for me to read. Haven't you got any detective stories?"

"Detective stories don't interest me."

"You're a damned fool then."

"I'm content that you should think so."

Every mail brought Walker a mass of periodical literature, papers from New Zealand and magazines from America, and it exasperated him that Mackintosh showed his contempt for these ephemeral publications. He had no patience with the books that absorbed Mackintosh's leisure and thought it only a pose that he read Gibbon's *Decline and Fall* or Burton's *Anatomy of Melancholy*. And since he had never learned to put any restraint on his tongue, he expressed his opinion of his assistant freely. Mackintosh began to see the real man, and under the boisterous good-humour he discerned a vulgar cunning which was hateful; he was vain and domineering, and it was strange that he had notwithstanding a shyness which made him dislike people who were not quite of his kidney. He judged others, naïvely, by their language, and if it was free from the oaths and the obscenity which made up the greater part of his own conversation, he looked upon them with suspicion. In the evening the two men played piquet. He played badly but vaingloriously, crowing over his opponent when he won and losing his temper when he lost. On rare occasions a couple of planters or traders would drive over to play bridge, and then Walker showed himself in what Mackintosh considered a characteristic light. He played regardless of his partner, calling up in his desire to play the hand, and argued interminably, beating down opposition by the loudness of his voice. He constantly revoked, and when he did so said with an ingratiating whine: "Oh, you wouldn't count it against an old man who can hardly see." Did he know that his opponents thought it as well to keep on the right side of him and hesitated to insist on the rigour of the game? Mackintosh watched him with an icy contempt. When the game was over, while they smoked their pipes and drank whisky, they would begin telling stories. Walker told with gusto the story of his marriage. He had got so drunk at the wedding feast that the bride had fled and he had never seen her since. He had had numberless adventures, commonplace and sordid, with the women of the island and he described them with a pride in his own prowess which was an offence to Mackintosh's fastidious ears. He was a gross, sensual old man. He thought Mackintosh a poor fellow because he would not share his promiscuous amours and remained sober when the company was drunk.

He despised him also for the orderliness with which he did his official work. Mackintosh liked to do everything just so. His desk was always tidy, his papers were always neatly docketed, he could put his hand on any document that was needed, and he had at his fingers' ends all the regulations that were required for the business of their administration.

"Fudge, fudge," said Walker. "I've run this island for twenty years without red tape, and I don't want it now."

"Does it make it any easier for you that when you want a letter you have to hunt half an hour for it?" answered Mackintosh.

"You're nothing but a damned official. But you're not a bad fellow; when you've been out here a year or two you'll be all right. What's wrong about you is that you won't drink. You wouldn't be a bad sort if you got soused once a week."

The curious thing was that Walker remained perfectly unconscious of the dislike for him which every month increased in the breast of his subordinate. Although he laughed at him, as he grew accustomed to him, he began almost to like him. He had a certain tolerance for the peculiarities of others, and he accepted Mackintosh as a queer fish. Perhaps he liked him, unconsciously, because he could chaff him. His humour consisted of coarse banter and he wanted a butt. Mackintosh's exactness, his morality, his sobriety, were all fruitful subjects; his Scots name gave an opportunity for the usual jokes about Scotland; he enjoyed himself thoroughly when two or three men were there and he could make them all laugh at the expense of Mackintosh. He would say ridiculous things about him to the natives, and Mackintosh, his knowledge of Samoan still imperfect, would see their unrestrained mirth when Walker had made an obscene reference to him. He smiled good-humouredly.

"I'll say this for you, Mac," Walker would say in his gruff loud voice, "you can take a joke."

"Was it a joke?" smiled Mackintosh. "I didn't know."

"Scots wha hae!" shouted Walker, with a bellow of laughter. "There's only one way to make a Scotchman see a joke and that's by a surgical operation."

Walker little knew that there was nothing Mackintosh could stand less than chaff. He would wake in the night, the breathless night of the rainy season, and brood sullenly over the gibe that Walker had uttered carelessly days before. It rankled. His heart swelled with rage, and he pictured to himself ways in which he might get even with the bully. He had tried answering him, but Walker had a gift of repartee, coarse and obvious, which gave him an advantage. The dullness of his intellect made him impervious to a delicate shaft. His self-satisfaction made it impossible to wound him. His loud voice, his bellow of laughter, were weapons against which Mackintosh had nothing to counter, and he learned that the wisest thing was never to betray his irritation. He learned to control himself. But his hatred grew till it was a monomania. He watched Walker with an insane vigilance. He fed his own self-esteem by every instance of meanness on Walker's part, by every exhibition of childish vanity, of cunning and of vulgarity. Walker ate greedily, noisily, filthily, and Mackintosh watched him with satisfaction. He took note of the foolish things he said and of his mistakes in grammar. He knew that Walker held him in small esteem, and he found a bitter satisfaction in his chief's opinion of him; it increased his own contempt for the narrow, complacent old man. And it gave him a singular pleasure to know that Walker was entirely unconscious of the hatred he felt for him. He was a fool who liked popularity, and he blandly fancied that everyone admired him. Once Mackintosh had overheard Walker speaking of him.

"He'll be all right when I've licked him into shape," he said. "He's a good dog and he loves his master."

Mackintosh silently, without a movement of his long, sallow face, laughed long and heartily.

But his hatred was not blind; on the contrary, it was peculiarly clear-sighted, and he judged Walker's capabilities with precision. He ruled his small kingdom with efficiency. He was just and honest. With opportunities to make money he was a poorer man than when he was first appointed to his post, and his only support for his old age was the pension which he expected when at last he retired from official life. His pride was that with an assistant and a half-caste clerk he was able to administer the island more competently than Upolu, the island of which Apia is the chief town, was administered with its army of functionaries. He had a few native policemen to sustain his authority, but he made no use of them. He governed by bluff and his Irish humour.

"They insisted on building a jail for me," he said. "What the devil do I want a jail for? I'm not going to put the natives in prison. If they do wrong I know how to deal with them."

One of his quarrels with the higher authorities at Apia was that he claimed entire jurisdiction over the natives of his island. Whatever their crimes he would not give them up to courts competent to deal with them, and several times an angry correspondence had passed between him and the governor at Upolu. For he looked upon the natives as his children. And that was the amazing thing about this coarse, vulgar, selfish man; he loved the island on which he had lived so long with passion, and he had for the natives a strange rough tenderness which was quite wonderful.

He loved to ride about the island on his old grey mare and he was never tired of its beauty. Sauntering along the grassy roads among the coconut trees he would stop every now and then to admire the loveliness of the scene. Now and then he would come upon a native village and stop while the headman brought him a bowl of kava. He would look at the little group of bell-shape huts with their high thatched roofs, like beehives, and a smile would spread over his fat face. His eyes rested happily on the spreading green of the bread-fruit trees.

"By George, it's like the garden of Eden."

Sometimes his rides took him along the coast and through the trees he had a glimpse of the wide sea, empty, with never a sail to disturb the loneliness; sometimes he climbed a hill so that a great stretch of country, with little villages nestling among the tall trees, was spread out before him like the kingdoms of the world, and he would sit there for an hour in an ecstasy of delight. But he had no words to express his feelings and to relieve them would utter an obscene jest; it was as though his emotion was so violent that he needed vulgarity to break the tension.

Mackintosh observed this sentiment with an icy disdain. Walker had always been a heavy drinker, he was proud of his capacity to see men half his age under the table when he spent a night in Apia, and he had the sentimentality of the toper. He could cry over the stories he read in his magazines and yet would refuse a loan to some trader in difficulties whom he had known for twenty years. He was close with his money. Once Mackintosh said to him:

"No one could accuse you of giving money away."

He took it as a compliment. His enthusiasm for nature was but the drivelling sensibility of the drunkard. Nor had Mackintosh any sympathy for his chief's feelings towards the natives. He loved them because they were in his power, as a selfish man loves his dog, and his mentality was on a level with theirs. Their humour was obscene and he was never at a loss for the lewd remark. He understood them and they understood him. He was proud of his influence over them. He looked upon them as his children and he mixed himself in all their affairs. But he was very jealous of his authority; if he ruled them with a rod of iron, brooking no contradiction, he would not suffer any of the white men on the island to take advantage of them. He watched the missionaries suspiciously and, if they did anything of which he disapproved, was able to make life so unendurable to them that if he could not get them removed they were glad to go of their own accord. His power over the natives was so great that on his word they would refuse labour and food to their pastor. On the other hand he showed the traders no favour. He took care that they should not cheat the natives; he saw that they got a fair reward for their work and their copra and that the traders made no extravagant profit on the wares they sold them. He was merciless to a bargain that he thought unfair. Sometimes the traders would complain at Apia that they did not get fair opportunities. They suffered for it. Walker then hesitated at no calumny, at no outrageous lie, to get even with them, and they found that if they wanted not only to live at peace, but to exist at all, they had to accept the situation on his own terms. More than once the store of a trader obnoxious to him had been burned down, and there was only the appositeness of the event to show that the administrator had instigated it. Once a Swedish half-caste, ruined by the burning, had gone to him and roundly accused him of arson. Walker laughed in his face.

"You dirty dog. Your mother was a native and you try to cheat the natives. If your rotten old store is burned down it's a judgment of Providence; that's what it is, a judgment of Providence. Get out."

And as the man was hustled out by two native policemen the administrator laughed fatly.

"A judgment of Providence."

And now Mackintosh watched him enter upon the day's work. He began with the sick, for Walker added doctoring to his other activities, and he had a small room behind the office full of drugs. An elderly man came forward, a man with a crop of curly grey hair, in a blue lava-lava, elaborately tattooed, with the skin of his body wrinkled like a wine-skin.

"What have you come for?" Walker asked him abruptly.

In a whining voice the man said that he could not eat without vomiting and that he had pains here and pains there.

"Go to the missionaries," said Walker. "You know that I only cure children."

"I have been to the missionaries and they do me no good."

"Then go home and prepare yourself to die. Have you lived so long and still want to go on living? You're a fool."

The man broke into querulous expostulation, but Walker, pointing to a woman with a sick child in her arms, told her to bring it to his desk. He asked her questions and looked at the child.

"I will give you medicine," he said. He turned to the half-caste clerk. "Go into the dispensary and bring me some calomel pills."

He made the child swallow one there and then and gave another to the mother.

"Take the child away and keep it warm. To-morrow it will be dead or better."

He leaned back in his chair and lit his pipe.

"Wonderful stuff, calomel. I've saved more lives with it than all the hospital doctors at Apia put together."

Walker was very proud of his skill, and with the dogmatism of ignorance had no patience with the members of the medical profession.

"The sort of case I like," he said, "is the one that all the doctors have given up as hopeless. When the doctors have said they can't cure you, I say to them, 'come to me.' Did I ever tell you about the fellow who had a cancer?"

"Frequently," said Mackintosh.

"I got him right in three months."

"You've never told me about the people you haven't cured."

He finished this part of the work and went on to the rest. It was a queer medley. There was a woman who could not get on with her husband and a man who complained that his wife had run away from him.

"Lucky dog," said Walker. "Most men wish their wives would too."

There was a long complicated quarrel about the ownership of a few yards of land. There was a dispute about the sharing out of a catch of fish. There was a complaint against a white trader because he had given short measure. Walker listened attentively to every case, made up his mind quickly, and gave his decision. Then he would listen to nothing more; if the complainant went on he was hustled out of the office by a policeman. Mackintosh listened to it all with sullen irritation. On the whole, perhaps, it might be admitted that rough justice was done, but it exasperated the assistant that his chief trusted his instinct rather than the evidence. He would not listen to reason. He browbeat the witnesses and when they did not see what he wished them to called them thieves and liars.

He left to the last a group of men who were sitting in the corner of the room. He had deliberately ignored them. The party consisted of an old chief, a tall, dignified man with short, white hair, in a new lava-lava, bearing a huge fly wisp as a badge of office, his son, and half a dozen of the important men of the village. Walker had had a feud with them and had beaten them. As was characteristic of him he meant now to rub in his victory, and because he had them down to profit by their helplessness. The facts were peculiar. Walker had a passion for building roads. When he had come to Talua there were but a few tracks here and there, but in course of time he had cut roads through the country, joining the villages together, and it was to this that a great part of the island's prosperity was due. Whereas in the old days it had been impossible to get the produce of the land, copra chiefly, down to the coast where it could be put on schooners or motor launches and so taken to Apia, now transport was easy and simple. His ambition was to make a road right round the island and a great part of it was already built.

"In two years I shall have done it, and then I can die or they can fire me, I don't care."

His roads were the joy of his heart and he made excursions constantly to see that they were kept in order. They were simple enough, wide tracks, grass-covered, cut through the scrub or through the plantations; but trees had to be rooted out, rocks dug up or blasted, and here and there levelling had been necessary. He was proud that he had surmounted by his own skill such difficulties as they presented. He rejoiced in his disposition of them so that they were not only convenient, but showed off the beauties of the island which his soul loved. When he spoke of his roads he was almost a poet. They meandered through those lovely scenes, and Walker had taken care that here and there they should run in a straight line, giving you a green vista through the tall trees, and here and there should turn and curve so that the heart was rested by the diversity. It was amazing that this coarse and sensual man should exercise so subtle an ingenuity to get the effects which his fancy suggested to him. He had used in making his roads all the fantastic skill of a Japanese gardener. He received a grant from headquarters for the work but took a curious pride in using but a small part of it, and the year before had spent only a hundred pounds of the thousand assigned to him.

"What do they want money for?" he boomed. "They'll only spend it on all kinds of muck they don't want; what the missionaries leave them, that is to say."

For no particular reason, except perhaps pride in the economy of his administration and the desire to contrast his efficiency with the wasteful methods of the authorities at Apia, he got the natives to do the work he wanted for wages that were almost nominal. It was owing to this that he had lately had difficulty with the village whose chief men now were come to see him. The chief's son had been in Upolu for a year and on coming back had told his people of the large sums that were paid at Apia for the public works. In long, idle talks he had inflamed their hearts with the desire for gain. He held out to them visions of vast wealth and they thought of the whisky they could buy—it was dear, since there was a law that it must not be sold to natives, and so it cost them double what the white man had to pay for it—they thought of the great sandalwood boxes in which they kept their treasures, and the scented soap and potted salmon, the luxuries for which the Kanaka will sell his soul; so that when the administrator sent for them and told them he wanted a road made from their village to a certain point along the coast and offered them twenty pounds, they asked him a hundred. The chief's son was called Manuma. He was a tall, handsome fellow, copper-coloured, with his fuzzy hair dyed red with lime, a wreath of red berries round his neck, and behind his ear a flower like a scarlet flame against his brown face. The upper part of his body was naked, but to show that he was no longer a savage, since he had lived in Apia, he wore a pair of dungarees instead of a lava-lava. He told them that if they held together the administrator would be obliged to accept their terms. His heart was set on building the road and when he found they would not work for less he would give them what they asked. But they must not move; whatever he said they must not abate their claim; they had asked a hundred and that they must keep to. When they mentioned the figure, Walker burst into a shout of his long, deep-voiced laughter. He told them not to make fools of themselves, but to set about the work at once. Because he was in a good humour that day he promised to give them a feast when the road was finished. But when he found that no attempt was made to start work, he went to the village and asked the men what silly game they were playing. Manuma had coached them well. They were quite calm, they did not attempt to argue—and argument is a passion with the Kanaka— they merely shrugged their shoulders: they would do it for a hundred pounds, and if he would not give them that they would do no work. He could please himself. They did not care. Then Walker flew into a passion. He was ugly then. His short fat neck swelled ominously, his red face grew purple, he foamed at the mouth. He set upon the natives with invective. He knew well how to wound and how to humiliate. He was terrifying. The older men grew pale and uneasy. They hesitated. If it had not been for Manuma, with his knowledge of the great world, and their dread of his ridicule, they would have yielded. It was Manuma who answered Walker.

"Pay us a hundred pounds and we will work."

Walker, shaking his fist at him, called him every name he could think of. He riddled him with scorn. Manuma sat still and smiled. There may have been more bravado than confidence in his smile, but he had to make a good show before the others. He repeated his words.

"Pay us a hundred pounds and we will work."

They thought that Walker would spring on him. It would not have been the first time that he had thrashed a native with his own hands; they knew his strength, and though Walker was three times the age of the young man and six inches shorter they did not doubt that he was more than a match for Manuma. No one had ever thought of resisting the savage onslaught of the administrator. But Walker said nothing. He chuckled.

"I am not going to waste my time with a pack of fools," he said. "Talk it over again. You know what I have offered. If you do not start in a week, take care."

He turned round and walked out of the chief's hut. He untied his old mare and it was typical of the relations between him and the natives that one of the elder men hung on to the off stirrup while Walker from a convenient boulder hoisted himself heavily into the saddle.

That same night when Walker according to his habit was strolling along the road that ran past his house, he heard something whizz past him and with a thud strike a tree. Something had been thrown at him. He ducked instinctively. With a shout, "Who's that?" he ran towards the place from which the missile had come and he heard the sound of a man escaping through the bush. He knew it was hopeless to pursue in the darkness, and besides he was soon out of breath, so he stopped and made his way back to the road. He looked about for what had been thrown, but could find nothing. It was quite dark. He went quickly back to the house and called Mackintosh and the Chinese boy.

"One of those devils has thrown something at me. Come along and let's find out what it was."

He told the boy to bring a lantern and the three of them made their way back to the place. They hunted about the ground, but could not find what they sought. Suddenly the boy gave a guttural cry. They turned to look. He held up the lantern, and there, sinister in the light that cut the surrounding darkness, was a long knife sticking into the trunk of a coconut tree. It had been thrown with such force that it required quite an effort to pull it out.

"By George, if he hadn't missed me I'd have been in a nice state."

Walker handled the knife. It was one of those knives, made in imitation of the sailor knives brought to the islands a hundred years before by the first white men, used to divide the coconuts in two so that the copra might be dried. It was a murderous weapon, and the blade, twelve inches long, was very sharp. Walker chuckled softly.

"The devil, the impudent devil."

He had no doubt it was Manuma who had flung the knife. He had escaped death by three inches. He was not angry. On the contrary, he was in high spirits; the adventure exhilarated him, and when they got back to the house, calling for drinks, he rubbed his hands gleefully.

"I'll make them pay for this!"

His little eyes twinkled. He blew himself out like a turkey-cock, and for the second time within half an hour insisted on telling Mackintosh every detail of the affair. Then he asked him to play piquet, and while they played he boasted of his intentions. Mackintosh listened with tightened lips.

"But why should you grind them down like this?" he asked. "Twenty pounds is precious little for the work you want them to do."

"They ought to be precious thankful I give them anything."

"Hang it all, it's not your own money. The government allots you a reasonable sum. They won't complain if you spend it."

"They're a bunch of fools at Apia."

Mackintosh saw that Walker's motive was merely vanity. He shrugged his shoulders.

"It won't do you much good to score off the fellows at Apia at the cost of your life."

"Bless you, they wouldn't hurt me, these people. They couldn't do without me. They worship me. Manuma is a fool. He only threw that knife to frighten me."

The next day Walker rode over again to the village. It was called Matautu. He did not get off his horse. When he reached the chief's house he saw that the men were sitting round the floor in a circle, talking, and he guessed they were discussing again the question of the road. The Samoan huts are formed in this way: trunks of slender trees are placed in a circle at intervals of perhaps five or six feet; a tall tree is set in the middle and from this downwards slopes the thatched roof. Venetian blinds of coconut leaves can be pulled down at night or when it is raining. Ordinarily the hut is open all round so that the breeze can blow through freely. Walker rode to the edge of the hut and called out to the chief.

"Oh, there, Tangatu, your son left his knife in a tree last night. I have brought it back to you."

He flung it down on the ground in the midst of the circle, and with a low burst of laughter ambled off.

On Monday he went out to see if they had started work. There was no sign of it. He rode through the village. The inhabitants were about their ordinary avocations. Some were weaving mats of the pandanus leaf, one old man was busy with a kava bowl, the children were playing, the women went about their household chores. Walker, a smile on his lips, came to the chief's house.

"*Talofa-li*," said the chief.

"*Talofa*," answered Walker.

Manuma was making a net. He sat with a cigarette between his lips and looked up at Walker with a smile of triumph.

"You have decided that you will not make the road."

The chief answered.

"Not unless you pay us one hundred pounds."

"You will regret it." He turned to Manuma. "And you, my lad, I shouldn't wonder if your back was very sore before you're much older."

He rode away chuckling. He left the natives vaguely uneasy. They feared the fat sinful old man, and neither the missionaries' abuse of him nor the scorn which Manuma had learnt in Apia made them forget that he had a devilish cunning and that no man had ever braved him without in the long run suffering for it. They found out within twenty-four hours what scheme he had devised. It was characteristic. For next morning a great band of men, women, and children came into the village and the chief men said that they had made a bargain with Walker to build the road. He had offered them twenty pounds and they had accepted. Now the cunning lay in this, that the Polynesians have rules of hospitality which have all the force of laws; an etiquette of absolute rigidity made it necessary for the people of the village not only to give lodging to the strangers, but to provide them with food and drink as long as they wished to stay. The inhabitants of Matautu were outwitted. Every morning the workers went out in a joyous band, cut down trees, blasted rocks, levelled here and there and then in the evening tramped back again, and ate and drank, ate heartily, danced, sang hymns, and enjoyed life. For them it was a picnic. But soon their hosts began to wear long faces; the strangers had enormous appetites, and the plantains and the bread-fruit vanished before their rapacity; the alligator-pear trees, whose fruit sent to Apia might sell for good money, were stripped bare. Ruin stared them in the face. And they then found that the strangers were working very slowly. Had they received a hint from Walker that they might take their time? At this rate by the time the road was finished there would not be a scrap of food in the village. And worse than this, they were a laughing-stock; when one or other of them went to some distant hamlet on an errand he found that the story had got there before him, and he was met with derisive laughter. There is nothing the Kanaka can endure less than ridicule. It was not long before much angry talk passed among the sufferers. Manuma was no longer a hero; he had to put up with a good deal of plain speaking, and one day what Walker had suggested came to pass: a heated argument turned into a quarrel and half a dozen of the young men set upon the chief's son and gave him such a beating that for a week he lay bruised and sore on the pandanus mats. He turned from side to side and could find no ease. Every day or two the administrator rode over on his old mare and watched the progress of the road. He was not a man to resist the temptation of taunting the fallen foe, and he missed no opportunity to rub into the shamed inhabitants of Matautu the bitterness of their humiliation. He broke their spirit. And one morning, putting their pride in their pockets—a figure of speech, since pockets they had not—they all set out with the strangers and started working on the road. It was urgent to get it done quickly if they wanted to save any food at all, and the whole village joined in. But they worked silently, with rage and mortification in their hearts, and even the children toiled in silence. The women wept as they carried away bundles of brushwood. When Walker saw them he laughed so much that he almost rolled out of his saddle. The news spread quickly and tickled the people of the island to death. This was the greatest joke of all, the crowning triumph of that cunning old white man whom no Kanaka had ever been able to circumvent; and they came from distant villages, with their wives and children, to look at the foolish folk who had refused twenty pounds to make the road and now were forced to work for nothing. But the harder they worked the more easily went the guests. Why should they hurry, when they were getting good food for nothing and the longer they took about the job the better the joke became? At last the wretched villagers could stand it no longer, and they were come this morning to beg the administrator to send the strangers back to their own homes. If he would do this they promised to finish the road themselves for nothing. For him it was victory complete and unqualified. They were humbled. A look of arrogant complacence spread over his large, naked face, and he seemed to swell in his chair like a great bullfrog. There was something sinister in his appearance, so that Mackintosh shivered with disgust. Then in his booming tones he began to speak.

"Is it for my good that I make the road? What benefit do you think I get out of it? It is for you, so that you can walk in comfort and carry your copra in comfort. I offered to pay you for your work, though it was for your own sake the work was done. I offered to pay you generously. Now *you* must pay. I will send the people of Manua back to their homes if you will finish the road and pay the twenty pounds that I have to pay them."

There was an outcry. They sought to reason with him. They told him they had not the money. But to everything they said he replied with brutal gibes. Then the clock struck.

"Dinner time," he said. "Turn them all out."

He raised himself heavily from his chair and walked out of the room. When Mackintosh followed him he found him already seated at table, a napkin tied round his neck, holding his knife and fork in readiness for the meal the Chinese cook was about to bring. He was in high spirits.

"I did 'em down fine," he said, as Mackintosh sat down. "I shan't have much trouble with the roads after this."

"I suppose you were joking," said Mackintosh icily.

"What do you mean by that?"

"You're not really going to make them pay twenty pounds?"

"You bet your life I am."

"I'm not sure you've got any right to."

"Ain't you? I guess I've got the right to do any damned thing I like on this island."

"I think you've bullied them quite enough."

Walker laughed fatly. He did not care what Mackintosh thought. "When I want your opinion I'll ask for it."

Mackintosh grew very white. He knew by bitter experience that he could do nothing but keep silence, and the violent effort at self-control made him sick and faint. He could not eat the food that was before him and with disgust he watched Walker shovel meat into his vast mouth. He was a dirty feeder, and to sit at table with him needed a strong stomach. Mackintosh shuddered. A tremendous desire seized him to humiliate that gross and cruel man; he would give anything in the world to see him in the dust, suffering as much as he had made others suffer. He had never loathed the bully with such loathing as now.

The day wore on. Mackintosh tried to sleep after dinner, but the passion in his heart prevented him; he tried to read, but the letters swam before his eyes. The sun beat down pitilessly, and he longed for rain; but he knew that rain would bring no coolness; it would only make it hotter and more steamy. He was a native of Aberdeen and his heart yearned suddenly for the icy winds that whistled through the granite streets of that city. Here he was a prisoner, imprisoned not only by that placid sea, but by his hatred for that horrible old man. He pressed his hands to his aching head. He would like to kill him. But he pulled himself together. He must do something to distract his mind, and since he could not read he thought he would set his private papers in order. It was a job which he had long meant to do and which he had constantly put off. He unlocked the drawer of his desk and took out a handful of letters. He caught sight of his revolver. An impulse, no sooner realised than set aside, to put a bullet through his head and so escape from the intolerable bondage of life flashed through his mind. He noticed that in the damp air the revolver was slightly rusted, and he got an oil rag and began to clean it. It was while he was thus occupied that he grew aware of someone slinking round the door. He looked up and called:

"Who is there?"

There was a moment's pause, then Manuma showed himself.

"What do you want?"

The chief's son stood for a moment, sullen and silent, and when he spoke it was with a strangled voice.

"We can't pay twenty pounds. We haven't the money."

"What am I to do?" said Mackintosh. "You heard what Mr. Walker said."

Manuma began to plead, half in Samoan and half in English. It was a sing-song whine, with the quavering intonations of a beggar, and it filled Mackintosh with disgust. It outraged him that the man should let himself be so crushed. He was a pitiful object.

"I can do nothing," said Mackintosh irritably. "You know that Mr. Walker is master here."

Manuma was silent again. He still stood in the doorway.

"I am sick," he said at last. "Give me some medicine."

"What is the matter with you?"

"I do not know. I am sick. I have pains in my body."

"Don't stand there;" said Mackintosh sharply. "Come in and let me look at you."

Manuma entered the little room and stood before the desk.

"I have pains here and here."

He put his hands to his loins and his face assumed an expression of pain. Suddenly Mackintosh grew conscious that the boy's eyes were resting on the revolver which he had laid on the desk when Manuma appeared in the doorway. There was a silence between the two which to Mackintosh was endless. He seemed to read the thoughts which were in the Kanaka's mind. His heart beat violently. And then he felt as though something possessed him so that he acted under the compulsion of a foreign will. Himself did not make the movements of his body, but a power that was strange to him. His throat was suddenly dry, and he put his hand to it mechanically in order to help his speech. He was impelled to avoid Manuma's eyes.

"Just wait here," he said, his voice sounded as though someone had seized him by the windpipe, "and I'll fetch you something from the dispensary."

He got up. Was it his fancy that he staggered a little? Manuma stood silently, and though he kept his eyes averted, Mackintosh knew that he was looking dully out of the door. It was this other person that possessed him that drove him out of the room, but it was himself that took a handful of muddled papers and threw them on the revolver in order to hide it from view. He went to the dispensary. He got a pill and poured out some blue draught into a small bottle, and then came out into the compound. He did not want to go back into his own bungalow, so he called to Manuma.

"Come here."

He gave him the drugs and instructions how to take them. He did not know what it was that made it impossible for him to look at the Kanaka. While he was speaking to him he kept his eyes on his shoulder. Manuma took the medicine and slunk out of the gate.

Mackintosh went into the dining-room and turned over once more the old newspapers. But he could not read them. The house was very still. Walker was upstairs in his room asleep, the Chinese cook was busy in the kitchen, the two policemen were out fishing. The silence that seemed to brood over the house was uncarthly, and there hammered in Mackintosh's head the question whether the revolver still lay where he had placed it. He could not bring himself to look. The uncertainty was horrible, but the certainty would be more horrible still. He sweated. At last he could stand the silence no longer, and he made up his mind to go down the road to the trader's, a man named Jervis, who had a store about a mile away. He was a half-caste, but even that amount of white blood made him possible to talk to. He wanted to get away from his bungalow, with the desk littered with untidy papers, and underneath them something, or nothing. He walked along the road. As he passed the fine hut of a chief a greeting was called out to him. Then he came to the store. Behind the counter sat the trader's daughter, a swarthy broad-featured girl in a pink blouse and a white drill skirt. Jervis hoped he would marry her. He had money, and he had told Mackintosh that his daughter's husband would be well-to-do. She flushed a little when she saw Mackintosh.

"Father's just unpacking some cases that have come in this morning. I'll tell him you're here."

He sat down and the girl went out behind the shop. In a moment her mother waddled in, a huge old woman, a chiefess, who owned much land in her own right; and gave him her hand. Her monstrous obesity was an offence, but she managed to convey an impression of dignity. She was cordial without obsequiousness; affable, but conscious of her station.

"You're quite a stranger, Mr. Mackintosh. Teresa was saying only this morning: 'Why, we never see Mr. Mackintosh now.' "

He shuddered a little as he thought of himself as that old native's son-in-law. It was notorious that she ruled her husband, notwithstanding his white blood, with a firm hand. Hers was the authority and hers the business head. She might be no more than Mrs. Jervis to the white people, but her father had been a chief of the blood royal, and his father and his father's father had ruled as kings. The trader came in, small beside his imposing wife, a dark man with a black beard going grey, in ducks, with handsome eyes and flashing teeth. He was very British, and his conversation was slangy, but you felt he spoke English as a foreign tongue; with his family he used the language of his native mother. He was a servile man, cringing and obsequious.

"Ah, Mr. Mackintosh, this is a joyful surprise. Get the whisky, Teresa; Mr. Mackintosh will have a gargle with us."

He gave all the latest news of Apia, watching his guest's eyes the while, so that he might know the welcome thing to say.

"And how is Walker? We've not seen him just lately. Mrs. Jervis is going to send him a sucking-pig one day this week."

"I saw him riding home this morning," said Teresa.

"Here's how," said Jervis, holding up his whisky.

Mackintosh drank. The two women sat and looked at him, Mrs. Jervis in her black Mother Hubbard, placid and haughty, and Teresa anxious to smile whenever she caught his eye, while the trader gossiped insufferably.

"They were saying in Apia it was about time Walker retired. He ain't so young as he was. Things have changed since he first come to the islands and he ain't changed with them."

"He'll go too far," said the old chiefess. "The natives aren't satisfied."

"That was a good joke about the road," laughed the trader. "When I told them about it in Apia they fair split their sides with laughing. Good old Walker."

Mackintosh looked at him savagely. What did he mean by talking of him in that fashion? To a half-caste trader he was Mr. Walker. It was on his tongue to utter a harsh rebuke for the impertinence. He did not know what held him back.

"When he goes I hope you'll take his place, Mr. Mackintosh," said Jervis. "We all like you on the island. You understand the natives. They're educated now, they must be treated differently to the old days. It wants an educated man to be administrator now. Walker was only a trader same as I am."

Teresa's eyes glistened.

"When the time comes if there's anything anyone can do here, you bet your bottom dollar we'll do it. I'd get all the chiefs to go over to Apia and make a petition."

Mackintosh felt horribly sick. It had not struck him that if anything happened to Walker it might be he who would succeed him. It was true that no one in his official position knew the island so well. He got up suddenly and scarcely taking his leave walked back to the compound. And now he went straight to his room. He took a quick look at his desk. He rummaged among the papers.

The revolver was not there.

His heart thumped violently against his ribs. He looked for the revolver everywhere. He hunted in the chairs and in the drawers. He looked desperately, and all the time he knew he would not find it. Suddenly he heard Walker's gruff, hearty voice.

"What the devil are you up to, Mac?"

He started. Walker was standing in the doorway and instinctively he turned round to hide what lay upon his desk.

"Tidying up?" quizzed Walker. "I've told 'em to put the grey in the trap. I'm going down to Tafoni to bathe. You'd better come along."

"All right," said Mackintosh.

So long as he was with Walker nothing could happen. The place they were bound for was about three miles away, and there was a fresh-water pool, separated by a thin barrier of rock from the sea, which the administrator had blasted out for the natives to bathe in. He had done this at spots round the island, wherever there was a spring; and the fresh water, compared with the sticky warmth of the sea, was cool and invigorating. They drove along the silent grassy road, splashing now and then through fords, where the sea had forced its way in, past a couple of native villages, the bell-shaped huts spaced out roomily and the white chapel in the middle, and at the third village they got out of the trap, tied up the horse, and walked down to the pool. They were accompanied by four or five girls and a dozen children. Soon they were all splashing about, shouting and laughing, while Walker, in a lava-lava, swam to and fro like an unwieldy porpoise. He made lewd jokes with the girls, and they amused themselves by diving under him and wriggling away when he tried to catch them. When he was tired he lay down on a rock, while the girls and children surrounded him; it was a happy family; and the old man, huge, with his crescent of white hair and his shining bald crown, looked like some old sea god. Once Mackintosh caught a queer soft look in his eyes.

"They're dear children," he said. "They look upon me as their father."

F

And then without a pause he turned to one of the girls and made an obscene remark which sent them all into fits of laughter. Mackintosh started to dress. With his thin legs and thin arms he made a grotesque figure, a sinister Don Quixote, and Walker began to make coarse jokes about him. They were acknowledged with little smothered laughs. Mackintosh struggled with his shirt. He knew he looked absurd, but he hated being laughed at. He stood silent and glowering.

"If you want to get back in time for dinner you ought to come soon."

"You're not a bad fellow, Mac. Only you're a fool. When you're doing one thing you always want to do another. That's not the way we live."

But all the same he raised himself slowly to his feet and began to put on his clothes. They sauntered back to the village, drank a bowl of kava with the chief, and then, after a joyful farewell from all the lazy villagers, drove home.

After dinner, according to his habit, Walker, lighting his cigar, prepared to go for a stroll. Mackintosh was suddenly seized with fear.

"Don't you think it's rather unwise to go out at night by yourself just now?"

Walker stared at him with his round blue eyes.

"What the devil do you mean?"

"Remember the knife the other night. You've got those fellows' backs up."

"Pooh! They wouldn't dare."

"Someone dared before."

"That was only a bluff. They wouldn't hurt me. They look upon me as a father. They know that whatever I do is for their own good."

Mackintosh watched him with contempt in his heart. The man's self-complacency outraged him, and yet something, he knew not what, made him insist.

"Remember what happened this morning. It wouldn't hurt you to stay at home just to-night. I'll play piquet with you."

"I'll play piquet with you when I come back. The Kanaka isn't born yet who can make me alter my plans."

"You'd better let me come with you."

"You stay where you are."

Mackintosh shrugged his shoulders. He had given the man full warning. If he did not heed it that was his own lookout. Walker put on his hat and went out. Mackintosh began to read; but then he thought of something; perhaps it would be as well to have his own whereabouts quite clear. He crossed over to the kitchen and, inventing some pretext, talked for a few minutes with the cook. Then he got out the gramophone and put a record on it, but while it ground out its melancholy tune, some comic song of a London music-hall, his ear was strained for a sound away there in the night. At his elbow the record reeled out its loudness, the words were raucous, but notwithstanding he seemed to be surrounded by an unearthly silence. He heard the dull roar of the breakers against the reef. He heard the breeze sigh, far up, in the leaves of the coconut trees. How long would it be? It was awful.

He heard a hoarse laugh.

"Wonders will never cease. It's not often you play yourself a tune, Mac."

Walker stood at the window, red-faced, bluff and jovial.

"Well, you see I'm alive and kicking. What were you playing for?"

Walker came in.

"Nerves a bit dicky, eh? Playing a tune to keep your pecker up?"

"I was playing your requiem."

"What the devil's that?"

" 'Alf o' bitter an' a pint of stout."

"A rattling good song too. I don't mind how often I hear it. Now I'm ready to take your money off you at piquet."

They played and Walker bullied his way to victory, bluffing his opponent, chaffing him, jeering at his mistakes, up to every dodge, browbeating him, exulting. Presently Mackintosh recovered his coolness, and standing outside himself, as it were, he was able to take a detached pleasure in watching the overbearing old man and in his own cold reserve. Somewhere Manuma sat quietly and awaited his opportunity.

Walker won game after game and pocketed his winnings at the end of the evening in high good-humour.

"You'll have to grow a little bit older before you stand much chance against me, Mac. The fact is I have a natural gift for cards."

"I don't know that there's much gift about it when I happen to deal you fourteen aces."

"Good cards come to good players," retorted Walker. "I'd have won if I'd had your hands."

He went on to tell long stories of the various occasions on which he had played cards with notorious sharpers and to their consternation had taken all their money from them. He boasted. He praised himself. And Mackintosh listened with absorption. He wanted now to feed his hatred; and everything Walker said, every gesture, made him more detestable. At last Walker got up.

"Well, I'm going to turn in," he said with a loud yawn. "I've got a long day to-morrow."

"What are you going to do?"

"I'm driving over to the other side of the island. I'll start at five, but I don't expect I shall get back to dinner till late."

They generally dined at seven.

"We'd better make it half-past seven then."

"I guess it would be as well."

Mackintosh watched him knock the ashes out of his pipe. His vitality was rude and exuberant. It was strange to think that death hung over him. A faint smile flickered in Mackintosh's cold, gloomy eyes.

"Would you like me to come with you?"

"What in God's name should I want that for? I'm using the mare and she'll have enough to do to carry me; she don't want to drag you over thirty miles of road."

"Perhaps you don't quite realise what the feeling is at Matautu. I think it would be safer if I came with you."

Walker burst into contemptuous laughter.

"You'd be a fine lot of use in a scrap. I'm not a great hand at getting the wind up."

Now the smile passed from Mackintosh's eyes to his lips. It distorted them painfully.

"*Quem deus vult perdere prius dementat.*"

"What the hell is that?" said Walker.

"Latin," answered Mackintosh as he went out.

And now he chuckled. His mood had changed. He had done all he could and the matter was in the hands of fate. He slept more soundly than he had done for weeks. When he awoke next morning he went out. After a good night he found a pleasant exhilaration in the freshness of the early air. The sea was a more vivid blue, the sky more brilliant, than on most days, the trade wind was fresh, and there was a ripple on the lagoon as the breeze brushed over it like velvet brushed the wrong way. He felt himself stronger and younger. He entered upon the day's work with zest. After luncheon he slept again, and as evening drew on he had the bay saddled and sauntered through the bush. He seemed to see it all with new eyes. He felt more normal. The extraordinary thing was that he was able to put Walker out of his mind altogether. So far as he was concerned he might never have existed.

He returned late, hot after his ride, and bathed again. Then he sat on the verandah, smoking his pipe, and looked at the day declining over the lagoon. In the sunset the lagoon, rosy and purple and green, was very beautiful. He felt at peace with the world and with himself. When the cook came out to say that dinner was ready and to ask whether he should wait, Mackintosh smiled at him with friendly eyes. He looked at his watch.

"It's half-past seven. Better not wait. One can't tell when the boss'll be back."

The boy nodded, and in a moment Mackintosh saw him carry across the yard a bowl of steaming soup. He got up lazily, went into the dining-room, and ate his dinner. Had it happened? The uncertainty was amusing and Mackintosh chuckled in the silence. The food did not seem so monotonous as usual, and even though there was Hamburger steak, the cook's invariable dish when his poor invention failed him, it tasted by some miracle succulent and spiced. After dinner he strolled over lazily to his bungalow to get a book. He liked the intense stillness, and now that the night had fallen the stars were blazing in the sky. He shouted for a lamp and in a moment the Chink pattered over on his bare feet, piercing the darkness with a ray of light. He put the lamp on the desk and noiselessly slipped out of the room. Mackintosh stood rooted to the floor, for there, half hidden by untidy papers, was his revolver. His heart throbbed painfully, and he broke into a sweat. It was done, then.

He took up the revolver with a shaking hand. Four of the chambers were empty. He paused a moment and looked suspiciously out into the night, but there was no one there. He quickly slipped four cartridges into the empty chambers and locked the revolver in his drawer.

He sat down to wait.

An hour passed, a second hour passed. There was nothing. He sat at his desk as though he were writing, but he neither wrote nor read. He merely listened. He strained his ears for a sound travelling from a far distance. At last he heard hesitating footsteps and knew it was the Chinese cook.

"Ah-Sung," he called.

The boy came to the door.

"Boss velly late," he said. "Dinner no good."

Mackintosh stared at him, wondering whether he knew what had happened, and whether, when he knew, he would realise on what terms he and Walker had been. He went about his work, sleek, silent, and smiling, and who could tell his thoughts?

"I expect he's had dinner on the way, but you must keep the soup hot at all events."

The words were hardly out of his mouth when the silence was suddenly broken into by a confusion, cries, and a rapid patter of naked feet. A number of natives ran into the compound, men and women and children; they crowded round Mackintosh and they all talked at once. They were unintelligible. They were excited and frightened and some of them were crying. Mackintosh pushed his way through them and went to the gateway. Though he had scarcely understood what they said he knew quite well what had happened. And as he reached the gate the dog-cart arrived. The old mare was being led by a tall Kanaka, and in the dog-cart crouched two men, trying to hold Walker up. A little crowd of natives surrounded it.

The mare was led into the yard and the natives surged in after it. Mackintosh shouted to them to stand back and the two policemen, appearing suddenly from God knows where, pushed them violently aside. By now he had managed to understand that some lads, who had been fishing, on their way back to their village had come across the cart on the home side of the ford. The mare was nuzzling about the herbage and in the darkness they could just see the great white bulk of the old man sunk between the seat and the dashboard. At first they thought he was drunk and they peered in, grinning, but then they heard him groan, and guessed that something was amiss. They ran to the village and called for help. It was when they returned, accompanied by half a hundred people, that they discovered Walker had been shot.

With a sudden thrill of horror Mackintosh asked himself whether he was already dead. The first thing at all events was to get him out of the cart, and that, owing to Walker's corpulence, was a difficult job. It took four strong men to lift him. They jolted him and he uttered a dull groan. He was still alive. At last they carried him into the house, up the stairs, and placed him on his bed. Then Mackintosh was able to see him, for in the yard, lit only by half a dozen hurricane lamps, everything had been obscured. Walker's white ducks were stained with blood, and the men who had carried him wiped their hands, red and sticky, on their lava-lavas. Mackintosh held up the lamp. He had not expected the old man to be so pale. His eyes were closed. He was breathing still, his pulse could be just felt, but it was obvious that he was dying. Mackintosh had not bargained for the shock of horror that convulsed him. He saw that the native clerk was there, and in a voice hoarse with fear told him to go into the dispensary and get what was necessary for a hypodermic injection. One of the policemen had brought up the whisky, and Mackintosh forced a little into the old man's mouth. The room was crowded with natives. They sat about the floor, speechless now and terrified, and every now and then one wailed aloud. It was very hot, but Mackintosh felt cold, his hands and his feet were like ice, and he had to make a violent effort not to tremble in all his limbs. He did not know what to do. He did not know if Walker was bleeding still, and if he was, how he could stop the bleeding.

The clerk brought the hypodermic needle.

"You give it to him," said Mackintosh. "You're more used to that sort of thing than I am."

His head ached horribly. It felt as though all sorts of little savage things were beating inside it, trying to get out. They watched for the effect of the injection. Presently Walker opened his eyes slowly. He did not seem to know where he was.

"Keep quiet," said Mackintosh. "You're at home. You're quite safe."

Walker's lips outlined a shadowy smile.

"They've got me," he whispered.

"I'll get Jervis to send his motor-boat to Apia at once. We'll get a doctor out by to-morrow afternoon."

There was a long pause before the old man answered.

"I shall be dead by then."

A ghastly expression passed over Mackintosh's pale face. He forced himself to laugh.

"What rot! You keep quiet and you'll be as right as rain."

"Give me a drink," said Walker. "A stiff one."

With shaking hand Mackintosh poured out whisky and water, half and half, and held the glass while Walker drank greedily. It seemed to restore him. He gave a long sigh and a little colour came into his great fleshy face. Mackintosh felt extraordinarily helpless. He stood and stared at the old man.

"If you'll tell me what to do I'll do it," he said.

"There's nothing to do. Just leave me alone. I'm done for."

He looked dreadfully pitiful as he lay on the great bed, a huge, bloated, old man; but so wan, so weak, it was heart-rending. As he rested, his mind seemed to grow clearer.

"You were right, Mac," he said presently. "You warned me."

"I wish to God I'd come with you."

"You're a good chap, Mac, only you don't drink."

There was another long silence, and it was clear that Walker was sinking. There was an internal hæmorrhage and even Mackintosh in his ignorance could not fail to see that his chief had but an hour or two to live. He stood by the side of the bed stock-still. For half an hour perhaps Walker lay with his eyes closed, then he opened them.

"They'll give you my job," he said, slowly. "Last time I was in Apia I told them you were all right. Finish my road. I want to think that'll be done. All round the island."

"I don't want your job. You'll get all right."

Walker shook his head wearily.

"I've had my day. Treat them fairly, that's the great thing. They're children. You must always remember that. You must be firm with them, but you must be kind. And you must be just. I've never made a bob out of them. I haven't saved a hundred pounds in twenty years. The road's the great thing. Get the road finished."

Something very like a sob was wrung from Mackintosh.

"You're a good fellow, Mac. I always liked you."

He closed his eyes, and Mackintosh thought that he would never open them again. His mouth was so dry that he had to get himself something to drink. The Chinese cook silently put a chair for him. He sat down by the side of the bed and waited. He did not know how long a time passed. The night was endless. Suddenly one of the men sitting there broke into uncontrollable sobbing, loudly, like a child, and Mackintosh grew aware that the room was crowded by this time with natives. They sat all over the floor on their haunches, men and women, staring at the bed.

"What are all these people doing here?" said Mackintosh. "They've got no right. Turn them out, turn them out, all of them."

His words seemed to rouse Walker, for he opened his eyes once more, and now they were all misty. He wanted to speak, but he was so weak that Mackintosh had to strain his ears to catch what he said.

"Let them stay. They're my children. They ought to be here."

Mackintosh turned to the natives.

"Stay where you are. He wants you. But be silent."

A faint smile came over the old man's white face.

"Come nearer," he said.

Mackintosh bent over him. His eyes were closed and the words he said were like a wind sighing through the fronds of the coconut trees.

"Give me another drink. I've got something to say."

This time Mackintosh gave him his whisky neat. Walker collected his strength in a final effort of will.

"Don't make a fuss about this. In 'ninety-five when there were troubles white men were killed, and the fleet came and shelled the villages. A lot of people were killed who'd had nothing to do with it. They're damned fools at Apia. If they make a fuss they'll only punish the wrong people. I don't want anyone punished."

He paused for a while to rest.

"You must say it was an accident. No one's to blame. Promise me that."

"I'll do anything you like," whispered Mackintosh.

"Good chap. One of the best. They're children. I'm their father. A father don't let his children get into trouble if he can help it."

A ghost of a chuckle came out of his throat. It was astonishingly weird and ghastly.

"You're a religious chap, Mac. What's that about forgiving them? You know."

For a while Mackintosh did not answer. His lips trembled.

"Forgive them, for they know not what they do?"

"That's right. Forgive them. I've loved them, you know, always loved them."

He sighed. His lips faintly moved, and now Mackintosh had to put his ears quite close to them in order to hear.

"Hold my hand," he said.

Mackintosh gave a gasp. His heart seemed wrenched. He took the old man's hand, so cold and weak, a coarse, rough hand, and held it in his own. And thus he sat until he nearly started out of his seat, for the silence was suddenly broken by a long rattle. It was terrible and unearthly. Walker was dead. Then the natives broke out with loud cries. The tears ran down their faces, and they beat their breasts.

Mackintosh disengaged his hand from the dead man's and staggering like one drunk with sleep he went out of the room. He went to the locked drawer in his writing-desk and took out the revolver. He walked down to the sea and walked into the lagoon; he waded out cautiously, so that he should not trip against a coral rock, till the water came to his arm-pits. Then he put a bullet through his head.

An hour later half a dozen slim brown sharks were splashing and struggling at the spot where he fell.

The Escape

I HAVE always been convinced that if a woman once made up her mind to marry a man nothing but instant flight could save him. Not always that; for once a friend of mine, seeing the inevitable loom menacingly before him, took ship from a certain port (with a toothbrush for all his luggage, so conscious was he of his danger and the necessity for immediate action) and spent a year travelling round the world; but when, thinking himself safe (women are fickle, he said, and in twelve months she will have forgotten all about me), he landed at the selfsame port the first person he saw gaily waving to him from the quay was the little lady from whom he had fled. I have only once known a man who in such circumstances managed to extricate himself. His name was Roger Charing. He was no longer young when he fell in love with Ruth Barlow and he had had sufficient experience to make him careful; but Ruth Barlow had a gift (or should I call it a quality?) that renders most men defenceless, and it was this that dispossessed Roger of his commonsense, his prudence and his worldly wisdom. He went down like a row of ninepins. This was the gift of pathos. Mrs. Barlow, for she was twice a widow, had splendid dark eyes and they were the most moving I ever saw; they seemed to be ever on the point of filling with tears; they suggested that the world was too much for her, and you felt that, poor dear, her sufferings had been more than anyone should be asked to bear. If, like Roger Charing, you were a strong, hefty fellow with plenty of money, it was almost inevitable that you should say to yourself: I must stand between the hazards of life and this helpless little thing, oh, how wonderful it would be to take the sadness out of those big and lovely eyes! I gathered from Roger that everyone had treated Mrs. Barlow very badly. She was apparently one of those unfortunate persons with whom nothing by any chance goes right. If she married a husband he beat her; if she employed a broker he cheated her; if she engaged a cook she drank. She never had a little lamb but it was sure to die.

When Roger told me that he had at last persuaded her to marry him, I wished him joy.

"I hope you'll be good friends," he said. "She's a little afraid of you, you know; she thinks you're callous."

"Upon my word I don't know why she should think that."

"You do like her, don't you?"

"Very much."

"She's had a rotten time, poor dear. I feel so dreadfully sorry for her."

"Yes," I said.

I couldn't say less. I knew she was stupid and I thought she was scheming. My own belief was that she was as hard as nails.

The first time I met her we had played bridge together and when she was my partner she twice trumped my best card. I behaved like an angel, but I confess that I thought if the tears were going to well up into anybody's eyes they should have been mine rather than hers. And when, having by the end of the evening lost a good deal of money to me, she said she would send me a cheque and never did, I could not but think that I and not she should have worn a pathetic expression when next we met.

Roger introduced her to his friends. He gave her lovely jewels. He took her here, there, and everywhere. Their marriage was announced for the immediate future. Roger was very happy. He was committing a good action and at the same time doing something he had very much a mind to. It is an uncommon situation and it is not surprising if he was a trifle more pleased with himself than was altogether becoming.

Then, on a sudden, he fell out of love. I do not know why. It could hardly have been that he grew tired of her conversation, for she had never had any conversation. Perhaps it was merely that this pathetic look of hers ceased to wring his heart-strings. His eyes were opened and he was once more the shrewd man of the world he had been. He became acutely conscious that Ruth Barlow had made up her mind to marry him and he swore a solemn oath that nothing would induce him to marry Ruth Barlow. But he was in a quandary. Now that he was in possession of his senses he saw with clearness the sort of woman he had to deal with and he was aware that, if he asked her to release him, she would (in her appealing way) assess her wounded feelings at an immoderately high figure. Besides, it is always awkward for a man to jilt a woman. People are apt to think he has behaved badly.

Roger kept his own counsel. He gave neither by word nor gesture an indication that his feelings towards Ruth Barlow had changed. He remained attentive to all her wishes; he took her to dine at restaurants, they went to the play together, he sent her flowers; he was sympathetic and charming. They had made up their minds that they would be married as soon as they found a house that suited them, for he lived in chambers and she in furnished rooms; and they set about looking at desirable residences. The agents sent Roger orders to view and he took Ruth to see a number of houses. It was very hard to find anything that was quite satisfactory. Roger applied to more agents. They visited house after house. They went over them thoroughly, examining them from the cellars in the basement to the attics under the roof. Sometimes they were too large and sometimes they were too small; sometimes they were too far from the centre of things and sometimes they were too close; sometimes they were too expensive and sometimes they wanted too many repairs; sometimes they were too stuffy and sometimes they were too airy; sometimes they were too dark and sometimes they were too bleak. Roger always found a fault that made the house unsuitable. Of course he was hard to please; he could not bear to ask his dear Ruth to live in any but the perfect house, and the perfect house wanted finding. House-hunting is a tiring and a tiresome business and presently Ruth began to grow peevish. Roger begged her to have patience; somewhere, surely, existed the very house they were looking for, and it only needed a little perseverance and they would find it. They looked at hundreds of houses; they climbed thousands of stairs; they inspected innumerable kitchens. Ruth was exhausted and more than once lost her temper.

"If you don't find a house soon," she said, "I shall have to reconsider my position. Why, if you go on like this we shan't be married for years."

"Don't say that," he answered, "I beseech you to have patience. I've just received some entirely new lists from agents I've only just heard of. There must be at least sixty houses on them."

They set out on the chase again. They looked at more houses and more houses. For two years they looked at houses. Ruth grew silent and scornful: her pathetic, beautiful eyes acquired an expression that was almost sullen. There are limits to human endurance. Mrs. Barlow had the patience of an angel, but at last she revolted.

"Do you want to marry me or do you not?" she asked him.

There was an unaccustomed hardness in her voice, but it did not affect the gentleness of his reply.

"Of course I do. We'll be married the very moment we find a house. By the way, I've just heard of something that might suit us."

"I don't feel well enough to look at any more houses just yet."

"Poor dear, I was afraid you were looking rather tired."

Ruth Barlow took to her bed. She would not see Roger and he had to content himself with calling at her lodgings to enquire and sending her flowers. He was as ever assiduous and gallant. Every day he wrote and told her that he had heard of another house for them to look at. A week passed and then he received the following letter:

Roger,
   I do not think you really love me.   I have found someone who is anxious to take care of me and I am going to be married to him to-day.

                                                                    Ruth.

He sent back his reply by special messenger:

Ruth,
   Your news shatters me.   I shall never get over the blow, but of course your happiness must be my first consideration.   I send you herewith seven orders to view; they arrived by this morning's post and I am quite sure you will find among them a house that will exactly suit you.

                                                                    Roger.

The Judgment Seat

THEY awaited their turn patiently, but patience was no new thing to them; they had practised it, all three of them, with grim determination, for thirty years. Their lives had been a long preparation for this moment and they looked forward to the issue now, if not with self-confidence, for that on so awful an occasion would have been misplaced, at all events with hope and courage. They had taken the strait and narrow path when the flowery meads of sin stretched all too invitingly before them; with heads held high, though with breaking hearts, they had resisted temptation; and now, their arduous journey done, they expected their reward. There was no need for them to speak, since each knew the others' thoughts, and they felt that in all three of them the same emotion of relief filled their bodiless souls with thanksgiving. With what anguish now would they have been wrung if they had yielded to the passion which then had seemed so nearly irresistible and what a madness it would have been if for a few short years of bliss they had sacrificed that Life Everlasting which with so bright a light at long last shone before them! They felt like men who with the skin of their teeth have escaped a sudden and violent death and touch their feet and hands and, scarce able to believe that they are still alive, look about them in amazement. They had done nothing with which they could reproach themselves and when presently their angels came and told them that the moment was come, they would advance, as they had passed through the world that was now so far behind, happily conscious that they had done their duty. They stood a little on one side, for the press was great. A terrible war was in progress and for years the soldiers of all nations, men in the full flush of their gallant youth, had marched in an interminable procession to the Judgment Seat; women and children too, their lives brought to a wretched end by violence or, more unhappily, by grief, disease, and starvation; and there was in the courts of heaven not a little confusion.

It was on account of this war, too, that these three wan, shivering ghosts stood in expectation of their doom. For John and Mary had been passengers on a ship which was sunk by the torpedo of a submarine; and Ruth, broken in health by the arduous work to which she had so nobly devoted herself, hearing of the death of the man whom she had loved with all her heart, sank beneath the blow and died. John, indeed, might have saved himself if he had not tried to save his wife; he hated her; he had hated her to the depths of his soul for thirty years; but he had always done his duty by her and now, in the moment of dreadful peril, it never occurred to him that he could do otherwise.

At last their angels took them by the hand and led them to the Presence. For a little while the Eternal took not the slightest notice of them. If the truth must be told he was in a bad humour. A moment before there had come up for judgment a philosopher, deceased full of years and honours, who had told the Eternal to his face that he did not believe in him. It was not this that would have disturbed the serenity of the King of Kings, this could only have made him smile; but the philosopher, taking perhaps an unfair advantage of the regrettable happenings just then upon Earth, had asked him how, considering them dispassionately, it was possible to reconcile his All-Power with his All-Goodness.

"No one can deny the fact of Evil," said the philosopher, sententiously. "Now, if God cannot prevent Evil he is not all-powerful, and if he can prevent it and will not, he is not all-good."

This argument was of course not new to the Omniscient, but he had always refused to consider the matter; for the fact is, though he knew everything, he did not know the answer to this. Even God cannot make two and two five. But the philosopher, pressing his advantage, and, as philosophers often will, drawing from a reasonable premise an unjustifiable inference—the philosopher had finished with a statement that in the circumstances was surely preposterous.

"I will not believe," he said, "in a God who is not All-Powerful and All-Good."

It was not then perhaps without relief that the Eternal turned his attention to the three shades who stood humbly and yet hopefully before him. The quick, with so short a time to live, when they talk of themselves, talk too much; but the dead, with eternity before them, are so verbose that only angels could listen to them with civility. But this in brief is the story that these three recounted. John and Mary had been happily married for five years and till John met Ruth they loved each other, as married couples for the most part do, with sincere affection and mutual respect. Ruth was eighteen, ten years younger than he was, a charming, graceful animal, with a sudden and all-conquering loveliness; she was as healthy in mind as she was in body, and, eager for the natural happiness of life, was capable of achieving that greatness which is beauty of soul. John fell in love with her and she with him. But it was no ordinary passion that seized them; it was something so overwhelming that they felt as if the whole long history of the world

signified only because it had led to the time and place that had
brought them together. They loved as Daphnis and Chloe or as
Paolo and Francesca. But after that first moment of ecstasy when
each discovered the other's love they were seized with dismay. They
were decent people and they respected themselves, the beliefs in
which they had been bred, and the society in which they lived.
How could he betray an innocent girl, and what had she to do with
a married man? Then they grew conscious that Mary was aware of
their love. The confident affection with which she had regarded
her husband was shaken; and there arose in her feelings of which she
would never have thought herself capable, jealousy and the fear that
he would desert her, anger because her possession of his heart was
threatened, and a strange hunger of the soul which was more painful
than love. She felt that she would die if he left her; and yet she knew
that if he loved it was because love had come to him, not because he
had sought it. She did not blame him. She prayed for strength;
she wept silent, bitter tears. John and Ruth saw her pine away before their eyes. The struggle was long and bitter. Sometimes their
hearts failed them and they felt that they could not resist the passion
that burned the marrow of their bones. They resisted. They wrestled
with evil as Jacob wrestled with the angel of God and at last they
conquered. With breaking hearts, but proud in their innocence,
they parted. They offered up to God, as it were a sacrifice, their
hopes of happiness, the joy of life and the beauty of the world.

Ruth had loved too passionately ever to love again and with a
stony heart she turned to God and to good works. She was inde-
fatigable. She tended the sick and assisted the poor. She founded
orphanages and managed charitable institutions. And little by little
her beauty which she cared for no longer left her and her face grew
as hard as her heart. Her religion was fierce and narrow; her very
kindness was cruel because it was founded not on love but on reason;
she became domineering, intolerant, and vindictive. And John,
resigned, but sullen and angry, dragged himself along the weary
years waiting for the release of death. Life lost its meaning to him;
he had made his effort and in conquering was conquered; the only
emotion that remained with him was the unceasing, secret hatred
with which he looked upon his wife. He used her with kindness and
consideration; he did everything that could be expected of a man
who was a Christian and a gentleman. He did his duty. Mary, a
good, faithful and (it must be confessed) exceptional wife, never
thought to reproach her husband for the madness that had seized
him; but all the same she could not forgive him for the sacrifice he
had made for her sake. She grew acid and querulous. Though she

hated herself for it, she could not refrain from saying the things that she knew would wound him. She would willingly have sacrificed her life for him, but she could not bear that he should enjoy a moment's happiness when she was so wretched that a hundred times she had wished she was dead. Well, now she was and so were they; grey and drab had life been, but that was passed; they had not sinned and now their reward was at hand.

They finished and there was silence. There was silence in all the courts of heaven. Go to hell were the words that came to the Eternal's lips, but he did not utter them, for they had a colloquial association that he rightly thought unfitting to the solemnity of the occasion. Nor indeed would such a decree have met the merits of the case. But his brows darkened. He asked himself if it was for this that he had made the rising sun shine on the boundless sea and the snow glitter on the mountain tops; was it for this that the brooks sang blithely as they hastened down the hillsides and the golden corn waved in the evening breeze?

"I sometimes think," said the Eternal, "that the stars never shine more brightly than when reflected in the muddy waters of a wayside ditch."

But the three shades stood before him and now that they had unfolded their unhappy story they could not but feel a certain satisfaction. It had been a bitter struggle, but they had done their duty. The Eternal blew lightly, he blew as a man might blow out a lighted match, and, behold! where the three poor souls had stood—was nothing. The Eternal annihilated them.

"I have often wondered why men think I attach so much importance to sexual irregularity," he said. "If they read my works more attentively they would see that I have always been sympathetic to that particular form of human frailty."

Then he turned to the philosopher, who was still waiting for a reply to his remarks.

"You cannot but allow," said the Eternal, "that on this occasion I have very happily combined my All-Power with my All-Goodness."

Mr. Know-All

I WAS prepared to dislike Max Kelada even before I knew him. The war had just finished and the passenger traffic in the ocean-going liners was heavy. Accommodation was very hard to get and you had to put up with whatever the agents chose to offer you. You could not hope for a cabin to yourself and I was thankful to be given one in which there were only two berths. But when I was told the name of my companion my heart sank. It suggested closed port-holes and the night air rigidly excluded. It was bad enough to share a cabin for fourteen days with anyone (I was going from San Francisco to Yokohama), but I should have looked upon it with less dismay if my fellow-passenger's name had been Smith or Brown.

When I went on board I found Mr. Kelada's luggage already below. I did not like the look of it; there were too many labels on the suitcases, and the wardrobe trunk was too big. He had unpacked his toilet things, and I observed that he was a patron of the excellent Monsieur Coty; for I saw on the washing-stand his scent, his hair-wash and his brilliantine. Mr. Kelada's brushes, ebony with his monogram in gold, would have been all the better for a scrub. I did not at all like Mr. Kelada. I made my way into the smoking-room. I called for a pack of cards and began to play patience. I had scarcely started before a man came up to me and asked me if he was right in thinking my name was so-and-so.

"I am Mr. Kelada," he added, with a smile that showed a row of flashing teeth, and sat down.

"Oh, yes, we're sharing a cabin, I think."

"Bit of luck, I call it. You never know who you're going to be put in with. I was jolly glad when I heard you were English. I'm all for us English sticking together when we're abroad, if you understand what I mean."

I blinked.

"Are you English?" I asked, perhaps tactlessly.

"Rather. You don't think I look like an American, do you? British to the backbone, that's what I am."

To prove it, Mr. Kelada took out of his pocket a passport and airily waved it under my nose.

King George has many strange subjects. Mr. Kelada was short and of a sturdy build, clean-shaven and dark-skinned, with a fleshy, hooked nose and very large, lustrous and liquid eyes. His long black hair was sleek and curly. He spoke with a fluency in which there was nothing English and his gestures were exuberant. I felt pretty sure that a closer inspection of that British passport would have betrayed the fact that Mr. Kelada was born under a bluer sky than is generally seen in England.

"What will you have?" he asked me.

I looked at him doubtfully. Prohibition was in force and to all appearances the ship was bone-dry. When I am not thirsty I do not know which I dislike more, ginger-ale or lemon-squash. But Mr. Kelada flashed an oriental smile at me.

"Whisky and soda or a dry Martini, you have only to say the word."

From each of his hip-pockets he fished a flask and laid them on the table before me. I chose the Martini, and calling the steward he ordered a tumbler of ice and a couple of glasses.

"A very good cocktail," I said.

"Well, there are plenty more where that came from, and if you've got any friends on board, you tell them you've got a pal who's got all the liquor in the world."

Mr. Kelada was chatty. He talked of New York and of San Francisco. He discussed plays, pictures, and politics. He was patri-otic. The Union Jack is an impressive piece of drapery, but when it is flourished by a gentleman from Alexandria or Beirut, I cannot but feel that it loses somewhat in dignity. Mr. Kelada was familiar. I do not wish to put on airs, but I cannot help feeling that it is seemly in a total stranger to put mister before my name when he addresses me. Mr. Kelada, doubtless to set me at my ease, used no such formality. I did not like Mr. Kelada. I had put aside the cards when he sat down, but now, thinking that for this first occasion our conversation had lasted long enough, I went on with my game.

"The three on the four," said Mr. Kelada.

There is nothing more exasperating when you are playing patience than to be told where to put the card you have turned up before you have had a chance to look for yourself.

"It's coming out, it's coming out," he cried. "The ten on the knave."

With rage and hatred in my heart I finished. Then he seized the pack.

"Do you like card tricks?"

"No, I hate card tricks," I answered.

"Well, I'll just show you this one."

He showed me three. Then I said I would go down to the dining-room and get my seat at table.

"Oh, that's all right," he said. "I've already taken a seat for you. I thought that as we were in the same state-room we might just as well sit at the same table."

I did not like Mr. Kelada.

I not only shared a cabin with him and ate three meals a day at the same table, but I could not walk round the deck without his joining me. It was impossible to snub him. It never occurred to him that he was not wanted. He was certain that you were as glad to see him as he was to see you. In your own house you might have kicked him downstairs and slammed the door in his face without the suspicion dawning on him that he was not a welcome visitor. He was a good mixer, and in three days knew everyone on board. He ran everything. He managed the sweeps, conducted the auctions, collected money for prizes at the sports, got up quoit and golf matches, organised the concert and arranged the fancy dress ball. He was everywhere and always. He was certainly the best-hated man in the ship. We called him Mr. Know-All, even to his face. He took it as a compliment. But it was at meal times that he was most intolerable. For the better part of an hour then he had us at his mercy. He was hearty, jovial, loquacious and argumentative. He knew everything better than anybody else, and it was an affront to his overweening vanity that you should disagree with him. He would not drop a subject, however unimportant, till he had brought you round to his way of thinking. The possibility that he could be mistaken never occurred to him. He was the chap who knew. We sat at the doctor's table. Mr. Kelada would certainly have had it all his own way, for the doctor was lazy and I was frigidly indifferent, except for a man called Ramsay who sat there also. He was as dogmatic as Mr. Kelada and resented bitterly the Levantine's cocksureness. The discussions they had were acrimonious and interminable.

Ramsay was in the American Consular Service, and was stationed at Kobe. He was a great heavy fellow from the Middle West, with loose fat under a tight skin, and he bulged out of his ready-made clothes. He was on his way back to resume his post, having been on a flying visit to New York to fetch his wife, who had been spending a year at home. Mrs. Ramsay was a very pretty little thing, with pleasant manners and a sense of humour. The Consular Service is ill paid, and she was dressed always very simply; but she knew how to wear her clothes. She achieved an effect of quiet distinction. I should not have paid any particular attention to her but that she possessed a quality that may be common enough in women, but nowadays is not obvious in their demeanour. You could not look at her without being struck by her modesty. It shone in her like a flower on a coat.

One evening at dinner the conversation by chance drifted to the subject of pearls. There had been in the papers a good deal of talk about the culture pearls which the cunning Japanese were making, and the doctor remarked that they must inevitably diminish the value of real ones. They were very good already; they would soon be perfect. Mr. Kelada, as was his habit, rushed the new topic. He told us all that was to be known about pearls. I do not believe Ramsay knew anything about them at all, but he could not resist the opportunity to have a fling at the Levantine, and in five minutes we were in the middle of a heated argument. I had seen Mr. Kelada vehement and voluble before, but never so voluble and vehement as now. At last something that Ramsay said stung him, for he thumped the table and shouted:

"Well, I ought to know what I am talking about. I'm going to Japan just to look into this Japanese pearl business. I'm in the trade and there's not a man in it who won't tell you that what I say about pearls goes. I know all the best pearls in the world, and what I don't know about pearls isn't worth knowing."

Here was news for us, for Mr. Kelada, with all his loquacity, had never told anyone what his business was. We only knew vaguely that he was going to Japan on some commercial errand. He looked round the table triumphantly.

"They'll never be able to get a culture pearl that an expert like me can't tell with half an eye." He pointed to a chain that Mrs. Ramsay wore. "You take my word for it, Mrs. Ramsay, that chain you're wearing will never be worth a cent less than it is now."

Mrs. Ramsay in her modest way flushed a little and slipped the chain inside her dress. Ramsay leaned forward. He gave us all a look and a smile flickered in his eyes.

"That's a pretty chain of Mrs. Ramsay's, isn't it?"

"I noticed it at once," answered Mr. Kelada. "Gee, I said to myself, those are pearls all right."

"I didn't buy it myself, of course. I'd be interested to know how much you think it cost."

"Oh, in the trade somewhere round fifteen thousand dollars. But if it was bought on Fifth Avenue I shouldn't be surprised to hear that anything up to thirty thousand was paid for it."

Ramsay smiled grimly.

"You'll be surprised to hear that Mrs. Ramsay bought that string at a department store the day before we left New York, for eighteen dollars."

Mr. Kelada flushed.

"Rot. It's not only real, but it's as fine a string for its size as I've ever seen."

"Will you bet on it? I'll bet you a hundred dollars it's imitation."

"Done."

"Oh, Elmer, you can't bet on a certainty," said Mrs. Ramsay. She had a little smile on her lips and her tone was gently deprecating.

"Can't I? If I get a chance of easy money like that I should be all sorts of a fool not to take it."

"But how can it be proved?" she continued. "It's only my word against Mr. Kelada's."

"Let me look at the chain, and if it's imitation I'll tell you quickly enough. I can afford to lose a hundred dollars," said Mr. Kelada.

"Take it off, dear. Let the gentleman look at it as much as he wants."

Mrs. Ramsay hesitated a moment. She put her hands to the clasp.

"I can't undo it," she said. "Mr. Kelada will just have to take my word for it."

I had a sudden suspicion that something unfortunate was about to occur, but I could think of nothing to say.

Ramsay jumped up.

"I'll undo it."

He handed the chain to Mr. Kelada. The Levantine took a magnifying glass from his pocket and closely examined it. A smile of triumph spread over his smooth and swarthy face. He handed back the chain. He was about to speak. Suddenly he caught sight of Mrs. Ramsay's face. It was so white that she looked as though she were about to faint. She was staring at him with wide and terrified eyes. They held a desperate appeal; it was so clear that I wondered why her husband did not see it.

Mr. Kelada stopped with his mouth open. He flushed deeply. You could almost *see* the effort he was making over himself.

"I was mistaken," he said. "It's a very good imitation, but of course as soon as I looked through my glass I saw that it wasn't real. I think eighteen dollars is just about as much as the damned thing's worth."

He took out his pocket-book and from it a hundred-dollar note. He handed it to Ramsay without a word.

"Perhaps that'll teach you not to be so cocksure another time, my young friend," said Ramsay as he took the note.

I noticed that Mr. Kelada's hands were trembling.

The story spread over the ship as stories do, and he had to put up with a good deal of chaff that evening. It was a fine joke that Mr. Know-All had been caught out. But Mrs. Ramsay retired to her state-room with a headache.

Next morning I got up and began to shave. Mr. Kelada lay on his bed smoking a cigarette. Suddenly there was a small scraping sound and I saw a letter pushed under the door. I opened the door and looked out. There was nobody there. I picked up the letter and saw that it was addressed to Max Kelada. The name was written in block letters. I handed it to him.

"Who's this from?" He opened it. "Oh!"

He took out of the envelope, not a letter, but a hundred-dollar note. He looked at me and again he reddened. He tore the envelope into little bits and gave them to me.

"Do you mind just throwing them out of the port-hole?"

I did as he asked, and then I looked at him with a smile.

"No one likes being made to look a perfect damned fool," he said.

"Were the pearls real?"

"If I had a pretty little wife I shouldn't let her spend a year in New York while I stayed at Kobe," said he.

At that moment I did not entirely dislike Mr. Kelada. He reached out for his pocket-book and carefully put in it the hundred-dollar note.

The Human Element

I seem never to find myself in Rome but at the dead season. I pass through in August or September on my way somewhere or other and spend a couple of days revisiting places or pictures that are endeared to me by old associations. It is very hot then and the inhabitants of the city spend their day interminably strolling up and down the Corso. The Caffé Nazionale is crowded with people sitting at little tables for long hours with an empty cup of coffee in front of them and a glass of water. In the Sistine Chapel you see blond and sunburned Germans, in knickerbockers and shirts open at the neck, who have walked down the dusty roads of Italy with knapsacks on their shoulders; and in St. Peter's little groups of the pious, tired but eager, who have come on pilgrimage (at an inclusive rate) from some distant country. They are under the charge of a priest and they speak strange tongues. The Hotel Plaza then is cool and restful. The public rooms are dark, silent, and spacious. In the lounge at tea-time the only persons are a young, smart officer and a woman with fine eyes, drinking iced lemonade, and they talk intimately, in low tones, with the unwearying fluency of their race. You go up to your room and read and write letters and come down again two hours later and they are still talking. Before dinner a few people saunter into the bar, but for the rest of the day it is empty and the barman has time to tell you of his mother in Switzerland and his experiences in New York. You discuss life and love and the high cost of liquor.

And on this occasion too I found that I had the hotel almost to myself. When the reception clerk took me to my room he told me that they were pretty full, but when, having bathed and changed, I came down again to the hall, the liftman, an old acquaintance, informed me that there were not more than a dozen people staying there. I was tired after a long and hot journey down Italy and had made up my mind to dine quietly in the hotel and go to bed early. It was late when I went into the dining-room, vast and brightly lit, but not more than three or four tables were occupied. I looked round me with satisfaction. It is very agreeable to find yourself alone in a great city which is yet not quite strange to you and in a large empty hotel. It gives you a delectable sense of freedom. I felt the wings of my spirit give a little flutter of delight. I had paused for ten minutes in the bar and had a dry Martini. I ordered myself a bottle of good red wine. My limbs were weary, but my soul re-

sponded wonderfully to food and drink and I began to feel a singular
lightness of heart. I ate my soup and my fish and pleasant thoughts
filled my mind. Scraps of dialogue occurred to me and my fancy
played happily with the persons of a novel I was then at work on.
I rolled a phrase on my tongue and it tasted better than the wine.
I began to think of the difficulty of describing the looks of people in
such a way as to make the reader see them as you see them. To me
it has always been one of the most difficult things in fiction. What
does the reader really get when you describe a face feature by feature ?
I should think nothing. And yet the plan some writers adopt of
taking a salient characteristic, a crooked smile or shifty eyes, and
emphasising that, though effective, avoids rather than solves the
problem. I looked about me and wondered how I would describe
the people at the tables round me. There was one man by himself
just opposite and for practice I asked myself in what way I should
treat him. He was a tall, spare fellow, and what I believe is generally
called loose-limbed. He wore a dinner jacket and a boiled shirt. He
had a rather long face and pale eyes; his hair was fairish and wavy,
but it was growing thin, and the baldness of his temples gave him a
certain nobility of brow. His features were undistinguished. His
mouth and nose were like everybody else's; he was clean-shaven; his
skin was naturally pale, but at the moment sunburned. His appearance suggested an intellectual but slightly commonplace distinction.
He looked as though he might have been a lawyer or a don who
played a pretty game of golf. I felt that he had good taste and was
well-read and would be a very agreeable guest at a luncheon-party
in Chelsea. But how the devil one was to describe him so as in a few
lines to give a vivid, interesting and accurate picture I could not
imagine. Perhaps it would be better to let all the rest go and dwell
only on that rather fatigued distinction which on the whole was the
most definite impression he gave. I looked at him reflectively.
Suddenly he leaned forwards and gave me a stiff but courtly little
bow. I have a ridiculous habit of flushing when I am taken aback
and now I felt my cheeks redden. I was startled. I had been staring
at him for several minutes as though he were a dummy. He must
have thought me extremely rude. I nodded with a good deal of
embarrassment and looked away. Fortunately at that moment the
waiter was handing me a dish. To the best of my belief I had never
seen the fellow before. I asked myself whether his bow was due to
my insistent stare, which made him think that he had met me
somewhere, or whether I had really run across him and completely
forgotten. I have a bad memory for faces and I had in this case
the excuse that he looked exactly like a great many other people.

You saw a dozen of him at every golf course round London on a fine Sunday.

He finished his dinner before me. He got up, but on his way out stopped at my table. He stretched out his hand.

"How d'you do?" he said. "I didn't recognise you when you first came in. I wasn't meaning to cut you."

He spoke in a pleasant voice with the tones cultivated at Oxford and copied by many who have never been there. It was evident that he knew me and evident too that he had no notion that I did not also know him. I had risen and since he was a good deal taller than I he looked down on me. He held himself with a sort of languor. He stooped a little, which added to the impression he gave me of having about him an air that was vaguely apologetic. His manner was a trifle condescending and at the same time a trifle shy.

"Won't you come and have your coffee with me?" he said. "I'm quite alone."

"Yes, I shall be glad to."

He left me and I still had no notion who he was or where I had met him. I had noticed one curious thing about him. Not once during the few sentences we exchanged, when we shook hands, or when with a nod he left me, did even the suspicion of a smile cross his face. Seeing him more closely I observed that he was in his way good-looking; his features were regular, his grey eyes were handsome, he had a slim figure; but it was a way that I found uninteresting. A silly woman would say he looked romantic. He reminded you of one of the knights of Burne-Jones though he was on a larger scale and there was no suggestion that he suffered from the chronic colitis that afflicted those unfortunate creatures. He was the sort of man whom you expected to look wonderful in fancy dress till you saw him in it and then you found that he looked absurd.

Presently I finished my dinner and went into the lounge. He was sitting in a large arm-chair and when he saw me he called a waiter. I sat down. The waiter came up and he ordered coffee and liqueurs. He spoke Italian very well. I was wondering by what means I could find out who he was without offending him. People are always a little disconcerted when you do not recognise them, they are so important to themselves, it is a shock to discover of what small importance they are to others. The excellence of his Italian recalled him to me. I remembered who he was and remembered at the same time that I did not like him. His name was Humphrey Carruthers. He was in the Foreign Office and he had a position of some importance. He was in charge of I know not what department. He had been attached to various embassies and I supposed that a sojourn in Rome accounted for his idiomatic Italian. It was stupid of me not to have seen at once that he was connected with the diplomatic service. He had all the marks of the profession. He had the supercilious courtesy that is so well calculated to put up the backs of the general public and the aloofness due to the consciousness the diplomat has that he is not as other men are, joined with the shyness occasioned by his uneasy feeling that other men do not quite realise it. I had known Carruthers for a good many years, but had met him infrequently, at luncheon-parties where I said no more than how do you do to him and at the opera where he gave me a cool nod. He was generally thought intelligent; he was certainly cultured. He could talk of all the right things. It was inexcusable of me not to have remembered him, for he had lately acquired a very considerable reputation as a writer of short stories. They had appeared first in one or other of those magazines that are founded now and then by well-disposed persons to give the intelligent reader something worthy of his attention and that die when their proprietors have lost as much money as they want to; and in their discreet and handsomely printed pages had excited as much attention as an exiguous circulation permitted. Then they were published in book form. They created a sensation. I have seldom read such unanimous praise in the weekly papers. Most of them gave the book a column and the Literary Supplement of *The Times* reviewed it not among the common ruck of novels but in a place by itself cheek by jowl with the memoirs of a distinguished statesman. The critics welcomed Humphrey Carruthers as a new star in the firmament. They praised his distinction, his subtlety, his delicate irony and his insight. They praised his style, his sense of beauty and his atmosphere. Here at last was a writer who had raised the short story from the depths into which in English-speaking countries it had fallen and here was work to which an Englishman could point with pride; it bore comparison with the best compositions in this manner of Finland, Russia, and Czecho-Slovakia.

Three years later Humphrey Carruthers brought out his second book and the critics commented on the interval with satisfaction. Here was no hack prostituting his talent for money! The praise it received was perhaps a little cooler than that which welcomed his first volume, the critics had had time to collect themselves, but it was enthusiastic enough to have delighted any common writer who earns his living by his pen and there was no doubt that his position in the world of letters was secure and honourable. The story that attracted most commendation was called *The Shaving Mop* and all the best critics pointed out with what beauty the author in three or four pages had laid bare the tragic soul of a barber's assistant.

But his best known story, which was also his longest, was called *Week End*. It gave its title to his first book. It narrated the adventures of a number of people who left Paddington Station on Saturday afternoon to stay with friends at Taplow and on Monday morning returned to London. It was so delicate that it was a little difficult to know exactly what happened. A young man, parliamentary secretary to a Cabinet Minister, very nearly proposed to a baronet's daughter, but didn't. Two or three others went on the river in a punt. They all talked a great deal in an allusive way, but none of them ever finished a sentence and what they meant was very subtly indicated by dots and dashes. There were a good many descriptions of flowers in the garden and a sensitive picture of the Thames under the rain. It was all seen through the eyes of the German governess and everyone agreed that Carruthers had conveyed her outlook on the situation with quite delicious humour.

I read both Humphrey Carruthers' books. I think it part of the writer's business to make himself aware of what is being written by his contemporaries. I am very willing to learn and I thought I might discover in them something that would be useful to me. I was disappointed. I like a story to have a beginning, a middle, and an end. I have a weakness for a point. I think atmosphere is all very well, but atmosphere without anything else is like a frame without a picture; it has not much significance. But it may be that I could not see the merit of Humphrey Carruthers on account of defects in myself, and if I have described his two most successful stories without enthusiasm the cause perhaps lies in my own wounded vanity. For I was perfectly conscious that Humphrey Carruthers looked upon me as a writer of no account. I am convinced that he had never read a word I had written. The popularity I enjoyed was sufficient to persuade him that there was no occasion for him to give me any of his attention. For a moment, such was the stir he created, it looked as though he might himself be faced with that ignominy, but it soon appeared that his exquisite work was above the heads of the public. One can never tell how large the intelligentsia is, but one can tell fairly well how many of its members are prepared to pay money to patronise the arts they cherish. The plays that are of too fine a quality to attract the patrons of the commercial theatre can count on an audience of ten thousand, and the books that demand from their readers more comprehension than can be expected from the common herd sell twelve hundred copies. For the intelligentsia, notwithstanding their sensitiveness to beauty, prefer to go to the theatre on the nod and to get a book from the library.

I am sure this did not distress Carruthers. He was an artist. He was also a clerk in the Foreign Office. His reputation as a writer was distinguished; he was not interested in the vulgar, and to sell well would possibly have damaged his career. I could not surmise what had induced him to invite me to have coffee with him. It is true he was alone, but I should have supposed he found his thoughts excellent company, and I could not believe he imagined that I had anything to say that would interest him. Nevertheless I could not but see that he was doing his dreary best to be affable. He reminded me of where we had last met and we talked for a moment of common friends in London. He asked me how I came to be in Rome at this season and I told him. He volunteered the information that he had arrived that morning from Brindisi. Our conversation did not go easily and I made up my mind that as soon as I civilly could I would get up and leave him. But presently I had an odd sensation, I hardly know what caused it, that he was conscious of this and was desperately anxious not to give me the opportunity. I was surprised. I gathered my wits about me. I noticed that whenever I paused he broke in with a new topic. He was trying to find something to interest me so that I should stay. He was straining every nerve to be agreeable. Surely he could not be lonely; with his diplomatic connections he must know plenty of people with whom he could have spent the evening. I wondered indeed that he was not dining at the Embassy; even though it was summer there must be someone there he knew. I noticed also that he never smiled. He talked with a sort of harsh eagerness as though he were afraid of a moment's silence and the sound of his voice shut out of his mind something that tortured him. It was very strange. Though I did not like him, though he meant nothing to me and to be with him irked me somewhat, I was against my will a trifle interested. I gave him a searching glance. I wondered if it was my fancy that I saw in those pale eyes of his the cowed look of a hunted dog and notwithstanding his neat features and his expression so civilly controlled, in his aspect something that suggested the grimace of a soul in pain. I could not understand. A dozen absurd notions flashed through my mind. I was not particularly sympathetic: like an old war horse scenting the fray I roused myself. I had been feeling very tired, but now I grew alert. My sensibilities put out tentacles. I was suddenly alive to every expression of his face and every gesture. I put aside the thought that had come to me that he had written a play and wanted my advice. These exquisite persons succumb strangely to the glamour of the footlights and they are not averse from getting a few tips from the craftsman whose competence they superciliously despise. No, it was not that. A single man in Rome, of æsthetic leanings, is liable to get into trouble, and I asked myself whether Carruthers had got into some difficulty to extricate himself from which the Embassy was the last place he could go to. The idealist, I have noticed, is apt at times to be imprudent in the affairs of the flesh. He sometimes finds love in places which the police inconveniently visit. I tittered in my heart. Even the gods laugh when a prig is caught in an equivocal situation.

Suddenly Carruthers said something that staggered me.

"I'm so desperately unhappy," he muttered.

He said it without warning. He obviously meant it. There was in his tone a sort of gasp. It might very well have been a sob. I cannot describe what a shock it was to me to hear him say those words. I felt as you do when you turn a corner of the street and on a sudden a great blast of wind meets you, takes your breath away, and nearly blows you off your feet. It was so unexpected. After all I hardly knew the fellow. We were not friends. I did not like him; he did not like me. I had never looked on him as quite human. It was amazing that a man so self-controlled, so urbane, accustomed to the usages of polite society, should break in upon a stranger with such a confession. I am naturally reticent. I should be ashamed, whatever I was suffering, to disclose my pain to another. I shivered. His weakness outraged me. For a moment I was filled with a passion of anger. How dared he thrust the anguish of his soul on me? I very nearly cried:

"What the hell do I care?"

But I didn't. He was sitting huddled up in the big arm-chair. The solemn nobility of his features, which reminded one of the marble statue of a Victorian statesman, had strangely crumpled and his face sagged. He looked almost as though he were going to cry. I hesitated. I faltered. I had flushed when he spoke and now I felt my face go white. He was a pitiable object.

"I'm awfully sorry," I said.

"Do you mind if I tell you about it?"

"No."

It was not the moment for many words. I suppose Carruthers was in the early forties. He was a well-made man, athletic in his way, and with a confident bearing. Now he looked twenty years older and strangely shrivelled. He reminded me of the dead soldiers I had seen during the war and how oddly small death had made them. I was embarrassed and looked away, but I felt his eyes claiming mine and I looked back.

"Do you know Betty Welldon-Burns?" he asked me.

"I used to meet her sometimes in London years ago. I've not seen her lately."

"She lives in Rhodes now, you know. I've just come from there. I've been staying with her."

"Oh?"

He hesitated.

"I'm afraid you'll think it awfully strange of me to talk to you like this. I'm at the end of my tether. If I don't talk to somebody I shall go off my head."

He had ordered double brandies with the coffee and now calling the waiter he ordered himself another. We were alone in the lounge. There was a little shaded lamp on the table between us. Because it was a public room he spoke in a low voice. The place gave one oddly enough a sense of intimacy. I cannot repeat all that Carruthers said to me in the words he said it; it would be impossible for me to remember them; it is more convenient for me to put it in my own fashion. Sometimes he could not bring himself to say a thing right out and I had to guess at what he meant. Sometimes he had not understood, and it seemed to me that in certain ways I saw the truth more clearly than he. Betty Welldon-Burns had a very keen sense of humour and he had none. I perceived a good deal that had escaped him.

I had met her a good many times, but I knew her chiefly from hearsay. In her day she had made a great stir in the little world of London and I had heard of her often before I met her. This was at a dance in Portland Place soon after the war. She was then already at the height of her celebrity. You could not open an illustrated paper without seeing in it a portrait of her, and her mad pranks were a staple of conversation. She was twenty-four. Her mother was dead, her father, the Duke of St. Erth, old and none too rich, spent most of the year in his Cornish castle and she lived in London with a widowed aunt. At the outbreak of the war she went to France. She was just eighteen. She was a nurse in a hospital at the Base and then drove a car. She acted in a theatrical tour designed to amuse the troops; she posed in tableaux at home for charitable purposes, held auctions for this object and that and sold flags in Piccadilly. Every one of her activities was widely advertised and in every new rôle she was profusely photographed. I suppose that she managed to have a very good time. But now that the war was over she was having her fling with a vengeance. Just then everybody a little lost his head. The young, relieved of the burden that for five years had oppressed them, indulged in one wild escapade after another. Betty took part in them all. Sometimes, for one reason or another, an account of them found its way into the newspapers and her name was always in the headline. At that time night clubs were in the first flush of their success and she was to be seen at them every night. She lived a life of hectic gaiety. It can only be described in a hackneyed phrase, because it was a hackneyed thing. The British public in its odd way took her to its heart and Lady Betty was a sufficient description of her throughout the British islands. Women mobbed her when she went to a wedding and the gallery applauded her at first nights as though she were a popular actress. Girls copied the way she did her hair and manufacturers of soap and face cream paid her money to use her photograph to advertise their wares.

Of course dull, stodgy people, the people who remembered and regretted the old order, disapproved of her. They sneered at her constant appearance in the limelight. They said she had an insane passion for self-advertisement. They said she was fast. They said she drank too much. They said she smoked too much. I will admit that nothing I had heard of her had predisposed me to think very well of her. I held cheap the women who seemed to look upon the war as an occasion to enjoy themselves and be talked about. I am bored by the papers in which you see photographs of persons in society walking in Cannes or playing golf at St. Andrews. I have always found the Bright Young People extremely tedious. The gay life seems dull and stupid to the onlooker, but the moralist is unwise to judge it harshly. It is as absurd to be angry with the young things who lead it as with a litter of puppies scampering aimlessly around, rolling one another over and chasing their tails. It is well to bear it with fortitude if they cause havoc in the flower beds or break a piece of china. Some of them will be drowned because their points are not up to the mark and the rest will grow up into well-behaved dogs. Their unruliness is due only to the vitality of youth.

And it was vitality that was Betty's most shining characteristic. The urge of life flowed through her with a radiance that dazzled you. I do not think I shall ever forget the impression she made on me at the party at which I first saw her. She was like a mænad. She danced with an abandon that made you laugh, so obvious was her intense enjoyment of the music and the movement of her young limbs. Her hair was brown, slightly disordered by the vigour of her gestures, but her eyes were deep blue, and her skin was milk and roses. She was a great beauty, but she had none of the coldness of great beauty. She laughed constantly and when she was not laughing she smiled and her eyes danced with the joy of living. She was like a milkmaid on the farmstead of the gods. She had the strength and health of the people; and yet the independence of her bearing, a sort of noble frankness of carriage, suggested the great lady. I do not quite know how to put the feeling she gave me, that though so

simple and unaffected she was not unconscious of her station. I
fancied that if occasion arose she could get on her dignity and be very
grand indeed. She was charming to everybody because, probably
without being quite aware of it, in the depths of her heart she felt
that the rest of the world was perfectly insignificant. I understood
why the factory girls in the East End adored her and why half a
million people who had never seen her except in a photograph looked
upon her with the intimacy of personal friendship. I was introduced
to her and she spent a few minutes talking to me. It was extraordinarily flattering to see the interest she showed in you; you knew she
could not really be so pleased to meet you as she seemed or so delighted with what you said, but it was very attractive. She had the
gift of being able to jump over the first difficult phases of acquaintance and you had not known her for five minutes before you felt you
had known her all her life. She was snatched away from me by someone who wanted to dance with her and she surrendered herself to her
partner's arms with just the same eager happiness as she had shown
when she sank into a chair by my side. I was surprised when I met
her at luncheon a fortnight later to find that she remembered exactly
what we had talked about during those noisy ten minutes at the
dance. A young woman with all the social graces.

I mentioned the incident to Carruthers.

"She was no fool," he said. "Very few people knew how intelligent she was. She wrote some very good poetry. Because she was so
gay, because she was so reckless and never cared a damn for anybody,
people thought she was scatter-brained. Far from it. She was as
clever as a monkey. You would never have thought she'd had the
time to read all the things she had. I don't suppose anyone knew
that side of her as well as I did. We used to take walks together, in
the country at week-ends, and in London we'd drive out to Rich-
mond Park and walk there, and talk. She loved flowers and trees
and grass. She was interested in everything. She had a lot of
information and a lot of sense. There was nothing she couldn't talk
about. Sometimes when we'd been for a walk in the afternoon
and we met at a night club and she'd had a couple of glasses of
champagne, that was enough to make her completely buffy, you
know, and she was the life and soul of the party, I couldn't help
thinking how amazed the rest of them would be if they knew how
seriously we'd been talking only a few hours before. It was an
extraordinary contrast. There seemed to be two entirely different
women in her."

Carruthers said all this without a smile. He spoke with the
melancholy he might have used if he had been speaking of some

G

person snatched from the pleasant company of the living by untimely death. He gave a deep sigh.

"I was madly in love with her. I proposed to her half a dozen times. Of course I knew I hadn't a chance, I was only a very junior clerk at the F.O., but I couldn't help myself. She refused me, but she was always frightfully nice about it. It never made any difference to our friendship. You see, she really liked me. I gave her something that other people didn't. I always thought that she was really fonder of me than of anybody. I was crazy about her."

"I don't suppose you were the only one," I said, having to say something.

"Far from it. She used to get dozens of love letters from men she'd never seen or heard of, farmers in Africa, miners, and policemen in Canada. All sorts of people proposed to her. She could have married anyone she liked."

"Even royalty, one heard."

"Yes, she said she couldn't stand the life. And then she married Jimmie Welldon-Burns."

"People were rather surprised, weren't they?"

"Did you ever know him?"

"No, I don't think so. I may have met him, but he left no impression on me."

"He wouldn't. He was the most insignificant fellow that ever breathed. His father was a big manufacturer up in the North. He'd made a lot of money during the war and bought a baronetcy. I believe he hadn't an aitch to his name. Jimmy was at Eton with me, they'd tried hard to make a gentleman of him, and in London after the war he was about a good deal. He was always willing to throw a party. No one ever paid any attention to him. He just paid the bill. He was the most crashing bore. You know, rather prim, terribly polite; he made you rather uncomfortable because he was so anxious not to do the wrong thing. He always wore his clothes as though he'd just put them on for the first time and they were a little tight for him."

When Carruthers innocently opened his *Times* one morning and casting his eyes down the fashionable intelligence of the day saw that a marriage had been arranged between Elizabeth, only daughter of the Duke of St. Erth, and James, eldest son of Sir John Welldon-Burns, Bart., he was dumbfounded. He rang Betty up and asked if it was true.

"Of course," she said.

He was so shocked that for the moment he found nothing to say. She went on speaking.

"He's bringing his family to luncheon to-day to meet father. I dare say it'll be a bit grim. You might stand me a cocktail at Claridge's to fortify me, will you?"

"At what time?" he asked.

"One."

"All right. I'll meet you there."

He was waiting for her when she came in. She walked with a sort of spring as though her eager feet itched to break into a dance. She was smiling. Her eyes shone with the joy that suffused her because she was alive and the world was such a pleasant place to live in. People recognising her whispered to one another as she came in. Carruthers really felt that she brought sunshine and the scent of flowers into the sober but rather overwhelming splendour of Claridge's lounge. He did not wait to say how do you do to her.

"Betty, you can't do it," he said. "It's simply out of the question."

"Why?"

"He's awful."

"I don't think he is. I think he's rather nice."

A waiter came up and took their order. Betty looked at Carruthers with those beautiful blue eyes of hers that managed to be at the same time so gay and so tender.

"He's such a frightful bounder, Betty."

"Oh, don't be so silly, Humphrey. He's just as good as anybody else. I think you're rather a snob."

"He's so dull."

"No, he's rather quiet. I don't know that I want a husband who's too brilliant. I think he'll make a very good background. He's quite good-looking and he has nice manners."

"My God, Betty."

"Oh, don't be idiotic, Humphrey."

"Are you going to pretend you're in love with him?"

"I think it would be tactful, don't you?"

"Why are you going to marry him?"

She looked at him coolly.

"He's got pots of money. I'm nearly twenty-six."

There was nothing much more to be said. He drove her back to her aunt's house. She had a very grand marriage, with dense crowds lining the approach to St. Margaret's, Westminster, presents from practically all the royal family, and the honeymoon was passed on the yacht her father-in-law had lent them. Carruthers applied for a post abroad and was sent to Rome (I was right in guessing that he had thus acquired his admirable Italian) and later to

Stockholm. Here he was counsellor and here he wrote the first of
his stories.

Perhaps Betty's marriage had disappointed the British public who
expected much greater things of her, perhaps only that as a young
married woman she no longer appealed to the popular sense of
romance; the fact was plain that she soon lost her place in the public
eye. You ceased to hear very much about her. Not long after the
marriage it was rumoured that she was going to have a baby and a
little later that she had had a miscarriage. She did not drop out of
society, I suppose she continued to see her friends, but her activities
were no longer spectacular. She was certainly but seldom seen any
more in those raffish assemblies where the members of a tarnished
aristocracy hob-nob with the hangers-on of the arts and flatter
themselves that they are being at once smart and cultured. People
said she was settling down. They wondered how she was getting on
with her husband and no sooner did they do this than they concluded
that she was not getting on very well. Presently gossip said that
Jimmie was drinking too much and then, a year or two later, one
heard that he had contracted tuberculosis. The Welldon-Burns'
spent a couple of winters in Switzerland. Then the news spread
that they had separated and Betty had gone to live in Rhodes. An
odd place to choose.

"It must be deadly," her friends said.

A few of them went to stay with her now and then and came back
with reports of the beauty of the island and the leisurely charm of the
life. But of course it was very lonely. It seemed strange that Betty,
with her brilliance and her energy, should be content to settle there.
She had bought a house. She knew no one but a few Italian officials,
there was indeed no one to know; but she seemed perfectly happy.
Her visitors could not make it out. But the life of London is busy and
memories are short. People ceased to concern themselves with her.
She was forgotten. Then, a few weeks before I met Humphrey
Carruthers in Rome, *The Times* announced the death of Sir James
Welldon-Burns, second baronet. His younger brother succeeded him
in the title. Betty had never had a child.

Carruthers continued to see her after the marriage. Whenever he
came to London they lunched together. She had the ability to take
up a friendship after a long separation as though no passage of
time had intervened, so that there was never any strangeness in
their meetings. Sometimes she asked him when he was going to
marry.

"You're getting on, you know, Humphrey. If you don't marry soon you'll get rather old-maidish."

"D'you recommend marriage?"

It was not a very kindly thing to say, because like everyone else he had heard that she was not getting on too well with her husband, but her remark piqued him.

"On the whole. I think probably an unsatisfactory marriage is better than no marriage at all."

"You know quite well that nothing would induce me to marry and you know why."

"Oh, my dear, you're not going to pretend that you're still in love with me?"

"I am."

"You are a damned fool."

"I don't care."

She smiled at him. Her eyes always had that look, partly bantering, partly tender, that gave him such a happy pain in his heart. Funny, he could almost localise it.

"You're rather sweet, Humphrey. You know I'm devoted to you, but I wouldn't marry you even if I were free."

When she left her husband and went to live in Rhodes Carruthers ceased to see her. She never came to England. They maintained an active correspondence.

"Her letters were wonderful," he said. "You seemed to hear her talking. They were just like her. Clever and witty, inconsequent and yet so shrewd."

He suggested coming to Rhodes for a few days, but she thought he had better not. He understood why. Everyone knew he had been madly in love with her. Everyone knew he was still. He did not know in what circumstances exactly the Welldon-Burns' had separated. It might be that there had been a good deal of bad feeling. Betty might think that his presence on the island would compromise her.

"She wrote a charming letter to me when my first book came out. You know I dedicated it to her. She was surprised that I had done anything so good. Everyone was very nice about it, and she was delighted with that. I think her pleasure was the chief thing that pleased me. After all I'm not a professional writer, you know: I don't attach much importance to literary success."

Fool, I thought, and liar. Did he think I had not noticed the self-satisfaction that consumed him on account of the favourable reception of his books? I did not blame him for feeling that, nothing could be more pardonable, but why be at such pains to deny it. But it was doubtless true that it was mostly for Betty's sake that he relished the notoriety they had brought him. He had a positive achievement to offer her. He could lay at her feet now not only his love, but a distinguished reputation. Betty was not very young any more, she was thirty-six; her marriage, her sojourn abroad, had changed things; she was no longer surrounded by suitors; she had lost the halo with which the public admiration had surrounded her. The distance between them was no longer insuperable. He alone had remained faithful through the years. It was absurd that she should continue to bury her beauty, her wit, her social grace in an island in a corner of the Mediterranean. He knew she was fond of him. She could hardly fail to be touched by his long devotion. And the life he had to offer her now was one that he knew would appeal to her. He made up his mind to ask her once more to marry him. He was able to get away towards the end of July. He wrote and said that he was going to spend his leave in the Greek islands and if she would be glad to see him he would stop off at Rhodes for a day or two, where he had heard the Italians had opened a very good hotel. He put his suggestion in this casual way out of delicacy. His training at the Foreign Office had taught him to eschew abruptness. He never willingly put himself in a position from which he could not if necessary withdraw with tact. Betty sent him a telegram in reply. She said it was too marvellous that he was coming to Rhodes and of course he must come and stay with her, for at least a fortnight, and he was to wire what boat he was coming by.

He was in a state of wild excitement when at last the ship he had taken at Brindisi steamed, soon after sunrise, into the neat and pretty harbour of Rhodes. He had hardly slept a wink all night and getting up early had watched the island loom grandly out of the dawn and the sun rise over the summer sea. Boats came out as the ship dropped her anchor. The gangway was lowered. Humphrey, leaning over the rail, watched the doctor and the port officials and the hotel couriers swarm up it. He was the only Englishman on board. His nationality was obvious. A man came on deck and immediately walked up to him.

"Are you Mr. Carruthers?"

"Yes."

He was about to smile and put out his hand, but he perceived in the twinkling of an eye that the person who addressed him, an Englishman like himself, was not a gentleman. Instinctively his manner, remaining exceedingly polite, became a trifle stiff. Of course Carruthers did not tell me this, but I see the scene so clearly that I have no hesitation in describing it.

"Her ladyship hopes you don't mind her not coming to meet you, but the boat got in so early and it's more than an hour's drive to where we live."

"Oh, of course. Her ladyship well?"

"Yes, thank you. Got your luggage ready?"

"Yes."

"If you'll show me where it is I'll tell one of these fellows to put it in a boat. You won't have any difficulty at the Customs. I've fixed that up all right, and then we'll get off. Have you had breakfast?"

"Yes, thank you."

The man was not quite sure of his aitches. Carruthers wondered who he was. You could not say he was uncivil, but he was certainly a little offhand. Carruthers knew that Betty had rather a large estate; perhaps he was her agent. He seemed very competent. He gave the porters instructions in fluent Greek and when they got in the boat and the boatmen asked for more money than he gave them, he said something that made them laugh and they shrugged their shoulders satisfied. The luggage was passed through the Customs without examination, Humphrey's guide shaking hands with the officials, and they went into a sunny place where a large yellow car was standing.

"Are you going to drive me?" asked Carruthers.

"I'm her ladyship's chauffeur."

"Oh, I see. I didn't know."

He was not dressed like a chauffeur. He wore white duck trousers and espadrilles on his bare feet, a white tennis shirt, with no tie and open at the neck, and a straw hat. Carruthers frowned. Betty oughtn't to let her chauffeur drive the car like that. It was true that he had had to get up before daybreak and it looked like being a hot drive up to the villa. Perhaps under ordinary conditions he wore uniform. Though not so tall as Carruthers, who was six feet one in his socks, he was not short; but he was broad-shouldered and squarely built, so that he looked stocky. He was not fat, but plump rather; he looked as though he had a hearty appetite and ate well. Young still, thirty perhaps or thirty-one, he had already a massive look and one day would be very beefy. Now he was a hefty fellow. He had a broad face deeply sunburned, a short thickish nose and a somewhat sullen look. He wore a short fair moustache. Oddly enough Carruthers had a vague feeling that he had seen him before.

"Have you been with her ladyship long?" he asked.

"Well, I have, in a manner of speaking."

Carruthers became a trifle stiffer. He did not quite like the manner in which the chauffeur spoke. He wondered why he did not say "sir" to him. He was afraid Betty had let him get a little above himself. It was like her to be a bit careless about such things. But it was a mistake. He'd give her a hint when he got a chance. Their eyes met for an instant and he could have sworn that there was a twinkle of amusement in the chauffeur's. Carruthers could not imagine why. He was not aware that there was anything amusing in him.

"That, I suppose, is the old city of the Knights," he said distantly, pointing to the battlemented walls.

"Yes. Her ladyship'll take you over. We get a rare lot of tourists here in the season."

Carruthers wished to be affable. He thought it would be nicer of him to offer to sit by the chauffeur rather than behind by himself and was just going to suggest it when the matter was taken out of his hands. The chauffeur told the porters to put Carruther's bags at the back, and settling himself at the wheel said:

"Now if you'll hop in we'll get along."

Carruthers sat down beside him and they set off along a white road that ran by the sea. In a few minutes they were in the open country. They drove in silence. Carruthers was a little on his dignity. He felt that the chauffeur was inclined to be familiar and he did not wish to give him occasion to be so. He flattered himself that he had a manner with him that put his inferiors in their place. He thought with sardonic grimness that it would not be long before the chauffeur would be calling him "sir". But the morning was lovely; the white road ran between olive groves and the farmhouses they passed now and then, with their white walls and flat roofs, had an Oriental look that took the fancy. And Betty was waiting for him. The love in his heart disposed him to kindliness towards all men and lighting himself a cigarette he thought it would be a generous act to offer the chauffeur one too. After all, Rhodes was very far away from England and the age was democratic. The chauffeur accepted the gift and stopped the car to light up.

"Have you got the baccy?" he asked suddenly.

"Have I got what?"

The chauffeur's face fell.

"Her ladyship wired to you to bring two pounds of Player's Navy Cut. That's why I fixed it up with the Customs people not to open your luggage."

"I never got the wire."

"Damn!"

"What on earth does her ladyship want with two pounds of Player's Navy Cut?"

He spoke with hauteur. He did not like the chauffeur's exclamation. The fellow gave him a sidelong glance in which Carruthers read a certain insolence.

"We can't get it here," he said briefly.

He threw away with what looked very like exasperation the Egyptian cigarette Carruthers had given him and started off again. He looked sulky. He said nothing more. Carruthers felt that his efforts at sociability had been a mistake. For the rest of the journey he ignored the chauffeur. He adopted the frigid manner that he had used so successfully as secretary at the Embassy when a member of the British public came to him for assistance. For some time they had been running up hill and now they came to a long low wall and then to an open gate. The chauffeur turned in.

"Have we arrived?" cried Carruthers.

"Sixty-five kilometres in fifty-seven minutes," said the chauffeur, a smile suddenly showing his fine white teeth. "Not so bad considering the road."

He sounded his klaxon shrilly. Carruthers was breathless with excitement. They drove up a narrow road through an olive grove, and came to a low, white, rambling house. Betty was standing at the door. He jumped out of the car and kissed her on both cheeks. For a moment he could not speak. But subconsciously he noticed that at the door stood an elderly butler in white ducks and a couple of footmen in the fustanellas of their country. They were smart and picturesque. Whatever Betty permitted her chauffeur it was evident that the house was run in the civilised style suited to her station. She led him through the hall, a large apartment with whitewashed walls in which he was vaguely conscious of handsome furniture, into the drawing-room. This also was large and low, with the same whitewashed walls, and he had immediately an impression of comfort and luxury.

"The first thing you must do is to come and look at my view," she said.

"The first thing I must do is to look at you."

She was dressed in white. Her arms, her face, her neck, were deeply burned by the sun; her eyes were bluer than he had ever seen them and the whiteness of her teeth was startling. She looked extremely well. She was very trim and neat. Her hair was waved, her nails were manicured; he had had a moment's anxiety that in the easy life she led on this romantic isle she had let herself go.

"Upon my word you look eighteen, Betty. How do you manage it?"

"Happiness," she smiled.

It gave him a momentary pang to hear her say this. He did not want her to be too happy. He wanted to give her happiness. But now she insisted on taking him out on the terrace. The drawing-room had five long windows that led out to it and from the terrace the olive-clad hill tumbled steeply to the sea. There was a tiny bay below in which a white boat, mirrored on the calm water, lay at anchor. On a further hill, round the corner, you saw the white houses of a Greek village and beyond it a huge grey crag surmounted by the battlements of a medieval castle.

"It was one of the strongholds of the Knights," she said. "I'll take you up there this evening."

The scene was quite lovely. It took your breath away. It was peaceful and yet it had a strange air of life. It moved you not to contemplation, but stirred you to activity.

"You've got the tobacco all right, I suppose."

He started.

"I'm afraid I haven't. I never got your wire."

"But I wired to the Embassy and I wired to the Excelsior."

"I stayed at the Plaza."

"What a bore! Albert'll be furious."

"Who is Albert?"

"He drove you out. Player's is the only tobacco he likes and he can't get it here."

"Oh, the chauffeur." He pointed to the boat that lay gleaming beneath them. "Is that the yacht I've heard about?"

"Yes."

It was a large caïque that Betty had bought, fitted with a motor auxiliary and smartened up. In it she wandered about the Greek islands. She had been as far north as Athens as and far south as Alexandria.

"We'll take you for a trip if you can spare the time," she said. "You ought to see Cos while you're here."

"Who runs it for you?"

"Of course I have a crew, but Albert chiefly. He's very clever with motors and all that."

He did not know why it gave him a vague discomfort to hear her speak of the chauffeur again. Carruthers wondered if she did not leave too much in his hands. It was a mistake to give a servant too much leeway.

"You know, I couldn't help thinking I'd seen Albert before somewhere. But I can't place him."

She smiled brightly, her eyes shining, with that sudden gaiety of hers that gave her face its delightful frankness.

"You ought to remember him. He was the second footman at Aunt Louise's. He must have opened the door to you hundreds of times."

Aunt Louise was the aunt with whom Betty had lived before her marriage.

"Oh, is that who he is? I suppose I must have seen him there without noticing him. How does he happen to be here?"

"He comes from our place at home. When I married he wanted to come with me, so I took him. He was Jimmie's valet for some time and then I sent him to some motor works, he was mad about cars, and eventually I took him on as my chauffeur. I don't know what I should do without him now."

"Don't you think it's rather a mistake to get too dependent on a servant?"

"I don't know. It never occurred to me."

Betty showed him the rooms that had been got ready for him, and when he had changed they strolled down to the beach. A dinghy was waiting for them and they rowed out to the caïque and bathed from there. The water was warm and they sunned themselves on the deck. The caïque was roomy, comfortable and luxurious. Betty showed him over and they came upon Albert tinkering with the engines. He was in filthy overalls, his hands were black and his face was smeared with grease.

"What's the matter, Albert?" said Betty.

He raised himself and faced her respectfully.

"Nothing, m'lady. I was just 'aving a look round."

"There are only two things Albert loves in the world. One is the car and the other's the yacht. Isn't that true, Albert?"

She gave him a gay smile and Albert's rather stolid face lit up. He showed his beautiful white teeth.

"That's true, m'lady."

"He sleeps on board, you know. We rigged up a very nice cabin for him aft."

Carruthers fell into the life very easily. Betty had bought the estate from a Turkish pasha exiled to Rhodes by Abdul Hamid and she had added a wing to the picturesque house. She had made a wild garden of the olive grove that surrounded it. It was planted with rosemary and lavender and asphodel, broom that she had had sent from England and the roses for which the island was famous. In the spring, she told him, the ground was carpeted with anemones. But when she showed him her property, telling him her plans and what alterations she had in mind, Carruthers could not help feeling a little uneasy.

"You talk as though you were going to live here all your life," he said.

"Perhaps I am," she smiled.

"What nonsense! At your age."

"I'm getting on for forty, old boy," she answered lightly.

He discovered with satisfaction that Betty had an excellent cook and it gratified his sense of propriety to dine with her in the splendid dining-room, with its Italian furniture, and be waited on by the dignified Greek butler and the two handsome footmen in their flamboyant uniforms. The house was furnished with taste; the rooms contained nothing that was not essential, but every piece was good. Betty lived in considerable state. When, the day after his arrival, the Governor with several members of his staff came over to dinner she displayed all the resources of the household. The Governor entering the house passed between a double row of flunkeys magnificent in their starched petticoats, embroidered jackets and velvet caps. It was almost a bodyguard. Carruthers liked the grand style. The dinner-party was very gay. Betty's Italian was fluent and Carruthers spoke it perfectly. The young officers in the Governor's suite were uncommonly smart in their uniforms. They were very attentive to Betty and she treated them with easy cordiality. She chaffed them. After dinner the gramophone was turned on and they danced with her one after the other.

When they were gone Carruthers asked her:

"Aren't they all madly in love with you?"

"I don't know about that. They hint occasionally at alliances permanent or otherwise, but they take it very good-naturedly when I decline with thanks."

They were not serious. The young ones were callow and the not so young were fat and bald. Whatever they might feel about her Carruthers could not for a moment believe that Betty would make a fool of herself with a middle-class Italian. But a day or two later a curious thing happened. He was in his rooms dressing for dinner; he heard a man's voice outside in the passage, he could not hear what was said or what language was spoken, and then ringing out suddenly Betty's laughter. It was a charming laugh, rippling and gay, like a young girl's, and it had a joyous abandon that was infectious. But whom could she be laughing with? It was not the way you would laugh with a servant. It had a curious intimacy. It may seem strange that Carruthers read all this into a peal of laughter, but it must be remembered that Carruthers was very subtle. His stories were remarkable for such touches.

When they met presently on the terrace and he was shaking a cocktail he sought to gratify his curiosity.

"What were you laughing your head off over just now? Has anyone been here?"

"No."

She looked at him with genuine surprise.

"I thought one of your Italian officers had come to pass the time of day."

"No."

Of course the passage of years had had its effect on Betty. She was beautiful, but her beauty was mature. She had always had assurance, but now she had repose; her serenity was a feature, like her blue eyes and her candid brow, that was part of her beauty. She seemed to be at peace with all the world; it rested you to be with her as it rested you to lie among the olives within sight of the wine-coloured sea. Though she was as gay and witty as ever, the seriousness which once he had been alone to know was now patent. No one could accuse her any longer of being scatterbrained; it was impossible not to perceive the fineness of her character. It had even nobility. That was not a trait it was usual to find in the modern woman and Carruthers said to himself that she was a throw-back; she reminded him of the great ladies of the eighteenth century. She had always had a feeling for literature, the poems she wrote as a girl were graceful and melodious, and he was more interested than surprised when she told him that she had undertaken a solid historical work. She was getting materials together for an account of the Knights of St. John in Rhodes. It was a story of romantic incidents. She took Carruthers to the city and showed him the noble battlements and together they wandered through austere and stately buildings. They strolled up the silent Street of the Knights with the lovely stone façades and the great coats of arms that recalled a dead chivalry. She had a surprise for him here. She had bought one of the old houses and with affectionate care had restored it to its old state. When you entered the little courtyard, with its carved stone stairway, you were taken back into the middle ages. It had a tiny walled garden in which a fig-tree grew and roses. It was small and secret and silent. The old knights had been in contact with the East long enough to have acquired Oriental ideas of privacy.

"When I'm tired of the villa I come here for two or three days and picnic. It's a relief sometimes not to be surrounded by people."

"But you're not alone here?"

"Practically."

There was a little parlour austerely furnished.

"What is this?" said Carruthers pointing with a smile to a copy of *The Sporting Times* that lay on a table.

"Oh, that's Albert's. I suppose he left it here when he came to meet you. He has *The Sporting Times* and the *News of the World* sent him every week. That is how he keeps abreast of the great world."

She smiled tolerantly. Next to the parlour was a bedroom with nothing much in it but a large bed.

"The house belonged to an Englishman. That's partly why I bought it. He was a Sir Giles Quern, and one of my ancestors married a Mary Quern who was a cousin of his. They were Cornish people."

Finding that she could not get on with her history without such a knowledge of Latin as would enable her to read the medieval documents with ease, Betty had set about learning the classical language. She troubled to acquire only the elements of grammar and then started, with a translation by her side, to read the authors that interested her. It is a very good method of learning a language and I have often wondered that it is not used in schools. It saves all the endless turning over of dictionaries and the fumbling search for meaning. After nine months Betty could read Latin as fluently as most of us can read French. It seemed a trifle ridiculous to Carruthers that this lovely, brilliant creature should take her work so seriously and yet he was moved; he would have liked to snatch her in his arms and kiss her, not at that moment as a woman, but as a precocious child whose cleverness suddenly enchants you. But later he reflected upon what she had told him. He was of course a very clever man, otherwise he could not have attained the position he held in the Foreign Office, and it would be silly to claim that those two books of his could have made so much stir without some merit; if I have made him look a bit of a fool it is only because I did not happen to like him, and if I have derided his stories it is merely because stories of that sort seem to me rather silly. He had tact and insight. He had a conviction that there was but one way to win her. She was in a groove and happy in it, her plans were definite; but her life at Rhodes was so well-ordered, so complete and satisfying, that for that very reason its hold over her could be combated. His chance was to arouse in her the restlessness that lies deep in the heart of the English. So he talked to Betty of England and London, their common friends and the painters, writers and musicians with whom his literary success had brought him acquaintance. He talked of the Bohemian parties in Chelsea, and of the opera, of trips to Paris *en bande* for a fancy-dress ball or to Berlin to see the new plays. He recalled to her imagination a life rich and easy, varied, cultured, intelligent and highly civilised. He tried to make her feel that she was stagnating in a backwater. The world was hurrying on, from one new and interesting phase to another, and she was standing still. They were living in a thrilling age and she was missing it. Of course he did not tell her this; he left her to infer it. He was amusing and spirited, he had an excellent memory for a good story, he was whimsical and gay. I know I have not made Humphrey Carruthers witty any more than I have shown Lady Betty brilliant. The reader must take my word for it that they were. Carruthers was generally reckoned an entertaining companion, and that is half the battle; people were willing to find him amusing and they vowed the things he said were marvellous. Of course his wit was social. It needed a particular company, who understood his allusions and shared his exclusive sense of humour. There are a score of journalists in Fleet Street who could knock spots off the most famous of the society wits; it is their business to be witty and brilliance is in their day's work. There are few of the society beauties whose photographs appear in the papers who could get a job at three pounds a week in the chorus of a song-and-dance show. Amateurs must be judged with tolerance. Carruthers knew that Betty enjoyed his society. They laughed a great deal together. The days passed in a flash.

"I shall miss you terribly when you go," she said in her frank way. "It's been a treat having you here. You are a sweet, Humphrey."

"Have you only just discovered it?"

He patted himself on the back. His tactics had been right. It was interesting to see how well his simple plan had worked. Like a charm. The vulgar might laugh at the Foreign Office, but there was no doubt it taught you how to deal with difficult people. Now he had but to choose his opportunity. He felt that Betty had never been more attached to him. He would wait till the end of his visit. Betty was emotional. She would be sorry that he was going. Rhodes would seem very dull without him. Whom would she have to talk to when he was gone? After dinner they usually sat on the terrace looking at the starry sea; the air was warm and balmy and vaguely scented: it was then he would ask her to marry him, on the eve of his departure. He felt it in his bones that she would accept him.

One morning when he had been in Rhodes a little over a week, he happened to be coming upstairs as Betty was walking along the passage.

"You've never shown me your room, Betty," he said.

"Haven't I? Come in and have a look now. It's rather nice."

She turned back and he followed her in. It was over the drawing-room and nearly as large. It was furnished in the Italian style, and as is the present way more like a sitting-room than a bedroom.

There were fine Paninis on the walls and one or two handsome cabinets. The bed was Venetian and beautifully painted.

"That's a couch of rather imposing dimensions for a widow lady," he said facetiously.

"It is enormous, isn't it? But it was so lovely, I had to buy it. It cost a fortune."

His eye took in the bed-table by the side. There were two or three books on it, a box of cigarettes, and on an ash-tray a briar pipe. Funny! What on earth had Betty got a pipe by her bed for?

"Do look at this *cassone*. Isn't the painting marvellous? I almost cried when I found it."

"I suppose that cost a fortune too."

"I daren't tell you what I paid."

When they were leaving the room he cast another glance at the bed-table. The pipe had vanished.

It was odd that Betty should have a pipe in her bedroom, she certainly didn't smoke one herself, and if she had would have made no secret of it, but of course there were a dozen reasonable explanations. It might be a present she was making to somebody, one of the Italians or even Albert, he had not been able to see if it was new or old, or it might be a pattern that she was going to ask him to take home to have others of the same sort sent out to her. After the moment's perplexity, not altogether unmingled with amusement, he put the matter out of his mind. They were going for a picnic that day, taking their luncheon with them, and Betty was driving him herself. They had arranged to go for a cruise of a couple of days before he left so that he should see Patmos and Cos, and Albert was busy with the engines of the caïque. They had a wonderful day. They visited a ruined castle and climbed a mountain on which grew asphodel, hyacinth and narcissus, and returned dead beat. They separated not long after dinner and Carruthers went to bed. He read for a little and then turned out his light. But he could not sleep. It was hot under his mosquito-net. He turned and tossed. Presently he thought he would go down to the little beach at the foot of the hill and bathe. It was not more than three minutes' walk. He put on his espadrilles and took a towel. The moon was full and he saw it shining on the sea through the olive-trees. But he was not alone to have thought that this radiant night would be lovely to bathe in, for just before he came out on to the beach sounds reached his ears. He muttered a little damn of vexation, some of Betty's servants were bathing, and he could not very well disturb them. The olive-trees came almost to the water's edge and undecided he stood in their shelter. He heard a voice that gave him a sudden start.

"Where's my towel?"

English. A woman waded out of the water and stood for a moment at its edge. From the darkness a man came forward with nothing but a towel round his loins. The woman was Betty. She was stark naked. The man wrapped a bath-robe round her and began drying her vigorously. She leaned on him while she put on first one shoe and then the other and to support her he placed his arm round her shoulders. The man was Albert.

Carruthers turned and fled up the hill. He stumbled blindly. Once he nearly fell. He was gasping like a wounded beast. When he got into his room he flung himself on the bed and clenched his fists and the dry, painful sobs that tore his chest broke into tears. He evidently had a violent attack of hysterics. It was all clear to him, clear with the ghastly vividness with which on a stormy night a flash of lightning can disclose a ravaged landscape, clear, horribly clear. The way the man had dried her and the way she leaned against him pointed not to passion, but to a long-continued intimacy, and the pipe by the bed-side, the pipe had a hideously conjugal air. It suggested the pipe a man might smoke while he was reading in bed before going to sleep. *The Sporting Times!* That was why she had that little house in the Street of the Knights, so that they could spend two or three days together in domestic familiarity. They were like an old married couple. Humphrey asked himself how long the hateful thing had lasted and suddenly he knew the answer; for years. Ten, twelve, fourteen; it had started when the young footman first came to London, he was a boy then and it was obvious enough that it was not he who had made the advances; all through those years when she was the idol of the British public, when everyone adored her and she could have married anyone she liked, she was living with the second footman at her aunt's house. She took him with her when she married. Why had she made that surprising marriage? And the still-born child that came before its time. Of course that was why she had married Jimmie Welldon-Burns, because she was going to have a child by Albert. Oh, shameless, shameless! And then, when Jimmie's health broke down she had made him take Albert as his valet. And what had Jimmie known and what had he suspected? He drank, that was what had started his tuberculosis; but why had he started drinking? Perhaps it was to still a suspicion that was so ugly that he could not face it. And it was to live with Albert that she had left Jimmie and it was to live with Albert that she had settled in Rhodes. Albert, his hands with their broken nails stained by his work on the motors, coarse of aspect and stocky, rather like a butcher with his high colour and clumsy strength, Albert not even very young any more and running to fat, uneducated and vulgar, with his common way of speaking. Albert, Albert, how could she?

Carruthers got up and drank some water. He threw himself into a chair. He could not bear his bed. He smoked cigarette after cigarette. He was a wreck in the morning. He had not slept at all. They brought him in his breakfast; he drank the coffee but could eat nothing. Presently there was a brisk knock on his door.

"Coming down to bathe, Humphrey?"

That cheerful voice sent the blood singing through his head. He braced himself and opened the door.

"I don't think I will to-day. I don't feel very well."

She gave him a look.

"Oh, my dear, you look all in. What's the matter with you?"

"I don't know. I think I must have got a touch of the sun."

His voice was dead and his eyes were tragic. She looked at him more closely. She did not say anything for a moment. He thought she went pale. *He knew.* Then a faintly mocking smile crossed her eyes; she thought the situation comic.

"Poor old boy, go and lie down, I'll send you in some aspirin. Perhaps you'll feel better at luncheon."

He lay in his darkened room. He would have given anything to get away then so that he need not set eyes on her again, but there was no means of that, the ship that was to take him back to Brindisi did not touch at Rhodes till the end of the week. He was a prisoner. And the next day they were to go to the islands. There was no escape from her there; in the caïque they would be in one another's pockets all day long. He couldn't face that. He was so ashamed. But she wasn't ashamed. At that moment when it had been plain to her that nothing was hidden from him any longer she had smiled. She was capable of telling him all about it. He could not bear that. That was too much. After all she couldn't be certain that he knew, at best she could only suspect; if he behaved as if nothing had happened, if at luncheon and during the days that remained he was as gay and jolly as usual she would think she had been mistaken. It was enough to know what he knew, he would not suffer the crowning humiliation of hearing from her own lips the disgraceful story. But at luncheon the first thing she said was:

"Isn't it a bore. Albert says something's gone wrong with the motor, we shan't be able to go on our trip after all. I daren't trust to sail at this time of the year. We might be becalmed for a week."

She spoke lightly and he answered in the same casual fashion.

"Oh, I'm sorry, but still I don't really care. It's so lovely here, I really didn't much want to go."

He told her that the aspirin had done him good and he felt much better; to the Greek butler and the two footmen in fustanellas it must have seemed that they talked as vivaciously as usual. That night the British consul came to dinner and the night after some Italian officers. Carruthers counted the days, he counted the hours. Oh, if the moment would only come when he could step on the ship and be free from the horror that every moment of the day obsessed him! He was growing so tired. But Betty's manner was so self-possessed that sometimes he asked himself if she really knew that he was aware of her secret. Was it the truth that she had told about the caïque and not, as had at once struck him, an excuse; and was it an accident that a succession of visitors prevented them from ever being alone together? The worst of having so much tact was that you never quite knew whether other people were acting naturally or being tactful too. When he looked at her, so easy and calm, so obviously happy, he could not believe the odious truth. And yet he had seen with his own eyes. And the future. What would her future be? It was horrible to think of. Sooner or later the truth must become notorious. And to think of Betty a mock and an outcast, in the power of a coarse and common man, growing older, losing her beauty; and the man was five years younger than she. One day he would take a mistress, one of her own maids, perhaps, with whom he would feel at home as he had never felt with the great lady, and what could she do then? What humiliation then must she be prepared to put up with! He might be cruel to her. He might beat her. Betty. Betty.

Carruthers wrung his hands. And on a sudden an idea came to him that filled him with a painful exaltation; he put it away from him, but it returned; it would not let him be. He must save her, he had loved her too much and too long to let her sink, sink as she was sinking; a passion of self-sacrifice welled up in him. Notwithstanding everything, though his love now was dead and he felt for her an almost physical repulsion, he would marry her. He laughed mirthlessly. What would his life be? He couldn't help that. He didn't matter. It was the only thing to do. He felt wonderfully uplifted, and yet very humble, for he was awed at the thought of the heights which the divine spirit of man could reach.

His ship was to sail on Saturday and on Thursday when the guests who had been dining left them, he said:

"I hope we're going to be alone to-morrow."

"As a matter of fact I've asked some Egyptians who spend the summer here. She's a sister of the ex-Khedive and very intelligent. I'm sure you'll like her."

"Well, it's my last evening. Couldn't we spend it alone?"

She gave him a glance. There was a faint amusement in her eyes, but his were grave.

"If you like. I can put them off."

"Then do."

He was to start early in the morning and his luggage was packed. Betty had told him not to dress, but he had answered that he preferred to. For the last time they sat down to dinner facing one another. The dining-room, with its shaded lights, was bare and formal, but the summer night flooding in through the great open windows gave it a sober richness. It had the effect of the private refectory in a convent to which a royal lady had retired in order to devote the remainder of her life to a piety not too austere. They had their coffee on the terrace. Carruthers drank a couple of liqueurs. He was feeling very nervous.

"Betty, my dear, I've got something I want to say to you," he began.

"Have you? I wouldn't say it if I were you."

She answered gently. She remained perfectly calm, watching him shrewdly, but with the glimmer of a smile in her blue eyes.

"I must."

She shrugged her shoulders and was silent. He was conscious that his voice trembled a little and he was angry with himself.

"You know I've been madly in love with you for many years. I don't know how many times I've asked you to marry me. But, after all, things change and people change too, don't they? We're neither of us so young as we were. Won't you marry me now, Betty?"

She gave him the smile that had always been such an attractive thing in her; it was so kindly, so frank, and still, still so wonderfully innocent.

"You're very sweet, Humphrey. It's awfully nice of you to ask me again. I can't tell you how touched I am. But you know, I'm a creature of habit, I've got in the habit of saying no to you now, and I can't change it."

"Why not?"

There was something aggressive in his tone, something almost ominous, that made her give him a quick look. Her face blanched with sudden anger, but she immediately controlled herself.

"Because I don't want to," she smiled.

"Are you going to marry anyone else?"

"I? No. Of course not."

For a moment she seemed to draw herself up as though a wave of ancestral pride swept through her and then she began to laugh. But whether she laughed at the thought that had passed through her mind or because something in Humphrey's proposal had amused her none but she could have told.

"Betty. I implore you to marry me."

"Never."

"You can't go on living this life."

He put into his voice all the anguish of his heart and his face was drawn and tortured. She smiled affectionately.

"Why not? Don't be such a donkey. You know I adore you, Humphrey, but you are rather an old woman."

"Betty. Betty."

Did she not see that it was for her sake that he wanted it? It was not love that made him speak, but human pity and shame. She got up.

"Don't be tiresome, Humphrey. You'd better go to bed, you know you have to be up with the lark. I shan't see you in the morning. Good-bye and God bless you. It's been wonderful having you here."

She kissed him on both cheeks.

Next morning, early, for he had to be on board at eight, when Carruthers stepped out of the front door he found Albert waiting for him in the car. He wore a singlet, duck trousers and a beret basque. Carruthers' luggage was in the back. He turned to the butler.

"Put my bags beside the chauffeur," he said. "I'll sit behind."

Albert made no remark. Carruthers got in and they drove off. When they arrived at the harbour, porters ran up. Albert got out of the car. Carruthers looked down at him from his great height.

"You need not see me on board. I can manage perfectly well by myself. Here's a tip for you."

He gave him a five-pound note. Albert flushed. He was taken aback, he would have liked to refuse it, but did not know how to, and the servility of years asserted itself. Perhaps he did not know what he said.

"Thank you, sir."

Carruthers gave him a curt nod and walked away. He had forced Betty's lover to call him "sir". It was as though he had struck her a blow across that smiling mouth of hers and flung in her face an opprobrious word. It filled him with a bitter satisfaction.

He shrugged his shoulders and I could see that even this small triumph now seemed vain. For a little while we were silent. There was nothing for me to say. Then he began again.

"I dare say you think it's very strange that I should tell you all this. I don't care. You know, I feel as if nothing mattered any more. I feel as if decency no longer existed in the world. Heaven knows, I'm not jealous. You can't be jealous unless you love and my love is dead. It was killed in a flash. After all those years. I can't think of her now without horror. What destroys me, what makes me so frightfully unhappy is to think of her unspeakable degradation."

So it has been said that it was not jealousy that caused Othello to kill Desdemona, but an agony that the creature that he believed angelic should be proved impure and worthless. What broke his noble heart was that virtue should so fall.

"I thought there was no one like her. I admired her so much. I admired her courage and her frankness, her intelligence and her love of beauty. She's just a sham and she's never been anything else."

"I wonder if that's true. Do you think any of us are all of a piece? Do you know what strikes me? I should have said that Albert was only the instrument, her toll to the solid earth, so to speak, that left her soul at liberty to range the empyrean. Perhaps the mere fact that he was so far below her gave her a sense of freedom in her relations with him that she would have lacked with a man of her own class. The spirit is very strange, it never soars so high as when the body has wallowed for a period in the gutter."

"Oh, don't talk such rot," he answered angrily.

"I don't think it is rot. I don't put it very well, but the idea's sound."

"Much good it does me. I'm broken and done for. I'm finished."

"Oh, nonsense. Why don't you write a story about it?"

"I?"

"You know, that's the great pull a writer has over other people. When something has made him terribly unhappy, and he's tortured and miserable, he can put it all into a story and it's astonishing what a comfort and relief it is."

"It would be monstrous. Betty was everything in the world to me. I couldn't do anything so caddish."

He paused for a little and I saw him reflect. I saw that notwithstanding the horror that my suggestion caused him he did for one minute look at the situation from the standpoint of the writer. He shook his head.

"Not for her sake, for mine. After all I have some self-respect. Besides, there's no story there."

The Happy Man

IT is a dangerous thing to order the lives of others and I have often wondered at the self-confidence of politicians, reformers and suchlike who are prepared to force upon their fellows measures that must alter their manners, habits and points of view. I have always hesitated to give advice, for how can one advise another how to act unless one knows that other as well as one knows oneself? Heaven knows, I know little enough of myself: I know nothing of others. We can only guess at the thoughts and emotions of our neighbours. Each one of us is a prisoner in a solitary tower and he communicates with the other prisoners, who form mankind, by conventional signs that have not quite the same meaning for them as for himself. And life, unfortunately, is something that you can lead but once; mistakes are often irreparable, and who am I that I should tell this one and that how he should lead it? Life is a difficult business and I have found it hard enough to make my own a complete and rounded thing; I have not been tempted to teach my neighbour what he should do with his. But there are men who flounder at the journey's start, the way before them is confused and hazardous, and on occasion, however unwillingly, I have been forced to point the finger of fate. Sometimes men have said to me, what shall I do with my life? and I have seen myself for a moment wrapped in the dark cloak of Destiny.

Once I know that I advised well.

I was a young man and I lived in a modest apartment in London near Victoria Station. Late one afternoon, when I was beginning to think that I had worked enough for that day, I heard a ring at the bell. I opened the door to a total stranger. He asked me my name; I told him. He asked if he might come in.

"Certainly."

I led him into my sitting-room and begged him to sit down. He seemed a trifle embarrassed. I offered him a cigarette and he had some difficulty in lighting it without letting go of his hat. When he had satisfactorily achieved this feat I asked him if I should not put it on a chair for him. He quickly did this and while doing it dropped his umbrella.

"I hope you don't mind my coming to see you like this," he said. "My name is Stephens and I am a doctor. You're in the medical, I believe?"

"Yes, but I don't practise."

"No, I know. I've just read a book of yours about Spain and I wanted to ask you about it."

"It's not a very good book, I'm afraid."

"The fact remains that you know something about Spain and there's no one else I know who does. And I thought perhaps you wouldn't mind giving me some information."

"I shall be very glad."

He was silent for a moment. He reached out for his hat and holding it in one hand absent-mindedly stroked it with the other. I surmised that it gave him confidence.

"I hope you won't think it very odd for a perfect stranger to talk to you like this." He gave an apologetic laugh. "I'm not going to tell you the story of my life."

When people say this to me I always know that it is precisely what they are going to do. I do not mind. In fact I rather like it.

"I was brought up by two old aunts. I've never been anywhere. I've never done anything. I've been married for six years. I have no children. I'm a medical officer at the Camberwell Infirmary. I can't stick it any more."

There was something very striking in the short, sharp sentences he used. They had a forcible ring. I had not given him more than a cursory glance, but now I looked at him with curiosity. He was a little man, thick-set and stout, of thirty perhaps, with a round red face from which shone small, dark and very bright eyes. His black hair was cropped close to a bullet-shaped head. He was dressed in a blue suit a good deal the worse for wear. It was baggy at the knees and the pockets bulged untidily.

"You know what the duties are of a medical officer in an infirmary. One day is pretty much like another. And that's all I've got to look forward to for the rest of my life. Do you think it's worth it?"

"It's a means of livelihood," I answered.

"Yes, I know. The money's pretty good."

"I don't exactly know why you've come to me."

"Well, I wanted to know whether you thought there would be any chance for an English doctor in Spain?"

"Why Spain?"

"I don't know, I just have a fancy for it."

"It's not like *Carmen*, you know."

"But there's sunshine there, and there's good wine, and there's colour, and there's air you can breathe. Let me say what I have to say straight out. I heard by accident that there was no English doctor in Seville. Do you think I could earn a living there? Is it madness to give up a good safe job for an uncertainty?"

"What does your wife think about it?"

"She's willing."

"It's a great risk."

"I know. But if you say take it, I will: if you say stay where you are, I'll stay."

He was looking at me intently with those bright dark eyes of his and I knew that he meant what he said. I reflected for a moment.

"Your whole future is concerned: you must decide for yourself. But this I can tell you: if you don't want money but are content to earn just enough to keep body and soul together, then go. For you will lead a wonderful life."

He left me, I thought about him for a day or two, and then forgot. The episode passed completely from my memory.

Many years later, fifteen at least, I happened to be in Seville and having some trifling indisposition asked the hotel porter whether there was an English doctor in the town. He said there was and gave me the address. I took a cab and as I drove up to the house a little fat man came out of it. He hesitated when he caught sight of me.

"Have you come to see me?" he said. "I'm the English doctor."

I explained my errand and he asked me to come in. He lived in an ordinary Spanish house, with a patio, and his consulting room which led out of it was littered with papers, books, medical appliances, and lumber. The sight of it would have startled a squeamish patient. We did our business and then I asked the doctor what his fee was. He shook his head and smiled.

"There's no fee."

"Why on earth not?"

"Don't you remember me? Why, I'm here because of something you said to me. You changed my whole life for me. I'm Stephens."

I had not the least notion what he was talking about. He reminded me of our interview, he repeated to me what we had said, and gradually, out of the night, a dim recollection of the incident came back to me.

"I was wondering if I'd ever see you again," he said, "I was wondering if ever I'd have a chance of thanking you for all you've done for me."

"It's been a success then?"

I looked at him. He was very fat now and bald, but his eyes twinkled gaily and his fleshy, red face bore an expression of perfect good-humour. The clothes he wore, terribly shabby they were, had been made obviously by a Spanish tailor and his hat was the wide-brimmed sombrero of the Spaniard. He looked to me as though he knew a good bottle of wine when he saw it. He had a dissipated, though entirely sympathetic, appearance. You might have hesitated to let him remove your appendix, but you could not have imagined a more delightful creature to drink a glass of wine with.

"Surely you were married?" I said.

"Yes. My wife didn't like Spain, she went back to Camberwell, she was more at home there."

"Oh, I'm sorry for that."

His black eyes flashed a bacchanalian smile. He really had some-what the look of a young Silenus.

"Life is full of compensations," he murmured.

The words were hardly out of his mouth when a Spanish woman, no longer in her first youth, but still boldly and voluptuously beauti-ful, appeared at the door. She spoke to him in Spanish, and I could not fail to perceive that she was the mistress of the house.

As he stood at the door to let me out he said to me:

"You told me when last I saw you that if I came here I should earn just enough money to keep body and soul together, but that I should lead a wonderful life. Well, I want to tell you that you were right. Poor I have been and poor I shall always be, but by heaven I've enjoyed myself. I wouldn't exchange the life I've had with that of any king in the world."

The Romantic Young Lady

ONE of the many inconveniences of real life is that it seldom gives you a complete story. Some incident has excited your interest, the people who are concerned in it are in the devil's own muddle, and you wonder what on earth will happen next. Well, generally nothing happens. The inevitable catastrophe you foresaw wasn't inevitable after all, and high tragedy, without any regard to artistic decency, dwindles into drawing-room comedy. Now, growing old has many disadvantages, but it has this compensation (among, let us admit, not a few others), that sometimes it gives you the opportunity of seeing what was the outcome of certain events you had witnessed long ago. You had given up the hope of ever knowing what was the end of the story, and then, when you least expected it, it is handed to you on a platter.

These reflections occurred to me when, having escorted the Marquesa de San Esteban to her car, I went back into the hotel and sat down again in the lounge. I ordered a cocktail, lit a cigarette and composed myself to order my recollections. The hotel was new and splendid, it was like every other first-class hotel in Europe, and I had been regretting that for the sake of its modern plumbing I had deserted the old-fashioned, picturesque Hotel de Madrid to which I generally went when I stayed in Seville. It was true that from my hotel I had a view of the noble river, the Guadalquivir, but that did not make up for the *thés dansants* that filled the bar-lounge two or three days a week with a fashionable crowd whose exuberant conversation almost drowned the strident din of a jazz orchestra.

I had been out all the afternoon, and coming in found myself in the midst of a seething mob. I went to the desk and asked for my key so that I might go straight up to my room. But the porter, handing it to me, said that a lady had been asking for me.

"For me?"

"She wants to see you very much. It's the Marquesa de San Esteban."

I knew no one of that name.

"It must be some mistake."

As I said the words, looking rather vaguely around, a lady came up to me with outstretched hands and a bright smile on her lips. To the best of my knowledge I had never seen her before in my life.

She seized my hands, both of them, and shook them warmly. She spoke in fluent French.

"How very nice to see you again after all these years. I saw by the paper that you were staying here and I said to myself: I must look him up. How many years is it since we danced together? I daren't think. Do you still dance? I do. And I'm a grandmother. I'm fat of course, I don't care, and it keeps me from getting fatter."

She talked with such a rush that it took my breath away to listen to her. She was a stout, more than middle-aged woman, very much made up, with dark red hair, obviously dyed, cut short; and she was dressed in the height of Parisian fashion, which never suits Spanish women very well. But she had a gay fruity laugh that made you feel you wanted to laugh too. It was quite obvious that she thoroughly enjoyed life. She was a fine figure of a woman and I could well believe that in youth she had been beautiful. But I could not place her.

"Come and drink a glass of champagne with me and we will talk of old times. Or will you have a cocktail? Our dear old Seville has changed, you see. *Thés dansants* and cocktails. It's just like Paris and London now. We've caught up. We're a civilised people."

She led me to a table near the space where they were dancing and we sat down. I could not go on pretending I was at ease; I thought I should only get into a fearful mess.

"It's terribly stupid of me, I'm afraid," I said, "but I don't seem able to remember ever having known anyone of your name in the old days in Seville."

"San Esteban?" she interrupted before I could go on. "Naturally. My husband came from Salamanca. He was in the diplomatic service. I'm a widow. You knew me as Pilar Carreon. Of course having my hair red changes me a little, but otherwise I don't think I've altered much."

"Not at all," I said quickly. "It was only the name that bothered me."

Of course now I remembered her, but I was concerned at the moment only with the effort to conceal from her the mingled consternation and amusement that filled me as I realised that the Pilar Carreon I had danced with at the Countess de Marbella's parties and at the Fair had turned into this stout, flaunting dowager. I could not get over it. But I had to watch my step. I wondered if she knew how well I recollected the story that had shaken Seville to its foundations, and I was glad when after she had finally bidden me an effusive farewell I was able to recall it at ease.

In those days, forty years ago, Seville had not become a

prosperous commercial city. It had quiet, white streets, paved with cobbles, with a multitude of churches on the belfries of which storks built their nests. Bull-fighters, students and loungers sauntered in the Sierpes all day long. Life was easy. This of course was before the time of motor-cars, and the Sevillan would live in penury, practising every possible economy, in order to have a carriage. For this luxury he was willing to sacrifice the necessities of life. Everyone who had any claim to gentility drove up and down the Delicias, the park-like gardens by the Guadalquivir, every blessed afternoon from five till seven. You saw carriages of all sorts from fashionable London victorias to old broken-down shays that seemed as though they would fall to pieces, magnificent horses and wretched hacks whose tragic end in the bull-ring was near at hand. But there was one equipage that could not fail to attract the stranger's attention. It was a victoria, very smart and new, drawn by two beautiful mules; and the coachman and the footman wore the national costume of Andalusia in pale grey. It was the most splendid turn-out Seville had ever known, and it belonged to the Countess de Marbella. She was a Frenchwoman married to a Spaniard, who had enthusiastically adopted the manners and customs of her husband's country, but with a Parisian elegance that gave them a peculiar distinction. The rest of the carriages went at a snail's pace so that their occupants could see and be seen, but the countess, behind her mules, dashed up between the two crawling lines at a fast trot, went to the end of the Delicias and back twice and then drove away. The proceeding savoured somewhat of royalty. When you looked at her gracefully seated in that swift victoria, her head handsomely poised, her hair of too brilliant a gold to be natural, you did not wonder that her French vivacity and determination had given her the position she held. She made the fashion. Her decrees were law. But the countess had too many adorers not to have as many enemies, and the most determined of these was the widowed Duchess de Dos Palos, whose birth and social consequence made her claim as a right the first place in Society which the Frenchwoman had won by grace, wit and character.

Now the duchess had an only daughter. This was Doña Pilar. She was twenty when I first knew her and she was very beautiful. She had magnificent eyes and a skin that, however hard you tried to find a less hackneyed way to describe it, you could only call peach-like. She was very slim, rather tall for a Spanish girl, with a red mouth and dazzlingly white teeth. She wore her abundant, shining black hair dressed very elaborately in the Spanish style of the period. She was infinitely alluring. The fire in her black eyes, the warmth of her smile, the seductiveness of her movements suggested so much passion that it really wasn't quite fair. She belonged to the generation which was straining to break the old conventions that had kept the Spanish girl of good family hidden away till it was time for her to be married. I often played tennis with her and I used to dance with her at the Countess de Marbella's parties. The duchess considered the Frenchwoman's parties, with champagne and a sit-down supper, ostentatious, and when she opened her own great house to Society, which was only twice a year, it was to give them lemonade and biscuits. But she bred fighting-bulls, as her husband had done, and on the occasions when the young bulls were tried out, she gave picnic luncheons to which her friends were asked, very gay and informal, but with a sort of feudal state which fascinated my romantic imagination. Once, when the duchess's bulls were to fight at a *corrida* in Seville, I rode in with them at night as one of the men escorting Doña Pilar, dressed in a costume that reminded one of a picture by Goya, who headed the cavalcade. It was a charming experience to ride through the night, on those prancing Andalusian horses, with the six bulls, surrounded by oxen, thundering along behind.

A good many men, rich or noble and sometimes both, had asked Doña Pilar's hand in marriage, but, notwithstanding her mother's remonstrances, she had refused them. The duchess had been married at fifteen and it seemed to her really indecent that her daughter at twenty should be still single. The duchess asked her what she was waiting for; it was absurd to be too difficult. It was her duty to marry. But Pilar was stubborn. She found reasons to reject every one of her suitors.

Then the truth came out.

During the daily drives in the Delicias which the duchess, accompanied by her daughter, took in a great old-fashioned landau, they passed the countess as she was twice swiftly driven up and down the promenade. The ladies were on such bad terms that they pretended not to see one another, but Pilar could not keep her eyes off that smart carriage and the two beautiful grey mules and, not wishing to catch the countess's somewhat ironic glance, her own fell on the coachman who drove her. He was the handsomest man in Seville and in his beautiful uniform he was a sight to see. Of course no one knew exactly what happened, but apparently the more Pilar looked at the coachman the more she liked the look of him, and somehow or other, for all this part of the story remained a mystery, the pair met. In Spain the classes are strangely mingled and the butler may have in his veins much nobler blood than the master. Pilar learnt, not I think without satisfaction, that the coachman belonged to the ancient

family of Leon, than which there is none in Andalusia more distinguished; and really so far as birth went there was little to choose
between them. Only her life had been passed in a ducal mansion,
while fate had forced him to earn his living on the box of a victoria.
Neither could regret this, since only in that exalted place could he
have attracted the attention of the most difficult young woman in
Seville. They fell madly in love with one another. It so happened
that just then a young man called the Marques de San Esteban,
whom they had met at San Sebastian the summer before, wrote to
the duchess and asked for Pilar's hand in marriage. He was extremely eligible and the two families had formed alliances from time
to time ever since the reign of Philip II. The duchess was determined
not to stand any more nonsense, and when she told Pilar of the proposal added that she had shilly-shallied long enough. She must
either marry him or she should go into a convent.

"I'm not going to do either the one or the other," said Pilar.

"What are you going to do then? I have given you a home long
enough."

"I'm going to marry José Leon."

"Who is he?"

Pilar hesitated for a moment and it may be, it is indeed to be
hoped, that she blushed a little.

"He's the countess's coachman."

"What countess?"

"The Countess de Marbella."

I remembered the duchess well and I am sure that when roused
she stuck at little. She raged, she implored, she cried, she argued.
There was a terrific scene. People said that she slapped her daughter
and pulled her hair, but I have an impression that Pilar in such a
pass was capable of hitting back. She repeated that she loved José
Leon and he loved her. She was determined to marry him. The
duchess called a family council. The matter was put before them
and it was decided that to save them all from disgrace Pilar should
be taken away to the country and kept there till she had recovered
from her infatuation. Pilar got wind of the scheme and put a stop
to it by slipping out of the window of her room one night when
everyone was asleep and going to live with her lover's parents. They
were respectable persons who inhabited a small apartment on the
unfashionable side of the Guadalquivir, in the quarter called Triana.

After that no concealment was possible. The fat was in the fire and
the clubs along the Sierpes buzzed with the scandal. Waiters were
kept busy bringing trays of little glasses of Manzanilla to the members
from the neighbouring wine-shops. They gossiped and laughed over

the scandal and Pilar's rejected suitors were the recipients of many congratulations. What an escape! The duchess was in despair. She could think of nothing better to do than go to the Archbishop, her trusted friend and former confessor, and beg him himself to reason with the infatuated girl. Pilar was summoned to the episcopal palace, and the good old man, used to intervening in family quarrels, did his utmost to show her the folly of her course. But she would not be persuaded. Nothing that anyone could say would induce her to forsake the man she loved. The duchess, waiting in an adjoining room, was sent for and made a final appeal to her daughter. In vain. Pilar returned to her humble lodging and the duchess in tears was left alone with the Archbishop. The Archbishop was no less astute than he was pious, and when he saw that the distracted woman was in a fit state to listen to him, advised her as a last resource to go to the Countess de Marbella. She was the cleverest woman in Seville and it might be that she could do something.

At first the duchess indignantly refused. She would never suffer the humiliation of appealing to her greatest enemy. Sooner might the ancient house of Dos Palos fall in ruin. The Archbishop was accustomed to dealing with tiresome women. He set himself with gentle cunning to induce her to change her mind and presently she consented to throw herself on the Frenchwoman's mercy. With rage in her heart she sent a message asking if she might see her, and that afternoon was ushered into her drawing-room. The countess of course had been one of the first to hear the story, but she listened to the unhappy mother as though she had not known a thing about it. She relished the situation enormously. It was the crowning triumph to have the vindictive duchess on her knees before her. But she was at heart a good-natured woman and she had a sense of humour.

"It's a most unfortunate situation," she said. "And I'm sorry that one of my servants should be the occasion of it. But I don't exactly see what I can do."

The duchess would have liked to slap her painted face and her voice trembled a little with the effort she made to control her anger.

"It is not for my own sake I'm asking you to help. It's for Pilar's. I know, we all know, that you are the cleverest woman in the city. It seemed to me, it seemed to the Archbishop, that if there was a way out, your quick wit would find it."

The countess knew she was being grossly flattered. She did not mind. She liked it.

"You must let me think."

"Of course, if he'd been a gentleman I could have sent for my son

H

and he would have killed him, but the Duke of Dos Palos cannot fight a duel with the Countess de Marbella's coachman."

"Perhaps not."

"In the old days it would have been so simple. I should merely have hired a couple of ruffians and had the brute's throat cut one night in the street. But with all these laws they have nowadays decent people have no way of protecting themselves from insult."

"I should deplore any method of settling the difficulty that deprived me of the services of an excellent coachman," murmured the countess.

"But if he marries my daughter he cannot continue to be your coachman," cried the duchess indignantly.

"Are you going to give Pilar an income for them to live on?"

"Me? Not a peseta. I told Pilar at once that she should get nothing from me. They can starve for all I care."

"Well, I should think rather than do that he will prefer to stay on as my coachman. There are very nice rooms over my stables."

The duchess went pale. The duchess went red.

"Forget all that has passed between us. Let us be friends. You can't expose me to such a humiliation. If I've ever done things to affront you I ask you on my knees to forgive me."

The duchess cried.

"Dry your eyes, Duchess," the Frenchwoman said at last. "I will do what I can."

"Is there anything you can do?"

"Perhaps. Is it true that Pilar has and will have no money of her own?"

"Not a penny if she marries without my consent."

The countess gave one of her brightest smiles.

"There is a common impression that southern people are romantic and northern people matter-of-fact. The reverse is true. It is the northerners who are incurably romantic. I have lived long enough among you Spaniards to know that you are nothing if not practical."

The duchess was too broken to resent openly these unpleasant remarks, but, oh, how she hated the woman! The Countess de Marbella rose to her feet.

"You shall hear from me in the course of the day."

She firmly dismissed her visitor.

The carriage was ordered for five o'clock and at ten minutes to, the countess, dressed for her drive, sent for José. When he came into the drawing-room, wearing his pale grey livery with such an air, she could not deny that he was very good to look upon. If he had not been her own coachman—well, it was not the moment for ideas of that sort. He stood before her, holding himself easily, but with a gallant swagger. There was nothing servile in his bearing.

"A Greek god," the countess murmured to herself. "It is only Andalusia that can produce such types." And then aloud: "I hear that you are going to marry the daughter of the Duchess of Dos Palos."

"If the countess does not object."

She shrugged her shoulders.

"Whoever you marry is a matter of complete indifference to me. You know of course that Doña Pilar will have no fortune."

"Yes, madam. I have a good place and I can keep my wife. I love her."

"I can't blame you for that. She is a beautiful girl. But I think it only right to tell you that I have a rooted objection to married coachmen. On your wedding-day you leave my service. That is all I had to say to you. You can go."

She began to look at the daily paper that had just arrived from Paris, but José, as she expected, did not stir. He stared down at the floor. Presently the countess looked up.

"What are you waiting for?"

"I never knew madam would send me away," he answered in a troubled tone.

"I have no doubt you'll find another place."

"Yes, but . . ."

"Well, what is it?" she asked sharply.

He sighed miserably.

"There's not a pair of mules in the whole of Spain to come up to ours. They're almost human beings. They understand every word I say to them."

The countess gave him a smile that would have turned the head of anyone who was not madly in love already.

"I'm afraid you must choose between me and your betrothed."

He shifted from one foot to the other. He put his hand to his pocket to get himself a cigarette, but then, remembering where he was, restrained the gesture. He glanced at the countess and that peculiar shrewd smile came over his face which those who have lived in Andalusia know so well.

"In that case, I can't hesitate. Pilar must see that this alters my position entirely. One can get a wife any day of the week, but a place like this is found only once in a lifetime. I should be a fool to throw it up for a woman."

That was the end of the adventure. José Leon continued to drive the Countess de Marbella, but she noticed when they sped up and down the Delicias that thenceforward as many eyes were turned on her handsome coachman as on her latest hat; and a year later Pilar married the Marques de San Esteban.

The Point of Honour

SOME years ago, being engaged on writing a book about Spain in the Golden Age, I had occasion to read again the plays of Calderon. Among others I read one called *El Medico de su Honra*, which means the Physician of his Honour. It is a cruel play and you can hardly read it without a shudder. But re-reading it, I was reminded of an encounter I had had many years before which has always remained in my memory as one of the strangest I have ever known. I was quite young then and I had gone to Seville on a short visit to see the celebration of the Feast of Corpus Christi. It was the height of summer and the heat was terrific. Great sail-cloths were drawn across the narrow streets, giving a grateful shade, but in the squares the sun beat down mercilessly. In the morning I watched the procession. It was splendid and impressive. The crowd knelt down as the Host was solemnly carried past, and the Civil Guards in full uniform stood at salute to do homage to the heavenly King. And in the afternoon I joined the dense throng which was making its way to the bull-ring. The cigarette girls and the sewing girls wore carnations in their dark hair and their young men were dressed in all their best. It was just after the Spanish–American war, and the short, embroidered jacket, the skin-tight trousers and the broad-brimmed, low-crowned hat were still worn. Sometimes the crowd was scattered by a picador on the wretched hack that would never survive the afternoon, and the rider, with conscious pride in his picturesque costume, exchanged pleasantries with the facetious. A long line of carriages, dilapidated and shabby, overfilled with *aficionados*, drove noisily along.

I went early, for it amused me to see the people gradually filling the vast arena. The cheaper seats in the sun were already packed, and it was a curious effect that the countless fans made, like the fluttering of a host of butterflies, as men and women restlessly fanned themselves. In the shade, where I was sitting, the places were taken more slowly, but even there, an hour before the fight began, one had to look rather carefully for a seat. Presently a man stopped in front of me and with a pleasant smile asked if I could make room for him. When he had settled down, I took a sidelong glance at him and noticed that he was well-dressed, in English clothes, and looked like a gentleman. He had beautiful hands, small but resolute, with thin, long fingers. Wanting a cigarette, I took out my case and thought it would be polite to offer him one. He accepted. He had evidently seen that I was a foreigner, for he thanked me in French.

"You are English?" he went on.

"Yes."

"How is it you haven't run away from the heat?"

I explained that I had come on purpose to see the Feast of Corpus Christi.

"After all, it's something you must come to Seville for."

Then I made some casual remark about the vast concourse of people.

"No one would imagine that Spain was bleeding from the loss of all that remained of her Empire and that her ancient glory is now nothing but a name."

"There's a great deal left."

"The sunshine, the blue sky, and the future."

He spoke dispassionately, as though the misfortunes of his fallen country were no concern of his. Not knowing what to reply, I remained silent. We waited. The boxes began to fill up. Ladies in their mantillas of black or white lace entered them and spread their Manila shawls over the balustrade so as to form a gay and many-coloured drapery. Now and then, when one of them was of particular beauty, a round of applause would greet her appearance and she would smile and bow without embarrassment. At last the president of the bull-fight made his entry, the band struck up, and the fighters, all glittering in their satin and gold and silver, marched swaggering across the ring. A minute later a great black bull charged in. Carried away by the horrible excitement of the contest, I noticed, notwithstanding, that my neighbour remained cool. When a man fell and only escaped by a miracle the horns of the furious beast, and with a gasp thousands sprang to their feet, he remained motionless. The bull was killed and the mules dragged out the huge carcass. I sank back exhausted.

"Do you like bull-fighting?" he asked me. "Most English do, though I have noticed that in their own country they say hard enough things about it."

"Can one like something that fills one with horror and loathing? Each time I come to a fight I swear I will never go to another. And yet I do."

"It's a curious passion that leads us to delight in the peril of others. Perhaps it's natural to the human race. The Romans had their gladiators and the moderns have their melodramas. It may be that it is an instinct in man to find pleasure in bloodshed and torture."

I did not answer directly.

"Don't you think that the bull-fight is the reason why human life is of so little account in Spain?"

"And do you think human life is of any great account?" he asked.

I gave him a quick look, for there was an ironical tone in his voice that no one could have missed, and I saw that his eyes were full of mockery. I flushed a little, for he made me on a sudden feel very young. I was surprised at the change of his expression. He had seemed rather an amiable man, with his large soft friendly eyes, but now his face bore a look of sardonic hauteur which was a trifle disquieting. I shrank back into my shell. We said little to one another during the rest of the afternoon, but when the last bull was killed and we all rose to our feet he shook hands with me and expressed the hope that we might meet again. It was a mere politeness and neither of us, I imagine, thought that there was even a remote possibility of it.

But quite by chance, two or three days later, we did. I was in a quarter of Seville that I did not know very well. I had been that afternoon to the palace of the Duke of Alba, which I knew had a fine garden and in one of the rooms a magnificent ceiling reputed to have been made by Moorish captives before the fall of Granada. It was not easy to gain admittance, but I wanted very much to see it and thought that now, in the height of summer when there were no tourists, with two or three pesetas I might be allowed in. I was disappointed. The man in charge told me that the house was under repair and no stranger could visit it without a written permission from the Duke's agent. So, having nothing else to do, I went to the royal garden of the Alcazar, the old palace of Don Pedro the Cruel, whose memory lives still among the people of Seville. It was very pleasant among the orange trees and cypresses. I had a book with me, a volume of Calderon, and I sat there for a while and read. Then I went for a stroll. In the older parts of Seville the streets are narrow and tortuous. It is delicious to wander along them under the awnings that stretch above, but not easy to find one's way. I lost mine. When I had just made up my mind that I had no notion in which direction to turn I saw a man walking towards me and recognised my acquaintance of the bull-ring. I stopped him and asked whether he could direct me. He remembered me.

"You'll never find your way," he smiled, turning round. "I'll walk a little with you until you can't mistake it."

I protested, but he would not listen. He assured me it was no trouble.

"You haven't gone away then?" he said.

"I'm leaving to-morrow. I've just been to the Duke of Alba's house. I wanted to see that Moorish ceiling of his, but they wouldn't let me in."

"Are you interested in Arabic art?"

"Well, yes. I've heard that that ceiling is one of the finest things in Seville."

"I think I could show you one as good."

"Where?"

He looked at me for a moment reflectively as though wondering what sort of a person I was. If he was, he evidently came to a satisfactory decision.

"If you have ten minutes to spare I will take you to it."

I thanked him warmly and we turned back and retraced our steps. We chatted of indifferent things till we came to a large house, washed in pale green, with the Arabic look of a prison, the windows on the street heavily barred, which so many houses in Seville have. My guide clapped his hands at the gateway and a servant looked out from a window into the patio, and pulled a cord.

"Whose house is this?"

"Mine."

I was surprised, for I knew how jealously Spaniards guarded their privacy and how little inclined they were to admit strangers into their houses. The heavy iron gate swung open and we walked into the courtyard; we crossed it and went through a narrow passage. Then I found myself suddenly in an enchanted garden. It was walled on three sides, with walls as high as houses; and their old red brick, softened by time, was covered with roses. They clad every inch in wanton, scented luxuriance. In the garden, growing wildly, as if the gardeners had striven in vain to curb the exuberance of nature, were palm-trees rising high into the air in their passionate desire for the sun, dark orange-trees and trees in flower whose names I did not know, and among them roses and more roses. The fourth wall was a Moorish loggia, with horseshoe arches heavily decorated with tracery, and when we entered this I saw the magnificent ceiling. It was like a little bit of the Alcazar, but it had not suffered the restorations that have taken all the charm from that palace, and the colours were exquisitely tender. It was a gem.

"Believe me, you need not regret that you have not been able to see the duke's house. Further, you can say that you have seen something that no other foreigner has seen within living memory."

"It's very kind of you to have shown it to me. I'm infinitely grateful."

He looked about him with a pride with which I could sympathise.

"It was built by one of my own ancestors in the time of Don Pedro the Cruel. It is very likely that the King himself more than once caroused under this ceiling with my ancestor."

I held out the book I was carrying.

"I've just been reading a play in which Don Pedro is one of the important characters."

"What is the book?"

I handed it to him and he glanced at the title. I looked about me.

"Of course, what adds to the beauty is that wonderful garden," I said. "The whole impression is awfully romantic."

The Spaniard was evidently pleased with my enthusiasm. He smiled. I had already noticed how grave his smile was. It hardly dispelled the habitual melancholy of his expression.

"Would you like to sit down for a few minutes and smoke a cigarette?"

"I should love to."

We walked out into the garden and came upon a lady sitting on a bench of Moorish tiles like those in the gardens of the Alcazar. She was working at some embroidery. She looked up quickly, evidently taken aback to see a stranger, and gave my companion an enquiring stare.

"Allow me to present you to my wife," he said.

The lady gravely bowed. She was very beautiful, with magnificent eyes, a straight nose with delicate nostrils, and a pale smooth skin. In her black hair, abundant as with most Spanish women, there was a broad white streak. Her face was quite unlined and she could not have been more than thirty.

"You have a very lovely garden, Señora," I said because I had to say something.

She gave it an indifferent glance.

"Yes, it is pretty."

I felt suddenly embarrassed. I did not expect her to show me any cordiality, and I could not blame her if she thought my intrusion merely a nuisance. There was something about her that I could not quite make out. It was not an active hostility. Absurd as it seemed, since she was a young woman and beautiful, I felt that there was something dead in her.

"Are you going to sit here?" she asked her husband.

"With your permission. Only for a few minutes."

"I won't disturb you."

She gathered her silks and the canvas on which she had been working and rose to her feet. When she stood up I saw that she was taller than Spanish women generally are. She gave me an unsmiling bow. She carried herself with a sort of royal composure and her gait

was stately. I was flippant in those days, and I remember saying to
myself that she was not the sort of girl you could very well think of
being silly with. We sat down on the multi-coloured bench and I
gave my host a cigarette. I held a match to it. He still had my
volume of Calderon in his hands, and now he idly turned the pages.

"Which of the plays have you been reading?"

"*El Medico de su Honra.*"

He gave me a look, and I thought I discerned in his large eyes a
sardonic glint.

"And what do you think of it?"

"I think it's revolting. The fact is, of course, that the idea is so
foreign to our modern notions."

"What idea?"

"The point of honour and all that sort of thing."

I should explain that the point of honour is the mainspring of
much of the Spanish drama. It is the nobleman's code that impels
a man to kill his wife, in cold blood, not only if she has been unfaithful to him, but even if, however little she was to blame, her conduct
has given rise to scandal. In this particular play there is an example
of this more deliberate than any I have ever read: the physician of
his honour takes vengeance on his wife, though aware that she is
innocent, simply as a matter of decorum.

"It's in the Spanish blood," said my friend. "The foreigner must
just take it or leave it."

"Oh, come, a lot of water has flowed down the Guadalquivir since
Calderon's day. You're not going to pretend that any man would
behave like that now."

"On the contrary, I pretend that even now a husband who finds
himself in such a humiliating and ridiculous position can only regain
his self-respect by the offender's death."

I did not answer. It seemed to me that he was pulling a romantic
gesture, and within me I murmured, Bosh. He gave me an ironic
smile.

"Have you ever heard of Don Pedro Aguria?"

"Never."

"The name is not unknown in Spanish history. An ancestor was
Admiral of Spain under Philip II and another was bosom friend to
Philip IV. By royal command he sat for his portrait to Velasquez."

My host hesitated a moment. He gave me a long, reflective stare
before he went on.

"Under the Philips the Agurias were rich, but by the time my
friend Don Pedro succeeded his father their circumstances were
much reduced. But still he was not poor, he had estates between

Cordova and Aguilar, and in Seville his house retained at least traces of its ancient splendour. The little world of Seville was astonished when he announced his engagement to Soledad, the daughter of the ruined Count of Acaba, for though her family was distinguished her father was an old scamp. He was crippled with debts, and the shifts he resorted to in order to keep his head above water were none too nice. But Soledad was beautiful and Don Pedro in love with her. They were married. He adored her with the vehement passion of which perhaps only a Spaniard is capable. But he discovered to his dismay that she did not love him. She was kind and gentle. She was a good wife and a good housekeeper. She was grateful to him. But that was all. He thought that when she had a child she would change, but the child came, and it made no difference. The barrier between them that he had felt from the beginning was still there. He suffered. At last he told himself that she had a character too noble, a spirit too delicate, to descend to earthly passion, and he resigned himself. She was too high above him for mortal love."

I moved a little uneasily in my seat. I thought the Spaniard was unduly rhetorical. He went on.

"You know that here in Seville the Opera House is open only for the six weeks after Easter, and since the Sevillans don't care very much for European music we go more to meet our friends than to listen to the singers. The Agurias had a box, like everybody else, and they went on the opening night of the season. *Tannhaüser* was being given. Don Pedro and his wife, like typical Spaniards, with nothing to do all day but always late, did not arrive till nearly the end of the first act. In the interval the Count of Acaba, Soledad's father, came into the box accompanied by a young officer of artillery whom Don Pedro had never seen before. But Soledad seemed to know him well.

" 'Here is Pepe Alvarez,' said the Count. 'He's just come back from Cuba and I insisted on bringing him to see you.''

"Soledad smiled and held out her hand, then introduced the new-comer to her husband.

" 'Pete is the son of the attorney at Carmona. We used to play together when we were children.'

"Carmona is a small town near Seville, and it was here that the Count had retired when his creditors in the city grew too trouble-some. The house he owned there was almost all that was left him of the fortune he had squandered. He lived in Seville now through Don Pedro's generosity. But Don Pedro did not like him and he bowed stiffly to the young officer. He guessed that his father the attorney and the count had been concerned together in transactions that were none too reputable. In a minute he left the box to talk with his cousin, the Duchess of Santaguador, whose box was opposite his own. A few days later he met Pepe Alvarez at his club in the Sierpes and had a chat with him. To his surprise he found him a very pleasant young fellow. He was full of his exploits in Cuba and he related them with humour.

"The six weeks about Easter and the great Fair are the gayest in Seville, and the world meets to exchange gossip and laughter, at one festivity after another. Pepe Alvarez with his good nature and high spirits was in great request and the Agurias met him constantly. Don Pedro saw that he amused Soledad. She was more vivacious when he was there, and her laughter, which he had so seldom heard, was a delight to him. Like other members of the aristocracy he took a booth for the Fair, where they danced, supped and drank champagne till dawn. Pepe Alvarez was always the life and soul of the parties.

"One night Don Pedro was dancing with the Duchess of Santaguador and they passed Soledad with Pepe Alvarez.

" 'Soledad is looking very beautiful this evening,' she remarked.

" 'And happy,' he replied.

" 'Is it true that once she was engaged to be married to Pepe Alvarez?'

" 'Of course not.'

"But the question startled him. He had known that Soledad and Pepe had known one another when they were children, but it had never crossed his mind that there could have been anything between them. The Count of Acaba, though a rogue, was a gentleman by birth, and it was inconceivable that he could have thought of marrying his daughter to the son of a provincial attorney. When they got home Don Pedro told his wife what the duchess had said and what he had replied.

" 'But I was engaged to Pepe,' she said.

" 'Why did you never tell me?'

" 'It was finished and done with. He was in Cuba. I never expected to see him again.'

" 'There must be people who know you were engaged to him.'

" 'I daresay. Does it matter?'

" 'Very much. You shouldn't have renewed your acquaintance with him when he returned.'

" 'Does that mean that you have no confidence in me?'

" 'Of course not. I have every confidence in you. All the same I wish you to discontinue it now.'

" 'And if I refuse?'

" 'I shall kill him.'

"They looked long into one another's eyes. Then she gave him a little bow and went to her room. Don Pedro sighed. He wondered whether she still loved Pepe Alvarez and whether it was on account of this that she had never loved him. But he would not allow himself to give way to the unworthy emotion of jealousy. He looked into his heart and was sure that it harboured no feeling of hatred for the young artilleryman. On the contrary, he liked him. This was not an affair of love or hate, but of honour. On a sudden he remembered that a few days before he went to his club he noticed that the conversation suddenly failed, and, looking back, he seemed to remember that several of the group who were sitting there and chatting eyed him curiously. Was it possible that he had been the subject of their conversation? He shivered a little at the thought.

"The Fair was drawing to its end, and when it was over the Agurias had arranged to go to Cordova, where Don Pedro had an estate which it was necessary for him to visit from time to time. He looked forward to the peace of a country life after the turmoil of Seville. The day after this conversation Soledad, saying she was not well, stayed in the house, and she did the same the day following. Don Pedro visited her in her room morning and evening and they talked of indifferent things. But on the third day his cousin Conchita de Santaguador was giving a ball. It was the last of the season and everyone in her exclusive set would be there. Soledad, saying she was still indisposed, announced that she would stay at home.

" 'Are you refusing to go because of our conversation of the other night?' Don Pedro asked.

" 'I have been thinking over what you said. I think your demand unreasonable, but I shall accede to it. The only way I can cease my friendship with Pepe is by not going to places where I am likely to meet him.' A tremor of pain passed over her lovely face. 'Perhaps it is best.'

" 'Do you love him still?'

" 'Yes.'

"Don Pedro felt himself go cold with anguish.

" 'Then why did you marry me?'

" 'Pepe was away, in Cuba, no one knew when he would come back. Perhaps never. My father said that I must marry you.'

" 'To save him from ruin?'

" 'From worse than ruin.'

" 'I am very sorry for you.'

" 'You have been kind to me. I have done everything in my power to prove to you that I am grateful.'

" 'And does Pepe love you?'"

"She shook her head and smiled sadly.

" 'Men are different. He's young. He's too gay to love anyone very long. No, to him I'm just the friend whom he used to play with when he was a child and flirt with when he was a boy. He can make jokes about the love he once had for me.'

"He took her hand and pressed it, then kissed it and left her. He went to the ball by himself. His friends were sorry to hear of Soledad's indisposition, but after expressing a proper sympathy devoted themselves to the evening's amusement. Don Pedro drifted into the card-room. There was room at a table, and he sat down to play *chemin de fer*. He played with extraordinary luck and made a good deal of money. One of the players laughingly asked where Soledad was that evening. Don Pedro saw another give him a startled glance, but he laughed and answered that she was safely in bed and asleep. Then an unlucky incident occurred. Some young man came into the room, and addressing an artillery officer who was playing asked where Pepe Alvarez was.

" 'Isn't he here?' said the officer.

" 'No.'

"An odd silence fell upon the party. Don Pedro exercised all his self-control to prevent his face from showing what he suddenly felt. The thought flashed through his mind that those men at the table suspected that Pepe was with Soledad, his wife. Oh, the shame! The indignity! He forced himself to go on playing for another hour and still he won. He could not go wrong. The game broke up and he returned to the ballroom. He went up to his cousin.

" 'I've hardly had a word with you,' he said. 'Come into another room and let us sit down for a little.'

" 'If you like.'

"The room, Conchita's boudoir, was empty.

" 'Where is Pepe Alvarez to-night?' he asked casually.

" 'I can't think.'

" 'You were expecting him?'

" 'Of course.'

"She was smiling as he was, but he noticed that she looked at him sharply. He dropped his mask of casualness and, though they were alone, lowered his voice.

" 'Conchita, I beseech you to tell me the truth. Are they saying that he is Soledad's lover?'

" 'Pedrito, what a monstrous question to put to me!'

"But he had seen the terror in her eyes and the sudden instinctive movement of her hand to her face.

" 'You've answered it.'

"He got up and left her. He went home and looking up from the patio saw a light in his wife's room. He went upstairs and knocked at the door. There was no answer, but he went in. To his surprise, for it was late, she was sitting up working at the embroidery upon which much of her time was spent.

" 'Why are you working at this hour?'

" 'I couldn't sleep, I couldn't read. I thought it would distract my mind if I worked.'

"He did not sit down.

" 'Soledad, I have something to tell you that must cause you pain. I must ask you to be brave. Pepe Alvarez was not at Conchita's to-night.'

" 'What is that to me?'

" 'It is unfortunate that you were not there either. Everyone at the ball thought that you were together.'

" 'That's preposterous.'

" 'I know, but that doesn't help matters. You could have opened the gate for him yourself and let him out, or you could have slipped out yourself without anyone seeing you go or come.'

" 'But do you believe it?'

" 'No. I agreed with you that the thing was preposterous. Where was Pepe Alvarez?'

" 'How do I know? How should I know?'

" 'It is very strange that he should not have come to the most brilliant party, the last party, of the season.'

"She was silent for a minute.

" 'The night after you spoke to me about him I wrote and told him that in view of the circumstances I thought it would be better if in future we saw no more of one another than could be helped. It may be that he did not go to the ball for the same reason that I did not.'

"They were silent for a while. He looked down at the ground, but he felt that her eyes were fixed on him. I should have told you before that Don Pedro possessed one accomplishment which raised him above his fellows, but at the same time was a drawback. He was the best shot in Andalusia. Everyone knew this and it would have been a brave man who ventured to offend him. A few days earlier there had been pigeon-shooting at Tablada, the wide common outside Seville along the Guadalquivir, and Don Pedro had carried all before him. Pepe Alvarez on the other hand had shown himself so indifferent a marksman that everyone had laughed at him. The young artilleryman had borne the chaff with good-humour. Cannon were his weapon, he said.

" 'What are you going to do?' Soledad asked.

" 'You know that there is only one thing I can do.'

"She understood. But she tried to treat what he said as a pleasantry.

" 'You're childish. We're not living any more in the sixteenth century.'

" 'I know. That is why I am talking to you now. If I have to challenge Pepe I shall kill him. I don't want to do that. If he will resign his commission and leave Spain I will do nothing.'

" 'How can he? Where is he to go?'

" 'He can go to South America. He may make his fortune.'

" 'Do you expect me to tell him that?'

" 'If you love him.'

" 'I love him too much to ask him to run away like a coward. How could he face life without honour?'

"Don Pedro laughed.

" 'What has Pepe Alvarez, the son of the attorney at Carmona, to do with honour?'

"She did not answer, but in her eyes he saw the fierce hatred she bore him. That look stabbed his heart, for he loved her, he loved her as passionately as ever.

"Next day he went to his club and joined a group who were sitting at the window looking out at the crowd passing up and down the Sierpes. Pepe Alvarez was in it. They were talking of last night's party.

" 'Where were you, Pepe?' someone asked.

" 'My mother was ill. I had to go to Carmona,' he answered. 'I was dreadfully disappointed, but perhaps it was all for the best.' He turned laughingly to Don Pedro. 'I hear you were in luck and won everybody's money.'

" 'When are you going to give us our revenge, Pedrito?' asked another.

" 'I'm afraid you'll have to wait for that,' he answered. 'I have to go to Cordova. I find that my attorney has been robbing me. I know that all attorneys are thieves, but I stupidly thought this one was honest.'

"He seemed to speak quite lightly, and it was as lightly that Pepe Alvarez put in his word.

" 'I think you exaggerate, Pedrito. Don't forget that my father is an attorney and he at least is honest.'

" 'I don't believe it for a minute,' laughed Don Pedro. 'I have no doubt that your father is as big a thief as any.'

"The insult was so unexpected and so unprovoked that for a moment Pepe Alvarez was staggered. The others were startled into sudden seriousness.

" 'What do you mean, Pedrito?'

" 'Exactly what I say.'

" 'It's a lie and you know it's a lie. You must withdraw that at once.'

"Don Pedro laughed.

" 'Of course I shall not withdraw. Your father is a thief and a rascal.'

"Pepe did the only thing he could do. He sprang from his chair and with his open hand hit Don Pedro in the face. The outcome was inevitable. Next day the two men met on the frontier of Portugal. Pepe Alvarez, the attorney's son, died like a gentleman with a bullet in his heart."

The Spaniard ended his story on such a casual note that for the first moment I hardly took it in. But when I did I was profoundly shocked.

"Barbarous," I said. "It was just cold-blooded murder."

My host got up.

"You're talking nonsense, my young friend. Don Pedro did the only thing he could do in the circumstances."

I left Seville next day, and from then till now have never been able to discover the name of the man who told me this strange story. I have often wondered whether the lady I saw, the lady with the pale face and the lock of white hair, was the unhappy Soledad.

The Poet

I AM not much interested in the celebrated and I have never had patience with the passion that afflicts so many to shake hands with the great ones of the earth. When it is proposed to me to meet some person distinguished above his fellows by his rank or his attainments, I seek for a civil excuse that may enable me to avoid the honour; and when my friend Diego Torre suggested giving me an introduction to Santa Aña I declined. But for once the excuse I made was sincere; Santa Aña was not only a great poet but also a romantic figure and it would have amused me to see in his decrepitude a man whose adventures (in Spain at least) were legendary; but I knew that he was old and ill and I could not believe that it would be anything but a nuisance to him to meet a stranger and a foreigner. Calisto de Santa Aña was the last descendant of the Grand School; in a world unsympathetic to Byronism he had led a Byronic existence and he had narrated his hazardous life in a series of poems that had brought him a fame unknown to his contemporaries. I am no judge of their value, for I read them first when I was three-and-twenty and then was enraptured by them; they had a passion, a heroic arrogance and a multi-coloured vitality that swept me off my feet, and to this day, so intermingled are those ringing lines and haunting cadences with the charming memories of my youth, I cannot read them without a beating heart. I am inclined to think that Calisto de Santa Aña deserves the reputation he enjoys among the Spanish-speaking peoples. In those days his verses were on the lips of all young men and my friends would talk to me endlessly of his wild ways, his vehement speeches (for he was a politician as well as a poet), his incisive wit and his amours. He was a rebel and sometimes an outlaw, daring and adventurous; but above all he was a lover. We knew all about his passion for this great actress or that divine singer—had we not read till we knew them by heart the burning sonnets in which he described his love, his anguish and his wrath?—and we were aware that an infanta of Spain, the proudest descendant of the Bourbons, having yielded to his entreaties, had taken the veil when he ceased to love her. When the Philips, her royal ancestors, tired of a mistress she entered a convent, for it was unfitting that one whom the King had loved should be loved by another, and was not Calisto de Santa Aña greater than any earthly king? We applauded the lady's romantic gesture; it was creditable to her and flattering to our poet.

But all this took place many years ago and for a quarter of a century Don Calisto, disdainfully withdrawing from a world that had nothing more to offer, had lived in seclusion in his native town of Ecija. It was when I announced my intention of going there (I had been spending a week or two in Seville) not because of him, but because it is a charming little Andalusian town with associations that endear it to me, that Diego Torre offered me this introduction. It appeared that Don Calisto allowed the younger men of letters occasionally to visit him and now and then would talk to them with the fire that had electrified his hearers in the great days of his prime.

"What does he look like now?" I asked.

"Magnificent."

"Have you a photograph of him?"

"I wish I had. He has refused to face the camera since he was thirty-five. He says he does not wish posterity to know him other than young."

I confess that I found this suggestion of vanity not a little touching. I knew that in early manhood he was of extraordinary beauty, and that moving sonnet of his written when he grew conscious that youth had for ever left him shows with what a bitter and sardonic pang he must have watched the passing of those looks that had been so fantastically admired.

But I refused my friend's offer; I was quite satisfied to read once more the poems I had known so well and for the rest I preferred to wander about the silent and sunswept streets of Ecija in freedom. It was with some consternation therefore that on the evening of my arrival I received a note from the great man himself. Diego Torre had written to him of my visit, he said, and it would give him great pleasure if I would call on him at eleven next morning. In the circumstances there was nothing for me to do but to present myself at his house at the appointed hour.

My hotel was in the Plaza and on that spring morning it was animated, but as soon as I left it I might have walked in a deserted city. The streets, the tortuous white streets, were empty but for a woman in black now and then who returned with measured steps from her devotions. Ecija is a town of churches and you can seldom go far without seeing a crumbling façade or a tower in which storks have built their nests. Once I paused to watch a string of little donkeys pass by. Their red caparisons were faded and they carried I know not what in their panniers. But Ecija has been a place of consequence in its day and many of these white houses have gateways of stone surmounted by imposing coats of arms, for to this remote spot flowed the riches of the New World and adventurers who had gathered wealth in the Americas spent here their declining years. It was in one of these houses that Don Calisto lived and as I stood at the *reja* after pulling the bell, I was pleased to think that he lived in such a fitting style. There was a dilapidated grandeur about the massive gateway that suited my impression of the flamboyant poet. Though I heard the bell peal through the house no one answered it and I rang a second and then a third time: at last an old woman with a heavy moustache came to the gate.

"What do you want?" she said.

She had fine black eyes, but a sullen look, and I supposed that it was she who took care of the old man. I gave her my card.

"I have an appointment with your master."

She opened the iron gateway and bade me enter. Asking me to wait she left me and went upstairs. The patio was pleasantly cool after the street. Its proportions were noble and you surmised that it had been built by some follower of the conquistadores; but the paint was tarnished, the tiles on the floor broken, and here and there great flakes of plaster had fallen away. There was about everything an air of poverty but not of squalor. I knew that Don Calisto was poor. Money had come to him easily at times but he had never attached any importance to it and had spent it profusely. It was plain that he lived now in a penury that he disdained to notice. In the middle of the patio was a table with a rocking-chair on each side of it, and on the table newspapers a fortnight old. I wondered what dreams occupied his fancy as he sat there on the warm summer nights, smoking cigarettes. On the walls under the colonnade were Spanish pictures, dark and bad, and here and there stood an ancient dusty *bargueño* and on it a mended lustre plate. By the side of a door hung a pair of old pistols, and I had a pleasant fancy that they were the weapons he had used when in the most celebrated of his many duels, for the sake of Pepa Montañez the dancer (now, I suppose, a toothless and raddled hag), he had killed the Duke of Dos Hermanos.

The scene, with its associations which I vaguely divined, so aptly fitted the romantic poet that I was overcome by the spirit of the place. Its noble indigence surrounded him with a glory as great as the magnificence of his youth; in him too there was the spirit of the old conquistadores, and it was becoming that he should finish his famous life in that ruined and magnificent house. Thus surely should a poet live and die. I had arrived cool enough and even somewhat bored at the prospect of my meeting, but now I began to grow a trifle nervous. I lit a cigarette. I had come at the time appointed and wondered what detained the old man. The silence was strangely disturbing. Ghosts of the past thronged the silent patio and an age

dead and gone gained a sort of shadowy life for me. The men of
that day had a passion and a wildness of spirit that are gone out of
the world for ever. We are no longer capable of their reckless deeds
or their theatrical heroics.

I heard a sound and my heart beat quickly. I was excited now
and when at last I saw him coming slowly down the stairs I caught
my breath. He held my card in his hand. He was a tall old man and
exceedingly thin, with a skin the colour of old ivory; his hair was
abundant and white, but his bushy eyebrows were dark still; they
made his great eyes flash with a more sombre fire. It was wonderful
that at his age those black eyes should still preserve their brilliance.
His nose was aquiline, his mouth close-set. His unsmiling eyes rested
on me as he approached and there was in them a look of cool
appraisal. He was dressed in black and in one hand held a broad-
brimmed hat. There was in his bearing assurance and dignity. He
was as I should have wished him to be and as I watched him I understood how he had swayed men's minds and touched their hearts. He
was every inch a poet.

He had reached the patio and came slowly towards me. He had
really the eyes of an eagle. It seemed to me a tremendous moment, for
there he stood, the heir of the great old Spanish poets, the magnificent
Herrera, the nostalgic and moving Fray Luis, Juan de la Cruz, the
mystic, and the crabbed and obscure Gongora. He was the last of
that long line and he trod in their steps not unworthily. Strangely
in my heart sang the lovely and tender song which is the most famous
of Don Calisto's lyrics.

I was abashed. It was fortunate for me that I had prepared
beforehand the phrase with which I meant to greet him.

"It is a wonderful honour, Maestro, for a foreigner such as I to
make the acquaintance of so great a poet."

A flicker of amusement passed through those piercing eyes and a
smile for an instant curved the lines of that stern mouth.

"I am not a poet, Señor, but a bristle merchant. You have made a
mistake, Don Calisto lives next door."

I had come to the wrong house.

The Mother

TWO or three people, hearing sounds of a quarrel in the patio, came out of their rooms and listened.

"It's the new lodger," said a woman. "She's having a row with the porter who brought her things."

It was a tenement house of two storeys, built round a patio, in a back street of La Macarena, which is the roughest quarter in Seville. The rooms were let to working men and the small functionaries with whom Spain is overrun, postmen, policemen, or tram conductors, and the place swarmed with children. There were twenty families there. They squabbled and made it up; they chattered their heads off; they helped one another when help was needed; for the Andalusians are good-natured people, and on the whole they got on well enough together. One room had been for some time unlet. A woman had taken it that morning, and an hour later had brought her bits and pieces, carrying as much as she could herself, a *gallego*— the Galicians are the general porters of Spain—laden with the rest.

But the quarrel was growing more violent, and the two women above, on the first floor, anxious not to miss a word, leant over the balcony.

They heard the newcomer's shrill voice raised in a torrent of abuse and the man's sullen interjections. The two women nudged one another.

"I shan't go till you pay me," he kept on saying.

"But I've paid you already. You said you'd do it for three reales."

"Never! You promised me four."

They were haggling over rather less than twopence halfpenny.

"Four reales for moving those few things? You're crazy."

She tried to push him away.

"I shan't go till you pay me," he repeated.

"I'll give you a penny more."

"I won't take it."

The dispute grew more and more noisy. The woman screamed at the porter and cursed him. She shook her fist in his face. At last he lost patience.

"Oh, all right, give me the penny and I'll go. I'm not going to waste time on a slut like you."

She paid him, and the man, throwing down her mattress, left her. She flung a filthy word at him as he went. She came out of the room

236

to drag the things in, and the two women in the balcony saw her face.

"*Carai*, what an evil face! She looks like a murderess."

A girl came up the stairs at that moment, and her mother called out: "Did you see her, Rosalia?"

"I asked the *gallego* where she came from, he says he brought the things from Triana. She promised him four reales and then wouldn't pay."

"Did he tell you her name?"

"He didn't know. But in Triana they called her La Cachirra."

The vixen appeared again to fetch a bundle she had forgotten. She glanced at the women in the balcony watching her unconcernedly, but said nothing. Rosalia shuddered.

"She frightens me."

La Cachirra was forty, haggard and very thin, with bony hands and fingers like a vulture's claws. Her cheeks were sunken and her skin wrinkled and yellow. When she opened her mouth, with its pale, heavy lips, she showed teeth that were pointed like those of a beast of prey. Her hair was black and coarse; she wore it in a clumsy knot, which seemed on the point of falling over her shoulders, and in front of each ear fell a straight wisp. Her eyes, deep-set in their sockets, large and black, shone fiercely. Her face bore an expression of such ferocity that no one dared come near to speak with her. She kept entirely to herself. The curiosity of the neighbours was aroused. They knew she was very poor, for her clothes were wretched. She went out every morning at six and did not return till night; but they could not even find out how she earned her living. They urged a policeman who lived in the house to make inquiries.

"As long as she doesn't break the peace, I have nothing to do with her," said he.

But in Seville scandal travels quickly and in a few days a mason who lived in an upper room brought the news that a friend in Triana knew her story. La Cachirra had only come out of prison one month before, and she had spent seven years there—for murder. She had lodged in a house in Triana, but the children, finding out what had happened, threw stones at her and called her names; and she, turning upon them with foul words and with blows, had filled the whole place with such tumult that the landlord gave her notice. Cursing him and all who had turned her out, La Cachirra one morning suddenly disappeared.

"And whom did she murder?" asked Rosalia.

"They say it was her lover," replied the mason.

"She can never have had one," said Rosalia, with a laugh of scorn.

"Santa Maria!" cried Pilar, her mother, "I hope she won't kill any of us. I said she looked like a murderess!"

Rosalia, shivering, crossed herself. At that moment La Cachirra came in from her day's work and a sudden oppression fell upon the talkers. They made a movement as if to huddle together and looked nervously at the wild-eyed woman. She seemed to see something ominous in their silence and gave them a rapid, suspicious glance. The policeman, to make conversation, bade her good-evening.

"*Buena sera*," she replied, with a scowl, and, passing quickly into her room, slammed the door.

They heard her lock it. The evil, sullen eyes had cast a gloom over them and they talked in whispers as if under a mischievous spell.

"She has the devil in her," said Rosalia.

"I'm glad you're here to protect us, Manuel," added her mother to the policeman.

But La Cachirra seemed indisposed to give trouble. She went her way, unbending, never addressing so much as a word to anyone, and brusquely cut short every attempt at friendliness. She felt that the neighbours had discovered her secret, the homicide and the long years of imprisonment; and the lines in her face grew sterner, the expression of her deep-set eyes more inhuman. But gradually the anxiety she had caused was dispelled. Even the garrulous Pilar ceased to pay attention to the silent gaunt figure who occasionally passed through the group sitting in the patio.

"I dare say the prison has sent her mad, they say it often does."

But one day an event occurred to revive the gossip. A youth came to the *reja*—the wrought-iron gate that serves as front door to the Sevillan house—and asked for Antonia Sanchez. Pilar, who was mending a skirt in the patio, looked up at her daughter and shrugged her shoulders.

"No one of that name lives here," she said.

"Yes, she does," the young man answered; then, after a pause: "They call her La Cachirra."

"Ah!" Rosalia opened the gate and pointed to the door. "She's in there."

"Thank you."

The youth gave her a smile. She was a pretty girl, with a high colour and fine bold eyes. A red carnation threw up the glossy blackness of her hair. Her breasts were full and the nipples were prominent under her blouse.

"Blessed be the mother that bore you," he said, using a hackneyed phrase.

"*Vaya Usted con Dios*, go you with God," answered Pilar.

He passed on and knocked at the door. The two women looked after him curiously.

"Who can he be?" asked Pilar. "La Cachirra's never had a visitor before."

There was no reply to his knocking, and he knocked again. They heard La Cachirra's rasping voice ask who was there.

"*Madre!*" he cried. "Mother."

There was a shriek. The door was burst open.

"Currito!"

The woman threw her arms round his neck and kissed him passionately. She fondled him and with a loving gesture stroked his face with both her hands. The girl and her mother who watched would never have thought her capable of such tenderness. At last, with little sobs of joy, she dragged him into her room.

"He's her son," said Rosalia, with surprise. "Who'd have thought it! And a fine fellow like that."

Currito had a lean face and white, even teeth; his hair was cut very close, shaved on the temples, and set on the scalp with a truly Andalusian perfection. The shadow of his precocious beard showed blue beneath his brown skin. And of course he was a dandy. He had the national love of fine clothes and his trousers were skin-tight; his short jacket and his frilled shirt were as new as new could be. He wore a broad-brimmed hat.

At last the door of La Cachirra's room was opened and she appeared, hanging on her son's arm.

"You'll come again next Sunday?" she asked.

"If nothing stops me."

He glanced at Rosalia and, having bidden his mother good-night, nodded to her also.

"*Vaya Usted con Dios!*" said she.

She gave him a smile and a flash of her dark eyes. La Cachirra intercepted the look; and the sullenness which her intense joy had driven away suddenly darkened her face like a thunder-cloud. She scowled fiercely at the handsome girl.

"Is that your son?" asked Pilar, when the youth was gone.

"Yes, he's my son," answered La Cachirra gruffly, going back to her room.

Nothing could soften her, and even when her heart was brimming over with happiness she repelled the overtures of friendship.

"He's a good-looking fellow," said Rosalia; and she thought of him more than once during the next few days.

It was a terrible love that La Cachirra had for her son. He was all she had in the world and she adored him with a fiery, jealous passion that demanded in return impossible devotion. She wished to be all in all to him. On account of his work they could not live together and it tortured her to imagine what he did when he was away from her. She could not bear him to look at a woman and she writhed at the bare idea that he might pay court to some girl. No amusement is more common in Seville than the long flirtation in which the maid sits at her window half the night long, guarded by iron bars, or stands at the gate, while her lover in the street pours his rapture into her willing ear. La Cachirra asked the boy if he had a *novia*, a sweetheart, aware that so attractive a youth must enjoy the smiles of women, and she knew he lied when he swore he spent his evenings at work. But his denials gave her a fierce delight.

When she saw Rosalia's provoking glance and Currito's answering smile, rage leapt to her throat. She had hated her neighbours before, because they were happy and she was wretched, because they knew her terrible secret; but now she hated them more, already fancying, half crazily, that they were conspiring to rob her of her son. On the following Sunday, in the afternoon, La Cachirra came out of her room, crossed the patio and stood at the gate. This was a proceeding so unusual that the neighbours commented upon it.

"Don't you know why she's there?" said Rosalia, with a stifled laugh. "Her precious son is coming, and she doesn't want us to see him."

"Does she think we'll eat him?"

Currito arrived and his mother took him quickly to her room.

"She's as jealous of him as if he was her lover," said Pilar.

Rosalia looked at the closed door, laughing again, and her shining eyes were filled with mischief. It occurred to her that it would be very amusing to have a word with Currito. Rosalia's white teeth gleamed at the thought of La Cachirra's anger. She stationed herself at the gate, so that the pair, when they came out, could not help crossing her; but La Cachirra, seeing the girl, moved to the other side of her son so that not even a glance should pass between them. Rosalia shrugged her shoulders.

"You won't beat me so easily as that," she thought.

The Sunday after, when La Cachirra took up her place at the gate, Rosalia went out into the street and strolled along in the direction from which she guessed he would come. In a minute she saw Currito, and walked on, elaborately ignoring him.

"Hola!" said he, stopping.

"Is it you? I thought you were afraid to speak to me."

"I'm afraid of nothing," he answered boastingly.

"Except mamma!"

She walked on, as if she wanted him to leave her; but she knew very well he would do no such thing.

"Where are you going?" he asked.

"What has that to do with you, Currito? Go to your mother, my son, or she'll beat you. You're afraid to look at me when she's with you."

"What nonsense."

"Well, *vaya Usted con Dios!* I have commissions."

He went off rather sheepishly, and Rosalia laughed to herself. She was in the courtyard once more when he passed through with La Cachirra on his way out; and this time, shamed into courage, he stopped and said good-night. La Cachirra turned red with anger.

"Come, Currito," she cried, with a rasping voice, "what are you waiting for?"

He went away, and the woman stopped a moment in front of Rosalia as if she were going to speak, but, with a visible effort, she restrained herself, and went back to her dark, silent room.

A few days later was the feast of San Isidoro, the patron saint of Seville, and to celebrate the holiday the mason and one or two others had put a string of Chinese lanterns in the patio. They glowed warmly in the clear summer night. The sky was soft against the shining stars. The people of the house were gathered in the middle of the patio, sitting on chairs; and the women, some with babies at their breasts, fanned themselves with little paper fans, interrupting their ceaseless chattering to fling a word of abuse at some older child who was making a nuisance of himself. The cool air was very pleasant after the day's breathless heat. Those who had been to the bull-fight were telling the less fortunate all about it. They described with precise detail a wonderful feat that Belmonte, the famous matador, had performed. With their vivid imaginations, the particulars gained every minute in variety and colour, so that it appeared that never in the history of Seville had there been a more excellent *corrida*. Everyone was present but La Cachirra, and in her room they saw the light of a solitary candle.

"And her son?"

"He's in there," answered Pilar. "I saw him pass an hour ago."

"He must be amusing himself," said Rosalia, with a laugh.

"Oh, don't bother about La Cachirra," said another. "Give us a dance, Rosalia."

"Yes, yes," they cried. "Go on, my girl. You dance."

In Spain they love dancing and they love to look at dancing. Years and years ago it was said that there was never a Spanish woman that was not born to dance.

The chairs were quickly set in a ring. The mason and the tram conductor fetched their guitars. Rosalia got her castanets, and stepping forward with another girl, began.

Currito, in the poky room, pricked up his ears when he heard the music.

"They're dancing," he said, and an itching shot down his limbs.

He looked through the curtain and saw the group in the mellow light of the Chinese lanterns. He saw the two girls dancing. Rosalia wore her Sunday clothes, and, as is customary, she was heavily powdered. A splendid carnation gleamed in her hair. Currito's heart beat quickly. Love in Spain grows fast, and he had thought often of the handsome girl since that day on which he first spoke to her. He moved towards the door.

"What are you doing?" asked La Cachirra.

"I'm going to look at them dance. You never wish me to amuse myself."

"It's Rosalia you want to see."

He pushed her away as she tried to stop him, and joined the group that watched the dancers. La Cachirra followed a step or two, and then stood, half hidden by the gloom, with fury gnawing at her heart. Rosalia saw him.

"Aren't you frightened to look at me?" she whispered, as she passed him.

The dancing had made her light-headed and she felt no fear of La Cachirra. When the measure ended and her partner sank into a chair, Rosalia marched up to Currito and stood in front of him, upright, with her head thrown back and her breast heaving with the rapid motion.

"Of course, you don't know how to dance," she said.

"Yes, I do."

"Well, come then."

She smiled provokingly, but he hesitated. He looked over his shoulder at his mother, whom he divined, rather than saw, in the darkness. Rosalia caught the glance and its meaning.

"Are you afraid?"

"What should I be afraid of?" he asked with a shrug of the shoulders.

He stepped into the ring. The guitarists strummed away and the onlookers rhythmically clapped their hands, punctuating the time with an occasional cry of Olé. A girl gave Currito a pair of castanets and the pair began to dance. They heard a little hiss, as of a serpent in the darkness, and Rosalia, quite reckless now, looked with a laugh at the face, ghastly white, that gleamed from the shadows. La Cachirra did not move. She watched the movements of the dance, the swaying of the bodies, the intricate steps; she saw Rosalia lean back with a graceful gesture and smile in Currito's face as he wound about her, clapping his castanets. Her eyes glowed like coals of fire and she felt them burning in the sockets; but no one noticed her, and she gave a groan of rage. The dance came to an end, and Rosalia, smiling with pleasure at the applause, told Currito she did not know he could dance so well.

La Cachirra flung herself into her room and bolted the door. She gave no answer when Currito came and bade her open.

"Well, I shall go home," he said.

Her heart bled with pain, but she would not speak. He was all she had, all she loved in the world; and yet she hated him. She could not sleep that night, but lay thinking, half-madly, that they were robbing her of her son. In the morning she did not go to work, but lay in wait for Rosalia. The girl came out at last, rather bedraggled after the night's festivities, and she started when La Cachirra suddenly faced her.

"What do you want with my son?"

"What do you mean?" replied Rosalia, assuming an expression of surprise.

La Cachirra quivered with passion and she bit her hand to keep herself quiet.

"Oh, you know what I mean. You're stealing him from me."

"Do you think I want your son? Keep him away from me. I can't help it if he runs after me wherever I go."

"That's a lie!"

"Ask him!" And now Rosalia's voice was so scornful that La Cachirra could hardly contain herself. "He waits an hour in the street to see me. Why don't you keep him to yourself?"

"You lie, you lie! You throw yourself in his way."

"If I wanted lovers I could get them without asking. I don't want the son of a murderess."

Then everything grew confused to La Cachirra; the blood leaped to her head and choked her eyes. She sprang at Rosalia and tore her hair. The girl gave a shrill cry and sought to defend herself, but immediately a passer-by wrenched them apart.

"If you don't leave Currito alone, I'll kill you!" cried La Cachirra.

"Do you think I'm frightened? Keep him from me if you can. You fool, don't you see that he loves me better than his eyes?"

"Now then, go away," said the man. "Don't answer her, Rosalia."

La Cachirra gave a little roar of passion, like a wild beast baulked of its prey, and pushed past into the street.

But the dance had left Currito madly in love with Rosalia, and all next day he thought of her red lips; the light of her eyes shone in his heart and filled him with enchantment. He passionately desired her. At nightfall he wandered towards the Macarena and presently found himself at her house. He waited in the darkness of the porch till he saw her in the patio. At the other end burned his mother's lonely light.

"Rosalia," he called in a low voice.

She turned, stifling a cry of surprise.

"Why are you here to-day?" she whispered, going towards him.

"I couldn't keep away from you."

"Why?" she smiled.

"Because I love you."

"Do you know your mother nearly killed me this morning?"

And with the embellishments necessary to the Andalusian temperament, she related the occurrence, omitting, however, the final taunt which had enraged La Cachirra beyond endurance.

"She's got the temper of the devil," said Currito; and then, with bravado: "I shall tell her that you're my sweetheart."

"She will be pleased," said Rosalia ironically.

"Will you come to the *reja* to-morrow?"

"Perhaps," she answered.

He gave a little chuckle, for he knew by her tone that she would. He swaggered even more than usual when he walked through the Sierpes on his way home. She was waiting for him when he came next day and, as is the way with lovers in Seville, they talked for hours under their breath, with the iron gate between them, and it never even occurred to Currito that it was a needless impediment. When he asked Rosalia if she loved him she answered with a little amorous sigh. They tried to see the passion that burnt hotly in one another's eyes. Then he went every night.

But fearing that his mother knew of his visits, Currito did not go to see her on the following Sunday. The wretched woman waited for him with an aching heart. She was ready to fall on her knees and beg him to forgive her, but then, when he did not come, she hated him; she would have liked to see him dead at her feet. Her heart sank when she thought that another week must pass before she could even hope to see him.

The week passed and still he did not come. She could not bear it. Anguish, anguish! She loved him as no sweetheart could ever love him. She told herself that this was Rosalia's doing and when she thought of her, rage filled her heart. At last Currito plucked up his courage and went to see his mother; but she had waited too long. It seemed as though her love was dead. She pushed him away when he wanted to kiss her.

"Why haven't you come before?"

"You locked the door on me. I thought you didn't want me!"

"Was it only that? Had you no other reason?"

"I've been busy," he said, shrugging his shoulders.

"Busy? An idle loafer like you. What have you been doing? You wouldn't have been too busy to come and see Rosalia."

"Why did you hit her?"

"How do you know I hit her? Have you seen her?" La Cachirra strode up to her son; her eyes flashed. "She called me a murderess."

"Well, what of it?"

"What of it?" she screamed, so that they heard her in the patio. "And if I am a murderess—it was for you. Yes, I killed Pepe Santi; but it was because he was beating you. It was for your sake that I lay in prison for seven years—for seven years. Oh, you fool, you think she cares for you, and every night she spends hours at the gate."

"I know," Currito answered with a grin.

La Cachirra started violently. She shot a puzzled look at him and then she understood. She gasped with pain and wrath; she clutched at her heart as though the agony were too intense to bear.

"You've been coming every night to the *reja* and you never came near me? Oh, how cruel! I've done everything in the world for you. Do you think I loved Pepe Santi? I endured his blows so that I could give you bread; and I killed him when he beat you. Oh, God, I only lived for you. But for the thought of you I would have died rather than suffer those years of prison."

"Come, woman, be reasonable. I'm twenty. What d'you expect? If it wasn't Rosalia it would be another."

"You beast. I hate you. Get out."

She pushed him violently to the door. Currito shrugged his shoulders.

"You needn't think I want to stay."

He walked jauntily through the patio and slammed the iron gate behind him. La Cachirra stalked to and fro in her tiny room. The hours passed slowly. For a long while she remained at the window, watching with the horrible steadfastness of a savage beast ready to spring. She stood motionless, repressing the convulsive restlessness that tore at her heart-strings. There was a clapping of hands at the *reja* as a signal that someone was without, and she peered forward with panting mouth, her fiery eyes almost starting from her head. But it was only the mason. She waited longer, and Pilar, Rosalia's mother, came in and walked slowly up the stairs to her room. La

Cachirra clutched at her throat to relieve the intolerable oppression of her breath. Still she waited. Now and then an extraordinary quiver travelled through all her limbs.

At last! There was a clap of light hands at the gate, and a voice above called out: "Who is it?"

"Peace!"

La Cachirra recognised Rosalia's voice. She gave a gasp of triumph. The door was opened from above, and Rosalia, entering, crossed the courtyard with a buoyant and easy step. The joy of life was in her every motion. She was about to put her foot on the stair when La Cachirra sprang forward and stopped her. She caught hold of her arm and the girl could not shake herself free.

"What do you want?" said Rosalia. "Let me pass."

"What have you been doing with my son?"

"Let me pass, or I shall call out."

"Is it true that you meet at the *reja* every night?"

"Mother, help! Antonio!" Rosalia cried out shrilly.

"Answer me."

"Well, if you want the truth, you can have it. He's going to marry me. He loves me, and I—I love him with all my heart." She turned on La Cachirra, trying to free herself from the vicious grip. "D'you think you can prevent us? D'you think he's frightened of you? He hates you, he told me so. He wishes you'd never come out of prison."

"He told you that?"

La Cachirra shrank back. Rosalia pursued the advantage.

"Yes, he told me that; and he told me much more. He told me that you murdered Pepe Santi; and that you were in prison for seven years; and he wished you were dead."

Rosalia hissed the words venomously, laughing with shrill voice when she saw the wretched woman shrink as though struck by palpable blows.

"And you ought to be proud that I don't refuse to marry the son of a murderess."

Then, giving La Cachirra a push, she leapt to the stairs; but the movement revived the woman, stunned by the horrible taunts, and with a cry of brutal rage she sprang upon Rosalia and caught her by the shoulders and dragged her down. Rosalia turned and hit her in the face. La Cachirra drew a knife from her bosom, and with an oath buried it in the girl's neck. Rosalia shrieked.

"Mother, she's killed me."

She fell to the bottom of the stairs and lay huddled up on the stone. Blood made a little pool on the ground.

Half a dozen doors were flung open at the despairing cry, and people rushed to seize La Cachirra; but she backed against the wall and faced them, with an expression of such ferocity on her face that no one dared approach her. The hesitation was momentary, but Pilar ran from the balcony shrieking, and the common attention for an instant was distracted. La Cachirra saw the opportunity and ran forward. She reached her room and locked and bolted the door behind her.

Suddenly the court was filled with people. Pilar with loud dreadful cries flung herself down on her daughter and would not let herself be dragged away. Someone rushed for a doctor and someone else went for the police. The crowd surged in from the street and collected round the door. The doctor hurried in with a black bag in his hand. When the police came a dozen people at once excitedly explained what had happened. They pointed to the door of La Cachirra's room, and the police broke in. There was a scuffle and they came out with La Cachirra handcuffed. The mob rushed forward, but the police surrounded her and with their scabbards beat the people off; but they shook their fists and hurled curses at her. She looked at them scornfully. She deigned to make no answer. Her eyes shone with triumph. The policemen led her through the patio and they passed by the body of Rosalia.

"Is she dead?" asked La Cachirra.

"Yes," the doctor answered gravely.

"Thanks be to God!" she said.

A Man from Glasgow

I T is not often that anyone entering a great city for the first time
has the luck to witness such an incident as engaged Shelley's attention when he drove into Naples. A youth ran out of a shop pursued
by a man armed with a knife. The man overtook him and with one
blow in the neck laid him dead on the road. Shelley had a tender
heart. He didn't look upon it as a bit of local colour; he was seized
with horror and indignation. But when he expressed his emotions
to a Calabrian priest who was travelling with him, a fellow of gigantic
strength and stature, the priest laughed heartily and attempted to
quiz him. Shelley says he never felt such an inclination to beat
anyone.

I have never seen anything so exciting as that, but the first time
I went to Algeciras I had an experience that seemed to me far from
ordinary. Algeciras was then an untidy, neglected town. I arrived
somewhat late at night and went to an inn on the quay. It was
rather shabby, but it had a fine view of Gibraltar, solid and matter-
of-fact, across the bay. The moon was full. The office was on the
first floor, and a slatternly maid, when I asked for a room, took me
upstairs. The landlord was playing cards. He seemed little pleased
to see me. He looked me up and down, curtly gave me a number,
and then, taking no further notice of me, went on with his game.

When the maid had shown me to my room I asked her what I could
have to eat.

"What you like," she answered.

I knew well enough the unreality of the seeming profusion.

"What have you got in the house?"

"You can have eggs and ham."

The look of the hotel had led me to guess that I should get little
else. The maid led me to a narrow room with white-washed walls
and a low ceiling in which was a long table laid already for the next
day's luncheon. With his back to the door sat a tall man, huddled
over a *brasero*, the round brass dish of hot ashes which is erroneously
supposed to give sufficient warmth for the temperate winter of
Andalusia. I sat down at table and waited for my scanty meal. I
gave the stranger an idle glance. He was looking at me, but meeting
my eyes he quickly turned away. I waited for my eggs. When at
last the maid brought them he looked up again.

"I want you to wake me in time for the first boat," he said.

248

"*Si, señor.*"

His accent told me that English was his native tongue, and the breadth of his build, his strongly marked features, led me to suppose him a northerner. The hardy Scot is far more often found in Spain than the Englishman. Whether you go to the rich mines of Rio Tinto, or to the bodegas of Jerez, to Seville or to Cadiz, it is the leisurely speech of beyond the Tweed that you hear. You will meet Scotsmen in the olive groves of Carmona, on the railway between Algeciras and Bobadilla, and even in the remote cork woods of Merida.

I finished eating and went over to the dish of burning ashes. It was midwinter and the windy passage across the bay had chilled my blood. The man pushed his chair away as I drew mine forwards. "Don't move," I said. "There's heaps of room for two."

I lit a cigar and offered one to him. In Spain the Havana from Gib is never unwelcome.

"I don't mind if I do," he said, stretching out his hand.

I recognised the singing speech of Glasgow. But the stranger was not talkative, and my efforts at conversation broke down before his monosyllables. We smoked in silence. He was even bigger than I had thought, with great broad shoulders and ungainly limbs; his face was sunburned, his hair short and grizzled. His features were hard; mouth, ears and nose were large and heavy and his skin much wrinkled. His blue eyes were pale. He was constantly pulling his ragged, grey moustache. It was a nervous gesture that I found faintly irritating. Presently I felt that he was looking at me, and the intensity of his stare grew so irksome that I glanced up expecting him, as before, to drop his eyes. He did, indeed, for a moment, but then raised them again. He inspected me from under his long, bushy eyebrows.

"Just come from Gib?" he asked suddenly.

"Yes."

"I'm going to-morrow—on my way home. Thank God."

He said the last two words so fiercely that I smiled.

"Don't you like Spain?"

"Oh, Spain's all right."

"Have you been here long?"

"Too long. Too long."

He spoke with a kind of gasp. I was surprised at the emotion my casual inquiry seemed to excite in him. He sprang to his feet and walked backwards and forwards. He stamped to and fro like a caged beast, pushing aside a chair that stood in his way, and now and again repeated the words in a groan. "Too long. Too long." I sat still.

I was embarrassed. To give myself countenance I stirred the *brasero* to bring the hotter ashes to the top, and he stood suddenly still, towering over me, as though my movement had brought back my existence to his notice. Then he sat down heavily in his chair.

"D'you think I'm queer?" he asked.

"Not more than most people," I smiled.

"You don't see anything strange in me?"

He leant forward as he spoke so that I might see him well.

"No."

"You'd say so if you did, wouldn't you?"

"I would."

I couldn't quite understand what all this meant. I wondered if he was drunk. For two or three minutes he didn't say anything and I had no wish to interrupt the silence.

"What's your name?" he asked suddenly.

I told him.

"Mine's Robert Morrison."

"Scotch?"

"Glasgow. I've been in this blasted country for years. Got any baccy?"

I gave him my pouch and he filled his pipe. He lit it from a piece of burning charcoal.

"I can't stay any longer. I've stayed too long. Too long."

He had an impulse to jump up again and walk up and down, but he resisted it, clinging to his chair. I saw on his face the effort he was making. I judged that his restlessness was due to chronic alcoholism. I find drunks very boring, and I made up my mind to take an early opportunity of slipping off to bed.

"I've been managing some olive groves," he went on. "I'm here working for the Glasgow and South of Spain Olive Oil Company Limited."

"Oh, yes."

"We've got a new process for refining oil, you know. Properly treated, Spanish oil is every bit as good as Lucca. And we can sell it cheaper."

He spoke in a dry, matter-of-fact, business-like way. He chose his words with Scotch precision. He seemed perfectly sober.

"You know, Ecija is more or less the centre of the olive trade, and we had a Spaniard there to look after the business. But I found he was robbing us right and left, so I had to turn him out. I used to live in Seville; it was more convenient for shipping the oil. However, I found I couldn't get a trustworthy man to be at Ecija, so last year I went there myself. D'you know it?"

"No."

"The firm has got a big estate two miles from the town, just outside the village of San Lorenzo, and it's got a fine house on it. It's on the crest of a hill, rather pretty to look at, all white, you know, and straggling, with a couple of storks perched on the roof. No one lived there, and I thought it would save the rent of a place in town if I did."

"It must have been a bit lonely," I remarked.

"It was."

Robert Morrison smoked on for a minute or two in silence. I wondered whether there was any point in what he was telling me. I looked at my watch.

"In a hurry?" he asked sharply.

"Not particularly. It's getting late."

"Well, what of it?"

"I suppose you didn't see many people?" I said, going back.

"Not many. I lived there with an old man and his wife who looked after me, and sometimes I used to go down to the village and play *tresillo* with Fernandez, the chemist, and one or two men who met at his shop. I used to shoot a bit and ride."

"It doesn't sound such a bad life to me."

"I'd been there two years last spring. By God, I've never known such heat as we had in May. No one could do a thing. The labourers just lay about in the shade and slept. Sheep died and some of the animals went mad. Even the oxen couldn't work. They stood around with their backs all humped up and gasped for breath. That blasted sun beat down and the glare was so awful, you felt your eyes would shoot out of your head. The earth cracked and crumbled, and the crops frizzled. The olives went to rack and ruin. It was simply hell. One couldn't get a wink of sleep. I went from room to room, trying to get a breath of air. Of course I kept the windows shut and had the floors watered, but that didn't do any good. The nights were just as hot as the days. It was like living in an oven.

"At last I thought I'd have a bed made up for me downstairs on the north side of the house in a room that was never used because in ordinary weather it was damp. I had an idea that I might get a few hours' sleep there at all events. Anyhow it was worth trying. But it was no damned good; it was a washout. I turned and tossed and my bed was so hot that I couldn't stand it. I got up and opened the doors that led to the verandah and walked out. It was a glorious night. The moon was so bright that I swear you could read a book by it. Did I tell you the house was on the crest of a hill? I leant against the parapet and looked at the olive-trees. It was like the sea.

I suppose that's what made me think of home. I thought of the cool breeze in the fir-trees and the racket of the streets in Glasgow. Believe it or not, I could smell them, and I could smell the sea. By God, I'd have given every bob I had in the world for an hour of that air. They say it's a foul climate in Glasgow. Don't you believe it. I like the rain and the grey sky and that yellow sea and the waves. I forgot that I was in Spain, in the middle of the olive country, and I opened my mouth and took a long breath as though I were breathing in the sea-fog.

"And then all of a sudden I heard a sound. It was a man's voice. Not loud, you know, low. It seemed to creep through the silence like—well, I don't know what it was like. It surprised me. I couldn't think who could be down there in the olives at that hour. It was past midnight. It was a chap laughing. A funny sort of laugh. I suppose you'd call it a chuckle. It seemed to crawl up the hill—disjointedly."

Morrison looked at me to see how I took the odd word he used to express a sensation that he didn't know how to describe.

"I mean, it seemed to shoot up in little jerks, something like shooting stones out of a pail. I leant forward and stared. With the full moon it was almost as light as day, but I'm dashed if I could see a thing. The sound stopped, but I kept on looking at where it had come from in case somebody moved. And in a minute it started off again, but louder. You couldn't have called it a chuckle any more, it was a real belly laugh. It just rang through the night. I wondered it didn't wake my servants. It sounded like someone who was roaring drunk.

" 'Who's there?' I shouted.

"The only answer I got was a roar of laughter. I don't mind telling you I was getting a bit annoyed. I had half a mind to go down and see what it was all about. I wasn't going to let some drunken swine kick up a row like that on my place in the middle of the night. And then suddenly there was a yell. By God, I was startled. Then cries. The man had laughed with a deep bass voice, but his cries were—shrill, like a pig having his throat cut.

" 'My God,' I cried.

"I jumped over the parapet and ran down towards the sound. I thought somebody was being killed. There was silence and then one piercing shriek. After that sobbing and moaning. I'll tell you what it sounded like, it sounded like someone at the point of death. There was a long groan and then nothing. Silence. I ran from place to place. I couldn't find anyone. At last I climbed the hill again and went back to my room.

"You can imagine how much sleep I got that night. As soon as it was light, I looked out of the window in the direction from which the row had come and I was surprised to see a little white house in a sort of dale among the olives. The ground on that side didn't belong to us and I'd never been through it. I hardly ever went to that part of the house and so I'd never seen the house before. I asked José who lived there. He told me that a madman had inhabited it, with his brother and a servant."

"Oh, was that the explanation?" I said. "Not a very nice neighbour."

The Scot bent over quickly and seized my wrist. He thrust his face into mine and his eyes were starting out of his head with terror.

"The madman had been dead for twenty years," he whispered.

He let go my wrist and leant back in his chair panting.

"I went down to the house and walked all round it. The windows were barred and shuttered and the door was locked. I knocked. I shook the handle and rang the bell. I heard it tinkle, but no one came. It was a two-storey house and I looked up. The shutters were tight closed, and there wasn't a sign of life anywhere."

"Well, what sort of condition was the house in?" I asked.

"Oh, rotten. The whitewash had worn off the walls and there was practically no paint left on the door or the shutters. Some of the tiles off the roof were lying on the ground. They looked as though they'd been blown away in a gale."

"Queer," I said.

"I went to my friend Fernandez, the chemist, and he told me the same story as José. I asked about the madman and Fernandez said that no one ever saw him. He was more or less comatose ordinarily, but now and then he had an attack of acute mania and then he could be heard from ever so far laughing his head off and then crying. It used to scare people. He died in one of his attacks and his keepers cleared out at once. No one had ever dared to live in the house since.

"I didn't tell Fernandez what I'd heard. I thought he'd only laugh at me. I stayed up that night and kept watch. But nothing happened. There wasn't a sound. I waited about till dawn and then I went to bed."

"And you never heard anything more?"

"Not for a month. The drought continued and I went on sleeping in the lumber-room at the back. One night I was fast asleep, when something seemed to happen to me; I don't exactly know how to describe it, it was a funny feeling as though someone had given me a little nudge, to warn me, and suddenly I was wide awake. I lay there in my bed and then in the same way as before I heard a long,

low gurgle, like a man enjoying an old joke. It came from away
down in the valley and it got louder. It was a great bellow of
laughter. I jumped out of bed and went to the window. My legs
began to tremble. It was horrible to stand there and listen to the
shouts of laughter that rang through the night. Then there was the
pause, and after that a shriek of pain and that ghastly sobbing. It
didn't sound human. I mean, you might have thought it was an
animal being tortured. I don't mind telling you I was scared stiff.
I couldn't have moved if I'd wanted to. After a time the sounds
stopped, not suddenly, but dying away little by little. I strained my
ears, but I couldn't hear a thing. I crept back to bed and hid my face.

"I remembered then that Fernandez had told me that the madman's attacks only came at intervals. The rest of the time he was
quite quiet. Apathetic, Fernandez said. I wondered if the fits of
mania came regularly. I reckoned out how long it had been between
the two attacks I'd heard. Twenty-eight days. It didn't take me
long to put two and two together; it was quite obvious that it was the
full moon that set him off. I'm not a nervous man really and I made
up my mind to get to the bottom of it, so I looked out in the calendar
which day the moon would be full next and that night I didn't go to
bed. I cleaned my revolver and loaded it. I prepared a lantern and
sat down on the parapet of my house to wait. I felt perfectly cool.
To tell you the truth, I was rather pleased with myself because I
didn't feel scared. There was a bit of a wind, and it whistled about
the roof. It rustled over the leaves of the olive-trees like waves
swishing on the pebbles of the beach. The moon shone on the white
walls of the house in the hollow. I felt particularly cheery.

"At last I heard a little sound, the sound I knew, and I almost
laughed. I was right; it was the full moon and the attacks came as
regular as clockwork. That was all to the good. I threw myself
over the wall into the olive grove and ran straight to the house.
The chuckling grew louder as I came near. I got to the house and
looked up. There was no light anywhere. I put my ears to the door
and listened. I heard the madman simply laughing his bloody head
off. I beat on the door with my fist and I pulled the bell. The sound
of it seemed to amuse him. He roared with laughter. I knocked
again, louder and louder, and the more I knocked the more he
laughed. Then I shouted at the top of my voice.

" 'Open the blasted door, or I'll break it down.'

"I stepped back and kicked the latch with all my might. I flung
myself at the door with the whole weight of my body. It cracked.
Then I put all my strength into it and the damned thing smashed
open.

Brunei brass whicl
been a present fror

"I thought it bet
have died of fever.

"You've put us i
frowning a little. "
of me not to have
in getting her to l
She said her father
we've known one a
the terms we've be
had confidence in
him the truth we n

"I must say I s
acidly.

"Of course I told
them what you tol

"I hope it didn't

"Really, my dea
exclaimed her fath

He rose from his
from force of habit

"It was my busir
myself I didn't see

"It doesn't look a
didn't even tell her

Millicent shrugge

"You might have
leen.

"Why? I didn't
nothing else to talk

"When the Bisho
the Heywoods shou

"All that's neith
you should certain
decided what was t
that in the long ru
hide them."

"Poor Harold," s
down her raddled cl
son-in-law to me.
thing?"

"The climate."

"I took the revolver out of my pocket and held my lantern in the other hand. The laughter sounded louder now that the door was opened. I stepped in. The stink nearly knocked me down. I mean, just think, the windows hadn't been opened for twenty years. The row was enough to raise the dead, but for a moment I didn't know where it was coming from. The walls seemed to throw the sound backwards and forwards. I pushed open a door by my side and went into a room. It was bare and white and there wasn't a stick of furniture in it. The sound was louder and I followed it. I went into another room, but there was nothing there. I opened a door and found myself at the foot of a staircase. The madman was laughing just over my head. I walked up, cautiously, you know, I wasn't taking any risks, and at the top of the stairs there was a passage. I walked along it, throwing my light ahead of me, and I came to a room at the end. I stopped. He was in there. I was only separated from the sound by a thin door.

"It was awful to hear it. A shiver passed through me and I cursed myself because I began to tremble. It wasn't like a human being at all. By Jove, I very nearly took to my heels and ran. I had to clench my teeth to force myself to stay. But I simply couldn't bring myself to turn the handle. And then the laughter was cut, cut with a knife you'd have said, and I heard a hiss of pain. I hadn't heard that before, it was too low to carry to my place, and then a gasp.

"'Ay!' I heard the man speak in Spanish. 'You're killing me. Take it away. O God, help me!'

"He screamed. The brutes were torturing him. I flung open the door and burst in. The draught blew a shutter back and the moon streamed in so bright that it dimmed my lantern. In my ears, as clearly as I hear you speak and as close, I heard the wretched chap's groans. It was awful, moaning and sobbing, and frightful gasps. No one could survive that. He was at the point of death. I tell you I heard his broken, choking cries right in my ears. And the room was empty."

Robert Morrison sank back in his chair. That huge solid man had strangely the look of a lay figure in a studio. You felt that if you pushed him he would fall over in a heap on to the floor.

"And then?" I asked.

He took a rather dirty handkerchief out of his pocket and wiped his forehead.

"I felt I didn't much want to sleep in that room on the north side, so, heat or no heat, I moved back to my own quarters. Well, exactly four weeks later, about two in the morning, I was waked up by the madman's chuckle. It was almost at my elbow. I don't mind telling

The light
advanced s
watched he
"Millicer
was playing
"Did you
Gladys H
"She tol
know."
Millicent
flowers in tl
"Have y
mother?" s
"Yes, she
Kathleen
"The Bis
home," she
Borneo, an
"He'll be
he know po
"Yes, he
He says he
Millicent
seemed str:
complete si
"Oh, Mi
you taken i
"Yes, I p
"I shoulc
Once mc
habit.
Kathleer
"Millicei
The wid
eyes, but h
"What d
"The Bis
Mrs. Ski
cating han
"Is it tr
"It is."
"But wh
Millicent

"Why don't you sit down, Kathleen? Surely there are plenty of chairs in the room."

Kathleen drew forward a chair and without a word seated herself. Mr. Skinner stopped in front of Millicent and faced her.

"Of course I see why you told us Harold had died of fever. I think it was a mistake, because that sort of thing is bound to come out sooner or later. I don't know how far what the Bishop has told the Heywoods coincides with the facts, but if you will take my advice you will tell us everything as circumstantially as you can, then we can see. We can't hope that it will go no further now that Canon Heywood and Gladys know. In a place like this people are bound to talk. It will make it easier for all of us if we at all events know the exact truth."

Mrs. Skinner and Kathleen thought he put the matter very well. They waited for Millicent's reply. She had listened with an impassive face; that sudden flush had disappeared and it was once more, as usual, pasty and sallow.

"I don't think you'll much like the truth if I tell it you," she said.

"You must know that you can count on our sympathy and understanding," said Kathleen gravely.

Millicent gave her a glance and the shadow of a smile flickered across her set mouth. She looked slowly at the three of them. Mrs. Skinner had an uneasy impression that she looked at them as though they were mannequins at a dressmaker's. She seemed to live in a different world from theirs and to have no connection with them.

"You know, I wasn't in love with Harold when I married him," she said reflectively.

Mrs. Skinner was on the point of making an exclamation when a rapid gesture of her husband, barely indicated, but after so many years of married life perfectly significant, stopped her. Millicent went on. She spoke with a level voice, slowly, and there was little change of expression in her tone.

"I was twenty-seven, and no one else seemed to want to marry me. It's true he was forty-four, and it seemed rather old, but he had a very good position, hadn't he? I wasn't likely to get a better chance."

Mrs. Skinner felt inclined to cry again, but she remembered the party.

"Of course I see now why you took his photograph away," she said dolefully.

"Don't, mother," exclaimed Kathleen.

It had been taken when he was engaged to Millicent and was a very good photograph of Harold. Mrs. Skinner had always thought him quite a fine man. He was heavily built, tall and perhaps a little

long speeches didn't irri
stately ways rather funn
years he never touched a
even able to joke about i
"Mr. Simpson had le1
called Francis.
" 'I'm a reformed dru
him once. 'If it hadn't l
ago. I've got the best wi
"You don't know wha
that all I'd gone through
She was silent. She th
on whose banks she had l
ing in the tremulous sur
low and swift, and scatte
sweet and pure and spri
a divine arpeggio, from
tween the green banks, v
happy thoughts of a con
"Then Joan fell ill. Fo
was no doctor nearer tha
the treatment of a nativ
took her down to the mou
of sea air. We stayed the
separated from Harold si
fishing village, on piles,
alone. I thought a great
once I knew that I loved
to fetch us back, because
mean a good deal to him
rowed up-stream the hea
go up-country to arrest a
He had been gone a coup
"I was surprised that
meet me; he was always v
used to say that husband a
as they treated acquain
business had prevented hi
bungalow stood. The aya
was strangely silent. The
could not make it out; I
soon and was out. I wei
ayah took her to the ser

too fat, but he held himself well, and his presence was imposing. He was inclined to be bald, even then, but men did go bald very early nowadays, and he said that topees, sun-helmets, you know, were very bad for the hair. He had a small dark moustache, and his face was deeply burned by the sun. Of course his best feature was his eyes; they were brown and large, like Joan's. His conversation was interesting. Kathleen said he was pompous, but Mrs. Skinner didn't think him so, she didn't mind it if a man laid down the law; and when she saw, as she very soon did, that he was attracted by Millicent she began to like him very much. He was always very attentive to Mrs. Skinner, and she listened as though she were really interested when he spoke of his district, and told her of the big game he had killed. Kathleen said he had a pretty good opinion of himself, but Mrs. Skinner came of a generation which accepted without question the good opinion that men had of themselves. Millicent saw very soon which way the wind blew, and though she said nothing to her mother, her mother knew that if Harold asked her she was going to accept him.

Harold was staying with some people who had been thirty years in Borneo and they spoke well of the country. There was no reason why a woman shouldn't live there comfortably; of course the children had to come home when they were seven; but Mrs. Skinner thought it unnecessary to trouble about that yet. She asked Harold to dine, and she told him they were always in to tea. He seemed to be at a loose end, and when his visit to his old friends was drawing to a close, she told him they would be very much pleased if he would come and spend a fortnight with them. It was towards the end of this that Harold and Millicent became engaged. They had a very pretty wedding, they went to Venice for their honeymoon, and then they started for the East. Millicent wrote from various ports at which the ship touched. She seemed happy.

"People were very nice to me at Kuala Solor," she said. Kuala Solor was the chief town of the state of Sembulu. "We stayed with the Resident and everyone asked us to dinner. Once or twice I heard men ask Harold to have a drink, but he refused; he said he had turned over a new leaf now he was a married man. I didn't know why they laughed. Mrs. Gray, the Resident's wife, told me they were all so glad Harold was married. She said it was dreadfully lonely for a bachelor on one of the outstations. When we left Kuala Solor Mrs. Gray said good-bye to me so funnily that I was quite surprised. It was as if she was solemnly putting Harold in my charge."

They listened to her in silence. Kathleen never took her eyes off

very much m
D.Ts.''
"Why didn'
"What wou
dismissed from
Joan? I had t
plain of. He v
me; I hadn't i
cause I wante
liquor from hir
sent from Kual
as a cat watch
while he had a
complaints wo
and that was
Mr. Gray wro
Harold. He st
for two or thr
And so it went
"Before we
careful. I didi
married. All t
we sailed I wa
very proud of
him better tha
child grow up
that at last I'd
him that I wou
take her away
when I said it.
cause I'd foun
"He told me
try. We made
tried so hard.
You know he v
humble, he wa
love me when
I'd hated him
drunk and tri
but now I got a
a queer, shy te
he was like a ch
months. He w

papaia, three cold fried eggs, Edam cheese, sliced thin, and a cup of black coffee. When he had eaten it, he smoked a large Dutch cigar, read the papers if he had not read them through and through already, and then dressed to go down to his office.

One morning while he was thus occupied his head boy came into his bedroom and told him that Tuan Jones wanted to know if he could see him. Mr. Gruyter was standing in front of a looking-glass. He had his trousers on and was admiring his smooth chest. He arched his back in order to throw it out and throw in his belly and with a good deal of satisfaction gave his breast three or four resounding slaps. It was a manly chest. When the boy brought the message he looked at his own eyes in the mirror and exchanged a slightly ironic smile with them. He asked himself what the devil his visitor could want. Evert Gruyter spoke English, Dutch and Malay with equal facility, but he thought in Dutch. He liked to do this. It seemed to him a pleasantly ribald language.

"Ask the tuan to wait and say I shall come directly." He put on his tunic, over his naked body, buttoned it up, and strutted into the sitting-room. The Rev. Owen Jones got up.

"Good-morning, Mr. Jones," said the Contrôleur. "Have you come in to have a peg with me before I start my day's work?"

Mr. Jones did not smile.

"I've come to see you upon a very distressing matter, Mr. Gruyter," he answered.

The Contrôleur was not disconcerted by his visitor's gravity nor depressed by his words. His little blue eyes beamed amiably.

"Sit down, my dear fellow, and have a cigar."

Mr. Gruyter knew quite well that the Rev. Owen Jones neither drank nor smoked, but it tickled something prankish in his nature to offer him a drink and a smoke whenever they met. Mr. Jones shook his head.

Mr. Jones was in charge of the Baptist Mission on the Alas Islands. His headquarters were at Baru, the largest of them, with the greatest population, but he had meeting-houses under the care of native helpers in several other islands of the group. He was a tall, thin, melancholy man, with a long face, sallow and drawn, of about forty. His brown hair was already white on the temples and it receded from the forehead. This gave him a look of somewhat vacuous intellectuality. Mr. Gruyter both disliked and respected him. He disliked him because he was narrow-minded and dogmatic. Himself a cheerful pagan who liked the good things of the flesh and was determined to get as many of them as his circumstances permitted, he had no patience with a man who disapproved of them all.

He thought the customs of the country suited its inhabitants and had
no patience with the missionary's energetic efforts to destroy a way
of life that for centuries had worked very well. He respected him
because he was honest, zealous and good. Mr. Jones, an Australian
of Welsh descent, was the only qualified doctor in the group and it
was a comfort to know that if you fell ill you need not rely only on a
Chinese practitioner, and none knew better than the Contrôleur
how useful to all Mr. Jones's skill had been and with what charity he
had given it. On the occasion of an epidemic of influenza the
missionary had done the work of ten men and no storm short of a
typhoon could prevent him from crossing to one island or another if
his help was needed.

He lived with his sister in a little white house about half a mile
from the village and when the Contrôleur had arrived, came on
board to meet him and begged him to stay till he could get his own
house in order. The Contrôleur had accepted and soon saw for
himself with what simplicity the couple lived. It was more than he
could stand. Tea at three sparse meals a day, and when he lit his
cigar Mr. Jones politely but firmly asked him to be good enough not
to smoke, since both his sister and he strongly disapproved of it. In
twenty-four hours Mr. Gruyter moved into his own house. He fled,
with panic in his heart, as though from a plague-stricken city. The
Contrôleur was fond of a joke and he liked to laugh; to be with a
man who took your nonsense in deadly earnest and never even
smiled at your best story was more than flesh and blood could stand.
The Rev. Owen Jones was a worthy man, but as a companion he
was impossible. His sister was worse. Neither had a sense of humour,
but whereas the missionary was of a melancholy turn, doing his duty
so conscientiously, with the obvious conviction that everything in the
world was hopeless, Miss Jones was resolutely cheerful. She grimly
looked on the bright side of things. With the ferocity of an avenging
angel she sought out the good in her fellow-men. Miss Jones taught
in the mission school and helped her brother in his medical work.
When he did operations she gave the anæsthetic and was matron,
dresser and nurse of the tiny hospital which on his own initiative
Mr. Jones had added to the mission. But the Contrôleur was an
obstinate little fellow and he never lost his capacity of extracting
amusement from the Rev. Owen's dour struggle with the infirmities
of human nature, and Miss Jones's ruthless optimism. He had to get
his fun where he could. The Dutch boats came in three times in two
months for a few hours and then he could have a good old crack with
the captain and chief engineer, and once in a blue moon a pearling
lugger came in from Thursday Island or Port Darwin and for two

moment to lose if she was to save the headman's life. Under the greatest difficulties, showing a native how to give the anæsthetic, she operated, and for the next three days nursed the patient with anxious assiduity. Everything went very well and she realised that her brother could not have made a better job of it. She waited long enough to take out the stitches and then prepared to go home. She could flatter herself that she had not wasted her time. She had given medical attention to such as needed it, she had strengthened the small Christian community in its faith, admonished such as were lax and cast the good seed in places where it might be hoped under divine providence to take root.

The launch, coming from one of the other islands, put in somewhat late in the afternoon, but it was full moon and they expected to reach Baru before midnight. They brought her things down to the wharf and the people who were seeing her off stood about repeating their thanks. Quite a little crowd collected. The launch was loaded with sacks of copra, but Miss Jones was used to its strong smell and it did not incommode her. She made herself as comfortable a place to sit in as she could, and waiting for the launch to start, chatted with her grateful flock. She was the only passenger. Suddenly a group of natives emerged from the trees that embowered the little village on the lagoon and she saw that among them was a white man. He wore a prison sarong and a baju. He had long red hair. She at once recognised Ginger Ted. A policeman was with him. They shook hands and Ginger Ted shook hands with the villagers who accompanied him. They bore bundles of fruit and a jar which Miss Jones guessed contained native spirit, and these they put in the launch. She discovered to her surprise that Ginger Ted was coming with her. His term was up and instructions had arrived that he was to be returned to Baru in the launch. He gave her a glance, but did not nod—indeed Miss Jones turned away her head—and stepped in. The mechanic started his engine and in a moment they were jug-jugging through the channel in the lagoon. Ginger Ted clambered on to a pile of sacks and lit a cigarette.

Miss Jones ignored him. Of course she knew him very well. Her heart sank when she thought that he was going to be once more in Baru, creating a scandal and drinking, a peril to the women and a thorn in the flesh of all decent people. She knew the steps her brother had taken to have him deported and she had no patience with the Contrôleur, who would not see a duty that stared him so plainly in the face. When they had crossed the bar and were in the open sea Ginger Ted took the stopper out of the jar of arak and putting his mouth to it took a long pull. Then he handed the jar to the two mechanics who formed the crew. One was a middle-aged man and the other a youth.

"I do not wish you to drink anything while we are on the journey," said Miss Jones sternly to the elder one.

He smiled at her and drank.

"A little arak can do no one any harm," he answered. He passed the jar to his companion, who drank also.

"If you drink again I shall complain to the Contrôleur," said Miss Jones.

The elder man said something she could not understand but which she suspected was very rude, and passed the jar back to Ginger Ted. They went along for an hour or more. The sea was like glass and the sun set radiantly. It set behind one of the islands and for a few minutes changed it into a mystic city of the skies. Miss Jones turned round to watch it and her heart was filled with gratitude for the beauty of the world.

"And only man is vile," she quoted to herself.

They went due east. In the distance was a little island which she knew they passed close by. It was uninhabited. A rocky islet thickly grown with virgin forest. The boatman lit his lamps. The night fell and immediately the sky was thick with stars. The moon had not yet risen. Suddenly there was a slight jar and the launch began to vibrate strangely. The engine rattled. The head mechanic, calling to his mate to take the helm, crept under the housing. They seemed to be going more slowly. The engine stopped. She asked the youth what was the matter, but he did not know. Ginger Ted got down from the top of the copra sacks and slipped under the housing. When he reappeared she would have liked to ask him what had happened, but her dignity prevented her. She sat still and occupied herself with her thoughts. There was a long swell and the launch rolled slightly. The mechanic emerged once more into view and started the engine. Though it rattled like mad they began to move. The launch vibrated from stem to stern. They went very slowly. Evidently something was amiss, but Miss Jones was exasperated rather than alarmed. The launch was supposed to do six knots, but now it was just crawling along; at that rate they would not get into Baru till long, long after midnight. The mechanic, still busy under the housing, shouted out something to the man at the helm. They spoke in Bugi, of which Miss Jones knew very little. But after a while she noticed that they had changed their course and seemed to be heading for the little uninhabited island a good deal to the lee of which they should have passed.

She held the largest scalpel in her closed fist. The moon allowed her to see where she was going. She looked for a place to hide. The thick forest came down to the very edge of the beach; but, afraid of its darkness (after all, she was but a woman), she dared not plunge into its depth. She did not know what animals lurked there or what dangerous snakes. Besides, her instinct told her that it was better to keep those three bad men in sight; then if they came towards her she would be prepared. Presently she found a little hollow. She looked round. They seemed to be occupied with their own affairs and they could not see her. She slipped in. There was a rock between them and her so that she was hidden from them and yet could watch them. She saw them go to and from the boat carrying things. She saw them build a fire. It lit them luridly and she saw them sit around it and eat, and she saw the jar of arak passed from one to the other. They were all going to get drunk. What would happen to her then? It might be that she could cope with Ginger Ted, though his strength terrified her, but against three she would be powerless. A mad idea came to her to go to Ginger Ted and fall on her knees before him and beg him to spare her. He must have some spark of decent feeling in him and she had always been so convinced that there was good even in the worst of men. He must have had a mother. Perhaps he had a sister. Ah, but how could you appeal to a man blinded with lust and drunk with arak? She began to feel terribly weak. She was afraid she was going to cry. That would never do. She needed all her self-control. She bit her lip. She watched them, like a tiger watching his prey; no, not like that, like a lamb watching three hungry wolves. She saw them put more wood on the fire, and Ginger Ted, in his sarong, silhouetted by the flames. Perhaps after he had had his will of her he would pass her on to the others. How could she go back to her brother when such a thing had happened to her? Of course he would be sympathetic, but would he ever feel quite the same to her again? It would break his heart. And perhaps he would think that she ought to have resisted more. For his sake perhaps it would be better if she said nothing about it. Naturally the men would say nothing. It would mean twenty years in prison for them. But then supposing she had a baby. Miss Jones instinctively clenched her hands with horror and nearly cut herself with the scalpel. Of course it would only infuriate them if she resisted.

"What shall I do?" she cried. "What have I done to deserve this?"

She flung herself down on her knees and prayed to God to save her. She prayed long and earnestly. She reminded God that she was a virgin and just mentioned, in case it had slipped the divine memory, how much St. Paul had valued that excellent state. And then she peeped round the rock again. The three men appeared to be smoking and the fire was dying down. Now was the time that Ginger Ted's lewd thoughts might be expected to turn to the woman who was at his mercy. She smothered a cry, for suddenly he got up and walked in her direction. She felt all her muscles grow taut, and though her heart was beating furiously she clenched the scalpel firmly in her hand. But it was for another purpose that Ginger Ted had got up. Miss Jones blushed and looked away. He strolled slowly back to the others and sitting down again raised the jar of arak to his lips. Miss Jones, crouching behind the rock, watched with straining eyes. The conversation round the fire grew less and presently she divined, rather than saw, that the two natives wrapped themselves in blankets and composed themselves to slumber. She understood. This was the moment Ginger Ted had been waiting for. When they were fast asleep he would get up cautiously and without a sound, in order not to wake the others, creep stealthily towards her. Was it that he was unwilling to share her with them or did he know that his deed was so dastardly that he did not wish them to know of it? After all, he was a white man and she was a white woman. He could not have sunk so low as to allow her to suffer the violence of natives. But his plan, which was so obvious to her, had given her an idea; when she saw him coming she would scream, she would scream so loudly that it would wake the two mechanics. She remembered now that the elder, though he had only one eye, had a kind face. But Ginger Ted did not move. She was feeling terribly tired. She began to fear that she would not have the strength now to resist him. She had gone through too much. She closed her eyes for a minute.

When she opened them it was broad daylight. She must have fallen asleep and, so shattered was she by emotion, have slept till long after dawn. It gave her quite a turn. She sought to rise, but something caught in her legs. She looked and found that she was covered with two empty copra sacks. Someone had come in the night and put them over her. Ginger Ted! She gave a little scream. The horrible thought flashed through her mind that he had outraged her in her sleep. No. It was impossible. And yet he had had her at his mercy. Defenceless. And he had spared her. She blushed furiously. She raised herself to her feet, feeling a little stiff, and arranged her disordered dress. The scalpel had fallen from her hand and she picked it up. She took the two copra sacks and emerged from her hiding-place. She walked towards the boat. It was floating in the shallow water of the lagoon.

"What the blazes does he mean?" he asked.

The Contrôleur laughed. He tried to control himself, but the more he did the more he laughed. He shook and you saw the folds of his fat belly ripple under the sarong. He leaned back in his long chair and rolled from side to side. He did not laugh only with his face, he laughed with his whole body, and even the muscles of his podgy legs shook with mirth. He held his aching ribs. Ginger Ted looked at him frowning, and because he did not understand what the joke was he grew angry. He seized one of the empty beer bottles by the neck.

"If you don't stop laughing, I'll break your bloody head open," he said.

The Contrôleur mopped his face. He swallowed a mouthful of beer. He sighed and groaned because his sides were hurting him.

"He's thanking you for having respected the virtue of Miss Jones," he spluttered at last.

"Me?" cried Ginger Ted.

The thought took quite a long time to travel through his head, but when at last he got it he flew into a violent rage. There flowed from his mouth such a stream of blasphemous obscenities as would have startled a marine.

"That old cow," he finished. "What does he take me for?"

"You have the reputation of being rather hot stuff with the girls, Ginger," giggled the little Contrôleur.

"I wouldn't touch her with the fag-end of a barge-pole. It never entered my head. The nerve. I'll wring his blasted neck. Look here, give me my money, I'm going to get drunk."

"I don't blame you," said the Contrôleur.

"That old cow," repeated Ginger Ted. "That old cow."

He was shocked and outraged. The suggestion really shattered his sense of decency.

The Contrôleur had the money at hand and having got Ginger Ted to sign the necessary papers gave it to him.

"Go and get drunk, Ginger Ted," he said, "but I warn you, if you get into mischief it'll be twelve months next time."

"I shan't get into mischief," said Ginger Ted sombrely. He was suffering from a sense of injury. "It's an insult," he shouted at the Contrôleur. "That's what it is, it's a bloody insult."

He lurched out of the house, and as he went he muttered to himself: "Dirty swine, dirty swine." Ginger Ted remained drunk for a week. Mr. Jones went to see the Contrôleur again.

"I'm very sorry to hear that poor fellow has taken up his evil course again," he said. "My sister and I are dreadfully disappointed.

I'm afraid it wasn't very wise to give him so much money at once."

"It was his own money. I had no right to keep it back."

"Not a legal right, perhaps, but surely a moral right."

He told the Contrôleur the story of that fearful night on the island. With her feminine instinct, Miss Jones had realised that the man, inflamed with lust, was determined to take advantage of her, and, resolved to defend herself to the last, had armed herself with a scalpel. He told the Contrôleur how she had prayed and wept and how she had hidden herself. Her agony was indescribable, and she knew that she could never have survived the shame. She rocked to and fro and every moment she thought he was coming. And there was no help anywhere and at last she had fallen asleep; she was tired out, poor thing, she had undergone more than any human being could stand, and then when she awoke she found that he had covered her with copra sacks. He had found her asleep, and surely it was her innocence, her very helplessness that had moved him, he hadn't the heart to touch her; he covered her gently with two copra sacks and crept silently away.

"It shows you that deep down in him there is something sterling. My sister feels it's our duty to save him. We must do something for him."

"Well, in your place I wouldn't try till he's got through all his money," said the Contrôleur, "and then if he's not in jail you can do what you like."

But Ginger Ted didn't want to be saved. About a fortnight after his release from prison he was sitting on a stool outside a Chinaman's shop looking vacantly down the street when he saw Miss Jones coming along. He stared at her for a minute and once more amazement seized him. He muttered to himself and there can be little doubt that his mutterings were disrespectful. But then he noticed that Miss Jones had seen him and he quickly turned his head away; he was conscious, notwithstanding, that she was looking at him. She was walking briskly, but she sensibly diminished her pace as she approached him. He got up quickly and went into the shop. He did not venture to come out for at least five minutes. Half an hour later Mr. Jones himself came along and he went straight up to Ginger Ted with outstretched hand.

"How do you do, Mr. Edward? My sister told me I should find you here."

Ginger Ted gave him a surly look and did not take the proffered hand. He made no answer.

"We'd be so very glad if you'd come to dinner with us next Sunday.

"I'm not going, if that's what you mean. Damned nerve."

"You must answer the letter."

"Well, I won't."

"Now look here, Ginger, you put on those new clothes and you come as a favour to me. I've got to go and, damn it all, you can't leave me in the lurch. It won't hurt you just once."

Ginger Ted looked at the Contrôleur suspiciously, but his face was serious and his manner sincere: he could not guess that within him the Dutchman bubbled with laughter.

"What the devil do they want me for?"

"I don't know. The pleasure of your society, I suppose."

"Will there be any booze?"

"No, but come up to my house at seven, and we'll have a tiddly before we go."

"Oh, all right," said Ginger Ted sulkily.

The Contrôleur rubbed his little fat hands with joy. He was expecting a great deal of amusement from the party. But when Thursday came and seven o'clock, Ginger Ted was dead drunk and Mr. Gruyter had to go alone. He told the missionary and his sister the plain truth. Mr. Jones shook his head.

"I'm afraid it's no good, Martha, the man's hopeless."

For a moment Miss Jones was silent and the Contrôleur saw two tears trickle down her long thin nose. She bit her lip.

"No one is hopeless. Everyone has some good in him. I shall pray for him every night. It would be wicked to doubt the power of God."

Perhaps Miss Jones was right in this, but the divine providence took a very funny way of effecting its ends. Ginger Ted began to drink more heavily than ever. He was so troublesome that even Mr. Gruyter lost patience with him. He made up his mind that he could not have the fellow on the islands any more and resolved to deport him on the next boat that touched at Baru. Then a man died under mysterious circumstances after having been for a trip to one of the islands and the Contrôleur learnt that there had been several deaths on the same island. He sent the Chinese who was the official doctor of the group to look into the matter, and very soon received intelligence that the deaths were due to cholera. Two more took place at Baru and the certainty was forced upon him that there was an epidemic.

The Contrôleur cursed freely. He cursed in Dutch, he cursed in English and he cursed in Malay. Then he drank a bottle of beer and smoked a cigar. After that he took thought. He knew the Chinese doctor would be useless. He was a nervous little man from Java and the natives would refuse to obey his orders. The Contrôleur was efficient and knew pretty well what must be done, but he could not do everything single-handed. He did not like Mr. Jones, but just then he was thankful that he was at hand, and he sent for him at once. He was accompanied by his sister.

"You know what I want to see you about, Mr. Jones," he said abruptly.

"Yes. I've been expecting a message from you. That is why my sister has come with me. We are ready to put all our resources at your disposal. I need not tell you that my sister is as competent as a man."

"I know. I shall be very glad of her assistance."

They set to without further delay to discuss the steps that must be taken. Hospital huts would have to be erected and quarantine stations. The inhabitants of the various villages on the islands must be forced to take proper precautions. In a good many cases the infected villages drew their water from the same well as the uninfected, and in each case this difficulty would have to be dealt with according to circumstances. It was necessary to send round people to give orders and make sure that they were carried out. Negligence must be ruthlessly punished. The worst of it was that the natives would not obey other natives, and orders given by native policemen, themselves unconvinced of their efficacy, would certainly be disregarded. It was advisable for Mr. Jones to stay at Baru, where the population was largest and his medical attention most wanted; and what with the official duties that forced him to keep in touch with his headquarters, it was impossible for Mr. Gruyter to visit all the other islands himself. Miss Jones must go; but the natives of some of the outlying islands were wild and treacherous; the Contrôleur had had a good deal of trouble with them. He did not like the idea of exposing her to danger.

"I'm not afraid," she said.

"I daresay. But if you have your throat cut I shall get into trouble, and besides, we're so short-handed I don't want to risk losing your help."

"Then let Mr. Wilson come with me. He knows the natives better than anyone and can speak all their dialects."

"Ginger Ted?" The Contrôleur stared at her. "He's just getting over an attack of D.Ts."

"I know," she answered.

"You know a great deal, Miss Jones."

Even though the moment was so serious Mr. Gruyter could not but smile. He gave her a sharp look, but she met it coolly.

"I don't mind having a cup of tea."

"A cup of what?"

"I'm on the wagon. Martha and I are going to be married."

"Ginger!"

The Contrôleur's eyes popped out of his head. He scratched his shaven pate.

"You can't marry Miss Jones," he said. "No one could marry Miss Jones."

"Well, I'm going to. That's what I've come to see you about. Owen's going to marry us in chapel, but we want to be married by Dutch law as well."

"A joke's a joke, Ginger. What's the idea?"

"She wanted it. She fell for me that night we spent on the island when the propeller broke. She's not a bad old girl when you get to know her. It's her last chance, if you understand what I mean, and I'd like to do something to oblige her. And she wants someone to take care of her, there's no doubt about that."

"Ginger, Ginger, before you can say knife she'll make you into a damned missionary."

"I don't know that I'd mind that so much if we had a little mission of our own. She says I'm a bloody marvel with the natives. She says I can do more with a native in five minutes than Owen can do in a year. She says she's never known anyone with the magnetism I have. It seems a pity to waste a gift like that."

The Contrôleur looked at him without speaking and slowly nodded his head three or four times. She'd nobbled him all right.

"I've converted seventeen already," said Ginger Ted.

"You? I didn't know you believed in Christianity."

"Well, I don't know that I did exactly, but when I talked to 'em and they just came into the fold like a lot of blasted sheep, well, it gave me quite a turn. Blimey, I said, I daresay there's something in it after all."

"You should have raped her, Ginger. I wouldn't have been hard on you. I wouldn't have given you more than three years and three years is soon over."

"Look here, Contrôleur, don't you ever let on that the thought never entered my head. Women are touchy, you know, and she'd be as sore as hell if she knew that."

"I guessed she'd got her eye on you, but I never thought it would come to this." The Controleur in an agitated manner walked up and down the verandah. "Listen to me, old boy," he said after an interval of reflection, "we've had some grand times together and a friend's a friend. I'll tell you what I'll do, I'll lend you the launch and you can go and hide on one of the islands till the next ship comes along and then I'll get 'em to slow down and take you on board. You've only got one chance now and that's to cut and run."

Ginger Ted shook his head.

"It's no good, Contrôleur, I know you mean well, but I'm going to marry the blasted woman, and that's that. You don't know the joy of bringing all them bleeding sinners to repentance, and Christ! that girl can make a treacle pudding. I haven't eaten a better one since I was a kid."

The Contrôleur was very much disturbed. The drunken scamp was his only companion on the islands and he did not want to lose him. He discovered that he had even a certain affection for him. Next day he went to see the missionary.

"What's this I hear about your sister marrying Ginger Ted?" he asked him. "It's the most extraordinary thing I've ever heard in my life."

"It's true nevertheless."

"You must do something about it. It's madness."

"My sister is of full age and entitled to do as she pleases."

"But you don't mean to tell me you approve of it. You know Ginger Ted. He's a bum and there are no two ways about it. Have you told her the risk she's running? I mean, bringing sinners to repentance and all that sort of thing's all right, but there are limits. And does the leopard ever change his spots?"

Then for the first time in his life the Contrôleur saw a twinkle in the missionary's eye.

"My sister is a very determined woman, Mr. Gruyter," he replied. "From that night they spent on the island he never had a chance."

The Contrôleur gasped. He was as surprised as the prophet when the Lord opened the mouth of the ass, and she said unto Balaam, What have I done unto thee, that thou hast smitten me these three times? Perhaps Mr. Jones was human after all.

"*Allejesus!*" muttered the Contrôleur.

Before anything more could be said Miss Jones swept into the room. She was radiant. She looked ten years younger. Her cheeks were flushed and her nose was hardly red at all.

"Have you come to congratulate me, Mr. Gruyter?" she cried, and her manner was sprightly and girlish. "You see, I was right after all. Everyone has some good in them. You don't know how splendid Edward has been all through this terrible time. He's a hero. He's a saint. Even I was surprised."

"I hope you'll be very happy, Miss Jones."

L

"I know I shall. Oh, it would be wicked of me to doubt it. For it is the Lord who has brought us together."

"Do you think so?"

"I know it. Don't you see? Except for the cholera Edward would never have found himself. Except for the cholera we should never have learnt to know one another. I have never seen the hand of God more plainly manifest."

The Contrôleur could not but think that it was rather a clumsy device to bring those two together that necessitated the death of six hundred innocent persons, but not being well versed in the ways of omnipotence he made no remark.

"You'll never guess where we're going for our honeymoon," said Miss Jones, perhaps a trifle archly.

"Java?"

"No, if you'll lend us the launch, we're going to that island where we were marooned. It has very tender recollections for both of us. It was there that I first guessed how fine and good Edward was. It's there I want him to have his reward."

The Contrôleur caught his breath. He left quickly, for he thought that unless he had a bottle of beer at once he would have a fit. He was never so shocked in his life.

Louise

I COULD never understand why Louise bothered with me. She disliked me and I knew that behind my back, in that gentle way of hers, she seldom lost the opportunity of saying a disagreeable thing about me. She had too much delicacy ever to make a direct statement, but with a hint and a sigh and a little flutter of her beautiful hands she was able to make her meaning plain. She was a mistress of cold praise. It was true that we had known one another almost intimately, for five-and-twenty years, but it was impossible for me to believe that she could be affected by the claims of old association. She thought me a coarse, brutal, cynical and vulgar fellow. I was puzzled at her not taking the obvious course and dropping me. She did nothing of the kind; indeed, she would not leave me alone; she was constantly asking me to lunch and dine with her and once or twice a year invited me to spend a week-end at her house in the country. At last I thought that I had discovered her motive. She had an uneasy suspicion that I did not believe in her; and if that was why she did not like me, it was also why she sought my acquaintance: it galled her that I alone should look upon her as a comic figure and she could not rest till I acknowledged myself mistaken and defeated. Perhaps she had an inkling that I saw the face behind the mask and because I alone held out was determined that sooner or later I too should take the mask for the face. I was never quite certain that she was a complete humbug. I wondered whether she fooled herself as thoroughly as she fooled the world or whether there was some spark of humour at the bottom of her heart. If there was it might be that she was attracted to me, as a pair of crooks might be attracted to one another, by the knowledge that we shared a secret that was hidden from everybody else.

I knew Louise before she married. She was then a frail, delicate girl with large and melancholy eyes. Her father and mother worshipped her with an anxious adoration, for some illness, scarlet fever I think, had left her with a weak heart and she had to take the greatest care of herself. When Tom Maitland proposed to her they were dismayed, for they were convinced that she was much too delicate for the strenuous state of marriage. But they were not too well off and Tom Maitland was rich. He promised to do everything in the world for Louise and finally they entrusted her to him as a sacred charge. Tom Maitland was a big, husky fellow, very good-looking

313

and a fine athlete. He doted on Louise. With her weak heart he could not hope to keep her with him long and he made up his mind to do everything he could to make her few years on earth happy. He gave up the games he excelled in, not because she wished him to, she was glad that he should play golf and hunt, but because by a coincidence she had a heart attack whenever he proposed to leave her for a day. If they had a difference of opinion she gave in to him at once, for she was the most submissive wife a man could have, but her heart failed her and she would be laid up, sweet and uncomplaining, for a week. He could not be such a brute as to cross her. Then they would have quite a little tussle about which should yield and it was only with difficulty that at last he persuaded her to have her own way. On one occasion seeing her walk eight miles on an expedition that she particularly wanted to make, I suggested to Tom Maitland that she was stronger than one would have thought. He shook his head and sighed.

"No, no, she's dreadfully delicate. She's been to all the best heart specialists in the world and they all say that her life hangs on a thread. But she has an unconquerable spirit."

He told her that I had remarked on her endurance.

"I shall pay for it to-morrow," she said to me in her plaintive way. "I shall be at death's door."

"I sometimes think that you're quite strong enough to do the things you want to," I murmured.

I had noticed that if a party was amusing she could dance till five in the morning, but if it was dull she felt very poorly and Tom had to take her home early. I am afraid she did not like my reply, for though she gave me a pathetic little smile I saw no amusement in her large blue eyes.

"You can't very well expect me to fall down dead just to please you," she answered.

Louise outlived her husband. He caught his death of cold one day when they were sailing and Louise needed all the rugs there were to keep her warm. He left her a comfortable fortune and a daughter. Louise was inconsolable. It was wonderful that she managed to survive the shock. Her friends expected her speedily to follow poor Tom Maitland to the grave. Indeed they already felt dreadfully sorry for Iris, her daughter, who would be left an orphan. They redoubled their attentions towards Louise. They would not let her stir a finger; they insisted on doing everything in the world to save her trouble. They had to, because if she was called upon to do anything tiresome or inconvenient her heart went back on her and there she was at death's door. She was entirely lost without a man to take care of her, she said, and she did not know how, with her delicate health, she was going to bring up her dear Iris. Her friends asked why she did not marry again. Oh, with her heart it was out of the question, though of course she knew that dear Tom would have wished her to, and perhaps it would be the best thing for Iris if she did; but who would want to be bothered with a wretched invalid like herself? Oddly enough more than one young man showed himself quite ready to undertake the charge and a year after Tom's death she allowed George Hobhouse to lead her to the altar. He was a fine, upstanding fellow and he was not at all badly off. I never saw anyone so grateful as he for the privilege of being allowed to take care of this frail little thing.

"I shan't live to trouble you long," she said.

He was a soldier and an ambitious one, but he resigned his commission. Louise's health forced her to spend the winter at Monte Carlo and the summer at Deauville. He hesitated a little at throwing up his career, and Louise at first would not hear of it; but at last she yielded as she always yielded, and he prepared to make his wife's last few years as happy as might be.

"It can't be very long now," she said. "I'll try not to be troublesome."

For the next two or three years Louise managed, notwithstanding her weak heart, to go beautifully dressed to all the most lively parties, to gamble very heavily, to dance and even to flirt with tall slim young men. But George Hobhouse had not the stamina of Louise's first husband and he had to brace himself now and then with a stiff drink for his day's work as Louise's second husband. It is possible that the habit would have grown on him, which Louise would not have liked at all, but very fortunately (for her) the war broke out. He rejoined his regiment and three months later was killed. It was a great shock to Louise. She felt, however, that in such a crisis she must not give way to a private grief; and if she had a heart attack nobody heard of it. In order to distract her mind she turned her villa at Monte Carlo into a hospital for convalescent officers. Her friends told her that she would never survive the strain.

"Of course it will kill me," she said, "I know that. But what does it matter? I must do my bit."

It didn't kill her. She had the time of her life. There was no convalescent home in France that was more popular. I met her by chance in Paris. She was lunching at the Ritz with a tall and very handsome young Frenchman. She explained that she was there on business connected with the hospital. She told me that the officers were too charming to her. They knew how delicate she was and they wouldn't let her do a single thing. They took care of her, well—as though they were all her husbands. She sighed.

"Poor George, who would ever have thought that I with my heart should survive him?"

"And poor Tom!" I said.

I don't know why she didn't like my saying that. She gave me her plaintive smile and her beautiful eyes filled with tears.

"You always speak as though you grudged me the few years that I can expect to live."

"By the way, your heart's much better, isn't it?"

"It'll never be better. I saw a specialist this morning and he said I must be prepared for the worst."

"Oh, well, you've been prepared for that for nearly twenty years now, haven't you?"

When the war came to an end Louise settled in London. She was now a woman of over forty, thin and frail still, with large eyes and pale cheeks, but she did not look a day more than twenty-five. Iris, who had been at school and was now grown up, came to live with her.

"She'll take care of me," said Louise. "Of course it'll be hard on her to live with such a great invalid as I am, but it can only be for such a little while, I'm sure she won't mind."

Iris was a nice girl. She had been brought up with the knowledge that her mother's health was precarious. As a child she had never been allowed to make a noise. She had always realised that her mother must on no account be upset. And though Louise told her now that she would not hear of her sacrificing herself for a tiresome old woman the girl simply would not listen. It wasn't a question of sacrificing herself, it was a happiness to do what she could for her poor dear mother. With a sigh her mother let her do a great deal.

"It pleases the child to think she's making herself useful," she said.

"Don't you think she ought to go out and about more?" I asked.

"That's what I'm always telling her. I can't get her to enjoy herself. Heaven knows, I never want anyone to put themselves out on my account."

And Iris, when I remonstrated with her, said: "Poor dear mother, she wants me to go and stay with friends and go to parties, but the moment I start off anywhere she has one of her heart attacks, so I much prefer to stay at home."

But presently she fell in love. A young friend of mine, a very good lad, asked her to marry him and she consented. I liked the child and was glad that she was to be given at last the chance to lead a life of her own. She had never seemed to suspect that such a thing was possible. But one day the young man came to me in great distress and told me that his marriage was indefinitely postponed. Iris felt that she could not desert her mother. Of course it was really no business of mine, but I made the opportunity to go and see Louise. She was always glad to receive her friends at teatime and now that she was older she cultivated the society of painters and writers.

"Well, I hear that Iris isn't going to be married," I said after a little.

"I don't know about that. She's not going to be married quite as soon as I could have wished. I've begged her on my bended knees not to consider me, but she absolutely refuses to leave me."

"Don't you think it's rather hard on her?"

"Dreadfully. Of course it can only be for a few months, but I hate the thought of anyone sacrificing themselves for me."

"My dear Louise, you've buried two husbands, I can't see the least reason why you shouldn't bury at least two more."

"Do you think that's funny?" she asked me in a tone that she made as offensive as she could.

"I suppose it's never struck you as strange that you're always strong enough to do anything you want to and that your weak heart only prevents you from doing things that bore you?"

"Oh, I know, I know what you've always thought of me. You've never believed that I had anything the matter with me, have you?"

I looked at her full and square.

"Never. I think you've carried out for twenty-five years a stupendous bluff. I think you're the most selfish and monstrous woman I have ever known. You ruined the lives of those two wretched men you married and now you're going to ruin the life of your daughter."

I should not have been surprised if Louise had had a heart attack then. I fully expected her to fly into a passion. She merely gave me a gentle smile.

"My poor friend, one of these days you'll be so dreadfully sorry you said this to me."

"Have you quite determined that Iris shall not marry this boy?"

"I've begged her to marry him. I know it'll kill me, but I don't mind. Nobody cares for me. I'm just a burden to everybody."

"Did you tell her it would kill you?"

"She made me."

"As if anyone ever made you do anything that you were not yourself quite determined to do."

"She can marry her young man to-morrow if she likes. If it kills me, it kills me."

"Well, let's risk it, shall we?"

"Haven't you got any compassion for me?"

"One can't pity anyone who amuses one as much as you amuse me," I answered.

A faint spot of colour appeared on Louise's pale cheeks and though she smiled still her eyes were hard and angry.

"Iris shall marry in a month's time," she said, "and if anything happens to me I hope you and she will be able to forgive yourselves."

Louise was as good as her word. A date was fixed, a trousseau of great magnificence was ordered, and invitations were issued. Iris and the very good lad were radiant. On the wedding-day, at ten o'clock in the morning, Louise, that devilish woman, had one of her heart attacks—and died. She died gently forgiving Iris for having killed her.

The Promise

MY wife is a very unpunctual woman, so when, having arranged to lunch with her at Claridge's, I arrived there ten minutes late and did not find her I was not surprised. I ordered a cocktail. It was the height of the season and there were but two or three vacant tables in the lounge. Some of the people after an early meal were drinking their coffee, others like myself were toying with a dry Martini; the women in their summer frocks looked gay and charming and the men debonair; but I could see no one whose appearance sufficiently interested me to occupy the quarter of an hour I was expecting to wait. They were slim and pleasant to look upon, well dressed and carelessly at ease, but they were for the most part of a pattern and I observed them with tolerance rather than with curiosity. But it was two o'clock and I felt hungry. My wife tells me that she can neither wear a turquoise nor a watch, for the turquoise turns green and the watch stops; and this she attributes to the malignity of fate. I have nothing to say about the turquoise, but I sometimes think the watch might go if she wound it. I was engaged with these reflections when an attendant came up and with that hushed significance that hotel attendants affect (as though their message held a more sinister meaning than their words suggested) told me that a lady had just telephoned to say that she had been detained and could not lunch with me.

I hesitated. It was not very amusing to eat in a crowded restaurant by oneself, but it was late to go to a club and I decided that I had better stay where I was. I strolled into the dining-room. It has never given me any particular satisfaction (as it appears to do to so many elegant persons) to be known by name to the head waiters of fashionable restaurants, but on this occasion I should certainly have been glad to be greeted by less stony an eye. The *maître d'hôtel* with a set and hostile face told me that every table was occupied. I looked helplessly round the large and stately room and on a sudden to my pleasure caught sight of someone I knew. Lady Elizabeth Vermont was an old friend. She smiled and noticing that she was alone I went up to her.

"Will you take pity on a hungry man and let me sit with you?" I asked.

"Oh, do. But I've nearly finished."

She was at a little table by the side of a massive column and when

I took my place I found that notwithstanding the crowd we sat almost in privacy.

"This is a bit of luck for me," I said. "I was on the point of fainting from hunger."

She had a very agreeable smile; it did not light up her face suddenly, but seemed rather to suffuse it by degrees with charm. It hesitated for a moment about her lips and then slowly travelled to those great shining eyes of hers and there softly lingered. No one surely could say that Elizabeth Vermont was cast in the common mould. I never knew her when she was a girl, but many have told me that then she was so lovely, it brought the tears to one's eyes, and I could well believe it; for now, though fifty, she was still incomparable. Her ravaged beauty made the fresh and blooming comeliness of youth a trifle insipid. I do not like these painted faces that look all alike; and I think women are foolish to dull their expression and obscure their personality with powder, rouge and lipstick. But Elizabeth Vermont painted not to imitate nature, but to improve it; you did not question the means but applauded the result. The flaunting boldness with which she used cosmetics increased rather than diminished the character of that perfect face. I suppose her hair was dyed; it was black and sleek and shining. She held herself upright as though she had never learned to loll and she was very slim. She wore a dress of black satin, the lines and simplicity of which were admirable, and about her neck was a long rope of pearls. Her only other jewel was an enormous emerald which guarded her wedding-ring, and its sombre fire emphasised the whiteness of her hand. But it was in her hands with their reddened nails that she most clearly betrayed her age; they had none of a girl's soft and dimpled roundness; and you could not but look at them with a certain dismay. Before very long they would look like the talons of a bird of prey.

Elizabeth Vermont was a remarkable woman. Of great birth, for she was the daughter of the seventh Duke of St. Erth, she married at the age of eighteen a very rich man and started at once upon a career of astounding extravagance, lewdness and dissipation. She was too proud to be cautious, too reckless to think of consequences, and within two years her husband in circumstances of appalling scandal divorced her. She married then one of the three co-respondents named in the case and eighteen months later ran away from him. Then followed a succession of lovers. She became notorious for her profligacy. Her startling beauty and her scandalous conduct held her in the public eye and it was never very long but that she gave the gossips something to talk about. Her name stank in the nostrils of decent people. She was a gambler, a spendthrift and a wanton. But though unfaithful to her lovers she was constant to her friends and there always remained a few who would never allow, whatever she did, that she was anything but a very nice woman. She had candour, high spirits and courage. She was never a hypocrite. She was generous and sincere. It was at this period of her life that I came to know her; for great ladies, now that religion is out of fashion, when they are very much blown upon take a flattering interest in the arts. When they receive the cold shoulder from members of their own class they condescend sometimes to the society of writers, painters and musicians. I found her an agreeable companion. She was one of those blessed persons who say quite fearlessly what they think (thus saving much useful time) and she had a ready wit. She was always willing to talk (with a diverting humour) of her lurid past. Her conversation, though uninstructed, was good, because, notwithstanding everything, she was an honest woman.

Then she did a very surprising thing. At the age of forty she married a boy of twenty-one. Her friends said it was the maddest act of all her life, and some who had stuck to her through thick and thin, now for the boy's sake, because he was nice and it seemed shameful thus to take advantage of his inexperience, refused to have anything more to do with her. It really was the limit. They prophesied disaster, for Elizabeth Vermont was incapable of sticking to any man for more than six months, nay, they hoped for it, since it seemed the only chance for the wretched youth that his wife should behave so scandalously that he must leave her. They were all wrong. I do not know whether time was responsible for a change of heart in her, or whether Peter Vermont's innocence and simple love touched her, but the fact remains that she made him an admirable wife. They were poor, and she was extravagant, but she became a thrifty housewife; she grew on a sudden so careful of her reputation that the tongue of scandal was silenced. His happiness seemed her only concern. No one could doubt that she loved him devotedly. After being the subject of so much conversation for so long Elizabeth Vermont ceased to be talked about. It looked as though her story were told. She was a changed woman, and I amused myself with the notion that when she was a very old lady, with many years of perfect respectability behind her, the past, the lurid past, would seem to belong not to her but to someone long since dead whom once she had vaguely known. For women have an enviable faculty of forgetting.

But who can tell what the fates have in store? In the twinkling of an eye all was changed. Peter Vermont, after ten years of an ideal marriage, fell madly in love with a girl called Barbara Canton. She was a nice girl, the youngest daughter of Lord Robert Canton who was at one time Under-Secretary for Foreign Affairs, and she was pretty in a fair and fluffy way. Of course she was not for a moment to be compared with Lady Elizabeth. Many people knew what had happened, but no one could tell whether Elizabeth Vermont had any inkling of it, and they wondered how she would meet a situation that was so foreign to her experience. It was always she who had discarded her lovers; none had deserted her. For my part I thought she would make short work of little Miss Canton; I knew her courage and her adroitness. All this was in my mind now while we chatted over our luncheon. There was nothing in her demeanour, as gay, charming and frank as usual, to suggest that anything troubled her. She talked as she always talked, lightly but with good sense and a lively perception of the ridiculous, of the various topics which the course of conversation brought forward. I enjoyed myself. I came to the conclusion that by some miracle she had no notion of Peter's changed feelings and I explained this to myself by the supposition that her love for him was so great, she could not conceive that his for her might be less.

We drank our coffee and smoked a couple of cigarettes, and she asked me the time.

"A quarter to three."

"I must ask for my bill."

"Won't you let me stand you lunch?"

"Of course," she smiled.

"Are you in a hurry?"

"I'm meeting Peter at three."

"Oh, how is he?"

"He's very well."

She gave a little smile, that tardy and delightful smile of hers, but I seemed to discern in it a certain mockery. For an instant she hesitated and she looked at me with deliberation.

"You like curious situations, don't you?" she said. "You'd never guess the errand I'm bound on. I rang up Peter this morning and asked him to meet me at three. I'm going to ask him to divorce me."

"You're not," I cried. I felt myself flush and did not know what to say. "I thought you got on so well together."

"Do you think it's likely that I shouldn't know what all the world knows? I'm really not such a fool as all that."

She was not a woman to whom it was possible to say what one did not believe and I could not pretend that I did not know what she meant. I remained silent for a second or two.

"Why should you allow yourself to be divorced?"

"Robert Canton is a stuffy old thing. I very much doubt if he'd let Barbara marry Peter if I divorced him. And for me, you know, it isn't of the smallest consequence: one divorce more or less . . ."

She shrugged her pretty shoulders.

"How do you know he wants to marry her?"

"He's head over ears in love with her."

"Has he told you so?"

"No. He doesn't even know that I know. He's been so wretched, poor darling. He's been trying so hard not to hurt my feelings."

"Perhaps it's only a momentary infatuation," I hazarded. "It may pass."

"Why should it? Barbara's young and pretty. She's quite nice. They're very well suited to one another. And besides, what good would it do if it did pass? They love each other now and the present in love is all that matters. I'm nineteen years older than Peter. If a man stops loving a woman old enough to be his mother do you think he'll ever come to love her again? You're a novelist, you must know more about human nature than that."

"Why should you make this sacrifice?"

"When he asked me to marry him ten years ago I promised him that when he wanted his release he should have it. You see, there was so great a disproportion between our ages I thought that was only fair."

"And are you going to keep a promise that he hasn't asked you to keep?"

She gave a little flutter of those long thin hands of hers and now I felt that there was something ominous in the dark glitter of that emerald.

"Oh, I must, you know. One must behave like a gentleman. To tell you the truth, that's why I'm lunching here to-day. It was at this table that he proposed to me; we were dining together, you know, and I was sitting just where I am now. The nuisance is that I'm just as much in love with him now as I was then." She paused for a minute and I could see that she clenched her teeth. "Well, I suppose I ought to go. Peter hates one to keep him waiting."

She gave me a sort of little helpless look and it struck me that she simply could not bring herself to rise from her chair. But she smiled and with an abrupt gesture sprang to her feet.

"Would you like me to come with you?"

"As far as the hotel door," she smiled.

We walked through the restaurant and the lounge and when we came to the entrance a porter swung round the revolving doors. I asked if she would like a taxi.

"No, I'd sooner walk, it's such a lovely day." She gave me her hand. "It's been so nice to see you. I shall go abroad to-morrow, but I expect to be in London all the autumn. Do ring me up."

She smiled and nodded and turned away. I watched her walk up Davies Street. The air was still bland and springlike and above the roofs little white clouds were sailing leisurely in a blue sky. She held herself very erect and the poise of her head was gallant. She was a slim and lovely figure so that people looked at her as they passed. I saw her bow graciously to some acquaintance who raised his hat, and I thought that never in a thousand years would it occur to him that she had a breaking heart. I repeat, she was a very honest woman.

A String of Beads

"WHAT a bit of luck that I'm placed next to you," said Laura, as we sat down to dinner.

"For me," I replied politely.

"That remains to be seen. I particularly wanted to have the chance of talking to you. I've got a story to tell you."

At this my heart sank a little.

"I'd sooner you talked about yourself," I answered. "Or even about me."

"Oh, but I must tell you the story. I think you'll be able to use it."

"If you must, you must. But let's look at the menu first."

"Don't you want me to?" she said, somewhat aggrieved. "I thought you'd be pleased."

"I am. You might have written a play and wanted to read me that."

"It happened to some friends of mine. It's perfectly true."

"That's no recommendation. A true story is never quite so true as an invented one."

"What does that mean?"

"Nothing very much," I admitted. "But I thought it sounded well."

"I wish you'd let me get on with it."

"I'm all attention. I'm not going to eat the soup. It's fattening."

She gave me a pinched look and then glanced at the menu. She uttered a little sigh.

"Oh, well, if you're going to deny yourself I suppose I must too. Heaven knows, I can't afford to take liberties with my figure."

"And yet is there any soup more heavenly than the sort of soup in which you put a great dollop of cream?"

"Bortsch," she sighed. "It's the only soup I really like."

"Never mind. Tell me your story and we'll forget about food till the fish comes."

"Well, I was actually there when it happened. I was dining with the Livingstones. Do you know the Livingstones?"

"No, I don't think I do."

"Well, you can ask them and they'll confirm every word I say. They'd asked their governess to come in to dinner because some woman had thrown them over at the last moment—you know how inconsiderate people are—and they would have been thirteen at table. Their governess was a Miss Robinson, quite a nice girl, young, you know, twenty or twenty-one, and rather pretty. Personally I would never engage a governess who was young and pretty. One never knows."

"But one hopes for the best."

Laura paid no attention to my remark.

"The chances are that she'll be thinking of young men instead of attending to her duties and then, just when she's got used to your ways, she'll want to go and get married. But Miss Robinson had excellent references, and I must allow that she was a very nice, respectable person. I believe in point of fact she was a clergyman's daughter.

"There was a man at dinner whom I don't suppose you've ever heard of, but who's quite a celebrity in his way. He's a Count Borselli and he knows more about precious stones than anyone in the world. He was sitting next to Mary Lyngate, who rather fancies herself on her pearls, and in the course of conversation she asked him what he thought of the string she was wearing. He said it was very pretty. She was rather piqued at this and told him it was valued at eight thousand pounds.

" 'Yes, it's worth that,' he said.

"Miss Robinson was sitting opposite to him. She was looking rather nice that evening. Of course I recognised her dress, it was one of Sophie's old ones; but if you hadn't known Miss Robinson was the governess you would never have suspected it.

" 'That's a very beautiful necklace that young lady has on,' said Borselli.

" 'Oh, but that's Mrs. Livingstone's governess,' said Mary Lyngate.

" 'I can't help that,' he said. 'She's wearing one of the finest strings of pearls for its size that I've ever seen in my life. It must be worth fifty thousand pounds.'

" 'Nonsense.'

" 'I give you my word it is.'

"Mary Lyngate leant over. She has rather a shrill voice.

" 'Miss Robinson, do you know what Count Borselli says?' she exclaimed. 'He says that string of pearls you're wearing is worth fifty thousand pounds.'

"Just at that moment there was a sort of pause in the conversation so that everybody heard. We all turned and looked at Miss Robinson. She flushed a little and laughed.

" 'Well, I made a very good bargain,' she said, 'because I paid fifteen shillings for it.'

" 'You certainly did.'

"We all laughed. It was of course absurd. We've all heard of wives palming off on their husbands as false a string of pearls that was real and expensive. The story is as old as the hills."

"Thank you," I said, thinking of a little narrative of my own.

"But it was too ridiculous to suppose that a governess would remain a governess if she owned a string of pearls worth fifty thousand pounds. It was obvious that the Count had made a bloomer. Then an extraordinary thing happened. The long arm of coincidence came in."

"It shouldn't," I retorted. "It's had too much exercise. Haven't you seen that charming book called *A Dictionary of English Usage*?"

"I wish you wouldn't interrupt just when I'm really getting to the exciting point."

But I had to do so again, for just then a young grilled salmon was insinuated round my left elbow.

"Mrs. Livingstone is giving us a heavenly dinner," I said.

"Is salmon fattening?" asked Laura.

"Very," I answered as I took a large helping.

"Bunk," she said.

"Go on," I begged her. "The long arm of coincidence was about to make a gesture."

"Well, at that very moment the butler bent over Miss Robinson and whispered something in her ear. I thought she turned a trifle pale. It's such a mistake not to wear rouge; you never know what tricks nature will play on you. She certainly looked startled. She leant forwards.

" 'Mrs. Livingstone, Dawson says there are two men in the hall who want to speak to me at once.'

" 'Well, you'd better go,' said Sophie Livingstone.

"Miss Robinson got up and left the room. Of course the same thought flashed through all our minds, but I said it first.

" 'I hope they haven't come to arrest her,' I said to Sophie. 'It would be too dreadful for you, my dear.'

" 'Are you sure it was a real necklace, Borselli?' she asked.

" 'Oh, quite.'

" 'She could hardly have had the nerve to wear it to-night if it were stolen,' I said.

"Sophie Livingstone turned as pale as death under her make-up, and I saw she was wondering if everything was all right in her jewel case. I only had on a little chain of diamonds, but instinctively I put my hand up to my neck to feel if it was still there.

" 'Don't talk nonsense,' said Mr. Livingstone. 'How on earth would Miss Robinson have had the chance of sneaking a valuable string of pearls?'

" 'She may be a receiver,' I said.

" 'Oh, but she had such wonderful references,' said Sophie.

" 'They always do,' I said."

I was positively forced to interrupt Laura once more.

"You don't seem to have been determined to take a very bright view of the case," I remarked.

"Of course I knew nothing against Miss Robinson, and I had every reason to think her a very nice girl, but it would have been rather thrilling to find out that she was a notorious thief and a well-known member of a gang of international crooks."

"Just like a film. I'm dreadfully afraid that it's only in films that exciting things like that happen."

"Well, we waited in breathless suspense. There was not a sound. I expected to hear a scuffle in the hall or at least a smothered shriek. I thought the silence very ominous. Then the door opened and Miss Robinson walked in. I noticed at once that the necklace was gone. I could see that she was pale and excited. She came back to the table, sat down and with a smile threw on it . . ."

"On what?"

"On the table, you fool. A string of pearls."

" 'There's my necklace,' she said.

"Count Borselli leant forwards.

" 'Oh, but those are false,' he said.

" 'I told you they were,' she laughed.

" 'That's not the same string that you had on a few moments ago,' he said.

"She shook her head and smiled mysteriously. We were all intrigued. I don't know that Sophie Livingstone was so very much pleased at her governess making herself the centre of interest like that and I thought there was a suspicion of tartness in her manner when she suggested that Miss Robinson had better explain. Well, Miss Robinson said that when she went into the hall she found two men who said they'd come from Jarrot's Stores. She'd bought her string there, as she said, for fifteen shillings, and she'd taken it back because the clasp was loose and had only fetched it that afternoon. The men said they had given her the wrong string. Someone left a string of real pearls to be re-strung and the assistant had made a mistake. Of course I can't understand how anyone could be so stupid as to take a really valuable string to Jarrot's, they aren't used to dealing with that sort of thing, and they wouldn't know real pearls from false; but you know what fools some women are. Anyhow, it was the string Miss Robinson was wearing, and it was valued at fifty thousand pounds. She naturally gave it back to them—she couldn't do anything else, I suppose, though it must have been a wrench—and they returned her own string to her; then they said that although of course they were under no obligation—you know the silly, pompous way men talk when they're trying to be businesslike—they were instructed, as a solatium or whatever you call it, to offer her a cheque for three hundred pounds. Miss Robinson actually showed it to us. She was as pleased as Punch."

"Well, it was a piece of luck, wasn't it?"

"You'd have thought so. As it turned out it was the ruin of her."

"Oh, how was that?"

"Well, when the time came for her to go on her holiday she told Sophie Livingstone that she'd made up her mind to go to Deauville for a month and blue the whole three hundred pounds. Of course Sophie tried to dissuade her, and begged her to put the money in the savings bank, but she wouldn't hear of it. She said she'd never had such a chance before and would never have it again and she meant for at least four weeks to live like a duchess. Sophie couldn't really do anything and so she gave way. She sold Miss Robinson a lot of clothes that she didn't want; she'd been wearing them all through the season and was sick to death of them; she says she gave them to her, but I don't suppose she quite did that—I dare say she sold them very cheap—and Miss Robinson started off, entirely alone, for Deauville. What do you think happened then?"

"I haven't a notion," I replied. "I hope she had the time of her life."

"Well, a week before she was due to come back she wrote to Sophie and said that she'd changed her plans and had entered another profession, and hoped that Mrs. Livingstone would forgive her if she didn't return. Of course poor Sophie was furious. What had actually happened was that Miss Robinson had picked up a rich Argentine in Deauville and had gone off to Paris with him. She's been in Paris ever since. I've seen her myself at Florence's, with bracelets right up to her elbow and ropes of pearls round her neck. Of course I cut her dead. They say she has a house in the Bois de Boulogne and I know she has a Rolls. She threw over the Argentine in a few months and then got hold of a Greek; I don't know who she's with now, but the long and short of it is that she's far and away the smartest cocotte in Paris."

"When you say she was ruined you use the word in a purely technical sense, I conclude," said I.

"I don't know what you mean by that," said Laura. "But don't you think you could make a story out of it?"

"Unfortunately I've already written a story about a pearl necklace. One can't go on writing stories about pearl necklaces."

"I've got half a mind to write it myself. Only, of course, I should change the end."

"Oh, how would you end it?"

"Well, I should have had her engaged to a bank clerk who had been badly knocked about in the war, with only one leg, say, or half his face shot away; and they'd be dreadfully poor and there would be no prospect of their marriage for years, and he would be putting all his savings into buying a little house in the suburbs, and they'd have arranged to marry when he had saved the last instalment. And then she takes him the three hundred pounds and they can hardly believe it, they're so happy, and he cries on her shoulder. He just cries like a child. And they get the little house in the suburbs and they marry, and they have his old mother to live with them, and he goes to the bank every day, and if she's careful not to have babies she can still go out as a daily governess, and he's often ill—with his wound, you know—and she nurses him, and it's all very pathetic and sweet and lovely."

"It sounds rather dull to me," I ventured.

"Yes, but moral," said Laura.

The Yellow Streak

THE two prahus were dropping easily down-stream, one a few yards ahead of the other, and in the first sat the two white men. After seven weeks on the rivers they were glad to know that they would lodge that night in a civilised house. To Izzart, who had been in Borneo since the war, the Dyak houses and their feasts were of course an old story; but Campion, though new to the country and at first amused by the strangeness, hankered too now for chairs to sit on and a bed to sleep in. The Dyaks were hospitable, but no one could say that there was much comfort to be found in their houses, and there was a monotony in the entertainment they offered a guest which presently grew somewhat wearisome. Every evening, as the travellers reached the landing-place, the headman, bearing a flag, and the more important members of the household came down to the river to fetch them. They were led up to the long-house—a village really under one roof, built on piles, to which access was obtained by climbing up the trunk of a tree rudely notched into steps—and to the beating of drums and gongs walked up and down the whole length of it in long procession. On both sides serried throngs of brown people sat on their haunches and stared silently as the white men passed. Clean mats were unrolled and the guests seated themselves. The headman brought a live chicken and, holding it by the legs, waved it three times over their heads, called the spirits loudly to witness and uttered an invocation. Then various persons brought eggs. Arak was drunk. A girl, a very small shy thing with the grace of a flower but with something hieratic in her immobile face, held a cup to the white man's lips till it was empty and then a great shout arose. The men began to dance, one after the other, each treading his little measure, with his shield and his parang, to the accompaniment of drum and gong. After this had gone on for some time the visitors were taken into one of the rooms that led off the long platform on which was led the common life of the household and found their supper prepared for them. The girls fed them with Chinese spoons. Then everyone grew a little drunk and they all talked till the early hours of the morning.

But now their journey was done and they were on their way to the coast. They had started at dawn. The river then was very shallow and ran clear and bright over a shingly bottom; the trees leaned over it so that above there was only a strip of blue sky; but now it had broadened out, and the men were poling no longer but paddling. The trees, bamboos, wild sago like huge bunches of ostrich feathers, trees with enormous leaves and trees with feathery foliage like the acacia, coconut trees and areca palms, with their long straight white stems, the trees on the banks were immensely and violently luxuriant. Here and there, gaunt and naked, was the bare skeleton of a tree struck by lightning or dead of old age, and its whiteness against all that green was vivid. Here and there, rival kings of the forest, tall trees soared above the common level of the jungle. Then there were the parasites; in the fork of two branches great tufts of lush green leaves, or flowering creepers that covered the spreading foliage like a bride's veil; sometimes they wound round a tall trunk, a sheath of splendour, and threw long flowering arms from branch to branch. There was something thrilling in the passionate wildness of that eager growth; it had the daring abandon of the nomad rioting in the train of the god.

The day wore on, and now the heat was no longer so oppressive. Campion looked at the shabby silver watch on his wrist. It could not be long now before they reached their destination.

"What sort of a chap is Hutchinson?" he asked.

"I don't know him. I believe he's a very good sort."

Hutchinson was the Resident in whose house they were to spend the night, and they had sent on a Dyak in a canoe to announce their arrival.

"Well, I hope he's got some whisky. I've drunk enough arak to last me a lifetime."

Campion was a mining engineer whom the Sultan on his way to England had met at Singapore, and finding him at a loose end had commissioned to go to Sembulu and see whether he could discover any mineral which might be profitably worked. He sent Willis, the Resident at Kuala Solor, instructions to afford him every facility, and Willis had put him in the care of Izzart because Izzart spoke both Malay and Dyak like a native. This was the third trip they had made into the interior, and now Campion was to go home with his reports. They were to catch the *Sultan Ahmed*, which was due to pass the mouth of the river at dawn on the next day but one, and with any luck should reach Kuala Solor on the same afternoon. They were both glad to get back to it. There was tennis and golf there, and the club with its billiard tables, food which was relatively good, and the comforts of civilisation. Izzart was glad, too, that he would have other society than Campion's. He gave him a sidelong glance. He was a little man with a big, bald head, and though certainly fifty, strong and wiry; he had quick, shining blue eyes and a stubbly, grey moustache. He was seldom without an old briar pipe between his broken and discoloured teeth. He was neither clean nor neat, his khaki shorts were ragged and his singlet torn; he was wearing now a battered topee. He had knocked about the world since he was eighteen and had been in South Africa, in China, and in Mexico. He was good company; he could tell a story well, and he was prepared to drink and drink again with anyone he met. They had got on very well together, but Izzart had never felt quite at home with him. Though they joked and laughed together, got drunk together, Izzart felt that there was no intimacy between them: for all the cordiality of their relations they remained nothing but acquaintances. He was very sensitive to the impression he made on others, and behind Campion's joviality he had felt a certain coolness; those shining blue eyes had summed him up; and it vaguely irritated Izzart that Campion had formed an opinion of him, and he did not quite know what it was. He was exasperated by the possibility that this common little man did not think entirely well of him. He desired to be liked and admired. He wanted to be popular. He wished the people he met to take an inordinate fancy to him, so that he could either reject them or a trifle condescendingly bestow his friendship on them. His inclination was to be familiar with all and sundry, but he was held back by the fear of a rebuff; sometimes he had been uneasily conscious that his effusiveness surprised the persons he lavished it on.

By some chance he had never met Hutchinson, though of course he knew all about him just as Hutchinson knew all about *him*, and they would have many common friends to talk of. Hutchinson had been at Winchester, and Izzart was glad that he could tell him that he had been at Harrow. . . .

The prahu rounded a bend in the river and suddenly, standing on a slight eminence, they saw the bungalow. In a few minutes they caught sight of the landing-stage and on it, among a little group of natives, a figure in white waving to them.

Hutchinson was a tall, stout man with a red face. His appearance led you to expect that he was breezy and self-confident, so that it was not a little surprising to discover quickly that he was diffident and even a trifle shy. When he shook hands with his guests—Izzart introduced himself and then Campion—and led them up the pathway to the bungalow, though he was plainly anxious to be civil it was not hard to see that he found it difficult to make conversation. He took them out on to the verandah and here they found on the table glasses and whisky and soda. They made themselves comfortable on long chairs. Izzart, conscious of Hutchinson's slight embarrassment with strangers, expanded; he was very hearty and voluble.

He began to speak of their common acquaintances at Kuala Solor, and he managed very soon to slip in casually the information that he had been at Harrow.

"You were at Winchester, weren't you?" he asked.

"Yes."

"I wonder if you knew George Parker. He was in my regiment. He was at Winchester. I daresay he was younger than you."

Izzart felt that it was a bond between them that they had been at these particular schools, and it excluded Campion, who obviously had enjoyed no such advantage. They drank two or three whiskies. Izzart in half an hour began to call his host Hutchie. He talked a good deal about "my regiment" in which he had got his company during the war, and what good fellows his brother officers were. He mentioned two or three names which could hardly be unknown to Hutchinson. They were not the sort of people that Campion was likely to have come across, and he was not sorry to administer to him a neat snub when he claimed acquaintance with someone he spoke of.

"Billie Meadows? I knew a fellow called Billie Meadows in Sinaloa many years ago," said Campion.

"Oh, I shouldn't think it could be the same," said Izzart, with a smile. "Billie's by way of being a peer of the realm. He's the Lord Meadows who races. Don't you remember, he owned Spring Carrots?"

Dinner time was approaching, and after a wash and brush-up they drank a couple of gin pahits. They sat down. Hutchinson had not been to Kuala Solor for the best part of a year, and had not seen another white man for three months. He was anxious to make the most of his visitors. He could give them no wine, but there was plenty of whisky and after dinner he brought out a precious bottle of Benedictine. They were very gay. They laughed and talked a great deal. Izzart was getting on famously. He thought he had never liked a fellow more than Hutchinson, and he pressed him to come down to Kuala Solor as soon as he could. They would have a wonderful beano. Campion was left out of the conversation by Izzart with the faintly malicious intention of putting him in his place, and by Hutchinson through shyness; and presently, after yawning a good deal, he said he would go to bed. Hutchinson showed him to his room and when he returned Izzart said to him:

"You don't want to turn in yet, do you?"

"Not on your life. Let's have another drink."

They sat and talked. They both grew a little drunk. Presently Hutchinson told Izzart that he lived with a Malay girl, and had a couple of children by her. He had told them to keep out of sight while Campion was there.

"I expect she's asleep now," said Hutchinson, with a glance at the door which Izzart knew led into his room, "but I'd like you to see the kiddies in the morning."

Just then a faint wail was heard and Hutchinson with a "Hulloa, the little devil's awake," went to the door and opened it. In a moment or two he came out of the room with a child in his arms. A woman followed him.

"He's cutting his teeth," said Hutchinson. "It makes him restless."

The woman wore a sarong and a thin white jacket and she was barefoot. She was young, with fine dark eyes, and she gave Izzart when he spoke to her a bright and pleasant smile. She sat down and lit a cigarette. She answered the civil questions Izzart put to her without embarrassment, but also without effusion. Hutchinson asked her if she would have a whisky and soda, but she refused. When the two men began to talk again in English she sat on quite quietly, faintly rocking herself in her chair, and occupied with none could tell what calm thoughts.

"She's a very good girl," said Hutchinson. "She looks after the house and she's no trouble. Of course it's the only thing to do in a place like this."

"I shall never do it myself," said Izzart. "After all, one may want to get married and then it means all sorts of botherations."

"But who wants to get married? What a life for a white woman. I wouldn't ask a white woman to live here for anything in the world."

"Of course it's a matter of taste. If I have any kiddies I'm going to see that they have a white mother."

Hutchinson looked down at the little dark-skinned child he held in his arms. He gave a faint smile.

"It's funny how you get to like them," he said. "When they're your own it doesn't seem to matter that they've got a touch of the tar-brush."

The woman gave the child a look, and getting up said she would take it back to bed.

"I should think we'd better all turn in," said Hutchinson. "God knows what the time is."

Izzart went to his room and threw open the shutters which his boy Hassan, whom he was travelling with, had closed. Blowing out the candle so that it should not attract the mosquitoes, he sat down at the window and looked at the soft night. The whisky he had drunk made him feel very wide awake, and he was not inclined to go to bed. He took off his ducks, put on a sarong and lit a cheroot. His good-humour was gone. It was the sight of Hutchinson looking fondly at the half-caste child which had upset him.

"They've got no right to have them," he said to himself. "They've got no chance in the world. Ever."

He passed his hands reflectively along his bare and hairy legs. He shuddered a little. Though he had done everything he could to develop the calves, his legs were like broomsticks. He hated them. He was uneasily conscious of them all the time. They were like a native's. Of course they were the very legs for a top-boot. In his uniform he had looked very well. He was a tall, powerful man, over six feet high, and he had a neat black moustache and neat black hair. His dark eyes were fine and mobile. He was a good-looking fellow and he knew it, and he dressed well, shabbily when shabbiness was good form, and smartly when the occasion demanded. He had loved the army, and it was a bitter blow to him when, at the end of the war, he could not remain in it. His ambitions were simple. He wanted to have two thousand a year, give smart little dinners, go to parties and wear a uniform. He hankered after London.

Of course his mother lived there, and his mother cramped his style. He wondered how on earth he could produce her if ever he got engaged to the girl of good family (with a little money) whom he was looking for to make his wife. Because his father had been dead so long and during the later part of his career was stationed in the most remote of the Malay States, Izzart felt fairly sure that no one in Sembulu knew anything about her, but he lived in terror lest someone, running across her in London, should write over to tell people that she was a half-caste. She had been a beautiful creature when Izzart's father, an engineer in the government service, had married her; but now she was a fat old woman with grey hair who sat about all day smoking cigarettes. Izzart was twelve years old when his father died and then he could speak Malay much more fluently than English. An aunt offered to pay for his education and Mrs. Izzart accompanied her son to England. She lived habitually in furnished apartments, and her rooms with their Oriental draperies and Malay silver were overheated and stuffy. She was for ever in trouble with her landladies because she would leave cigarette-ends about. Izzart hated the way she made friends with them: she would be shockingly familiar with them for a time, then there would be a falling-out, and after a violent scene she would flounce out of the house. Her only amusement was the pictures, and to these she went every day in the week. At home she wore an old and tawdry dressing-gown, but when she went out she dressed herself—but, oh, how untidily—in extravagant colours, so that it was a mortification to her dapper son. He quarrelled with her frequently, she made him impatient and he was ashamed of her; and yet he felt for her a deep tenderness; it was almost a physical bond between them, something stronger than the ordinary feeling of mother and son, so that notwithstanding the failings that exasperated him she was the only person in the world with whom he felt entirely at home.

It was owing to his father's position and his own knowledge of Malay, for his mother always spoke it to him, that after the war, finding himself with nothing to do, he had managed to enter the service of the Sultan of Sembulu. He had been a success. He played games well, he was strong and a good athlete; in the rest-house at Kuala Solor were the cups which he had won at Harrow for running and jumping, and to these he had added since others for golf and tennis. With his abundant fund of small-talk he was an asset at parties and his cheeriness made things go. He ought to have been happy and he was wretched. He wanted so much to be popular, and he had an impression, stronger than ever at this moment, that popularity escaped him. He wondered whether by any chance the men at Kuala Solor with whom he was so hail-fellow-well-met suspected that he had native blood in him. He knew very well what to expect if they ever found out. They wouldn't say he was gay and friendly then, they would say he was damned familiar; and they would say he was inefficient and careless, as the half-castes were, and when he talked of marrying a white woman they would snigger. Oh, it was so unfair! What difference could it make, that drop of native blood in his veins, and yet because of it they would always be on the watch for the expected failure at the critical moment. Everyone knew that you couldn't rely on Eurasians, sooner or later they would let you down; he knew it too, but now he asked himself whether they didn't fail because failure was expected of them. They were never given a chance, poor devils.

But a cock crew loudly. It must be very late and he was beginning to feel chilly. He got into bed. When Hassan brought him his tea next morning he had a racking headache, and when he went in to breakfast he could not look at the porridge and the bacon and eggs which were set before him. Hutchinson too was feeling none too well.

"I fancy we made rather a night of it," said his host, with a smile to conceal his faint embarrassment.

"I feel like hell," said Izzart.

"I'm going to breakfast off a whisky and soda myself," added Hutchinson.

Izzart asked for nothing better, and it was with distaste that they watched Campion eat with healthy appetite a substantial meal. Campion chaffed them.

"By God, Izzart, you're looking green about the gills," he said. "I never saw such a filthy colour."

Izzart flushed. His swarthiness was always a sensitive point with him. But he forced himself to give a cheery laugh.

"You see, I had a Spanish grandmother," he answered, "and when I'm under the weather it always comes out. I remember at Harrow I fought a boy and licked him, because he called me a damned half-caste."

"You are dark," said Hutchinson. "Do Malays ever ask you if you have any native blood in you?"

"Yes, damn their impudence."

A boat with their kit had started early in the morning in order to get to the mouth of the river before them, and tell the skipper of the *Sultan Ahmed*, if by chance he arrived before he was due, that they were on their way. Campion and Izzart were to set out immediately after tiffin in order to arrive at the place where they were to spend the night before the Bore passed. A Bore is a tidal wave that, by reason of a peculiarity in the lie of the land, surges up certain rivers, and there happened to be one on the river on which they were travelling. Hutchinson had talked to them of it the night before and Campion, who had never seen such a thing, was much interested.

"This is one of the best in Borneo. It's worth looking at," said Hutchinson.

He told them how the natives, waiting the moment, rode it and were borne up the river on its crest at a breathless and terrifying speed. He had done it once himself.

"Never no more for me," he said. "I was scared out of my wits."

"I should like to try it once," said Izzart.

"It's exciting enough, but my word, when you're in a flimsy dug-out and you know that if the native doesn't get the right moment you'll be flung in that seething torrent and you won't have a chance in a million . . . no, it's not my idea of sport."

"I've shot a good many rapids in my day," said Campion.

"Rapids be damned. You wait till you see the Bore. It's one of the most terrifying things I know. D'you know that at least a dozen natives are drowned in it in this river alone every year?"

They lounged about on the verandah most of the morning and Hutchinson showed them the court-house. Then gin pahits were served. They drank two or three. Izzart began to feel himself, and when at length tiffin was ready he found that he had an excellent appetite. Hutchinson had boasted of his Malay curry and when the steaming, succulent dishes were placed before them they all set to ravenously. Hutchinson pressed them to drink.

"You've got nothing to do but sleep. Why shouldn't you get drunk?"

He could not bear to let them go so soon, it was good after so long to have white men to talk to, and he lingered over the meal. He urged them to eat. They would have a filthy meal that night at the long-house and nothing to drink but arak. They had better make hay while the sun shone. Campion suggested once or twice that they should start, but Hutchinson, and Izzart too, for now he was feeling very happy and comfortable, assured him there was plenty of time. Hutchinson sent for his precious bottle of Benedictine. They had made a hole in it last night; they might as well finish it before they went.

When at last he walked down with them to the river they were all very merry and none of them was quite steady on his legs. Over the middle of the boat was an attap awning, and under this Hutchinson had had a mattress laid. The crew were prisoners who had been marched down from the jail to row the white men, and they wore dingy sarongs with the prison mark. They waited at their oars. Izzart and Campion shook hands with Hutchinson and threw themselves down on the mattress. The boat pushed off. The turbid river, wide and placid, glistened in the heat of that brilliant afternoon like polished brass. In the distance ahead of them they could see the bank with its tangle of green trees. They felt drowsy, but Izzart at least found a curious enjoyment in resisting for a little while the heaviness that was creeping over him, and he made up his mind that he would not let himself fall asleep till he had finished his cheroot. At last the stub began to burn his fingers and he flung it into the river.

"I'm going to have a wonderful snooze," he said.

"What about the Bore?" asked Campion.

"Oh, that's all right. We needn't worry about that."

He gave a long and noisy yawn. His limbs felt like lead. He had one moment in which he was conscious of his delicious drowsiness and then he knew nothing more. Suddenly he was awakened by Campion shaking him.

"I say, what's that?"

"What's what?"

He spoke irritably, for sleep was still heavy upon him, but with his eyes he followed Campion's gesture. He could hear nothing, but a good way off he saw two or three white-crested waves following one another. They did not look very alarming.

"Oh, I suppose that's the Bore."

"What are we going to do about it?" cried Campion.

Izzart was scarcely yet quite awake. He smiled at the concern in Campion's voice.

"Don't worry. These fellows know all about it. They know exactly what to do. We may get a bit splashed."

But while they were saying these few words the Bore came nearer, very quickly, with a roar like the roar of an angry sea, and Izzart saw that the waves were much higher than he had thought. He did not like the look of them and he tightened his belt so that his shorts should not slip down if the boat were upset. In a moment the waves were upon them. It was a great wall of water that seemed to tower over them, and it might have been ten or twelve feet high, but you could measure it only with your horror. It was quite plain that no boat could weather it. The first wave dashed over them, drenching them all, half filling the boat with water, and then immediately another wave struck them. The boatmen began to shout. They pulled madly at their oars and the steersman yelled an order. But in that surging torrent they were helpless, and it was frightening to see how soon they lost all control of the boat. The force of the water turned it broadside on and it was carried along, helter skelter, upon the crest of the Bore. Another great wave dashed over them and the boat began to sink. Izzart and Campion scrambled out of the covered place in which they had been lying and suddenly the boat gave way under their feet and they found themselves struggling in the water. It surged and stormed around them. Izzart's first impulse was to swim for the shore, but his boy, Hassan, shouted to him to cling to the boat. For a minute or two they all did this.

"Are you all right?" Campion shouted to him.

"Yes, enjoying the bath," said Izzart.

He imagined that the waves would pass by as the Bore ascended the river, and in a few minutes at the outside they would find themselves in calm water once more. He forgot that they were being carried along on its crest. The waves dashed over them. They clung to the gunwale and the base of the structure which supported the attap awning. Then a larger wave caught the boat and it turned over, falling upon them so that they lost their hold; there seemed nothing but a slippery bottom to cling to and Izzart's hands slithered helplessly on the greasy surface. But the boat continued to turn and he made a desperate grab at the gunwale, only to feel it slip out of his hands as the turn went on, then he caught the framework of the awning, and still it turned, turned slowly right round and once more he sought for a hand-hold on the bottom. The boat went round and round with a horrible regularity. He thought this must be because everyone was clinging to one side of it, and he tried to make the crew go round to the other. He could not make them understand. Everyone was shouting and the waves beat against them with a dull and angry roar. Each time the boat rolled over on them Izzart was pushed under water, only to come up again as the gunwale and the framework of the awning gave him something to cling to. The struggle was awful. Presently he began to get terribly out of breath, and he felt his strength leaving him. He knew that he could not hold on much longer, but he did not feel frightened, for his fatigue by now was so great that he did not very much care what happened. Hassan was by his side and he told him he was growing very tired. He thought the best thing was to make a dash for the shore, it did not look more than sixty yards away, but Hassan begged him not to. Still they were being carried along amid those seething, pounding waves. The boat went round and round and they scrambled over it like squirrels in a cage. Izzart swallowed a lot of water. He felt he was very nearly done. Hassan could not help him, but it was a comfort that he was there, for Izzart knew that his boy, used to the water all his life, was a powerful swimmer. Then, Izzart did not know why, for a minute or two the boat held bottom downwards, so that he was able to hold on to the gunwale. It was a precious thing to be able to get his breath. At that moment two dug-outs, with Malays in them riding the Bore, passed swiftly by them. They shouted for help, but the Malays averted their faces and went on. They saw the white men, and did not want to be concerned in any trouble that might befall them. It was agonising to see them go past, callous and indifferent in their safety. But on a sudden the boat rolled round again, round and round, slowly, and the miserable, exhausting scramble repeated itself. It took the heart out of you. But the short respite had helped Izzart, and he was able to struggle a little longer. Then once more he found himself so terribly out of breath that he thought his chest would burst. His strength was all gone, and he did not know now whether he had enough to try to swim for the shore. Suddenly he heard a cry.

"Izart, Izzart. Help. Help."

It was Campion's voice. It was a scream of agony. It sent a shock all through Izzart's nerves. Campion, Campion, what did he care for Campion? Fear seized him, a blind animal fear, and it gave him a new strength. He did not answer.

"Help me, quick, quick," he said to Hassan.

Hassan understood him at once. By a miracle one of the oars was floating quite close to them and he pushed it into Izzart's reach. He placed a hand under Izzart's arm and they struck away from the boat. Izzart's heart was pounding and his breath came with difficulty. He felt horribly weak. The waves beat in his face. The bank looked dreadfully far away. He did not think he could ever reach it. Suddenly the boy cried that he could touch bottom and Izzart put down his legs; but he could feel nothing; he swam a few more exhausted strokes, his eyes fixed on the bank, and then, trying again, felt his feet sink into thick mud. He was thankful. He floundered on and there was the bank within reach of his hands, black mud in which he sank to his knees: he scrambled up, desperate to get out of the cruel water, and when he came to the top he found a little flat with tall rank grass all about it. He and Hassan sank down on it and lay for a while stretched out like dead men. They were so tired that they could not move. They were covered with black mud from head to foot.

But presently Izzart's mind began to work, and a pang of anguish on a sudden shook him. Campion was drowned. It was awful. He did not know how he was going to explain the disaster when he got back to Kuala Solor. They would blame him for it; he ought to have remembered the Bore and told the steersman to make for the bank and tie up the boat when he saw it coming. It wasn't his fault, it was the steersman's, he knew the river; why in God's name hadn't he had the sense to get into safety? How could he have expected that it was possible to ride that horrible torrent? Izzart's limbs shook as he remembered the wall of seething water that rushed down upon them. He must get the body and take it back to Kuala Solor. He wondered whether any of the crew were drowned too. He felt too weak to move, but Hassan now rose and wrang the water out of his sarong; he looked over the river and quickly turned to Izzart.

"Tuan, a boat is coming."

The lalang grass prevented Izzart from seeing anything.

"Shout to them," he said.

Hassan slipped out of view and made his way along the branch of a tree that overhung the water; he cried out and waved. Presently Izzart heard voices. There was a rapid conversation between the boy and the occupants of the boat, and then the boy came back.

"They saw us capsize, Tuan," he said, "and they came as soon as the Bore passed. There's a long-house on the other side. If you will cross the river they will give us sarongs and food and we can sleep there."

Izzart for a moment felt that he could not again trust himself on the face of the treacherous water.

"What about the other tuan?" he asked.

"They do not know."

"If he's drowned they must find the body."

"Another boat has gone up-stream."

Izzart did not know what to do. He was numb. Hassan put his arm round his shoulder and raised him to his feet. He made his way through the thick grass to the edge of the water, and there he saw a dug-out with two Dyaks in it. The river now once more was calm and sluggish; the great wave had passed on and no one would have dreamed that so short a while before the placid surface was like a stormy sea. The Dyaks repeated to him what they had already told the boy. Izzart could not bring himself to speak. He felt that if he said a word he would burst out crying. Hassan helped him to get in, and the Dyaks began to pull across. He fearfully wanted something to smoke, but his cigarettes and his matches, both in a hip-pocket, were soaking. The passage of the river seemed endless. The night fell and when they reached the bank the first stars were shining. He stepped ashore and one of the Dyaks took him up to the long-house. But Hassan seized the paddle he had dropped and with the other pushed out into the stream. Two or three men and some children came down to meet Izzart and he climbed to the house amid a babel of conversation. He went up the ladder and was led with greetings and excited comment to the space where the young men slept. Rattan mats were hurriedly laid to make him a couch and he sank down on them. Someone brought him a jar of arak and he took a long drink; it was rough and fiery, burning his throat, but it warmed his heart. He slipped off his shirt and trousers and put on a dry sarong which someone lent him. By chance he caught sight of the yellow new moon lying on her back, and it gave him a keen, almost a sensual, pleasure. He could not help thinking that he might at that moment be a corpse floating up the river with the tide. The moon had never looked to him more lovely. He began to feel hungry and he asked for rice. One of the women went into a room to prepare it. He was more himself now, and he began to think again of the explanations he would make at Kuala Solor. No one could really blame him because he had gone to sleep; he certainly wasn't drunk, Hutchinson would bear him out there, and how was he to suspect that the steersman would be such a damned fool? It was just rotten luck. But he couldn't think of Campion without a shudder. At last a platter of rice was brought him, and he was just about to start eating when a man ran hurriedly along and came up to him.

M

"The tuan's come," he cried.

"What tuan?"

He jumped up. There was a commotion about the doorway and he stepped forward. Hassan was coming quickly towards him out of the darkness, and then he heard a voice.

"Izzart. Are you there?"

Campion advanced towards him.

"Well, here we are again. By God, that was a pretty near thing, wasn't it? You seem to have made yourself nice and comfortable. My heavens, I could do with a drink."

His dank clothes clung round him, and he was muddy and dishevelled. But he was in excellent spirits.

"I didn't know where the hell they were bringing me. I'd made up my mind that I should have to spend the night on the bank. I thought you were drowned."

"Here's some arak," said Izzart.

Campion put his mouth to the jar and drank and spluttered and drank again.

"Muck, but by God it's strong." He looked at Izzart with a grin of his broken and discoloured teeth. "I say, old man, you look as though you'd be all the better for a wash."

"I'll wash later."

"All right, so will I. Tell them to get me a sarong. How did you get out?" He did not wait for an answer. "I thought I was done for. I owe my life to these two sportsmen here." He indicated with a cheery nod two of the Dyak prisoners whom Izzart vaguely recognised as having been part of their crew. "They were hanging on to that blasted boat on each side of me and somehow they cottoned on to it that I was down and out. I couldn't have lasted another minute. They made signs to me that we could risk having a shot at getting to the bank, but I didn't think I had the strength. By George, I've never been so blown in all my life. I don't know how they managed it, but somehow they got hold of the mattress we'd been lying on, and they made it into a roll. They're sportsmen they are. I don't know why they didn't just save themselves without bothering about me. They gave it me. I thought it a damned poor lifebelt, but I saw the force of the proverb about a drowning man clutching at a straw. I caught hold of the damned thing and between them somehow or other they dragged me ashore."

The danger from which he had escaped made Campion excited and voluble; but Izzart hardly listened to what he said. He heard once more, as distinctly as though the words rang now through the air, Campion's agonised cry for help, and he felt sick with terror

The blind panic raced down his nerves. Campion was talking still, but was he talking to conceal his thoughts? Izzart looked into those bright blue eyes and sought to read the sense behind the flow of words. Was there a hard glint in them or something of cynical mockery? Did he know that Izzart, leaving him to his fate, had cut and run? He flushed deeply. After all, what was there that he could have done? At such a moment it was each for himself and the devil take the hindmost. But what would they say in Kuala Solor if Campion told them that Izzart had deserted him? He ought to have stayed, he wished now with all his heart that he had, but then, then it was stronger than himself, he couldn't. Could anyone blame him? No one who had seen that fierce and seething torrent. Oh, the water and the exhaustion, so that he could have cried!

"If you're as hungry as I am you'd better have a tuck in at this rice," he said.

Campion ate voraciously, but when Izzart had taken a mouthful or two he found that he had no appetite. Campion talked and talked. Izzart listened suspiciously. He felt that he must be alert and he drank more arak. He began to feel a little drunk.

"I shall get into the devil of a row at K.S." he said tentatively.

"I don't know why."

"I was told off to look after you. They won't think it was very clever of me to let you get nearly drowned."

"It wasn't your fault. It was the fault of the damned fool of a steersman. After all, the important thing is that we're saved. By George, I thought I was finished once. I shouted out to you. I don't know if you heard me."

"No, I didn't hear anything. There was such a devil of a row, wasn't there?"

"Perhaps you'd got away before. I don't know exactly when you did get away."

Izzart looked at him sharply. Was it his fancy that there was an odd look in Campion's eyes?

"There was such an awful confusion," he said. "I was just about down and out. My boy threw me over an oar. He gave me to understand you were all right. He told me you'd got ashore."

The oar! He ought to have given Campion the oar and told Hassan, the strong swimmer, to give *him* his help. Was it his fancy again that Campion gave him a quick and searching glance?

"I wish I could have been of more use to you," said Izzart.

"Oh, I'm sure you had enough to do to look after yourself," answered Campion.

The headman brought them cups of arak, and they both drank

a great deal. Izzart's head began to spin and he suggested that they should turn in. Beds had been prepared for them and mosquito nets fixed. They were to set out at dawn on the rest of their journey down the river. Campion's bed was next to his, and in a few minutes he heard him snoring. He had fallen asleep the moment he lay down The young men of the long-house and the prisoners of the boat's crew went on talking late into the night. Izzart's head now was aching horribly and he could not think. When Hassan roused him a day broke it seemed to him that he had not slept at all. Their clothes had been washed and dried, but they were bedraggled objects a they walked along the narrow pathway to the river where the prahu was waiting for them. They rowed leisurely. The morning wa lovely and the great stretch of placid water gleamed in the early light.

"By George, it's fine to be alive," said Campion.

He was grubby and unshaved. He took long breaths, and hi twisted mouth was half open with a grin. You could tell that h found the air singularly good to breathe. He was delighted with the blue sky and the sunshine and the greenness of the trees. Izzar hated him. He was sure that this morning there was a difference in his manner. He did not know what to do. He had a mind to throw himself on his mercy. He had behaved like a cad, but he was sorry he would give anything to have the chance again, but anyone migh have done what he did, and if Campion gave him away he wa ruined. He could never stay in Sembulu; his name would be mud i Borneo and the Straits Settlements. If he made his confession to Campion he could surely get Campion to promise to hold his tongue But would he keep his promise? He looked at him, a shifty littl man: how could he be relied on? Izzart thought of what he had sai the night before. It wasn't the truth, of course, but who could know that? At all events who could prove that he hadn't honestly though that Campion was safe? Whatever Campion said, it was only hi word against Izzart's; he could laugh and shrug his shoulders an say that Campion had lost his head and didn't know what he wa talking about. Besides, it wasn't certain that Campion hadn' accepted his story; in the frightful struggle for life he could be ver sure of nothing. He had a temptation to go back to the subject, bu was afraid if he did that he would excite suspicion in Campion' mind. He *must* hold his tongue. That was his only chance of safety And when they got to K.S. he would get in his story first.

"I should be completely happy now," said Campion, "if I onl had something to smoke."

"We shall be able to get some stinkers on board."

Campion gave a little laugh.

"Human beings are very unreasonable," he said. "At the first moment I was so glad to be alive that I thought of nothing else, but now I'm beginning to regret the loss of my notes and my photographs and my shaving tackle."

Izzart formulated the thought which had lurked at the back of his mind, but which all through the night he had refused to admit into his consciousness.

"I wish to God he'd been drowned. Then I'd have been safe."

"There she is," cried Campion suddenly.

Izzart looked round. They were at the mouth of the river and there was the *Sultan Ahmed* waiting for them. Izzart's heart sank: he had forgotten that she had an English skipper and that he would have to be told the story of their adventure. What would Campion say? The skipper was called Bredon, and Izzart had met him often at Kuala Solor. He was a little bluff man, with a black moustache, and a breezy manner.

"Hurry up," he called out to them, as they rowed up, "I've been waiting for you since dawn." But when they climbed on board his face fell. "Hulloa, what's the matter with you?"

"Give us a drink and you shall hear all about it," said Campion, with his crooked grin.

"Come along."

They sat down under the awning. On a table were glasses, a bottle of whisky and soda-water. The skipper gave an order and in a few minutes they were noisily under way.

"We were caught in the Bore," said Izzart.

He felt he must say something. His mouth was horribly dry notwithstanding the drink.

"Were you, by Jove? You're lucky not to have been drowned. What happened?"

He addressed himself to Izzart because he knew him, but it was Campion who answered. He related the whole incident, accurately, and Izzart listened with strained attention. Campion spoke in the plural when he told the early part of the story, and then, as he came to the moment when they were thrown into the water, changed to the singular. At first it was what *they* had done and now it was what happened to *him*. He left Izzart out of it. Izzart did not know whether to be relieved or alarmed. Why did he not mention him? Was it because in that mortal struggle for life he had thought of nothing but himself or—did he *know*?

"And what happened to you?" said Captain Bredon, turning to Izzart.

Izzart was about to answer when Campion spoke.

"Until I got over to the other side of the river I thought he was drowned. I don't know how he got out. I expect he hardly knows himself."

"It was touch and go," said Izzart with a laugh.

Why had Campion said that? He caught his eye. He was sure now that there was a gleam of amusement in it. It was awful not to be certain. He was frightened. He was ashamed. He wondered if he could not so guide the conversation, either now or later, as to ask Campion whether that was the story he was going to tell in Kuala Solor. There was nothing in it to excite anyone's suspicions. But if nobody else knew, Campion knew. He could have killed him.

"Well, I think you're both of you damned lucky to be alive," said the skipper.

It was but a short run to Kuala Solor, and as they steamed up the Sembulu river Izzart moodily watched the banks. On each side were the mangroves and the nipahs washed by the water, and behind, the dense green of the jungle; here and there, among fruit trees, were Malay houses on piles. Night fell as they docked. Goring, of the police, came on board and shook hands with them. He was living at the rest-house just then, and as he set about his work of seeing the native passengers he told them they would find another man, Porter by name, staying there too. They would all meet at dinner. The boys took charge of their kit, and Campion and Izzart strolled along. They bathed and changed, and at half-past eight the four of them assembled in the common-room for gin pahits.

"I say, what's this Bredon tells me about your being nearly drowned?" said Goring as he came in.

Izzart felt himself flush, but before he could answer Campion broke in, and it seemed certain to Izzart that he spoke in order to give the story as he chose. He felt hot with shame. Not a word was spoken in disparagement of him, not a word was said of him at all; he wondered if those two men who listened, Goring and Porter, thought it strange that he should be left out. He looked at Campion intently as he proceeded with his narration; he told it rather humorously; he did not disguise the danger in which they had been, but he made a joke of it, so that the two listeners laughed at the quandary in which they found themselves.

"A thing that's tickled me since," said Campion, "is that when I got over to the other bank I was black with mud from head to foot. I felt I really ought to jump in the river and have a wash, but you know I felt I'd been in that damned river as much as ever I wanted, and I said to myself: No, by George, I'll go dirty. And when I got into the long-house and saw Izzart as black as I was, I knew he'd felt just like I did."

They laughed and Izzart forced himself to laugh too. He noticed that Campion had told the story in precisely the same words as he had used when he told it to the skipper of the *Sultan Ahmed*. There could be only one explanation of that: he knew, he knew everything, and had made up his mind exactly what story to tell. The ingenuity with which Campion gave the facts and yet left out what must be to Izzart's discredit was devilish. But why was he holding his hand? It wasn't in him not to feel contempt and resentment for the man who had callously deserted him in that moment of dreadful peril. Suddenly, in a flash of inspiration Izzart understood: he was keeping the truth to tell to Willis, the Resident. Izzart had gooseflesh as he thought of confronting Willis. He could deny, but would his denials serve him? Willis was no fool, and he would get at Hassan; Hassan could not be trusted to be silent; Hassan would give him away. Then he would be done for. Willis would suggest that he had better go home.

He had a racking headache, and after dinner he went to his room, for he wanted to be alone so that he could devise a plan of action. And then a thought came to him which made him go hot and cold: he knew that the secret which he had guarded so long was a secret to nobody. He was on a sudden certain of it. Why should he have those bright eyes and that swarthy skin? Why should he speak Malay with such ease and have learned Dyak so quickly? Of course they knew. What a fool he was ever to think that they believed that story of his, about the Spanish grandmother! They must have laughed up their sleeves when he told it, and behind his back they had called him a damned nigger. And now another thought came to him, torturing, and he asked himself whether it was on account of that wretched drop of native blood in him that when he heard Campion cry out his nerve failed him. After all, anyone might at that moment have been seized with panic; and why in God's name should he sacrifice his life to save a man's whom he cared nothing for? It was insane. But of course in K.S. they would say it was only what they expected; they would make no allowances.

At last he went to bed, but when, after tossing about recklessly for God knows how long, he fell asleep, he was awakened by a fearful dream; he seemed to be once more in that raging torrent, with the boat turning, turning; and then there was the desperate clutching at the gunwale, and the agony as it slipped out of his hands, and the water that roared over him. He was wide awake before dawn. His only chance was to see Willis and get his story in first; and he thought over carefully what he was going to say, and chose the very words he meant to use.

He got up early, and in order not to see Campion went out without breakfast. He walked along the high road till such time as he knew the Resident would be in his office, and then walked back again. He sent in his name and was ushered into Willis's room. He was a little elderly man with thin grey hair and a long yellow face.

"I'm glad to see you back safe and sound," he said, shaking hands with Izzart. "What's this I hear about your being nearly drowned?"

Izzart, in clean ducks, his topee spotless, was a fine figure of a man. His black hair was neatly brushed, and his moustache was trimmed. He had an upright and soldierly bearing.

"I thought I'd better come and tell you at once, sir, as you told me to look after Campion."

"Fire away."

Izzart told his story. He made light of the danger. He gave Willis to understand that it had not been very great. They would never have been upset if they had not started so late.

"I tried to get Campion away earlier, but he'd had two or three drinks and the fact is, he didn't want to move."

"Was he tight?"

"I don't know about that," smiled Izzart good-humouredly. "I shouldn't say he was cold sober."

He went on with his story. He managed to insinuate that Campion had lost his head a little. Of course it was a very frightening business to a man who wasn't a decent swimmer: he, Izzart, had been more concerned for Campion than for himself; he knew the only chance was to keep cool, and the moment they were upset he saw that Campion had got the wind up.

"You can't blame him for that," said the Resident.

"Of course I did everything I possibly could for him, sir, but the fact is, there wasn't anything much I could do."

"Well, the great thing is that you both escaped. It would have been very awkward for all of us if he'd been drowned."

"I thought I'd better come and tell you the facts before you saw Campion, sir. I fancy he's inclined to talk rather wildly about it. There's no use exaggerating."

"On the whole your stories agree pretty well," said Willis, with a little smile.

Izzart looked at him blankly.

"Haven't you seen Campion this morning? I heard from Goring that there'd been some trouble, and I looked in last night on my way home from the Fort after dinner. You'd already gone to bed."

Izzart felt himself trembling, and he made a great effort to preserve his composure.

"By the way, you got away first, didn't you?"

"I don't really know, sir. You see, there was a lot of confusion."

"You must have if you got over to the other side before he did."

"I suppose I did then."

"Well, thanks for coming to tell me," said Willis, rising from his chair.

As he did so he knocked some books on the floor. They fell with a sudden thud. The unexpected sound made Izzart start violently, and he gave a gasp. The Resident looked at him quickly.

"I say, your nerves are in a pretty state."

Izzart could not control his trembling.

"I'm very sorry, sir," he murmured.

"I expect it's been a shock. You'd better take it easy for a few days. Why don't you get the doctor to give you something?"

"I didn't sleep very well last night."

The Resident nodded as though he understood. Izzart left the room, and as he passed out some man he knew stopped and congratulated him on his escape. They all knew of it. He walked back to the rest-house. And as he walked, he repeated to himself the story he had told the Resident. Was it really the same story that Campion had told? He had never suspected that the Resident had already heard it from Campion. What a fool he had been to go to bed! He should never have let Campion out of his sight. Why had the Resident listened without telling him that he already knew? Now Izzart cursed himself for having suggested that Campion was drunk and had lost his head. He had said this in order to discredit him, but he knew now that it was a stupid thing to do. And why had Willis said that about his having got away first? Perhaps he was holding his hand too; perhaps he was going to make inquiries; Willis was very shrewd. But what exactly had Campion said? He must know that; at whatever cost he must know. Izzart's mind was seething, so that he felt he could hardly keep a hold on his thoughts, but he must keep calm. He felt like a hunted animal. He did not believe that Willis liked him; once or twice in the office he had blamed him because he was careless; perhaps he was just waiting till he got all the facts. Izzart was almost hysterical.

He entered the rest-house and there, sitting on a long chair, with his legs stretched out, was Campion. He was reading the papers which had arrived during their absence in the jungle. Izzart felt a blind rush of hatred well up in him as he looked at the little, shabby man who held him in the hollow of his hand.

"Hulloa," said Campion, looking up. "Where have you been?"

To Izzart it seemed that there was in his eyes a mocking irony. He clenched his hands, and his breath came fast.

"What have you been saying to Willis about me?" he asked abruptly.

The tone in which he put the unexpected question was so harsh that Campion gave him a glance of faint surprise.

"I don't think I've been saying anything very much about you. Why?"

"He came here last night."

Izzart looked at him intently. His brows were drawn together in an angry frown as he tried to read Campion's thoughts.

"I told him you'd gone to bed with a headache. He wanted to know about our mishap."

"I've just seen him."

Izzart walked up and down the large and shaded room; now, though it was still early, the sun was hot and dazzling. He felt himself in a net. He was blind with rage; he could have seized Campion by the throat and strangled him, and yet, because he did not know what he had to fight against, he felt himself powerless. He was tired and ill, and his nerves were shaken. On a sudden the anger which had given him a sort of strength left him, and he was filled with despondency. It was as though water and not blood ran through his veins; his heart sank and his knees seemed to give way. He felt that if he did not take care, he would begin to cry. He was dreadfully sorry for himself.

"Damn you, I wish to God I'd never set eyes on you," he cried pitifully.

"What on earth's the matter?" asked Campion, with astonishment.

"Oh, don't pretend. We've been pretending for two days, and I'm fed up with it." His voice rose shrilly, it sounded odd in that robust and powerful man. "I'm fed up with it. I cut and run. I left you to drown. I know I behaved like a skunk. I couldn't help it."

Campion rose slowly from his chair.

"What *are* you talking about?"

His tone was so genuinely surprised that it gave Izzart a start. A cold shiver ran down his spine.

"When you called for help I was panic-stricken. I just caught hold of an oar and got Hassan to help me get away."

"That was the most sensible thing you could do."

"I couldn't help you. There wasn't a thing I could do."

"Of course not. It was damned silly of me to shout. It was waste of breath, and breath was the very thing I wanted."

"Do you mean to say you didn't know?"

"When those fellows got me the mattress, I thought you were still clinging to the boat. I had an idea that I got away before you did."

Izzart put both his hands to his head, and gave a hoarse cry of despair.

"My God, what a fool I've been."

The two men stood for a while staring at one another. The silence seemed endless.

"What are you going to do now?" asked Izzart at last.

"Oh, my dear fellow, don't worry. I've been frightened too often myself to blame anyone who shows the white feather. I'm not going to tell a soul."

"Yes, but you *know*."

"I promise you, you can trust me. Besides, my job's done here and I'm going home. I want to catch the next boat to Singapore." There was a pause, and Campion looked for a while reflectively at Izzart. "There's only one thing I'd like to ask you: I've made a good many friends here, and there are one or two things I'm a little sensitive about; when you tell the story of our upset, I should be grateful if you wouldn't make out that I had behaved badly. I wouldn't like the fellows here to think that I'd lost my nerve."

Izzart flushed darkly. He remembered what he had said to the Resident. It almost looked as though Campion had been listening over his shoulder. He cleared his throat.

"I don't know why you think I should do that."

Campion chuckled good-naturedly, and his blue eyes were gay with amusement.

"The yellow streak," he replied, and then, with a grin that showed his broken and discoloured teeth: "Have a cheroot, dear boy."

The Force of Circumstance

SHE was sitting on the verandah waiting for her husband to come in for luncheon. The Malay boy had drawn the blinds when the morning lost its freshness, but she had partly raised one of them so that she could look at the river. Under the breathless sun of midday it had the white pallor of death. A native was paddling along in a dug-out so small that it hardly showed above the surface of the water. The colours of the day were ashy and wan. They were but the various tones of the heat. (It was like an Eastern melody, in the minor key, which exacerbates the nerves by its ambiguous monotony; and the ear awaits impatiently a resolution, but waits in vain.) The cicadas sang their grating song with a frenzied energy; it was as continual and monotonous as the rustling of a brook over the stones; but on a sudden it was drowned by the loud singing of a bird, mellifluous and rich; and for an instant, with a catch at her heart, she thought of the English blackbird.

Then she heard her husband's step on the gravel path behind the bungalow, the path that led to the court-house in which he had been working, and she rose from her chair to greet him. He ran up the short flight of steps, for the bungalow was built on piles, and at the door the boy was waiting to take his topee. He came into the room which served them as a dining-room and parlour, and his eyes lit up with pleasure as he saw her.

"Hulloa, Doris. Hungry?"

"Ravenous."

"It'll only take me a minute to have a bath and then I'm ready."

"Be quick," she smiled.

He disappeared into his dressing-room and she heard him whistling cheerily while, with the carelessness with which she was always remonstrating, he tore off his clothes and flung them on the floor. He was twenty-nine, but he was still a school-boy; he would never grow up. That was why she had fallen in love with him, perhaps, for no amount of affection could persuade her that he was good-looking. He was a little round man, with a red face like the full moon, and blue eyes. He was rather pimply. She had examined him carefully and had been forced to confess to him that he had not a single feature which she could praise. She had told him often that he wasn't her type at all.

"I never said I was a beauty," he laughed.

"I can't think what it is I see in you."

But of course she knew perfectly well. He was a gay, jolly little man, who took nothing very solemnly, and he was constantly laughing. He made her laugh too. He found life an amusing rather than a serious business, and he had a charming smile. When she was with him she felt happy and good-tempered. And the deep affection which she saw in those merry blue eyes of his touched her. It was very satisfactory to be loved like that. Once, sitting on his knees, during their honeymoon she had taken his face in her hands and said to him:

"You're an ugly, little fat man, Guy, but you've got charm. I can't help loving you."

A wave of emotion swept over her and her eyes filled with tears. She saw his face contorted for a moment with the extremity of his feeling and his voice was a little shaky when he answered.

"It's a terrible thing for me to have married a woman who's mentally deficient," he said.

She chuckled. It was the characteristic answer which she would have liked him to make.

It was hard to realise that nine months ago she had never even heard of him. She had met him at a small place by the seaside where she was spending a month's holiday with her mother. Doris was secretary to a member of parliament. Guy was home on leave. They were staying at the same hotel, and he quickly told her all about himself. He was born in Sembulu, where his father had served for thirty years under the second Sultan, and on leaving school he had entered the same service. He was devoted to the country.

"After all, England's a foreign land to me," he told her. "My home's Sembulu."

And now it was her home too. He asked her to marry him at the end of the month's holiday. She had known he was going to, and had decided to refuse him. She was her widowed mother's only child and she could not go so far away from her, but when the moment came she did not quite know what happened to her, she was carried off her feet by an unexpected emotion, and she accepted him. They had been settled now for four months in the little outstation of which he was in charge. She was very happy.

She told him once that she had quite made up her mind to refuse him.

"Are you sorry you didn't?" he asked, with a merry smile in his twinkling blue eyes.

"I should have been a perfect fool if I had. What a bit of luck that fate or chance or whatever it was stepped in and took the matter entirely out of my hands!"

Now she heard Guy clatter down the steps to the bath-house. He was a noisy fellow and even with bare feet he could not be quiet. But he uttered an exclamation. He said two or three words in the local dialect and she could not understand. Then she heard someone speaking to him, not aloud, but in a sibilant whisper. Really it was too bad of people to waylay him when he was going to have his bath. He spoke again and though his voice was low she could hear that he was vexed. The other voice was raised now; it was a woman's. Doris supposed it was someone who had a complaint to make. It was like a Malay woman to come in that surreptitious way. But she was evidently getting very little from Guy, for she heard him say: Get out. That at all events she understood, and then she heard him bolt the door. There was a sound of the water he was throwing over himself (the bathing arrangements still amused her, the bath-houses were under the bedrooms, on the ground; you had a large tub of water and you sluiced yourself with a little tin pail) and in a couple of minutes he was back again in the dining-room. His hair was still wet. They sat down to luncheon.

"It's lucky I'm not a suspicious or a jealous person," she laughed. "I don't know that I should altogether approve of your having animated conversations with ladies while you're having your bath."

His face, usually so cheerful, had borne a sullen look when he came in, but now it brightened.

"I wasn't exactly pleased to see her."

"So I judged by the tone of your voice. In fact, I thought you were rather short with the young person."

"Damned cheek, waylaying me like that!"

"What did she want?"

"Oh, I don't know. It's a woman from the kampong. She's had a row with her husband or something."

"I wonder if it's the same one who was hanging about this morning."

He frowned a little.

"Was there someone hanging about?"

"Yes, I went into your dressing-room to see that everything was nice and tidy, and then I went down to the bath-house. I saw someone slink out of the door as I went down the steps and when I looked out I saw a woman standing there."

"Did you speak to her?"

"I asked her what she wanted and she said something, but I couldn't understand."

"I'm not going to have all sorts of stray people prowling about here," he said. "They've got no right to come."

He smiled, but Doris, with the quick perception of a woman in love, noticed that he smiled only with his lips, not as usual with his eyes also, and wondered what it was that troubled him.

"What have you been doing this morning?" he asked.

"Oh, nothing much. I went for a little walk."

"Through the kampong?"

"Yes. I saw a man send a chained monkey up a tree to pick coconuts, which rather thrilled me."

"It's rather a lark, isn't it?"

"Oh, Guy, there were two little boys watching him who were much whiter than the others. I wondered if they were half-castes. I spoke to them, but they didn't know a word of English."

"There are two or three half-caste children in the kampong," he answered.

"Who do they belong to?"

"Their mother is one of the village girls."

"Who is their father?"

"Oh, my dear, that's the sort of question we think it a little dangerous to ask out here." He paused. "A lot of fellows have native wives, and then when they go home or marry they pension them off and send them back to their village."

Doris was silent. The indifference with which he spoke seemed a little callous to her. There was almost a frown on her frank, open, pretty English face when she replied.

"But what about the children?"

"I have no doubt they're properly provided for. Within his means, a man generally sees that there's enough money to have them decently educated. They get jobs as clerks in a government office, you know; they're all right."

She gave him a slightly rueful smile.

"You can't expect me to think it's a very good system."

"You mustn't be too hard," he smiled back.

"I'm not hard. But I'm thankful you never had a Malay wife. I should have hated it. Just think if those two little brats were yours."

The boy changed their plates. There was never much variety in their menu. They started luncheon with river fish, dull and insipid, so that a good deal of tomato ketchup was needed to make it palatable, and then went on to some kind of stew. Guy poured Worcester Sauce over it.

"The old Sultan didn't think it was a white woman's country," he said presently. "He rather encouraged people to—keep house with native girls. Of course things have changed now. The country's perfectly quiet and I suppose we know better how to cope with the climate."

"But, Guy, the eldest of those boys wasn't more than seven or eight and the other was about five."

"It's awfully lonely on an outstation. Why, often one doesn't see another white man for six months on end. A fellow comes out here when he's only a boy." He gave her that charming smile of his which transfigured his round, plain face. "There are excuses, you know."

She always found that smile irresistible. It was his best argument. Her eyes grew once more soft and tender.

"I'm sure there are." She stretched her hand across the little table and put it on his. "I'm very lucky to have caught you so young. Honestly, it would upset me dreadfully if I were told that you had lived like that."

He took her hand and pressed it.

"Are you happy here, darling?"

"Desperately."

She looked very cool and fresh in her linen frock. The heat did not distress her. She had no more than the prettiness of youth, though her brown eyes were fine; but she had a pleasing frankness of expression, and her dark, short hair was neat and glossy. She gave you the impression of a girl of spirit and you felt sure that the member of parliament for whom she worked had in her a very competent secretary.

"I loved the country at once," she said. "Although I'm alone so much I don't think I've ever once felt lonely."

Of course she had read novels about the Malay Archipelago and she had formed an impression of a sombre land with great ominous rivers and a silent, impenetrable jungle. When the little coasting steamer set them down at the mouth of the river, where a large boat, manned by a dozen Dyaks, was waiting to take them to the station, her breath was taken away by the beauty, friendly rather than awe-inspiring, of the scene. It had a gaiety, like the joyful singing of birds in the trees, which she had never expected. On each bank of the river were mangroves and nipah palms, and behind them the dense green of the forest. In the distance stretched blue mountains, range upon range, as far as the eye could see. She had no sense of confinement nor of gloom, but rather of openness and wide spaces where the exultant fancy could wander with delight. The green glittered in the sunshine and the sky was blithe and cheerful. The gracious land seemed to offer her a smiling welcome.

They rowed on, hugging a bank, and high overhead flew a pair of doves. A flash of colour, like a living jewel, dashed across their path. It was a kingfisher. Two monkeys, with their dangling tails, sat side by side on a branch. On the horizon, over there on the other side of the broad and turbid river, beyond the jungle, was a row of little white clouds, the only clouds in the sky, and they looked like a row of ballet-girls, dressed in white, waiting at the back of the stage, alert and merry, for the curtain to go up. Her heart was filled with joy; and now, remembering it all, her eyes rested on her husband with a grateful, assured affection.

And what fun it had been to arrange their living-room! It was very big. On the floor, when she arrived, was a torn and dirty matting; on the walls of unpainted wood hung (much too high up) photogravures of Academy pictures, Dyak shields and parangs. The tables were covered with Dyak cloth in sombre colours, and on them stood pieces of Brunei brass-ware, much in need of cleaning, empty cigarette tins and bits of Malay silver. There was a rough wooden shelf with cheap editions of novels and a number of old travel books in battered leather; and another shelf was crowded with empty bottles. It was a bachelor's room, untidy but stiff; and though it amused her she found it intolerably pathetic. It was a dreary, comfortless life that Guy had led there, and she threw her arms round his neck and kissed him.

"You poor darling," she laughed.

She had deft hands and she soon made the room habitable. She arranged this and that, and what she could not do with she turned out. Her wedding-presents helped. Now the room was friendly and comfortable. In glass vases were lovely orchids and in great bowls huge masses of flowering shrubs. She felt an inordinate pride because it was her house (she had never in her life lived in anything but a poky flat) and she had made it charming for him.

"Are you pleased with me?" she asked when she had finished.

"Quite," he smiled.

The deliberate understatement was much to her mind. How jolly it was that they should understand each other so well! They were both of them shy of displaying emotion, and it was only at rare moments that they used with one another anything but ironic banter.

They finished luncheon and he threw himself into a long chair to have a sleep. She went towards her room. She was a little surprised that he drew her to him as she passed and, making her bend down, kissed her lips. They were not in the habit of exchanging embraces at odd hours of the day.

"A full tummy is making you sentimental, my poor lamb," she chaffed him.

"Get out and don't let me see you again for at least two hours."

"Don't snore."

She left him. They had risen at dawn and in five minutes were fast asleep.

Doris was awakened by the sound of her husband's splashing in the bath-house. The walls of the bungalow were like a sounding-board and not a thing that one of them did escaped the other. She felt too lazy to move, but she heard the boy bring the tea things in, so she jumped up and ran down into her own bath-house. The water, not cold but cool, was deliciously refreshing. When she came into the sitting-room Guy was taking the rackets out of the press, for they played tennis in the short cool of the evening. The night fell at six.

The tennis-court was two or three hundred yards from the bungalow and after tea, anxious not to lose time, they strolled down to it.

"Oh, look," said Doris, "there's that girl that I saw this morning."

Guy turned quickly. His eyes rested for a moment on a native woman, but he did not speak.

"What a pretty sarong she's got," said Doris. "I wonder where it comes from."

They passed her. She was slight and small, with the large, dark, starry eyes of her race and a mass of raven hair. She did not stir as they went by, but stared at them strangely. Doris saw then that she was not quite so young as she had at first thought. Her features were a trifle heavy and her skin was dark, but she was very pretty. She held a small child in her arms. Doris smiled a little as she saw it, but no answering smile moved the woman's lips. Her face remained impassive. She did not look at Guy, she looked only at Doris, and he walked on as though he did not see her. Doris turned to him.

"Isn't that baby a duck?"

"I didn't notice."

She was puzzled by the look of his face. It was deathly white, and the pimples which not a little distressed her were more than commonly red.

"Did you notice her hands and feet? She might be a duchess."

"All natives have good hands and feet," he answered, but not jovially as was his wont; it was as though he forced himself to speak.

But Doris was not intrigued.

"Who is she, d'you know?"

"She's one of the girls in the kampong."

They had reached the court now. When Guy went up to the net to see that it was taut he looked back. The girl was still standing where they had passed her. Their eyes met.

"Shall I serve?" said Doris.

"Yes, you've got the balls on your side."

He played very badly. Generally he gave her fifteen and beat her, but to-day she won easily. And he played silently. Generally he was a noisy player, shouting all the time, cursing his foolishness when he missed a ball and chaffing her when he placed one out of her reach.

"You're off your game, young man," she cried.

"Not a bit," he said.

He began to slam the balls, trying to beat her, and sent one after the other into the net. She had never seen him with that set face. Was it possible that he was a little out of temper because he was not playing well? The light fell, and they ceased to play. The woman whom they had passed stood in exactly the same position as when they came and once more, with expressionless face, she watched them go.

The blinds on the verandah were raised now and on the table between their two long chairs were bottles and soda-water. This was the hour at which they had the first drink of the day and Guy mixed a couple of gin slings. The river stretched widely before them and on the further bank the jungle was wrapped in the mystery of the approaching night. A native was silently rowing up-stream, standing at the bow of the boat, with two oars.

"I played like a fool," said Guy, breaking a silence. "I'm feeling a bit under the weather."

"I'm sorry. You're not going to have fever, are you?"

"Oh, no. I shall be all right to-morrow."

Darkness closed in upon them. The frogs croaked loudly and now and then they heard a few short notes from some singing bird of the night. Fireflies flitted across the verandah and they made the trees that surrounded it look like Christmas trees lit with tiny candles. They sparkled softly. Doris thought she heard a little sigh. It vaguely disturbed her. Guy was always so full of gaiety.

"What is it, old man?" she said gently. "Tell mother."

"Nothing. Time for another drink," he answered breezily.

Next day he was as cheerful as ever and the mail came. The coasting steamer passed the mouth of the river twice a month, once on its way to the coalfields and once on its way back. On the outward journey it brought mail, which Guy sent a boat down to fetch. Its arrival was the excitement of their uneventful lives. For the first day or two they skimmed rapidly all that had come, letters, English papers and papers from Singapore, magazines and books, leaving for the ensuing weeks a more exact perusal. They snatched the illustrated papers from one another. If Doris had not been so absorbed she might have noticed that there was a change in Guy. She would have found it hard to describe and harder still to explain. There was in his eyes a sort of watchfulness and in his mouth a slight droop of anxiety.

Then, perhaps a week later, one morning when she was sitting in the shaded room studying a Malay grammar (for she was industriously learning the language) she heard a commotion in the compound. She heard the house boy's voice, he was speaking angrily, the voice of another man, perhaps it was the water-carrier's, and then a woman's, shrill and vituperative. There was a scuffle. She went to the window and opened the shutters. The water-carrier had hold of a woman's arm and was dragging her along, while the house boy was pushing her from behind with both hands. Doris recognised her at once as the woman she had seen one morning loitering in the compound and later in the day outside the tennis-court. She was holding a baby against her breast. All three were shouting angrily.

"Stop," cried Doris. "What are you doing?"

At the sound of her voice the water-carrier let go suddenly and the woman, still pushed from behind, fell to the ground. There was a sudden silence and the house boy looked sullenly into space. The water-carrier hesitated a moment and then slunk away. The woman raised herself slowly to her feet, arranged the baby on her arm, and stood impassive, staring at Doris. The boy said something to her which Doris could not have heard even if she had understood; the woman by no change of face showed that his words meant anything to her; but she slowly strolled away. The boy followed her to the gate of the compound. Doris called to him as he walked back, but he pretended not to hear. She was growing angry now and she called more sharply.

"Come here at once," she cried.

Sullenly, avoiding her wrathful glance, he came towards the bungalow. He came in and stood at the door. He looked at her sulkily.

"What were you doing with that woman?" she asked abruptly.

"Tuan say she no come here."

"You mustn't treat a woman like that. I won't have it. I shall tell the tuan exactly what I saw."

The boy did not answer. He looked away, but she felt that he was watching her through his long eyelashes. She dismissed him.

"That'll do."

Without a word he turned and went back to the servants' quarters. She was exasperated and she found it impossible to give her attention once more to the Malay exercises. In a little while the boy came in to lay the cloth for luncheon. On a sudden he went to the door.

"What is it?" she asked.

"Tuan just coming."

He went out to take Guy's hat from him. His quick ears had caught the footsteps before they were audible to her. Guy did not as usual come up the steps immediately; he paused, and Doris at once surmised that the boy had gone down to meet him in order to tell him of the morning's incident. She shrugged her shoulders. The boy evidently wanted to get his story in first. But she was astonished when Guy came in. His face was ashy.

"Guy, what on earth's the matter?"

He flushed a sudden hot red.

"Nothing. Why?"

She was so taken aback that she let him pass into his room without a word of what she had meant to speak of at once. It took him longer than usual to have his bath and change his clothes and luncheon was served when he came in.

"Guy," she said, as they sat down, "that woman we saw the other day was here again this morning."

"So I've heard," he answered.

"The boys were treating her brutally. I had to stop them. You must really speak to them about it."

Though the Malay understood every word she said, he made no sign that he heard. He handed her the toast.

"She's been told not to come here. I gave instructions that if she showed herself again she was to be turned out."

"Were they obliged to be so rough?"

"She refused to go. I don't think they were any rougher than they could help."

"It was horrible to see a woman treated like that. She had a baby in her arms."

"Hardly a baby. It's three years old."

"How d'you know?"

"I know all about her. She hasn't the least right to come here pestering everybody."

"What does she want?"

"She wants to do exactly what she did. She wants to make a disturbance."

For a little while Doris did not speak. She was surprised at her husband's tone. He spoke tersely. He spoke as though all this were no concern of hers. She thought him a little unkind. He was nervous and irritable.

"I doubt if we shall be able to play tennis this afternoon," he said. "It looks to me as though we were going to have a storm."

The rain was falling when she awoke and it was impossible to go out. During tea Guy was silent and abstracted. She got her sewing and began to work. Guy sat down to read such of the English papers as he had not yet gone through from cover to cover; but he was restless; he walked up and down the large room and then went out on the verandah. He looked at the steady rain. What was he thinking of? Doris was vaguely uneasy.

It was not till after dinner that he spoke. During the simple meal he had exerted himself to be his usual gay self, but the exertion was apparent. The rain had ceased and the night was starry. They sat on the verandah. In order not to attract insects they had put out the lamp in the sitting-room. At their feet, with a mighty, formidable sluggishness, silent, mysterious and fatal, flowed the river. It had the terrible deliberation and the relentlessness of destiny.

"Doris, I've got something to say to you," he said suddenly.

His voice was very strange. Was it her fancy that he had difficulty in keeping it quite steady? She felt a little pang in her heart because he was in distress, and she put her hand gently into his. He drew it away.

"It's rather a long story. I'm afraid it's not a very nice one and I find it rather difficult to tell. I'm going to ask you not to interrupt me, or to say anything, till I've finished."

In the darkness she could not see his face, but she felt that it was haggard. She did not answer. He spoke in a voice so low that it hardly broke the silence of the night.

"I was only eighteen when I came out here. I came straight from school. I spent three months in Kuala Solor, and then I was sent to a station up the Sembulu river. Of course there was a Resident there and his wife. I lived in the court-house, but I used to have my meals with them and spend the evening with them. I had an awfully good time. Then the fellow who was here fell ill and had to go home. We were short of men on account of the war and I was put in charge of this place. Of course I was very young, but I spoke the language like a native, and they remembered my father. I was as pleased as Punch to be on my own."

He was silent while he knocked the ashes out of his pipe and refilled it. When he lit a match Doris, without looking at him, noticed that his hand was unsteady.

"I'd never been alone before. Of course at home there'd been father and mother and generally an assistant. And then at school naturally there were always fellows about. On the way out, on the boat, there were people all the time, and at K.S., and the same at my first post. The people there were almost like my own people. I seemed always to live in a crowd. I like people. I'm a noisy blighter. I like to have a good time. All sorts of things make me laugh and you must have somebody to laugh with. But it was different here. Of course it was all right in the day time; I had my work and I could talk to the Dyaks. Although they were head-hunters in those days and now and then I had a bit of trouble with them, they were an awfully decent lot of fellows. I got on very well with them. Of course I should have liked a white man to gas to, but they were better than nothing, and it was easier for me because they didn't look upon me quite as a stranger. I liked the work too. It was rather lonely in the evening to sit on the verandah and drink a gin and bitters by myself, but I could read. And the boys were about. My own boy was called Abdul. He'd known my father. When I got tired of reading I could give him a shout and have a bit of a jaw with him.

"It was the nights that did for me. After dinner the boys shut up and went away to sleep in the kampong. I was all alone. There wasn't a sound in the bungalow except now and then the croak of the chik-chak. It used to come out of the silence, suddenly, so that it made me jump. Over in the kampong I heard the sound of a gong or fire-crackers. They were having a good time, they weren't so far away, but I had to stay where I was. I was tired of reading. I couldn't have been more of a prisoner if I'd been in jail. Night after night it was the same. I tried drinking three or four whiskies, but it's poor fun drinking alone, and it didn't cheer me up; it only made me feel rather rotten next day. I tried going to bed immediately after dinner, but I couldn't sleep. I used to lie in bed, getting hotter and hotter, and more wide awake, till I didn't know what to do with myself. By George, those nights were long. D'you know, I got so low, I was so sorry for myself that sometimes—it makes me laugh now when I think of it, but I was only nineteen and a half—sometimes I used to cry.

"Then, one evening, after dinner, Abdul had cleared away and was just going off, when he gave a little cough. He said, wasn't I lonely in the house all night by myself? 'Oh, no, that's all right,' I said. I didn't want him to know what a damned fool I was, but I expect he knew all right. He stood there without speaking, and I knew he wanted to say something to me. 'What is it?' I said. 'Spit it out.' Then he said that if I'd like to have a girl to come and live with me he knew one who was willing. She was a very good girl and he could recommend her. She'd be no trouble and it would be someone to have about the bungalow. She'd mend my things for me. . . . I felt awfully low. It had been raining all day and I hadn't been able to get any exercise. I knew I shouldn't sleep for hours. It wouldn't cost me very much money, he said, her people were poor and they'd be quite satisfied with a small present. Two hundred Straits dollars. 'You look,' he said. 'If you don't like her you send her away.' I asked him where she was. 'She's here,' he said. 'I call her.' He went to the door. She'd been waiting on the steps with her mother. They came in and sat down on the floor. I gave them some sweets. She was shy, of course, but cool enough, and when I said something to her she gave me a smile. She was very young, hardly more than a child, they said she was fifteen. She was awfully pretty, and she had her best clothes on. We began to talk. She didn't say much, but she laughed a lot when I chaffed her. Abdul said I'd find she had plenty to say for herself when she got to know me. He told her to come and sit by me. She giggled and refused, but her mother told her to come, and I made room for her on the chair. She blushed and laughed, but she came, and then she snuggled up to me. The boy laughed too. 'You see, she's taken to you already,' he said. 'Do you want her to stay?' he asked. 'Do you want to?' I said to her. She hid her face, laughing, on my shoulder. She was very soft and small. 'Very well,' I said, 'let her stay.' "

Guy leaned forward and helped himself to a whisky and soda.

"May I speak now?" asked Doris.

"Wait a minute, I haven't finished yet. I wasn't in love with her, not even at the beginning. I only took her so as to have somebody about the bungalow. I think I should have gone mad if I hadn't, or else taken to drink. I was at the end of my tether. I was too young to be quite alone. I was never in love with anyone but you." He hesitated a moment. "She lived here till I went home last year on leave. It's the woman you've seen hanging about."

"Yes, I guessed that. She had a baby in her arms. Is that your child?"

"Yes. It's a little girl."

"Is it the only one?"

"You saw the two small boys the other day in the kampong. You mentioned them."

"She has three children then?"

"Yes."

"It's quite a family you've got."

She felt the sudden gesture which her remark forced from him, but he did not speak.

"Didn't she know that you were married till you suddenly turned up here with a wife?" asked Doris.

"She knew I was going to be married."

"When?"

"I sent her back to the village before I left here. I told her it was all over. I gave her what I'd promised. She always knew it was only a temporary arrangement. I was fed up with it. I told her I was going to marry a white woman."

"But you hadn't even seen me then."

"No, I know. But I'd made up my mind to marry when I was home." He chuckled in his old manner. "I don't mind telling you that I was getting rather despondent about it when I met you. I fell in love with you at first sight and then I knew it was either you or nobody."

"Why didn't you tell me? Don't you think it would have been only fair to give me a chance of judging for myself? It might have occurred to you that it would be rather a shock to a girl to find out that her husband had lived for ten years with another girl and had three children."

"I couldn't expect you to understand. The circumstances out here are peculiar. It's the regular thing. Five men out of six do it. I thought perhaps it would shock you and I didn't want to lose you. You see, I was most awfully in love with you. I am now, darling. There was no reason that you should ever know. I didn't expect to come back here. One seldom goes back to the same station after home leave. When we came here I offered her money if she'd go to some other village. First she said she would and then she changed her mind."

"Why have you told me now?"

"She's been making the most awful scenes. I don't know how she found out that you knew nothing about it. As soon as she did she began to blackmail me. I've had to give her an awful lot of money. I gave orders that she wasn't to be allowed in the compound. This morning she made that scene just to attract your attention. She wanted to frighten me. It couldn't go on like that. I thought the only thing was to make a clean breast of it."

There was a long silence as he finished. At last he put his hand on hers.

"You do understand, Doris, don't you? I know I've been to blame."

She did not move her hand. He felt it cold beneath his.

"Is she jealous?"

"I daresay there were all sorts of perks when she was living here, and I don't suppose she much likes not getting them any longer. But she was never in love with me any more than I was in love with her. Native women never do really care for white men, you know."

"And the children?"

"Oh, the children are all right. I've provided for them. As soon as the boys are old enough I shall send them to school at Singapore."

"Do they mean nothing to you at all?"

He hesitated.

"I want to be quite frank with you. I should be sorry if anything happened to them. When the first one was expected I thought I'd be much fonder of it than I ever had been of its mother. I suppose I should have been if it had been white. Of course, when it was a baby it was rather funny and touching, but I had no particular feeling that it was mine. I think that's what it is; you see, I have no sense of their belonging to me. I've reproached myself sometimes, because it seemed rather unnatural, but the honest truth is that they're no more to me than if they were somebody else's children. Of course a lot of slush is talked about children by people who haven't got any."

Now she had heard everything. He waited for her to speak, but she said nothing. She sat motionless.

"Is there anything more you want to ask me, Doris?" he said at last.

"No, I've got rather a headache. I think I shall go to bed." Her voice was as steady as ever. "I don't quite know what to say. Of course it's been all very unexpected. You must give me a little time to think."

"Are you very angry with me?"

"No. Not at all. Only—only I must be left to myself for a while. Don't move. I'm going to bed."

She rose from her long chair and put her hand on his shoulder.

"It's so very hot to-night. I wish you'd sleep in your dressing-room. Good-night."

She was gone. He heard her lock the door of her bedroom.

She was pale next day and he could see that she had not slept. There was no bitterness in her manner, she talked as usual, but without ease; she spoke of this and that as though she were making conversation with a stranger. They had never had a quarrel, but it seemed to Guy that so would she talk if they had had a disagreement and the subsequent reconciliation had left her still wounded. The look in her eyes puzzled him; he seemed to read in them a strange fear. Immediately after dinner she said:

"I'm not feeling very well to-night. I think I shall go straight to bed."

"Oh, my poor darling, I'm so sorry," he cried.

"It's nothing. I shall be all right in a day or two."

"I shall come in and say good-night to you later."

"No, don't do that. I shall try and get straight off to sleep."

"Well, then, kiss me before you go."

He saw that she flushed. For an instant she seemed to hesitate; then, with averted eyes, she leaned towards him. He took her in his arms and sought her lips, but she turned her face away and he kissed her cheek. She left him quickly and again he heard the key turn softly in the lock of her door. He flung himself heavily on the chair. He tried to read, but his ear was attentive to the smallest sound in his wife's room. She had said she was going to bed, but he did not hear her move. The silence in there made him unaccountably nervous. Shading the lamp with his hand he saw that there was a glimmer under her door; she had not put out her light. What on earth was she doing? He put down his book. It would not have surprised him if she had been angry and had made him a scene, or if she had cried; he could have coped with that; but her calmness frightened him. And then what was that fear which he had seen so plainly in her eyes? He thought once more over all he had said to her on the previous night. He didn't know how else he could have put it. After all, the chief point was that he'd done the same as everybody else, and it was all over long before he met her. Of course as things turned out he had been a fool, but anyone could be wise after the event. He put his hand to his heart. Funny how it hurt him there.

"I suppose that's the sort of thing people mean when they say they're heartbroken," he said to himself. "I wonder how long it's going on like this?"

Should he knock at the door and tell her he must speak to her? It was better to have it out. He *must* make her understand. But the silence scared him. Not a sound! Perhaps it was better to leave her alone. Of course it had been a shock. He must give her as long as she wanted. After all, she knew how devotedly he loved her. Patience, that was the only thing; perhaps she was fighting it out with herself; he must give her time; he must have patience.

Next morning he asked her if she had slept better.

"Yes, much," she said.

"Are you very angry with me?" he asked piteously.

She looked at him with candid, open eyes.

"Not a bit."

"Oh, my dear, I'm so glad. I've been a brute and a beast. I know it's been hateful for you. But do forgive me. I've been so miserable."

"I do forgive you. I don't even blame you."

He gave her a little rueful smile, and there was in his eyes the look of a whipped dog.

"I haven't much liked sleeping by myself the last two nights."

She glanced away. Her face grew a trifle paler.

"I've had the bed in my room taken away. It took up so much space. I've had a little camp bed put there instead."

"My dear, what are you talking about?"

Now she looked at him steadily.

"I'm not going to live with you as your wife again."

"Never?"

She shook her head. He looked at her in a puzzled way. He could hardly believe he had heard aright and his heart began to beat painfully.

"But that's awfully unfair to me, Doris."

"Don't you think it was a little unfair to me to bring me out here in the circumstances?"

"But you just said you didn't blame me."

"That's quite true. But the other's different. I can't do it."

"But how are we going to live together like that?"

She stared at the floor. She seemed to ponder deeply.

"When you wanted to kiss me on the lips last night I—it almost made me sick."

"Doris."

She looked at him suddenly and her eyes were cold and hostile.

"That bed I slept on, is that the bed in which she had her children?" She saw him flush deeply. "Oh, it's horrible. How could you?" She wrung her hands, and her twisting, tortured fingers looked like little writhing snakes. But she made a great effort and controlled herself. "My mind is quite made up. I don't want to be unkind to you, but there are some things that you can't ask me to do. I've thought it all over. I've been thinking of nothing else since you told me, night and day, till I'm exhausted. My first instinct was to get up and go. At once. The steamer will be here in two or three days."

"Doesn't it mean anything to you that I love you?"

"Oh, I know you love me. I'm not going to do that. I want to give us both a chance. I have loved you so, Guy." Her voice broke, but she did not cry. "I don't want to be unreasonable. Heaven knows, I don't want to be unkind. Guy, will you give me time?"

"I don't know quite what you mean."

"I just want you to leave me alone. I'm frightened by the feelings that I have."

He had been right then; she was afraid.

"What feelings?"

"Please don't ask me. I don't want to say anything to wound you. Perhaps I shall get over them. Heaven knows, I want to. I'll try, I promise you. I'll try. Give me six months. I'll do everything in the world for you, but just that one thing." She made a little gesture of appeal. "There's no reason why we shouldn't be happy enough together. If you really love me you'll—you'll have patience."

He sighed deeply.

"Very well," he said. "Naturally I don't want to force you to do anything you don't like. It shall be as you say."

He sat heavily for a little, as though, on a sudden grown old, it was an effort to move; then he got up.

"I'll be getting along to the office."

He took his topee and went out.

A month passed. Women conceal their feelings better than men and a stranger visiting them would never have guessed that Doris was in any way troubled. But in Guy the strain was obvious; his round, good-natured face was drawn, and in his eyes was a hungry, harassed look. He watched Doris. She was gay and she chaffed him as she had been used to do; they played tennis together; they chatted about one thing and another. But it was evident that she was merely playing a part, and at last, unable to contain himself, he tried to speak again of his connections with the Malay woman.

"Oh, Guy, there's no object in going back on all that," she answered breezily. "We've said all we had to say about it and I don't blame you for anything."

"Why do you punish me then?"

"My poor boy, I don't want to punish you. It's not my fault if . . ." she shrugged her shoulders. "Human nature is very odd."

"I don't understand."

"Don't try."

The words might have been harsh, but she softened them with a pleasant, friendly smile. Every night when she went to bed she leaned over Guy and lightly kissed his cheek. Her lips only touched it. It was as though a moth had just brushed his face in its flight.

A second month passed, then a third, and suddenly the six months which had seemed so interminable were over. Guy asked himself whether she remembered. He gave a strained attention now to everything she said, to every look on her face and to every gesture of her hands. She remained impenetrable. She had asked him to give her six months; well, he had.

The coasting steamer passed the mouth of the river, dropped their mail, and went on its way. Guy busily wrote the letters which it would pick up on the return journey. Two or three days passed by. It was a Tuesday and the prahu was to start at dawn on Thursday to await the steamer. Except at meal time when Doris exerted herself to make conversation they had not of late talked very much together; and after dinner as usual they took their books and began to read; but when the boy had finished clearing away and was gone for the night Doris put down hers.

"Guy, I have something I want to say to you," she murmured.

His heart gave a sudden thud against his ribs and he felt himself change colour.

"Oh, my dear, don't look like that, it's not so very terrible," she laughed.

But he thought her voice trembled a little.

"Well?"

"I want you to do something for me."

"My darling, I'll do anything in the world for you."

He put out his hand to take hers, but she drew it away.

"I want you to let me go home."

"You?" he cried, aghast. "When? Why?"

"I've borne it as long as I can. I'm at the end of my tether."

"How long do you want to go for? For always?"

"I don't know. I think so." She gathered determination. "Yes, for always."

"Oh, my God!"

His voice broke and she thought he was going to cry.

"Oh, Guy, don't blame me. It really is not my fault. I can't help myself."

"You asked me for six months. I accepted your terms. You can't say I've made a nuisance of myself."

"No, no."

"I've tried not to let you see what a rotten time I was having."

"I know. I'm very grateful to you. You've been awfully kind to me. Listen, Guy, I want to tell you again that I don't blame you for a single thing you did. After all, you were only a boy, and you did no more than the others; I know what the loneliness is here. Oh, my dear, I'm so dreadfully sorry for you. I knew all that from the beginning. That's why I asked you for six months. My commonsense tells me that I'm making a mountain out of a molehill. I'm unreasonable; I'm being unfair to you. But, you see, commonsense has nothing to do with it; my whole soul is in revolt. When I see the woman and her children in the village I just feel my legs shaking.

Everything in this house; when I think of that bed I slept in it gives me goose-flesh. . . . You don't know what I've endured."

"I think I've persuaded her to go away. And I've applied for a transfer."

"That wouldn't help. She'll be there always. You belong to them, you don't belong to me. I think perhaps I could have stood it if there'd only been one child, but three; and the boys are quite big boys. For ten years you lived with her." And now she came out with what she had been working up to. She was desperate. "It's a physical thing, I can't help it, it's stronger than I am. I think of those thin black arms of hers round you and it fills me with a physical nausea. I think of you holding those little black babies in your arms. Oh, it's loathsome. The touch of you is odious to me. Each night, when I've kissed you, I've had to brace myself up to it, I've had to clench my hands and force myself to touch your cheek." Now she was clasping and unclasping her fingers in a nervous agony, and her voice was out of control. "I know it's I who am to blame now. I'm a silly, hysterical woman. I thought I'd get over it. I can't, and now I never shall. I've brought it all on myself; I'm willing to take the consequences; if you say I must stay here, I'll stay, but if I stay I shall die. I beseech you to let me go."

And now the tears which she had restrained so long overflowed and she wept broken-heartedly. He had never seen her cry before.

"Of course I don't want to keep you here against your will," he said hoarsely.

Exhausted, she leaned back in her chair. Her features were all twisted and awry. It was horribly painful to see the abandonment of grief on that face which was habitually so placid.

"I'm so sorry, Guy. I've broken your life, but I've broken mine too. And we might have been so happy."

"When do you want to go? On Thursday?"

"Yes."

She looked at him piteously. He buried his face in his hands. At last he looked up.

"I'm tired out," he muttered.

"May I go?"

"Yes."

For two minutes perhaps they sat there without a word. She started when the chik-chak gave its piercing, hoarse and strangely human cry. Guy rose and went out on to the verandah. He leaned against the rail and looked at the softly flowing water. He heard Doris go into her room.

Next morning, up earlier than usual, he went to her door and knocked.

"Yes?"

"I have to go up-river to-day. I shan't be back till late."

"All right."

She understood. He had arranged to be away all day in order not to be about while she was packing. It was heartbreaking work. When she had packed her clothes she looked round the sitting-room at the things that belonged to her. It seemed dreadful to take them. She left everything but the photograph of her mother. Guy did not come in till ten o'clock at night.

"I'm sorry I couldn't get back to dinner," he said. "The headman at the village I had to go to had a lot of things for me to attend to."

She saw his eyes wander about the room and notice that her mother's photograph no longer stood in its place.

"Is everything quite ready?" he asked. "I've ordered the boatman to be at the steps at dawn."

"I told the boy to wake me at five."

"I'd better give you some money." He went to his desk and wrote out a cheque. He took some notes from a drawer. "Here's some cash to take you as far as Singapore and at Singapore you'll be able to change the cheque."

"Thank you."

"Would you like me to come to the mouth of the river with you?"

"Oh, I think it would be better if we said good-bye here."

"All right. I think I shall turn in. I've had a long day and I'm dead beat."

He did not even touch her hand. He went into his room. In a few minutes she heard him throw himself on his bed. For a little while she sat looking for the last time round that room in which she had been so happy and so miserable. She sighed deeply. She got up and went into her own room. Everything was packed except the one or two things she needed for the night.

It was dark when the boy awakened them. They dressed hurriedly and when they were ready breakfast was waiting for them. Presently they heard the boat row up to the landing-stage below the bungalow, and then the servants carried down her luggage. It was a poor pretence they made of eating. The darkness thinned away and the river was ghostly. It was not yet day, but it was no longer night. In the silence the voices of the natives at the landing-stage were very clear. Guy glanced at his wife's untouched plate.

"If you've finished we might stroll down. I think you ought to be starting."

She did not answer. She rose from the table. She went into her room to see that nothing had been forgotten and then side by side with him walked down the steps. A little winding path led them to the river. At the landing-stage the native guards in their smart uniform were lined up and they presented arms as Guy and Doris passed. The head boatman gave her his hand as she stepped into the boat. She turned and looked at Guy. She wanted desperately to say one last word of comfort, once more to ask for his forgiveness, but she seemed to be struck dumb.

He stretched out his hand.

"Well, good-bye, I hope you'll have a jolly journey."

They shook hands.

Guy nodded to the head boatman and the boat pushed off. The dawn now was creeping along the river mistily, but the night lurked still in the dark trees of the jungle. He stood at the landing-stage till the boat was lost in the shadows of the morning. With a sigh he turned away. He nodded absent-mindedly when the guard once more presented arms. But when he reached the bungalow he called the boy. He went round the room picking out everything that had belonged to Doris.

"Pack all these things up," he said. "It's no good leaving them about."

Then he sat down on the verandah and watched the day advance gradually like a bitter, an unmerited and an overwhelming sorrow. At last he looked at his watch. It was time for him to go to the office.

In the afternoon he could not sleep, his head ached miserably, so he took his gun and went for a tramp in the jungle. He shot nothing, but he walked in order to tire himself out. Towards sunset he came back and had two or three drinks, and then it was time to dress for dinner. There wasn't much use in dressing now; he might just as well be comfortable; he put on a loose native jacket and a sarong. That was what he had been accustomed to wear before Doris came. He was barefoot. He ate his dinner listlessly and the boy cleared away and went. He sat down to read the *Tatler*. The bungalow was very silent. He could not read and let the paper fall on his knees. He was exhausted. He could not think and his mind was strangely vacant. The chik-chak was noisy that night and its hoarse and sudden cry seemed to mock him. You could hardly believe that this reverberating sound came from so small a throat. Presently he heard a discreet cough.

"Who's there?" he cried.

There was a pause. He looked at the door. The chik-chak

N

laughed harshly. A small boy sidled in and stood on the threshold.
It was a little half-caste boy in a tattered singlet and a sarong. It
was the elder of his two sons.

"What do you want?" said Guy.

The boy came forward into the room and sat down, tucking his
legs away under him.

"Who told you to come here?"

"My mother sent me. She says, do you want anything?"

Guy looked at the boy intently. The boy said nothing more. He
sat and waited, his eyes cast down shyly. Then Guy in deep and
bitter reflection buried his face in his hands. What was the use? It
was finished. Finished! He surrendered. He sat back in his chair
and sighed deeply.

"Tell your mother to pack up her things and yours. She can come
back."

"When?" asked the boy, impassively.

Hot tears trickled down Guy's funny, round spotty face.

"To-night."

Flotsam and Jetsam

NORMAN GRANGE was a rubber-planter. He was up before day-break to take the roll-call of his labour and then walked over the estate to see that the tapping was properly done. This duty performed, he came home, bathed and changed, and now with his wife opposite him he was eating the substantial meal, half breakfast and half luncheon, which in Borneo is called brunch. He read as he ate. The dining-room was dingy. The worn electro-plate, the shabby cruet, the chipped dishes betokened poverty, but a poverty accepted with apathy. A few flowers would have brightened the table, but there was apparently no one to care how things looked. When Grange had finished he belched, filled his pipe and lit it, rose from the table and went out on to the verandah. He took no more notice of his wife than if she had not been there. He lay down in a long rattan chair and went on reading. Mrs. Grange reached over for a tin of cigarettes and smoked while she sipped her tea. Suddenly she looked out, for the house boy came up the steps and accompanied by two men went up to her husband. One was a Dyak and the other Chinese. Strangers seldom came and she could not imagine what they wanted. She got up and went to the door to listen. Though she had lived in Borneo for so many years she knew no more Malay than was necessary to get along with the boys, and she only vaguely understood what was said. She gathered from her husband's tone that something had happened to annoy him. He seemed to be asking questions first of the Chink and then of the Dyak; it looked as though they were pressing him to do something he didn't want to do; at length, however, with a frown on his face he raised himself from his chair and followed by the men walked down the steps. Curious to see where he was going she slipped out on to the verandah. He had taken the path that led down to the river. She shrugged her thin shoulders and went to her room. Presently she gave a violent start, for she heard her husband call her.

"Vesta."

She came out.

"Get a bed ready. There's a white man in a prahu at the landing-stage. He's damned ill."

"Who is he?"

"How the hell should I know? They're just bringing him up."

"We can't have anyone to stay here."

"Shut up and do as I tell you."

He left her on that and again went down to the river. Mrs. Grange called the boy and told him to put sheets on the bed in the spare room. Then she stood at the top of the steps and waited. In a little while she saw her husband coming back and behind him a huddle of Dyaks carrying a man on a mattress. She stood aside to let them pass and caught a glimpse of a white face.

"What shall I do?" she asked her husband.

"Get out and keep quiet."

"Polite, aren't you?"

The sick man was taken into the room, and in two or three minutes the Dyaks and Grange came out.

"I'm going to see about his kit. I'll have it brought up. His boy's looking after him and there's no cause for you to butt in!"

"What's the matter with him?"

"Malaria. His boatmen are afraid he's going to die and won't take him on. His name's Skelton."

"He isn't going to die, is he?"

"If he does we'll bury him."

But Skelton didn't die. He woke next morning to find himself in a room, in bed and under a mosquito-net. He couldn't think where he was. It was a cheap iron bed and the mattress was hard, but to lie on it was a relief after the discomfort of the prahu. He could see nothing of the room but a chest of drawers, roughly made by a native carpenter, and a wooden chair. Opposite was a doorway, with a blind down, and this he guessed led on to a verandah.

"Kong," he called.

The blind was drawn aside and his boy came in. The Chinaman's face broke into a grin when he saw that his master was free from fever.

"You more better, Tuan. Velly glad."

"Where the devil am I?"

Kong explained.

"Luggage all right?" asked Skelton.

"Yes, him all right."

"What's the name of this fellow—the tuan whose house this is?"

"Mr. Norman Glange."

To confirm what he said he showed Skelton a little book in which the owner's name was written. It was Grange. Skelton noticed that the book was Bacon's *Essays*. It was curious to find it in a planter's house away up a river in Borneo.

"Tell him I'd be glad to see him."

"Tuan out. Him come presently."

"What about my having a wash? And by God, I want a shave."

He tried to get out of bed, but his head swam and with a bewildered cry he sank back. But Kong shaved and washed him, and changed the shorts and singlet in which he had been lying ever since he fell ill for a sarong and a baju. After that he was glad to lie still. But presently Kong came in and said that the tuan of the house was back. There was a knock on the door and a large stoutish man stepped in.

"I hear you're better," he said.

"Oh, much. It's terribly kind of you to have taken me in like this. It seems awful, planting myself on you."

Grange answered a trifle harshly.

"That's all right. You were pretty bad, you know. No wonder those Dyaks wanted to get rid of you."

"I don't want to impose myself on you longer than I need. If I could hire a launch here, or a prahu, I could get off this afternoon."

"There's no launch to hire. You'd better stay a bit. You must be as weak as a rat."

"I'm afraid I shall be a frightful bother."

"I don't see why. You've got your own boy and he'll look after you."

Grange had just come in from his round of the estate and wore dirty shorts, a khaki shirt open at the neck and an old, battered terai hat. He looked as shabby as a beachcomber. He took off his hat to wipe his sweating brow; he had close-cropped grey hair; his face was red, a broad, fleshy face, with a large mouth under a stubble of grey moustache, a short, pugnacious nose and small, mean eyes.

"I wonder if you could let me have something to read," said Skelton.

"What sort of thing?"

"I don't mind so long as it's lightish."

"I'm not much of a novel reader myself, but I'll send you in two or three books. My wife can provide you with novels. They'll be trash, because that's all she reads. But it may suit you."

With a nod he withdrew. Not a very likeable man. But he was obviously very poor, the room in which Skelton lay, something in Grange's appearance, indicated that; he was probably manager of an estate on a cut salary, and it was not unlikely that the expense of a guest and his servant was unwelcome. Living in that remote spot, and so seeing white men but seldom, it might be that he was ill at ease with strangers. Some people improve unbelievably on acquaintance. But his hard, shifty little eyes were disconcerting; they gave the lie to the red face and the massive frame which otherwise might have persuaded you that this was a jolly sort of fellow with whom you could quickly make friends.

After a while the house boy came in with a parcel of books. There were half a dozen novels by authors he had never heard of, and a glance told him they were slop; these must be Mrs. Grange's; and then there was a Boswell's *Johnson*, Borrow's *Lavengro* and Lamb's *Essays*. It was an odd choice. They were not the books you would have expected to find in a planter's house. In most planter's houses there is not more than a shelf or two of books and for the most part they're detective stories. Skelton had a disinterested curiosity in human creatures, and he amused himself now by trying to make out from the books Norman Grange had sent, from the look of him and from the few words they had exchanged, what sort of a man he could be. Skelton was a little surprised that his host did not come to see him again that day; it looked as though he were going to content himself with giving his uninvited guest board and lodging, but were not sufficiently interested in him to seek his company. Next morning he felt well enough to get up, and with Kong's help settled himself in a long chair on the verandah. It badly needed a coat of paint. The bungalow stood on the brow of a hill, about fifty yards from the river; and on the opposite bank, looking very small across that great stretch of water, you could see native houses on piles nestling among the greenery. Skelton had not yet the activity of mind to read steadily, and after a page or two, his thoughts wandering, he found himself content to watch idly the sluggish flow of the turbid stream. Suddenly he heard a step. He saw a little elderly woman come towards him, and knowing that this must be Mrs. Grange tried to get up.

"Don't move," she said. "I only came to see if you had everything you wanted."

She wore a blue cotton dress, simple enough, but more suited to a young girl than to a woman of her age; her short hair was tousled, as though on getting out of bed she had scarcely troubled to pass a comb through it, and dyed a vivid yellow, but badly, and the roots showed white. Her skin was raddled and dry, and there was a great dab of rouge on each cheek-bone, put on however so clumsily that you could not for a moment take it for a natural colour, and a smear of lipstick on her mouth. But the strangest thing about her was a tic she had that made her jerk her head as though she were beckoning you to an inner room. It seemed to come at regular intervals, perhaps three times a minute, and her left hand was in almost constant movement; it was not quite a tremble, it was a rapid twirl as though she wanted to draw your attention to something behind her back. Skelton was startled by her appearance and embarrassed by her tic.

"I hope I'm not making myself too great a nuisance," he said. "I think I shall be well enough to make a move to-morrow or the day after."

"It's not often we see anybody in a place like this, you know. It's a treat to have someone to talk to."

"Won't you sit down? I'll tell my boy to bring you a chair."

"Norman said I was to leave you alone."

"I haven't spoken to a white person for two years. I've been longing for a good old talk."

Her head twitched violently, more quickly than usual, and her hand gave that queer spasmodic gesture.

"He won't be back for another hour. I'll get a chair."

Skelton told her who he was and what he had been doing, but he discovered that she had questioned his boy and already knew all about him.

"You must be crazy to get back to England?" she asked.

"I shan't be sorry."

Suddenly Mrs. Grange seemed to be attacked by what one could only describe as a nerve storm. Her head twitched so madly, her hand shook with such fury, that it was disconcerting. You could only look away.

"I haven't been to England for sixteen years," she said.

"You don't mean that? Why, I thought all you planters went home every five years at the longest."

"We can't afford it; we're broke to the wide. Norman put all the money he had into this plantation, and it hasn't really paid for years. It only just brings in enough to keep us from starvation. Of course it doesn't matter to Norman. He isn't English really."

"He looks English enough."

"He was born in Sarawak. His father was in the government service. If he's anything he's a native of Borneo."

Then, without warning, she began to cry. It was horribly painful to see the tears running down the raddled, painted cheeks of that woman with the constant tic. Skelton knew neither what to say nor what to do. He did what was probably the best thing, he kept silent. She dried her eyes.

"You must think me a silly old fool. I sometimes wonder that after all these years I can still cry. I suppose it's in my nature. I always could cry very easy when I was on the stage."

"Oh, were you on the stage?"

"Yes, before I married. That's how I met Norman. We were

playing in Singapore and he was there on holiday. I don't suppose
I shall ever see England any more. I shall stay here till I die and
every day of my life I shall look at that beastly river. I shall never
get away now. Never."

"How did you happen to find yourself in Singapore?"

"Well, it was soon after the war, I couldn't get anything to suit me
in London, I'd been on the stage a good many years and I was fed
up with playing small parts; the agents told me a fellow called
Victor Palace was taking a company out East. His wife was playing
lead, but I could play seconds. They'd got half a dozen plays,
comedies, you know, and farces. The salary wasn't much, but they
were going to Egypt and India, the Malay States and China and
then down to Australia. It was a chance to see the world and I
accepted. We didn't do badly in Cairo and I think we made money
in India, but Burma wasn't much good, and Siam was worse;
Penang was a disaster and so were the rest of the Malay States. Well,
one day Victor called us together and said he was bust, he hadn't got
the money for our fares on to Hong Kong, and the tour was a wash-
out and he was very sorry but we'd have to get back home as best we
could. Of course we told him he couldn't do that to us. You never
heard such a row. Well, the long and short of it was that he said we
could have the scenery and the props if we thought they was any
good to us, but as to money it was no use asking for it because he
damned well hadn't got it. And next day we found out that him and
his wife, without saying a word to anybody, had got on a French
boat and skipped. I was in a rare state, I can tell you. I had a few
pounds I'd saved out of me salary, and that was all; somebody told
me if we was absolutely stranded the government would have to send
us home, but only steerage, and I didn't much fancy that. We got
the Press to put our plight before the public and someone came along
with the proposition that we should give a benefit performance.
Well, we did, but it wasn't much without Victor or his wife, and by
the time we'd paid the expenses we weren't any better off than we'd
been before. I was at my wits' end, I don't mind telling you. It
was then that Norman proposed to me. The funny thing is that I
hardly knew him. He'd taken me for a drive round the island and
we'd had tea two or three times at the Europe and danced. Men
don't often do things for you without wanting something in return,
and I thought he expected to get a little bit of fun, but I'd had a
good deal of experience and I thought he'd be clever if he got round
me. But when he asked me to marry him, well, I was so surprised,
I couldn't hardly believe me own ears. He said he'd got his own
estate in Borneo and it only wanted a little patience and he'd make a

packet. And it was on the banks of a fine river and all round was the jungle. He made it sound very romantic. I was getting on, you know, I was thirty, it wasn't going to be any easier to get work as time went on, and it was tempting to have a house of me own and all that. Never to have to hang around agents' offices no more. Never to have to lay awake no more and wonder how you was going to pay next week's rent. He wasn't a bad-looking chap in those days, brown and big and virile. No one could say I was willing to marry anybody just to . . ." Suddenly she stopped. "There he is. Don't say you've seen me."

She picked up the chair she had been sitting in and quickly slipped away with it into the house. Skelton was bewildered. Her grotesque appearance, the painful tears, her story told with that incessant twitching; and then her obvious fear when she heard her husband's voice in the compound, and her hurried escape; he could make nothing of it.

In a few minutes Norman Grange stumped along the verandah.

"I hear you're better," he said.

"Much, thanks."

"If you care to join us at brunch I'll have a place laid for you."

"I'd like it very much."

"All right. I'm just going to have a bath and a change."

He walked away. Presently a boy came along and told Skelton his tuan was waiting for him. Skelton followed him into a small sitting-room, with the jalousies drawn to keep out the heat, an uncomfortable, overcrowded room with a medley of furniture, English and Chinese, and occasional tables littered with worthless junk. It was neither cosy nor cool. Grange had changed into a sarong and baju and in the native dress looked coarse but powerful. He introduced Skelton to his wife. She shook hands with him as though she had never seen him before and uttered a few polite words of greeting. The boy announced that their meal was ready and they went into the dining-room.

"I hear that you've been in this bloody country for some time," said Grange.

"Two years. I'm an anthropologist and I wanted to study the manners and customs of tribes that haven't had any contact with civilisation."

Skelton felt that he should tell his host how it had come about that he had been forced to accept a hospitality which he could not but feel was grudgingly offered. After leaving the village that had been his headquarters he had journeyed by land for ten days till he reached the river. There he had engaged a couple of prahus, one for himself and his luggage and the other for Kong, his Chinese servant, and the camp equipment, to take him to the coast. The long trek across country had been hard going and he found it very comfortable to lie on a mattress under an awning of rattan matting and take his ease. All the time he had been away Skelton had been in perfect health, and as he travelled down the river he could not but think that he was very lucky; but even as the thought passed through his mind, it occurred to him that if he happened just then to congratulate himself on his good fortune in this respect, it was because he did not feel quite so well as usual. It was true that he had been forced to drink a great deal of arak the night before at the long-house where he had put up, but he was used to it and that hardly accounted for his headache. He had a general sense of malaise. He was wearing nothing but shorts and a singlet, and he felt chilly; it was curious because the sun was shining fiercely and when he put his hand on the gunwale of the prahu the heat was hardly bearable. If he had had a coat handy he would have put it on. He grew colder and colder and presently his teeth began to chatter; he huddled up on his mattress, shivering all over in a desperate effort to get warm. He could not fail to guess what was the matter.

"Christ," he groaned. "Malaria."

He called the headman, who was steering the prahu.

"Get Kong."

The headman shouted to the second prahu and ordered his own paddlers to stop. In a moment the two boats were side by side and Kong stepped in.

"I've got fever, Kong," gasped Skelton. "Get me the medicine chest, and for God's sake, blankets. I'm freezing to death."

Kong gave his master a big dose of quinine and piled on him what coverings they had. They started off again.

Skelton was too ill to be taken ashore when they tied up for the night and so passed it in the prahu. All next day and the day after he was very ill. Sometimes one or other of the crew came and looked at him, and often the headman stayed for quite a long while staring at him thoughtfully.

"How many days to the coast?" Skelton asked the boy.

"Four, five." He paused for a minute. "Headman, he no go coast. He say, he wantchee go home."

"Tell him to go to hell."

"Headman say, you velly sick, you die. If you die and he go coast he catchee trouble."

"I'm not thinking of dying," said Skelton. "I shall be all right. It's just an ordinary go of malaria."

Kong did not answer. The silence irritated Skelton. He knew that the Chinese had something in mind that he did not like to say.

"Spit it out, you fool," he cried.

Skelton's heart sank when Kong told him the truth. When they reached their resting-place that night the headman was going to demand his money and slip away with the two prahus before dawn. He was too frightened to carry a dying man farther. Skelton had no strength to take the determined attitude that might have availed him; he could only hope by the offer of more money to persuade the headman to carry out his agreement. The day passed in long arguments between Kong and the headman, but when they tied up for the night the headman came to Skelton and told him sulkily that he would go no farther. There was a long-house near-by where he might get lodging till he grew better. He began to unload the baggage. Skelton refused to move. He got Kong to give him his revolver and swore to shoot anyone who came near him.

Kong, the crew and the headman went up to the long-house and Skelton was left alone. Hour after hour he lay there, the fever burning his body and his mouth parched, while muddled thoughts hammered away in his brain. Then there were lights and the sound of men talking. The Chinese boy came with the headman and another man, whom Skelton had not yet seen, from the neighbouring long-house. He did his best to understand what Kong was telling him. It appeared that a few hours down-stream there lived a white man, and to his house, if that would satisfy Skelton, the headman was willing to take him.

"More better you say yes," said Kong. "Maybe white man has launch, then we go down to coast chop-chop."

"Who is he?"

"Planter," said Kong. "This fellow say, him have rubber estate."

Skelton was too tired to argue further. All he wanted just then was to sleep. He accepted the compromise.

"To tell you the truth," he finished, "I don't remember much more till I woke up yesterday morning to find myself an uninvited guest in your house."

"I don't blame those Dyaks, you know," said Grange. "When I came down to the prahu and saw you, I thought you were for it."

Mrs. Grange sat silent while Skelton told his story, her head and her hand twitching regularly, as though by the action of some invisible clockwork, but when her husband addressed her, asking for the Worcester Sauce, and that was the only time he spoke to her, she was seized with such a paroxysm of involuntary movement that it was horrible to see. She passed him what he asked for without a word. Skelton got an uncomfortable impression that she was terrified of Grange. It was odd, because to all appearance he was not a bad sort. He was knowledgeable and far from stupid; and though you could not have said that his manner was cordial, it was plain that he was ready to be of what service he could.

They finished their meal and separated to rest through the heat of the day.

"See you again at six for a sun-downer," said George.

When Skelton had had a good sleep, a bath and a read, he went out on to the verandah. Mrs. Grange came up to him. It looked as though she had been waiting.

"He's back from the office. Don't think it's funny if I don't speak to you. If he thought I liked having you here he'd turn you out to-morrow."

She said these words in a whisper and slipped back into the house. Skelton was startled. It was a strange house he had come into in a strange manner. He went into the overcrowded sitting-room and there found his host. He had been worried by the evident poverty of the establishment and he felt that the Granges could ill afford even the small expense he must be putting them to. But he had already formed the impression that Grange was a quick-tempered, susceptible man and he did not know how he would take an offer to help. He made up his mind to risk it.

"Look here," he said to him, "it looks as though I might have to inflict myself on you for several days, I'd be so much more comfortable if you'd let me pay for my board and lodging."

"Oh, that's all right, your lodging costs nothing, the house belongs to the mortgagees, and your board doesn't come to much."

"Well, there are drinks anyway and I've had to come down on your stores of tobacco and cigarettes."

"It's not more than once a year that anyone comes up here, and then it's only the D.O. or someone like that—besides, when one's as broke as I am nothing matters much."

"Well, then, will you take my camp equipment? I shan't be wanting it any more, and if you'd like one of my guns, I'd be only too glad to leave it with you."

Grange hesitated. There was a glimmer of cupidity in those small, cunning eyes of his.

"If you'd let me have one of your guns you'd pay for your board and lodging over and over again."

"That's settled, then."

They began to talk over the whisky and sparkler with which,

following the Eastern habit, they celebrated the setting of the sun. Discovering that they both played chess they had a game. Mrs. Grange did not join them till dinner. The meal was dull. An insipid soup, a tasteless river fish, a tough piece of steak and a caramel pudding. Norman Grange and Skelton drank beer; Mrs. Grange water. She never of her own will uttered a word. Skelton had again the uncomfortable impression that she was scared to death of her husband. Once or twice, Skelton from common politeness sought to bring her into the conversation, addressing himself to her, telling her a story or asking her a question, but it evidently distressed her so much, her head twitched so violently, her hand was agitated by gestures so spasmodic that he thought it kinder not to insist. When the meal was over she got up.

"I'll leave you gentlemen to your port," she said.

Both the men got up as she left the room. It was rather absurd, and somehow sinister, to see this social pretence in those poverty-stricken surroundings on a Borneo river.

"I may add that there is no port. There might be a little Benedictine left."

"Oh, don't bother."

They talked for a while and Grange began to yawn. He got up every morning before sunrise and by nine o'clock at night could hardly keep his eyes open.

"Well, I'm going to turn in," he said.

He nodded to Skelton and without further ceremony left him. Skelton went to bed, but he could not sleep. Though the heat was oppressive, it was not the heat that kept him awake. There was something horrible about that house and those two people who lived in it. He didn't know what it was that affected him with this peculiar uneasiness, but this he knew, that he would be heartily thankful to be out of it and away from them. Grange had talked a good deal about himself, but he knew no more of him than he had learned at first glance. To all appearances he was just the commonplace planter who had fallen upon evil days. He had bought his land immediately after the war and had planted trees; but by the time they were bearing the slump had come and since then it had been a constant struggle to keep going. The estate and the house were heavily mortgaged, and now that rubber was once more selling profitably all he made went to the mortgagees. That was an old story in Malaya. What made Grange somewhat unusual was that he was a man without a country. Born in Borneo, he had lived there with his parents till he was old enough to go to school in England; at seventeen he had come back and had never left it since except to go to Mesopotamia during the war. England meant nothing to him. He had neither relations nor friends there. Most planters, like civil servants, have come from England, go back on leave now and then, and look forward to settling down there when they retire. But what had England to offer Norman Grange?

"I was born here," he said, "and I shall die here. I'm a stranger in England. I don't like their ways over there and I don't understand the things they talk about. And yet I'm a stranger here too. To the Malays and the Chinese I'm a white man, though I speak Malay as well as they do, and a white man I shall always be." Then he said a significant thing. "Of course if I'd had any sense I'd have married a Malay girl and had half a dozen half-caste kids. That's the only solution really for us chaps who were born and bred here."

Grange's bitterness was greater than could be explained by his financial embarrassment. He had little good to say of any of the white men in the colony. He seemed to think that they despised him because he was native-born. He was a sour, disappointed fellow, and a conceited one. He had shown Skelton his books. There were not many of them, but they were the best on the whole that English literature can show; he had read them over and over again; but it looked as though he had learnt from them neither charity nor loving-kindness, it looked as though their beauty had left him unmoved; and to know them so well had only made him self-complacent. His exterior, which was so hearty and English, seemed to have little relation to the man within; you could not resist the suspicion that it masked a very sinister being.

Early next morning, to enjoy the cool of the day, Skelton, with his pipe and a book, was sitting on the verandah outside his room. He was still very weak, but felt much better. In a little while Mrs. Grange joined him. She held in her hand a large album.

"I thought I'd like to show you some of me old photos and me notices. You mustn't think I always looked like what I do now. He's off on his round and he won't be back for two or three hours yet."

Mrs. Grange, in the same blue dress she had worn the day before, her hair as untidy, appeared strangely excited.

"It's all I have to remind me of the past. Sometimes when I can't bear life any more I look at my album."

She sat by Skelton's side as he turned the pages. The notices were from provincial papers, and the references to Mrs. Grange, whose stage name had been apparently Vesta Blaise, were carefully underlined. From the photographs you could see that she had been pretty enough in an undistinguished way. She had acted in musical comedy and revue, in farce and comedy, and taking the photographs and the notices together it was easy to tell that here had been the common, dreary, rather vulgar career of the girl with no particular talent who has taken to the stage on the strength of a pretty face and a good figure. Her head twitching, her hand shaking, Mrs. Grange looked at the photographs and read the notices with as much interest as if she had never seen them before.

"You've got to have influence on the stage, and I never had any," she said. "If I'd only had my chance I know I'd have made good. I had bad luck, there's no doubt about that."

It was all sordid and somewhat pathetic.

"I daresay you're better off as you are," said Skelton.

She snatched the book from him and shut it with a bang. She had a paroxysm so violent that it was really frightening to look at her.

"What d'you mean by that? What d'you know about the life I lead here? I'd have killed myself years ago only I know he wants me to die. That's the only way I can get back on him, by living, and I'm going to live; I'm going to live as long as he does. Oh, I hate him. I've often thought I'd poison him, but I was afraid. I didn't know how to do it really, and if he died the Chinks would foreclose and I'd be turned out. And where should I go then? I haven't a friend in the world."

Skelton was aghast. It flashed through his mind that she was crazy. He hadn't a notion what to say. She gave him a keen look.

"I suppose it surprises you to hear me talk like that. I mean it, you know, every word of it. He'd like to kill me too, but he daren't either. And he knows how to do it all right. He knows how the Malays kill people. He was born here. There's nothing he doesn't know about the country."

Skelton forced himself to speak.

"You know, Mrs. Grange, I'm a total stranger. Don't you think it's rather unwise to tell me all sorts of things there's no need for me to know? After all, you live a very solitary life. I daresay you get on one another's nerves. Now that things are looking up perhaps you'll be able to take a trip to England."

"I don't want to go to England. I'd be ashamed to let them see me like I am now. D'you know how old I am? Forty-six. I look sixty and I know it. That's why I showed you those photos, so as you might see I wasn't always like what I am now. Oh, my God, how I've wasted my life! They talk of the romance of the East. They can have it. I'd rather be a dresser in a provincial theatre, I'd rather be one of the sweepers that keep it clean, than what I am now. Until I came here I'd never been alone in me life, I'd always lived in a crowd; you don't know what it is to have nobody to talk to from year's end to year's end. To have to keep it all bottled up. How would you like to see no one, week in and week out, day after day for sixteen years, except the man you hate most in the world? How would you like to live for sixteen years with a man who hates you so he can't bear to look at you?"

"Oh, come, it can't be as bad as that."

"I'm telling you the truth. Why should I tell you a lie? I shall never see you again; what do I care what you think of me? And if you tell them what I've said when you get down to the coast, what's the odds? They'll say: 'God, you don't mean to say you stayed with those people? I pity you. He's an outsider and she's crazy; got a tic; they say it looks as if she was always trying to wipe the blood off her dress. They were mixed up in a damned funny business, but no one ever really knew the ins and outs of it; it all happened a long time ago and the country was pretty wild in those days.' A damned funny business and no mistake. I'd tell you for two pins. That would be a bit of dirt for them at the club. You wouldn't have to pay for a drink for days. Damn them. Oh, Christ, how I hate this country. I hate that river. I hate this house. I hate that damned rubber. I loathe the filthy natives. And that's all I've got to look forward to till I die—till I die without a doctor to take care of me, without a friend to hold me hand."

She began to cry hysterically. Mrs. Grange had spoken with a dramatic intensity of which Skelton would never have thought her capable. Her coarse irony was as painful as her anguish. Skelton was young, he was not yet thirty, and he did not know how to deal with the difficult situation. But he could not keep silent.

"I'm terribly sorry, Mrs. Grange. I wish I could do something to help you."

"I'm not asking for your help. No one can help me."

Skelton was distressed. From what she said he could not but suspect that she had been concerned in a mysterious and perhaps dreadful occurrence, and it might be that to tell him about it without fear of the consequences was just the relief she needed.

"I don't want to butt into what's no business of mine, but, Mrs. Grange, if you think it would ease your mind to tell me—what you were referring to just now, I mean what you said was a damned funny business, I promise you on my word of honour that I'll never repeat it to a living soul."

She stopped crying quite suddenly and gave him a long, intent look. She hesitated. He had an impression that the desire to speak was almost irresistible. But she shook her head and sighed.

"It wouldn't do any good. Nothing can do me any good."

She got up and abruptly left him.

The two men sat down to brunch by themselves.

"My wife asks you to excuse her," said Grange. "She's got one of her sick headaches and she's staying in bed to-day."

"Oh, I'm sorry."

Skelton had a notion that in the searching look that Grange gave him was mistrust and animosity. It flashed through his mind that somehow he had discovered that Mrs. Grange had been talking to him and perhaps had said things that should have been left unsaid. Skelton made an effort at conversation, but his host was taciturn, and they ended the meal in a silence that was only broken by Grange when he got up.

"You seem pretty fit to-day and I don't suppose you want to stay in this God-forsaken place longer than you must. I've sent over the river to arrange for a couple of prahus to take you down to the coast. They'll be here at six to-morrow morning."

Skelton felt sure then that he was right; Grange knew or guessed that his wife had spoken too freely, and he wanted to be rid as soon as possible of the dangerous visitor.

"That's terribly kind of you," Skelton answered, smiling. "I'm as fit as a fiddle."

But in Grange's eyes was no answering smile. They were coldly hostile.

"We might have another game of chess later on," said he.

"All right. When d'you get back from your office?"

"I haven't got much to do there to-day. I shall be about the house."

Skelton wondered if it were only his fancy that there was something very like a threat in the tone in which Grange uttered these words. It looked as though he were going to make sure that his wife and Skelton should not again be left alone. Mrs. Grange did not come to dinner. They drank their coffee and smoked their cheroots. Then Grange, pushing back his chair, said:

"You've got to make an early start to-morrow. I daresay you'd like to turn in. I shall have started out on my round by the time you go, so I'll say good-bye to you now."

"Let me get my guns. I want you to take the one you like best."

"I'll tell the boy to fetch them."

The guns were brought and Grange made his choice. He gave no sign that he was pleased with the handsome gift.

"You quite understand that this gun's worth a damned sight more than what your food and drink and smoke have run me into?" he said.

"For all I know you saved my life. I don't think an old gun is an over-generous return for that."

"Oh, well, if you like to look at it that way, I suppose it's your own business. Thank you very much all the same."

They shook hands and parted.

Next morning, while the baggage was being stowed away in the prahus, Skelton asked the house boy whether, before starting, he could say good-bye to Mrs. Grange. The house boy said he would go and see. He waited a little while. Mrs. Grange came out of her room on to the verandah. She was wearing a pink dressing-gown, shabby, rumpled and none too clean, of Japanese silk, heavily trimmed with cheap lace. The powder was thick on her face, her cheeks were rouged and her lips scarlet with lipstick. Her head seemed to twitch more violently than usual and her hand was agitated by that strange gesture. When first Skelton saw it he had thought that it suggested a wish to call attention to something behind her back, but now, after what she had told him yesterday, it did indeed look as though she were constantly trying to brush something off her dress. Blood, she had said.

"I didn't want to go without thanking you for all your kindness to me," he said.

"Oh, that's all right."

"Well, good-bye."

"I'll walk down with you to the landing-stage."

They hadn't far to go. The boatmen were still arranging the luggage. Skelton looked across the river where you could see some native houses.

"I suppose these men come from over there. It looks quite a village."

"No, only those few houses. There used to be a rubber estate there, but the company went broke and it was abandoned."

"D'you ever go over there?"

"Me?" cried Mrs. Grange. Her voice rose shrill and her head, her hand, were on a sudden convulsed by a paroxysm of involuntary movement. "No. Why should I?"

Skelton could not imagine why that simple question, asked merely for something to say, should so greatly upset her. But by now all was in order and he shook hands with her. He stepped into the boat and comfortably settled down. They pushed off. He waved to Mrs. Grange. As the boat slid into the current she cried out with a harsh, strident scream:

"Give my regards to Leicester Square."

Skelton heaved a great sigh of relief as with their powerful strokes the paddlers took him farther and farther away from that dreadful house and from those two unhappy and yet repellent people. He was glad now that Mrs. Grange had not told him the story that was on the tip of her tongue to tell. He did not want some tragic tale of sin or folly to connect him with them in a recollection that he could not escape. He wanted to forget them as one forgets a bad dream.

But Mrs. Grange watched the two prahus till a bend of the river took them out of sight. She walked slowly up to the house and went into her bedroom. The light was dim because the blinds were drawn to keep out the heat, but she sat down at her dressing-table and stared at herself in the glass. Norman had had the dressing-table made for her soon after they were married. It had been made by a native carpenter, of course, and they had had the mirror sent from Singapore, but it was made to her own design, of the exact size and shape she wanted, with plenty of room for all her toilet things and her make-up. It was the dressing-table she had hankered after for donkey's years and had never had. She remembered still how pleased she was when she first had it. She threw her arms round her husband's neck and kissed him.

"Oh, Norman, you are good to me," she said. "I'm a lucky little girl to have caught a chap like you, aren't I?"

But then everything delighted her. She was amused by the river life and the life of the jungle, the teeming growth of the forest, the birds with their gay plumage and the brilliant butterflies. She set about giving the house a woman's touch; she put out all her own photographs and she got vases to put flowers in; she routed around and got a lot of knick-knacks to place here and there. "They make a room look homey," she said. She wasn't in love with Norman, but she liked him all right; and it was lovely to be married; it was lovely to have nothing to do from morning till night, except play the gramophone, or patience, and read novels. It was lovely to think one hadn't got to bother about one's future. Of course it was a bit lonely sometimes, but Norman said she'd get used to that, and he'd promised that in a year, or two at the outside, he'd take her to England for three months. It would be a lark to show him off to her friends. She felt that what had caught him was the glamour of the stage and she'd made herself out a good deal more successful than she really had been. She wanted him to realise that she'd made a sacrifice when she'd thrown up her career to become a planter's wife. She'd claimed acquaintance with a good many stars that in point of fact she'd never even spoken to. That would need a bit of handling when they went home, but she'd manage it; after all, poor Norman knew no more about the stage than a babe unborn, if she couldn't cod a simple fellow like that, after twelve years on the stage, well, she'd wasted her time, that's all she could say. Things went all right the first year. At one moment she thought she was going to have a baby. They were both disappointed when it turned out not to be true. Then she began to grow bored. It seemed to her that she'd done the same damned thing day after day for ever and it frightened her to think that she'd have to go on doing the same damned thing day after day for ever more. Norman said he couldn't leave the plantation that year. They had a bit of a scene. It was then that he'd said something that scared her.

"I hate England," he said. "If I had my way I'd never set foot in the damned country again."

Living this lonely life Mrs. Grange got into the habit of talking out loud to herself. Shut up in her room she could be heard chattering away hour after hour; and now, dipping the puff in her powder and plastering her face with it, she addressed her reflection in the mirror exactly as though she were talking to another person.

"That ought to have warned me. I should have insisted on going by myself, and who knows, I might have got a job when I got to London. With all the experience I had and everything. Then I'd have written to him and said I wasn't coming back." Her thoughts turned to Skelton. "Pity I didn't tell him," she continued. "I had half a mind to. P'raps he was right, p'raps it would have eased me mind. I wonder what he'd have said." She imitated his Oxford accent. "I'm so terribly sorry, Mrs. Grange. I wish I could help you." She gave a chuckle which was almost a sob. "I'd have liked to tell him about Jack. Oh, Jack."

It was when they had been married for two years that they got a neighbour. The price of rubber at that time was so high that new estates were being put under cultivation and one of the big companies had bought a great tract of land on the opposite bank of the river. It was a rich company and everything was done on a lavish scale. The manager they had put in had a launch at his disposal so that it was no trouble for him to pop over and have a drink whenever he felt inclined. Jack Carr his name was. He was quite a different sort of chap from Norman; for one thing he was a gentleman, he'd been to a public school and a university; he was about thirty-five, tall, not beefy like Norman, but slight, he had the sort of figure that looked lovely in evening dress; and he had crisply curling hair and a laughing look in his eyes. Just her type. She took to him at once. It was a treat, having someone you could talk about London to, and the theatre. He was gay and easy. He made the sort of jokes you could understand. In a week or two she felt more at home with him than she did with her husband after two years. There had always been something about Norman that she hadn't quite been able to get to the bottom of. He was crazy about her, of course, and he'd told her a lot about himself, but she had a funny feeling that there was something he kept from her, not because he wanted to, but—well you couldn't hardly explain it, because it was so alien, you might say, that he couldn't put it into words. Later, when she knew Jack better, she mentioned it to him, and Jack said it was because he was country-born; even though he hadn't a drop of native blood in his veins, something of the country had gone to the making of him so that he wasn't white really; he had an Eastern streak in him. However hard he tried he could never be quite English.

She chattered away aloud, in that empty house, for the two boys, the cook and the house boy, were in their own quarters, and the sound of her voice, ringing along the wooden floors, piercing the wooden walls, was like the uncanny, unhuman gibber of new wine fermenting in a vat. She spoke just as though Skelton were there, but so incoherently that if he had been, he would have had difficulty in following the story she told. It did not take her long to discover that Jack Carr wanted her. She was excited. She'd never been promiscuous, but in all those years she'd been on the stage naturally there'd been episodes. You couldn't hardly have put up with being on tour month after month if you didn't have a bit of fun sometimes. Of course now she wasn't going to give in too easily, she didn't want to make herself cheap, but what with the life she led, she'd be a fool if she missed the chance; and as far as Norman was concerned, well, what the eye didn't see the heart didn't grieve over. They understood one another all right, Jack and her; they knew it was bound to happen sooner or later, it was only a matter of waiting for the opportunity; and the opportunity came. But then something happened that they hadn't bargained for: they fell madly in love with one another. If Mrs. Grange really had been telling the story to Skelton it might have seemed as unlikely to him as it did to them. They were two very ordinary people, he a jolly, good-natured, commonplace planter, and she a small-part actress far from clever, not even very young, with nothing to recommend her but a neat figure and a prettyish face. What started as a casual affair turned without warning into a devastating passion, and neither of them was of a texture to sustain its exorbitant compulsion. They longed to be with one another; they were restless and miserable apart. She'd been finding Norman a bore for some time, but she'd put up with him because he was her husband; now he irritated her to frenzy because he stood between her and Jack. There was no question of their going off together, Jack Carr had nothing but his salary, and he couldn't throw up a job he'd been only too glad to get. It was difficult for them to meet. They had to run awful risks. Perhaps the chances they had to take, the obstacles they had to surmount, were fuel to their love; a year passed and it was as overwhelming as at the beginning; it was a year of agony and bliss, of fear and thrill. Then she discovered that she was pregnant. She had no doubt that Jack Carr was the father and she was wildly happy. It was true life was difficult, so difficult sometimes that she felt she just couldn't cope with it, but there'd be a baby, his baby, and that would make everything easy. She was going to Kuching for her confinement. It happened about then that Jack Carr had to go to Singapore on business and was to be away for several weeks; but he promised to get back before she left and he said he'd send word by a native the moment he arrived. When at last the message came she felt sick with the anguish of her joy. She had never wanted him so badly.

"I hear that Jack is back," she told her husband at dinner. "I shall go over to-morrow morning and get the things he promised to bring me."

"I wouldn't do that. He's pretty sure to drop in towards sundown and he'll bring them himself."

"I can't wait. I'm crazy to have them."

"All right. Have it your own way."

She couldn't help talking about him. For some time now they had seemed to have little to say to one another, Norman and she, but that night, in high spirits, she chattered away as she had done during the first months of their marriage. She always rose early, at six, and next morning she went down to the river and had a bathe. There was a little dent in the bank just there, with a tiny sandy beach, and it was delicious to splash about in the cool, transparent water. A kingfisher stood on the branch of a tree overhanging the pool and its reflection was brilliantly blue in the water. Lovely. She had a cup of tea and then stepped into a dug-out. A boy paddled her across the river. It took a good half-hour. As they got near she scanned the bank; Jack knew she would come at the earliest opportunity; he must be on the lookout. Ah, there he was. The delicious pain in her heart was almost unbearable. He came down to the landing-stage and helped her to get out of the boat. They walked hand in hand up the pathway and when they were out of sight of the boy who had paddled her over and of prying eyes from the house, they stopped. He put his arms round her and she yielded with ecstasy to his embrace. She clung to him. His mouth sought hers. In that kiss was all the agony of their separation and all the bliss of their reunion. The miracle of love transfused them so that they were unconscious of time and place. They were not human any more, but two spirits united by a divine fire. No thought passed through their minds. No words issued from their lips. Suddenly there was a brutal shock, like a blow, and immediately, almost simultaneously, a deafening noise. Horrified, not understanding, she clung to Jack more tightly and his grip on her was spasmodic, so that she gasped; then she felt that he was bearing her over.

"Jack."

She tried to hold him up. His weight was too great for her and as he fell to the ground she fell with him. Then she gave a great cry, for she felt a gush of heat, and his blood sputtered over her. She began to scream. A rough hand seized her and dragged her to her feet. It was Norman. She was distraught. She could not understand.

"Norman, what have you done?"

"I've killed him."

She stared at him stupidly. She pushed him aside.

"Jack. Jack."

"Shut up. I'll go and get help. It was an accident."

He walked quickly up the pathway. She fell to her knees and took Jack's head in her arms.

"Darling," she moaned. "Oh, my darling."

Norman came back with some coolies and they carried him up to the house. That night she had a miscarriage and was so ill that for days it looked as if she would die. When she recovered she had the nervous tic that she'd had ever since. She expected that Norman would send her away; but he didn't, he had to keep her to allay suspicion. There was some talk among the natives, and after a while the District Officer came up and asked a lot of questions; but the natives were frightened of Norman, and the D.O. could get nothing out of them. The Dyak boy who paddled her over had vanished. Norman said something had gone wrong with his gun and Jack was looking at it to see what was the matter and it went off. They bury people quickly in that country and by the time they might have dug him up there wouldn't have been much left to show that Norman's story wasn't true. The D.O. hadn't been satisfied.

"It all looks damned fishy to me," he said, "but in the absence of any evidence, I suppose I must accept your version."

She would have given anything to get away, but with that nervous affliction she had no ghost of a chance any longer of earning a living. She had to stay—or starve; and Norman had to keep her—or hang.

Nothing had happened since then and now nothing ever would happen. The endless years one after another dragged out their weary length.

Mrs. Grange on a sudden stopped talking. Her sharp ears had caught the sound of a footstep on the path and she knew that Norman was back from his round. Her head twitching furiously, her hand agitated by that sinister, uncontrollable gesture, she looked in the untidy mess of her dressing-table for her precious lipstick. She smeared it on her lips, and then, she didn't know why, on a freakish impulse daubed it all over her nose till she looked like a red-nose comedian in a music-hall. She looked at herself in the glass and burst out laughing.

"To hell with life!" she shouted.

The Alien Corn

I HAD known the Blands a long time before I discovered that they had any connection with Ferdy Rabenstein. Ferdy must have been nearly fifty when I first knew him and at the time of which I write he was well over seventy. He had altered little. His hair, coarse but abundant and curly, was white, but he had kept his figure and held himself as gallantly as ever. It was not hard to believe that in youth he had been as beautiful as people said. He had still his fine Semitic profile and the lustrous black eyes that had caused havoc in so many a Gentile breast. He was very tall, lean, with an oval face and a clear skin. He wore his clothes very well and in evening dress, even now, he was one of the handsomest men I had ever seen. He wore then large black pearls in his shirt-front and platinum and sapphire rings on his fingers. Perhaps he was rather flashy, but you felt it was so much in character that it would have ill become him to be anything else.

"After all, I am an Oriental," he said. "I can carry a certain barbaric magnificence."

I have often thought that Ferdy Rabenstein would make an admirable subject for a biography. He was not a great man, but within the limits he set himself he made of his life a work of art. It was a masterpiece in little, like a Persian miniature, and derived its interest from its perfection. Unfortunately the materials are scanty. They would consist of letters that may very well have been destroyed and the recollections of people who are old now and will soon be dead. His memory is extraordinary, but he would never write his memoirs, for he looks upon his past as a source of purely private entertainment; and he is a man of the most perfect discretion. Nor do I know anyone who could do justice to the subject but Max Beerbohm. There is no one else in this hard world of to-day who can look upon the trivial with such tender sympathy and wring such a delicate pathos from futility. I wonder that Max, who must have known Ferdy much better than I, and long before, was never tempted to exercise his exquisite fancy on such a theme. He was born for Max to write about. And who should have illustrated the elegant book that I see in my mind's eye but Aubrey Beardsley? Thus would have been erected a monument of triple brass and the ephemera imprisoned to succeeding ages in the amber's translucency.

Ferdy's conquests were social and his venue was the great world.

He was born in South Africa and did not come to England till he was twenty. For some time he was on the Stock Exchange, but on the death of his father he inherited a considerable fortune, and retiring from business devoted himself to the life of a man about town. At that period English society was still a closed body and it was not easy for a Jew to force its barriers, but to Ferdy they fell like the walls of Jericho. He was handsome, he was rich, he was a sportsman and he was good company. He had a house in Curzon Street, furnished with the most beautiful French furniture, and a French chef, and a brougham. It would be interesting to know the first steps in his wonderful career: they are lost in the dark absym of time. When I first met him he had been long established as one of the smartest men in London: this was at a very grand house in Norfolk to which I had been asked as a promising young novelist by the hostess who took an interest in letters, but the company was very distinguished and I was over-awed. We were sixteen, and I felt shy and alone among these Cabinet Ministers, great ladies and peers of the realm who talked of people and things of which I knew nothing. They were civil to me, but indifferent, and I was conscious that I was somewhat of a burden to my hostess. Ferdy saved me. He sat with me, walked with me and talked with me. He discovered that I was a writer and we discussed the drama and the novel; he learnt that I had lived much on the Continent and he talked to me pleasantly of France, Germany and Spain. He seemed really to seek my society. He gave me the flattering impression that he and I stood apart from the other members of the company and by our conversation upon affairs of the spirit made that of the rest of them, the political situation, the scandal of somebody's divorce and the growing disinclination of pheasants to be killed, seem a little ridiculous. But if Ferdy had at the bottom of his heart a feeling of ever so faint a contempt for the hearty British gentry that surrounded us I am sure that it was only to me that he allowed an inkling of it to appear; and looking back I cannot but wonder whether it was not after all a suave and very delicate compliment that he paid me. I think of course that he liked to exercise his charm and I dare say the obvious pleasure his conversation gave me gratified him, but he could have had no motive for taking so much trouble over an obscure novelist other than his real interest in art and letters. I felt that he and I at bottom were equally alien in that company, I because I was a writer and he because he was a Jew, but I envied the ease with which he bore himself. He was completely at home. Everyone called him Ferdy. He seemed to be always in good spirits. He was never at a loss for a quip, a jest or a repartee. They liked him in that house because he made them laugh but never made them uncomfortable by talking over their heads. He brought a faint savour of Oriental romance into their lives, but so cleverly that they only felt more English. You could never be dull when he was by and with him present you were safe from the fear of the devastating silences that sometimes overwhelm a British company. A pause looked inevitable and Ferdy Rabenstein had broken into a topic that interested everyone. An invaluable asset to any party. He had an inexhaustible fund of Jewish stories. He was a very good mimic and he assumed the Yiddish accent and reproduced the Jewish gestures to perfection; his head sank into his body, his face grew cunning, his voice oily, and he was a rabbi or an old clothes merchant or a smart commercial traveller or a fat procuress in Frankfort. It was as good as a play. Because he was himself a Jew and insisted on it you laughed without reserve, but for my own part not without an under-current of discomfort. I was not quite sure of a sense of humour that made such cruel fun of his own race. I discovered afterwards that Jewish stories were his speciality and I seldom met him anywhere without hearing him tell sooner or later the last he had heard.

But the best story he told me on this occasion was not a Jewish one. It struck me so that I have never forgotten it, but for one reason or another I have never had occasion to tell it again. I give it here because it is a curious little incident concerning persons whose names at least will live in the social history of the Victorian Era and I think it would be a pity if it were lost. He told me then that once when quite a young man he was staying in the country in a house where Mrs. Langtry, at that time at the height of her beauty and astounding reputation, was also a guest. It happened to be within driving distance of that in which lived the Duchess of Somerset, who had been Queen of Beauty at the Eglinton Tournament, and knowing her slightly, it occurred to him that it would be interesting to bring the two women together. He suggested it to Mrs. Langtry, who was willing, and forthwith wrote to the Duchess asking if he might bring the celebrated beauty to call on her. It was fitting, he said, that the loveliest woman of this generation (this was in the 'eighties) should pay her respects to the loveliest woman of the last. "Bring her by all means," answered the Duchess, "but I warn you that it will be a shock to her." They drove over in a carriage and pair, Mrs. Langtry in a close-fitting blue bonnet with long satin strings, which showed the fine shape of her head and made her blue eyes even bluer, and were received by a little ugly old hag who looked with irony out of her beady eyes at the radiant beauty who had come to see her. They had tea, they talked and they drove home again. Mrs. Langtry was very silent and when Ferdy looked at her he saw that she was quietly weeping. When they got back to the house she went to her room and would not come down to dinner that night. For the first time she had realised that beauty dies.

Ferdy asked me for my address and a few days after I got back to London invited me to dinner. There were only six of us, an American woman married to an English peer, a Swedish painter, an actress and a well-known critic. We ate very good food and drank excellent wine. The conversation was easy and intelligent. After dinner Ferdy was persuaded to play the piano. He only played Viennese waltzes, I discovered later that they were his speciality, and the light, tuneful and sensual music seemed to accord well with his discreet flamboyance. He played without affectation, with a lilt, and he had a graceful touch. This was the first of a good many dinners I had with him, he would ask me two or three times a year, and as time passed I met him more and more frequently at other people's houses. I rose in the world and perhaps he came down a little. Of late years I had sometimes found him at parties where other Jews were and I fancied that I read in his shining liquid eyes, resting for a moment on these members of his race, a certain good-natured amusement at the thought of what the world was coming to. There were people who said he was a snob, but I do not think he was; it just happened that in his early days he had never met any but the great. He had a real passion for art and in his commerce with those that produced it was at his best. With them he had never that faint air of persiflage which when he was with very grand persons made you suspect that he was never quite the dupe of their grandeur. His taste was perfect and many of his friends were glad to avail themselves of his knowledge. He was one of the first to value old furniture and he rescued many a priceless piece from the attics of ancestral mansions and gave it an honourable place in the drawing-room. It amused him to saunter round the auction rooms and he was always willing to give his advice to great ladies who desired at once to acquire a beautiful thing and make a profitable investment. He was rich and good-natured. He liked to patronise the arts and would take a great deal of trouble to get commissions for some young painter whose talent he admired or an engagement to play at a rich man's house for a violinist who could in no other way get a hearing. But he never let his rich man down. His taste was too good to deceive and civil though he might be to the mediocre he would not lift a finger to help them. His own musical parties, very small and carefully chosen, were a treat.

He never married.

"I am a man of the world," he said, "and I flatter myself that I have no prejudices, *tous les goûts sont dans la nature*, but I do not think I could bring myself to marry a Gentile. There's no harm in going to the opera in a dinner-jacket, but it just would never occur to me to do so."

"Then why didn't you marry a Jewess?"

(I did not hear this conversation, but the lively and audacious creature who thus tackled him told me of it.)

"Oh, my dear, our women are so prolific. I could not bear the thought of peopling the world with a little Ikey and a little Jacob and a little Rebecca and a little Leah and a little Rachel."

But he had had affairs of note and the glamour of past romance still clung to him. He was in his youth of an amorous complexion. I have met old ladies who told me that he was irresistible, and when in reminiscent mood they talked to me of this woman and that who had completely lost her head over him, I divined that, such was his beauty, they could not find it in their hearts to blame them. It was interesting to hear of great ladies that I had read of in the memoirs of the day or had met as respectable dowagers garrulous over their grandsons at Eton or making a mess of a hand at bridge and bethink myself that they had been consumed with sinful passion for the handsome Jew. Ferdy's most notorious amour was with the Duchess of Hereford, the loveliest, the most gallant and dashing of the beauties of the end of Queen Victoria's reign. It lasted for twenty years. He had doubtless flirtations meanwhile, but their relations were stable and recognised. It was proof of his marvellous tact that when at last they ended he exchanged an ageing mistress for a loyal friend. I remember meeting the pair not so very long ago at luncheon. She was an old woman, tall and of a commanding presence, but with a mask of paint on a ravaged face. We were lunching at the Carlton and Ferdy, our host, came a few minutes late. He offered us a cocktail and the Duchess told him we had already had one.

"Ah, I wondered why your eyes were so doubly bright," he said.

The old raddled woman flushed with pleasure.

My youth passed, I grew middle-aged, I wondered how soon I must begin to describe myself as elderly; I wrote books and plays, I travelled, I underwent experiences, I fell in love and out of it; and still I kept meeting Ferdy at parties. War broke out and was waged, millions of men were killed and the face of the world was changed. Ferdy did not like the war. He was too old to take part in it, and his German name was awkward, but he was discreet and took care not to expose himself to humiliation. His old friends were faithful to him and he lived in a dignified but not too strict seclusion. But then peace came and with courage he set himself to making the best of changed conditions. Society was mixed now, parties were rowdy, but Ferdy fitted himself to the new life. He still told his funny Jewish stories, he still played charmingly the waltzes of Strauss, he still went round auction rooms and told the new rich what they ought to buy. I went to live abroad, but whenever I was in London I saw Ferdy and now there was something a little uncanny in him. He did not give in. He had never known a day's illness. He seemed never to grow tired. He still dressed beautifully. He was interested in everybody. His mind was alert and people asked him to dinner, not for old times' sake, but because he was worth his salt. He still gave charming little concerts at his house in Curzon Street.

It was when he invited me to one of these that I made the discovery that started the recollections of him I have here set down. We were dining at a house in Hill Street, a large party, and the women having gone upstairs Ferdy and I found ourselves side by side. He told me that Lea Makart was coming to play for him on the following Friday evening and he would be glad if I would come.

"I'm awfully sorry," I said, "but I'm going down to the Blands."

"What Blands?"

"They live in Sussex at a place called Tilby."

"I didn't know you knew them."

He looked at me rather strangely. He smiled. I didn't know what amused him.

"Oh, yes, I've known them for years. It's a very nice house to stay at."

"Adolph is my nephew."

"Sir Adolphus?"

"It suggests one of the bucks of the Regency, doesn't it? But I will not conceal from you that he was named Adolf."

"Everyone I know calls him Freddy."

"I know, and I understand that Miriam, his wife, only answers to the name of Muriel."

"How does he happen to be your nephew?"

"Because Hannah Rabenstein, my sister, married Alfons Bleikogel, who ended life as Sir Alfred Bland, first Baronet, and Adolf, their only son, in due course became Sir Adolphus Bland, second Baronet."

"Then Freddy Bland's mother, the Lady Bland who lives in Portland Place, is your sister?"

"Yes, my sister Hannah. She was the eldest of the family. She's eighty, but in full possession of her faculties and a remarkable woman."

"I've never met her."

"I think your friends the Blands would just as soon you didn't. She has never lost her German accent."

"Do you never see them?" I asked.

"I haven't spoken to them for twenty years. I am such a Jew and they are so English." He smiled. "I could never remember that their names were Freddy and Muriel. I used to come out with an Adolf or a Miriam at awkward moments. And they didn't like my stories. It was better that we should not meet. When the war broke out and I would not change my name it was the last straw. It was too late, I could never have accustomed my friends to think of me as anything but Ferdy Rabenstein: I was quite content. I was not ambitious to be a Smith, a Brown or a Robinson."

Though he spoke facetiously, there was in his tone the faintest possible derision and I felt, hardly felt even, the sensation was so shadowy, that, as it had often vaguely seemed to me before, there was in the depth of his impenetrable heart a cynical contempt for the Gentiles he had conquered.

"Then you don't know the two boys?" I said.

"No."

"The eldest is called George, you know. I don't think he's so clever as Harry, the other one, but he's an engaging youth. I think you'd like him."

"Where is he now?"

"Well, he's just been sent down from Oxford. I suppose he's at home. Harry's still at Eton."

"Why don't you bring George to lunch with me?"

"I'll ask him. I should think he'd love to come."

"It has reached my ears that he's been a little troublesome."

"Oh, I don't know. He wouldn't go into the army, which is what they wanted. They rather fancied the Guards. And so he went to Oxford instead. He didn't work and he spent a great deal of money and he painted the town red. It was all quite normal."

"What was he sent down for?"

"I don't know. Nothing of any consequence."

At that moment our host rose and we went upstairs. When Ferdy bade me good-night he asked me not to forget about his great-nephew.

"Ring me up," he said. "Wednesday would suit me. Or Friday."

Next day I went down to Tilby. It was an Elizabethan mansion standing in a spacious park, in which roamed fallow deer, and from its windows you had wide views of rolling downs. It seemed to me that as far as the eye could reach the land belonged to the Blands.

His tenants must have found Sir Adolphus a wonderful landlord, for I never saw farms kept in such order, the barns and cow-sheds were spick and span and the pigsties were a picture; the public-houses looked like old English water-colours and the cottages he had built on the estate combined admirably picturesqueness and convenience. It must have cost him a pot of money to run the place on these lines. Fortunately he had it. The park with its grand old trees (and its nine-hole golf course) was tended like a garden, and the wide-stretching gardens were the pride of the neighbourhood. The magnificent house, with its steep roofs and mullioned windows, had been restored by the most celebrated architect in England and furnished by Lady Bland, with taste and knowledge, in a style that perfectly fitted it.

"Of course it's very simple," she said. "Just an English house in the country."

The dining-room was adorned with old English sporting pictures and the Chippendale chairs were of incredible value. In the drawing-room were portraits by Reynolds and Gainsborough and landscapes by Old Crome and Richard Wilson. Even in my bedroom with its four-post bed were water-colours by Birket Foster. It was very beautiful and a treat to stay there, but though it would have distressed Muriel Bland beyond anything to know it, it entirely missed oddly enough the effect she had sought. It did not give you for a moment the impression of an English house. You had the feeling that every object had been bought with a careful eye to the general scheme. You missed the dull Academy portraits that hung in the dining-room beside a Carlo Dolci that an ancestor had brought back from the grand tour, and the water-colours painted by a great-aunt that cluttered up the drawing-room so engagingly. There was no ugly Victorian sofa that had always been there and that it never occurred to anybody to take away and no needlework chairs that an unmarried daughter had so painstakingly worked at about the time of the Great Exhibition. There was beauty but no sentiment.

And yet how comfortable it was and how well looked after you were! And what a cordial greeting the Blands gave you! They seemed really to like people. They were generous and kindly. They were never happier than when they were entertaining the county, and though they had not owned the property for more than twenty years they had established themselves firmly in the favour of their neighbours. Except perhaps in their splendour and the competent way in which the estate was run there was nothing to suggest that they had not been settled there for centuries.

Freddy had been at Eton and Oxford. He was now in the early

fifties. He was quiet in manner, courtly, very clever, I imagine, but a trifle reserved. He had great elegance, but it was not an English elegance; he had grey hair and a short pointed grey beard, fine dark eyes and an aquiline nose. He was just above middle height; I don't think you would have taken him for a Jew, but rather for a foreign diplomat of some distinction. He was a man of character, but gave you, strangely enough, notwithstanding the success he had had in life, an impression of faint melancholy. His successes had been financial and political; in the world of sport, for all his perseverance, he had never shone. For many years he had followed hounds, but he was a bad rider and I think it must have been a relief to him when he could persuade himself that middle age and pressure of business forced him to give up hunting. He had excellent shooting and gave grand parties for it, but he was a poor shot; and despite the course in his park he never succeeded in being more than an indifferent golfer. He knew only too well how much these things meant in England and his incapacity was a bitter disappointment to him. However George would make up for it.

George was scratch at golf, and though tennis was not his game he played much better than the average; the Blands had had him taught to shoot as soon as he was old enough to hold a gun and he was a fine shot; they had put him on a pony when he was two and Freddy, watching him mount his horse, knew that out hunting when the boy came to a fence he felt exhilaration and not that sickening feeling in the pit of his stomach which, though he had chased the fox with such determination, had always made the sport a torture to him. George was so tall and slim, his curly hair, of a palish brown, was so fine, his eyes were so blue, he was the perfect type of the young Englishman. He had the engaging candour of the breed. His nose was straight, though perhaps a trifle fleshy, and his lips were perhaps a little full and sensual, but he had beautiful teeth, and his smooth skin was like ivory. George was the apple of his father's eye. He did not like Harry, his second son, so well. He was rather stocky, broad-shouldered and strong for his age, but his black eyes, shining with cleverness, his coarse dark hair and his big nose revealed his race. Freddy was severe with him, and often impatient, but with George he was all indulgence. Harry would go into the business, he had brains and push, but George was the heir. George would be an English gentleman.

George had offered to motor me down in the roadster his father had given him as a birthday present. He drove very fast and we arrived before the rest of the guests. The Blands were sitting on the lawn and tea was laid out under a magnificent cedar.

o

"By the way," I said presently, "I saw Ferdy Rabenstein the other day and he wants me to bring George to lunch with him."

I had not mentioned the invitation to George on the way because I thought that if there had been a family coldness I had better address his parents as well.

"Who in God's name is Ferdy Rabenstein?" said George.

How brief is human glory! A generation back such a question would have seemed grotesque.

"He's by way of being your great-uncle," I replied.

A glance had passed from father to mother when I first spoke.

"He's a horrid old man," said Muriel.

"I don't think it's in the least necessary for George to resume relationships that were definitely severed before he was born," said Freddy with decision.

"Anyhow I've delivered the message," said I, feeling somewhat snubbed.

"I don't want to see the old blighter," said George.

The conversation was broken off by the arrival of other guests and in a little while George went off to play golf with one of his Oxford friends.

It was not till next day that the matter was referred to again. I had played an unsatisfactory round with Freddy Bland in the morning and several sets of what is known as country-house tennis in the afternoon and was sitting alone with Muriel on the terrace. In England we have so much bad weather that it is only fair that a beautiful day should be more beautiful than anywhere in the world and this June evening was perfect. The blue sky was cloudless and the air was balmy; before us stretched green rolling downs, and woods, and in the distance you saw the red roofs of a little village and the grey tower of the village church. It was a day when to be alive was sufficient happiness. Detached lines of poetry hovered vaguely in my memory. Muriel and I had been chatting desultorily.

"I hope you didn't think it rather horrid of us to refuse to let George lunch with Ferdy," she said suddenly. "He's such a fearful snob, isn't he?"

"D'you think so? He's always been very nice to me."

"We haven't been on speaking terms for twenty years. Freddy never forgave him for his behaviour during the war. So unpatriotic, I thought, and one really must draw the line somewhere. You know, he absolutely refused to drop his horrible German name. With Freddy in Parliament and running munitions and all that sort of thing it was quite impossible. I don't know why he should want to see George. He can't mean anything to him."

"He's an old man. George and Harry are his great-nephews. He must leave his money to someone."

"We'd rather not have his money," said Muriel coldly.

Of course I didn't care a row of pins whether George went to lunch with Ferdy Rabenstein, and I was quite willing to let the matter drop, but evidently the Blands had talked it over and Muriel felt that some explanation was due to me.

"Of course you know that Freddy has Jewish blood in him," she said.

She looked at me sharply. Muriel was rather a big blonde woman and she spent a great deal of time trying to keep down the corpulence to which she was predisposed. She had been very pretty when young and even now was a comely person; but her round blue eyes, slightly prominent, her fleshy nose, the shape of her face and the back of her neck, her exuberant manner, betrayed her race. No Englishwoman, however fair-haired, ever looked like that. And yet her observation was designed to make me take it for granted that she was a Gentile. I answered discreetly:

"So many people have nowadays."

"I know. But there's no reason to dwell on it, is there? After all, we're absolutely English; no one could be more English than George, in appearance and manner and everything; I mean, he's such a fine sportsman and all that sort of thing, I can't see any object in his knowing Jews just because they happen to be distant connections of his."

"It's very difficult in England now not to know Jews, isn't it?"

"Oh, I know, in London one does meet a good many, and I think some of them are very nice. They're so artistic. I don't go so far as to say that Freddy and I deliberately avoid them, of course I wouldn't do that, but it just happens that we don't really know any of them very well. And down here, there simply aren't any to know."

I could not but admire the convincing manner in which she spoke. It would not have surprised me to be told that she really believed every word she said.

"You say that Ferdy might leave George his money. Well, I don't believe it's so very much anyway; it was quite a comfortable fortune before the war, but that's nothing nowadays. Besides we're hoping that George will go in for politics when he's a little older, and I don't think it would do him any good in the constituency to inherit money from a Mr. Rabenstein."

"Is George interested in politics?" I asked, to change the conversation.

"Oh, I do hope so. After all, there's the family constituency waiting for him. It's a safe Conservative seat and one can't expect Freddy to go on with the grind of the House of Commons indefinitely."

Muriel was grand. She talked already of the constituency as though twenty generations of Blands had sat for it. Her remark, however, was my first intimation that Freddy's ambition was not satisfied.

"I suppose Freddy would go to the House of Lords when George was old enough to stand."

"We've done a good deal for the party," said Muriel.

Muriel was a Catholic and she often told you that she had been educated in a convent—"Such sweet women, those nuns, I always said that if I had a daughter I should have sent her to a convent too"—but she liked her servants to be Church of England, and on Sunday evenings we had what was called supper because the fish was cold and there was ice-cream, so that they could go to church, and we were waited on by two footmen instead of four. It was still light when we finished and Freddy and I, smoking our cigars, walked up and down the terrace in the gloaming. I suppose Muriel had told him of her conversation with me, and it may be that his refusal to let George see his great-uncle still troubled him, but being subtler than she he attacked the question more indirectly. He told me that he had been very much worried about George. It had been a great disappointment that he had refused to go into the army.

"I should have thought he'd have loved the life," he said.

"And he would certainly have looked marvellous in his Guards uniform."

"He would, wouldn't he?" returned Freddy, ingenuously. "I wonder he could resist that."

He had been completely idle at Oxford; although his father had given him a very large allowance, he had got monstrously into debt; and now he had been sent down. But though he spoke so tartly I could see that he was not a little proud of his scapegrace son, and he loved him with oh, such an unEnglish love, and in his heart it flattered him that George had cut such a dash.

"Why should you worry?" I said. "You don't really care if George has a degree or not."

Freddy chuckled.

"No, I don't suppose I do really. I always think the only important thing about Oxford is that people know you were there, and I dare say that George isn't any wilder than the other young men in his set. It's the future I'm thinking of. He's so damned idle. He doesn't seem to want to do anything but have a good time."

"He's young, you know."

"He's not interested in politics, and though he's so good at games he's not even very keen on sport. He seems to spend most of his time strumming the piano."

"That's a harmless amusement."

"Oh, yes, I don't mind that, but he can't go on loafing indefinitely. You see, all this will be his one day." Freddy gave a sweeping gesture that seemed to embrace the whole county, but I knew that he did not own it all yet. "I'm very anxious that he should be fit to assume his responsibilities. His mother is very ambitious for him, but I only want him to be an English gentleman."

Freddy gave me a sidelong glance as though he wanted to say something but hesitated in case I thought it ridiculous; but there is one advantage in being a writer that, since people look upon you as of no account, they will often say things to you that they would not to their equals. He thought he would risk it.

"You know, I've got an idea that nowhere in the world now is the Greek ideal of life so perfectly cultivated as by the English country gentleman living on his estates. I think his life has the beauty of a work of art."

I could not but smile when I reflected that it was impossible for the English country gentleman in these days to do anything of the sort without a packet of money safely invested in American Bonds, but I smiled with sympathy. I thought it rather touching that this Jewish financier should cherish so romantic a dream.

"I want him to be a good landlord. I want him to take his part in the affairs of the country. I want him to be a thorough sportsman."

"Poor mutt," I thought, but said: "Well, what are your plans for George now?"

"I think he has a fancy for the diplomatic service. He's suggested going to Germany to learn the language."

"A very good idea, I should have thought."

"For some reason he's got it into his head that he wants to go to Munich."

"A nice place."

Next day I went back to London and shortly after my arrival rang up Ferdy.

"I'm sorry, but George isn't able to come to lunch on Wednesday."

"What about Friday?"

"Friday's no good either." I thought it useless to beat about the bush. "The fact is, his people aren't keen on his lunching with you."

There was a moment's silence. Then:

"I see. Well, will you come on Wednesday anyway?"

"Yes, I'd like to," I answered.

So on Wednesday at half-past one I strolled round to Curzon Street. Ferdy received me with the somewhat elaborate graciousness that he cultivated. He made no reference to the Blands. We sat in the drawing-room and I could not help reflecting what an eye for beautiful objects that family had. The room was more crowded than the fashion of to-day approves and the gold snuff-boxes in vitrines, the French china, appealed to a taste that was not mine; but they were no doubt choice pieces; and the Louis XV suite, with its beautiful *petit point*, must have been worth an enormous lot of money. The pictures on the walls by Lancret, Pater and Watteau did not greatly interest me, but I recognised their intrinsic excellence. It was a proper setting for this aged man of the world. It fitted his period. Suddenly the door opened and George was announced. Ferdy saw my surprise and gave me a little smile of triumph.

"I'm very glad you were able to come after all," he said as he shook George's hand.

I saw him in a glance take in his great-nephew whom he saw to-day for the first time. George was very well dressed. He wore a short black coat, striped trousers and the grey double-breasted waistcoat which at that time was the mode. You could only wear it with elegance if you were tall and thin and your belly was slightly concave. I felt sure that Ferdy knew exactly who George's tailor was and what haberdasher he went to and approved of them. George, so smart and trim, wearing his clothes so beautifully, certainly looked very handsome. We went down to luncheon. Ferdy had the social graces at his fingers' ends and he put the boy at his ease, but I saw that he was carefully appraising him; then, I do not know why, he began to tell some of his Jewish stories. He told them with gusto and with his wonderful mimicry. I saw George flush, and though he laughed at them, I could see that it was with embarrassment. I wondered what on earth had induced Ferdy to be so tactless. But he was watching George and he told story after story. It looked as though he would never stop. I wondered if for some reason I could not grasp he was taking a malicious pleasure in the boy's obvious discomfiture. At last we went upstairs and to make things easier I asked Ferdy to play the piano. He played us three or four little waltzes. He had lost none of his exquisite lightness nor his sense of their lilting rhythm. Then he turned to George.

"Do you play?" he asked him.

"A little."

"Won't you play something?"

"I'm afraid I only play classical music. I don't think it would interest you."

Ferdy smiled slightly, but did not insist. I said it was time for me to go and George accompanied me.

"What a filthy old Jew," he said as soon as we were in the street. "I hated those stories of his."

"They're his great stunt. He always tells them."

"Would you if you were a Jew?"

I shrugged my shoulders.

"How is it you came to lunch after all?" I asked George.

He chuckled. He was a light-hearted creature, with a sense of humour, and he shook off the slight irritation his great-uncle had caused him.

"He went to see Granny. You don't know Granny, do you?"

"No."

"She treats daddy like a kid in Etons. Granny said I was to go to lunch with great-uncle Ferdy and what Granny says goes."

"I see."

A week or two later George went to Munich to learn German. I happened then to go on a journey and it was not till the following spring that I was again in London. Soon after my arrival I found myself sitting next to Muriel Bland at dinner. I asked after George.

"He's still in Germany," she said.

"I see in the papers that you're going to have a great beano at Tilby for his coming of age."

"We're going to entertain the tenants and they're making George a presentation."

She was less exuberant than usual, but I did not pay much attention to the fact. She led a strenuous life and it might be that she was tired. I knew she liked to talk of her son, so I continued.

"I suppose George has been having a grand time in Germany," I said.

She did not answer for a moment and I gave her a glance. I was surprised to see that her eyes were filled with tears.

"I'm afraid George has gone mad," she said.

"What *do* you mean?"

"We've been so frightfully worried. Freddy's so angry, he won't even discuss it. I don't know what we're going to do."

Of course it immediately occurred to me that George, who, I supposed, like most young Englishmen sent to learn the language, had been put with a German family, had fallen in love with the daughter of the house and wanted to marry her. I had a pretty strong suspicion that the Blands were intent on his making a very grand marriage.

"Why, what's happened?" I asked.

"He wants to become a pianist."

"A what?"

"A professional pianist."

"What on earth put that idea in his head?"

"Heaven knows. We didn't know anything about it. We thought he was working for his exam. I went out to see him. I thought I'd like to know that he was getting on all right. Oh, my dear. He looks like nothing on earth. And he used to be so smart; I could have cried. He told me he wasn't going in for the exam. and had never had any intention of doing so; he'd only suggested the diplomatic service so that we'd let him go to Germany and he'd be able to study music."

"But has he any talent?"

"Oh, that's neither here nor there. Even if he had the genius of Paderewski we couldn't have George traipsing around the country playing at concerts. No one can deny that I'm very artistic, and so is Freddy, we love music and we've always known a lot of artists, but George will have a very great position, it's out of the question. We've set our hearts on his going into Parliament. He'll be very rich one day. There's nothing he can't aspire to."

"Did you point all that out to him?"

"Of course I did. He laughed at me. I told him he'd break his father's heart. He said his father could always fall back on Harry. Of course I'm devoted to Harry, and he's as clever as a monkey, but it was always understood that he was to go into the business; even though I am his mother I can see that he hasn't got the advantages that George has. Do you know what he said to me? He said that if his father would settle five pounds a week on him he would resign everything in Harry's favour and Harry could be his father's heir and succeed to the baronetcy and everything. It's too ridiculous. He said that if the Crown Prince of Roumania could abdicate a throne he didn't see why he couldn't abdicate a baronetcy. But you can't do that. Nothing can prevent him from being third baronet and if Freddy should be granted a peerage from succeeding to it at Freddy's death. Do you know, he even wants to drop the name of Bland and take some horrible German name."

I could not help asking what.

"Bleikogel or something like that," she answered.

That was a name I recognised. I remembered Ferdy telling me that Hannah Rabenstein had married Alfons Bleikogel who became eventually Sir Alfred Bland, first Baronet. It was all very strange. I wondered what had happened to the charming and so typically English boy whom I had seen only a few months before.

"Of course when I came home and told Freddy he was furious. I've never seen him so angry. He foamed at the mouth. He wired to George to come back immediately and George wired back to say he couldn't on account of his work."

"Is he working?"

"From morning till night. That's the maddening part of it. He never did a stroke of work in his life. Freddy used to say he was born idle."

"H'm."

"Then Freddy wired to say that if he didn't come he'd stop his allowance and George wired back: 'Stop it.' That put the lid on. You don't know what Freddy can be when his back is up."

I knew that Freddy had inherited a large fortune, but I knew also that he had immensely increased it, and I could well imagine that behind the courteous and amiable Squire of Tilby there was a ruthless man of affairs. He had been used to having his own way and I could believe that when crossed he would be hard and cruel.

"We'd been making George a very handsome allowance, but you know how frightfully extravagant he was. We didn't think he'd be able to hold out long and in point of fact within a month he wrote to Ferdy and asked him to lend him a hundred pounds. Ferdy went to my mother-in-law, she's his sister, you know, and asked her what it meant. Though they hadn't spoken for twenty years Freddy went to see him and begged him not to send George a penny, and he promised he wouldn't. I don't know how George has been making both ends meet. I'm sure Freddy's right, but I can't help being rather worried. If I hadn't given Freddy my word of honour that I wouldn't send him anything I think I'd have slipped a few notes in a letter in case of accident. I mean, it's awful to think that perhaps he hasn't got enough to eat."

"It'll do him no harm to go short for a bit."

"We were in an awful hole, you know. We'd made all sorts of preparations for his coming of age, and I'd issued hundreds of invitations. Suddenly George said he wouldn't come. I was simply frantic. I wrote and wired. I would have gone over to Germany only Freddy wouldn't let me. I practically went down on my bended knees to George. I begged him not to put us in such a humiliating position. I mean, it's the sort of thing it's so difficult to explain. Then my mother-in-law stepped in. You don't know her, do you? She's an extraordinary old woman. You'd never think she was Freddy's mother. She was German originally, but of very good family."

"Oh?"

"To tell you the truth I'm rather frightened of her. She tackled Freddy and then she wrote to George herself. She said that if he'd come home for his twenty-first birthday she'd pay any debts he had in Munich and we'd all give a patient hearing to anything he had to say. He agreed to that and we're expecting him one day next week. But I'm not looking forward to it, I can tell you."

She gave a deep sigh. When we were walking upstairs after dinner Freddy addressed me.

"I see Muriel has been telling you about George. The damned fool! I have no patience with him. Fancy wanting to be a pianist. It's so ungentlemanly."

"He's very young, you know," I said soothingly.

"He's had things too easy for him. I've been much too indulgent. There's never been a thing he wanted that I haven't given him. I'll learn him."

The Blands had a discreet apprehension of the uses of advertisement and I gathered from the papers that the celebrations at Tilby of George's twenty-first birthday were conducted in accordance with the usage of English county families. There was a dinner-party and a ball for the gentry and a collation and a dance in marquees on the lawn for the tenants. Expensive bands were brought down from London. In the illustrated papers were pictures of George surrounded by his family being presented with a solid silver tea-set by the tenantry. They had subscribed to have his portrait painted, but since his absence from the country had made it impossible for him to sit, the tea-service had been substituted. I read in the columns of the gossip writers that his father had given him a hunter, his mother a gramophone that changed its own records, his grandmother the dowager Lady Bland an *Encyclopædia Britannica* and his great-uncle Ferdinand Rabenstein a *Virgin and Child* by Pellegrino da Modena. I could not help observing that these gifts were bulky and not readily convertible into cash. From Ferdy's presence at the festivities I concluded that George's unaccountable vagary had effected a reconciliation between uncle and nephew. I was right. Ferdy did not at all like the notion of his great-nephew becoming a professional pianist. At the first hint of danger to its prestige the family drew together and a united front was presented to oppose George's designs. Since I was not there I only know from hearsay what happened when the birthday celebrations were over. Ferdy told me something and so did Muriel, and later George gave me his version. The Blands had very much the impression that when George came home and found himself occupying the centre of the stage, when, surrounded by splendour, he saw for himself once more how much it meant to be the heir of a great estate, he would weaken. They surrounded him with love. They flattered him. They hung on his words. They counted on the goodness of his heart and thought that if they were very kind to him he would not have the courage to cause them pain. They seemed to take it for granted that he had no intention of going back to Germany and in conversation included him in all their plans. George did not say very much. He seemed to be enjoying himself. He did not open a piano. Things looked as though they were going very well. Peace descended on the troubled house. Then one day at luncheon when they were discussing a garden-party to which they had all been asked for one day of the following week, George said pleasantly:

"Don't count on me. I shan't be here."

"Oh, George, why not?" asked his mother.

"I must get back to my work. I'm leaving for Munich on Monday."

There was an awful pause. Everyone looked for something to say, but was afraid of saying the wrong thing, and at last it seemed impossible to break it. Luncheon was finished in silence. Then George went into the garden and the others, old Lady Bland and Ferdy, Muriel and Sir Adolphus, into the morning-room. There was a family council. Muriel wept. Freddy flew into a temper. Presently from the drawing-room they heard the sound of someone playing a nocturne of Chopin. It was George. It was as though now he had announced his decision he had gone for comfort, rest and strength to the instrument he loved. Freddy sprang to his feet.

"Stop that noise," he said. "I won't have him play the piano in my house."

Muriel rang for a servant and gave him a message.

"Will you tell Mr. Bland that her ladyship has a bad headache and would he mind not playing the piano."

Ferdy, the man of the world, was deputed to have a talk with George. He was authorised to make him certain promises if he would give up the idea of becoming a pianist. If he did not wish to go into the diplomatic service his father would not insist, but if he would stand for Parliament he was prepared to pay his election expenses, give him a flat in London and make him an allowance of five thousand a year. I must say it was a handsome offer. I do not know what Ferdy said to the boy. I suppose he painted to him the life that a young man could lead in London on such an income. I am sure he made it very alluring. It availed nothing. All George asked was five pounds a week to be able to continue his studies and to be left alone. He was indifferent to the position that he might some day enjoy. He didn't want to hunt. He didn't want to shoot. He didn't want to be a Member of Parliament. He didn't want to be a millionaire. He didn't want to be a baronet. He didn't want to be a peer. Ferdy left him defeated and in a state of considerable exasperation.

After dinner that evening there was a battle royal. Freddy was a quick-tempered man, unused to opposition, and he gave George the rough side of his tongue. I gather that it was very rough indeed. The women who sought to restrain his violence were sternly silenced. Perhaps for the first time in his life Freddy would not listen to his mother. George was obstinate and sullen. He had made up his mind and if his father didn't like it he could lump it. Freddy was peremptory. He forbade George to go back to Germany. George answered that he was twenty-one and his own master. He would go where he chose. Freddy swore he would not give him a penny.

"All right, I'll earn money."

"You! You've never done a stroke of work in your life. What do you expect to do to earn money?"

"Sell old clothes," grinned George.

There was a gasp from all of them. Muriel was so taken aback that she said a stupid thing.

"Like a Jew?"

"Well, aren't I a Jew? And aren't you a Jewess and isn't daddy a Jew? We're all Jews, the whole gang of us, and everyone knows it and what the hell's the good of pretending we're not?"

Then a very dreadful thing happened. Freddy burst suddenly into tears. I'm afraid he didn't behave very much like Sir Adolphus Bland, Bart., M.P., and the good old English gentleman he so much wanted to be, but like an emotional Adolf Bleikogel who loved his son and wept with mortification because the great hopes he had set on him were brought to nothing and the ambition of his life was frustrated. He cried noisily with great loud sobs and pulled his beard and beat his breast and rocked to and fro. Then they all began to cry, old Lady Bland and Muriel, and Ferdy, who sniffed and blew his nose and wiped the tears streaming down his face, and even George cried. Of course it was very painful, but to our rough Anglo-Saxon temperament I am afraid it must seem also a trifle ridiculous. No one tried to console anybody else. They just sobbed and sobbed. It broke up the party.

But it had no result on the situation. George remained obdurate. His father would not speak to him. There were more scenes. Muriel sought to excite his pity; he was deaf to her piteous entreaties, he did not seem to mind if he broke her heart, he did not care two hoots if he killed his father. Ferdy appealed to him as a sportsman and a man of the world. George was flippant and indeed personally offensive. Old Lady Bland with her guttural German accent and strong common-sense argued with him, but he would not listen to reason. It was she, however, who at last found a way out. She made George acknowledge that it was no use to throw away all the beautiful things the world laid at his feet unless he had talent. Of course he thought he had, but he might be mistaken. It was not worth while to be a second-rate pianist. His only excuse, his only justification, was genius. If he had genius his family had no right to stand in his way.

"You can't expect me to show genius already," said George. "I shall have to work for years."

"Are you sure you are prepared for that?"

"It's my only wish in the world. I'll work like a dog. I only want to be given my chance."

This was the proposition she made. His father was determined to give him nothing and obviously they could not let the boy starve. He had mentioned five pounds a week. Well, she was willing to give him that herself. He could go back to Germany and study for two years. At the end of that time he must come back and they would get some competent and disinterested person to hear him play, and if then that person said he showed promise of becoming a first-rate pianist no further obstacles would be placed in his way. He would be given every advantage, help and encouragement. If on the other hand that person decided that his natural gifts were not such as to ensure ultimate success he must promise faithfully to give up all thoughts of making music his profession and in every way accede to his father's wishes. George could hardly believe his ears.

"Do you mean that, Granny?"

"I do."

"But will daddy agree?"

"I vill see dat he does," she answered.

George seized her in his arms and impetuously kissed her on both cheeks.

"Darling," he cried.

"Ah, but de promise?"

He gave her his solemn word of honour that he would faithfully abide by the terms of the arrangement. Two days later he went back to Germany. Though his father consented unwillingly to his going, and indeed could not help doing so, he would not be reconciled to him and when he left refused to say good-bye to him. I imagine that in no manner could he have caused himself such pain. I permit myself a trite remark. It is strange that men, inhabitants for so short a

while of an alien and inhuman world, should go out of their way to
cause themselves so much unhappiness.

George had stipulated that during his two years of study his family
should not visit him, so that when Muriel heard some months before
he was due to come home that I was passing through Munich on
my way to Vienna, whither business called me, it was not unnatural
that she should ask me to look him up. She was anxious to have
first-hand information about him. She gave me George's address and
I wrote ahead, telling him I was spending a day in Munich, and
asked him to lunch with me. His answer awaited me at the hotel.
He said he worked all day and could not spare the time to lunch
with me, but if I would come to his studio about six he would like to
show me that and if I had nothing better to do would love to spend
the evening with me. So soon after six I went to the address he gave
me. He lived on the second floor of a large block of flats and when I
came to his door I heard the sound of piano-playing. It stopped
when I rang and George opened the door for me. I hardly recognised
him. He had grown very fat. His hair was extremely long, it curled
all over his head in picturesque confusion; and he had certainly not
shaved for three days. He wore a grimy pair of Oxford bags, a tennis
shirt and slippers. He was not very clean and his finger-nails were
rimmed with black. It was a startling change from the spruce, slim
youth so elegantly dressed in such beautiful clothes that I had last
seen. I could not but think it would be a shock to Ferdy to see him
now. The studio was large and bare; on the walls were three or four
unframed canvases of a highly cubist nature, there were several arm-
chairs much the worse for wear, and a grand piano. Books were
littered about and old newspapers and art magazines. It was dirty
and untidy and there was a frowzy smell of stale beer and stale smoke.
  "Do you live here alone?" I asked.
  "Yes, I have a woman who comes in twice a week and cleans up.
But I make my own breakfast and lunch."
  "Can you cook?"
  "Oh, I only have bread and cheese and a bottle of beer for lunch.
I dine at a *Bierstube*."
  It was pleasant to discover that he was very glad to see me. He
seemed in great spirits and extremely happy. He asked after his
relations and we talked of one thing and another. He had a lesson
twice a week and for the rest of the time practised. He told me that
he worked ten hours a day.
  "That's a change," I said.
  He laughed.

"Daddy said I was born tired. I wasn't really lazy. I didn't see the use of working at things that bored me."

I asked him how he was getting on with the piano. He seemed to be satisfied with his progress and I begged him to play to me.

"Oh, not now, I'm all in, I've been at it all day. Let's go out and dine and come back here later and then I'll play. I generally go to the same place, there are several students I know there, and it's rather fun."

Presently we set out. He put on socks and shoes and a very old golf coat, and we walked together through the wide quiet streets. It was a brisk cold day. His step was buoyant. He looked round him with a sigh of delight.

"I love Munich," he said. "It's the only city in the world where there's art in the very air you breathe. After all, art is the only thing that matters, isn't it? I loathe the idea of going home."

"All the same I'm afraid you'll have to."

"I know. I'll go all right, but I'm not going to think about it till the time comes."

"When you do, you might do worse than get a haircut. If you don't mind my saying so you look almost too artistic to be convincing."

"You English, you're such Philistines," he said.

He took me to a rather large restaurant in a side street, crowded even at that early hour with people dining and furnished heavily in the German medieval style. A table covered with a red cloth, well away from the air, was reserved for George and his friends and when we went to it four or five youths were at it. There was a Pole studying Oriental languages, a student of philosophy, a painter (I suppose the author of George's cubist pictures), a Swede, and a young man who introduced himself to me, clicking his heels, as Hans Reiting, *Dichter*, namely Hans Reiting, poet. Not one of them was more than twenty-two and I felt a trifle out of it. They all addressed George as *du* and I noticed that his German was extremely fluent. I had not spoken it for some time and mine was rusty, so that I could not take much part in the lively conversation. But nevertheless I thoroughly enjoyed myself. They ate sparingly, but drank a good deal of beer. They talked of art and women. They were very revolutionary and though gay very much in earnest. They were contemptuous of everyone you had ever heard of, and the only point on which they all agreed was that in this topsy-turvy world only the vulgar could hope for success. They argued points of technique with animation, and contradicted one another, and shouted and were obscene. They had a grand time.

At about eleven George and I walked back to his studio. Munich
is a city that frolics demurely and except about the Marienplatz the
streets were still and empty. When we got in he took off his coat and
said:

"Now I'll play to you."

I sat in one of the dilapidated arm-chairs and a broken spring
stuck into my behind, but I made myself as comfortable as I could.
George played Chopin. I know very little of music and that is one
of the reasons for which I have found this story difficult to write.
When I go to a concert at the Queen's Hall and in the intervals read
the programme it is all Greek to me. I know nothing of harmony
and counterpoint. I shall never forget how humiliated I felt once
when, having come to Munich for a Wagner Festival, I went to a
wonderful performance of *Tristan und Isolde* and never heard a note
of it. The first few bars sent me off and I began to think of what I was
writing, my characters leapt into life and I heard their long conversations, I suffered their pains and was a party to their joy; the years
swept by and all sorts of things happened to me, the spring brought
me its rapture and in the winter I was cold and hungry; and I loved
and I hated and I died. I suppose there were intervals in which I
walked round and round the garden and probably ate *Schinken-
Brödchen* and drank beer, but I have no recollection of them. The
only thing I know is that when the curtain for the last time fell I woke
with a start. I had had a wonderful time, but I could not help thinking it was very stupid of me to come such a long way and spend
so much money if I couldn't pay attention to what I heard and
saw.

I knew most of the things George played. They were the familiar
pieces of concert programmes. He played with a great deal of dash.
Then he played Beethoven's *Appassionata*. I used to play it myself
when I played the piano (very badly) in my far distant youth and I
still knew every note of it. Of course it is a classic and a great work,
it would be foolish to deny it, but I confess that at this time of day it
leaves me cold. It is like *Paradise Lost*, splendid, but a trifle stolid.
This too George played with vigour. He sweated profusely. At first
I could not make out what was the matter with his playing, something did not seem to me quite right, and then it struck me that the
two hands did not exactly synchronise, so that there was ever so
slight an interval between the bass and the treble; but I repeat, I am
ignorant of these things; what disconcerted me might have been
merely the effect of his having drunk a good deal of beer that evening or indeed only my fancy. I said all I could think of to praise
him.

"Of course I know I need a lot more work. I'm only a beginner, but I know I can do it. I feel it in my bones. It'll take me ten years, but then I shall be a pianist."

He was tired and came away from the piano. It was after midnight and I suggested going, but he would not hear of it. He opened a couple of bottles of beer and lit his pipe. He wanted to talk.

"Are you happy here?" I asked him.

"Very," he answered gravely. "I'd like to stay for ever. I've never had such fun in my life. This evening, for instance. Wasn't it grand?"

"It was very jolly. But one can't go on leading the student's life. Your friends here will grow older and go away."

"Others'll come. There are always students here and people like that."

"Yes, but you'll grow older too. Is there anything more lamentable than the middle-aged man who tries to go on living the undergraduate's life? The old fellow who wants to be a boy among boys, and tries to persuade himself that they'll accept him as one of themselves—how ridiculous he is. It can't be done."

"I feel so at home here. My poor father wants me to be an English gentleman. It gives me gooseflesh. I'm not a sportsman. I don't care a damn for hunting and shooting and playing cricket. I was only acting."

"You gave a very natural performance."

"It wasn't till I came here that I knew it wasn't real. I loved Eton, and Oxford was a riot, but all the same I knew I didn't belong. I played the part all right, because acting's in my blood, but there was always something in me that wasn't satisfied. The house in Grosvenor Square is a freehold and daddy paid a hundred and eighty thousand pounds for Tilby; I don't know if you understand what I mean, I felt they were just furnished houses we'd taken for the season and one of these days we'd pack up and the real owners would come back."

I listened to him attentively, but I wondered how much he was describing what he had obscurely felt and how much he imagined now in his changed circumstances that he had felt.

"I used to hate hearing great-uncle Ferdy tell his Jewish stories. I thought it so damned mean. I understand now; it was a safety valve. My God, the strain of being a man about town. It's easier for daddy, he can play the old English squire at Tilby, but in the City he can be himself. He's all right. I've taken the make-up off and my stage clothes and at last I can be my real self too. What a relief! You know, I don't like English people. I never really know where I

am with you. You're so dull and conventional. You never let yourselves go. There's no freedom in you, freedom of the soul, and you're
such funks. There's nothing in the world you're so frightened of as
doing the wrong thing."

"Don't forget that you're English yourself, George," I murmured.
He laughed.

"I? I'm not English. I haven't got a drop of English blood in me.
I'm a Jew and you know it, and a German Jew into the bargain. I
don't want to be English. I want to be a Jew. My friends are Jews.
You don't know how much more easy I feel with them. I can be myself. We did everything we could to avoid Jews at home; Mummy,
because she was blonde, thought she could get away with it and pretended she was a Gentile. What rot! D'you know, I have a lot of fun
wandering about the Jewish parts of Munich and looking at the
people. I went to Frankfort once, there are a lot of them there, and I
walked about and looked at the frowzy old men with their hooked
noses and the fat women with their false hair. I felt such a sympathy
for them, I felt I belonged to them, I could have kissed them. When
they looked at me I wondered if they knew that I was one of them.
I wish to God I knew Yiddish. I'd like to become friends with them,
and go into their houses and eat Kosher food and all that sort of
thing. I wanted to go to a synagogue, but I was afraid I'd do the
wrong thing and be kicked out. I like the smell of the Ghetto and the
sense of life, and the mystery and the dust and the squalor and the
romance. I shall never get the longing for it out of my head now.
That's the real thing. All the rest is only pretence."

"You'll break your father's heart," I said.

"It's his or mine. Why can't he let me go? There's Harry. Harry
would love to be squire of Tilby. He'd be an English gentleman all
right. You know, mummy's set her heart on my marrying a Christian. Harry would love to. He'll found the good old English family
all right. After all, I ask so little. I only want five pounds a week,
and they can keep the title and the park and the Gainsboroughs and
the whole bag of tricks."

"Well, the fact remains that you gave your solemn word of honour
to go back after two years."

"I'll go back all right," he said sullenly. "Lea Makart has promised to come and hear me play."

"What'll you do if she says you're no good?"

"Shoot myself," he said gaily.

"What nonsense," I answered in the same tone.

"Do *you* feel at home in England?"

"No," I said, "but then I don't feel at home anywhere else."

But he was quite naturally not interested in me.

"I loathe the idea of going back. Now that I know what life has to offer I wouldn't be an English country gentleman for anything in the world. My God, the boredom of it!"

"Money's a very nice thing and I've always understood it's very pleasant to be an English peer."

"Money means nothing to me. I want none of the things it can buy, and I don't happen to be a snob."

It was growing very late and I had to get up early next day. It seemed unnecessary for me to pay too much attention to what George said. It was the sort of nonsense a young man might very well indulge in when thrown suddenly among painters and poets. Art is strong wine and needs a strong head to carry it. The divine fire burns most efficiently in those who temper its fury with horse sense. After all, George was not twenty-three yet. Time teaches. And when all was said and done his future was no concern of mine. I bade him good-night and walked back to my hotel. The stars were shining in the indifferent sky. I left Munich in the morning.

I did not tell Muriel on my return to London what George had said to me, or what he looked like, but contented myself with assuring her that he was well and happy, working very hard, and seemed to be leading a virtuous and sober life. Six months later he came home. Muriel asked me to go down to Tilby for the week-end: Ferdy was bringing Lea Makart to hear George play and he particularly wished me to be there. I accepted. Muriel met me at the station.

"How did you find George?" I asked.

"He's very fat, but he seems in great spirits. I think he's pleased to be back again. He's been very sweet to his father."

"I'm glad of that."

"Oh, my dear, I do hope Lea Makart will say he's no good. It'll be such a relief to all of us."

"I'm afraid it'll be a terrible disappointment to him."

"Life is full of disappointments," said Muriel crisply. "But one learns to put up with them."

I gave her a smile of amusement. We were sitting in a Rolls, and there was a footman as well as a chauffeur on the box. She wore a string of pearls that had probably cost forty thousand pounds. I recollected that in the birthday honours Sir Adolphus Bland had not been one of the three gentlemen on whom the King had been pleased to confer a peerage.

Lea Makart was able to make only a flying visit. She was playing that evening at Brighton and would motor over to Tilby on the Sunday morning for luncheon. She was returning to London the same day because she had a concert in Manchester on the Monday. George was to play in the course of the afternoon.

"He's practising very hard," his mother told me. "That's why he didn't come with me to meet you."

We turned in at the park gates and drove up the imposing avenue of elms that led to the house. I found that there was no party.

I met the dowager Lady Bland for the first time. I had always been curious to see her. I had had in my mind's eye a somewhat sensational picture of an old, old Jewish woman who lived alone in her grand house in Portland Place and, with a finger in every pie, ruled her family with a despotic hand. She did not disappoint me. She was of a commanding presence, rather tall, and stout without being corpulent. Her countenance was markedly Hebraic. She wore a rather heavy moustache and a wig of a peculiarly metallic brown. Her dress was very grand, of black brocade, and she had a row of large diamond stars on her breast and round her neck a chain of diamonds. Diamond rings gleamed on her wrinkled hands. She spoke in a rather loud harsh voice and with a strong German accent. When I was introduced to her she fixed me with shining eyes. She summed me up with despatch and to my fancy at all events made no attempt to conceal from me that the judgment she formed was unfavourable.

"You have known my brother Ferdinand for many years, is it not so?" she said, rolling a guttural R. "My brother Ferdinand has always moved in very good society. Where is Sir Adolphus, Muriel? Does he know your guest is arrived? And will you not send for George? If he does not know his pieces by now he will not know them by to-morrow."

Muriel explained that Freddy was finishing a round of golf with his secretary and that she had had George told I was there. Lady Bland looked as though she thought Muriel's replies highly unsatisfactory and turned again to me.

"My daughter-in-law tells me you have been in Italy?"

"Yes, I've only just come back."

"It is a beautiful country. How is the King?"

I said I did not know.

"I used to know him when he was a little boy. He was not very strong then. His mother, Queen Margherita, was a great friend of mine. They thought he would never marry. The Duchess of Aosta was very angry when he fell in love with the Princess of Montenegro."

She seemed to belong to some long-past period of history, but she was very alert and I imagine that little escaped her beady eyes. Freddy, very spruce in plus-fours, presently came in. It was amusing and yet a little touching to see this grey-bearded man, as a rule somewhat domineering, so obviously on his best behaviour with the old lady. He called her Mamma. Then George came in. He was as fat as ever, but he had taken my advice and had his hair cut; he was losing his boyish looks, but he was a powerful and well-set-up young man. It was good to see the pleasure he took in his tea. He ate quantities of sandwiches and great hunks of cake. He had still a boy's appetite. His father watched him with a tender smile and as I looked at him I could not be surprised at the attachment which they all so obviously felt for him. He had an ingenuousness, a charm and an enthusiasm which were certainly very pleasant. There was about him a generosity of demeanour, a frankness and a natural cordiality which could not but make people take to him. I do not know whether it was owing to a hint from his grandmother or merely of his own good nature, but it was plain that he was going out of his way to be nice to his father; and in his father's soft eyes, in the way he hung upon the boy's words, in his pleased, proud and happy look, you felt how bitterly the estrangement of the last two years had weighed on him. He adored George.

We played golf in the morning, a three-ball match, since Muriel, having to go to Mass, could not join us, and at one Ferdy arrived in Lea Makart's car. We sat down to luncheon. Of course Lea Makart's reputation was well known to me. She was acknowledged to be the greatest woman pianist in Europe. She was a very old friend of Ferdy's, who with his interest and patronage had greatly helped her at the beginning of her career, and it was he who had arranged for her to come and give her opinion of George's chances. At one time I went as often as I could to hear her play. She had no affectations; she played as a bird sings, without any appearance of effort, very naturally, and the silvery notes dripped from her light fingers in a curiously spontaneous manner, so that it gave you the impression that she was improvising those complicated rhythms. They used to tell me that her technique was wonderful. I could never make up my mind how much the delight her playing gave me was due to her person. In those days she was the most ethereal thing you could imagine, and it was surprising that a creature so sylphlike should be capable of so much power. She was very slight, pale, with enormous eyes and magnificent black hair, and at the piano she had a child-like wistfulness that was most appealing. She was very beautiful in a hardly human way and when she played, a little smile on her closed lips, she seemed to be remembering things she had heard in another world. Now, however, a woman in the early forties, she was sylphlike no more; she was stout and her face had broadened; she had no longer that lovely remoteness, but the authority of her long succession of triumphs. She was brisk, business-like and somewhat overwhelming. Her vitality lit her with a natural spotlight as his sanctity surrounds the saint with a halo. She was not interested in anything very much but her own affairs, but since she had humour and knew the world she was able to invest them with gaiety. She held the conversation, but did not absorb it. George talked little. Every now and then she gave him a glance, but did not try to draw him in. I was the only Gentile at the table. All but old Lady Bland spoke perfect English, yet I could not help feeling that they did not speak like English people; I think they rounded their vowels more than we do, they certainly spoke louder, and the words seemed not to fall, but to gush from their lips. I think if I had been in another room where I could hear the tone but not the words of their speech I should have thought it was in a foreign language that they were conversing. The effect was slightly disconcerting.

Lea Makart wished to set out for London at about six, so it was arranged that George should play at four. Whatever the result of the audition, I felt that I, a stranger in the circle which her departure must render exclusively domestic, would be in the way and so, pretending an early engagement in town next morning, I asked her if she would take me with her in her car.

At a little before four we all wandered into the drawing-room. Old Lady Bland sat on a sofa with Ferdy; Freddy, Muriel and I made ourselves comfortable in arm-chairs; and Lea Makart sat by herself. She chose instinctively a high-backed Jacobean chair that had somewhat the air of a throne, and in a yellow dress, with her olive skin, she looked very handsome. She had magnificent eyes. She was very much made up and her mouth was scarlet.

George gave no sign of nervousness. He was already seated at the piano when I went in with his father and mother, and he watched us quietly settling ourselves down. He gave me the shadow of a smile. When he saw that we were all at our ease he began to play. He played Chopin. He played two waltzes that were familiar to me, a polonaise and an *étude*. He played with a great deal of brio. I wish I knew music well enough to give an exact description of his playing. It had strength, and a youthful exuberance, but I felt that he missed what to me is the peculiar charm of Chopin, the tenderness, the nervous melancholy, the wistful gaiety and the slightly faded romance that reminds me always of an Early Victorian keepsake. And again I had the vague sensation, so slight that it almost escaped me, that the two hands did not quite synchronise. I looked at Ferdy and saw him give his sister a look of faint surprise, Muriel's eyes were fixed on the pianist, but presently she dropped them and for the rest of the time stared at the floor. His father looked at him too, and his eyes were steadfast, but unless I was much mistaken he went pale and his face betrayed something like dismay. Music was in the blood of all of them, all their lives they had heard the greatest pianists in the world, and they judged with instinctive precision. The only person whose face betrayed no emotion was Lea Makart. She listened very attentively. She was as still as an image in a niche.

At last he stopped and turning round on his seat faced her. He did not speak.

"What is it you want me to tell you?" she asked.

They looked into one another's eyes.

"I want you to tell me whether I have any chance of becoming in time a pianist in the first rank."

"Not in a thousand years."

For a moment there was dead silence. Freddy's head sank and he looked down at the carpet at his feet. His wife put out her hand and took his. But George continued to look steadily at Lea Makart.

"Ferdy has told me the circumstances," she said at last. "Don't think I'm influenced by them. Nothing of this is very important." She made a great sweeping gesture that took in the magnificent room with the beautiful things it contained and all of us. "If I thought you had in you the makings of an artist I shouldn't hesitate to beseech you to give up everything for art's sake. Art is the only thing that matters. In comparison with art, wealth and rank and power are not worth a straw." She gave us a look so sincere that it was void of insolence. "We are the only people who count. We give the world significance. You are only our raw material."

I was not too pleased to be included with the rest under that heading, but that is neither here nor there.

"Of course I can see that you've worked very hard. Don't think it's been wasted. It will always be a pleasure to you to be able to play the piano and it will enable you to appreciate great playing as no ordinary person can hope to do. Look at your hands. They're not a pianist's hands."

Involuntarily I glanced at George's hands. I had never noticed them before. I was astounded to see how podgy they were and how short and stumpy the fingers.

"Your ear is not quite perfect. I don't think you can ever hope to be more than a very competent amateur. In art the difference between the amateur and the professional is immeasurable."

George did not reply. Except for his pallor no one would have known that he was listening to the blasting of all his hopes. The silence that fell was quite awful. Lea Makart's eyes suddenly filled with tears.

"But don't take my opinion alone," she said. "After all, I'm not infallible. Ask somebody else. You know how good and generous Paderewski is. I'll write to him about you and you can go down and play to him. I'm sure he'll hear you."

George now gave a little smile. He had very good manners and whatever he was feeling did not want to make the situation too difficult for others.

"I don't think that's necessary, I am content to accept your verdict. To tell you the truth it's not so very different from my master's in Munich."

He got up from the piano and lit a cigarette. It eased the strain. The others moved a little in their chairs. Lea Makart smiled at George.

"Shall I play to you?" she said.

"Yes, do."

She got up and went to the piano. She took off the rings with which her fingers were laden. She played Bach. I do not know the names of the pieces, but I recognised the stiff ceremonial of the frenchified little German courts and the sober, thrifty comfort of the burghers, and the dancing on the village green, the green trees that looked like Christmas trees, and the sunlight on the wide German country, and a tender cosiness; and in my nostrils there was a warm scent of the soil and I was conscious of a sturdy strength that seemed to have its roots deep in mother earth, and of an elemental power that was timeless and had no home in space. She played beautifully, with a soft brilliance that made you think of the full moon shining at dusk in the summer sky. With another part of me I watched the others and I saw how intensely they were conscious of the experience. They were rapt. I wished with all my heart that I could get from music the wonderful exaltation that possessed them. She stopped, a smile hovered on her lips, and she put on her rings. George gave a little chuckle.

"That clinches it, I fancy," he said.

The servants brought in tea and after tea Lea Makart and I bade the company farewell and got into the car. We drove up to London. She talked all the way, if not brilliantly at all events with immense gusto; she told me of her early years in Manchester and of the struggle of her beginnings. She was very interesting. She never even mentioned George; the episode was of no consequence, it was finished and she thought of it no more.

We little knew what was happening at Tilby. When we left George went out on the terrace and presently his father joined him. Freddy had won the day, but he was not happy. With his more than feminine sensitiveness he felt all that George was feeling, and George's anguish simply broke his heart. He had never loved his son more than then. When he appeared George greeted him with a little smile. Freddy's voice broke. In a sudden and overwhelming emotion he found it in him to surrender the fruits of his victory.

"Look here, old boy," he said, "I can't bear to think that you've had such a disappointment. Would you like to go back to Munich for another year and then see?"

George shook his head.

"No, it wouldn't be any good. I've had my chance. Let's call it a day."

"Try not to take it too hard."

"You see, the only thing in the world I want is to be a pianist. And there's nothing doing. It's a bit thick if you come to think of it."

George, trying so hard to be brave, smiled wanly.

"Would you like to go round the world? You can get one of your Oxford pals to go with you and I'll pay all the expenses. You've been working very hard for a long time."

"Thanks awfully, daddy, we'll talk about it. I'm just going for a stroll now."

"Shall I come with you?"

"I'd rather go alone."

Then George did a strange thing. He put his arm round his father's neck, and kissed him on the lips. He gave a funny little moved laugh and walked away. Freddy went back to the drawing-room. His mother, Ferdy and Muriel were sitting there.

"Freddy, why don't you marry the boy?" said the old lady. "He is twenty-three. It would take his mind off his troubles and when he is married and has a baby he will soon settle down like everybody else."

"Whom is he to marry, mamma?" asked Sir Adolphus, smiling.

"That's not so difficult. Lady Frielinghausen came to see me the other day with her daughter Violet. She is a very nice maiden and she will have money of her own. Lady Frielinghausen gave me to understand that her Sir Jacob would come down very handsome if Violet made a good match."

Muriel flushed.

"I hate Lady Frielinghausen. George is much too young to marry. He can afford to marry anyone he likes."

Old Lady Bland gave her daughter a strange look.

"You are a very foolish girl, Miriam," she said, using the name Muriel had long discarded. "As long as I am here I shall not allow you to commit a foolishness."

She knew as well as if Muriel had said it in so many words that she wanted George to marry a Gentile, but she knew also that so long as she was alive neither Freddy nor his wife would dare to suggest it.

But George did not go for a walk. Perhaps because the shooting season was about to open he took it into his head to go into the gun-room. He began to clean the gun that his mother had given him on his twentieth birthday. No one had used it since he went to Germany. Suddenly the servants were startled by a report. When they went into the gun-room they found George lying on the floor shot through the heart. Apparently the gun had been loaded and George while playing about with it had accidentally shot himself. One reads of such accidents in the paper often.

The Creative Impulse

I SUPPOSE that very few people know how Mrs. Albert Forrester came to write *The Achilles Statue*; and since it has been acclaimed as one of the great novels of our time I cannot but think that a brief account of the circumstances that gave it birth must be of interest to all serious students of literature; and indeed, if, as the critics say, this is a book that will live, the following narrative, serving a better purpose than to divert an idle hour, may be regarded by the historian of the future as a curious footnote to the literary annals of our day.

Everyone of course remembers the success that attended the publication of *The Achilles Statue*. Month after month printers were kept busy printing, binders were kept busy binding, edition after edition; and the publishers, both in England and America, were hard put to it to fulfil the pressing orders of the booksellers. It was promptly translated into every European tongue and it has been recently announced that it will soon be possible to read it in Japanese and in Urdu. But it had previously appeared serially in magazines on both sides of the Atlantic and from the editors of these Mrs. Albert Forrester's agent had wrung a sum that can only be described as thumping. A dramatisation of the work was made, which ran for a season in New York, and there is little doubt that when the play is produced in London it will have an equal success. The film rights have been sold at a great price. Though the amount that Mrs. Albert Forrester is reputed (in literary circles) to have made is probably exaggerated, there can be no doubt that she will have earned enough money from this one book to save her for the rest of her life from any financial anxiety.

It is not often that a book meets with equal favour from the public and the critics, and that she, of all persons, had (if I may so put it) squared the circle must have proved the more gratifying to Mrs. Albert Forrester, since, though she had received the commendation of the critics in no grudging terms (and indeed had come to look upon it as her due), the public had always remained strangely insensible to her merit. Each work she published, a slender volume beautifully printed and bound in white buckram, was hailed as a masterpiece, always to the length of a column, and in the weekly reviews which you see only in the dusty library of a very long-established club even to the extent of a page; and all well-read persons read and praised it. But well-read persons apparently do not buy books, and

433

she did not sell. It was indeed a scandal that so distinguished an author, with an imagination so delicate and a style so exquisite, should remain neglected of the vulgar. In America she was almost completely unknown; and though Mr. Carl van Vechten had written an article berating the public for its obtuseness, the public remained callous. Her agent, a warm admirer of her genius, had blackmailed an American publisher into taking two of her books by refusing, unless he did so, to let him have others (trashy novels doubtless) that he badly wanted, and they had been duly published. The reception they received from the press was flattering and showed that in America the best minds were sensitive to her talent; but when it came to the third book the American publisher (in the coarse way publishers have) told the agent that any money he had to spare he preferred to spend on synthetic gin.

Since *The Achilles Statue* Mrs. Albert Forrester's previous books have been republished (and Mr. Carl van Vechten has written another article pointing out sadly, but firmly, that he had drawn the attention of the reading world to the merits of this exceptional writer fully fifteen years ago), and they have been so widely advertised that they can scarcely have escaped the cultured reader's attention. It is unnecessary, therefore, for me to give an account of them; and it would certainly be no more than cold potatoes after those two subtle articles by Mr. Carl van Vechten. Mrs. Albert Forrester began to write early. Her first work (a volume of elegies) appeared when she was a maiden of eighteen; and from then on she published, every two or three years, for she had too exalted a conception of her art to hurry her production, a volume either of verse or prose. When *The Achilles Statue* was written she had reached the respectable age of fifty-seven, so that it will be readily surmised that the number of her works was considerable. She had given the world half a dozen volumes of verse, published under Latin titles, such as *Felicitas, Pax Maris* and *Aes Triplex*, all of the graver kind, for her muse, disinclined to skip on a light, fantastic toe, trod a somewhat solemn measure. She remained faithful to the Elegy, and the Sonnet claimed much of her attention; but her chief distinction was to revive the Ode, a form of poetry that the poets of the present day somewhat neglect; and it may be asserted with confidence that her *Ode to President Fallières* will find a place in every anthology of English verse. It is admirable not only for the noble sonority of its rhythms, but also for its felicitous description of the pleasant land of France. Mrs. Albert Forrester wrote of the valley of the Loire with its memories of du Bellay, of Chartres and the jewelled windows of its cathedral, of the sun-swept cities of Provence, with a sympathy all the more remarkable since she had never penetrated further into France than Boulogne, which she visited shortly after her marriage on an excursion steamer from Margate. But the physical mortification of being extremely seasick and the intellectual humiliation of discovering that the inhabitants of that popular seaside resort could not understand her fluent and idiomatic French made her determine not to expose herself a second time to experiences that were at once undignified and unpleasant; and she never again embarked on the treacherous element which she, however, sang (*Pax Maris*) in numbers both grave and sweet.

There are some fine passages too in the *Ode to Woodrow Wilson*, and I regret that, owing to a change in her sentiments towards that no doubt excellent man, the author decided not to reprint it. But I think it must be admitted that Mrs. Albert Forrester's most distinguished work was in prose. She wrote several volumes of brief, but perfectly constructed, essays on such subjects as Autumn in Sussex, Queen Victoria, Death, Spring in Norfolk, Georgian Architecture, Monsieur de Diaghileff and Dante; she also wrote works, both erudite and whimsical, on the Jesuit Architecture of the XVIIth Century and on the Literary Aspect of the Hundred Years War. It was her prose that gained her that body of devoted admirers, fit though few, as with her rare gift of phrase she herself put it, that proclaimed her the greatest master of the English language that this century has seen. She admitted herself that it was her style, sonorous yet racy, polished yet eloquent, that was her strong point; and it was only in her prose that she had occasion to exhibit the delicious, but restrained, humour that her readers found so irresistible. It was not a humour of ideas, nor even a humour of words; it was much more subtle than that, it was a humour of punctuation: in a flash of inspiration she had discovered the comic possibilities of the semi-colon, and of this she had made abundant and exquisite use. She was able to place it in such a way that if you were a person of culture with a keen sense of humour, you did not exactly laugh through a horse-collar, but you giggled delightedly, and the greater your culture the more delightedly you giggled. Her friends said that it made every other form of humour coarse and exaggerated. Several writers had tried to imitate her; but in vain: whatever else you might say about Mrs. Albert Forrester you were bound to admit that she was able to get every ounce of humour out of the semi-colon and no one else could get within a mile of her.

Mrs. Albert Forrester lived in a flat not far from the Marble Arch, which combined the advantage of a good address and a moderate rent. It had a handsome drawing-room on the street and a large bedroom for Mrs. Albert Forrester, a darkish dining-room at the back and a small poky bedroom, next door to the kitchen, for Mr. Albert Forrester, who paid the rent. It was in the handsome drawing-room that Mrs. Albert Forrester every Tuesday afternoon received her friends. It was a severe and chaste apartment. On the walls was a paper designed by William Morris himself and on this, in plain black frames, mezzotints collected before mezzotints grew expensive; the furniture was of the Chippendale period, but for the roll-top desk, vaguely Louis XVI in character, at which Mrs. Albert Forrester wrote her works. This was pointed out to visitors the first time they came to see her, and there were few who looked at it without emotion. The carpet was thick and the lights discreet. Mrs. Albert Forrester sat in a straight-backed grandfather's chair covered with red damask. There was nothing ostentatious about it, but since it was the only comfortable chair in the room it set her apart as it were and above her guests. Tea was dispensed by a female of uncertain age, silent and colourless, who was never introduced to anyone but who was known to look upon it as a privilege to be allowed to save Mrs. Albert Forrester from the irksome duty of pouring out tea. She was thus able to devote herself entirely to conversation, and it must be admitted that her conversation was excellent. It was not sprightly; and since it is difficult to indicate punctuation in speech it may have seemed to some slightly lacking in humour, but it was of wide range, solid, instructive and interesting. Mrs. Albert Forrester was well acquainted with social science, jurisprudence and theology. She had read much and her memory was retentive. She had a pretty gift for quotation, which is a serviceable substitute for wit, and having for thirty years known more or less intimately a great many distinguished people, she had a great many interesting anecdotes to tell, which she placed with tact and which she did not repeat more than was pardonable. Mrs. Albert Forrester had the gift of attracting the most varied persons and you were liable at one and the same time to meet in her drawing-room an ex-Prime Minister, a newspaper proprietor and the ambassador of a First Class Power. I always imagined that these great people came because they thought that here they rubbed shoulders with Bohemia, but with a Bohemia sufficiently neat and clean for them to be in no danger that the dirt would come off on them. Mrs. Albert Forrester was deeply interested in politics and I myself heard a Cabinet Minister tell her frankly that she had a masculine intelligence. She had been opposed to Female Suffrage, but when it was at last granted to women she began to dally with the idea of going into Parliament. Her difficulty was that she did not know which party to choose.

"After all," she said, with a playful shrug of her somewhat massive shoulders, "I cannot form a party of one."

Like many serious patriots, in her inability to know for certain which way the cat would jump she held her political opinions in suspense; but of late she had been definitely turning towards Labour as the best hope of the country, and if a safe seat were offered her it was felt fairly certain that she would not hesitate to come out into the open as a champion of the oppressed proletariat.

Her drawing-room was always open to foreigners, to Czecho-Slovaks, Italians and Frenchmen if they were distinguished and to Americans even if they were obscure. But she was not a snob and you seldom met there a duke unless he was of a peculiarly serious turn and a peeress only if in addition to her rank she had the passport of some small social solecism such as having been divorced, written a novel or forged a cheque, which might give her claim on Mrs. Albert Forrester's catholic sympathies. She did not much care for painters, who were shy and silent; and musicians did not interest her: even if they consented to play, and if they were celebrated they were too often reluctant, their music was a hindrance to conversation: if people wanted music they could go to a concert; for her part she preferred the more subtle music of the soul. But her hospitality to writers, especially if they were promising and little known, was warm and constant. She had an eye for budding talent and there were few of the famous writers who from time to time drank a dish of tea with her whose first efforts she had not encouraged and whose early steps she had not guided. Her own position was too well assured for her to be capable of envy, and she had heard the word genius attached to her name too often to feel a trace of jealousy because the talents of others brought them a material success that was denied to her.

Mrs. Albert Forrester, confident in the judgment of posterity, could afford to be disinterested. With these elements then it is no wonder that she had succeeded in creating something as near the French Salon of the Eighteenth Century as our barbarous nation has ever reached. To be invited to "eat a bun and drink a cup of tea on Tuesday" was a privilege that few failed to recognise; and when you sat on your Chippendale chair in the discreetly lit but austere room, you could not but feel that you were living literary history. The American Ambassador once said to Mrs. Albert Forrester:

"A cup of tea with you, Mrs. Forrester, is one of the richest intellectual treats which it has ever been my lot to enjoy."

It was indeed on occasion a trifle overwhelming. Mrs. Albert Forrester's taste was so perfect, she so inevitably admired the right thing and made the just observation about it, that sometimes you almost gasped for air. For my part I found it prudent to fortify myself with a cocktail or two before I exposed myself to the rarefied atmosphere of her society. Indeed, I very nearly found myself for ever excluded from it, for one afternoon, presenting myself at the door, instead of asking the maid who opened it: "Is Mrs. Forrester at home?" I asked: "Is there Divine Service to-day?"

Of course it was said in pure inadvertence, but it was unfortunate that the maid sniggered and one of Mrs. Albert Forrester's most devoted admirers, Ellen Hannaway, happened to be at the moment in the hall taking off her goloshes. She told my hostess what I had said before I got into the drawing-room, and as I entered Mrs. Albert Forrester fixed me with an eagle eye.

"Why did you ask if there was Divine Service to-day?" she inquired.

I explained that I was absent-minded, but Mrs. Albert Forrester held me with a gaze that I can only describe as compelling.

"Do you mean to suggest that my parties are . . ." she searched for a word. "Sacramental?"

I did not know what she meant, but did not like to show my ignorance before so many other clever people, and I decided that the only thing was to seize my trowel and the butter.

"Your parties are like you, dear lady, perfectly beautiful and perfectly divine."

A little tremor passed through Mrs. Albert Forrester's substantial frame. She was like a man who enters suddenly a room filled with hyacinths; the perfume is so intoxicating that he almost staggers. But she relented.

"If you were trying to be facetious," she said, "I should prefer you to exercise your facetiousness on my guests rather than on my maids. . . . Miss Warren will give you some tea."

Mrs. Albert Forrester dismissed me with a wave of the hand, but she did not dismiss the subject, since for the next two or three years whenever she introduced me to someone she never failed to add:

"You must make the most of him, he only comes here as a penance. When he comes to the door he always asks: Is there Divine Service to-day? So amusing, isn't he?"

But Mrs. Albert Forrester did not confine herself to weekly tea-parties: every Saturday she gave a luncheon of eight persons; this according to her opinion being the perfect number for general conversation and her dining-room conveniently holding no more. If Mrs. Albert Forrester flattered herself upon anything it was not that her knowledge of English prosody was unique, but that her luncheons were celebrated. She chose her guests with care and an invitation to one of them was more than a compliment, it was a consecration. Over the luncheon-table it was possible to keep the conversation on a higher level than in the mixed company of a tea-party and few can have left her dining-room without taking away with them an enhanced belief in Mrs. Albert Forrester's ability and a brighter faith in human nature. She only asked men, since, stout enthusiast for her sex as she was and glad to see women on other occasions, she could not but realise that they were inclined at table to talk exclusively to their next-door neighbours and thus hinder the general exchange of ideas that made her own parties an entertainment not only of the body but of the soul. For it must be said that Mrs. Albert Forrester gave you uncommonly good food, excellent wine and a first-rate cigar. Now to anyone who has partaken of literary hospitality this must appear very remarkable, since literary persons for the most part think highly and live plainly; their minds are occupied with the things of the spirit and they do not notice that the roast mutton is underdone and the potatoes cold: the beer is all right, but the wine has a sobering effect, and it is unwise to touch the coffee. Mrs. Albert Forrester was pleased enough to receive compliments on the fare she provided.

"If people do me the honour to break bread with me," she said, "it is only fair that I should give them as good food as they can get at home."

But if the flattery was excessive she deprecated it.

"You really embarrass me when you give me a meed of praise which is not my due. You must praise Mrs. Bulfinch."

"Who is Mrs. Bulfinch?"

"My cook."

"She's a treasure then, but you're not going to ask me to believe that she's responsible for the wine."

"Is it good? I'm terribly ignorant of such things; I put myself entirely in the hands of my wine merchant."

But if mention was made of the cigars Mrs. Albert Forrester beamed.

"Ah, for them you must compliment Albert. It is Albert who chooses the cigars and I am given to understand that no one knows more about a cigar than Albert."

She looked at her husband, who sat at the end of the table, with the proud bright eyes of a pedigree hen (a Buff Orpington for choice) looking at her only chick. Then there was a quick flutter of conversation as the guests, anxious to be civil to their host and relieved at length to find an occasion, expressed their appreciation of his peculiar merit.

P

"You're very kind," he said. "I'm glad you like them."

Then he would give a little discourse on cigars, explaining the excellencies he sought and regretting the deterioration in quality which had followed on the commercialisation of the industry. Mrs. Albert Forrester listened to him with a complacent smile, and it was plain that she enjoyed this little triumph of his. Of course you cannot go on talking of cigars indefinitely and as soon as she perceived that her guests were growing restive she broached a topic of more general, and it may be of more significant, interest. Albert subsided into silence. But he had had his moment.

It was Albert who made Mrs. Forrester's luncheons to some less attractive than her tea-parties, for Albert was a bore; but though without doubt perfectly conscious of the fact, she made a point that he should come to them and in fact had fixed upon Saturdays (for the rest of the week he was busy) in order that he should be able to. Mrs. Albert Forrester felt that her husband's presence on these festive occasions was an unavoidable debt that she paid to her own self-respect. She would never by a negligence admit to the world that she had married a man who was not spiritually her equal, and it may be that in the silent watches of the night she asked herself where indeed such could have been found. Mrs. Albert Forrester's friends were troubled by no such reticence and they said it was dreadful that such a woman should be burdened with such a man. They asked each other how she had ever come to marry him and (being mostly celibate) answered despairingly that no one ever knew why anybody married anybody else.

It was not that Albert was a verbose and aggressive bore; he did not buttonhole you with interminable stories or pester you with pointless jokes; he did not crucify you on a platitude or hamstring you with a commonplace; he was just dull. A cipher. Clifford Boyleston, for whom the French Romantics had no secrets and who was himself a writer of merit, had said that when you looked into a room into which Albert had just gone there was nobody there. This was thought very clever by Mrs. Albert Forrester's friends and Rose Waterford, the well-known novelist and the most fearless of women, had ventured to repeat it to Mrs. Albert Forrester. Though she pretended to be annoyed, she had not been able to prevent the smile that rose to her lips. Her behaviour towards Albert could not but increase the respect in which her friends held her. She insisted that whatever in their secret hearts they thought of him, they should treat him with the decorum that was due to her husband. Her own demeanour was admirable. If he chanced to make an observation she listened to him with a pleasant expression and when he fetched her a book that she wanted or gave her his pencil to make a note of an idea that had occurred to her, she always thanked him. Nor would she allow her friends pointedly to neglect him, and though, being a woman of tact, she saw that it would be asking too much of the world if she took him about with her always, and she went out much alone, yet her friends knew that she expected them to ask him to dinner at least once a year. He always accompanied her to public banquets when she was going to make a speech, and if she delivered a lecture she took care that he should have a seat on the platform.

Albert was, I believe, of average height, but perhaps because you never thought of him except in connection with his wife (of imposing dimensions) you only thought of him as a little man. He was spare and frail and looked older than his age. This was the same as his wife's. His hair, which he kept very short, was white and meagre, and he wore a stubby white moustache; his was a face, thin and lined, without a noticeable feature; and his blue eyes, which once might have been attractive, were now pale and tired. He was always very neatly dressed in pepper-and-salt trousers, which he chose always of the same pattern, a black coat and a grey tie with a small pearl pin in it. He was perfectly unobtrusive, and when he stood in Mrs. Albert Forrester's drawing-room to receive the guests whom she had asked to luncheon you noticed him as little as you noticed the quiet and gentlemanly furniture. He was well-mannered and it was with a pleasant, courteous smile that he shook hands with them.

"How do you do? I'm very glad to see you," he said if they were friends of some standing. "Keeping well, I hope?"

But if they were strangers of distinction coming for the first time to the house, he went to the door as they entered the drawing-room and said :

"I am Mrs. Albert Forrester's husband. I will introduce you to my wife."

Then he led the visitor to where Mrs. Albert Forrester stood, with her back to the light, and she with a glad and eager gesture advanced to make the stranger welcome.

It was agreeable to see the demure pride he took in his wife's literary reputation and the self-effacement with which he furthered her interests. He was always there when he was wanted and never when he wasn't. His tact, if not deliberate, was instinctive. Mrs. Albert Forrester was the first to acknowledge his merits.

"I really don't know what I should do without him," she said. "He's invaluable to me. I read him everything I write and his criticisms are often very useful."

"Molière and his cook," said Miss Waterford.

"Is that funny, dear Rose?" asked Mrs. Forrester, somewhat acidly.

When Mrs. Albert Forrester did not approve of a remark, she had a way that put many persons to confusion of asking you whether it was a joke which she was too dense to see. But it was impossible to embarrass Miss Waterford. She was a lady who in the course of a long life had had many affairs, but only one passion, and this was for printer's ink. Mrs. Albert Forrester tolerated rather than approved her.

"Come, come, my dear," she replied, "you know very well that he wouldn't exist without you. He wouldn't know us. It must be wonderful to him to come in contact with all the best brains and the most distinguished people of our day."

"It may be that the bee would perish without the hive which shelters it, but the bee nevertheless has a significance of its own."

And since Mrs. Albert Forrester's friends, though they knew all about art and literature, knew little about natural history, they had no reply to this observation. She went on:

"He doesn't interfere with me. He knows subconsciously when I don't want to be disturbed and, indeed, when I am following out a train of thought I find his presence in the room a comfort rather than a hindrance to me."

"Like a Persian cat," said Miss Waterford.

"But like a very well-trained, well-bred, and well-mannered Persian cat," answered Mrs. Forrester severely, thus putting Miss Waterford in her place.

But Mrs. Albert Forrester had not finished with her husband.

"We who belong to the intelligentsia," she said, "are apt to live in a world too exclusively our own. We are interested in the abstract rather than in the concrete, and sometimes I think that we survey the bustling world of human affairs in too detached a manner and from too serene a height. Do you not think that we stand in danger of becoming a little inhuman? I shall always be grateful to Albert because he keeps me in contact with the man in the street."

It was on account of this remark, to which none of her friends could deny the rare insight and subtlety that characterised so many of her utterances, that for some time Albert was known in her immediate circle as The Man in the Street. But this was only for a while, and it was forgotten. He then became known as The Philatelist. It was Clifford Boyleston, with his wicked wit, who invented the name. One day, his poor brain exhausted by the effort to sustain a conversation with Albert, he had asked in desperation:

"Do you collect stamps?"

"No," answered Albert mildly. "I'm afraid I don't."

But Clifford Boyleston had no sooner asked the question than he saw its possibilities. He had written a book on Baudelaire's aunt by marriage, which had attracted the attention of all who were interested in French literature, and was well known in his exhaustive studies of the French spirit to have absorbed a goodly share of the Gallic quickness and the Gallic brilliancy. He paid no attention to Albert's disclaimer, but at the first opportunity informed Mrs. Albert Forrester's friends that he had at last discovered Albert's secret. He collected stamps. He never met him afterwards without asking him: "Well, Mr. Forrester, how is the stamp collection?" Or: "Have you been buying any stamps since I saw you last?"

It mattered little that Albert continued to deny that he collected stamps, the invention was too apt not to be made the most of; Mrs. Albert Forrester's friends insisted that he did, and they seldom spoke to him without asking him how he was getting on. Even Mrs. Albert Forrester, when she was in a specially gay humour, would sometimes speak of her husband as The Philatelist. The name really did seem to fit Albert like a glove. Sometimes they spoke of him thus to his face and they could not but appreciate the good nature with which he took it; he smiled unresentfully and presently did not even protest that they were mistaken.

Of course Mrs. Albert Forrester had too keen a social sense to jeopardise the success of her luncheons by allowing her more distinguished guests to sit on either side of Albert. She took care that only her older and more intimate friends should do this, and when the appointed victims came in she would say to them:

"I know you won't mind sitting by Albert, will you?"

They could only say that they would be delighted, but if their faces too plainly expressed their dismay she would pat their hands playfully and add:

"Next time you shall sit by me. Albert is so shy with strangers and you know so well how to deal with him."

They did: they simply ignored him. So far as they were concerned the chair in which he sat might as well have been empty. There was no sign that it annoyed him to be taken no notice of by persons who after all were eating food he paid for, since the earnings of Mrs. Forrester could certainly not have provided her guests with spring salmon and forced asparagus. He sat quiet and silent, and if he opened his mouth it was only to give a direction to one of the maids. If a guest were new to him he would let his eyes rest on him in a stare that would have been embarrassing if it had not been so child-like. He seemed to be asking himself what this strange creature was; but what answer his mild scrutiny gave him he never revealed.

When the conversation grew animated he would look from one speaker to the other, but again you could not tell from his thin, lined face what he thought of the fantastic notions that were bandied across the table.

Clifford Boyleston said that all the wit and wisdom he heard passed over his head like water over a duck's back. He had given up trying to understand and now only made a semblance of listening. But Harry Oakland, the versatile critic, said that Albert was taking it all in; he found it all too, too marvellous, and with his poor, muddled brain he was trying desperately to make head or tail of the wonderful things he heard. Of course in the City he must boast of the distinguished persons he knew, perhaps there he was a light of learning and letters, an authority on the ideal; it would be perfectly divine to hear what he made of it all. Harry Oakland was one of Mrs. Albert Forrester's staunchest admirers, and had written a brilliant and subtle essay on her style. With his refined and even beautiful features he looked like a San Sebastian who had had an accident with a hair-restorer; for he was uncommonly hirsute. He was a very young man, not thirty, but he had been in turn a dramatic critic, and a critic of fiction, a musical critic and a critic of painting. But he was getting a little tired of art and threatened to devote his talents in future to the criticism of sport.

Albert, I should explain, was in the City and it was a misfortune that Mrs. Forrester's friends thought she bore with meritorious fortitude that he was not even rich. There would have been something romantic in it if he had been a merchant prince who held the fate of nations in his hand or sent argosies, laden with rare spices, to those ports of the Levant the names of which have provided many a poet with so rich and rare a rhyme. But Albert was only a currant merchant and was supposed to make no more than just enabled Mrs. Albert Forrester to conduct her life with distinction and even with liberality. Since his occupation kept him in his office till six o'clock he never managed to get to Mrs. Albert Forrester's Tuesdays till the most important visitors were gone. By the time he arrived, there were seldom more than three or four of her more intimate friends in the drawing-room, discussing with freedom and humour the guests who had departed, and when they heard Albert's key in the front door they realised with one accord that it was late. In a moment he opened the door in his hesitating way and looked mildly in. Mrs. Albert Forrester greeted him with a bright smile.

"Come in, Albert, come in. I think you know everybody here."

Albert entered and shook hands with his wife's friends.

"Have you just come from the City?" she asked eagerly, though she knew there was nowhere else he could have come from. "Would you like a cup of tea?"

"No, thank you, my dear. I had tea in my office."

Mrs. Albert Forrester smiled still more brightly and the rest of the company thought she was perfectly wonderful with him.

"Ah, but I know you like a second cup. I will pour it out for you myself."

She went to the tea-table and, forgetting that the tea had been stewing for an hour and a half and was stone cold, poured him out a cup and added milk and sugar. Albert took it with a word of thanks, and meekly stirred it, but when Mrs. Forrester resumed the conversation which his appearance had interrupted, without tasting it put it quietly down. His arrival was the signal for the party finally to break up and one by one the remaining guests took their departure. On one occasion, however, the conversation was so absorbing and the point at issue so important that Mrs. Albert Forrester would not hear of their going.

"It must be settled once for all. And after all," she remarked in a manner that for her was almost arch, "this is a matter on which Albert may have something to say. Let us have the benefit of his opinion."

It was when women were beginning to cut their hair and the subject of discussion was whether Mrs. Albert Forrester should or should not shingle. Mrs. Albert Forrester was a woman of authoritative presence. She was large-boned and her bones were well covered; had she not been so tall and strong it might have suggested itself to you that she was corpulent. But she carried her weight gallantly. Her features were a little larger than life-size and it was this that gave her face doubtless the look of virile intellectuality that it certainly possessed. Her skin was dark and you might have thought that she had in her veins some trace of Levantine blood: she admitted that she could not but think there was in her a gypsy strain and that would account, she felt, for the wild and lawless passion that sometimes characterised her poetry. Her eyes were large and black and bright, her nose like the great Duke of Wellington's, but more fleshy, and her chin square and determined. She had a big mouth, with full red lips, which owed nothing to cosmetics, for of these Mrs. Albert Forrester had never deigned to make use; and her hair, thick, solid and grey, was piled on the top of her head in such a manner as to increase her already commanding height. She was in appearance an imposing, not to say an alarming, female.

She was always very suitably dressed in rich materials of sombre hue and she looked every inch a woman of letters; but in her discreet way (being after all human and susceptible to vanity) she followed the fashions and the cut of her gowns was modish. I think for some time she had hankered to shingle her hair, but she thought it more becoming to do it at the solicitation of her friends than on her own initiative.

"Oh, you must, you must," said Harry Oakland, in his eager, boyish way. "You'd look too, too wonderful."

Clifford Boyleston, who was now writing a book on Madame de Maintenon, was doubtful. He thought it a dangerous experiment.

"I think," he said, wiping his eye-glasses with a cambric handkerchief, "I think when one has made a type one should stick to it. What would Louis XIV have been without his wig?"

"I'm hesitating," said Mrs. Forrester. "After all, we must move with the times. I am of my day and I do not wish to lag behind. America, as Wilhelm Meister said, is here and now." She turned brightly to Albert. "What does my lord and master say about it? What is your opinion, Albert? To shingle or not to shingle, that is the question."

"I'm afraid my opinion is not of great importance, my dear," he answered mildly.

"To me it is of the greatest importance," answered Mrs. Albert Forrester, flatteringly.

She could not but see how beautifully her friends thought she treated The Philatelist.

"I insist," she proceeded, "I insist. No one knows me as you do, Albert. Will it suit me?"

"It might," he answered. "My only fear is that with your— statuesque appearance short hair would perhaps suggest—well, shall we say, the Isle of Greece where burning Sappho loved and sung."

There was a moment's embarrassed pause. Rose Waterford smothered a giggle, but the others preserved a stony silence. Mrs. Forrester's smile froze on her lips. Albert had dropped a brick.

"I always thought Byron a very mediocre poet," said Mrs. Albert Forrester at last.

The company broke up. Mrs. Albert Forrester did not shingle, nor indeed was the matter ever again referred to.

It was towards the end of another of Mrs. Albert Forrester's Tuesdays that the event occurred that had so great an influence on her literary career.

It had been one of her most successful parties. The leader of the Labour Party had been there and Mrs. Albert Forrester had gone as far as she could without definitely committing herself to intimate to him that she was prepared to throw in her lot with Labour. The time was ripe and if she was ever to adopt a political career she must come to a decision. A member of the French Academy had been brought by Clifford Boyleston and, though she knew he was wholly unacquainted with English, it had gratified her to receive his affable compliment on her ornate and yet pellucid style. The American Ambassador had been there and a young Russian prince whose authentic Romanoff blood alone prevented him from looking a gigolo. A duchess who had recently divorced her duke and married a jockey had been very gracious; and her strawberry leaves, albeit sere and yellow, undoubtedly added tone to the assembly. There had been quite a galaxy of literary lights. But now all, all were gone but Clifford Boyleston, Harry Oakland, Rose Waterford, Oscar Charles and Simmons. Oscar Charles was a little, gnome-like crea- ture, young but with the wizened face of a cunning monkey, with gold spectacles, who earned his living in a government office but spent his leisure in the pursuit of literature. He wrote little articles for the sixpenny weeklies and had a spirited contempt for the world in general. Mrs. Albert Forrester liked him, thinking he had talent, but though he always expressed the keenest admiration for her style (it was indeed he who had named her the mistress of the semi-colon), his acerbity was so general that she also somewhat feared him. Simmons was her agent; a round-faced man who wore glasses so strong that his eyes behind them looked strange and misshapen. They reminded you of the eyes of some uncouth crustacean that you had seen in an aquarium. He came regularly to Mrs. Albert For- rester's parties, partly because he had the greatest admiration for her genius and partly because it was convenient for him to meet prospective clients in her drawing-room.

Mrs. Albert Forrester, for whom he had long laboured with but a trifling recompense, was not sorry to put him in the way of earning an honest penny, and she took care to introduce him, with warm ex- pressions of gratitude, to anyone who might be supposed to have literary wares to sell. It was not without pride that she remembered that the notorious and vastly lucrative memoirs of Lady St. Swithin had been first mooted in her drawing-room.

They sat in a circle of which Mrs. Albert Forrester was the centre and discussed brightly and, it must be confessed, somewhat malici- ously the various persons who had been that day present. Miss Warren, the pallid female who had stood for two hours at the tea- table, was walking silently round the room collecting cups that had been left here and there. She had some vague employment, but was always able to get off in order to pour out tea for Mrs. Albert Forrester, and in the evening she typed Mrs. Albert Forrester's manuscripts. Mrs. Albert Forrester did not pay her for this, thinking quite rightly that as it was she did a great deal for the poor thing; but she gave her the seats for the cinema that were sent her for nothing and often presented her with articles of clothing for which she had no further use.

Mrs. Albert Forrester in her rather deep, full voice was talking in a steady flow and the rest were listening to her with attention. She was in good form and the words that poured from her lips could have gone straight down on paper without alteration. Suddenly there was a noise in the passage as though something heavy had fallen and then the sound of an altercation.

Mrs. Albert Forrester stopped and a slight frown darkened her really noble brow.

"I should have thought they knew by now that I will not have this devastating racket in the flat. Would you mind ringing the bell, Miss Warren, and asking what is the reason of this tumult?"

Miss Warren rang the bell and in a moment the maid appeared. Miss Warren at the door, in order not to interrupt Mrs. Albert Forrester, spoke to her in undertones. But Mrs. Albert Forrester somewhat irritably interrupted herself.

"Well, Carter, what is it? Is the house falling down or has the Red Revolution at last broken out?"

"If you please, ma'am, it's the new cook's box," answered the maid. "The porter dropped it as he was bringing it in and the cook got all upset about it."

"What do you mean by 'the new cook'?"

"Mrs. Bulfinch went away this afternoon, ma'am," said the maid.

Mrs. Albert Forrester stared at her.

"This is the first I've heard of it. Had Mrs. Bulfinch given notice? The moment Mr. Forrester comes in tell him that I wish to speak to him."

"Very good, ma'am."

The maid went out and Miss Warren slowly returned to the tea-table. Mechanically, though nobody wanted them, she poured out several cups of tea.

"What a catastrophe!" cried Miss Waterford.

"You must get her back," said Clifford Boyleston. "She's a treasure, that woman, a remarkable cook, and she gets better and better every day."

But at that moment the maid came in again with a letter on a small plated salver and handed it to her mistress.

"What is this?" said Mrs. Albert Forrester.

"Mr. Forrester said I was to give you this letter when you asked for him, ma'am," said the maid.

"Where is Mr. Forrester then?"

"Mr. Forrester's gone, ma'am," answered the maid as though the question surprised her.

"Gone? That'll do. You can go."

The maid left the room and Mrs. Albert Forrester, with a look of perplexity on her large face, opened the letter. Rose Waterford has told me that her first thought was that Albert, fearful of his wife's displeasure at the departure of Mrs. Bulfinch, had thrown himself in the Thames. Mrs. Albert Forrester read the letter and a look of consternation crossed her face.

"Oh, monstrous," she cried. "Monstrous! Monstrous!"

"What is it, Mrs. Forrester?"

Mrs. Albert Forrester pawed the carpet with her foot like a restive, high-spirited horse pawing the ground, and crossing her arms with a gesture that is indescribable (but that you sometimes see in a fish-wife who is going to make the very devil of a scene) bent her looks upon her curious and excessively startled friends.

"Albert has eloped with the cook."

There was a gasp of dismay. Then something terrible happened. Miss Warren, who was standing behind the tea-table, suddenly choked. Miss Warren, who never opened her mouth and whom no one ever spoke to, Miss Warren, whom not one of them, though he had seen her every week for three years, would have recognised in the street, Miss Warren suddenly burst into uncontrollable laughter. With one accord, aghast, they turned and stared at her. They felt as Balaam must have felt when his ass broke into speech. She positively shrieked with laughter. There was a nameless horror about the sight, as though something had on a sudden gone wrong with a natural phenomenon, and you were just as startled as though the chairs and tables without warning began to skip about the floor in an antic dance. Miss Warren tried to contain herself, but the more she tried the more pitilessly the laughter shook her, and seizing a handkerchief she stuffed it in her mouth and hurried from the room. The door slammed behind her.

"Hysteria," said Clifford Boyleston.

"Pure hysteria, of course," said Harry Oakland.

But Mrs. Albert Forrester said nothing.

The letter had dropped at her feet and Simmons, the agent, picked it up and handed it to her. She would not take it.

"Read it," she said. "Read it aloud."

Mr. Simmons pushed his spectacles up on his forehead and holding the letter very close to his eyes read as follows:

My Dear,

Mrs. Bulfinch is in need of a change and has decided to leave, and as I do not feel inclined to stay on here without her I am going too. I have had all the literature I can stand and I am fed up with art.

Mrs. Bulfinch does not care about marriage, but if you care to divorce me she is willing to marry me. I hope you will find the new cook satisfactory. She has excellent references. It may save you trouble if I inform you that Mrs. Bulfinch and I are living at 411, Kennington Road, S.E.

Albert.

No one spoke. Mr. Simmons slipped his spectacles back on to the bridge of his nose. The fact was that none of them, brilliant as they were and accustomed to find topics of conversation to suit every occasion, could think of an appropriate remark. Mrs. Albert Forrester was not the kind of woman to whom you could offer condolences and each was too much afraid of the others' ridicule to venture upon the obvious. At last Clifford Boyleston came bravely to the rescue.

"One doesn't know what to say," he observed.

There was another silence and then Rose Waterford spoke.

"What does Mrs. Bulfinch look like?" she asked.

"How should I know?" answered Mrs. Albert Forrester, somewhat peevishly. "I have never looked at her. Albert always engaged the servants, she just came in for a moment so that I could see if her aura was satisfactory."

"But you must have seen her every morning when you did the housekeeping."

"Albert did the housekeeping. It was his own wish, so that I might be free to devote myself to my work. In this life one has to limit oneself."

"Did Albert order your luncheons?" asked Clifford Boyleston.

"Naturally. It was his province."

Clifford Boyleston slightly raised his eyebrows. What a fool he had been never to guess that it was Albert who was responsible for Mrs. Forrester's beautiful food! And of course it was owing to him that the excellent Chablis was always just sufficiently chilled to run coolly over the tongue, but never so cold as to lose its bouquet and its savour.

"He certainly knew good food and good wine."

"I always told you he had his points," answered Mrs. Albert Forrester, as though he were reproaching her. "You all laughed at him. You would not believe me when I told you that I owed a great deal to him."

There was no answer to this and once more silence, heavy and ominous, fell on the party. Suddenly Mr. Simmons flung a bomb-shell.

"You must get him back."

So great was her surprise that if Mrs. Albert Forrester had not been standing against the chimney-piece she would undoubtedly have staggered two paces to the rear.

"What on earth do you mean?" she cried. "I will never see him again as long as I live. Take him back? Never. Not even if he came and begged me on his bended knees."

"I didn't say take him back; I said, get him back."

But Mrs. Albert Forrester paid no attention to the misplaced inter-ruption.

"I have done everything for him. What would he be without me? I ask you. I have given him a position which never in his remotest dreams could he have aspired to."

None could deny that there was something magnificent in the indignation of Mrs. Albert Forrester, but it appeared to have little effect on Mr. Simmons.

"What are you going to live on?"

Mrs. Albert Forrester flung him a glance totally devoid of amia-bility.

"God will provide," she answered in freezing tones.

"I think it very unlikely," he returned.

Mrs. Albert Forrester shrugged her shoulders. She wore an out-raged expression. But Mr. Simmons made himself as comfortable as he could on his chair and lit a cigarette.

"You know you have no warmer admirer of your art than me," he said.

"Than I," corrected Clifford Boyleston.

"Or than you," went on Mr. Simmons blandly. "We all agree that there is no one writing now whom you need fear comparison with. Both in prose and verse you are absolutely first class. And your style—well, everyone knows your style."

"The opulence of Sir Thomas Browne with the limpidity of Car-dinal Newman," said Clifford Boyleston. "The raciness of John Dryden with the precision of Jonathan Swift."

The only sign that Mrs. Albert Forrester heard was the smile that hesitated for a brief moment at the corners of her tragic mouth.

"And you have humour."

"Is there anyone in the world," cried Miss Waterford, "who can put such a wealth of wit and satire and comic observation into a semi-colon?"

"But the fact remains that you don't sell," pursued Mr. Simmons imperturbably. "I've handled your work for twenty years and I tell you frankly that I shouldn't have grown fat on my commission, but I've handled it because now and again I like to do what I can for good work. I've always believed in you and I've hoped that sooner or later we might get the public to swallow you. But if you think you can make your living by writing the sort of stuff you do I'm bound to tell you that you haven't a chance."

"I have come into the world too late," said Mrs. Albert Forrester. "I should have lived in the eighteenth century when the wealthy patron rewarded a dedication with a hundred guineas."

"What do you suppose the currant business brings in?"

Mrs. Albert Forrester gave a little sigh.

"A pittance. Albert always told me he made about twelve hundred a year."

"He must be a very good manager. But you couldn't expect him on that income to allow you very much. Take my word for it, there's only one thing for you to do and that's to get him back."

"I would rather live in a garret. Do you think I'm going to submit to the affront he has put upon me? Would you have me battle for his affections with my cook? Do not forget that there is one thing which is more valuable to a woman like me than her ease and that is her dignity."

"I was just coming to that," said Mr. Simmons coldly.

He glanced at the others and those strange, lopsided eyes of his looked more than ever monstrous and fish-like.

"There is no doubt in my mind," he went on, "that you have a very distinguished and almost unique position in the world of letters. You stand for something quite apart. You never prostituted your genius for filthy lucre and you have held high the banner of pure art. You're thinking of going into Parliament. I don't think much of politics myself, but there's no denying that it would be a good advertisement and if you get in I daresay we could get you a lecture tour in America on the strength of it. You have ideals and this I can say, that even the people who've never read a word you've written respect you. But in your position there's one thing you can't afford to be and that's a joke."

Mrs. Albert Forrester gave a distinct start.

"What on earth do you mean by that?"

"I know nothing about Mrs. Bulfinch and for all I know she's a very respectable woman, but the fact remains that a man doesn't run away with his cook without making his wife ridiculous. If it had been a dancer or a lady of title I daresay it wouldn't have done you any harm, but a cook would finish you. In a week you'd have all London laughing at you, and if there's one thing that kills an author or a politician it is ridicule. You must get your husband back and you must get him back pretty damned quick."

A dark flush settled on Mrs. Albert Forrester's face, but she did not immediately reply. In her ears there rang on a sudden the outrageous and unaccountable laughter that had sent Miss Warren flying from the room.

"We're all friends here and you can count on our discretion."

Mrs. Forrester looked at her friends and she thought that in Rose Waterford's eyes there was already a malicious gleam. On the wizened face of Oscar Charles was a whimsical look. She wished that in a moment of abandon she had not betrayed her secret. Mr. Simmons, however, knew the literary world and allowed his eyes to rest on the company.

"After all you are the centre and head of their set. Your husband has not only run away from you but also from them. It's not too good for them either. The fact is that Albert Forrester has made you all look a lot of damned fools."

"All," said Clifford Boyleston. "We're all in the same boat. He's quite right, Mrs. Forrester, The Philatelist must come back."

"*Et tu, Brute.*"

Mr. Simmons did not understand Latin and if he had would probably not have been moved by Mrs. Albert Forrester's exclamation. He cleared his throat.

"My suggestion is that Mrs. Albert Forrester should go and see him to-morrow, fortunately we have his address, and beg him to reconsider his decision. I don't know what sort of things a woman says on these occasions, but Mrs. Forrester has tact and imagination and she must say them. If Mr. Forrester makes any conditions she must accept them. She must leave no stone unturned."

"If you play your cards well there is no reason why you shouldn't bring him back here with you to-morrow evening," said Rose Waterford lightly.

"Will you do it, Mrs. Forrester?"

For two minutes, at least, turned away from them, she stared at the empty fireplace; then, drawing herself to her full height, she faced them.

"For my art's sake, not for mine. I will not allow the ribald laughter of the Philistine to besmirch all that I hold good and true and beautiful."

"Capital," said Mr. Simmons, rising to his feet, "I'll look in on my way home to-morrow and I hope to find you and Mr. Forrester billing and cooing side by side like a pair of turtle-doves."

He took his leave, and the others, anxious not to be left alone with Mrs. Albert Forrester and her agitation, in a body followed his example.

It was latish in the afternoon next day when Mrs. Albert Forrester, imposing in black silk and a velvet toque, set out from her flat in order to get a bus from the Marble Arch that would take her to Victoria Station. Mr. Simmons had explained to her by telephone how to reach the Kennington Road with expedition and economy. She neither felt nor looked like Delilah. At Victoria she took the tram that runs down the Vauxhall Bridge Road. When she crossed the river she found herself in a part of London more noisy, sordid and bustling than that to which she was accustomed, but she was too much occupied with her thoughts to notice the varied scene. She was relieved to find that the tram went along the Kennington Road and asked the conductor to put her down a few doors from the house she sought. When it did and rumbled on leaving her alone in the busy street, she felt strangely lost, like a traveller in an eastern tale set down by a djinn in an unknown city. She walked slowly, looking to right and left, and notwithstanding the emotions of indignation and embarrassment that fought for the possession of her somewhat opulent bosom, she could not but reflect that here was the material for a very pretty piece of prose. The little houses held about them the feeling of a bygone age when here it was still almost country, and Mrs. Albert Forrester registered in her retentive memory a note that she must look into the literary associations of the Kennington Road. Number four hundred and eleven was one of a row of shabby houses that stood some way back from the street; in front of it was a narrow strip of shabby grass, and a paved way led up to a latticed wooden porch that badly needed a coat of paint. This and the straggling, stunted creeper that grew over the front of the house gave it a falsely rural air which was strange and even sinister in that road down which thundered a tumultuous traffic. There was something equivocal about the house that suggested that here lived women to whom a life of pleasure had brought an inadequate reward.

The door was opened by a scraggy girl of fifteen with long legs and a tousled head.

"Does Mrs. Bulfinch live here, do you know?"

"You've rung the wrong bell. Second floor." The girl pointed to the stairs and at the same time screamed shrilly: "Mrs. Bulfinch, a party to see you. Mrs. Bulfinch."

Mrs. Albert Forrester walked up the dingy stairs. They were covered with torn carpet. She walked slowly, for she did not wish to get out of breath. A door opened as she reached the second floor and she recognised her cook.

"Good-afternoon, Bulfinch," said Mrs. Albert Forrester, with dignity. "I wish to see your master."

Mrs. Bulfinch hesitated for the shadow of a second, then held the door wide open.

"Come in, ma'am." She turned her head. "Albert, here's Mrs. Forrester to see you."

Mrs. Forrester stepped by quickly and there was Albert sitting by the fire in a leather-covered, but rather shabby, arm-chair, with his feet in slippers, and in shirt-sleeves. He was reading the evening paper and smoking a cigar. He rose to his feet as Mrs. Albert Forrester came in. Mrs. Bulfinch followed her visitor into the room and closed the door.

"How are you, my dear?" said Albert cheerfully. "Keeping well, I hope."

"You'd better put on your coat, Albert," said Mrs. Bulfinch. "What *will* Mrs. Forrester think of you, finding you like that? I never."

She took the coat, which was hanging on a peg, and helped him into it; and like a woman familiar with the peculiarities of masculine dress pulled down his waistcoat so that it should not ride over his collar.

"I received your letter, Albert," said Mrs. Forrester.

"I supposed you had, or you wouldn't have known my address, would you?"

"Won't you sit down, ma'am?" said Mrs. Bulfinch, deftly dusting a chair, part of a suite covered in plum-coloured velvet, and pushing it forwards.

Mrs. Albert Forrester with a slight bow seated herself.

"I should have preferred to see you alone, Albert," she said.

His eyes twinkled.

"Since anything you have to say concerns Mrs. Bulfinch as much as it concerns me I think it much better that she should be present."

"As you wish."

Mrs. Bulfinch drew up a chair and sat down. Mrs. Albert Forrester had never seen her before but with a large apron over a print dress. She was wearing now an open-work blouse of white silk, a black skirt, and high-heeled patent-leather shoes with silver buckles. She was a woman of about five-and-forty, with reddish hair and a reddish face, not pretty, but with a good-natured look, and buxom. She reminded Mrs. Albert Forrester of a serving wench, somewhat overblown, in a jolly picture by an old Dutch master.

"Well, my dear, what have you to say to me?" asked Albert.

Mrs. Albert Forrester gave him her brightest and most affable smile. Her great black eyes shone with tolerant good-humour.

"Of course you know that this is perfectly absurd, Albert. I think you must be out of your mind."

"Do you, my dear? Fancy that."

"I'm not angry with you, I'm only amused, but a joke's a joke and should not be carried too far. I've come to take you home."

"Was my letter not quite clear?"

"Perfectly. I ask no questions and I will make no reproaches. We will look upon this as a momentary aberration and say no more about it."

"Nothing will induce me ever to live with you again, my dear," said Albert in, however, a perfectly friendly fashion.

"You're not serious?"

"Quite."

"Do you love this woman?"

Mrs. Albert Forrester still smiled with an eager and somewhat metallic brightness. She was determined to take the matter lightly. With her intimate sense of values she realised that the scene was comic. Albert looked at Mrs. Bulfinch and a smile broke out on his withered face.

"We get on very well together, don't we, old girl?"

"Not so bad," said Mrs. Bulfinch.

Mrs. Albert Forrester raised her eyebrows; her husband had never in all their married life called *her* "old girl": nor indeed would she have wished it.

"If Bulfinch has any regard or respect for you she must know that the thing is impossible. After the life you've led and the society you've moved in she can hardly expect to make you permanently happy in miserable furnished lodgings."

"They're not furnished lodgings, ma'am," said Mrs. Bulfinch. "It's all me own furniture. You see, I'm very independent-like and I've always liked to have a home of me own. So I keep these rooms on whether I'm in a situation or whether I'm not, and so I always have some place to go back to."

"And a very nice cosy little place it is," said Albert.

Mrs. Albert Forrester looked about her. There was a kitchen range in the fireplace on which a kettle was simmering and on the mantelshelf was a black marble clock flanked by black marble candelabra. There was a large table covered with a red cloth, a dresser, and a sewing-machine. On the walls were photographs and framed pictures from Christmas supplements. A door at the back, covered with a red plush portière, led into what, considering the size of the house, Mrs. Albert Forrester (who in her leisure moments had made a somewhat extensive study of architecture) could not but conclude was the only bedroom. Mrs. Bulfinch and Albert lived in a contiguity that allowed no doubt about their relations.

"Have you not been happy with me, Albert?" asked Mrs. Forrester in a deeper tone.

"We've been married for thirty-five years, my dear. It's too long. It's a great deal too long. You're a good woman in your way, but you don't suit me. You're literary and I'm not. You're artistic and I'm not."

"I've always taken care to make you share in all my interests. I've taken great pains that you shouldn't be overshadowed by my success. You can't say that I've ever left you out of things."

"You're a wonderful writer, I don't deny it for a moment, but the truth is I don't like the books you write."

"That, if I may be permitted to say so, merely shows that you have very bad taste. All the best critics admit their power and their charm."

"And I don't like your friends. Let me tell you a secret, my dear. Often at your parties I've had an almost irresistible impulse to take off all my clothes just to see what would happen."

"Nothing would have happened," said Mrs. Albert Forrester with a slight frown. "I should merely have sent for the doctor."

"Besides you haven't the figure for that, Albert," said Mrs. Bulfinch.

Mr. Simmons had hinted to Mrs. Albert Forrester that if the need arose she must not hesitate to use the allurements of her sex in order to bring back her erring husband to the conjugal roof, but she did not in the least know how to do this. It would have been easier, she could not but reflect, had she been in evening dress.

"Does the fidelity of five-and-thirty years count for nothing? I have never looked at another man, Albert. I'm used to you. I shall be lost without you."

"I've left all my menus with the new cook, ma'am. You've only got to tell her how many to luncheon and she'll manage," said Mrs. Bulfinch. "She's very reliable and she has as light a hand with pastry as anyone I ever knew."

Mrs. Albert Forrester began to be discouraged. Mrs. Bulfinch's remark, well-meant no doubt, made it difficult to bring the conversation on to the plane on which emotion could be natural.

"I'm afraid you're only wasting your time, my dear," said Albert. "My decision is irrevocable. I'm not very young any more and I want someone to take care of me. I shall of course make you as good an allowance as I can. Corinne wants me to retire."

"Who is Corinne?" asked Mrs. Forrester with the utmost surprise.

"It's my name," said Mrs. Bulfinch. "My mother was half French."

"That explains a great deal," replied Mrs. Forrester, pursing her lips, for though she admired the literature of our neighbours she knew that their morals left much to be desired.

"What I say is, Albert's worked long enough, and it's about time he started enjoying himself. I've got a little bit of property at Clacton-on-Sea. It's a very healthy neighbourhood and the air is wonderful. We could live there very comfortable. And what with the beach and the pier there's always something to do. They're a very nice lot of people down there. If you don't interfere with nobody, nobody'll interfere with you."

"I discussed the matter with my partners to-day and they're willing to buy me out. It means a certain sacrifice. When everything is settled I shall have an income of nine hundred pounds a year. There are three of us, so it gives us just three hundred a year apiece."

"How am I to live on that?" cried Mrs. Albert Forrester. "I have my position to keep up."

"You have a fluent, a fertile and a distinguished pen, my dear."

Mrs. Albert Forrester impatiently shrugged her shoulders.

"You know very well that my books don't bring me in anything but reputation. The publishers always say that they lose by them and in fact they only publish them because it gives them prestige."

It was then that Mrs. Bulfinch had the idea that was to have consequences of such magnitude.

"Why don't you write a good thrilling detective story?" she asked.

"Me?" exclaimed Mrs. Albert Forrester, for the first time in her life regardless of grammar.

"It's not a bad idea," said Albert. "It's not a bad idea at all."

"I should have the critics down on me like a thousand of bricks."

"I'm not so sure of that. Give the highbrow the chance of being lowbrow without demeaning himself and he'll be so grateful to you, he won't know what to do."

"For this relief much thanks," murmured Mrs. Albert Forrester reflectively.

"My dear, the critics'll eat it. And written in your beautiful English they won't be afraid to call it a masterpeice."

"The idea is preposterous. It's absolutely foreign to my genius. I could never hope to please the masses."

"Why not? The masses want to read good stuff, but they dislike being bored. They all know your name, but they don't read you because you bore them. The fact is, my dear, you're dull."

"I don't know how you can say that, Albert," replied Mrs. Albert Forrester, with as little resentment as the equator might feel if someone called it chilly. "Everyone knows and acknowledges that I have an exquisite sense of humour and there is nobody who can extract so much good wholesome fun from a semi-colon as I can."

"If you can give the masses a good thrilling story and let them think at the same time that they are improving their minds you'll make a fortune."

"I've never read a detective story in my life," said Mrs. Albert Forrester. "I once heard of a Mr. Barnes of New York and I was told that he had written a book called *The Mystery of a Hansom Cab*. But I never read it."

"Of course you have to have the knack," said Mrs. Bulfinch. "The first thing to remember is that you don't want any love-making, it's out of place in a detective story, what you want is murder, and sleuth-hounds, and you don't want to be able to guess who done it till the last page."

"But you must play fair with your reader, my dear," said Albert. "It always annoys me when suspicion has been thrown on the secretary or the lady of title and it turns out to be the second footman who's never done more than say, 'The carriage is at the door.' Puzzle your reader as much as you can, but don't make a fool of him."

"I love a good detective story," said Mrs. Bulfinch. "Give me a lady in evening dress, just streaming with diamonds, lying on the library floor with a dagger in her heart, and I know I'm going to have a treat."

"There's no accounting for tastes," said Albert. "Personally, I prefer a respectable family solicitor, with side-whiskers, gold watch-chain, and a benign appearance, lying dead in Hyde Park."

"With his throat cut?" asked Mrs. Bulfinch eagerly.

"No, stabbed in the back. There's something peculiarly attractive to the reader in the murder of a middle-aged gentleman of spotless reputation. It is pleasant to think that the most apparently blameless of us have a mystery in our lives."

"I see what you mean, Albert," said Mrs. Bulfinch. "He was the repository of a fatal secret."

"We can give you all the tips, my dear," said Albert, smiling mildly at Mrs. Albert Forrester. "I've read hundreds of detective stories."

"You!"

"That's what first brought Corinne and me together. I used to pass them on to her when I'd finished them."

"Many's the time I've heard him switch off the electric light as the dawn was creeping through the window and I couldn't help smiling to myself as I said: 'There, he's finished it at last, now he can have a good sleep.'"

Mrs. Albert Forrester rose to her feet. She drew herself up.

"Now I see what a gulf separates us," she said, and her fine contralto shook a little. "You have been surrounded for thirty years with all that was best in English literature and you read hundreds of detective novels."

"Hundreds and hundreds," interrupted Albert with a smile of satisfaction.

"I came here willing to make any reasonable concession so that you should come back to your home, but now I wish it no longer. You have shown me that we have nothing in common and never had. There is an abyss between us."

"Very well, my dear," said Albert gently, "I will submit to your decision. But you think over the detective story."

"I will arise and go now," she murmured, "and go to Innisfree."

"I'll just show you downstairs," said Mrs. Bulfinch. "One has to be careful of the carpet if one doesn't exactly know where the holes are."

With dignity, but not without circumspection, Mrs. Albert Forrester walked downstairs and when Mrs. Bulfinch opened the door and asked her if she would like a taxi she shook her head.

"I shall take the tram."

"You need not be afraid that I won't take good care of Mr. Forrester, ma'am," said Mrs. Bulfinch pleasantly. "He shall have every comfort. I nursed Mr. Bulfinch for three years during his last illness and there's very little I don't know about invalids. Not that Mr. Forrester isn't very strong and active for his years. And of course he'll have a hobby. I always think a man should have a hobby. He's going to collect postage-stamps."

Mrs. Albert Forrester gave a little start of surprise. But just then a tram came in sight and, as a woman (even the greatest of them) will, she hurried at the risk of her life into the middle of the road and waved frantically. It stopped and she climbed in. She did not know how she was going to face Mr. Simmons. He would be waiting for her when she got home. Clifford Boyleston would probably be there too. They would all be there and she would have to tell them that she had miserably failed. At that moment she had no warm feeling of friendship for her little group of devoted admirers. Wondering what the time was, she looked up at the man sitting opposite her to see whether he was the kind of person she could modestly ask, and suddenly started; for sitting there was a middle-aged gentleman of the most respectable appearance, with side-whiskers, a benign expression and a gold watch-chain. It was the very man whom Albert had described lying dead in Hyde Park and she could not but jump to the conclusion that he was a family solicitor. The coincidence was extraordinary and really it looked as though the hand of fate were beckoning to her. He wore a silk hat, a black coat and pepper-and-salt trousers, he was somewhat corpulent, of a powerful build, and by his side was a despatch-case. When the tram was half-way down the Vauxhall Bridge Road he asked the conductor to stop and she saw him go down a small, mean street. Why? Ah, why? When it reached Victoria, so deeply immersed in thought was she, until the conductor somewhat roughly told her where she was, she did not move. Edgar Allan Poe had written detective stories. She took a bus. She sat inside, buried in reflection, but when it arrived at Hyde Park Corner she suddenly made up her mind to get out. She couldn't sit still any longer. She felt she must walk. She entered the gates, walking slowly, and looked about her with an air that was at once intent and abstracted. Yes, there was Edgar Allan Poe; no one could deny that. After all he had invented the genre, and everyone knew how great his influence had been on the Parnassians. Or was it the Symbolists? Never mind. Baudelaire and all that. As she passed the Achilles Statue she stopped for a minute and looked at it with raised eyebrows.

At length she reached her flat and opening the door saw several hats in the hall. They were all there. She went into the drawing-room.

"Here she is at last," cried Miss Waterford.

Mrs. Albert Forrester advanced, smiling with animation, and shook the proffered hands. Mr. Simmons and Clifford Boyleston were there, Harry Oakland and Oscar Charles.

"Oh, you poor things, have you had no tea?" she cried brightly. "I haven't an idea what the time is, but I know I'm fearfully late."

"Well?" they said. "Well?"

"My dears, I've got something quite wonderful to tell you. I've had an inspiration. Why should the devil have all the best tunes?"

"What *do* you mean?"

She paused in order to give full effect to the surprise she was going

to spring upon them. Then she flung it at them without preamble.
"I'M GOING TO WRITE A DETECTIVE STORY."
They stared at her with open mouths. She held up her hand to
prevent them from interrupting her, but indeed no one had the
smallest intention of doing so.

"I am going to raise the detective story to the dignity of Art. It
came to me suddenly in Hyde Park. It's a murder story and I shall
give the solution on the very last page. I shall write it in an im-
peccable English, and since it's occurred to me lately that perhaps
I've exhausted the possibilities of the semi-colon, I am going to take
up the colon. No one yet has explored its potentialities. Humour
and mystery are what I aim at. I shall call it *The Achilles Statue*."

"What a title!" cried Mr. Simmons, recovering himself before any
of the others. "I can sell the serial rights on the title and your name
alone."

"But what about Albert?" asked Clifford Boyleston.

"Albert?" echoed Mrs. Forrester. "Albert?"

She looked at him as though for the life of her she could not think
what he was talking about. Then she gave a little cry as if she had
suddenly remembered.

"Albert! I knew I'd gone out on some errand and it absolutely
slipped my memory. I was walking through Hyde Park and I had
this inspiration. What a fool you'll all think me!"

"Then you haven't seen Albert?"

"My dear, I forgot all about him." She gave an amused laugh.
"Let Albert keep his cook. I can't bother about Albert now. Albert
belongs to the semi-colon period. I am going to write a detective
story."

"My dear, you're too, too wonderful," said Harry Oakland.

Virtue

THERE are few things better than a good Havana. When I was young and very poor and smoked a cigar only when somebody gave me one, I determined that if ever I had money I would smoke a cigar every day after luncheon and after dinner. This is the only resolution of my youth that I have kept. It is the only ambition I have achieved that has never been embittered by disillusion. I like a cigar that is mild, but full-flavoured, neither so small that it is finished before you have become aware of it nor so large as to be irksome, rolled so that it draws without consciousness of effort on your part, with a leaf so firm that it doesn't become messy on your lips and in such condition that it keeps its savour to the very end. But when you have taken the last pull and put down the shapeless stump and watched the final cloud of smoke dwindle blue in the surrounding air it is impossible, if you have a sensitive nature, not to feel a certain melancholy at the thought of all the labour, the care and pains that have gone, the thought, the trouble, the complicated organisation that have been required to provide you with half an hour's delight. For this men have sweltered long years under tropical suns and ships have scoured the seven seas. These reflections become more poignant still when you are eating a dozen oysters (with half a bottle of dry white wine) and they become almost unbearable when it comes to a lamb cutlet. For these are animals and there is something that inspires awe in the thought that since the surface of the earth became capable of supporting life from generation to generation for millions upon millions of years creatures have come into existence to end at last upon a plate of crushed ice or on a silver grill. It may be that a sluggish fancy cannot grasp the dreadful solemnity of eating an oyster and evolution has taught us that the bivalve has through the ages kept itself to itself in a manner that inevitably alienates sympathy. There is an aloofness in it that is offensive to the aspiring spirit of man and a self-complacency that is obnoxious to his vanity. But I do not know how anyone can look upon a lamb cutlet without thoughts too deep for tears: here man himself has taken a hand and the history of the race is bound up with the tender morsel on your plate.

And sometimes even the fate of human beings is curious to consider. It is strange to look upon this man or that, the quiet ordinary persons of every day, the bank clerk, the dustman, the middle-aged girl in the second row of the chorus, and think of the interminable history behind them and of the long, long series of hazards by which from the primeval slime the course of events has brought them at this moment to such and such a place. When such tremendous vicissitudes have been needed to get them here at all one would have thought some huge significance must be attached to them; one would have thought that what befell them must matter a little to the Life Spirit or whatever else it is that has produced them. An accident befalls them. The thread is broken. The story that began with the world is finished abruptly and it looks as though it meant nothing at all. A tale told by an idiot. And is it not odd that this event, of an importance so dramatic, may be brought about by a cause so trivial?

An incident of no moment, that might easily not have happened, has consequences that are incalculable. It looks as though blind chance ruled all things. Our smallest actions may affect profoundly the whole lives of people who have nothing to do with us. The story I have to tell would never have happened if one day I had not walked across the street. Life is really very fantastic and one has to have a peculiar sense of humour to see the fun of it.

I was strolling down Bond Street one spring morning and having nothing much to do till lunch-time thought I would look in at Sotheby's, the auction rooms, to see whether there was anything on show that interested me. There was a block in the traffic and I threaded my way through the cars. When I reached the other side I ran into a man I had known in Borneo coming out of a hatter's.

"Hullo, Morton," I said. "When did you come home?"

"I've been back about a week."

He was a District Officer. The Governor had given me a letter of introduction to him and I wrote and told him I meant to spend a week at the place he lived at and should like to put up at the government rest-house. He met me on the ship when I arrived and asked me to stay with him. I demurred. I did not see how I could spend a week with a total stranger, I did not want to put him to the expense of my board, and besides I thought I should have more freedom if I were on my own. He would not listen to me.

"I've got plenty of room," he said, "and the rest-house is beastly. I haven't spoken to a white man for six months and I'm fed to the teeth with my own company."

But when Morton had got me and his launch had landed us at the bungalow and he had offered me a drink he did not in the least know what to do with me. He was seized on a sudden with shyness and his conversation, which had been fluent and ready, ran dry. I did my best to make him feel at home (it was the least I could do, considering that it was his own house) and asked him if he had any new records. He turned on the gramophone and the sound of rag-time gave him confidence.

His bungalow overlooked the river and his living-room was a large verandah. It was furnished in the impersonal fashion that characterised the dwellings of government officials who were moved here and there at little notice according to the exigencies of the service. There were native hats as ornaments on the walls and the horns of animals, blow-pipes and spears. In the book-shelf were detective novels and old magazines. There was a cottage piano with yellow keys. It was very untidy, but not uncomfortable.

Unfortunately I cannot very well remember what he looked like. He was young, twenty-eight, I learnt later, and he had a boyish and attractive smile. I spent an agreeable week with him. We went up and down the river and we climbed a mountain. We had tiffin one day with some planters who lived twenty miles away and every evening we went to the club. The only members were the managers of a kutch factory and his assistants, but they were not on speaking terms with one another and it was only on Morton's representations that they must not let him down when he had a visitor that we could get up a rubber of bridge. The atmosphere was strained. We came back to dinner, listened to the gramophone and went to bed. Morton had little office work and one would have thought the time hung heavy on his hands, but he had energy and high spirits; it was his first post of the sort and he was happy to be independent. His only anxiety was lest he should be transferred before he had finished a road he was building. This was the joy of his heart. It was his own idea and he had wheedled the government into giving him the money to make it; he had surveyed the country himself and traced the path. He had solved unaided the technical problems that presented themselves. Every morning, before he went to his office, he drove out in a rickety old Ford to where the coolies were working and watched the progress that had been made since the day before. He thought of nothing else. He dreamt of it at night. He reckoned that it would be finished in a year and he did not want to take his leave till then. He could not have worked with more zest if he had been a painter or a sculptor creating a work of art. I think it was this eagerness that made me take a fancy to him. I liked his zeal. I liked his ingenuousness. And I was impressed by the passion for achievement that made him indifferent to the solitariness of his life, to promotion and even to the thought of going home. I forget how long the road was, fifteen or twenty miles, I think, and I forget what purpose it was to serve. I don't believe Morton cared very much. His passion was the artist's and his triumph was the triumph of man over nature. He learnt as he went along. He had the jungle to contend against, torrential rains that destroyed the labour of weeks, accidents of topography; he had to collect his labour and hold it together; he had inadequate funds. His imagination sustained him. His labours gained a sort of epic quality and the vicissitudes of the work were a great saga that unrolled itself with an infinity of episodes.

His only complaint was that the day was too short. He had office duties, he was judge and tax collector, father and mother (at twenty-eight) of the people in his district; he had now and then to make tours that took him away from home. Unless he was on the spot nothing was done. He would have liked to be there twenty-four hours a day driving the reluctant coolies to further effort. It so happened that shortly before I arrived an incident had occurred that filled him with jubilation. He had offered a contract to a Chinese to make a certain section of the road and the Chinese had asked more than Morton could afford to pay. Notwithstanding interminable discussions they had been unable to arrive at an agreement and Morton with rage in his heart saw his work held up. He was at his wits' end. Then going down to his office one morning, he heard that there had been a row in one of the Chinese gambling houses the night before. A coolie had been badly wounded and his assailant was under arrest. This assailant was the contractor. He was brought into court, the evidence was clear and Morton sentenced him to eighteen months' hard labour.

"Now he'll have to build the blasted road for nothing," said Morton, his eyes glistening when he told me the story.

We saw the fellow at work one morning, in the prison sarong, unconcerned. He was taking his misfortunes in good part.

"I've told him I'll remit the rest of his sentence when the road's finished," said Morton, "and he's as pleased as Punch. Bit of a snip for me, eh, what?"

When I left Morton I asked him to let me know when he came to England and he promised to write to me as soon as he landed. On the spur of the moment one gives these invitations and one is perfectly sincere about them. But when one is taken at one's word a slight dismay seizes one. People are so different at home from what they are abroad. There they are easy, cordial and natural. They have interesting things to tell you. They are immensely kind. You are anxious when your turn comes to do something in return for the hospitality you have received. But it is not easy. The persons who were so entertaining in their own surroundings are very dull in yours.

They are constrained and shy. You introduce them to your friends and your friends find them a crashing bore. They do their best to be civil, but sigh with relief when the strangers go and the conversation can once more run easily in its accustomed channels. I think the residents in far places early in their careers understand the situation pretty well, as the result maybe of bitter and humiliating experiences, for I have found that they seldom take advantage of the invitation which on some outstation on the edge of the jungle has been so cordially extended to them and by them as cordially accepted. But Morton was different. He was a young man and single. It is generally the wives that are the difficulty; other women look at their drab clothes, in a glance take in their provincial air, and freeze them with their indifference. But a man can play bridge and tennis, and dance. Morton had charm. I had had no doubt that in a day or two he would find his feet.

"Why didn't you let me know you were back?" I asked him.

"I thought you wouldn't want to be bothered with me," he smiled.

"What nonsense!"

Of course now as we stood in Bond Street on the kerb and chatted for a minute he looked strange to me. I had never seen him in anything but khaki shorts and a tennis shirt, except when we got back from the club at night and he put on a pyjama jacket and a sarong for dinner. It is as comfortable a form of evening dress as has ever been devised. He looked a bit awkward in his blue serge suit. His face against a white collar was very brown.

"How about the road?" I asked him.

"Finished. I was afraid I'd have to postpone my leave, we struck one or two snags towards the end, but I made 'em hustle and the day before I left I drove the Ford to the end and back without stopping."

I laughed. His pleasure was charming.

"What have you been doing with yourself in London?"

"Buying clothes."

"Been having a good time?"

"Marvellous. A bit lonely, you know, but I don't mind that. I've been to a show every night. The Palmers, you know, I think you met them in Sarawak, were going to be in town and we were going to do the play together, but they had to go to Scotland because her mother's ill."

His words, said so breezily, cut me to the quick. His was the common experience. It was heartbreaking. For months, for long months before it was due, these people planned their leave and when they got off the ship they were in such spirits they could hardly contain themselves. London. Shops and clubs and theatres and restaurants. London. They were going to have the time of their lives. London. It swallowed them. A strange turbulent city, not hostile but indifferent, and they were lost in it. They had no friends. They had nothing in common with the acquaintances they made. They were more lonely than in the jungle. It was a relief when at a theatre they ran across someone they had known in the East (and perhaps been bored stiff by or disliked) and they could fix up an evening together and have a good laugh and tell one another what a grand time they were having and talk of common friends and at last confide to one another a little shyly that they would not be sorry when their leave was up and they were once again in harness. They went to see their families and of course they were glad to see them, but it wasn't the same as it had been, they did feel a bit out of it, and when you came down to brass tacks the life people led in England was deadly. It was grand fun to come home, but you couldn't live there any more, and sometimes you thought of your bungalow overlooking the river and your tours of the district and what a lark it was to run over once in a blue moon to Sandakan or Kuching or Singapore.

And because I remembered what Morton had looked forward to when, the road finished and off his chest, he went on leave I could not but feel a pang when I thought of him dining by himself in a dismal club where he knew nobody or alone in a restaurant in Soho and then going off to see a play with no one by his side with whom he could enjoy it and no one to have a drink with during the interval. And at the same time I reflected that even if I had known he was in London I could have done nothing much for him, for during the last week I had not had a moment free. That very evening I was dining with friends and going to a play, and the next day I was going abroad.

"What are you doing to-night?" I asked him.

"I'm going to the Pavilion. It's packed jammed full, but there's a fellow over the road who's wonderful and he's got me a ticket that had been returned. You can often get one seat, you know, when you can't get two."

"Why don't you come and have supper with me? I'm taking some people to the Haymarket and we're going on to Ciro's afterwards."

"I'd love to."

We arranged to meet at eleven and I left him to keep an engagement.

I was afraid the friends I had asked him to meet would not amuse

Morton very much, for they were distinctly middle-aged, but I could not think of anyone young that at this season of the year I should be likely to get hold of at the last moment. None of the girls I knew would thank me for asking her to supper to dance with a shy young man from Malaya. I could trust the Bishops to do their best for him, and after all it must be jollier for him to have supper in a club with a good band where he could see pretty women dancing than to go home to bed at eleven because he had nowhere else in the world to go. I had known Charlie Bishop first when I was a medical student. He was then a thin little fellow with sandy hair and blunt features; he had fine eyes, dark and gleaming, but he wore spectacles. He had a round, merry, red face. He was very fond of the girls. I suppose he had a way with him, for with no money and no looks, he managed to pick up a succession of young persons who gratified his roving desires. He was clever and bumptious, argumentative and quick-tempered. He had a caustic tongue. Looking back, I should say he was a rather disagreeable young man, but I do not think he was a bore. Now, half-way through the fifties, he was inclined to be stout and he was very bald, but his eyes behind the gold-rimmed spectacles were still bright and alert. He was dogmatic and somewhat conceited, argumentative still and caustic, but he was good-natured and amusing. After you have known a person so long his idiosyncrasies cease to trouble you. You accept them as you accept your own physical defects. He was by profession a pathologist and now and then he sent me a slim book he had just published. It was severe and extremely technical and grimly illustrated with photographs of bacteria. I did not read it. I gathered from what I sometimes heard that Charlie's views on the subjects with which he dealt were unsound. I do not believe that he was very popular with the other members of his profession, he made no secret of the fact that he looked upon them as a set of incompetent idiots; but he had his job, it brought him in six or eight hundred a year, I think, and he was completely indifferent to other people's opinion of him.

I liked Charlie Bishop because I had known him for thirty years, but I liked Margery, his wife, because she was very nice. I was extremely surprised when he told me he was going to be married. He was hard on forty at the time and so fickle in his affections that I had made up my mind he would remain single. He was very fond of women, but he was not in the least sentimental, and his aims were loose. His views on the female sex would in these idealistic days be thought crude. He knew what he wanted and he asked for it, and if he couldn't get it for love or money he shrugged his shoulders and went his way. To be brief, he did not look to women to gratify his ideal but to provide him with fornication. It was odd that though small and plain he found so many who were prepared to grant his wishes. For his spiritual needs he found satisfaction in unicellular organisms. He had always been a man who spoke to the point, and when he told me he was going to marry a young woman called Margery Hobson I did not hesitate to ask him why. He grinned.

"Three reasons. First, she won't let me go to bed with her without. Second, she makes me laugh like a hyena. And third, she's alone in the world, without a single relation, and she must have someone to take care of her."

"The first reason is just swank and the second is eyewash. The third is the real one and it means that she's got you by the short hairs."

His eyes gleamed softly behind his large spectacles.

"I shouldn't be surprised if you weren't dead right."

"She's not only got you by the short hairs but you're as pleased as Punch that she has."

"Come and lunch to-morrow and have a look at her. She's easy on the eye."

Charlie was a member of a cock-and-hen club which at that time I used a good deal and we arranged to lunch there. I found Margery a very attractive young woman. She was then just under thirty. She was a lady. I noticed the fact with satisfaction, but with a certain astonishment, for it had not escaped my notice that Charlie was attracted as a rule by women whose breeding left something to be desired. She was not beautiful, but comely, with fine dark hair and fine eyes, a good colour and a look of health. She had a pleasant frankness and an air of candour that were very taking. She looked honest, simple and dependable. I took an immediate liking to her. She was easy to talk to and though she did not say anything very brilliant she understood what other people were talking about; she was quick to see a joke and she was not shy. She gave you the impression of being competent and business-like. She had a happy placidity that suggested a good temper and an excellent digestion.

They seemed extremely pleased with one another. I had asked myself when I first saw her why Margery was marrying this irritable little man, baldish already and by no means young, but I discovered very soon that it was because she was in love with him. They chaffed one another a good deal and laughed a lot and every now and then their eyes met more significantly and they seemed to exchange a little private message. It was really rather touching.

A week later they were married at a registrar's office. It was a very successful marriage. Looking back now after sixteen years I could not but chuckle sympathetically at the thought of the lark they had made of their life together. I had never known a more devoted couple. They had never had very much money. They never seemed to want any. They had no ambitions. Their life was a picnic that never came to an end. They lived in the smallest flat I ever saw, in Panton Street, a small bedroom, a small sitting-room and a bathroom that served also as a kitchen. But they had no sense of home, they ate their meals in restaurants, and only had breakfast in the flat. It was merely a place to sleep in. It was comfortable, though a third person coming in for a whisky and soda crowded it, and Margery with the help of a charwoman kept it as neat as Charlie's untidiness permitted, but there was not a single thing in it that had a personal note. They had a tiny car and whenever Charlie had a holiday they took it across the Channel and started off, with a bag each for all their luggage, to drive wherever the fancy took them. Breakdowns never disturbed them, bad weather was part of the fun, a puncture was no end of a joke and if they lost their way and had to sleep out in the open they thought they were having the time of their lives.

Charlie continued to be irascible and contentious, but nothing he did ever disturbed Margery's lovely placidity. She could calm him with a word. She still made him laugh. She typed his monographs on obscure bacteria and corrected the proofs of his articles in the scientific magazines. Once I asked them if they ever quarrelled.

"No," she said, "we never seem to have anything to quarrel about. Charlie has the temper of an angel."

"Nonsense," I said, "he's an overbearing, aggressive and cantankerous fellow. He always has been."

She looked at him and giggled and I saw that she thought I was being funny.

"Let him rave," said Charlie. "He's an ignorant fool and he uses words of whose meaning he hasn't the smallest idea."

They were sweet together. They were very happy in one another's company and were never apart if they could help it. Even after the long time they had been married Charlie used to get into the car every day at luncheon-time to come west and meet Margery at a restaurant. People used to laugh at them, not unkindly, but perhaps with a little catch in the throat, because when they were asked to go and spend a week-end in the country Margery would write to the hostess and say they would like to come if they could be given a double bed. They had slept together for so many years that neither of them could sleep alone. It was often a trifle awkward. Husbands and wives as a rule not only demanded separate rooms, but were

Q

inclined to be peevish if asked to share the same bathroom. Modern houses were not arranged for domestic couples, but among their friends it became an understood thing that if you wanted the Bishops you must give them a room with a double bed. Some people of course thought it a little indecent, and it was never convenient, but they were a pleasant pair to have to stay and it was worth while to put up with their crankiness. Charlie was always full of spirits and in his caustic way extremely amusing and Margery was peaceful and easy. They were no trouble to entertain. Nothing pleased them more than to be left to go out together for a long ramble in the country.

When a man marries, his wife sooner or later estranges him from his old friends, but Margery on the contrary increased Charlie's intimacy with them. By making him more tolerant she made him a more agreeable companion. They gave you the impression not of a married couple, but, rather amusingly, of two middle-aged bachelors living together; and when Margery, as was the rule, found herself the only woman among half a dozen men, ribald, argumentative and gay, she was not a bar to good-fellowship but an asset. Whenever I was in England I saw them. They generally dined at the club of which I have spoken and if I happened to be alone I joined them.

When we met that evening for a snack before going to the play I told them I had asked Morton to come to supper.

"I'm afraid you'll find him rather dull," I said. "But he's a very decent sort of boy and he was awfully kind to me when I was in Borneo."

"Why didn't you let me know sooner?" cried Margery. "I'd have brought a girl along."

"What do you want a girl for?" said Charlie. "There'll be you."

"I don't think it can be much fun for a young man to dance with a woman of my advanced years," said Margery.

"Rot. What's your age got to do with it?" He turned to me. "Have you ever danced with anyone who danced better?"

I had, but she certainly danced very well. She was light on her feet and she had a good sense of rhythm.

"Never," I said heartily.

Morton was waiting for us when we reached Ciro's. He looked very sunburned in his evening clothes. Perhaps it was because I knew that they had been wrapped away in a tin box with moth balls for four years that I felt he did not look quite at home in them. He was certainly more at ease in khaki shorts. Charlie Bishop was a good talker and liked to hear himself speak. Morton was shy. I

gave him a cocktail and ordered some champagne. I had a feeling
that he would be glad to dance, but was not quite sure whether it
would occur to him to ask Margery. I was acutely conscious that we
all belonged to another generation.

"I think I should tell you that Mrs. Bishop is a beautiful dancer,"
I said.

"Is she?" He flushed a little. "Will you dance with me?"

She got up and they took the floor. She was looking peculiarly
nice that evening, not at all smart, and I do not think her plain black
dress had cost more than six guineas, but she looked a lady. She
had the advantage of having extremely good legs and at that time
skirts were still being worn very short. I suppose she had a little
make-up on, but in contrast with the other women there she looked
very natural. Shingled hair suited her; it was not even touched with
white and it had an attractive sheen. She was not a pretty woman,
but her kindliness, her wholesome air, her good health gave you, if
not the illusion that she was, at least the feeling that it didn't at all
matter. When she came back to the table her eyes were bright and
she had a heightened colour.

"How does he dance?" asked her husband.

"Divinely."

"You're very easy to dance with," said Morton.

Charlie went on with his discourse. He had a sardonic humour
and he was interesting because he was himself so interested in what
he said. But he spoke of things that Morton knew nothing about and
though he listened with a civil show of interest I could see that he was
too much excited by the gaiety of the scene, the music and the
champagne to give his attention to conversation. When the music
struck up again his eyes immediately sought Margery's. Charles
caught the look and smiled.

"Dance with him, Margery. Good for my figure to see you take
exercise."

They set off again and for a moment Charlie watched her with
fond eyes.

"Margery's having the time of her life. She loves dancing and it
makes me puff and blow. Not a bad youth."

My little party was quite a success and when Morton and I,
having taken leave of the Bishops, walked together towards Piccadilly
Circus he thanked me warmly. He had really enjoyed himself. I
said good-bye to him. Next morning I went abroad.

I was sorry not to have been able to do more for Morton and I
knew that when I returned he would be on his way back to Borneo.

I gave him a passing thought now and then, but by the autumn when I got home he had slipped my memory. After I had been in London a week or so I happened to drop in one night at the club to which Charlie Bishop also belonged. He was sitting with three or four men I knew and I went up. I had not seen any of them since my return. One of them, a man called Bill Marsh, whose wife, Janet, was a great friend of mine, asked me to have a drink.

"Where have you sprung from?" asked Charlie. "Haven't seen you about lately."

I noticed at once that he was drunk. I was astonished. Charlie had always liked his liquor, but he carried it well and never exceeded. In years gone by, when we were very young, he got tight occasionally, but probably more than anything to show what a great fellow he was, and it is unfair to bring up against a man the excesses of his youth. But I remembered that Charlie had never been very nice when he was drunk: his natural aggressiveness was exaggerated then and he talked too much and too loud; he was very apt to be quarrelsome. He was very dogmatic now, laying down the law and refusing to listen to any of the objections his rash statements called forth. The others knew he was drunk and were struggling between the irritation his cantankerousness aroused in them and the good-natured tolerance which they felt his condition demanded. He was not an agreeable object. A man of that age, bald and fattish, with spectacles, is disgusting drunk. He was generally rather dapper, but he was untidy now and there was tobacco ash all over him. Charlie called the waiter and ordered another whisky. The waiter had been at the club for thirty years.

"You've got one in front of you, sir."

"Mind your own damned business," said Charlie Bishop. "Bring me a double whisky right away or I'll report you to the secretary for insolence."

"Very good, sir," said the waiter.

Charlie emptied his glass at a gulp, but his hand was unsteady and he spilled some of the whisky over himself.

"Well, Charlie, old boy, we'd better be toddling along," said Bill Marsh. He turned to me. "Charlie's staying with us for a bit."

I was more surprised still. But I felt that something was wrong and thought it safer not to say anything.

"I'm ready," said Charlie. "I'll just have another drink before I go. I shall have a better night if I do."

It did not look to me as though the party would break up for some time, so I got up and announced that I meant to stroll home.

"I say," said Bill, as I was about to go, "you wouldn't come and dine with us to-morrow night, would you, just me and Janet and Charlie?"

"Yes, I'll come with pleasure," I said.

It was evident that something was up.

The Marshes lived in a terrace on the East side of Regent's Park. The maid who opened the door for me asked me to go in to Mr. Marsh's study. He was waiting for me there.

"I thought I'd better have a word with you before you went upstairs," he said as he shook hands with me. "You know Margery's left Charlie?"

"No!"

"He's taken it very hard. Janet thought it was so awful for him alone in that beastly little flat that we asked him to stay here for a bit. We've done everything we could for him. He's been drinking like a fish. He hasn't slept a wink for a fortnight."

"But she hasn't left him for good?"

I was astounded.

"Yes. She's crazy about a fellow called Morton."

"Morton. Who's he?"

It never struck me it was my friend from Borneo.

"Damn it all, you introduced him and a pretty piece of work you did. Let's go upstairs. I thought I'd better put you wise."

He opened the door and we went out. I was thoroughly confused.

"But look here," I said.

"Ask Janet. She knows the whole thing. It beats me. I've got no patience with Margery, and he must be a mess."

He preceded me into the drawing-room. Janet Marsh rose as I entered and came forward to greet me. Charlie was sitting at the window, reading the evening paper; he put it aside as I went up to him and shook his hand. He was quite sober and he spoke in his usual rather perky manner, but I noticed that he looked very ill. We had a glass of sherry and went down to dinner. Janet was a woman of spirit. She was tall and fair and good to look at. She kept the conversation going with alertness. When she left us to drink a glass of port it was with instructions not to stay more than ten minutes. Bill, as a rule somewhat taciturn, exerted himself now to talk. I tumbled to the game. I was hampered by my ignorance of what exactly had happened, but it was plain that the Marshes wanted to prevent Charlie from brooding, and I did my best to interest him. He seemed willing to play his part, he was always fond of holding forth, and he discussed, from the pathologist's standpoint, a murder that was just then absorbing the public. But he spoke without life. He was an empty shell, and one had the feeling that though for the sake of his host he forced himself to speak, his thoughts were else-where. It was a relief when a knocking on the floor above indicated to us that Janet was getting impatient. This was an occasion when a woman's presence eased the situation. We went upstairs and played family bridge. When it was time for me to go Charlie said he would walk with me as far as the Marylebone Road.

"Oh, Charlie, it's so late, you'd much better go to bed," said Janet.

"I shall sleep better if I have a stroll before turning in," he replied.

She gave him a worried look. You cannot forbid a middle-aged professor of pathology from going for a little walk if he wants to. She glanced brightly at her husband.

"I daresay it'll do Bill no harm."

I think the remark was tactless. Women are often a little too managing. Charlie gave her a sullen look.

"There's absolutely no need to drag Bill out," he said with some firmness.

"I haven't the smallest intention of coming," said Bill, smiling. "I'm tired out and I'm going to hit the hay."

I fancy we left Bill Marsh and his wife to a little argument.

"They've been frightfully kind to me," said Charlie, as we walked along by the railings. "I don't know what I should have done with-out them. I haven't slept for a fortnight."

I expressed regret but did not ask the reason, and we walked for a little in silence. I presumed that he had come with me in order to talk to me of what had happened, but I felt that he must take his own time. I was anxious to show my sympathy, but afraid of saying the wrong thing; I did not want to seem eager to extract confidences from him. I did not know how to give him a lead. I was sure he did not want one. He was not a man given to beating about the bush. I imagined that he was choosing his words. We reached the corner.

"You'll be able to get a taxi at the church," he said. "I'll walk on a bit further. Good-night."

He nodded and slouched off. I was taken aback. There was nothing for me to do but to stroll on till I found a cab. I was having my bath next morning when a telephone call dragged me out of it, and with a towel round my wet body I took up the receiver. It was Janet.

"Well, what do you think of it all?" she said. "You seem to have kept Charlie up pretty late last night. I heard him come home at three."

"He left me at the Marylebone Road," I answered. "He said nothing to me at all."

"Didn't he?"

There was something in Janet's voice that suggested that she was prepared to have a long talk with me. I suspected she had a telephone by the side of her bed.

"Look here," I said quickly. "I'm having my bath."

"Oh, have you got a telephone in your bathroom?" she answered eagerly, and I think with envy.

"No, I haven't." I was abrupt and firm. "And I'm dripping all over the carpet."

"Oh!" I felt disappointment in her tone and a trace of irritation. "Well, when can I see you? Can you come here at twelve?"

It was inconvenient, but I was not prepared to start an argument.

"Yes, good-bye."

I rang off before she could say anything more. In heaven when the blessed use the telephone they will say what they have to say and not a word beside.

I was devoted to Janet, but I knew that there was nothing that thrilled her more than the misfortunes of her friends. She was only too anxious to help them, but she wanted to be in the thick of their difficulties. She was the friend in adversity. Other people's business was meat and drink to her. You could not enter upon a love affair without finding her somehow your confidante nor be mixed up in a divorce case without discovering that she too had a finger in the pie. Withal she was a very nice woman. I could not help then chuckling in my heart when at noon I was shown in to Janet's drawing-room and observed the subdued eagerness with which she received me. She was very much upset by the catastrophe that had befallen the Bishops, but it was exciting, and she was tickled to death to have someone fresh to whom she could tell all about it. Janet had just that business-like expectancy that a mother has when she is discussing with the family doctor her married daughter's first confinement. Janet was conscious that the matter was very serious, and she would not for a moment have been thought to regard it flippantly, but she was determined to get every ounce of value out of it.

"I mean, no one could have been more horrified than I was when Margery told me she'd finally made up her mind to leave Charlie," she said, speaking with the fluency of a person who has said the same thing in the same words a dozen times at least. "They were the most devoted couple I'd ever known. It was a perfect marriage. They got on like a house on fire. Of course Bill and I are devoted to one another, but we have awful rows now and then. I mean, I could kill him sometimes."

"I don't care a hang about your relations with Bill," I said. "Tell me about the Bishops. That's what I've come here for."

"I simply felt I must see you. After all you're the only person who can explain it."

"Oh, God, don't go on like that. Until Bill told me last night I didn't know a thing about it."

"That was my idea. It suddenly dawned on me that perhaps you didn't know and I thought you might put your foot in it too awfully."

"Supposing you began at the beginning," I said.

"Well, you're the beginning. After all you started the trouble. You introduced the young man. That's why I was so crazy to see you. You know all about him. I never saw him. All I know is what Margery has told me about him."

"At what time are you lunching?" I asked.

"Half-past one."

"So am I. Get on with the story."

But my remark had given Janet an idea.

"Look here, will you get out of your luncheon if I get out of mine? We could have a snack here. I'm sure there's some cold meat in the house, and then we needn't hurry. I don't have to be at the hair-dresser's till three."

"No, no, no," I said. "I hate the notion of that. I shall leave here at twenty minutes past one at the latest."

"Then I shall just have to race through it. What do *you* think of Gerry?"

"Who's Gerry?"

"Gerry Morton. His name's Gerald."

"How should I know that?"

"You stayed with him. Weren't there any letters lying about?"

"I daresay, but I didn't happen to read them," I answered somewhat tartly.

"Oh, don't be so stupid. I meant the envelopes. What's he like?"

"All right. Rather the Kipling type, you know. Very keen on his work. Hearty. Empire-builder and all that sort of thing."

"I don't mean that," cried Janet, not without impatience. "I mean, what does he look like?"

"More or less like everybody else, I think. Of course I should recognise him if I saw him again, but I can't picture him to myself very distinctly. He looks clean."

"Oh, my God," said Janet. "Are you a novelist or are you not? What's the colour of his eyes?"

"I don't know."

"You must know. You can't spend a week with anyone without knowing if their eyes are blue or brown. Is he fair or dark?"

"Neither."

"Is he tall or short?"

"Average, I should say."

"Are you trying to irritate me?"

"No. He's just ordinary. There's nothing in him to attract your attention. He's neither plain nor good-looking. He looks quite decent. He looks a gentleman."

"Margery says he has a charming smile and a lovely figure."

"I dare say."

"He's absolutely crazy about her."

"What makes you think that?" I asked dryly.

"I've seen his letters."

"Do you mean to say she's shown them to you?"

"Why, of course."

It is always difficult for a man to stomach the want of reticence that women betray in their private affairs. They have no shame. They will talk to one another without embarrassment of the most intimate matters. Modesty is a masculine virtue. But though a man may know this theoretically, each time he is confronted with women's lack of reserve he suffers a new shock. I wondered what Morton would think if he knew that not only were his letters read by Janet Marsh as well as by Margery, but that she had been kept posted from day to day with the progress of his infatuation. According to Janet he had fallen in love with Margery at first sight. The morning after they had met at my little supper party at Ciro's he had rung up and asked her to come and have tea with him at some place where they could dance. While I listened to Janet's story I was conscious of course that she was giving me Margery's view of the circumstances and I kept an open mind. I was interested to observe that Janet's sympathies were with Margery. It was true that when Margery left her husband it was her idea that Charlie should come to them for two or three weeks rather than stay on in miserable loneliness in the deserted flat and she had been extraordinarily kind to him. She lunched with him almost every day, because he had been accustomed to lunch every day with Margery; she took him for walks in Regent's Park and made Bill play golf with him on Sundays. She listened with wonderful patience to the story of his unhappiness and did what she could to console him. She was terribly sorry for him. But all the same she was definitely on Margery's side and when I expressed my disapproval of her she came down on me like a thousand of bricks. The affair thrilled her. She had been in it from the beginning when Margery, smiling, flattered and a little doubtful, came and told her that she had a young man to the final scene when Margery, exasperated and distraught, announced that she could not stand the strain any more and had packed her things and moved out of the flat.

"Of course, at first I couldn't believe my ears," she said. "You know how Charlie and Margery were. They simply lived in one another's pockets. One couldn't help laughing at them, they were so devoted to one another. I never thought him a very nice little man and heaven knows he wasn't very attractive physically, but one couldn't help liking him because he was so awfully nice to Margery. I rather envied her sometimes. They had no money and they lived in a hugger-mugger sort of way, but they were frightfully happy. Of course I never thought anything would come of it. Margery was rather amused. 'Naturally I don't take it very seriously,' she told me, 'but it is rather fun to have a young man at my time of life. I haven't had any flowers sent me for years. I had to tell him not to send any more because Charlie would think it so silly. He doesn't know a soul in London and he loves dancing and he says I dance like a dream. It's miserable for him going to the theatre by himself all the time and we've done two or three matinees together. It's pathetic to see how grateful he is when I say I'll go out with him.' 'I must say,' I said, 'he sounds rather a lamb.' 'He is,' she said. 'I knew you'd understand. You don't blame me, do you?' 'Of course not, darling,' I said, 'surely you know me better than that. I'd do just the same in your place.' "

Margery made no secret of her outings with Morton and her husband chaffed her good-naturedly about her beau. But he thought him a very civil, pleasant-spoken young man and was glad that Margery had someone to play with while he was busy. It never occurred to him to be jealous. The three of them dined together several times and went to a show. But presently Gerry Morton begged Margery to spend an evening with him alone; she said it was impossible, but he was persuasive, he gave her no peace; and at last she went to Janet and asked her to ring up Charlie one day and ask him to come to dinner and make a fourth at bridge. Charlie would never go anywhere without his wife, but the Marshes were old friends, and Janet made a point of it. She invented some cock-and-bull story that made it seem important that he should consent. Next day Margery and she met. The evening had been wonderful. They had dined at Maidenhead and danced there and then had driven home through the summer night.

"He says he's crazy about me," Margery told her.

"Did he kiss you?" asked Janet.

"Of course," Margery chuckled. "Don't be silly, Janet. He is awfully sweet and, you know, he has such a nice nature. Of course I don't believe half the things he says to me."

"My dear, you're not going to fall in love with him."

"I have," said Margery.

"Darling, isn't it going to be rather awkward?"

"Oh, it won't last. After all he's going back to Borneo in the autumn."

"Well, one can't deny that it's made you look years younger."

"I know, and I feel years younger."

Soon they were meeting every day. They met in the morning and walked in the Park together or went to a picture gallery. They separated for Margery to lunch with her husband and after lunch met again and motored into the country or to some place on the river. Margery did not tell her husband. She very naturally thought he would not understand.

"How was it you never met Morton?" I asked Janet.

"Oh, she didn't want me to. You see, we belong to the same generation, Margery and I. I quite understand that."

"I see."

"Of course I did everything I could. When she went out with Gerry she was always supposed to be with me."

I am a person who likes to cross a "t" and dot an "i".

"Were they having an affair?" I asked.

"Oh, no. Margery isn't that sort of woman at all."

"How do you know?"

"She would have told me."

"I suppose she would."

"Of course I asked her. But she denied it point-blank and I'm sure she was telling me the truth. There's never been anything of that sort between them at all."

"It seems rather odd to me."

"Well, you see, Margery is a very good woman."

I shrugged my shoulders.

"She was absolutely loyal to Charlie. She wouldn't have deceived him for anything in the world. She couldn't bear the thought of having any secret from him. As soon as she knew she was in love with Gerry she wanted to tell Charlie. Of course I begged her not to. I told her it wouldn't do any good and it would only make Charlie miserable. And after all, the boy was going away in a couple of months, it didn't seem much good to make a lot of fuss about a thing that couldn't possibly last."

But Gerry's imminent departure was the cause of the crash. The Bishops had arranged to go abroad as usual and proposed to motor through Belgium, Holland and the North of Germany. Charlie was busy with maps and guides. He collected information from friends about hotels and roads. He looked forward to his holiday with the bubbling excitement of a schoolboy. Margery listened to him discussing it with a sinking heart. They were to be away four weeks and in September Gerry was sailing. She could not bear to lose so much of the short time that remained to them and the thought of the motor tour filled her with exasperation. As the interval grew shorter and shorter she grew more and more nervous. At last she decided that there was only one thing to do.

"Charlie, I don't want to come on this trip," she interrupted him suddenly, one day when he was talking to her of some restaurant he had just heard of. "I wish you'd get someone else to go with you."

He looked at her blankly. She was startled at what she had said and her lips trembled a little.

"Why, what's the matter?"

"Nothing's the matter. I don't feel like it. I want to be by myself for a bit."

"Are you ill?"

She saw the sudden fear in his eyes. His concern drove her beyond her endurance.

"No. I've never been better in my life. I'm in love."

"You? Whom with?"

"Gerry."

He looked at her in amazement. He could not believe his ears. She mistook his expression.

"It's no good blaming me. I can't help it. He's going away in a few weeks. I'm not going to waste the little time he has left."

He burst out laughing.

"Margery, how can you make such a damned fool of yourself? You're old enough to be his mother."

She flushed.

"He's just as much in love with me as I am with him."

"Has he told you so?"

"A thousand times."

"He's a bloody liar, that's all."

He chuckled. His fat stomach rippled with mirth. He thought it a huge joke. I daresay Charlie did not treat his wife in the proper way. Janet seemed to think he should have been tender and compassionate. *He should have understood.* I saw the scene that was in her mind's eye, the stiff upper lip, the silent sorrow, and the final renunciation. Women are always sensitive to the beauty of the self-sacrifice of others. Janet would have sympathised also if he had flown into a violent passion, broken one or two pieces of furniture (which he would have had to replace), or given Margery a sock in the jaw. But to laugh at her was unpardonable. I did not point out that it is very difficult for a rather stout and not very tall professor of pathology, aged fifty-five, to act all of a sudden like a cave-man. Anyhow, the excursion to Holland was given up and the Bishops stayed in London through August. They were not very happy. They lunched and dined together every day because they had been in the habit of doing so for so many years and the rest of the time Margery spent with Gerry. The hours she passed with him made up for all she had to put up with and she had to put up with a good deal. Charlie had a ribald and sarcastic humour and he made himself very funny at her expense and at Gerry's. He persisted in refusing to take the matter seriously. He was vexed with Margery for being so silly, but apparently it never occurred to him that she might have been unfaithful to him. I commented upon this to Janet.

"He never suspected it even," she said. "He knew Margery much too well."

The weeks passed and at last Gerry sailed. He went from Tilbury and Margery saw him off. When she came back she cried for forty-eight hours. Charlie watched her with increasing exasperation. His nerves were much frayed.

"Look here, Margery," he said at last, "I've been very patient with you, but now you must pull yourself together. This is getting past a joke."

"Why can't you leave me alone?" she cried. "I've lost everything that made life lovely to me."

"Don't be such a fool," he said.

I do not know what else he said. But he was unwise enough to tell her what he thought of Gerry and I gather that the picture he drew was virulent. It started the first violent scene they had ever had. She had borne Charlie's jibes when she knew that she would see Gerry in an hour or next day, but now that she had lost him for ever she could bear them no longer. She had held herself in for weeks: now she flung her self-control to the winds. Perhaps she never knew exactly what she said to Charlie. He had always been irascible and at last he hit her. They were both frightened when he had. He seized a hat and flung out of the flat. During all that miserable time they had shared the same bed, but when he came back, in the middle of the night, he found that she had made herself up a shake-down on the sofa in the sitting-room.

"You can't sleep there," he said. "Don't be so silly. Come to bed."

"No, I won't, let me alone."

For the rest of the night they wrangled, but she had her way and now made up her bed every night on the sofa. But in that tiny flat they could not get away from one another; they could not even get out of sight or out of hearing of one another. They had lived in such intimacy for so many years that it was an instinct for them to be together. He tried to reason with her. He thought her incredibly stupid and argued with her interminably in the effort to show her how wrong-headed she was. He could not leave her alone. He would not let her sleep, and he talked half through the night till they were both exhausted. He thought he could talk her out of love. For two or three days at a time they would not speak to one another. Then one day, coming home, he found her crying bitterly; the sight of her tears distracted him; he told her how much he loved her and sought to move her by the recollection of all the happy years they had spent together. He wanted to let bygones be bygones. He promised never to refer to Gerry again. Could they not forget the nightmare they had been through? But the thought of all that a reconciliation implied revolted her. She told him she had a racking headache and asked him to give her a sleeping draught. She pretended to be still asleep when he went out next morning, but the moment he was gone she packed up her things and left. She had a few trinkets that she had inherited and by selling them she got a little money. She took a room at a cheap boarding-house and kept her address a secret from Charlie.

It was when he found she had left him that he went all to pieces. The shock of her flight broke him. He told Janet that his loneliness was intolerable. He wrote to Margery imploring her to come back, and asked Janet to intercede for him; he was willing to promise anything; he abased himself. Margery was obdurate.

"Do you think she'll ever go back?" I asked Janet.

"She says not."

I had to leave then, for it was nearly half-past one and I was bound for the other end of London.

Two or three days later I got a telephone message from Margery asking if I could see her. She suggested coming to my rooms. I asked her to tea. I tried to be nice to her; her affairs were no business of mine, but in my heart I thought her a very silly woman and I dare say my manner was cold. She had never been handsome and the passing years had changed her little. She had still those fine dark eyes and her face was astonishingly unlined. She was very simply dressed and if she wore make-up it was so cunningly put on that I did not perceive it. She had still the charm she had always had of perfect naturalness and of a kindly humour.

"I want you to do something for me if you will," she began without beating about the bush.

"What is it?"

"Charlie is leaving the Marshes to-day and going back to the flat. I'm afraid his first few days there will be rather difficult; it would be awfully nice of you if you'd ask him to dinner or something."

"I'll have a look at my book."

"I'm told he's been drinking heavily. It's such a pity. I wish you could give him a hint."

"I understand he's had some domestic worries of late," I said, perhaps acidly.

Margery flushed. She gave me a pained look. She winced as though I had struck her.

"Of course you've known him ever so much longer than you've known me. It's natural that you should take his part."

"My dear, to tell you the truth I've known him all these years chiefly on your account. I have never very much liked him, but I thought you were awfully nice."

She smiled at me and her smile was very sweet. She knew that I meant what I said.

"Do you think I was a good wife to him?"

"Perfect."

"He used to put people's backs up. A lot of people didn't like him, but I never found him difficult."

"He was awfully fond of you."

"I know. We had a wonderful time together. For sixteen years we were perfectly happy." She paused and looked down. "I had to leave him. It became quite impossible. That cat-and-dog life we were leading was too awful."

"I never see why two persons should go on living together if they don't want to."

"You see, it was awful for us. We'd always lived in such close intimacy. We could never get away from one another. At the end I hated the sight of him."

"I don't suppose the situation was easy for either of you."

"It wasn't my fault that I fell in love. You see, it was quite a different love from the one I'd felt for Charlie. There was always something maternal in that and protective. I was so much more reasonable than he was. He was unmanageable, but I could always manage him. Gerry was different." Her voice grew soft and her face was transfigured with glory. "He gave me back my youth. I was a girl to him and I could depend on his strength and be safe in his care."

"He seemed to me a very nice lad," I said slowly. "I imagine he'll do well. He was very young for the job he had when I ran across him. He's only twenty-nine now, isn't he?"

She smiled softly. She knew quite well what I meant.

"I never made any secret of my age to him. He says it doesn't matter."

I knew this was true. She was not the woman to have lied about her age. She had found a sort of fierce delight in telling him the truth about herself.

"How old are you?"

"Forty-four."

"What are you going to do now?"

"I've written to Gerry and told him I've left Charlie. As soon as I hear from him I'm going out to join him."

I was staggered.

"You know, it's a very primitive little colony he's living in. I'm afraid you'll find your position rather awkward."

"He made me promise that if I found my life impossible after he left I'd go to him."

"Are you sure you're wise to attach so much importance to the things a young man says when he's in love?"

Again that really beautiful look of exaltation came into her face.

"Yes, when the young man happens to be Gerry."

My heart sank. I was silent for a moment. Then I told her the story of the road Gerry Morton had built. I dramatised it, and I think I made it rather effective.

"What did you tell me that for?" she asked when I finished.

"I thought it rather a good story."

She shook her head and smiled.

"No, you wanted to show me that he was very young and enthusiastic, and so keen on his work that he hadn't much time to waste on other interests. I wouldn't interfere with his work. You don't know him as I do. He's incredibly romantic. He looks upon himself as a pioneer. I've caught from him something of his excitement at the idea of taking part in the opening up of a new country. It *is* rather splendid, isn't it? It makes life here seem very humdrum and commonplace. But of course it's very lonely there. Even the companionship of a middle-aged woman may be worth having."

"Are you proposing to marry him?" I asked.

"I leave myself in his hands. I want to do nothing that he does not wish."

She spoke with so much simplicity, there was something so touching in her self-surrender, that when she left me I no longer felt angry with her. Of course I thought her very foolish, but if the folly of men made one angry one would pass one's life in a state of chronic ire. I thought all would come right. She said Gerry was romantic. He was, but the romantics in this workaday world only get away with their nonsense because they have at bottom a shrewd sense of reality: the mugs are the people who take their vapourings at their face value. The English are romantic; that is why other nations think them hypocritical; they are not: they set out in all sincerity for the Kingdom of God, but the journey is arduous and they have reason to pick up any gilt-edged investment that offers itself by the way. The British soul, like Wellington's armies, marches on its belly. I supposed that Gerry would go through a bad quarter of an hour when he received Margery's letter. My sympathies were not deeply engaged in the matter and I was only curious to see how he would extricate himself from the pass he was in. I thought Margery would suffer a bitter disappointment; well, that would do her no great harm, and then she would go back to her husband and I had no doubt the pair of them, chastened, would live in peace, quiet and happiness for the rest of their lives.

The event was different. It happened that it was quite impossible for me to make any sort of engagement with Charlie Bishop for some days, but I wrote to him and asked him to dine with me one evening in the following week. I proposed, though with misgiving, that we should go to a play; I knew he was drinking like a fish, and when tight he was noisy. I hoped he would not make a nuisance of himself in the theatre. We arranged to meet at our club and dine at seven because the piece we were going to began at a quarter past eight. I arrived. I waited. He did not come. I rang up his flat, but could get no reply, so concluded that he was on his way. I hate missing the beginning of a play and I waited impatiently in the hall so that when he came we could go straight upstairs. To save time I had ordered dinner. The clock pointed to half-past seven, then a quarter to eight; I did not see why I should wait for him any longer, so walked up to the dining-room and ate my dinner alone. He did not appear. I put a call through from the dining-room to the Marshes and presently was told by a waiter that Bill Marsh was at the end of the wire.

"I say, do you know anything about Charlie Bishop?" I said. "We were dining together and going to a play and he hasn't turned up."

"He died this afternoon."

"What?"

My exclamation was so startled that two or three people within earshot looked up. The dining-room was full and the waiters were hurrying to and fro. The telephone was on the cashier's desk and a wine waiter came up with a bottle of hock and two long-stemmed glasses on a tray and gave the cashier a chit. The portly steward showing two men to a table jostled me.

"Where are you speaking from?" asked Bill.

I suppose he heard the clatter that surrounded me. When I told him he asked me if I could come round as soon as I had finished my dinner. Janet wanted to speak to me.

"I'll come at once," I said.

I found Janet and Bill sitting in the drawing-room. He was reading the paper and she was playing patience. She came forward swiftly when the maid showed me in. She walked with a sort of spring, crouching a little, on silent feet, llike a panther stalking his prey. I saw at once that she was in her element. She gave me her hand and turned her face away to hide her eyes brimming with tears. Her voice was low and tragic.

"I brought Margery here and put her to bed. The doctor has given her a sedative. She's all in. Isn't it awful?" She gave a sound that was something between a gasp and a sob. "I don't know why these things always happen to me."

The Bishops had never kept a servant but a charwoman went in every morning, cleaned the flat and washed up the breakfast things. She had her own key. That morning she had gone in as usual and done the sitting-room. Since his wife had left him Charlie's hours had been irregular and she was not surprised to find him asleep. But the time passed and she knew he had his work to go to. She went to the bedroom door and knocked. There was no answer. She thought she heard him groaning. She opened the door softly. He was lying in bed, on his back, and was breathing stertorously. He did not wake. She called him. Something about him frightened her. She went to the flat on the same landing. It was occupied by a journalist. He was still in bed when she rang, and opened the door to her in pyjamas.

"Beg pardon, sir," she said, "but would you just come and 'ave a look at my gentleman. I don't think he's well."

The journalist walked across the landing and into Charlie's flat. There was an empty bottle of veronal by the bed.

"I think you'd better fetch a policeman," he said.

A policeman came and rang through to the police station for an ambulance. They took Charlie to Charing Cross Hospital. He never recovered consciousness. Margery was with him at the end.

"Of course there'll have to be an inquest," said Janet. "But it's quite obvious what happened. He'd been sleeping awfully badly for the last three or four weeks and I suppose he'd been taking veronal. He must have taken an overdose by accident."

"Is that what Margery thinks?" I asked.

"She's too upset to think anything, but I told her I was positive he hadn't committed suicide. I mean, he wasn't that sort of a man. Am I right, Bill?"

"Yes, dear," he answered.

"Did he leave any letter?"

"No, nothing. Oddly enough Margery got a letter from him this morning, well, hardly a letter, just a line. 'I'm so lonely without you, darling.' That's all. But of course that means nothing and she's promised to say nothing about it at the inquest. I mean, what is the use of putting ideas in people's heads? Everyone knows that you never can tell with veronal, I wouldn't take it myself for anything in the world, and it was quite obviously an accident. Am I right, Bill?"

"Yes, dear," he answered.

I saw that Janet was quite determined to believe that Charlie Bishop had not committed suicide, but how far in her heart she believed what she wanted to believe I was not sufficiently expert in female psychology to know. And of course it might be that she was right. It is unreasonable to suppose that a middle-aged scientist should kill himself because his middle-aged wife leaves him and it is extremely plausible that, exasperated by sleeplessness, and in all probability far from sober, he took a larger dose of the sleeping-draught than he realised. Anyhow that was the view the coroner took of the matter. It was indicated to him that of late Charles Bishop had given way to habits of intemperance which had caused his wife to leave him, and it was quite obvious that nothing was further from his thoughts than to put an end to himself. The coroner expressed his sympathy with the widow and commented very strongly on the dangers of sleeping-draughts.

I hate funerals, but Janet begged me to go to Charlie's. Several of his colleagues at the hospital had intimated their desire to come, but at Margery's wish they were dissuaded; and Janet and Bill, Margery and I were the only persons who attended it. We were to fetch the hearse from the mortuary and they offered to call for me on their way. I was on the look-out for the car and when I saw it drive up went downstairs, but Bill got out and met me just inside the door.

"Half a minute," he said. "I've got something to say to you. Janet wants you to come back afterwards and have tea. She says it's no good Margery moping and after tea we'll play a few rubbers of bridge. Can you come?"

"Like this?" I asked.

I had a tail coat on and a black tie and my evening dress trousers.

"Oh, that's all right. It'll take Margery's mind off."

"Very well."

But we did not play bridge after all. Janet, with her fair hair, was very smart in her deep mourning and she played the part of the sympathetic friend with amazing skill. She cried a little, wiping her eyes delicately so as not to disturb the black on her eyelashes, and when Margery sobbed broken-heartedly put her arm tenderly through hers. She was a very present help in trouble. We returned to the house. There was a telegram for Margery. She took it and went upstairs. I presumed it was a message of condolence from one of Charlie's friends who had just heard of his death. Bill went to change and Janet and I went up to the drawing-room and got the bridge table out. She took off her hat and put it on the piano.

"It's no good being hypocritical," she said. "Of course Margery has been frightfully upset, but she must pull herself together now. A rubber of bridge will help her to get back to her normal state. Naturally I'm dreadfully sorry about poor Charlie, but as far as he was concerned I don't believe he'd ever have got over Margery's leaving him and one can't deny that it has made things much easier for her. She wired to Gerry this morning."

"What about?"

"To tell him about poor Charlie."

At that moment the maid came to the room.

"Will you go up to Mrs. Bishop, please, ma'am? She wants to see you."

"Yes, of course."

She went out of the room quickly and I was left alone. Bill joined me presently and we had a drink. At last Janet came back. She handed a telegram to me. It read as follows:

For God's sake await letter. Gerry.

"What do you think it means?" she asked me.

"What it says," I replied.

"Idiot! Of course I've told Margery that it doesn't mean anything, but she's rather worried. It must have crossed her cable telling him that Charles was dead. I don't think she feels very much like bridge after all. I mean, it would be rather bad form to play on the very day her husband has been buried."

"Quite," I said.

"Of course he may wire in answer to the cable. He's sure to do that, isn't he? The only thing we can do now is to sit tight and wait for his letter."

I saw no object in continuing the conversation. I left. In a couple of days Janet rang me up to tell me that Margery had received a telegram of condolence from Morton. She repeated it to me.

Dreadfully distressed to hear sad news. Deeply sympathise with your great grief. Love. Gerry.

"What do you think of it?" she asked me.

"I think it's very proper."

"Of course he couldn't say he was as pleased as Punch, could he?"

"Not with any delicacy."

"And he did put in *love*."

I imagined how those women had examined the two telegrams from every point of view and scrutinised every word to press from it every possible shade of meaning. I almost heard their interminable conversations.

"I don't know what'll happen to Margery if he lets her down now," Janet went on. "Of course it remains to be seen if he's a gentleman."

"Rot," I said and rang off quickly.

In the course of the following days I dined with the Marshes a couple of times. Margery looked tired. I guessed that she awaited the letter that was on the way with sickening anxiety. Grief and fear had worn her to a shadow, she seemed very fragile now and she had acquired a spiritual look that I had never seen in her before. She was very gentle, very grateful for every kindness shown her, and in her smile, unsure and a little timid, was an infinite pathos. Her helplessness was very appealing. But Morton was several thousand miles away. Then one morning Janet rang me up.

"The letter has come. Margery says I can show it to you. Will you come round?"

Her tense voice told me everything. When I arrived Janet gave it to me. I read it. It was a very careful letter and I guessed that Morton had written it a good many times. It was very kind and he had evidently taken great pains to avoid saying anything that could possibly wound Margery; but what transpired was his terror. It was obvious that he was shaking in his shoes. He had felt apparently that the best way to cope with the situation was to be mildly facetious and he made very good fun of the white people in the colony. What would they say if Margery suddenly turned up? He would be given the order of the boot pretty damn quick. People thought the East was free and easy; it wasn't, it was more suburban than Clapham. He loved Margery far too much to bear the thoughts of those horrible women out there turning up their noses at her. And besides he had been sent to a station ten days from anywhere; she couldn't live in his bungalow exactly and of course there wasn't a hotel, and his work took him out into the jungle for days at a time. It was no place for a woman anyhow. He told her how much she meant to him, but she mustn't bother about him and he couldn't help thinking it would be better if she went back to her husband. He would never forgive himself if he thought he had come between her and Charlie. Yes, I am quite sure it had been a difficult letter to write.

"Of course he didn't know then that Charlie was dead. I've told Margery that changes everything."

"Does she agree with you?"

"I think she's being rather unreasonable. What do you make of the letter?"

"Well, it's quite plain that he doesn't want her."

"He wanted her badly enough two months ago."

"It's astonishing what a change of air and a change of scene will do for you. It must seem to him already like a year since he left London. He's back among his old friends and his old interests. My dear, it's no good Margery kidding herself; the life there has taken him back and there's no place for her."

"I've advised her to ignore the letter and go straight out to him."

"I hope she's too sensible to expose herself to a very terrible rebuff."

"But then what's to happen to her? Oh, it's too cruel. She's the best woman in the world. She has real goodness."

"It's funny if you come to think of it, it's her goodness that has caused all the trouble. Why on earth didn't she have an affair with Morton? Charlie would have known nothing about it and wouldn't have been a penny the worse. She and Morton could have had a grand time and when he went away they could have parted with the consciousness that a pleasant episode had come to a graceful end. It would have been a jolly recollection, and she could have gone back to Charlie satisfied and rested and continued to make him the excellent wife she had always been."

Janet pursed her lips. She gave me a look of disdain.

"There is such a thing as virtue, you know."

"Virtue be damned. A virtue that only causes havoc and unhappiness is worth nothing. You can call it virtue if you like. I call it cowardice."

"The thought of being unfaithful to Charlie while she was living with him revolted her. There are women like that, you know."

"Good gracious, she could have remained faithful to him in spirit while she was being unfaithful to him in the flesh. That is a feat of legerdemain that women find it easy to accomplish."

"What an odious cynic you are."

"If it's cynical to look truth in the face and exercise common-sense in the affairs of life, then certainly I'm a cynic and odious if you like. Let's face it, Margery's a middle-aged woman, Charlie was fifty-five and they'd been married for sixteen years. It was natural enough that she should lose her head over a young man who made a fuss of her. But don't call it love. It was physiology. She was a fool to take anything he said seriously. It wasn't himself speaking, it was his starved sex, he'd suffered from sexual starvation, at least as far as white women are concerned, for four years; it's monstrous that she should seek to ruin his life by holding him to the wild promises he made then. It was an accident that Margery took his fancy; he wanted her, and because he couldn't get her wanted her more. I dare say he thought it love; believe me, it was only letch. If they'd gone to bed together Charlie would be alive to-day. It's her damned virtue that caused the whole trouble."

"How stupid you are. Don't you see that she couldn't help herself? She just doesn't happen to be a loose woman."

"I prefer a loose woman to a selfish one and a wanton to a fool."

"Oh, shut up. I didn't ask you to come here in order to make yourself absolutely beastly."

"What did you ask me to come here for?"

"Gerry is your friend. You introduced him to Margery. If she's in the soup it's on his account. But *you* are the cause of the whole trouble. It's your duty to write to him and tell him he must do the right thing by her."

"I'm damned if I will," I said.

"Then you'd better go."

I started to do so.

"Well, at all events it's a mercy that Charlie's life was insured," said Janet.

Then I turned on her.

"And you have the nerve to call me a cynic."

I will not repeat the opprobrious word I flung at her as I slammed the door behind me. But Janet is all the same a very nice woman. I often think it would be great fun to be married to her.

The Man with the Scar

IT was on account of the scar that I first noticed him, for it ran, broad and red, in a great crescent from his temple to his chin. It must have been due to a formidable wound and I wondered whether this had been caused by a sabre or by a fragment of shell. It was unexpected on that round, fat and good-humoured face. He had small and undistinguished features, and his expression was artless. His face went oddly with his corpulent body. He was a powerful man of more than common height. I never saw him in anything but a very shabby grey suit, a khaki shirt and a battered sombrero. He was far from clean. He used to come into the Palace Hotel at Guatemala City every day at cocktail time and strolling leisurely round the bar offer lottery tickets for sale. If this was the way he made his living it must have been a poor one for I never saw anyone buy, but now and then I saw him offered a drink. He never refused it. He threaded his way among the tables with a sort of rolling walk as though he were accustomed to traverse long distances on foot, paused at each table, with a little smile mentioned the numbers he had for sale and then, when no notice was taken of him, with the same smile passed on. I think he was for the most part a trifle the worse for liquor.

I was standing at the bar one evening, my foot on the rail, with an acquaintance—they make a very good dry Martini at the Palace Hotel in Guatemala City—when the man with the scar came up. I shook my head as for the twentieth time since my arrival he held out for my inspection his lottery tickets. But my companion nodded affably.

"*Qué tal, general?* How is life?"

"Not so bad. Business is none too good, but it might be worse."

"What will you have, general?"

"A brandy."

He tossed it down and put the glass back on the bar. He nodded to my acquaintance.

"*Gracias. Hasta luego.*"

Then he turned away and offered his tickets to the men who were standing next to us.

"Who is your friend?" I asked. "That's a terrific scar on his face."

"It doesn't add to his beauty, does it? He's an exile from Nicaragua. He's a ruffian of course and a bandit, but not a bad fellow. I

494

give him a few *pesos* now and then. He was a revolutionary general, and if his ammunition hadn't given out he'd have upset the government and be Minister of War now instead of selling lottery tickets in Guatemala. They captured him, along with his staff, such as it was, and tried him by court-martial. Such things are rather summary in these countries, you know, and he was sentenced to be shot at dawn. I guess he knew what was coming to him when he was caught. He spent the night in gaol and he and the others, there were five of them altogether, passed the time playing poker. They used matches for chips. He told me he'd never had such a run of bad luck in his life; they were playing with a short pack, Jacks to open, but he never held a card; he never improved more than half a dozen times in the whole sitting and no sooner did he buy a new stack than he lost it. When day broke and the soldiers came into the cell to fetch them for execution he had lost more matches than a reasonable man could use in a lifetime.

"They were led into the patio of the gaol and placed against a wall, the five of them side by side, with the firing party facing them. There was a pause and our friend asked the officer in charge of them what the devil they were keeping him waiting for. The officer said that the general commanding the government troops wished to attend the execution and they awaited his arrival.

" 'Then I have time to smoke another cigarette,' said our friend. 'He was always unpunctual.'

"But he had barely lit it when the general—it was San Ignacio, by the way: I don't know whether you ever met him—followed by his A.D.C. came into the patio. The usual formalities were performed and San Ignacio asked the condemned men whether there was anything they wished before the execution took place. Four of the five shook their heads, but our friend spoke.

" 'Yes, I should like to say good-bye to my wife.'

" '*Bueno*,' said the general, 'I have no objection to that. Where is she?'

" 'She is waiting at the prison door.'

" 'Then it will not cause a delay of more than five minutes.'

" 'Hardly that, *Señor General*,' said our friend.

" 'Have him placed on one side.'

"Two soldiers advanced and between them the condemned rebel walked to the spot indicated. The officer in command of the firing squad on a nod from the general gave an order, there was a ragged report, and the four men fell. They fell strangely, not together, but one after the other, with movements that were almost grotesque, as though they were puppets in a toy theatre. The officer went up to them and into one who was still alive emptied two barrels of his revolver. Our friend finished his cigarette and threw away the stub.

"There was a little stir at the gateway. A woman came into the patio, with quick steps, and then, her hand on her heart, stopped suddenly. She gave a cry and with outstretched arms ran forward.

" '*Caramba*,' said the general.

"She was in black, with a veil over her hair, and her face was dead white. She was hardly more than a girl, a slim creature, with little regular features and enormous eyes. But they were distraught with anguish. Her loveliness was such that as she ran, her mouth slightly open and the agony of her face beautiful, a gasp of surprise was wrung from those indifferent soldiers who looked at her.

"The rebel advanced a step or two to meet her. She flung herself into his arms and with a hoarse cry of passion: *alma de mi corazón*, soul of my heart, he pressed his lips to hers. And at the same moment he drew a knife from his ragged shirt—I haven't a notion how he managed to retain possession of it—and stabbed her in the neck. The blood spurted from the cut vein and dyed his shirt. Then he flung his arms round her and once more pressed his lips to hers.

"It happened so quickly that many did not know what had occurred, but from the others burst a cry of horror; they sprang forward and seized him. They loosened his grasp and the girl would have fallen if the A.D.C. had not caught her. She was unconscious. They laid her on the ground and with dismay on their faces stood round watching her. The rebel knew where he was striking and it was impossible to staunch the blood. In a moment the A.D.C. who had been kneeling by her side rose.

" 'She's dead,' he whispered.

"The rebel crossed himself.

" 'Why did you do it?' asked the general.

" 'I loved her.'

"A sort of sigh passed through those men crowded together and they looked with strange faces at the murderer. The general stared at him for a while in silence.

" 'It was a noble gesture,' he said at last. 'I cannot execute this man. Take my car and have him led to the frontier. *Señor*, I offer you the homage which is due from one brave man to another.'

"A murmur of approbation broke from those who listened. The A.D.C. tapped the rebel on the shoulder, and between the two soldiers without a word he marched to the waiting car."

My friend stopped and for a little I was silent. I must explain that he was a Guatemalecan and spoke to me in Spanish. I have translated what he told me as well as I could, but I have made no attempt to tone down his rather high-flown language. To tell the truth I think it suits the story.

"But how then did he get the scar?" I asked at length.

"Oh, that was due to a bottle that burst when I was opening it. A bottle of ginger ale."

"I never liked it," said I.

The Closed Shop

NOTHING would induce me to tell the name of the happy country in which the incidents occurred that I am constrained to relate; but I see no harm in admitting that it is a free and independent state on the continent of America. This is vague enough in all conscience and can give rise to no diplomatic incident. Now the president of this free and independent state had an eye to a pretty woman and there came to his capital, a wide and sunny town with a plaza, a cathedral that was not without dignity and a few old Spanish houses, a young person from Michigan of such a pleasing aspect that his heart went out to her. He lost no time in declaring his passion and was gratified to learn that it was returned, but he was mortified to discover that the young person regarded his possession of a wife and her possession of a husband as a bar to their union. She had a feminine weakness for marriage. Though it seemed unreasonable to the president, he was not the man to refuse a pretty woman the gratification of her whim and promised to make such arrangements as would enable him to offer her wedlock. He called his attorneys together and put the matter before them. He had long thought, he said, that for a progressive country their marriage laws were remarkably out of date and he proposed therefore radically to amend them. The attorneys retired and after a brief interval devised a divorce law that was satisfactory to the president. But the state of which I write was always careful to do things in a constitutional way, for it was a highly civilised, democratic and reputable country. A president who respects himself and his oath of office cannot promulgate a law, even if it is to his own interest, without adhering to certain forms, and these things take time; the president had barely signed the decree that made the new divorce law valid when a revolution broke out and he was very unfortunately hanged on a lamp-post in the plaza in front of the cathedral that was not without dignity. The young person of pleasing aspect left town in a hurry, but the law remained. Its terms were simple. On the payment of one hundred dollars gold and after a residence of thirty days a man could divorce his wife or a wife her husband without even apprising the other party of the intended step. Your wife might tell you that she was going to spend a month with her aged mother and one morning at breakfast when you looked through your mail you might receive a letter from her informing you that she had divorced you and was already married to another.

Now it was not long before the happy news spread here and there that at a reasonable distance from New York was a country, the capital of which had an equable climate and tolerable accommodation, where a woman could release herself, expeditiously and with economy, from the irksome bonds of matrimony. The fact that the operation could be performed without the husband's knowledge saved her from those preliminary and acrimonious discussions that are so wearing to the nerves. Every woman knows that however much a man may argue about a proposition he will generally accept a fact with resignation. Tell him you want a Rolls-Royce and he will say he can't afford it, but buy it and he will sign his cheque like a lamb. So in a very short time beautiful women in considerable numbers began to come down to the pleasant, sunny town; tired business women and women of fashion, women of pleasure and women of leisure; they came from New York, Chicago and San Francisco, they came from Georgia and they came from Dakota, they came from all the states in the Union. The passenger accommodation on the ships of the United Fruit Line was only just adequate to the demand, and if you wanted a stateroom to yourself you had to engage it six months in advance. Prosperity descended upon the capital of this enterprising state and in a very little while there was not a lawyer in it who did not own a Ford car. Don Agosto, the proprietor of the Grand Hotel, went to the expense of building several bathrooms, but he did not grudge it; he was making a fortune, and he never passed the lamp-post on which the outgoing president had been hanged without giving it a jaunty wave of his hand.

"He was a great man," he said. "One day they will erect a statue to him."

I have spoken as though it were only women who availed themselves of this convenient and reasonable law, and this might indicate that in the United States it is they rather than men who desire release from the impediment of Holy Matrimony. I have no reason to believe that this is so. Though it was women in great majority who travelled to this country to get a divorce, I ascribe this to the fact that it is always easy for them to get away for six weeks (a week there, a week back and thirty days to establish a domicile) but it is difficult for men to leave their affairs so long. It is true that they could go there during their summer holidays, but then the heat is somewhat oppressive; and besides, there are no golf links: it is reasonable enough to suppose that many a man will hesitate to divorce his wife when he can only do it at the cost of a month's golf. There were of course two or three males spending their thirty days at the Grand Hotel, but they were generally, for a reason that is obscure, commercial travellers. I can but imagine that by the nature of their avocations they were able at one and the same time to pursue freedom and profit.

Be this as it may, the fact remains that the inmates of the Grand Hotel were for the most part women, and very gay it was in the patio at luncheon and at dinner when they sat at little square tables under the arches discussing their matrimonial troubles and drinking champagne. Don Agosto did a roaring trade with the generals and colonels (there were more generals than colonels in the army of this state), the lawyers, bankers, merchants and the young sparks of the town who came to look at these beautiful creatures. But the perfect is seldom realised in this world. There is always something that is not quite right and women engaged in getting rid of their husbands are very properly in an agitated condition. It makes them at times hard to please. Now it must be confessed that this delightful little city, notwithstanding its manifold advantages, somewhat lacked places of amusement. There was but one cinema and this showed films that had been wandering too long from their happy home in Hollywood. In the daytime you could have consultations with your lawyer, polish your nails and do a little shopping, but the evenings were intolerable. There were many complaints that thirty days were a long time and more than one impatient young thing asked her lawyer why they didn't put a little pep into their law and do the whole job in eight and forty hours. Don Agosto, however, was a man of resource and presently he had an inspiration: he engaged a troupe of wandering Guatemalecans who played the marimba. There is no music in the world that sets the toes so irresistibly tingling and in a little while everyone in the patio began dancing. It is of course obvious that twenty-five beautiful women cannot dance with three commercial travellers, but there were all these generals and colonels and there were all the young sparks of the town. They danced divinely and they had great liquid black eyes. The hours flew, the days tripped one upon the heels of the other so quickly that the month passed before you realised it, and more than one of Don Agosto's guests when she bade him farewell confessed that she would willingly have stayed longer. Don Agosto was radiant. He liked to see people enjoy themselves. The marimba band was worth twice the money he paid for it, and it did his heart good to see his ladies dance with the gallant officers and the young men of the town. Since Don Agosto was thrifty he always turned off the electric light on the stairs and in the passages at ten o'clock at night and the gallant officers and the young men of the town improved their English wonderfully.

Everything went as merrily as a marriage bell, if I may use a phrase that, however hackneyed, in this connection is irresistible, till one day Madame Coralie came to the conclusion that she had had enough of it. For one man's meat is another man's poison. She dressed herself and went to call on her friend Carmencita. After she had in a few voluble words stated the purpose of her visit, Carmencita called a maid and told her to run and fetch La Gorda. They had a matter of importance which they wished to discuss with her. La Gorda, a woman of ample proportions with a heavy moustache, soon joined them and over a bottle of Malaga the three of them held a momentous conversation. The result of it was that they indited a letter to the president asking for an audience. The new president was a hefty young man in the early thirties who, a few years before, had been a stevedore in the employment of an American firm, and he had risen to his present exalted station by a natural eloquence and an effective use of his gun when he wanted to make a point or emphasise a statement. When one of his secretaries placed the letter before him he laughed.

"What do those three old faggots want with me?"

But he was a good-natured fellow and accessible. He did not forget that he had been elected by the people, as one of the people, to protect the people. He had also during his early youth been employed for some months by Madame Coralie to run errands. He told his secretary that he would see them at ten o'clock next morning. They went at the appointed hour to the palace and were led up a noble stairway to the audience chamber; the official who conducted them knocked softly on the door; a barred judas was opened and a suspicious eye appeared. The president had no intention of suffering the fate of his predecessor if he could help it and no matter who his visitors were did not receive them without precaution. The official gave the three ladies' names, the door was opened, but not too wide, and they slipped in. It was a handsome room and various secretaries at little tables, in their shirt-sleeves and with a revolver on each hip, were busy typing. One or two other young men, heavily armed, were lying on sofas reading the papers and smoking cigarettes. The president, also in his shirt-sleeves, with a revolver in his belt, was standing with his thumbs in the sleeve-holes of his waistcoat. He was tall and stout, of a handsome and even dignified presence.

"*Qué tal?*" he cried, jovially, with a flash of his white teeth. "What brings you here, *señoras?*"

"How well you're looking, Don Manuel," said La Gorda. "You are a fine figure of a man."

He shook hands with them, and his staff, ceasing their strenuous activity, leaned back and cordially waved their hands to the three ladies. They were old friends and the greetings, if a trifle sardonic, were hearty. I must disclose the fact now (which I could without doubt do in a manner so discreet that I might be misunderstood; but if you have to say something you may just as well say it plainly as not) that these three ladies were the Madams of the three principal brothels in the capital of this free and independent state. La Gorda and Carmencita were of Spanish origin and were very decently dressed in black, with black silk shawls over their heads, but Madame Coralie was French and she wore a toque. They were all of mature age and of modest demeanour.

The president made them sit down, and offered them madeira and cigarettes, but they refused.

"No, thank you, Don Manuel," said Madame Coralie. "It is on business that we have come to see you."

"Well, what can I do for you?"

La Gorda and Carmencita looked at Madame Coralie and Madame Coralie looked at La Gorda and Carmencita. They nodded and she saw that they expected her to be their spokeswoman.

"Well, Don Manuel, it is like this. We are three women who have worked hard for many years and not a breath of scandal has ever tarnished our good names. There are not in all the Americas three more distinguished houses than ours and they are a credit to this beautiful city. Why, only last year I spent five hundred dollars to supply my *sala principal* with plate-glass mirrors. We have always been respectable and we have paid our taxes with regularity. It is hard now that the fruits of our labours should be snatched away from us. I do not hesitate to say that after so many years of honest and conscientious attention to business it is unjust that we should have to submit to such treatment."

The president was astounded.

"But, Coralie, my dear, I do not know what you mean. Has any-one dared to claim money from you that the law does not sanction or that I know nothing about?"

He gave his secretaries a suspicious glance. They tried to look innocent, but though they were, only succeeded in looking uneasy.

"It is the law we complain of. Ruin stares us in the face."

"Ruin?"

"So long as this new divorce law is in existence we can do no business and we may just as well shut up our beautiful houses."

Then Madame Coralie explained in a manner so frank that I prefer to paraphrase her speech that owing to this invasion of the town by beautiful ladies from a foreign land the three elegant houses on which she and her two friends paid rates and taxes were utterly deserted. The young men of fashion preferred to spend their evenings at the Grand Hotel where they received for soft words entertainment which at the regular establishments they could only have got for hard cash.

"You cannot blame them," said the president.

"I don't," cried Madame Coralie. "I blame the women. They have no right to come and take the bread out of our mouths. Don Manuel, you are one of the people, you are not one of these aristocrats; what will the country say if you allow us to be driven out of business by blacklegs? I ask you is it just, is it honest?"

"But what can I do?" said the president. "I cannot lock them up in their rooms for thirty days. How am I to blame if these foreigners have no sense of decency?"

"It's different for a poor girl," said La Gorda. "She has her way to make. But that these women do that sort of thing when they're not obliged to, no, that I shall never understand."

"It is a bad and wicked law," said Carmencita.

The president sprang to his feet and threw his arms akimbo.

"You are not going to ask me to abrogate a law that has brought peace and plenty to this country. I am of the people and I was elected by the people, and the prosperity of my fatherland is very near my heart. Divorce is our staple industry and the law shall be repealed only over my dead body."

"Oh, *Maria Santissima*, that it should come to this," said Carmencita. "And me with two daughters in a convent in New Orleans. Ah, in this business one often has unpleasantness, but I always consoled myself by thinking that my daughters would marry well, and when the time came for me to retire they would inherit my business. Do you think I can keep them in a convent in New Orleans for nothing?"

"And who is going to keep my son at Harvard if I have to close my house, Don Manuel?" asked La Gorda.

"As for myself," said Madame Coralie, "I do not care. I shall return to France. My dear mother is eighty-seven years of age and she cannot live very much longer. It will be a comfort to her if I spend her last remaining years by her side. But it is the injustice of it that hurts. You have spent many happy evenings in my house, Don Manuel, and I am wounded that you should let us be treated like this. Did you not tell me yourself that it was the proudest day of your life when you entered as an honoured guest the house in which you had once been employed as errand boy?"

"I do not deny it. I stood champagne all round." Don Manuel

R

walked up and down the large hall, shrugging his shoulders as he went, and now and then, deep in thought, he gesticulated. "I am of the people, elected by the people," he cried, "and the fact is, these women are blacklegs." He turned to his secretaries with a dramatic gesture. "It is a stain on my administration. It is against all my principles to allow unskilled foreign labour to take the bread out of the mouths of honest and industrious people. These ladies are quite right to come to me and appeal for my protection. I will not allow the scandal to continue."

It was of course a pointed and effective speech, but all who heard it knew that it left things exactly where they were. Madame Coralie powdered her nose and gave it, a commanding organ, a brief look in her pocket mirror.

"Of course I know what human nature is," she said, "and I can well understand that time hangs heavily on the hands of these creatures."

"We could build a golf-course," hazarded one of the secretaries. "It is true that this would only occupy them by day."

"If they want men why can't they bring them with them?" said La Gorda.

"*Caramba!*" cried the president, and with that stood on a sudden quite still. "There is the solution."

He had not reached his exalted station without being a man of insight and resource. He beamed.

"We will amend the law. Men shall come in as before without let or hindrance, but women only accompanied by their husbands or with their written consent." He saw the look of consternation which his secretaries gave him, and he waved his hand. "But the immigration authorities shall receive instructions to interpret the word husband with the widest latitude."

"*Maria Santissima!*" cried Madame Coralie. "If they come with a friend he will take care that no one else interferes with them and our customers will return to the houses where for so long they have been so hospitably entertained. Don Manuel, you are a great man and one of these days they will erect a statue to you."

It is often the simplest expedients that settle the most formidable difficulties. The law was briefly amended according to the terms of Don Manuel's suggestion and, whereas prosperity continued to pour its blessings on the wide and sunny capital of this free and independent state, Madame Coralie was enabled profitably to pursue her useful avocations, Carmencita's two daughters completed their expensive education in the convent at New Orleans, and La Gorda's son successfully graduated at Harvard.

The Bum

GOD knows how often I had lamented that I had not half the time I needed to do half the things I wanted. I could not remember when last I had had a moment to myself. I had often amused my fancy with the prospect of just one week's complete idleness. Most of us when not busy working are busy playing; we ride, play tennis or golf, swim or gamble; but I saw myself doing nothing at all. I would lounge through the morning, dawdle through the afternoon and loaf through the evening. My mind would be a slate and each passing hour a sponge that wiped out the scribblings written on it by the world of sense. Time, because it is so fleeting, time, because it is beyond recall, is the most precious of human goods and to squander it is the most delicate form of dissipation in which man can indulge. Cleopatra dissolved in wine a priceless pearl, but she gave it to Antony to drink; when you waste the brief golden hours you take the beaker in which the gem is melted and dash its contents to the ground. The gesture is grand and like all grand gestures absurd. That of course is its excuse. In the week I promised myself I should naturally read, for to the habitual reader reading is a drug of which he is the slave; deprive him of printed matter and he grows nervous, moody and restless; then, like the alcoholic bereft of brandy who will drink shellac or methylated spirit, he will make do with the advertisements of a paper five years old; he will make do with a telephone directory. But the professional writer is seldom a disinterested reader. I wished my reading to be but another form of idleness. I made up my mind that if the happy day arrived when I could enjoy untroubled leisure I would complete an enterprise that had always tempted me, but which hitherto, like an explorer making reconnaissances into an undiscovered country, I had done little more than enter upon: I would read the entire works of Nick Carter.

But I had always fancied myself choosing my moment with surroundings to my liking, not having it forced upon me; and when I was suddenly faced with nothing to do and had to make the best of it (like a steamship acquaintance whom in the wide waste of the Pacific Ocean you have invited to stay with you in London and who turns up without warning and with all his luggage) I was not a little taken aback. I had come to Vera Cruz from Mexico City to catch one of the Ward Company's white cool ships to Yucatan; and found to my dismay that, a dock strike having been declared over-night, my ship would not put in. I was stuck in Vera Cruz. I took a room in the Hotel Diligencias overlooking the plaza, and spent the morning looking at the sights of the town. I wandered down side streets and peeped into quaint courts. I sauntered through the parish church; it is picturesque with its gargoyles and flying buttresses, and the salt wind and the blazing sun have patined its harsh and massive walls with the mellowness of age; its cupola is covered with white and blue tiles. Then I found that I had seen all that was to be seen and I sat down in the coolness of the arcade that surrounded the square and ordered a drink. The sun beat down on the plaza with a merciless splendour. The coco-palms drooped dusty and bedraggled. Great black buzzards perched on them for a moment uneasily, swooped to the ground to gather some bit of offal, and then with lumbering wings flew up to the church tower. I watched the people crossing the square; negroes, Indians, Creoles and Spanish, the motley people of the Spanish Main; and they varied in colour from ebony to ivory. As the morning wore on, the tables around me filled up, chiefly with men, who had come to have a drink before luncheon, for the most part in white ducks, but some notwithstanding the heat in the dark clothes of professional respectability. A small band, a guitarist, a blind fiddler and a harpist, played rag-time and after every other tune the guitarist came round with a plate. I had already bought the local paper and I was adamant to the newsvendors who pertinaciously sought to sell me more copies of the same sheet. I refused, oh, twenty times at least, the solicitations of grimy urchins who wanted to shine my spotless shoes; and having come to the end of my small change I could only shake my head at the beggars who importuned me. They gave one no peace. Little Indian women, in shapeless rags, each one with a baby tied in the shawl on her back, held out skinny hands and in a whimper recited a dismal screed; blind men were led up to my table by small boys; the maimed, the halt, the deformed exhibited the sores and the monstrosities with which nature or accident had afflicted them; and half naked, underfed children whined endlessly their demand for coppers. But these kept their eyes open for the fat policeman who would suddenly dart out on them with a thong and give them a sharp cut on the back or over the head. Then they would scamper, only to return again when, exhausted by the exercise of so much energy, he relapsed into lethargy.

But suddenly my attention was attracted by a beggar who, unlike the rest of them and indeed the people sitting round me, swarthy and black-haired, had hair and beard of a red so vivid that it was startling. His beard was ragged and his long mop of hair looked as though it had not been brushed for months. He wore only a pair of trousers and a cotton singlet, but they were tatters, grimy and foul, that barely held together. I have never seen anyone so thin; his legs, his naked arms were but skin and bone and through the rents of his singlet you saw every rib of his wasted body; you could count the bones of his dust-covered feet. Of that starveling band he was easily the most abject. He was not old, he could not well have been more than forty, and I could not but ask myself what had brought him to this pass. It was absurd to think that he would not have worked if work he had been able to get. He was the only one of the beggars who did not speak. The rest of them poured forth their litany of woe and if it did not bring the alms they asked continued until an impatient word from you chased them away. He said nothing. I suppose he felt that his look of destitution was all the appeal he needed. He did not even hold out his hand, he merely looked at you, but with such wretchedness in his eyes, such despair in his attitude, it was dreadful; he stood on and on, silent and immobile, gazing steadfastly, and then, if you took no notice of him, he moved slowly to the next table. If he was given nothing he showed neither disappointment nor anger. If someone offered him a coin he stepped forward a little, stretched out his claw-like hand, took it without a word of thanks and impassively went his way. I had nothing to give him and when he came to me, so that he should not wait in vain, I shook my head.

"*Dispense Usted por Dios,*" I said, using the polite Castilian formula with which the Spaniards refuse a beggar.

But he paid no attention to what I said. He stood in front of me, for as long as he stood at the other tables, looking at me with tragic eyes. I have never seen such a wreck of humanity. There was something terrifying in his appearance. He did not look quite sane. At length he passed on.

It was one o'clock and I had lunch. When I awoke from my siesta it was still very hot, but towards evening a breath of air coming in through the windows which I had at last ventured to open tempted me into the plaza. I sat down under my arcade and ordered a long drink. Presently people in greater numbers filtered into the open space from the surrounding streets, the tables in the restaurants round it filled up, and in the kiosk in the middle the band began to play. The crowd grew thicker. On the free benches people sat huddled together like dark grapes clustered on a stalk. There was a lively hum of conversation. The big black buzzards flew screeching overhead, swooping down when they saw something to pick up, or scurrying away from under the feet of the passers-by. As twilight descended they swarmed, it seemed from all parts of the town, towards the church tower; they circled heavily about it and hoarsely crying, squabbling and jangling, settled themselves uneasily to roost. And again bootblacks begged me to have my shoes cleaned, newsboys pressed dank papers upon me, beggars whined their plaintive demand for alms. I saw once more that strange, red-bearded fellow and watched him stand motionless, with the crushed and piteous air, before one table after another. He did not stop before mine. I supposed he remembered me from the morning and having failed to get anything from me then thought it useless to try again. You do not often see a red-haired Mexican, and because it was only in Russia that I had seen men of so destitute a mien I asked myself if he was by chance a Russian. It accorded well enough with the Russian fecklessness that he should have allowed himself to sink to such a depth of degradation. Yet he had not a Russian face; his emaciated features were clear-cut, and his blue eyes were not set in the head in a Russian manner; I wondered if he could be a sailor, English, Scandinavian or American, who had deserted his ship and by degrees sunk to this pitiful condition. He disappeared. Since there was nothing else to do, I stayed on till I got hungry, and when I had eaten came back. I sat on till the thinning crowd suggested it was bed-time. I confess that the day had seemed long and I wondered how many similar days I should be forced to spend there.

But I woke after a little while and could not get to sleep again. My room was stifling. I opened the shutters and looked out at the church. There was no moon, but the bright stars faintly lit its outline. The buzzards were closely packed on the cross above the cupola and on the edges of the tower, and now and then they moved a little. The effect was uncanny. And then, I have no notion why, that red scarecrow recurred to my mind and I had suddenly a strange feeling that I had seen him before. It was so vivid that it drove away from me the possibility of sleep. I felt sure that I had come across him, but when and where I could not tell. I tried to picture the surroundings in which he might take his place, but I could see no more than a dim figure against a background of fog. As the dawn approached it grew a little cooler and I was able to sleep.

I spent my second day at Vera Cruz as I had spent the first. But I watched for the coming of the red-haired beggar, and as he stood at the tables near mine I examined him with attention. I felt certain now that I had seen him somewhere. I even felt certain that I had known him and talked to him, but I still could recall none of the circumstances. Once more he passed my table without stopping and when his eyes met mine I looked in them for some gleam of recollection. Nothing. I wondered if I had made a mistake and thought I had seen him in the same way as sometimes, by some queer motion of the brain, in the act of doing something you are convinced that you are repeating an action that you have done at some past time. I could not get out of my head the impression that at some moment he had entered into my life. I racked my brains. I was sure now that he was either English or American. But I was shy of addressing him. I went over in my mind the possible occasions when I might have met him. Not to be able to place him exasperated me as it does when you try to remember a name that is on the tip of your tongue and yet eludes you. The day wore on.

Another day came, another morning, another evening. It was Sunday and the plaza was more crowded than ever. The tables under the arcade were packed. As usual the red-haired beggar came along, a terrifying figure in his silence, his threadbare rags and his pitiful distress. He was standing in front of a table only two from mine, mutely beseeching, but without a gesture. Then I saw the policeman who at intervals tried to protect the public from the importunities of all these beggars sneak round a column and give him a resounding whack with his thong. His thin body winced, but he made no protest and showed no resentment; he seemed to accept the stinging blow as in the ordinary course of things and with his slow movements slunk away into the gathering night of the plaza. But the cruel stripe had whipped my memory and suddenly I remembered.

Not his name, that escaped me still, but everything else. He must have recognised me, for I have not changed very much in twenty years, and that was why after that first morning he had never paused in front of my table. Yes, it was twenty years since I had known him. I was spending a winter in Rome and every evening I used to dine in a restaurant in the Via Sistina where you got excellent macaroni and a good bottle of wine. It was frequented by a little band of English and American art students, and one or two writers; and we used to stay late into the night engaged in interminable arguments upon art and literature. He used to come in with a young painter who was a friend of his. He was only a boy then, he could not have been more than twenty-two; and with his blue eyes, straight nose and red hair he was pleasing to look at. I remembered that he spoke a great deal of Central America, he had had a job with the American Fruit Company, but had thrown it over because he wanted to be a writer. He was not popular among us because he was arrogant and we were none of us old enough to take the arrogance of youth with tolerance. He thought us poor fish and did not hesitate to tell us so. He would not show us his work, because our praise meant nothing to him and he despised our censure. His vanity was enormous. It irritated us; but some of us were uneasily aware that it might perhaps be justified. Was it possible that the intense consciousness of genius that he had, rested on no grounds? He had sacrificed everything to be a writer. He was so certain of himself that he infected some of his friends with his own assurance.

I recalled his high spirits, his vitality, his confidence in the future and his disinterestedness. It was impossible that it was the same man, and yet I was sure of it. I stood up, paid for my drink and went out into the plaza to find him. My thoughts were in a turmoil. I was aghast. I had thought of him now and then and idly wondered what had become of him. I could never have imagined that he was reduced to this frightful misery. There are hundreds, thousands of youths who enter upon the hard calling of the arts with extravagant hopes; but for the most part they come to terms with their mediocrity and find somewhere in life a niche where they can escape starvation. This was awful. I asked myself what had happened. What hopes deferred had broken his spirit, what disappointments shattered him and what lost illusions ground him to the dust? I asked myself if nothing could be done. I walked round the plaza. He was not in the arcades. There was no hope of finding him in the crowd that circled round the bandstand. The light was waning and I was afraid I had lost him. Then I passed the church and saw him sitting on the steps. I cannot describe what a lamentable object he looked. Life had taken him, rent him on its racks, torn him limb from limb, and then flung him, a bleeding wreck, on the stone steps of that church. I went up to him.

"Do you remember Rome?" I said.

He did not move. He did not answer. He took no more notice of me than if I were not standing before him. He did not look at me. His vacant blue eyes rested on the buzzards that were screaming and tearing at some object at the bottom of the steps. I did not know what to do. I took a yellow-backed note out of my pocket and pressed it in his hand. He did not give it a glance. But his hand moved a little, the thin claw-like fingers closed on the note and scrunched it up; he made it into a little ball and then edging it on to his thumb flicked it into the air so that it fell among the jangling buzzards. I turned my head instinctively and saw one of them seize it in his beak and fly off followed by two others screaming behind it. When I looked back the man was gone.

I stayed three more days in Vera Cruz. I never saw him again.

The Dream

IT chanced that in August, 1917, the work upon which I was then engaged obliged me to go from New York to Petrograd and I was instructed for safety's sake to travel by way of Vladivostok. I landed there in the morning and passed an idle day as best I could. The trans-Siberian train was due to start, so far as I remember, at about nine in the evening. I dined at the station restaurant by myself. It was crowded and I shared a small table with a man whose appearance entertained me. He was a Russian, a tall fellow, but amazingly stout, and he had so vast a paunch that he was obliged to sit well away from the table. His hands, small for his size, were buried in rolls of fat. His hair, long, dark and thin, was brushed carefully across his crown in order to conceal his baldness, and his huge sallow face, with its enormous double chin, clean-shaven, gave you an impression of indecent nakedness. His nose was small, a funny little button upon that mass of flesh, and his black shining eyes were small too. But he had a large, red and sensual mouth. He was dressed neatly enough in a black suit. It was not worn but shabby; it looked as if it had been neither pressed nor brushed since he had had it.

The service was bad and it was almost impossible to attract the attention of a waiter. We soon got into conversation. The Russian spoke good and fluent English. His accent was marked but not tiresome. He asked me many questions about myself and my plans, which—my occupation at the time making caution necessary—I answered with a show of frankness but with dissimulation. I told him I was a journalist. He asked me whether I wrote fiction and when I confessed that in my leisure moments I did, he began to talk of the later Russian novelists. He spoke intelligently. It was plain that he was a man of education.

By this time we had persuaded the waiter to bring us some cabbage soup, and my acquaintance pulled a small bottle of vodka from his pocket which he invited me to share. I do not know whether it was the vodka or the natural loquaciousness of his race that made him communicative, but presently he told me, unasked, a good deal about himself. He was of noble birth, it appeared, a lawyer by profession, and a radical. Some trouble with the authorities had made it necessary for him to be much abroad, but now he was on his way home. Business had detained him at Vladivostok, but he expected to start for Moscow in a week and if I went there he would be charmed to see me.

"Are you married?" he asked me.

I did not see what business it was of his, but I told him that I was. He sighed a little.

"I am a widower," he said. "My wife was a Swiss, a native of Geneva. She was a very cultivated woman. She spoke English, German and Italian perfectly. French, of course, was her native tongue. Her Russian was much above the average for a foreigner. She had scarcely the trace of an accent."

He called a waiter who was passing with a tray full of dishes and asked him, I suppose—for then I knew hardly any Russian—how much longer we were going to wait for the next course. The waiter, with a rapid but presumably reassuring exclamation, hurried on, and my friend sighed.

"Since the revolution the waiting in restaurants has become abominable."

He lighted his twentieth cigarette and I, looking at my watch, wondered whether I should get a square meal before it was time for me to start.

"My wife was a very remarkable woman," he continued. "She taught languages at one of the best schools for the daughters of noblemen in Petrograd. For a good many years we lived together on perfectly friendly terms. She was, however, of a jealous temperament and unfortunately she loved me to distraction."

It was difficult for me to keep a straight face. He was one of the ugliest men I had ever seen. There is sometimes a certain charm in the rubicund and jovial fat man, but this saturnine obesity was repulsive.

"I do not pretend that I was faithful to her. She was not young when I married her and we had been married for ten years. She was small and thin, and she had a bad complexion. She had a bitter tongue. She was a woman who suffered from a fury of possession, and she could not bear me to be attracted to anyone but her. She was jealous not only of the women I knew, but of my friends, my cat and my books. On one occasion in my absence she gave away a coat of mine merely because I liked none of my coats so well. But I am of an equable temperament. I will not deny that she bored me, but I accepted her acrimonious disposition as an act of God and no more thought of rebelling against it than I would against bad weather or a cold in the head. I denied her accusations as long as it was possible to deny them, and when it was impossible I shrugged my shoulders and smoked a cigarette.

"The constant scenes she made me did not very much affect me. I led my own life. Sometimes, indeed, I wondered whether it was passionate love she felt for me or passionate hate. It seemed to me that love and hate were very near allied.

"So we might have continued to the end of the chapter if one night a very curious thing had not happened. I was awakened by a piercing scream from my wife. Startled, I asked her what was the matter. She told me that she had had a fearful nightmare; she had dreamt that I was trying to kill her. We lived at the top of a large house and the well round which the stairs climbed was broad. She had dreamt that just as we had arrived at our own floor I had caught hold of her and attempted to throw her over the balusters. It was six storeys to the stone floor at the bottom and it meant certain death.

"She was much shaken. I did my best to soothe her. But next morning, and for two or three days after, she referred to the subject again and, notwithstanding my laughter, I saw that it dwelt in her mind. I could not help thinking of it either, for this dream showed me something that I had never suspected. She thought I hated her, she thought I would gladly be rid of her; she knew of course that she was insufferable, and at some time or other the idea had evidently occurred to her that I was capable of murdering her. The thoughts of men are incalculable and ideas enter our minds that we should be ashamed to confess. Sometimes I had wished that she might run away with a lover, sometimes that a painless and sudden death might give me my freedom; but never, never had the idea come to me that I might deliberately rid myself of an intolerable burden.

"The dream made an extraordinary impression upon both of us. It frightened my wife, and she became for a little less bitter and more tolerant. But when I walked up the stairs to our apartment it was impossible for me not to look over the balusters and reflect how easy it would be to do what she had dreamt. The balusters were dangerously low. A quick gesture and the thing was done. It was hard to put the thought out of my mind. Then some months later my wife awakened me one night. I was very tired and I was exasperated. She was white and trembling. She had had the dream again. She burst into tears and asked me if I hated her. I swore by all the saints of the Russian calendar that I loved her. At last she went to sleep again. It was more than I could do. I lay awake. I seemed to see her falling down the well of the stairs, and I heard her shriek and the thud as she struck the stone floor. I could not help shivering."

The Russian stopped and beads of sweat stood on his forehead. He had told the story well and fluently so that I had listened with attention. There was still some vodka in the bottle; he poured it out and swallowed it at a gulp.

"And how did your wife eventually die?" I asked after a pause.

He took out a dirty handkerchief and wiped his forehead.

"By an extraordinary coincidence she was found late one night at the bottom of the stairs with her neck broken."

"Who found her?"

"She was found by one of the lodgers who came in shortly after the catastrophe."

"And where were you?"

I cannot describe the look he gave me of malicious cunning. His little black eyes sparkled.

"I was spending the evening with a friend of mine. I did not come in till an hour later."

At that moment the waiter brought us the dish of meat that we had ordered, and the Russian fell upon it with good appetite. He shovelled the food into his mouth in enormous mouthfuls.

I was taken aback. Had he really been telling me in this hardly veiled manner that he had murdered his wife? That obese and sluggish man did not look like a murderer; I could not believe that he would have had the courage. Or was he making a sardonic joke at my expense?

In a few minutes it was time for me to go and catch my train. I left him and I have not seen him since. But I have never been able to make up my mind whether he was serious or jesting.

The Treasure

RICHARD HARENGER was a happy man. Notwithstanding what
the pessimists, from Ecclesiastes onwards, have said, this is not
so rare a thing to find in this unhappy world, but Richard Harenger
knew it, and that is a very rare thing indeed. The golden mean
which the ancients so highly prized is out of fashion, and those who
follow it must put up with polite derision from those who see no
merit in self-restraint and no virtue in common-sense. Richard
Harenger shrugged a polite and amused shoulder. Let others live
dangerously, let others burn with a hard gemlike flame, let others
stake their fortunes on the turn of a card, walk the tight-rope that
leads to glory or the grave, or hazard their lives for a cause, a passion
or an adventure. He neither envied the fame their exploits brought
them nor wasted his pity on them when their efforts ended in
disaster.

But it must not be inferred from this that Richard Harenger was
a selfish or a callous man. He was neither. He was considerate and
of a generous disposition. He was always ready to oblige a friend
and he was sufficiently well off to be able to indulge himself in the
pleasure of helping others. He had some money of his own and he
occupied in the Home Office a position that brought him an adequate
stipend. The work suited him. It was regular, responsible and
pleasant. Every day when he left the office he went to his club to play
bridge for a couple of hours, and on Saturdays and Sundays he
played golf. He went abroad for his holidays, staying at good hotels,
and visited churches, galleries and museums. He was a regular
first-nighter. He dined out a good deal. His friends liked him. He
was easy to talk to. He was well-read, knowledgeable and amusing.
He was besides of a personable exterior, not remarkably handsome,
but tall, slim and erect of carriage, with a lean, intelligent face; his
hair was growing thin, for he was now approaching the age of fifty,
but his brown eyes retained their smile and his teeth were all his own.
He had from nature a good constitution and he had always taken
care of himself. There was no reason in the world why he should
not be a happy man, and if there had been in him a trace of self-
complacency he might have claimed that he deserved to be.

He had the good fortune even to sail safely through those perilous,
unquiet straits of marriage in which so many wise and good men
have made shipwreck. Married for love in the early twenties, his

wife and he, after some years of almost perfect felicity, had drifted gradually apart. Neither of them wished to marry anyone else, so there was no question of divorce (which indeed Richard Harenger's situation in the government service made undesirable), but for convenience sake, with the help of the family lawyer, they arranged a separation which left them free to lead their lives as each one wished without interference from the other. They parted with mutual expressions of respect and good will.

Richard Harenger sold his house in St. John's Wood and took a flat within convenient walking distance of Whitehall. It had a sitting-room which he lined with his books, a dining-room into which his Chippendale furniture just fitted, a nice-sized bedroom for himself, and beyond the kitchen a couple of maids' rooms. He brought his cook, whom he had had for many years, from St. John's Wood, but needing no longer so large a staff dismissed the rest of the servants and applied at a registry office for a house-parlourmaid. He knew exactly what he wanted and he explained his needs to the superintendent of the agency with precision. He wanted a maid who was not too young, first because young women are flighty and secondly because, though he was of mature age and a man of principle, people would talk, the porter and the tradesmen if nobody else, and both for the sake of his own reputation and that of the young person he considered that the applicant should have reached years of discretion. Besides that he wanted a maid who could clean silver well. He had always had a fancy for old silver, and it was reasonable to demand that the forks and spoons that had been used by a woman of quality under the reign of Queen Anne should be treated with tenderness and respect. He was of a hospitable nature and liked to give at least once a week little dinners of not less than four people and not more than eight. He could trust his cook to send in a meal that his guests would take pleasure in eating and he desired his parlourmaid to wait with neatness and dispatch. Then he needed a perfect valet. He dressed well, in a manner that suited his age and condition, and he liked his clothes to be properly looked after. The parlourmaid he was looking for must be able to press trousers and iron a tie, and he was very particular that his shoes should be well shone. He had small feet and he took a good deal of trouble to have well-cut shoes. He had a large supply and he insisted that they should be treed up the moment he took them off. Finally the flat must be kept clean and tidy. It was of course understood that any applicant for the post must be of irreproachable character, sober, honest, reliable and of a pleasing exterior. In return for this he was prepared to offer good wages, reasonable liberty and ample holidays.

The superintendent listened without batting an eyelash and, telling him that she was quite sure she could suit him, sent him a string of candidates which proved that she had not paid the smallest attention to a word he said. He saw them all personally. Some were obviously inefficient, some looked fast, some were too old, others too young, some lacked the presence he thought essential; there was not one to whom he was inclined even to give a trial. He was a kindly, polite man and he declined their services with a smile and a pleasant expression of regret. He did not lose patience. He was prepared to interview house-parlourmaids till he found one who was suitable.

Now it is a funny thing about life, if you refuse to accept anything but the best you very often get it: if you utterly decline to make do with what you can get, then somehow or other you are very likely to get what you want. It is as though fate said, this man's a perfect fool, he's asking for perfection, and then just out of her feminine wilfulness flung it in his lap. One day the porter of the flats said to Richard Harenger out of a blue sky:

"I hear you're lookin' for a house-parlourmaid, sir. There's someone I know lookin' for a situation as might do."

"Can you recommend her personally?"

Richard Harenger had the sound opinion that one servant's recommendation of another was worth much more than that of an employer.

"I can vouch for her respectability. She's been in some very good situations."

"I shall be coming in to dress about seven. If that's convenient to her I could see her then."

"Very good, sir. I'll see that she's told."

He had not been in more than five minutes when the cook, having answered a ring at the front door, came in and told him that the person the porter had spoken to him about had called.

"Show her in," he said.

He turned on some more light so that he could see what the applicant looked like and, getting up, stood with his back to the fireplace. A woman came in and stood just inside the door in a respectful attitude.

"Good-evening," he said. "What is your name?"

"Pritchard, sir."

"How old are you?"

"Thirty-five, sir."

"Well, that's a reasonable age."

He gave his cigarette a puff and looked at her reflectively. She was on the tall side, nearly as tall as he, but he guessed that she wore high heels. Her black dress fitted her station. She held herself well. She had good features and a rather high colour.

"Will you take off your hat?" he asked.

She did so and he saw that she had pale brown hair. It was neatly and becomingly dressed. She looked strong and healthy. She was neither fat nor thin. In a proper uniform she would look very presentable. She was not inconveniently handsome, but she was certainly a comely, in another class of life you might almost have said a handsome, woman. He proceeded to ask her a number of questions. Her answers were satisfactory. She had left her last place for an adequate reason. She had been trained under a butler and appeared to be well acquainted with her duties. In her last place she had been head parlourmaid of three, but she did not mind undertaking the work of the flat single-handed. She had valeted a gentleman before who had sent her to a tailor's to learn how to press clothes. She was a little shy, but neither timid nor ill-at-ease. Richard asked her his questions in his amiable, leisurely way and she answered them with modest composure. He was considerably impressed. He asked her what references she could give. They seemed extremely satisfactory.

"Now look here," he said, "I'm very much inclined to engage you. But I hate changes, I've had my cook for twelve years: if you suit me and the place suits you I hope you'll stay. I mean, I don't want you to come to me in three or four months and say that you're leaving to get married."

"There's not much fear of that, sir. I'm a widow. I don't believe marriage is much catch for anyone in my position, sir. My husband never did a stroke of work from the day I married him to the day he died, and I had to keep him. What I want now is a good home."

"I'm inclined to agree with you," he smiled. "Marriage is a very good thing, but I think it's a mistake to make a habit of it."

She very properly made no reply to this, but waited for him to announce his decision. She did not seem anxious about it. He reflected that if she was as competent as she appeared she must be well aware that she would have no difficulty in finding a place. He told her what wages he was offering and these seemed to be satisfactory to her. He gave her the necessary information about the place, but she gave him to understand that she was already apprised of this, and he received the impression, which amused rather than disconcerted him, that she had made certain enquiries about him before applying for the situation. It showed prudence on her part and good sense.

"When would you be able to come in if I engaged you? I haven't got anybody at the moment. The cook's managing as best she can with a char, but I should like to get settled as soon as possible."

"Well, sir, I was going to give myself a week's holiday, but if it's a matter of obliging a gentleman I don't mind giving that up. I could come in to-morrow if it was convenient."

Richard Harenger gave her his attractive smile.

"I shouldn't like you to do without a holiday that I dare say you've been looking forward to. I can very well go on like this for another week. Go and have your holiday and come to me when it's over."

"Thank you very much, sir. Would it do if I came in to-morrow week?"

"Quite well."

When she left, Richard Harenger felt he had done a good day's work. It looked as though he had found exactly what he was after. He rang for the cook and told her he had engaged a house-parlour-maid at last.

"I think you'll like her, sir," she said. "She came in and 'ad a talk with me this afternoon. I could see at once she knew her duties. And she's not one of them flighty ones."

"We can but try, Mrs. Jeddy. I hope you gave me a good character."

"Well, I said you was particular, sir. I said you was a gentleman as liked things just so."

"I admit that."

"She said she didn't mind that. She said she liked a gentleman as knew what was what. She said there's no satisfaction in doing things proper if nobody notices. I expect you'll find she'll take a rare lot of pride in her work."

"That's what I want her to do. I think we might go farther and fare worse."

"Well, sir, there is that to it, of course. And the proof of the pudding's the eating. But if you ask my opinion I think she's going to be a real treasure."

And that is precisely what Pritchard turned out. No man was ever better served. The way she shone shoes was marvellous, and he set out of a fine morning for his walk to the office with a more jaunty step because you could almost see yourself reflected in them. She looked after his clothes with such attention that his colleagues began to chaff him about being the best-dressed man in the Civil Service. One day, coming home unexpectedly, he found a line of socks and handkerchiefs hung up to dry in the bathroom. He called Pritchard.

"D'you wash my socks and handkerchiefs yourself, Pritchard? I should have thought you had enough to do without that."

"They do ruin them so at the laundry, sir. I prefer to do them at home if you have no objection."

She knew exactly what he should wear on every occasion, and without asking him was aware whether she should put out a dinner jacket and a black tie in the evening or a dress coat and a white one. When he was going to a party where decorations were to be worn he found his neat little row of medals automatically affixed to the lapel of his coat. He soon ceased to choose every morning from his wardrobe the tie he wanted, for he found that she put out for him without fail the one he would have himself selected. Her taste was perfect. He supposed she read his letters, for she always knew what his movements were, and if he had forgotten at what hour he had an engagement he had no need to look in his book, for Pritchard could tell him. She knew exactly what tone to use with persons with whom she conversed on the telephone. Except with tradesmen, with whom she was apt to be peremptory, she was always polite, but there was a distinct difference in her manner if she was addressing one of Mr. Harenger's literary friends or the wife of a Cabinet Minister. She knew by instinct with whom he wished to speak and with whom he didn't. From his sitting-room he sometimes heard her with placid sincerity assuring a caller that he was out, and then she would come in and tell him that So-and-So had rung up, but she thought he wouldn't wish to be disturbed.

"Quite right, Pritchard," he smiled.

"I knew she only wanted to bother you about that concert," said Pritchard.

His friends made appointments with him through her, and she would tell him what she had done on his return in the evening.

"Mrs. Soames rang up, sir, and asked if you would lunch with her on Thursday, the eighth, but I said you were very sorry but you were lunching with Lady Versinder. Mr. Oakley rang up and asked if you'd go to a cocktail party at the Savoy next Tuesday at six. I said you would if you possibly could, but you might have to go to the dentist's."

"Quite right."

"I thought you could see when the time came, sir."

She kept the flat like a new pin. On one occasion soon after she entered his service, Richard coming back from a holiday took out a book from his shelves and at once noticed that it had been dusted. He rang the bell.

"I forgot to tell you when I went away under no circumstances ever to touch my books. When books are taken out to be dusted they're never put back in the right place. I don't mind my books being dirty, but I hate not being able to find them."

"I'm very sorry, sir," said Pritchard. "I know some gentlemen are very particular and I took care to put back every book exactly where I took it from."

Richard Harenger gave his books a glance. So far as he could see every one was in its accustomed place. He smiled.

"I apologise, Pritchard."

"They were in a muck, sir. I mean, you couldn't open one without getting your hands black with dust."

She certainly kept his silver as he had never had it kept before. He felt called upon to give her a special word of praise.

"Most of it's Queen Anne and George I, you know," he explained.

"Yes, I know, sir. When you've got something good like that to look after it's a pleasure to keep it like it should be."

"You certainly have a knack for it. I never knew a butler who kept his silver as well as you do."

"Men haven't the patience women have," she replied modestly.

As soon as he thought Pritchard had settled down in the place he resumed the little dinners he was fond of giving once a week. He had already discovered that she knew how to wait at table, but it was with a warm sense of complacency that he realised then how competently she could manage a party. She was quick, silent and watchful. A guest had hardly felt the need of something before Pritchard was at his elbow offering him what he wanted. She soon learned the tastes of his more intimate friends and remembered that one liked water instead of soda with his whisky and that another particularly fancied the knuckle end of a leg of lamb. She knew exactly how cold a hock should be not to ruin its taste and how long claret should have stood in the room to bring out its bouquet. It was a pleasure to see her pour out a bottle of burgundy in such a fashion as not to disturb the grounds. On one occasion she did not serve the wine Richard had ordered. He somewhat sharply pointed this out to her.

"I opened the bottle, sir, and it was slightly corked. So I got the Chambertin, as I thought it was safer."

"Quite right, Pritchard."

Presently he left this matter entirely in her hands, for he discovered that she knew perfectly what wines his guests would like. Without orders from him she would provide the best in his cellar and his oldest brandy if she thought they were the sort of people who knew what they were drinking. She had no belief in the palate of women, and when they were of the party was apt to serve the champagne which had to be drunk before it went off. She had the English servant's instinctive knowledge of social differences and neither rank nor money blinded her to the fact that someone was not a gentleman, but she had favourites among his friends, and when someone she particularly liked was dining, with the air of a cat that has swallowed a canary she would pour out for him a bottle of a wine that Harenger kept for very special occasions. It amused him.

"You've got on the right side of Pritchard, old boy," he exclaimed. "There aren't many people she gives this wine to."

Pritchard became an institution. She was known very soon to be the perfect parlourmaid. People envied Harenger the possession of her as they envied nothing else that he had. She was worth her weight in gold. Her price was above rubies. Richard Harenger beamed with self-complacency when they praised her.

"Good masters make good servants," he said gaily.

One evening, when they were sitting over their port and she had left the room, they were talking about her.

"It'll be an awful blow when she leaves you."

"Why should she leave me? One or two people have tried to get her away from me, but she turned them down. She knows where she's well off."

"She'll get married one of these days."

"I don't think she's that sort."

"She's a good-looking woman."

"Yes, she has quite a decent presence."

"What are you talking about? She's a very handsome creature. In another class of life she'd be a well-known society beauty with her photograph in all the papers."

At that moment Pritchard came in with the coffee. Richard Harenger looked at her. After seeing her every day, off and on, for four years it was now—my word, how time flies—he had really forgotten what she looked like. She did not seem to have changed much since he had first seen her. She was no stouter than then, she still had the high colour, and her regular features bore the same expression which was at once intent and vacuous. The black uniform suited her. She left the room.

"She's a paragon and there's no doubt about it."

"I know she is," answered Harenger. "She's perfection. I should be lost without her. And the strange thing is that I don't very much like her."

"Why not?"

"I think she bores me a little. You see, she has no conversation.

I've often tried to talk to her. She answers when I speak to her, but that's all. In four years she's never volunteered a remark of her own. I know absolutely nothing about her. I don't know if she likes me or if she's completely indifferent to me. She's an automaton. I respect her, I appreciate her, I trust her. She has every quality in the world and I've often wondered why it is that with all that I'm so completely indifferent to her. I think it must be that she is entirely devoid of charm."

They left it at that.

Two or three days after this, since it was Pritchard's night out and he had no engagement, Richard Harenger dined by himself at his club. A page-boy came to him and told him that they had just rung up from his flat to say that he had gone out without his keys and should they be brought along to him in a taxi? He put his hand to his pocket. It was a fact. By a singular chance he had forgotten to replace them when he had changed into a blue serge suit before coming out to dinner. His intention had been to play bridge, but it was an off-night at the club and there seemed little chance of a decent game; it occurred to him that it would be a good opportunity to see a picture that he had heard talked about, so he sent back the message by the page that he would call for the keys himself in half an hour.

He rang at the door of his flat and it was opened by Pritchard. She had the keys in her hand.

"What are you doing here, Pritchard?" he asked. "It's your night out, isn't it?"

"Yes, sir. But I didn't care about going, so I told Mrs. Jeddy she could go instead."

"You ought to get out when you have the chance," he said, with his usual thoughtfulness. "It's not good for you to be cooped up here all the time."

"I get out now and then on an errand, but I haven't been out in the evening for the last month."

"Why on earth not?"

"Well, it's not very cheerful going out by yourself, and somehow I don't know anyone just now that I'm particularly keen on going out with."

"You ought to have a bit of fun now and then. It's good for you."

"I've got out of the habit of it somehow."

"Look here, I'm just going to the cinema. Would you like to come along with me?"

He spoke in kindliness, on the spur of the moment, and the moment he had said the words half regretted them.

"Yes, sir, I'd like to," said Pritchard.

"Run along then and put on a hat."

"I shan't be a minute."

She disappeared and he went into the sitting-room and lit a cigarette. He was a little amused at what he was doing, and pleased too; it was nice to be able to make someone happy with so little trouble to himself. It was characteristic of Pritchard that she had shown neither surprise nor hesitation. She kept him waiting about five minutes, and when she came back he noticed that she had changed her dress. She wore a blue frock in what he supposed was artificial silk, a small black hat with a blue brooch on it, and a silver fox round her neck. He was a trifle relieved to see that she looked neither shabby nor showy. It would never occur to anyone who happened to see them that this was a distinguished official in the Home Office taking his housemaid to the pictures.

"I'm sorry to have kept you waiting, sir."

"It doesn't matter at all," he said graciously.

He opened the front door for her and she went out before him. He remembered the familiar anecdote of Louis XIV and the courtier and appreciated the fact that she had not hesitated to precede him. The cinema for which they were bound was at no great distance from Mr. Harenger's flat and they walked there. He talked about the weather and the state of the roads and Adolf Hitler. Pritchard made suitable replies. They arrived just as Mickey the Mouse was starting and this put them in a good humour. During the four years she had been in his service Richard Harenger had hardly ever seen Pritchard even smile, and now it diverted him vastly to hear her peal upon peal of joyous laughter. He enjoyed her pleasure. Then the principal attraction was thrown on the screen. It was a good picture and they both watched it with breathless excitement. Taking his cigarette-case out to help himself he automatically offered it to Pritchard.

"Thank you, sir," she said, taking one.

He lit it for her. Her eyes were on the screen and she was almost unconscious of his action. When the picture was finished they streamed out with the crowd into the street. They walked back towards the flat. It was a fine starry night.

"Did you like it?" he said.

"Like anything, sir. It was a real treat."

A thought occurred to him.

"By the way, did you have any supper to-night?"

"No, sir, I didn't have time."

"Aren't you starving?"

"I'll have a bit of bread and cheese when I get in and I'll make meself a cup of cocoa."

"That sounds rather grim." There was a feeling of gaiety in the air, and the people who poured past them, one way and another, seemed filled with a pleasant elation. In for a penny, in for a pound, he said to himself. "Look here, would you like to come and have a bit of supper with me somewhere?"

"If you'd like to, sir."

"Come on."

He hailed a cab. He was feeling very philanthropic and it was not a feeling that he disliked at all. He told the driver to go to a restaurant in Oxford Street which was gay, but at which he was confident there was no chance of meeting anyone he knew. There was an orchestra and people danced. It would amuse Pritchard to see them. When they sat down a waiter came up to them.

"They've got a set supper here," he said, thinking that was what she would like. "I suggest we have that. What would you like to drink? A little white wine?"

"What I really fancy is a glass of ginger beer," she said.

Richard Harenger ordered himself a whisky and soda. She ate the supper with hearty appetite, and though Harenger was not hungry, to put her at her ease he ate too. The picture they had just seen gave them something to talk about. It was quite true what they had said the other night, Pritchard was not a bad-looking woman, and even if someone had seen them together he would not have minded. It would make rather a good story for his friends when he told them how he had taken the incomparable Pritchard to the cinema and then afterwards to supper. Pritchard was looking at the dancers with a faint smile on her lips.

"Do you like dancing?" he said.

"I used to be a rare one for it when I was a girl. I never danced much after I was married. My husband was a bit shorter than me and somehow I never think it looks well unless the gentleman's taller, if you know what I mean. I suppose I shall be getting too old for it soon."

Richard was certainly taller than his parlourmaid. They would look all right. He was fond of dancing and he danced well. But he hesitated. He did not want to embarrass Pritchard by asking her to dance with him. It was better not to go too far perhaps. And yet what did it matter? It was a drab life she led. She was so sensible, if she thought it a mistake he was pretty sure she would find a decent excuse.

"Would you like to take a turn, Pritchard?" he said, as the band struck up again.

"I'm terribly out of practice, sir."

"What does that matter?"

"If you don't mind, sir," she answered coolly, rising from her seat. She was not in the least shy. She was only afraid that she would not be able to follow his step. They moved on to the floor. He found she danced very well.

"Why, you dance perfectly, Pritchard," he said.

"It's coming back to me."

Although she was a big woman she was light on her feet and she had a natural sense of rhythm. She was very pleasant to dance with. He gave a glance at the mirrors that lined the walls and he could not help reflecting that they looked very well together. Their eyes met in the mirror; he wondered whether she was thinking that too. They had two more dances and then Richard Harenger suggested that they should go. He paid the bill and they walked out. He noticed that she threaded her way through the crowd without a trace of self-consciousness. They got into a taxi and in ten minutes were at home.

"I'll go up the back way, sir," said Pritchard.

"There's no need to do that. Come up in the lift with me."

He took her up, giving the night-porter an icy glance, so that he should not think it strange that he came back at that somewhat late hour with his parlourmaid, and with his latch-key let her into the flat.

"Well, good-night, sir," she said. "Thank you very much. It's been a real treat for me."

"Thank *you*, Pritchard. I should have had a very dull evening by myself. I hope you've enjoyed your outing."

"That I have, sir, more than I can say."

It had been a success. Richard Harenger was satisfied with himself. It was a kindly thing for him to have done. It was a very agreeable sensation to give anyone so much real pleasure. His benevolence warmed him and for a moment he felt a great love in his heart for the whole human race.

"Good-night, Pritchard," he said, and because he felt happy and good he put his arm round her waist and kissed her on the lips.

Her lips were very soft. They lingered on his and she returned his kiss. It was the warm, hearty embrace of a healthy woman in the prime of life. He found it very pleasant and he held her to him a little more closely. She put her arms round his neck.

As a general rule he did not wake till Pritchard came in with his letters, but next morning he woke at half-past seven. He had a curious sensation that he did not recognise. He was accustomed to sleep with two pillows under his head and he suddenly grew aware of the fact that he had only one. Then he remembered and with a start looked round. The other pillow was beside his own. Thank God, no sleeping head rested there, but it was plain that one had. His heart sank. He broke out into a cold sweat.

"My God, what a fool I've been!" he cried out loud.

How could he have done anything so stupid? What on earth had come over him? He was the last man to play about with servant girls. What a disgraceful thing to do! At his age and in his position. He had not heard Pritchard slip away. He must have been asleep. It wasn't even as if he'd liked her very much. She wasn't his type. And, as he had said the other night, she rather bored him. Even now he only knew her as Pritchard. He had no notion what her first name was. What madness! And what was to happen now? The position was impossible. It was obvious he couldn't keep her, and yet to send her away for what was his fault as much as hers seemed shockingly unfair. How idiotic to lose the best parlourmaid a man ever had just for an hour's folly!

"It's that damned kindness of heart of mine," he groaned.

He would never find anyone else to look after his clothes so admirably or clean the silver so well. She knew all his friends' telephone numbers and she understood wine. But of course she must go. She must see for herself that after what had happened things could never be the same. He would make her a handsome present and give her an excellent reference. At any minute she would be coming in now. Would she be arch, would she be familiar? Or would she put on airs? Perhaps even she wouldn't trouble to come in with his letters. It would be awful if he had to ring the bell and Mrs. Jeddy came in and said: Pritchard's not up yet, sir, she's having a lie in after last night.

"What a fool I've been! What a contemptible cad!"

There was a knock at the door. He was sick with anxiety.

"Come in."

Richard Harenger was a very unhappy man.

Pritchard came in as the clock struck. She wore the print dress she was in the habit of wearing during the early part of the day.

"Good-morning, sir," she said.

"Good-morning."

She drew the curtains and handed him his letters and the papers. Her face was impassive. She looked exactly as she always looked. Her movements had the same competent deliberation that they always had. She neither avoided Richard's glance nor sought it.

"Will you wear your grey, sir? It came back from the tailor's yesterday."

"Yes."

He pretended to read his letters, but he watched her from under his eyelashes. Her back was turned to him. She took his vest and drawers and folded them over a chair. She took the studs out of the shirt he had worn the day before and studded a clean one. She put out some clean socks for him and placed them on the seat of a chair with the suspenders to match by the side. Then she put out his grey suit and attached the braces to the back buttons of the trousers. She opened his wardrobe and after a moment's reflection chose a tie to go with the suit. She collected on her arm the suit of the day before and picked up the shoes.

"Will you have breakfast now, sir, or will you have your bath first?"

"I'll have breakfast now," he said.

"Very good, sir."

With her slow quiet movements, unruffled, she left the room. Her face bore that rather serious, deferential, vacuous look it always bore. What had happened might have been a dream. Nothing in Pritchard's demeanour suggested that she had the smallest recollection of the night before. He gave a sigh of relief. It was going to be all right. She need not go, she need not go. Pritchard was the perfect parlourmaid. He knew that never by word nor gesture would she ever refer to the fact that for a moment their relations had been other than those of master and servant. Richard Harenger was a very happy man.

The Colonel's Lady

All this happened two or three years before the outbreak of the war.

The Peregrines were having breakfast. Though they were alone and the table was long they sat at opposite ends of it. From the walls George Peregrine's ancestors, painted by the fashionable painters of the day, looked down upon them. The butler brought in the morning post. There were several letters for the colonel, business letters, *The Times* and a small parcel for his wife Evie. He looked at his letters and then, opening *The Times*, began to read it. They finished breakfast and rose from the table. He noticed that his wife hadn't opened the parcel.

"What's that?" he asked.

"Only some books."

"Shall I open them for you?"

"If you like."

He hated to cut string and so with some difficulty untied the knots.

"But they're all the same," he said when he had unwrapped the parcel. "What on earth d'you want six copies of the same book for?" He opened one of them. "Poetry." Then he looked at the title page. *When Pyramids Decay*, he read, by E. K. Hamilton. Eva Katherine Hamilton: that was his wife's maiden name. He looked at her with smiling surprise. "Have you written a book, Evie? You are a slyboots."

"I didn't think it would interest you very much. Would you like a copy?"

"Well, you know poetry isn't much in my line, but—yes, I'd like a copy; I'll read it. I'll take it along to my study. I've got a lot to do this morning."

He gathered up *The Times*, his letters and the book, and went out. His study was a large and comfortable room, with a big desk, leather arm-chairs and what he called "trophies of the chase" on the walls. On the bookshelves were works of reference, books on farming, gardening, fishing and shooting, and books on the last war, in which he had won an M.C. and a D.S.O. For before his marriage he had been in the Welsh Guards. At the end of the war he retired and settled down to the life of a country gentleman in the spacious house, some twenty miles from Sheffield, which one of his forebears had built in the reign of George III. George Peregrine had an estate of some fifteen hundred acres which he managed with ability; he was a Justice of the Peace and performed his duties conscientiously. During the season he rode to hounds two days a week. He was a good shot, a golfer and though now a little over fifty could still play a hard game of tennis. He could describe himself with propriety as an all-round sportsman.

He had been putting on weight lately, but was still a fine figure of a man; tall, with grey curly hair, only just beginning to grow thin on the crown, frank blue eyes, good features and a high colour. He was a public-spirited man, chairman of any number of local organisations and, as became his class and station, a loyal member of the Conservative Party. He looked upon it as his duty to see to the welfare of the people on his estate and it was a satisfaction to him to know that Evie could be trusted to tend the sick and succour the poor. He had built a cottage hospital on the outskirts of the village and paid the wages of a nurse out of his own pocket. All he asked of the recipients of his bounty was that at elections, county or general, they should vote for his candidate. He was a friendly man, affable to his inferiors, considerate with his tenants and popular with the neighbouring gentry. He would have been pleased and at the same time slightly embarrassed if someone had told him he was a jolly good fellow. That was what he wanted to be. He desired no higher praise.

It was hard luck that he had no children. He would have been an excellent father, kindly but strict, and would have brought up his sons as gentlemen's sons should be brought up, sent them to Eton, you know, taught them to fish, shoot and ride. As it was, his heir was a nephew, son of his brother killed in a motor accident, not a bad boy, but not a chip off the old block, no, sir, far from it; and would you believe it, his fool of a mother was sending him to a co-educational school. Evie had been a sad disappointment to him. Of course she was a lady, and she had a bit of money of her own; she managed the house uncommonly well and she was a good hostess. The village people adored her. She had been a pretty little thing when he had married her, with a creamy skin, light brown hair and a trim figure, healthy too and not a bad tennis player; he couldn't understand why she'd had no children; of course she was faded now, she must be getting on for five and forty; her skin was drab, her hair had lost its sheen and she was as thin as a rail. She was always neat and suitably dressed, but she didn't seem to bother how she looked, she wore no make-up and didn't even use lipstick; sometimes at night when she dolled herself up for a party you could tell that once she'd been quite attractive, but ordinarily she was—well, the sort of woman you simply didn't notice. A nice woman, of course, a good wife, and it wasn't her fault if she was barren, but it was tough on a fellow who wanted an heir of his own loins; she hadn't any vitality, that's what was the matter with her. He supposed he'd been in love with her when he asked her to marry him, at least sufficiently in love for a man who wanted to marry and settle down, but with time he discovered that they had nothing much in common. She didn't care about hunting, and fishing bored her. Naturally they'd drifted apart. He had to do her the justice to admit that she'd never bothered him. There'd been no scenes. They had no quarrels. She seemed to take it for granted that he should go his own way. When he went up to London now and then she never wanted to come with him. He had a girl there, well, she wasn't exactly a girl, she was thirty-five if she was a day, but she was blonde and luscious and he only had to wire ahead of time and they'd dine, do a show and spend the night together. Well, a man, a healthy normal man had to have some fun in his life. The thought crossed his mind that if Evie hadn't been such a good woman she'd have been a better wife; but it was not the sort of thought that he welcomed and he put it away from him.

George Peregrine finished his *Times* and being a considerate fellow rang the bell and told the butler to take it to Evie. Then he looked at his watch. It was half-past ten and at eleven he had an appointment with one of his tenants. He had half an hour to spare.

"I'd better have a look at Evie's book," he said to himself.

He took it up with a smile. Evie had a lot of highbrow books in her sitting-room, not the sort of books that interested him, but if they amused her he had no objection to her reading them. He noticed that the volume he now held in his hand contained no more than ninety pages. That was all to the good. He shared Edgar Allan Poe's opinion that poems should be short. But as he turned the pages he noticed that several of Evie's had long lines of irregular length and didn't rhyme. He didn't like that. At his first school, when he was a little boy, he remembered learning a poem that began: *The boy stood on the burning deck*, and later, at Eton, one that started: *Ruin seize thee, ruthless king*; and then there was *Henry V*; they'd had to take that, one half. He stared at Evie's pages with consternation.

"That's not what I call poetry," he said.

Fortunately it wasn't all like that. Interspersed with the pieces that looked so odd, lines of three or four words and then a line of ten or fifteen, there were little poems, quite short, that rhymed, thank God, with the lines all the same length. Several of the pages were just headed with the word *Sonnet*, and out of curiosity he counted the lines; there were fourteen of them. He read them. They seemed all right, but he didn't quite know what they were all about. He repeated to himself: *Ruin seize thee, ruthless king*.

"Poor Evie," he sighed.

At that moment the farmer he was expecting was ushered into the study, and putting the book down he made him welcome. They embarked on their business.

"I read your book, Evie," he said as they sat down to lunch. "Jolly good. Did it cost you a packet to have it printed?"

"No, I was lucky. I sent it to a publisher and he took it."

"Not much money in poetry, my dear," he said in his good-natured, hearty way.

"No, I don't suppose there is. What did Bannock want to see you about this morning?"

Bannock was the tenant who had interrupted his reading of Evie's poems.

"He's asked me to advance the money for a pedigree bull he wants to buy. He's a good man and I've half a mind to do it."

George Peregrine saw that Evie didn't want to talk about her book and he was not sorry to change the subject. He was glad she had used her maiden name on the title page; he didn't suppose anyone would ever hear about the book, but he was proud of his own unusual name and he wouldn't have liked it if some damned penny-a-liner had made fun of Evie's effort in one of the papers.

During the few weeks that followed he thought it tactful not to ask Evie any questions about her venture into verse, and she never referred to it. It might have been a discreditable incident that they had silently agreed not to mention. But then a strange thing happened. He had to go to London on business and he took Daphne out to dinner. That was the name of the girl with whom he was in the habit of passing a few agreeable hours whenever he went to town.

"Oh, George," she said, "is that your wife who's written a book they're all talking about?"

"What on earth d'you mean?"

"Well, there's a fellow I know who's a critic. He took me out to dinner the other night and he had a book with him. 'Got anything for me to read?' I said. 'What's that?' 'Oh, I don't think that's your cup of tea,' he said. 'It's poetry. I've just been reviewing it.' 'No poetry for me,' I said. 'It's about the hottest stuff I ever read,' he said. "Selling like hot cakes. And it's damned good.' "

"Who's the book by?" asked George.

"A woman called Hamilton. My friend told me that wasn't her real name. He said her real name was Peregrine. 'Funny,' I said, 'I know a fellow called Peregrine.' 'Colonel in the army,' he said. 'Lives near Sheffield.' "

"I'd just as soon you didn't talk about me to your friends," said George with a frown of vexation.

"Keep your shirt on, dearie. Who d'you take me for? I just said: 'It's not the same one.' " Daphne giggled. "My friend said: 'They say he's a regular Colonel Blimp.' "

George had a keen sense of humour.

"You could tell them better than that," he laughed. "If my wife had written a book I'd be the first to know about it, wouldn't I?"

"I suppose you would."

Anyhow the matter didn't interest her and when the colonel began to talk of other things she forgot about it. He put it out of his mind too. There was nothing to it, he decided, and that silly fool of a critic had just been pulling Daphne's leg. He was amused at the thought of her tackling that book because she had been told it was hot stuff and then finding it just a lot of bosh cut up into unequal lines.

He was a member of several clubs and next day he thought he'd lunch at one in St. James's Street. He was catching a train back to Sheffield early in the afternoon. He was sitting in a comfortable arm-chair having a glass of sherry before going into the dining-room when an old friend came up to him.

"Well, old boy, how's life?" he said. "How d'you like being the husband of a celebrity?"

George Peregrine looked at his friend. He thought he saw an amused twinkle in his eyes.

"I don't know what you're talking about," he answered.

"Come off it, George. Everyone knows E. K. Hamilton is your wife. Not often a book of verse has a success like that. Look here, Henry Dashwood is lunching with me. He'd like to meet you."

"Who the devil is Henry Dashwood and why should he want to meet me?"

"Oh, my dear fellow, what do you do with yourself all the time in the country? Henry's about the best critic we've got. He wrote a wonderful review of Evie's book. D'you mean to say she didn't show it you?"

Before George could answer his friend had called a man over. A tall, thin man, with a high forehead, a beard, a long nose and a stoop, just the sort of man whom George was prepared to dislike at first sight. Introductions were effected. Henry Dashwood sat down.

"Is Mrs. Peregrine in London by any chance? I should very much like to meet her," he said.

"No, my wife doesn't like London. She prefers the country," said George stiffly.

"She wrote me a very nice letter about my review. I was pleased. You know, we critics get more kicks than halfpence. I was simply bowled over by her book. It's so fresh and original, very modern without being obscure. She seems to be as much at her ease in free verse as in the classical metres." Then because he was a critic he thought he could criticise. "Sometimes her ear is a trifle at fault, but you can say the same of Emily Dickinson. There are several of those short lyrics of hers that might have been written by Landor."

All this was gibberish to George Peregrine. The man was nothing but a disgusting highbrow. But the colonel had good manners and he answered with proper civility: Henry Dashwood went on as though he hadn't spoken.

"But what makes the book so outstanding is the passion that throbs in every line. So many of these young poets are so anæmic, cold, bloodless, dully intellectual, but here you have real naked, earthy passion; of course deep, sincere emotion like that is tragic——ah, my dear Colonel, how right Heine was when he said that the poet makes little songs out of his great sorrows. You know, now and then, as I read and re-read those heart-rending pages I thought of Sappho."

This was too much for George Peregrine and he got up.

"Well, it's jolly nice of you to say such nice things about my wife's little book. I'm sure she'll be delighted. But I must bolt, I've got to catch a train and I want to get a bite of lunch."

"Damned fool," he said irritably to himself as he walked upstairs to the dining-room.

He got home in time for dinner and after Evie had gone to bed he went into his study and looked for her book. He thought he'd just glance through it again to see for himself what they were making such a fuss about, but he couldn't find it. Evie must have taken it away.

"Silly," he muttered.

He'd told her he thought it jolly good. What more could a fellow be expected to say? Well, it didn't matter. He lit his pipe and read the *Field* till he felt sleepy. But a week or so later it happened that he had to go into Sheffield for the day. He lunched there at his club. He had nearly finished when the Duke of Haverel came in. This was the great local magnate and of course the colonel knew him, but only to say how d'you do to; and he was surprised when the Duke stopped at his table.

"We're so sorry your wife couldn't come to us for the week-end," he said, with a sort of shy cordiality. "We're expecting rather a nice lot of people."

George was taken aback. He guessed that the Haverels had asked him and Evie over for the week-end and Evie, without saying a word to him about it, had refused. He had the presence of mind to say he was sorry too.

"Better luck next time," said the Duke pleasantly and moved on.

Colonel Peregrine was very angry and when he got home he said to his wife:

"Look here, what's this about being asked over to Haverel? Why on earth did you say we couldn't go? We've never been asked before and it's the best shooting in the county."

"I didn't think of that. I thought it would only bore you."

"Damn it all, you might at least have asked me if I wanted to go."

"I'm sorry."

He looked at her closely. There was something in her expression that he didn't quite understand. He frowned.

"I suppose *I* was asked?" he barked.

Evie flushed a little.

"Well, in point of fact you weren't."

"I call it damned rude of them to ask you without asking me."

"I suppose they thought it wasn't your kind of party. The Duchess is rather fond of writers and people like that, you know. She's having Henry Dashwood, the critic, and for some reason he wants to meet me."

"It was damned nice of you to refuse, Evie."

"It's the least I could do," she smiled. She hesitated a moment. "George, my publishers want to give a little dinner-party for me one day towards the end of the month and of course they want you to come too."

"Oh, I don't think that's quite my mark. I'll come up to London with you if you like. I'll find someone to dine with."

Daphne.

"I expect it'll be very dull, but they're making rather a point of it. And the day after, the American publisher who's taken my book

s

is giving a cocktail party at Claridge's. I'll like you to come to that if you don't mind."

"Sounds like a crashing bore, but if you really want me to come I'll come."

"It would be sweet of you."

George Peregrine was dazed by the cocktail party. There were a lot of people. Some of them didn't look so bad, a few of the women were decently turned out, but the men seemed to him pretty awful. He was introduced to everyone as Colonel Peregrine, E. K. Hamilton's husband, you know. The men didn't seem to have anything to say to him, but the women gushed.

"You *must* be proud of your wife. Isn't it *wonderful?* You know, I read it right through at a sitting, I simply couldn't put it down, and when I'd finished I started again at the beginning and read it through a second time. I was simply *thrilled.*"

The English publisher said to him:

"We've not had a success like this with a book of verse for twenty years. I've never seen such reviews."

The American publisher said to him:

"It's swell. It'll be a smash hit in America. You wait and see."

The American publisher had sent Evie a great spray of orchids. Damned ridiculous, thought George. As they came in, people were taken up to Evie, and it was evident that they said flattering things to her, which she took with a pleasant smile and a word or two of thanks. She was a trifle flushed with the excitement, but seemed quite at her ease. Though he thought the whole thing a lot of stuff and nonsense George noted with approval that his wife was carrying it off in just the right way.

"Well, there's one thing," he said to himself, "you can see she's a lady and that's a damned sight more than you can say of anyone else here."

He drank a good many cocktails. But there was one thing that bothered him. He had a notion that some of the people he was introduced to looked at him in rather a funny sort of way, he couldn't quite make out what it meant, and once when he strolled by two women who were sitting together on a sofa he had the impression that they were talking about him and after he passed he was almost certain they tittered. He was very glad when the party came to an end.

In the taxi on their way back to their hotel Evie said to him:

"You were wonderful, dear. You made quite a hit. The girls simply raved about you: they thought you so handsome."

"Girls," he said bitterly. "Old hags."

"Were you so bored, dear?"

"Stiff."

She pressed his hand in a gesture of sympathy.

"I hope you won't mind if we wait and go down by the afternoon train. I've got some things to do in the morning."

"No, that's all right. Shopping?"

"I do want to buy one or two things, but I've got to go and be photographed. I hate the idea, but they think I ought to be. For America, you know."

He said nothing. But he thought. He thought it would be a shock to the American public when they saw the portrait of the homely, desiccated little woman who was his wife. He'd always been under the impression that they liked glamour in America.

He went on thinking, and next morning when Evie had gone out he went to his club and up to the library. There he looked up recent numbers of *The Times Literary Supplement*, *The New Statesman* and *The Spectator*. Presently he found reviews of Evie's book. He didn't read them very carefully, but enough to see that they were extremely favourable. Then he went to the bookseller's in Piccadilly where he occasionally bought books. He'd made up his mind that he had to read this damned thing of Evie's properly, but he didn't want to ask her what she'd done with the copy she'd given him. He'd buy one for himself. Before going in he looked in the window and the first thing he saw was a display of *When Pyramids Decay*. Damned silly title! He went in. A young man came forward and asked if he could help him.

"No, I'm just having a look round." It embarrassed him to ask for Evie's book and he thought he'd find it for himself and then take it to the salesman. But he couldn't see it anywhere and at last, finding the young man near him, he said in a carefully casual tone: "By the way, have you got a book called *When Pyramids Decay*?"

"The new edition came in this morning. I'll get a copy."

In a moment the young man returned with it. He was a short, rather stout young man, with a shock of untidy carroty hair and spectacles. George Peregrine, tall, upstanding, very military, towered over him.

"Is this a new edition then?" he asked.

"Yes, sir. The fifth. It might be a novel the way it's selling."

George Peregrine hesitated a moment.

"Why d'you suppose it's such a success? I've always been told no one reads poetry."

"Well, it's good, you know. I've read it meself." The young

man, though obviously cultured, had a slight Cockney accent, and George quite instinctively adopted a patronising attitude. "It's the story they like. Sexy, you know, but tragic."

George frowned a little. He was coming to the conclusion that the young man was rather impertinent. No one had told him anything about there being a story in the damned book and he had not gathered that from reading the reviews. The young man went on:

"Of course it's only a flash in the pan, if you know what I mean. The way I look at it, she was sort of inspired like by a personal experience, like Housman was with *The Shropshire Lad*. She'll never write anything else."

"How much is the book?" said George coldly to stop his chatter.

"You needn't wrap it up, I'll just slip it into my pocket."

The November morning was raw and he was wearing a greatcoat.

At the station he bought the evening papers and magazines and he and Evie settled themselves comfortably in opposite corners of a first-class carriage and read. At five o'clock they went along to the restaurant car to have tea and chatted a little. They arrived. They drove home in the car which was waiting for them. They bathed, dressed for dinner, and after dinner Evie, saying she was tired out, went to bed. She kissed him, as was her habit, on the forehead. Then he went into the hall, took Evie's book out of his greatcoat pocket and going into the study began to read it. He didn't read verse very easily and though he read with attention, every word of it, the impression he received was far from clear. Then he began at the beginning again and read it a second time. He read with increasing malaise, but he was not a stupid man and when he had finished he had a distinct understanding of what it was all about. Part of the book was in free verse, part in conventional metres, but the story it related was coherent and plain to the meanest intelligence. It was the story of a passionate love affair between an older woman, married, and a young man. George Peregrine made out the steps of it as easily as if he had been doing a sum in simple addition.

Written in the first person, it began with the tremulous surprise of the woman, past her youth, when it dawned upon her that the young man was in love with her. She hesitated to believe it. She thought she must be deceiving herself. And she was terrified when on a sudden she discovered that she was passionately in love with him. She told herself it was absurd; with the disparity of age between them nothing but unhappiness could come to her if she yielded to her emotion. She tried to prevent him from speaking, but the day came when he told her that he loved her and forced her to tell him that she loved him too. He begged her to run away with him. She couldn't leave her husband, her home; and what life could they look forward to, she an ageing women, he so young? How could she expect his love to last? She begged him to have mercy on her. But his love was impetuous. He wanted her, he wanted her with all his heart, and at last, trembling, afraid, desirous, she yielded to him. Then there was a period of ecstatic happiness. The world, the dull, humdrum world of every day, blazed with glory. Love songs flowed from her pen. The woman worshipped the young, virile body of her lover. George flushed darkly when she praised his broad chest and slim flanks, the beauty of his legs and the flatness of his belly.

Hot stuff, Daphne's friend had said. It was that all right. Disgusting.

There were sad little pieces in which she lamented the emptiness of her life when as must happen he left her, but they ended with a cry that all she had to suffer would be worth it for the bliss that for a while had been hers. She wrote of the long, tremulous nights they passed together and the languor that lulled them to sleep in one another's arms. She wrote of the rapture of brief stolen moments when, braving all danger, their passion overwhelmed them and they surrendered to its call.

She thought it would be an affair of a few weeks, but miraculously it lasted. One of the poems referred to three years having gone by without lessening the love that filled their hearts. It looked as though he continued to press her to go away with him, far away, to a hill town in Italy, a Greek island, a walled city in Tunisia, so that they could be together always, for in another of the poems she besought him to let things be as they were. Their happiness was precarious. Perhaps it was owing to the difficulties they had to encounter and the rarity of their meetings that their love had retained for so long its first enchanting ardour. Then on a sudden the young man died. How, when or where George could not discover. There followed a long, heartbroken cry of bitter grief, grief she could not indulge in, grief that had to be hidden. She had to be cheerful, give dinner-parties and go out to dinner, behave as she had always behaved, though the light had gone out of her life and she was bowed down with anguish. The last poem of all was a set of four short stanzas in which the writer, sadly resigned to her loss, thanked the dark powers that rule man's destiny that she had been privileged at least for a while to enjoy the greatest happiness that we poor human beings can ever hope to know.

It was three o'clock in the morning when George Peregrine finally put the book down. It had seemed to him that he heard Evie's voice in every line, over and over again he came upon turns of phrase he had heard her use, there were details that were as familiar to him as to her: there was no doubt about it; it was her own story she had told, and it was as plain as anything could be that she had had a lover and her lover had died. It was not anger so much that he felt, nor horror or dismay, though he was dismayed and he was horrified, but amazement. It was as inconceivable that Evie should have had a love affair, and a wildly passionate one at that, as that the trout in a glass case over the chimney piece in his study, the finest he had ever caught, should suddenly wag its tail. He understood now the meaning of the amused look he had seen in the eyes of that man he had spoken to at the club, he understood why Daphne when she was talking about the book had seemed to be enjoying a private joke, and why those two women at the cocktail party had tittered when he strolled past them.

He broke out into a sweat. Then on a sudden he was seized with fury and he jumped up to go and awake Evie and ask her sternly for an explanation. But he stopped at the door. After all, what proof had he? A book. He remembered that he'd told Evie he thought it jolly good. True, he hadn't read it, but he'd pretended he had. He would look a perfect fool if he had to admit that.

"I must watch my step," he muttered.

He made up his mind to wait for two or three days and think it all over. Then he'd decide what to do. He went to bed, but he couldn't sleep for a long time.

"Evie," he kept on saying to himself. "Evie, of all people."

They met at breakfast next morning as usual. Evie was as she always was, quiet, demure and self-possessed, a middle-aged woman who made no effort to look younger than she was, a woman who had nothing of what he still called It. He looked at her as he hadn't looked at her for years. She had her usual placid serenity. Her pale blue eyes were untroubled. There was no sign of guilt on her candid brow. She made the same little casual remarks she always made.

"It's nice to get back to the country again after those two hectic days in London. What are you going to do this morning?"

It was incomprehensible.

Three days later he went to see his solicitor. Henry Blane was an old friend of George's as well as his lawyer. He had a place not far from Peregrine's and for years they had shot over one another's preserves. For two days a week he was a country gentleman and for the other five a busy lawyer in Sheffield. He was a tall, robust fellow, with a boisterous manner and a jovial laugh, which suggested that he liked to be looked upon essentially as a sportsman and a good fellow and only incidentally as a lawyer. But he was shrewd and worldly-wise.

"Well, George, what's brought you here today?" he boomed as the colonel was shown into his office. "Have a good time in London? I'm taking my missus up for a few days next week. How's Evie?"

"It's about Evie I've come to see you," said Peregrine, giving him a suspicious look. "Have you read her book?"

His sensitivity had been sharpened during those last days of troubled thought and he was conscious of a faint change in the lawyer's expression. It was as though he were suddenly on his guard.

"Yes, I've read it. Great success, isn't it? Fancy Evie breaking out into poetry. Wonders will never cease."

George Peregrine was inclined to lose his temper.

"It's made me look a perfect damned fool."

"Oh, what nonsense, George! There's no harm in Evie's writing a book. You ought to be jolly proud of her."

"Don't talk such rot. It's her own story. You know it and everyone else knows it. I suppose I'm the only one who doesn't know who her lover was."

"There is such a thing as imagination, old boy. There's no reason to suppose the whole thing isn't made up."

"Look here, Henry, we've known one another all our lives. We've had all sorts of good times together. Be honest with me. Can you look me in the face and tell me you believe it's a made-up story?"

Harry Blane moved uneasily in his chair. He was disturbed by the distress in old George's voice.

"You've got no right to ask me a question like that. Ask Evie."

"I daren't," George answered after an anguished pause. "I'm afraid she'd tell me the truth."

There was an uncomfortable silence.

"Who was the chap?"

Harry Blane looked at him straight in the eye.

"I don't know, and if I did I wouldn't tell you."

"You swine. Don't you see what a position I'm in? Do you think it's very pleasant to be made absolutely ridiculous?"

The lawyer lit a cigarette and for some moments silently puffed it.

"I don't see what I can do for you," he said at last.

"You've got some private detectives you employ, I suppose. I want you to put them on the job and let them find everything out."

"It's not very pretty to put detectives on one's wife, old boy; and besides, taking for granted for a moment that Evie had an affair, it was a good many years ago and I don't suppose it would be possible to find out a thing. They seem to have covered their tracks pretty carefully."

"I don't care. You put the detectives on. I want to know the truth."

"I won't, George. If you're determined to do that you'd better consult someone else. And look here, even if you got evidence that Evie had been unfaithful to you what would you do with it? You'd look rather silly divorcing your wife because she'd committed adultery ten years ago."

"At all events I could have it out with her."

"You can do that now, but you know just as well as I do that if you do she'll leave you. D'you want her to do that?"

George gave him an unhappy look.

"I don't know. I always thought she'd been a damned good wife to me. She runs the house perfectly, we never have any servant trouble; she's done wonders with the garden and she's splendid with all the village people. But damn it, I have my self-respect to think of. How can I go on living with her when I know that she was grossly unfaithful to me?"

"Have you always been faithful to her?"

"More or less, you know. After all, we've been married for nearly twenty-four years and Evie was never much for bed."

The solicitor slightly raised his eyebrows, but George was too intent on what he was saying to notice.

"I don't deny that I've had a bit of fun now and then. A man wants it. Women are different."

"We only have men's word for that," said Harry Blane, with a faint smile.

"Evie's absolutely the last woman I'd have suspected of kicking over the traces. I mean, she's a very fastidious, reticent woman. What on earth made her write the damned book?"

"I suppose it was a very poignant experience and perhaps it was a relief to her to get it off her chest like that."

"Well, if she had to write it why the devil didn't she write it under an assumed name?"

"She used her maiden name. I suppose she thought that was enough, and it would have been if the book hadn't had this amazing boom."

George Peregrine and the lawyer were sitting opposite one another with a desk between them. George, his elbow on the desk, his cheek on his hand, frowned at his thought.

"It's so rotten not to know what sort of a chap he was. One can't even tell if he was by way of being a gentleman. I mean, for all I know he may have been a farm-hand or a clerk in a lawyer's office."

Harry Blane did not permit himself to smile and when he answered there was in his eyes a kindly, tolerant look.

"Knowing Evie so well I think the probabilities are that he was all right. Anyhow I'm sure he wasn't a clerk in my office."

"It's been a shock to me," the colonel sighed. "I thought she was fond of me. She couldn't have written that book unless she hated me."

"Oh, I don't believe that. I don't think she's capable of hatred."

"You're not going to pretend that she loves me?"

"No."

"Well, what does she feel for me?"

Harry Blane leaned back in his swivel chair and looked at George reflectively.

"Indifference, I should say."

The colonel gave a little shudder and reddened.

"After all, you're not in love with her, are you?"

George Peregrine did not answer directly.

"It's been a great blow to me not to have any children, but I've never let her see that I think she's let me down. I've always been kind to her. Within reasonable limits I've tried to do my duty by her."

The lawyer passed a large hand over his mouth to conceal the smile that trembled on his lips.

"It's been such an awful shock to me," Peregrine went on. "Damn it all, even ten years ago Evie was no chicken and God knows, she wasn't much to look at. It's so ugly." He sighed deeply. "What would *you* do in my place?"

"Nothing."

George Peregrine drew himself bolt upright in his chair and he looked at Harry with the stern set face that he must have worn when he inspected his regiment.

"I can't overlook a thing like this. I've been made a laughing-stock. I can never hold up my head again."

"Nonsense," said the lawyer sharply, and then in a pleasant, kindly manner: "Listen, old boy: the man's dead; it all happened a long while back. Forget it. Talk to people about Evie's book, rave about it, tell 'em how proud you are of her. Behave as though you had so much confidence in her, you *knew* she could never have been unfaithful to you. The world moves so quickly and people's memories are so short. They'll forget."

"I shan't forget."

"You're both middle-aged people. She probably does a great deal more for you than you think and you'd be awfully lonely without her. I don't think it matters if you don't forget. It'll be all to the good if you can get it into that thick head of yours that there's a lot more in Evie than you ever had the gumption to see."

"Damn it all, you talk as if *I* was to blame."

"No, I don't think you were to blame, but I'm not so sure that Evie was either. I don't suppose she wanted to fall in love with this boy. D'you remember those verses right at the end? The impression they gave me was that though she was shattered by his death, in a strange sort of way she welcomed it. All through she'd been aware of the fragility of the tie that bound them. He died in the full flush of his first love and had never known that love so seldom endures; he'd only known its bliss and beauty. In her own bitter grief she found solace in the thought that he'd been spared all sorrow."

"All that's a bit above my head, old boy. I see more or less what you mean."

George Peregrine stared unhappily at the inkstand on the desk. He was silent and the lawyer looked at him with curious, yet sympathetic eyes.

"Do you realise what courage she must have had never by a sign to show how dreadfully unhappy she was?" he said gently.

Colonel Peregrine sighed.

"I'm broken. I suppose you're right; it's no good crying over spilt milk and it would only make things worse if I made a fuss."

"Well?"

George Peregrine gave a pitiful little smile.

"I'll take your advice. I'll do nothing. Let them think me a damned fool and to hell with them. The truth is, I don't know what I'd do without Evie. But I'll tell you what, there's one thing I shall never understand till my dying day: What in the name of heaven did the fellow ever see in her?"

Miss King

IT was not till the beginning of September that Ashenden, a writer by profession, who had been abroad at the outbreak of the war, managed to get back to England. He chanced soon after his arrival to go to a party and was there introduced to a middle-aged colonel whose name he did not catch. He had some talk with him. As he was about to leave, this officer came up to him and asked:

"I say, I wonder if you'd mind coming to see me. I'd rather like to have a chat with you."

"Certainly," said Ashenden. "Whenever you like."

"What about to-morrow at eleven?"

"All right."

"I'll just write down my address. Have you a card on you?"

Ashenden gave him one and on this the colonel scribbled in pencil the name of the street and the number of a house. When Ashenden walked along next morning to keep his appointment he found himself in a street of rather vulgar red-brick houses in a part of London that had once been fashionable, but was now fallen in the esteem of the house-hunter who wanted a good address. On the house at which Ashenden had been asked to call there was a board up to announce that it was for sale, the shutters were closed and there was no sign that anyone lived in it. He rang the bell and the door was opened by a non-commissioned officer so promptly that he was startled. He was not asked his business, but led immediately into a long room at the back, once evidently a dining-room, the florid decoration of which looked oddly out of keeping with the office furniture, shabby and sparse, that was in it. It gave Ashenden the impression of a room in which the brokers had taken possession. The Colonel, who was known in the Intelligence Department, as Ashenden later discovered, by the letter R., rose when he came in and shook hands with him. He was a man somewhat above the middle height, lean, with a yellow, deeply-lined face, thin grey hair and a toothbrush moustache. The thing immediately noticeable about him was the closeness with which his blue eyes were set. He only just escaped a squint. They were hard and cruel eyes, and very wary; and they gave him a cunning, shifty look. He was a man that you could neither like nor trust at first sight. His manner was pleasant and cordial.

He asked Ashenden a good many questions and then, without

545

further to-do, suggested that he had particular qualifications for the secret service. Ashenden was acquainted with several European languages and his profession was excellent cover; on the pretext that he was writing a book he could without attracting attention visit any neutral country. It was while they were discussing this point that R. said:

"You know, you ought to get material that would be very useful to you in your work."

"I shouldn't mind that," said Ashenden.

"I'll tell you an incident that occurred only the other day and I can vouch for its truth. I thought at the time it would make a damned good story. One of the French ministers went down to Nice to recover from a cold and he had some very important documents with him that he kept in a despatch-case. They were very important indeed. Well, a day or two after he arrived he picked up a yellow-haired lady at some restaurant or other where there was dancing, and he got very friendly with her. To cut a long story short, he took her back to his hotel—of course it was a very imprudent thing to do—and when he came to himself in the morning the lady and the despatch-case had disappeared. They had one or two drinks up in his room and his theory is that when his back was turned the woman slipped a drug into his glass."

R. finished and looked at Ashenden with a gleam in his close-set eyes.

"Dramatic, isn't it?" he asked.

"Do you mean to say that happened the other day?"

"The week before last."

"Impossible," cried Ashenden. "Why, we've been putting that incident on the stage for sixty years, we've written it in a thousand novels. Do you mean to say that life has only just caught up with us?"

R. was a trifle disconcerted.

"Well, if necessary, I could give you names and dates, and believe me, the Allies have been put to no end of trouble by the loss of the documents that the despatch-case contained."

"Well, sir, if you can't do better than that in the secret service," sighed Ashenden, "I'm afraid that as a source of inspiration to the writer of fiction it's a wash-out. We really *can't* write that story much longer."

It did not take them long to settle things and when Ashenden rose to go he had already made careful note of his instructions. He was to start for Geneva next day. The last words that R. said to him, with a casualness that made them impressive, were:

"There's just one thing I think you ought to know before you take on this job. And don't forget it. If you do well you'll get no thanks and if you get into trouble you'll get no help. Does that suit you?"

"Perfectly."

"Then I'll wish you good-afternoon."

Ashenden was on his way back to Geneva. The night was stormy and the wind blew cold from the mountains, but the stodgy little steamer plodded sturdily through the choppy waters of the lake. A scudding rain, just turning into sleet, swept the deck in angry gusts, like a nagging woman who cannot leave a subject alone. Ashenden had been to France in order to write and despatch a report. A day or two before, about five in the afternoon, an Indian agent of his had come to see him in his rooms; it was only by a lucky chance that he was in, for he had no appointment with him, and the agent's instructions were to come to the hotel only in a case of urgent importance. He told Ashenden that a Bengali in the German service had recently come from Berlin with a black cane trunk in which were a number of documents interesting to the British Government. At that time the Central Powers were doing their best to foment such an agitation in India as would make it necessary for Great Britain to keep their troops in the country and perhaps send others from France. It had been found possible to get the Bengali arrested in Berne on a charge that would keep him out of harm's way for a while, but the black cane trunk could not be fou d. Ashenden's agent was a very brave and very clever fellow and he mixed freely with such of his countrymen as were disaffected to the interests of Great Britain. He had just discovered that the Bengali before going to Berne had, for greater safety, left the trunk in the cloak-room at Zürich station, and now that he was in gaol, awaiting trial, was unable to get the *bulletin* by which it might be obtained into the hands of any of his confederates. It was a matter of great urgency for the German Intelligence Department to secure the contents of the trunk without delay, and since it was impossible for them to get hold of it by the ordinary official means, they had decided to break into the station that very night and steal it. It was a bold and ingenious scheme and Ashenden felt a pleasant exhilaration (for a great deal of his work was uncommonly dull) when he heard of it. He recognised the dashing and unscrupulous touch of the head of the German secret service at Berne. But the burglary was arranged for two o'clock on the following morning and there was not a moment to lose. He could trust neither the telegraph nor the telephone to communicate with the British officer at Berne, and since the Indian agent could not go (he was taking his life in his hands by coming to see Ashenden and if he were noticed leaving his room it might easily be that he would be found one day floating in the lake with a knife thrust in his back), there was nothing for it but to go himself.

There was a train to Berne that he could just catch and he put on his hat and coat as he ran downstairs. He jumped into a cab. Four hours later he rang the bell of the headquarters of the Intelligence Department. His name was unknown there but to one person, and it was for him that Ashenden asked. A tall tired-looking man, whom he had not met before, came out and without a word led him into an office. Ashenden told him his errand. The tall man looked at his watch.

"It's too late for us to do anything ourselves. We couldn't possibly get to Zürich in time."

He reflected.

"We'll put the Swiss authorities on the job. They can telephone and when your friends attempt their little burglary, I have no doubt they'll find the station well guarded. Anyhow, you had better get back to Geneva."

He shook hands with Ashenden and showed him out. Ashenden was well aware that he would never know what happened then. Being no more than a tiny rivet in a vast and complicated machine, he never had the advantage of seeing a completed action. He was concerned with the beginning or the end of it, perhaps, or with some incident in the middle, but what his own doings led to he had seldom a chance of discovering. It was as unsatisfactory as those modern novels that give you a number of unrelated episodes and expect you by piecing them together to construct in your mind a connected narrative.

Notwithstanding his fur coat and his muffler, Ashenden was chilled to the bone. It was warm in the saloon and there were good lights to read by, but he thought it better not to sit there in case some habitual traveller, recognising him, wondered why he made these constant journeys between Geneva in Switzerland and Thonon in France; and so, making the best of what shelter could be found, he passed the tedious time in the darkness of the deck. He looked in the direction of Geneva, but could see no lights, and the sleet, turning to snow, prevented him from recognising the landmarks. Lake Leman, on fine days so trim and pretty, artificial like a piece of water in a French garden, in this tempestuous weather was as secret and as menacing as the sea. He made up his mind that, on getting back to his hotel, he would have a fire lit in his sitting-room, a hot bath, and dinner comfortably by the fireside in pyjamas and a dressing-gown. The prospect of spending an evening by himself with his pipe and a book was so agreeable that it made the misery of that journey across the lake positively worth while. Two sailors tramped past him heavily, their heads bent down to save themselves from the sleet that blew in their faces, and one of them shouted to him: *Nous arrivons*; they went to the side and withdrew a bar to allow passage for the gangway, and looking again Ashenden through the howling darkness saw mistily the lights of the quay. A welcome sight. In two or three minutes the steamer was made fast and Ashenden, muffled to the eyes, joined himself to the little knot of passengers that waited to step ashore. Though he made the journey so often—it was his duty to cross the lake into France once a week to deliver his reports and to receive instructions—he had always a faint sense of trepidation when he stood among the crowd at the gangway and waited to land. There was nothing on his passport to show that he had been in France; the steamer went round the lake touching French soil at two places, but going from Switzerland to Switzerland, so that his journey might have been to Vevey or to Lausanne; but he could never be sure that the secret police had not taken note of him, and if he had been followed and seen to land in France, the fact that there was no stamp on his passport would be difficult to explain. Of course he had his story ready, but he well knew that it was not a very convincing one, and though it might be impossible for the Swiss authorities to prove that he was anything but a casual traveller, he might nevertheless spend two or three days in gaol, which would be uncomfortable, and then be firmly conducted to the frontier, which would be mortifying. The Swiss knew well that their country was the scene of all manner of intrigues; agents of the secret service, spies, revolutionaries and agitators infested the hotels of the principal towns and, jealous of their neutrality, they were determined to prevent conduct that might embroil them with any of the belligerent powers.

There were as usual two police officers on the quay to watch the passengers disembark and Ashenden, walking past them with as unconcerned an air as he could assume, was relieved when he had got safely by. The darkness swallowed him up and he stepped out briskly for his hotel. The wild weather with a scornful gesture had swept all the neatness from the trim promenade. The shops were closed and Ashenden passed only an occasional pedestrian who sidled along, scrunched up, as though he fled from the blind wrath of the unknown. You had a feeling in that black and bitter night

that civilisation, ashamed of its artificiality, cowered before the
fury of elemental things. It was hail now that blew in Ashenden's
face and the pavement was wet and slippery so that he had to walk
with caution. The hotel faced the lake. When he reached it and a
page-boy opened the door for him, he entered the hall with a flurry
of wind that sent the papers on the porter's desk flying into the air.
Ashenden was dazzled by the light. He stopped to ask the porter
if there were letters for him. There was nothing, and he was about
to get into the lift when the porter told him that two gentlemen
were waiting in his room to see him. Ashenden had no friends in
Geneva.

"Oh?" he answered, not a little surprised. "Who are they?"

He had taken care to get on friendly terms with the porter and
his tips for trifling services had been generous. The porter gave a
discreet smile.

"There is no harm in telling you. I think they are members of the
police."

"What do they want?" asked Ashenden.

"They did not say. They asked me where you were, and I told
them you had gone for a walk. They said they would wait till you
came back."

"How long have they been there?"

"An hour."

Ashenden's heart sank, but he took care not to let his face betray
his concern.

"I'll go up and see them," he said. The liftman stood aside to
let him step into the lift, but Ashenden shook his head. "I'm so
cold," he said, "I'll walk up."

He wished to give himself a moment to think, but as he ascended
the three flights slowly his feet were like lead. There could be small
doubt why two police officers were so bent upon seeing him. He
felt on a sudden dreadfully tired. He did not feel he could cope
with a multitude of questions. And if he were arrested as a secret
agent he must at least spend the night in a cell. He longed more than
ever for a hot bath and a pleasant dinner by his fireside. He had
half a mind to turn tail and walk out of the hotel, leaving everything
behind him; he had his passport in his pocket and he knew by
heart the hours at which trains started for the frontier: before the
Swiss authorities had made up their minds what to do he would be
in safety. But he continued to trudge upstairs. He did not like the
notion of abandoning his job so easily; he had been sent to Geneva,
knowing the risks, to do work of a certain kind, and it seemed to
him that he had better go through with it. Of course it would not

be very nice to spend two years in a Swiss prison, but the chance of this was, like assassination to kings, one of the inconveniences of his profession. He reached the landing of the third floor and walked to his room. Ashenden had in him, it seems, a strain of flippancy (on account of which, indeed, the critics had often reproached him) and as he stood for a moment outside the door his predicament appeared to him on a sudden rather droll. His spirits went up and he determined to brazen the thing out. It was with a genuine smile on his lips that he turned the handle and entering the room faced his visitors.

"Good evening, gentlemen," said he.

The room was brightly lit, for all the lights were on, and a fire burned in the hearth. The air was grey with smoke, since the strangers, finding it long to wait for him, had been smoking strong and inexpensive cigars. They sat in their greatcoats and bowler-hats as though they had only just that moment come in; but the ashes in the little tray on the table would alone have suggested that they had been long enough there to make themselves familiar with their surroundings. They were two powerful men, with black moustaches, on the stout side, heavily built, and they reminded Ashenden of Fafner and Fasolt, the giants in *The Rhinegold*; their clumsy boots, the massive way they sat in their chairs and the ponderous alertness of their expression made it obvious that they were members of the detective force. Ashenden gave his room an enveloping glance. He was a neat creature and saw at once that his things, though not in disorder, were not as he had left them. He guessed that an examination had been made of his effects. That did not disturb him, for he kept in his room no document that would compromise him; his code he had learned by heart and destroyed before leaving England, and such communications as reached him from Germany were handed to him by third parties and transmitted without delay to the proper places. There was nothing he need fear in a search, but the impression that it had been made confirmed his suspicion that he had been denounced to the authorities as a secret agent.

"What can I do for you, gentlemen?" he asked affably. "It's warm in here, wouldn't you like to take off your coats—and hats?"

It faintly irritated him that they should sit there with their hats on.

"We're only staying a minute," said one of them. "We were passing and as the *concierge* said you would be in at once, we thought we would wait."

He did not remove his hat. Ashenden unwrapped his scarf and disembarrassed himself of his heavy coat.

"Won't you have a cigar?" he asked, offering the box to the two detectives in turn.

"I don't mind if I do," said the first, Fafner, taking one, upon which the second, Fasolt, helped himself without a word, even of thanks.

The name on the box appeared to have a singular effect on their manners, for both now took off their hats.

"You must have had a very disagreeable walk in this bad weather," said Fafner, as he bit half an inch off the end of his cigar and spat it in the fire-place.

Now, it was Ashenden's principle (a good one in life as well as in the Intelligence Department) always to tell as much of the truth as he conveniently could; so he answered as follows:

"What do you take me for? I wouldn't go out in such weather if I could help it. I had to go to Vevey to-day to see an invalid friend and I came back by boat. It was bitter on the lake."

"We come from the police," said Fafner casually.

Ashenden thought they must consider him a perfect idiot if they imagined he had not guessed that, but it was not a piece of information to which it was discreet to reply with a pleasantry.

"Oh, really," he said.

"Have you your passport on you?"

"Yes. In these war-times I think a foreigner is wise always to keep his passport on him."

"Very wise."

Ashenden handed the man the nice new passport, which gave no information about his movements other than that he had come from London three months before and had since then crossed no frontier. The detective looked at it carefully and passed it on to his colleague.

"It appears to be all in order," he said.

Ashenden, standing in front of the fire to warm himself, a cigarette between his lips, made no reply. He watched the detectives warily, but with an expression, he flattered himself, of amiable unconcern. Fasolt handed back the passport to Fafner, who tapped it reflectively with a thick forefinger.

"The chief of police told us to come here," he said, and Ashenden was conscious that both of them now looked at him with attention, "to make a few inquiries of you."

Ashenden knew that when you have nothing apposite to say it is better to hold your tongue; and when a man has made a remark that calls to his mind for an answer, he is apt to find silence a trifle disconcerting. Ashenden waited for the detective to proceed. He was not quite sure, but it seemed to him that he hesitated.

"It appears that there have been a good many complaints lately of the noise that people make when they come out of the Casino late at night. We wish to know if you personally have been troubled by the disturbance. It is evident that as your rooms look on the lake and the revellers pass your windows, if the noise is serious, you must have heard it."

For an instant Ashenden was dumbfounded. What balderdash was this the detective was talking to him (boom, boom, he heard the big drum as the giant lumbered on the scene), and why on earth should the chief of police send to him to find out if his beauty sleep had been disturbed by vociferous gamblers? It looked very like a trap. But nothing is so foolish as to ascribe profundity to what on the surface is merely inept; it is a pitfall into which many an ingenuous reviewer has fallen headlong. Ashenden had a confident belief in the stupidity of the human animal, which in the course of his life had stood him in good stead. It flashed across him that if the detective asked him such a question it was because he had no shadow of proof that he was engaged in any illegal practice. It was clear that he had been denounced, but no evidence had been offered, and the search of his rooms had been fruitless. But what a silly excuse was this to make for a visit and what a poverty of invention it showed! Ashenden immediately thought of three reasons the detectives might have given for seeking an interview with him and he wished that he were on terms sufficiently familiar with them to make the suggestions. This was really an insult to the intelligence. These men were even stupider than he thought; but Ashenden had always a soft corner in his heart for the stupid and now he looked upon them with a feeling of unexpected kindliness. He would have liked to pat them gently. But he answered the question with gravity.

"To tell you the truth, I am a very sound sleeper (the result doubtless of a pure heart and an easy conscience), and I have never heard a thing."

Ashenden looked at them for the faint smile that he thought his remark deserved, but their countenances remained stolid. Ashenden, as well as an agent of the British Government, was a humorist, and he stifled the beginnings of a sigh. He assumed a slightly imposing air and adopted a more serious tone.

"But even if I had been awakened by noisy people I should not dream of complaining. At a time when there is so much trouble, misery and unhappiness in the world, I cannot but think it very wrong to disturb the amusement of persons who are lucky enough to be able to amuse themselves."

"*En effet*," said the detective. "But the fact remains that people have been disturbed and the chief of police thought the matter should be inquired into."

His colleague, who had hitherto preserved a silence that was positively sphinx-like, now broke it.

"I notice by your passport that you are an author, *monsieur*," he said.

Ashenden in reaction from his previous perturbation was feeling exceedingly debonair and he answered with good-humour:

"It is true. It is a profession full of tribulation, but it has now and then its compensations."

"*La gloire*," said Fafner politely.

"Or shall we say notoriety?" hazarded Ashenden.

"And what are you doing in Geneva?"

The question was put so pleasantly that Ashenden felt it behoved him to be on his guard. A police officer amiable is more dangerous to the wise than a police officer aggressive.

"I am writing a play," said Ashenden.

He waved his hand to the papers on his table. Four eyes followed his gesture. A casual glance told him that the detectives had looked and taken note of his manuscripts.

"And why should you write a play here rather than in your own country?"

Ashenden smiled upon them with even more affability than before, since this was a question for which he had long since been prepared, and it was a relief to give the answer. He was curious to see how it would go down.

"*Mais, monsieur*, there is the war. My country is in turmoil, it would be impossible to sit there quietly and write a play."

"Is it a comedy or a tragedy?"

"Oh, a comedy, and a light one at that," replied Ashenden. "The artist needs peace and quietness. How do you expect him to preserve that detachment of spirit that is demanded by creative work unless he can have perfect tranquillity? Switzerland has the good fortune to be neutral, and it seemed to me that in Geneva I should find the very surroundings I wanted."

Fafner nodded slightly to Fasolt, but whether to indicate that he thought Ashenden an imbecile or whether in sympathy with his desire for a safe retreat from a turbulent world, Ashenden had no means of knowing. Anyhow the detective evidently came to the conclusion that he could learn nothing from talking to Ashenden, for his remarks grew more desultory and in a few minutes he rose to go.

When Ashenden, having warmly shaken their hands, closed the door behind the pair he heaved a great sigh of relief. He turned on the water for his bath, as hot as he thought he could possibly bear it, and as he undressed reflected comfortably over his escape.

The day before, an incident had occurred that had left him on his guard. There was in his service a Swiss, known in the Intelligence Department as Bernard, who had recently come from Germany, and Ashenden, desiring to see him, had instructed him to go to a certain café at a certain time. Since he had not seen him before, so that there might be no mistake he had informed him through an intermediary what question himself would ask and what reply he was to give. He chose the luncheon hour for the meeting, since then the café was unlikely to be crowded, and it chanced that on entering he saw but one man of about the age he knew Bernard to be. He was by himself, and going up to him Ashenden casually put to him the pre-arranged question. The pre-arranged answer was given, and sitting down beside him, Ashenden ordered himself a Dubonnet. The spy was a stocky little fellow, shabbily dressed, with a bullet-shaped head, close-cropped, fair, with shifty blue eyes and a sallow skin. He did not inspire confidence, and but that Ashenden knew by experience how hard it was to find men willing to go into Germany he would have been surprised that his predecessor had engaged him. He was a German-Swiss and spoke French with a strong accent. He immediately asked for his wages and these Ashenden passed over to him in an envelope. They were in Swiss francs. He gave a general account of his stay in Germany and answered Ashenden's careful questions. He was by calling a waiter and had found a job in a restaurant near one of the Rhine bridges, which gave him good opportunity to get the information that was required of him. His reasons for coming to Switzerland for a few days were plausible and there could be no difficulty in his crossing the frontier on his return. Ashenden expressed his satisfaction with his behaviour, gave him his orders and was prepared to finish the interview.

"Very good," said Bernard. "But before I go back to Germany I want two thousand francs."

"Do you?"

"Yes, and I want them now, before you leave this café. It's a sum I have to pay, and I've got to have it."

"I'm afraid I can't give it to you."

A scowl made the man's face even more unpleasant to look at than it was before.

"You've got to."

"What makes you think that?"

The spy leaned forward and, not raising his voice, but speaking so that only Ashenden could hear, burst out angrily:

"Do you think that I'm going on risking my life for that beggarly sum you give me? Not ten days ago a man was caught at Mainz and shot. Was that one of your men?"

"We haven't got anyone at Mainz," said Ashenden, carelessly, and for all he knew it was true. He had been puzzled not to receive his usual communications from that place and Bernard's information might afford the explanation. "You knew exactly what you were to get when you took on the job, and if you weren't satisfied you needn't have taken it. I have no authority to give you a penny more."

"Do you see what I've got here?" said Bernard.

He took a small revolver out of his pocket and fingered it significantly.

"What are you going to do with it? Pawn it?"

With an angry shrug of his shoulders he put it back in his pocket. Ashenden reflected that had he known anything of the technique of the theatre Bernard would have been aware that it was useless to make a gesture that had no ulterior meaning.

"You refuse to give me the money?"

"Certainly."

The spy's manner, which at first had been obsequious, was now somewhat truculent, but he kept his head and never for a moment raised his voice. Ashenden could see that Bernard, however big a ruffian, was a reliable agent, and he made up his mind to suggest to R. that his salary should be raised. The scene diverted him. A little way off two fat citizens of Geneva, with black beards, were playing dominoes, and on the other side a young man with spectacles was with great rapidity writing sheet after sheet of an immensely long letter. A Swiss family (who knows, perhaps Robinson by name), consisting of a father and mother and four children, were sitting round a table making the best of two small cups of coffee. The *caissière* behind the counter, an imposing brunette with a large bust encased in black silk, was reading the local paper. The surroundings made the melodramatic scene in which Ashenden was engaged perfectly grotesque. His own play seemed to him much more real.

Bernard smiled. His smile was not engaging.

"Do you know that I have only to go to the police and tell them about you to have you arrested? Do you know what a Swiss prison is like?"

"No, I've often wondered lately. Do you?"

"Yes, and you wouldn't much like it."

One of the things that had bothered Ashenden was the possibility that he would be arrested before he finished his play. He disliked the notion of leaving it half done for an indefinite period. He did not know whether he would be treated as a political prisoner or as a common criminal and he had a mind to ask Bernard whether in the latter case (the only one Bernard was likely to know anything about) he would be allowed writing materials. He was afraid Bernard would think the inquiry an attempt to laugh at him. But he was feeling comparatively at ease and was able to answer Bernard's threat without heat.

"You could of course get me sentenced to two years' imprisonment."

"At least."

"No, that is the maximum, I understand, and I think it is quite enough. I won't conceal from you that I should find it extremely disagreeable. But not nearly so disagreeable as you would."

"What could you do?"

"Oh, we'd get you somehow. And after all, the war won't last for ever. You are a waiter, you want your freedom of action. I promise you that if I get into any trouble, you will never be admitted into any of the Allied countries for the rest of your life. I can't help thinking it would cramp your style."

Bernard did not reply, but looked down sulkily at the marble-topped table. Ashenden thought this was the moment to pay for the drinks and go.

"Think it over, Bernard," he said. "If you want to go back to your job, you have your instructions, and your usual wages shall be paid through the usual channels."

The spy shrugged his shoulders, and Ashenden, though not knowing in the least what was the result of their conversation, felt that it behoved him to walk out with dignity. He did so.

And now as he carefully put one foot into the bath, wondering if he could bear it, he asked himself what Bernard had in the end decided on. The water was just not scalding and he gradually let himself down into it. On the whole it seemed to him that the spy had thought it would be as well to go straight, and the source of his denunciation must be looked for elsewhere. Perhaps in the hotel itself. Ashenden lay back, and as his body grew used to the heat of the water he gave a sigh of satisfaction.

"Really," he reflected, "there are moments in life when all this to-do that has led from the primeval slime to myself seems almost worth while."

Ashenden could not but think he was lucky to have wriggled out of the fix he had found himself in that afternoon. Had he been arrested and in due course sentenced, R., shrugging his shoulders, would merely have called him a damned fool and set about looking for someone to take his place. Already Ashenden knew his chief well enough to be aware that when he had told him that if he got into trouble he need look for no help he meant exactly what he said.

Ashenden, lying comfortably in his bath, was glad to think that in all probability he would be able to finish his play in peace. The police had drawn a blank and though they might watch him from now on with some care it was unlikely that they would take a further step until he had at least roughed out his third act. It behoved him to be prudent (only a fortnight ago his colleague at Lausanne had been sentenced to a term of imprisonment), but it would be foolish to be alarmed: his predecessor in Geneva, seeing himself, with an exaggerated sense of his own importance, shadowed from morning till night, had been so affected by the nervous strain that it had been found necessary to withdraw him. Twice a week Ashenden had to go to the market to receive instructions that were brought to him by an old peasant woman from French Savoy who sold butter and eggs. She came in with the other market-women and the search at the frontier was perfunctory. It was barely dawn when they crossed and the officials were only too glad to have done quickly with these chattering noisy women and get back to their warm fires and their cigars. Indeed this old lady looked so bland and innocent, with her corpulence, her fat red face, and her smiling good-natured mouth, it would have been a very astute detective who could imagine that if he took the trouble to put his hand deep down between those voluminous breasts of hers, he would find a little piece of paper that would land in the dock an honest old woman (who kept her son out of the trenches by taking the risk) and an English writer approaching middle age. Ashenden went to the market about nine when the housewives of Geneva for the most part had done their provisioning, stopped in front of the basket by the side of which, rain or wind, hot or cold, sat that indomitable creature and bought half a pound of butter. She slipped the note into his hand when he was given change for ten francs and he sauntered away. His only moment of risk was when he walked back to his hotel with the paper in his pocket, and after this scare he made up his mind to shorten as much as possible the period during which it could be found on him.

Ashenden sighed, for the water was no longer quite so hot; he

could not reach the tap with his hand nor could he turn it with his
toes (as every properly regulated tap should turn) and if he got up
enough to add more hot water he might just as well get out altogether. On the other hand he could not pull out the plug with his
foot in order to empty the bath and so force himself to get out, nor
could he find in himself the will-power to step out of it like a man.
He had often heard people tell him that he possessed character and
he reflected that people judge hastily in the affairs of life because
they judge on insufficient evidence: they had never seen him in a
hot, but diminishingly hot, bath. His mind, however, wandered
back to his play, and telling himself jokes and repartees that he knew
by bitter experience would never look so neat on paper nor sound
so well on the stage as they did then, he abstracted his mind from
the fact that his bath was growing almost tepid, when he heard a
knock at the door. Since he did not want anyone to enter, he had
the presence of mind not to say come in, but the knocking was
repeated.

"Who is it?" he cried irascibly.

"A letter."

"Come in, then. Wait a minute."

Ashenden heard his bedroom door open and getting out of the
bath flung a towel round him and went in. A page-boy was waiting
with a note. It needed only a verbal answer. It was from a lady
staying in the hotel asking him to play bridge after dinner and was
signed in the continental fashion Baronne de Higgins. Ashenden,
longing for a cosy meal in his own room, in slippers and with a
book leaned up against a reading-lamp, was about to refuse when
it occurred to him that in the circumstances it might be discreet to
show himself in the dining-room that night. It was absurd to suppose that in the hotel the news would not have spread that he had
been visited by the police and it would be as well to prove to his
fellow-guests that he was not disconcerted. It had passed through
his mind that it might be someone in the hotel who had denounced
him and indeed the name of the sprightly baroness had not failed to
suggest itself to him. If it was she who had given him away there
would be a certain humour in playing bridge with her. He gave the
boy a message that he would be pleased to come and proceeded
slowly to don his evening clothes.

The Baroness von Higgins was an Austrian, who on settling in
Geneva during the first winter of the war had found it convenient
to make her name look as French as possible. She spoke English
and French perfectly. Her surname, so far from Teutonic, she owed
to her grandfather, a Yorkshire stable-boy, who had been taken over

to Austria by a Prince Blankenstein early in the nineteenth century. He had had a charming and romantic career; a very good-looking man, he attracted the attention of one of the arch-duchesses and then made such good use of his opportunities that he ended his life as a baron and minister plenipotentiary to an Italian court. The baroness, his only descendant, after an unhappy marriage, the particulars of which she was fond of relating to her acquaintance, had resumed her maiden name. She mentioned not infrequently the fact that her grandfather had been an ambassador, but never that he had been a stable-boy, and Ashenden had learned this interesting detail from Vienna; for as he grew friendly with her he had thought it necessary to get a few particulars about her past, and he knew among other things that her private income did not permit her to live on the somewhat lavish scale on which she was living in Geneva. Since she had so many advantages for espionage, it was fairly safe to suppose that an alert secret service had enlisted her services and Ashenden took it for granted that she was engaged somehow on the same kind of work as himself. It increased if anything the cordiality of his relations with her.

When he went into the dining-room it was already full. He sat down at his table and feeling jaunty after his adventure ordered himself (at the expense of the British Government) a bottle of champagne. The baroness gave him a flashing, brilliant smile. She was a woman of more than forty, but in a hard and glittering manner extremely beautiful. She was a high-coloured blonde with golden hair of a metallic lustre, lovely no doubt but not attractive, and Ashenden had from the first reflected that it was not the sort of hair you would like to find in your soup. She had fine features, blue eyes, a straight nose, and a pink and white skin, but her skin was stretched over her bones a trifle tightly; she was generously *décolletée* and her white and ample bosom had the quality of marble. There was nothing in her appearance to suggest the yielding tenderness that the susceptible find so alluring. She was magnificently gowned, but scantily bejewelled, so that Ashenden, who knew something of these matters, concluded that the superior authority had given her *carte blanche* at a dressmaker's but had not thought it prudent or necessary to provide her with rings or pearls. She was notwithstanding so showy that but for R.'s story of the minister, Ashenden would have thought the sight of her alone must have aroused in anyone on whom she desired to exercise her wiles the sense of prudence.

While he waited for his dinner to be served, Ashenden cast his eyes over the company. Most of the persons gathered were old friends by sight. At that time Geneva was a hot-bed of intrigue and its home was the hotel at which Ashenden was staying. There were Frenchmen there, Italians and Russians, Turks, Rumanians, Greeks and Egyptians. Some had fled their country, some doubtless represented it. There was a Bulgarian, an agent of Ashenden's, whom for greater safety he had never even spoken to in Geneva; he was dining that night with two fellow-countrymen and in a day or so, if he was not killed in the interval, might have a very interesting communication to make. Then there was a little German prostitute, with china-blue eyes and a doll-like face, who made frequent journeys along the lake and up to Berne, and in the exercise of her profession got little titbits of information over which doubtless they pondered with deliberation in Berlin. She was of course of a different class from the baroness and hunted much easier game. But Ashenden was surprised to catch sight of Count von Holzminden and wondered what on earth he was doing there. This was the German agent in Vevey and he came over to Geneva only on occasion. Once Ashenden had seen him in the old quarter of the city, with its silent houses and deserted streets, talking at a corner to a man whose appearance very much suggested the spy and he would have given a great deal to hear what they said to one another. It had amused him to come across the Count, for in London before the war he had known him fairly well. He was of a great family and indeed related to the Hohenzollerns. He was fond of England; he danced well, rode well and shot well; people said he was more English than the English. He was a tall, thin fellow, in well-cut clothes, with a close-cropped Prussian head, and that peculiar bend of the body as though he were just about to bow to a royalty that you feel, rather than see, in those who have spent their lives about a court. He had charming manners and was much interested in the Fine Arts. But now Ashenden and he pretended they had never seen one another before. Each of course knew on what work the other was engaged and Ashenden had had a mind to chaff him about it— it seemed absurd, when he had dined with a man off and on for years and played cards with him, to act as though he did not know him from Adam—but refrained in case the German looked upon his behaviour as further proof of the British frivolity in face of war. Ashenden was perplexed: Holzminden had never set foot in that hotel before and it was unlikely that he had done so now without good reason.

Ashenden asked himself whether this event had anything to do with the unusual presence in the dining-room of Prince Ali. At that juncture it was imprudent to ascribe any occurrence, however accidental it looked, to the hazard of coincidence. Prince Ali was an Egyptian, a near relation of the Khedive, who had fled his country when the Khedive was deposed. He was a bitter enemy of the English and was known to be actively engaged in stirring up trouble in Egypt. The week before, the Khedive in great secrecy had passed three days at the hotel and the pair of them had held constant meetings in the prince's apartments. He was a little fat man with a heavy black moustache. He was living with his two daughters and a certain pasha, Mustapha by name, who was his secretary and managed his affairs. The four of them were now dining together; they drank a great deal of champagne, but sat in a stolid silence. The two princesses were emancipated young women who spent their nights dancing in restaurants with the bloods of Geneva. They were short and stout, with fine black eyes and heavy sallow faces; and they were dressed with a rich loudness that suggested the Fish-market at Cairo rather than the Rue de la Paix. His Highness usually ate upstairs but the princesses dined every evening in the public dining-room: they were chaperoned vaguely by a little old Englishwoman, a Miss King, who had been their governess; but she sat at a table by herself and they appeared to pay no attention to her. Once Ashenden, going along a corridor, had come upon the elder of the two fat princesses berating the governess in French with a violence that took his breath away. She was shouting at the top of her voice and suddenly smacked the old woman's face. When she caught sight of Ashenden she gave him a furious look and flinging into her room slammed the door. He walked on as though he had noticed nothing.

On his arrival Ashenden had tried to scrape acquaintance with Miss King, but she had received his advances not merely with frigidity but with churlishness. He had begun by taking off his hat when he met her, and she had given him a stiff bow, then he had addressed her and she had answered with such brevity that it was evident that she wished to have nothing much to do with him. But it was not his business to be discouraged, so with what assurance he could muster he took the first opportunity to enter into conversation with her. She drew herself up and said in French, but with an English accent:

"I don't wish to make acquaintance with strangers."

She turned her back on him and, next time he saw her, cut him dead.

She was a tiny woman, just a few little bones in a bag of wrinkled skin, and her face was deeply furrowed. It was obvious that she wore a wig, it was of a mousy brown, very elaborate and not always set quite straight, and she was heavily made up, with great patches of scarlet on her withered cheeks and brilliantly red lips. She dressed fantastically in gay clothes that looked as though they had been bought higgledy-piggledy from an old-clothes shop, and in the day-time she wore enormous, extravagantly girlish hats. She tripped along in very small smart shoes with very high heels. Her appearance was so gruesome that it created consternation rather than amusement. People turned in the street and stared at her with open mouths.

Ashenden was told that Miss King had not been to England since she was first engaged as governess of the prince's mother and he could not but be amazed to think of all she must have seen during those long years in the harems of Cairo. It was impossible to guess how old she was. How many of those short Eastern lives must have run their course under her eyes and what dark secrets must she have known! Ashenden wondered where she came from; an exile from her own country for so long, she must possess in it neither family nor friends: he knew her sentiments were anti-English and if she had answered him so rudely he surmised that she had been told to be on her guard against him. She never spoke anything but French. Ashenden wondered what it was she thought of as she sat there, at luncheon and dinner by herself. He wondered if she ever read. After meals she went straight upstairs and was never seen in the public sitting-rooms. He wondered what she thought of those two emancipated princesses who wore garish frocks and danced with strange men in second-rate cafés. But when Miss King passed him on her way out of the dining-room it seemed to Ashenden that her mask of a face scowled. She appeared actively to dislike him. Her gaze met his and the pair of them looked at one another for a moment; he imagined that she tried to put into her stare an unspoken insult. It would have been pleasantly absurd in that painted, withered visage if it had not been for some reason rather oddly pathetic.

But now the Baroness de Higgins, having finished her dinner, gathered up her handkerchief and her bag, and with waiters bowing on either side sailed down the spacious room. She stopped at Ashenden's table. She looked magnificent.

"I'm so glad you can play bridge to-night," she said in perfect English, with no more than a trace of German accent. "Will you come to my sitting-room when you are ready and have your coffee?"

"What a lovely dress," said Ashenden.

"It is frightful. I have nothing to wear, I don't know what I shall do now that I cannot go to Paris. Those horrible Prussians," and her r's grew guttural as she raised her voice, "why did they want to drag my poor country into this terrible war?"

She gave a sigh, and a flashing smile, and sailed on. Ashenden was among the last to finish and when he left the dining-room it was almost empty. As he walked past Count Holzminden, Ashenden, feeling very gay, hazarded the shadow of a wink. The German agent could not be quite sure of it and if he suspected it might rack his brains to discover what mystery it portended. Ashenden walked up to the second floor and knocked at the baroness's door.

"*Entrez, entrez,*" she said and flung it open.

She shook both his hands with cordiality and drew him into the room. He saw that the two persons who were to make the four had already arrived. They were Prince Ali and his secretary. Ashenden was astounded.

"Allow me to introduce Mr. Ashenden to Your Highness," said the baroness, speaking in her fluent French.

Ashenden bowed and took the proffered hand. The prince gave him a quick look, but did not speak. Madame de Higgins went on:

"I do not know if you have met the Pasha."

"I am delighted to make your acquaintance, Mr. Ashenden," said the prince's secretary, warmly shaking his hand. "Our beautiful baroness has talked to us of your bridge and His Highness is devoted to the game. *N'est ce pas, Altesse?*"

"*Oui, oui,*" said the prince.

Mustapha Pasha was a huge fat fellow, of forty-five perhaps, with large mobile eyes and a big black moustache. He wore a dinner jacket with a large diamond in his shirt-front and the *tarboosh* of his country. He was exceedingly voluble, and the words tumbled out of his mouth tumultuously, like marbles out of a bag. He took pains to be extremely civil to Ashenden. The prince sat in silence, looking at Ashenden quietly from under his heavy eyelids. He seemed shy.

"I have not seen you at the club, *Monsieur,*" said the pasha. "Do you not like baccarat?"

"I play but seldom."

"The baroness, who has read everything, tells me that you are a remarkable writer. Unfortunately I do not read English."

The baroness paid Ashenden some very fulsome compliments to which he listened with a proper and grateful politeness, and then, having provided her guests with coffee and liqueurs, she produced the cards. Ashenden could not but wonder why he had been asked to play. He had (he flattered himself) few illusions about himself, and so far as bridge was concerned none. He knew that he was a good player of the second class, but he had played often enough with the best players in the world to know that he was not in the same street with them. The game played now was contract, with which he was not very familiar, and the stakes were high; but the game was obviously but a pretext and Ashenden had no notion what other game was being played under the rose. It might be that knowing he was a British agent the prince and his secretary had desired to see him in order to find out what sort of person he was. Ashenden had felt for a day or two that something was in the air and this meeting confirmed his suspicions, but he had not the faintest notion of what nature this something was. His spies had told him of late nothing that signified. He was now persuaded that he owed that visit of the Swiss police to the kindly intervention of the baroness and it looked as though the bridge-party had been arranged when it was discovered that the detectives had been able to do nothing. The notion was mysterious, but diverting, and as Ashenden played one rubber after another, joining in the incessant conversation, he watched what was said by himself no less closely than what was said by the others. The war was spoken of a good deal and the baroness and the pasha expressed very anti-German sentiments. The baroness's heart was in England, whence her family (the stable-boy from Yorkshire) had sprung, and the pasha looked upon Paris as his spiritual home. When the pasha talked of Montmartre and its life by night the prince was roused from his silence.

"*C'est une bien belle ville, Paris,*" he said.

"The Prince has a beautiful apartment there," said his secretary, "with beautiful pictures and life-sized statues."

Ashenden explained that he had the greatest sympathy for the national aspirations of Egypt and that he looked upon Vienna as the most pleasing capital in Europe. He was as friendly to them as they were to him. But if they were under the impression that they would get any information out of him that they had not already seen in the Swiss papers he had a notion that they were mistaken. At one moment he had a suspicion that he was being sounded upon the possibility of selling himself. It was done so discreetly that he could not be quite sure, but he had a feeling that a suggestion floated in the air that a clever writer could do his country a good turn and make a vast amount of money for himself if he cared to enter into an arrangement that would bring to a troubled world the peace that every humane man must so sincerely desire. It was plain that nothing very much would be said that first evening, but Ashenden as evasively as he could, more by general amiability than by words, tried to indicate that he was willing to hear more of the subject. While he talked with the pasha and the beautiful Austrian, he was conscious that the watchful eyes of Prince Ali were upon him, and had an uneasy suspicion that they read too much of his thoughts. He felt rather than knew that the prince was an able and astute man. It was possible that after he left them the prince would tell the other two that they were wasting their time and there was nothing to be done with Ashenden.

Soon after midnight, a rubber having been finished, the prince rose from the table.

"It is getting late," he said, "and Mr. Ashenden has doubtless much to do to-morrow. We must not keep him up."

Ashenden looked upon this as a signal to take himself off. He left the three together to discuss the situation and retired not a little mystified. He could only trust that they were no less puzzled than he. When he got to his room he suddenly realised that he was dog-tired. He could hardly keep his eyes open while he undressed, and the moment he flung himself into bed he fell asleep.

He would have sworn that he had not been asleep five minutes when he was dragged back to wakefulness by a knocking at the door. He listened for a moment.

"Who is it?"

"It's the maid. Open. I have something to say to you."

Cursing, Ashenden turned on his light, ran a hand through his thinning and rumpled hair (for like Julius Cæsar he disliked exposing an unbecoming baldness) and unlocked and opened the door. Outside it stood a tousled Swiss maid. She wore no apron and looked as though she had thrown on her clothes in a hurry.

"The old English lady, the governess of the Egyptian princesses, is dying and she wants to see you."

"Me?" said Ashenden. "It's impossible. I don't know her. She was all right this evening."

He was confused and spoke his thoughts as they came to him.

"She asks for you. The doctor says, will you come. She cannot last much longer."

"It must be a mistake. She can't want me."

"She said your name and the number of your room. She says quick, quick."

Ashenden shrugged his shoulders. He went back into his room to put on slippers and a dressing-gown, and as an after-thought dropped a small revolver into his pocket. Ashenden believed much more in his acuteness than in a firearm, which is apt to go off at the wrong time and make a noise, but there are moments when it gives you confidence to feel your fingers round its butt, and this sudden summons seemed to him exceedingly mysterious. It was ridiculous to suppose that those two cordial stout Egyptian gentlemen were laying some kind of trap for him, but in the work upon which Ashenden was engaged the dullness of routine was apt now and again to slip quite shamelessly into the melodrama of the sixties. Just as passion will make use brazenly of the hackneyed phrase, so will chance show itself insensitive to the triteness of the literary convention.

Miss King's room was two floors higher than Ashenden's, and as he accompanied the chamber-maid along the corridor and up the stairs he asked her what was the matter with the old governess. She was flurried and stupid.

"I think she has had a stroke. I don't know. The night-porter woke me and said Monsieur Bridet wanted me to get up at once."

Monsieur Bridet was the assistant-manager.

"What is the time?" asked Ashenden.

"It must be three o'clock."

They arrived at Miss King's door and the maid knocked. It was opened by Monsieur Bridet. He had evidently been roused from his sleep; he wore slippers on his bare feet, grey trousers and a frock-coat over his pyjamas. He looked absurd. His hair as a rule plastered neatly on his head stood on end. He was extremely apologetic.

"A thousand excuses for disturbing you, Monsieur Ashenden, but she kept asking for you and the doctor said you should be sent for."

"It doesn't matter at all."

Ashenden walked in. It was a small back-room and all the lights were on. The windows were closed and the curtains drawn. It was intensely hot. The doctor, a bearded, grizzled Swiss, was standing at the bedside. Monsieur Bridet, notwithstanding his costume and his evident harassment, found in himself the presence of mind to remain the attentive manager, and with ceremony effected the proper introduction.

"This is Mr. Ashenden, for whom Miss King has been asking. Dr. Arbos of the Faculty of Medicine of Geneva."

Without a word the doctor pointed to the bed. On it lay Miss King. It gave Ashenden a shock to look at her. She wore a large white cotton nightcap (on entering Ashenden had noticed the brown wig on a stand on the dressing-table) tied under the chin and a white, voluminous nightdress that came high up in the neck. Nightcap and nightdress belonged to a past age and reminded you of Cruikshank's illustrations to the novels of Charles Dickens. Her face was greasy still with the cream she had used before going to bed to remove her make-up, but she had removed it summarily and there were streaks of black on her eyebrows and of red on her cheeks.

T

She looked very small, lying in the bed, no larger than a child, and immensely old.

"She must be well over eighty," thought Ashenden.

She did not look human, but like a doll, the caricature of an old, old witch that an ironic toymaker had amused himself with modelling. She lay perfectly still on her back, the tiny little body hardly marked under the flatness of the blanket, her face even smaller than usual because she had removed her teeth; and you would have thought she was dead but for the black eyes, strangely large in the shrunken mask, that stared unblinkingly. Ashenden thought their expression changed when she saw him.

"Well, Miss King, I'm sorry to see you like this," he said with forced cheerfulness.

"She cannot speak," said the doctor. "She had another little stroke when the maid went to fetch you. I have just given her an injection. She may partly recover the use of her tongue in a little while. She has something to say to you."

"I will gladly wait," said Ashenden.

He fancied that in those dark eyes he saw a look of relief. For a moment or two the four of them stood round the bed and stared at the dying woman.

"Well, if there is nothing I can do, I may just as well go back to bed," said Monsieur Bridet then.

"*Allez, mon ami,*" said the doctor. "You can do nothing."

Monsieur Bridet turned to Ashenden.

"May I have a word with you?" he asked.

"Certainly."

The doctor noticed a sudden fear in Miss King's eyes.

"Do not be alarmed," he said kindly. "Monsieur Ashenden is not going. He will stay as long as you wish."

The assistant-manager took Ashenden to the door and partly closed it so that those within should not hear his undertones.

"I can count on your discretion, Monsieur Ashenden, can I not? It is a very disagreeable thing to have anyone die in a hotel. The other guests do not like it and we must do all we can to prevent their knowing. I shall have the body removed the first possible moment and I shall be extremely obliged if you will not say that there has been a death."

"You can have every confidence in me," said Ashenden.

"It is very unfortunate that the manager should be away for the night. I am afraid he will be exceedingly displeased. Of course if it had been possible I would have sent for an ambulance and had her taken to the hospital, but the doctor said she might die before we got her downstairs and absolutely refused to let me. It is not my fault if she dies in the hotel."

"Death so often chooses its moments without consideration," murmured Ashenden.

"After all she is an old woman, she should have died years ago. What did this Egyptian prince want to have a governess of that age for? He ought to have sent her back to her own country. These Orientals, they are always giving trouble."

"Where is the prince now?" asked Ashenden. "She has been in his service for many years. Ought you not to wake him?"

"He is not in the hotel. He went out with his secretary. He may be playing baccarat. I do not know. Anyhow I cannot send all over Geneva to find him."

"And the princesses?"

"They have not come in. They seldom return to the hotel till dawn. They are mad about dancing. I do not know where they are; in any case they would not thank me for dragging them away from their diversions because their governess has had a stroke. I know what they are. The night-porter will tell them when they arrive and then they can please themselves. She does not want them. When the night-porter fetched me and I went into her room I asked where His Highness was and she cried with all her strength: no, no."

"She could talk then?"

"Yes, after a fashion, but the thing that surprised me was that she spoke in English. She always insisted on talking French. You know, she hated the English."

"What did she want with me?"

"That I cannot tell you. She said she had something that she must say to you at once. It is funny, she knew the number of your room. At first when she asked for you I would not let them send. I cannot have my clients disturbed in the middle of the night because a crazy old woman asks for them. You have the right to your sleep, I imagine. But when the doctor came he insisted. She gave us no peace and when I said she must wait till morning she cried."

Ashenden looked at the assistant-manager. He seemed to find nothing at all touching in the scene he related.

"The doctor asked who you were and when I told him he said that perhaps she wished to see you because you were a compatriot."

"Perhaps," said Ashenden dryly.

"Well, I shall try to get a little sleep. I shall give the night-porter orders to wake me when everything is over. Fortunately the nights are long now and if everything goes well we may be able to get the body away before it is light."

Ashenden went back into the room and immediately the dark eyes of the dying woman fixed upon him. He felt that it was incumbent upon him to say something, but as he spoke he reflected on the foolish way in which one speaks to the sick.

"I'm afraid you're feeling very ill, Miss King."

It seemed to him that a flash of anger crossed her eyes and Ashenden could not but imagine that she was exasperated by his futile words.

"You do not mind waiting?" asked the doctor.

"Of course not."

It appeared that the night-porter had been roused by the ringing of the telephone from Miss King's room, but on listening could get no one to speak. The bell continued to ring, so he went upstairs and knocked at the door. He entered with his pass-key and found Miss King lying on the floor. The telephone had fallen too. It looked as though, feeling ill, she had taken off the receiver to call for help and then collapsed. The night-porter hurried to fetch the assistant-manager and together they had lifted her back into bed. Then the maid was wakened and the doctor sent for. It gave Ashenden a queer feeling to listen to the doctor giving him these facts in Miss King's hearing. He spoke as though she could not understand his French. He spoke as though she were already dead.

Then the doctor said:

"Well, there is really nothing more that I can do. It is useless for me to stay. I can be rung up if there is any change."

Ashenden, knowing that Miss King might remain in that condition for hours, shrugged his shoulders.

"Very well!"

The doctor patted her raddled cheek as though she were a child.

"You must try to sleep. I will come back in the morning."

He picked up his despatch-case in which he had his medical appliances, washed his hands and shuffled himself into a heavy coat. Ashenden accompanied him to the door and as he shook hands the doctor gave his prognosis in a pout of his bearded mouth. Ashenden, coming back, looked at the maid. She sat on the edge of a chair, uneasily, as though in the presence of death she feared to presume. Her broad, ugly face was bloated with fatigue.

"There's no use in your staying up," Ashenden said to her. "Why don't you go to bed?"

"*Monsieur* wouldn't like to remain here alone. Somebody must stay with him."

"But good heavens, why? You have your day's work to do to-morrow."

"In any case I have to get up at five."

"Then try to get a little sleep now. You can give me a look in when you get up. *Allez.*"

She rose heavily to her feet.

"As the gentleman wishes. But I will stay very willingly."

Ashenden smiled and shook his head.

"*Bonsoir, ma pauvre mademoiselle,*" said the maid.

She went out and Ashenden was left alone. He sat by the bedside and again his eyes met Miss King's. It was embarrassing to encounter that unshrinking stare.

"Don't worry yourself, Miss King. You've had a slight stroke. I'm sure your speech will come back to you in a minute."

He felt certain then that he saw in those dark eyes a desperate effort to speak. He could not be mistaken. The mind was shaken by desire, but the paralysed body was incapable of obedience. For her disappointment expressed itself quite plainly, tears came to her eyes and ran down her cheeks. Ashenden took out his handkerchief and dried them.

"Don't distress yourself, Miss King. Have a little patience and I'm sure you'll be able to say anything you want."

He did not know if it was his fancy that he read in her eyes now the despairing thought that she had not the time to wait. Perhaps it was only that he ascribed to her the notions that came to himself. On the dressing-table were the governess's poor little toilet things, silver-backed embossed brushes and a silver mirror, in a corner stood a shabby black trunk and on the top of the wardrobe a large hat-box in shiny leather. It all looked poor and mean in that trim hotel room, with its suite in highly varnished rose-wood. The glare was intolerable.

"Wouldn't you be more comfortable if I turned out some of the lights?" asked Ashenden.

He put out all the lamps but the one by the bedside and then sat down again. He had a longing to smoke. Once more his eyes were held by those other eyes in which was all that remained alive of that old, old, woman. He felt certain that she had something that she wanted urgently to say to him. But what was it? What was it? Perhaps she had asked him only because, feeling death near, she had had a sudden yearning, she the exile of so many years, to die with someone of her own people, so long forgotten, by her side. That was what the doctor thought. But why should she have sent for him? There were other English people in the hotel. There was an old pair, a retired Indian Civilian and his wife, to whom it seemed more natural that she should turn. No one could be more of a stranger to her than Ashenden.

"Have you got something to say to me, Miss King?"

He tried to read an answer in her eyes. They continued to stare at him meaningly, but what the meaning was he had no notion.

"Don't be afraid I shall go. I will stay as long as you want me."

Nothing, nothing. The black eyes, and as he looked at them they seemed to glow mysteriously as though there were fires behind them, the eyes continued to hold him with that insistent stare. Then Ashenden asked himself if she had sent for him because she knew that he was a British agent. Was it possible that at that last moment she had had some unexpected revulsion of feeling from everything that had signified to her for so many years? Perhaps at the moment of death a love for her country, a love that had been dead for half a century, awakened again in her—("I'm silly to fancy these idiotic things," thought Ashenden, "it's cheap and tawdry fiction.")—and she had been seized with a desire to do something for what was after all her own. No one was quite himself just then and patriotism (in peace-time an attitude best left to politicians, publicists and fools, but in the dark days of war an emotion that can wring the heart-strings), patriotism made one do odd things. It was curious that she had been unwilling to see the prince and his daughters. Did she on a sudden hate them? Did she feel a traitor on their account and now at the last hour wish to make amends? ("It's all very improbable, she's just a silly old maid who ought to have died years ago.") But you couldn't ignore the improbable. Ashenden, his common-sense protesting, became strangely convinced that she had some secret that she wished to impart to him. She had sent for him knowing who he was because he could make use of it. She was dying and feared nothing. But was it really important? Ashenden leaned forward trying more eagerly to read what her eyes had to say. Perhaps it was only some trivial thing that was important only in her addled old brain. Ashenden was sick of the people who saw spies in every inoffensive passer-by and plots in the most innocent combination of circumstances. It was a hundred to one that if Miss King recovered her speech she would tell him something that could be of no use to anybody.

But how much must that old woman know! With her sharp eyes and sharp ears she must have had the chance to discover matters that were closely hidden from persons that seemed less insignificant. Ashenden thought again how he had the impression that something of real consequence was being prepared round about him. It was curious that Holzminden should have come to the hotel that day; and why had Prince Ali and the pasha, those wild gamblers, wasted an evening in playing contract-bridge with him? It might be that some new plan was in question, it might be that the very greatest affairs were afoot, and perhaps what the old woman had to say might make all the difference in the world. It might mean defeat or victory. It might mean anything. And there she lay powerless to speak. For a long time Ashenden stared at her in silence.

"Has it got anything to do with the war, Miss King?" he said on a sudden, loudly.

Something passed through her eyes and a tremor shot across her little old face. It was a distinct movement. Something strange and horrible was happening and Ashenden held his breath. The tiny frail body was suddenly convulsed and that old woman, as though by a final desperate effort of will, raised herself up in the bed. Ashenden sprang forward to support her.

"England," she said, just that one word, in a harsh cracked voice, and fell back in his arms.

When he laid her down on the pillow, he saw that she was dead.

The Hairless Mexican

"Do you like macaroni?" said R.

"What do you mean by macaroni?" answered Ashenden. "It is like asking me if I like poetry. I like Keats and Wordsworth and Verlaine and Goethe. When you say macaroni, do you mean *spaghetti, tagliatelli, vermicelli, fettucini, tufali, farfalli*, or just macaroni?"

"Macaroni," replied R., a man of few words.

"I like all simple things, boiled eggs, oysters and caviare, *truite au bleu*, grilled salmon, roast lamb (the saddle by preference), cold grouse, treacle tart and rice pudding. But of all simple things the only one I can eat day in and day out, not only without disgust but with the eagerness of an appetite unimpaired by excess, is macaroni."

"I am glad of that because I want you to go down to Italy."

Ashenden had come from Geneva to meet R. at Lyons and having got there before him had spent the afternoon wandering about the dull, busy and prosaic streets of that thriving city. They were sitting now in a restaurant on the *place* to which Ashenden had taken R. on his arrival because it was reputed to give you the best food in that part of France. But since in so crowded a resort (for the Lyonese like a good dinner) you never knew what inquisitive ears were pricked up to catch any useful piece of information that might fall from your lips, they had contented themselves with talking of indifferent things. They had reached the end of an admirable repast.

"Have another glass of brandy?" said R.

"No, thank you," answered Ashenden, who was of an abstemious turn.

"One should do what one can to mitigate the rigours of war," remarked R. as he took the bottle and poured out a glass for himself and another for Ashenden.

Ashenden, thinking it would be affectation to protest, let the gesture pass, but felt bound to remonstrate with his chief on the unseemly manner in which he held the bottle.

"In my youth I was always taught that you should take a woman by the waist and a bottle by the neck," he murmured.

"I am glad you told me. I shall continue to hold a bottle by the waist and give women a wide berth."

Ashenden did not know what to reply to this and so remained silent. He sipped his brandy and R. called for his bill. It was true that he was an important person, with power to make or mar quite

574

a large number of his fellows, and his opinions were listened to by those who held in their hands the fate of empires; but he could never face the business of tipping a waiter without an embarrassment that was obvious in his demeanour. He was tortured by the fear of making a fool of himself by giving too much or of exciting the waiter's icy scorn by giving too little. When the bill came he passed some hundred-franc notes over to Ashenden and said:

"Pay him, will you? I can never understand French figures."

The groom brought them their hats and coats.

"Would you like to go back to the hotel?" asked Ashenden.

"We might as well."

It was early in the year, but the weather had suddenly turned warm, and they walked with their coats over their arms. Ashenden knowing that R. liked a sitting-room had engaged one for him and to this, when they reached the hotel, they went. The hotel was old-fashioned and the sitting-room was vast. It was furnished with a heavy mahogany suite upholstered in green velvet and the chairs were set primly round a large table. On the walls, covered with a dingy paper, were large steel engravings of the battles of Napoleon, and from the ceiling hung an enormous chandelier once used for gas, but now fitted with electric bulbs. It flooded the cheerless room with a cold, hard light.

"This is very nice," said R., as they went in.

"Not exactly cosy," suggested Ashenden.

"No, but it looks as though it were the best room in the place. It all looks very *good* to me."

He drew one of the green velvet chairs away from the table and, sitting down, lit a cigar. He loosened his belt and unbuttoned his tunic.

"I always thought I liked a cheroot better than anything," he said, "but since the war I've taken quite a fancy to Havanas. Oh well, I suppose it can't last for ever." The corners of his mouth flickered with the beginning of a smile. "It's an ill wind that blows nobody any good."

Ashenden took two chairs, one to sit on and one for his feet, and when R. saw him he said: "That's not a bad idea," and swinging another chair out from the table with a sigh of relief put his boots on it.

"What room is that next door?" he asked.

"That's your bedroom."

"And on the other side?"

"A banqueting hall."

R. got up and strolled slowly about the room and when he passed the windows, as though in idle curiosity, peeped through the heavy rep curtains that covered them, and then returning to his chair once more comfortably put his feet up.

"It's just as well not to take any more risk than one need," he said.

He looked at Ashenden reflectively. There was a slight smile on his thin lips, but the pale eyes, too closely set together, remained cold and steely. R.'s stare would have been embarrassing if Ashenden had not been used to it. He knew that R. was considering how he would broach the subject that he had in mind. The silence must have lasted for two or three minutes.

"I'm expecting a fellow to come and see me to-night," he said at last. "His train gets in about ten." He gave his wrist-watch a glance. "He's known as the Hairless Mexican."

"Why?"

"Because he's hairless and because he's a Mexican."

"The explanation seems perfectly satisfactory," said Ashenden.

"He'll tell you all about himself. He talks nineteen to the dozen. He was on his uppers when I came across him. It appears that he was mixed up in some revolution in Mexico and had to get out with nothing but the clothes he stood up in. They were rather the worse for wear when I found him. If you want to please him you call him General. He claims to have been a general in Huerta's army, at least I think it was Huerta; anyhow he says that if things had gone right he would be Minister of War now and no end of a big bug. I've found him very useful. Not a bad chap. The only thing I really have against him is that he will use scent."

"And where do I come in?" asked Ashenden.

"He's going down to Italy. I've got rather a ticklish job for him to do and I want you to stand by. I'm not keen on trusting him with a lot of money. He's a gambler and he's a bit too fond of the girls. I suppose you came from Geneva on your Ashenden passport?"

"Yes."

"I've got another for you, a diplomatic one, by the way, in the name of Somerville with visas for France and Italy. I think you and he had better travel together. He's an amusing cove when he gets going, and I think you ought to know one another."

"What is the job?"

"I haven't yet quite made up my mind how much it's desirable for you to know about it."

Ashenden did not reply. They eyed one another in a detached manner, as though they were strangers who sat together in a railway carriage and each wondered who and what the other was.

"In your place I'd leave the General to do most of the talking. I wouldn't tell him more about yourself than you find absolutely necessary. He won't ask you any questions, I can promise you that, I think he's by way of being a gentleman after his own fashion."

"By the way, what is his real name?"

"I always call him Manuel, I don't know that he likes it very much, his name is Manuel Carmona."

"I gather by what you have not said that he's an unmitigated scoundrel."

R. smiled with his pale blue eyes.

"I don't know that I'd go quite so far as that. He hasn't had the advantages of a public-school education. His ideas of playing the game are not quite the same as yours or mine. I don't know that I'd leave a gold cigarette-case about when he was in the neighbourhood, but if he lost money to you at poker and had pinched your cigarette case he would immediately pawn it to pay you. If he had half a chance he'd seduce your wife, but if you were up against it he'd share his last crust with you. The tears will run down his face when he hears Gounod's 'Ave Maria' on the gramophone, but if you insult his dignity he'll shoot you like a dog. It appears that in Mexico it's an insult to get between a man and his drink and he told me himself that once when a Dutchman who didn't know passed between him and the bar he whipped out his revolver and shot him dead."

"Did nothing happen to him?"

"No, it appears that he belongs to one of the best families. The matter was hushed up and it was announced in the papers that the Dutchman had committed suicide. He did practically. I don't believe the Hairless Mexican has a great respect for human life."

Ashenden, who had been looking intently at R., started a little and he watched more carefully than ever his chief's tired, lined and yellow face. He knew that he did not make this remark for nothing.

"Of course a lot of nonsense is talked about the value of human life. You might just as well say that the counters you use at poker have an intrinsic value; their value is what you like to make it; for a general giving battle, men are merely counters and he's a fool if he allows himself for sentimental reasons to look upon them as human beings."

"But, you see, they're counters that feel and think and if they believe they're being squandered they are quite capable of refusing to be used any more."

"Anyhow, that's neither here nor there. We've had information that a man called Constantine Andreadi is on his way from Constantinople with certain documents that we want to get hold of. He's a Greek. He's an agent of Enver Pasha and Enver has great confidence in him. He's given him verbal messages that are too secret and too important to be put on paper. He's sailing from the Piræus, on a boat called the *Ithaca*, and will land at Brindisi on his way to Rome. He's to deliver his despatches at the German Embassy and impart what he has to say personally to the ambassador."

"I see."

At this time Italy was still neutral; the Central Powers were straining every nerve to keep her so; the Allies were doing what they could to induce her to declare war on their side.

"We don't want to get into any trouble with the Italian authorities, it might be fatal, but we've got to prevent Andreadi from getting to Rome."

"At any cost?" asked Ashenden.

"Money's no object," answered R., his lips twisting into a sardonic smile.

"What do you propose to do?"

"I don't think you need bother your head about that."

"I have a fertile imagination," said Ashenden.

"I want you to go down to Naples with the Hairless Mexican. He's very keen on getting back to Cuba. It appears that his friends are organising a show and he wants to be as near at hand as possible so that he can hop over to Mexico when things are ripe. He needs cash. I've brought money down with me, in American dollars, and I shall give it to you to-night. You'd better carry it on your person."

"Is it much?"

"It's a good deal, but I thought it would be easier for you if it wasn't bulky, so I've got it in thousand-dollar notes. You will give the Hairless Mexican the notes in return for the documents that Andreadi is bringing."

A question sprang to Ashenden's lips, but he did not ask it. He asked another instead.

"Does this fellow understand what he has to do?"

"Perfectly."

There was a knock at the door. It opened and the Hairless Mexican stood before them.

"I have arrived. Good evening, Colonel. I am enchanted to see you."

R. got up.

"Had a nice journey, Manuel? This is Mr. Somerville, who's going to Naples with you, General Carmona."

"Pleased to meet you, sir."

He shook Ashenden's hand with such force that he winced.

"Your hands are like iron, General," he murmured.

The Mexican gave them a glance.

"I had them manicured this morning. I do not think they were very well done. I like my nails much more highly polished."

They were cut to a point, stained bright red, and to Ashenden's mind shone like mirrors. Though it was not cold the General wore a fur coat with an astrakhan collar and with his every movement a wave of perfume was wafted to your nose.

"Take off your coat, General, and have a cigar," said R.

The Hairless Mexican was a tall man, and though thinnish gave you the impression of being very powerful; he was smartly dressed in a blue serge suit, with a silk handkerchief neatly tucked in the breast pocket of his coat, and he wore a gold bracelet on his wrist. His features were good, but a little larger than life-size, and his eyes were brown and lustrous. He was quite hairless. His yellow skin had the smoothness of a woman's and he had no eyebrows nor eyelashes; he wore a pale brown wig, rather long, and the locks were arranged in artistic disorder. This and the unwrinkled sallow face, combined with his dandified dress, gave him an appearance that was at first glance a trifle horrifying He was repulsive and ridiculous, but you could not take your eyes from him. There was a sinister fascination in his strangeness.

He sat down and hitched up his trousers so that they should not bag at the knee.

"Well, Manuel, have you been breaking any hearts to-day?" said R. with his sardonic joviality.

The General turned to Ashenden.

"Our good friend, the Colonel, envies me my successes with the fair sex. I tell him he can have just as many as I if he will only listen to me. Confidence, that is all you need. If you never fear a rebuff you will never have one."

"Nonsense, Manuel, one has to have your way with the girls. There's something about you that they can't resist."

The Hairless Mexican laughed with a self-satisfaction that he did not try to disguise. He spoke English very well, with a Spanish accent, but with an American intonation.

"But since you ask me, Colonel, I don't mind telling you that I got into conversation on the train with a little woman who was coming to Lyons to see her mother-in-law. She was not very young and she was thinner than I like a woman to be, but she was possible, and she helped me to pass an agreeable hour."

"Well, let's get to business," said R.

"I am at your service, Colonel." He gave Ashenden a glance. "Is Mr. Somerville a military man?"

"No," said R., "he's an author."

"It takes all sorts to make a world, as you say. I am happy to make your acquaintance, Mr. Somerville. I can tell you many stories that will interest you; I am sure that we shall get on well together. You have a sympathetic air. I am very sensitive to that. To tell you the truth I am nothing but a bundle of nerves and if I am with a person who is antipathetic to me I go all to pieces."

"I hope we shall have a pleasant journey," said Ashenden.

"When does our friend arrive at Brindisi?" asked the Mexican, turning to R.

"He sails from the Piræus in the *Ithaca* on the fourteenth. It's probably some old tub, but you'd better get down to Brindisi in good time."

"I agree with you."

R. got up and with his hands in his pockets sat on the edge of the table. In his rather shabby uniform, his tunic unbuttoned, he looked a slovenly creature beside the neat and well-dressed Mexican.

"Mr. Somerville knows practically nothing of the errand on which you are going and I do not desire you to tell him anything. I think you had much better keep your own counsel. He is instructed to give you the funds you need for your work, but your actions are your own affair. If you need his advice of course you can ask for it."

"I seldom ask other people's advice and never take it."

"And should you make a mess of things I trust you to keep Mr. Somerville out of it. He must on no account be compromised."

"I am a man of honour, Colonel," answered the Hairless Mexican with dignity, "and I would sooner let myself be cut in a thousand pieces than betray my friends."

"That is what I have already told Mr. Somerville. On the other hand, if everything pans out O.K. Mr. Somerville is instructed to give you the sum we agreed on in return for the papers I spoke to you about. In what manner you get them is no business of his."

"That goes without saying. There is only one thing I wish to make quite plain; Mr. Somerville understands of course that I have not accepted the mission with which you have entrusted me on account of the money?"

"Quite," replied R. gravely, looking him straight in the eyes.

"I am with the Allies body and soul, I cannot forgive the Germans for outraging the neutrality of Belgium, and if I accept the money that you have offered me it is because I am first and foremost a patriot. I can trust Mr. Somerville implicitly, I suppose?"

R. nodded. The Mexican turned to Ashenden.

"An expedition is being arranged to free my unhappy country

from the tyrants that exploit and ruin it and every penny that I receive will go on guns and cartridges. For myself I have no need of
money; I am a soldier and I can live on a crust and a few olives.
There are only three occupations that befit a gentleman, war, cards
and women; it costs nothing to sling a rifle over your shoulder and
take to the mountains—and that is real warfare, not this manœuv-
ring of battalions and firing of great guns—women love me for myself, and I generally win at cards."

Ashenden found the flamboyance of this strange creature, with
his scented handkerchief and his gold bracelet, very much to his
taste. This was far from being just the man in the street (whose
tyranny we rail at but in the end submit to) and to the amateur of
the baroque in human nature he was a rarity to be considered with
delight. He was a purple patch on two legs. Notwithstanding his
wig and his hairless big face, he had undoubtedly an air; he was
absurd, but he did not give you the impression that he was a man
to be trifled with. His self-complacency was magnificent.

"Where is your kit, Manuel?" asked R.

It was possible that a frown for an instant darkened the Mexican's
brow at the abrupt question that seemed a little contemptuously to
brush to one side his eloquent statement, but he gave no other sign
of displeasure. Ashenden suspected that he thought the Colonel a
barbarian insensitive to the finer emotions.

"I left it at the station."

"Mr. Somerville has a diplomatic passport so that he can get it
through with his own things at the frontier without examination if
you like."

"I have very little, a few suits and some linen, but perhaps it would
be as well if Mr. Somerville would take charge of it. I bought half
a dozen suits of silk pyjamas before I left Paris."

"And what about you?" asked R., turning to Ashenden.

"I've only got one bag. It's in my room."

"You'd better have it taken to the station while there's someone
about. Your train goes at one ten."

"Oh?"

This was the first Ashenden had heard that they were to start that
night.

"I think you'd better get down to Naples as soon as possible."

"Very well."

R. got up.

"I'm going to bed. I don't know what you fellows want to
do."

"I shall take a walk about Lyons," said the Hairless Mexican. "I am interested in life. Lend me a hundred francs, Colonel, will you? I have no change on me."

R. took out his pocket-book and gave the General the note he asked for. Then to Ashenden:

"What are you going to do? Wait here?"

"No," said Ashenden, "I shall go to the station and read."

"You'd both of you better have a whisky and soda before you go, hadn't you? What about it, Manuel?"

"It is very kind of you, but I never drink anything but champagne and brandy."

"Mixed?" asked R. dryly.

"Not necessarily," returned the other with gravity.

R. ordered brandy and soda and when it came, whereas he and Ashenden helped themselves to both, the Hairless Mexican poured himself out three parts of a tumbler of neat brandy and swallowed it in two noisy gulps. He rose to his feet and put on his coat with the astrakhan collar, seized in one hand his bold black hat and, with the gesture of a romantic actor giving up the girl he loves to one more worthy of her, held out the other to R.

"Well, Colonel, I will bid you good-night and pleasant dreams. I do not expect that we shall meet again so soon."

"Don't make a hash of things, Manuel, and if you do, keep your mouth shut."

"They tell me that in one of your colleges where the sons of gentlemen are trained to become naval officers it is written in letters of gold: There is no such word as impossible in the British Navy. I do not know the meaning of the word failure."

"It has a good many synonyms," retorted R.

"I will meet you at the station, Mr. Somerville," said the Hairless Mexican, and with a flourish left them.

R. looked at Ashenden with that little smile of his that always made his face look so dangerously shrewd.

"Well, what d'you think of him?"

"You've got me beat," said Ashenden. "Is he a mountebank? He seems as vain as a peacock. And with that frightful appearance can he really be the lady's man he pretends? What makes you think you can trust him?"

R. gave a low chuckle and he washed his thin, old hands with imaginary soap.

"I thought you'd like him. He's quite a character, isn't he? I think we can trust him." R.'s eyes suddenly grew opaque. "I don't believe it would pay him to double-cross us." He paused for a moment. "Anyhow, we've got to risk it. I'll give you the tickets and the money and then you can take yourself off; I'm all in and I want to go to bed."

Ten minutes later Ashenden set out for the station with his bag on a porter's shoulder.

Having nearly two hours to wait he made himself comfortable in the waiting-room. The light was good and he read a novel. When the time drew near for the arrival of the train from Paris that was to take them direct to Rome and the Hairless Mexican did not appear, Ashenden, beginning to grow a trifle anxious, went out on the platform to look for him. Ashenden suffered from that distressing malady known as train fever: an hour before his train was due he began to have apprehensions lest he should miss it; he was impatient with the porters who would never bring his luggage down from his room in time and he could not understand why the hotel bus cut it so fine; a block in the street would drive him to frenzy and the languid movements of the station porters infuriate him. The whole world seemed in a horrid plot to delay him; people got in his way as he passed through the barriers; others, a long string of them, were at the ticket-office getting tickets for other trains than his and they counted their change with exasperating care; his luggage took an interminable time to register; and then if he was travelling with friends they would go to buy newspapers, or would take a walk along the platform, and he was certain they would be left behind, they would stop to talk to a casual stranger or suddenly be seized with a desire to telephone and disappear at a run. In fact the universe conspired to make him miss every train he wanted to take and he was not happy unless he was settled in his corner, his things on the rack above him, with a good half-hour to spare. Sometimes by arriving at the station too soon he had caught an earlier train than the one he had meant to, but that was nerve-racking and caused him all the anguish of very nearly missing it.

The Rome express was signalled and there was no sign of the Hairless Mexican; it came in and he was not to be seen. Ashenden became more and more harassed. He walked quickly up and down the platform, looked in all the waiting-rooms, went to the *consigne* where the luggage was left; he could not find him. There were no sleeping-cars, but a number of people got out and he took two seats in a first-class carriage. He stood by the door, looking up and down the platform and up at the clock; it was useless to go if his travelling companion did not turn up, and Ashenden made up his mind to take his things out of the carriage as the porter cried *en voiture*; but, by George! he would give the brute hell when he found him. There were three minutes more, then two minutes, then one; at that late hour there were few persons about and all who were travelling had taken their seats. Then he saw the Hairless Mexican, followed by two porters with his luggage and accompanied by a man in a bowler-hat, walk leisurely on to the platform. He caught sight of Ashenden and waved to him.

"Ah, my dear fellow, there you are, I wondered what had become of you."

"Good God, man, hurry up or we shall miss the train."

"I never miss a train. Have you got good seats? The *chef de gare* has gone for the night; this is his assistant."

The man in the bowler-hat took it off when Ashenden nodded to him.

"But this is an ordinary carriage. I am afraid I could not travel in that." He turned to the stationmaster's assistant with an affable smile. "You must do better for me than that, *mon cher*."

"*Certainement, mon général*, I will put you into a *salon-lit*. Of course." The assistant stationmaster led them along the train and opened the door of an empty compartment where there were two beds. The Mexican eyed it with satisfaction and watched the porters arrange the luggage.

"That will do very well. I am much obliged to you." He held out his hand to the man in the bowler-hat. "I shall not forget you and next time I see the Minister I will tell him with what civility you have treated me."

"You are too good, General. I shall be very grateful."

A whistle was blown and the train started.

"This is better than an ordinary first-class carriage, I think, Mr. Somerville," said the Mexican. "A good traveller should learn how to make the best of things."

But Ashenden was still extremely cross.

"I don't know why the devil you wanted to cut it so fine. We should have looked a pair of damned fools if we'd missed the train."

"My dear fellow, there was never the smallest chance of that. When I arrived I told the stationmaster that I was General Carmona, Commander-in-Chief of the Mexican Army, and that I had to stop off in Lyons for a few hours to hold a conference with the British Field-Marshal. I asked him to hold the train for me if I was delayed and suggested that my government might see its way to conferring an order on him. I have been to Lyons before, I like the girls here; they have not the chic of the Parisians, but they have something, there is no denying that they have something. Will you have a mouthful of brandy before you go to sleep?"

"No, thank you," said Ashenden morosely.

"I always drink a glass before going to bed, it settles the nerves."

He looked in his suit-case and without difficulty found a bottle. He put it to his lips and had a long drink, wiped his mouth with the back of his hand and lit a cigarette. Then he took off his boots and lay down. Ashenden dimmed the light.

"I have never yet made up my mind," said the Hairless Mexican reflectively, "whether it is pleasanter to go to sleep with the kisses of a beautiful woman on your mouth or with a cigarette between your lips. Have you ever been to Mexico? I will tell you about Mexico to-morrow. Good-night."

Soon Ashenden heard from his steady breathing that he was asleep and in a little while himself dozed off. Presently he woke. The Mexican, deep in slumber, lay motionless; he had taken off his fur coat and was using it as a blanket; he still wore his wig. Suddenly there was a jolt and the train with a noisy grinding of brakes stopped; in the twinkling of an eye, before Ashenden could realise that anything had happened, the Mexican was on his feet with his hand to his hip.

"What is it?" he cried.

"Nothing. Probably only a signal against us."

The Mexican sat down heavily on his bed. Ashenden turned on the light.

"You wake quickly for such a sound sleeper," he said.

"You have to in my profession."

Ashenden would have liked to ask him whether this was murder, conspiracy or commanding armies, but was not sure that it would be discreet. The General opened his bag and took out the bottle.

"Will you have a nip?" he asked. "There is nothing like it when you wake suddenly in the night."

When Ashenden refused he put the bottle once more to his lips and poured a considerable quantity of liquor down his throat. He sighed and lit a cigarette. Although Ashenden had seen him now drink nearly a bottle of brandy, and it was probable that he had had a good deal more when he was going about the town, he was certainly quite sober. Neither in his manner nor in his speech was there any indication that he had drunk during the evening anything but lemonade.

The train started and Ashenden again fell asleep. When he awoke it was morning and turning round lazily he saw that the Mexican was awake too. He was smoking a cigarette. The floor by his side was strewn with burnt-out butts and the air was thick and grey. He had begged Ashenden not to insist on opening a window, for he said the night air was dangerous.

"I did not get up, because I was afraid of waking you. Will you do your toilet first or shall I?"

"I'm in no hurry," said Ashenden.

"I am an old campaigner, it will not take me long. Do you wash your teeth every day?"

"Yes," said Ashenden.

"So do I. It is a habit I learned in New York. I always think that a fine set of teeth are an adornment to a man."

There was a wash-basin in the compartment and the General scrubbed his teeth, with gurglings and garglings, energetically. Then he got a bottle of eau-de-Cologne from his bag, poured some of it on a towel and rubbed it over his face and hands. He took a comb and carefully arranged his wig; either it had not moved in the night or else he had set it straight before Ashenden awoke. He got another bottle out of the bag, with a spray attached to it, and squeezing a bulb covered his shirt and coat with a fine cloud of scent, did the same to his handkerchief, and then with a beaming face, like a man who has done his duty by the world and is well pleased, turned to Ashenden and said:

"Now I am ready to brave the day. I will leave my things for you, you need not be afraid of the eau-de-Cologne, it is the best you can get in Paris."

"Thank you very much," said Ashenden. "All I want is soap and water."

"Water? I never use water except when I have a bath. Nothing can be worse for the skin."

When they approached the frontier, Ashenden, remembering the General's instructive gesture when he was suddenly awakened in the night, said to him:

"If you've got a revolver on you I think you'd better give it to me. With my diplomatic passport they're not likely to search me, but they might take it into their heads to go through you and we don't want to have any bothers."

"It is hardly a weapon, it is only a toy," returned the Mexican, taking out of his hip-pocket a fully loaded revolver of formidable dimensions. "I do not like parting with it even for an hour, it gives me the feeling that I am not fully dressed. But you are quite right, we do not want to take any risks; I will give you my knife as well. I would always rather use a knife than a revolver; I think it is a more elegant weapon."

"I dare say it is only a matter of habit," answered Ashenden. "Perhaps you are more at home with a knife."

"Anyone can pull a trigger, but it needs a man to use a knife."

To Ashenden it looked as though it were in a single movement that he tore open his waistcoat and from his belt snatched and opened a long knife of murderous aspect. He handed it to Ashenden with a pleased smile on his large, ugly and naked face.

"There's a pretty piece of work for you, Mr. Somerville. I've never seen a better bit of steel in my life, it takes an edge like a razor and it's strong; you can cut a cigarette-paper with it and you can hew down an oak. There is nothing to get out of order and when it is closed it might be the knife a schoolboy uses to cut notches in his desk."

He shut it with a click and Ashenden put it along with the revolver in his pocket.

"Have you anything else?"

"My hands," replied the Mexican with arrogance, "but those I dare say the Custom officials will not make trouble about."

Ashenden remembered the iron grip he had given him when they shook hands and slightly shuddered. They were large and long and smooth; there was not a hair on them or on the wrists, and with the pointed, rosy, manicured nails there was really something sinister about them.

Ashenden and General Carmona went through the formalities at the frontier independently and when they returned to their carriage Ashenden handed back to his companion the revolver and the knife. He sighed.

"Now I feel more comfortable. What do you say to a game of cards?"

"I should like it," said Ashenden.

The Hairless Mexican opened his bag again and from a corner extracted a greasy pack of French cards. He asked Ashenden whether he played *écarté* and when Ashenden told him that he did not suggested piquet. This was a game that Ashenden was not unfamiliar with, so they settled the stakes and began. Since both were in favour of quick action, they played the game of four hands, doubling the first and last. Ashenden had good enough cards, but the General seemed notwithstanding always to have better. Ashenden kept his eyes open and he was not careless of the possibility that his antagonist might correct the inequalities of chance, but he saw nothing to suggest that everything was not above board. He lost game after game. He was capoted and rubiconed. The score against him mounted up and up till he had lost something like a thousand francs, which at that time was a tidy sum. The General smoked innumerable cigarettes. He made them himself with a twist of the finger, a lick of his tongue and incredible celerity. At last he flung himself against the back of his seat.

"By the way, my friend, does the British Government pay your card losses when you are on a mission?" he asked.

"It certainly doesn't."

"Well, I think you have lost enough. If it went down on your expense account I would have proposed playing till we reached Rome, but you are sympathetic to me. If it is your own money I do not want to win any more of it."

He picked up the cards and put them aside. Ashenden somewhat ruefully took out a number of notes and handed them to the Mexican. He counted them and with his usual neatness put them carefully folded into his pocket-book. Then, leaning forward, he patted Ashenden almost affectionately on the knee.

"I like you, you are modest and unassuming, you have not the arrogance of your countrymen, and I am sure that you will take my advice in the spirit in which it is meant. Do not play piquet with people you don't know."

Ashenden was somewhat mortified and perhaps his face showed it, for the Mexican seized his hand.

"My dear fellow, I have not hurt your feelings? I would not do that for the world. You do not play piquet worse than most piquet players. It is not that. If we were going to be together longer I would teach you how to win at cards. One plays cards to win money and there is no sense in losing."

"I thought it was only in love and war that all things were fair," said Ashenden, with a chuckle.

"Ah, I am glad to see you smile. That is the way to take a loss. I see that you have good humour and good sense. You will go far in life. When I get back to Mexico and am in possession of my estates again you must come and stay with me. I will treat you like a king. You shall ride my best horses, we will go to bull-fights together, and if there are girls you fancy you have only to say the word and you shall have them."

He began telling Ashenden of the vast territories, the *haciendas* and the mines in Mexico, of which he had been dispossessed. He told him of the feudal state in which he lived. It did not matter whether what he said was true or not, for those sonorous phrases of his were fruity with the rich-distilled perfumes of romance. He described a spacious life that seemed to belong to another age and his eloquent gestures brought before the mind's eye tawny distances and vast green plantations, great herds of cattle and in the moonlit night the song of the blind singers that melted in the air and the twanging of guitars.

"Everything I lost, everything. In Paris I was driven to earn a pittance by giving Spanish lessons or showing Americans—*Americanos del Norte*, I mean—the night life of the city. I who have flung away a thousand *duros* on a dinner have been forced to beg my bread like a blind Indian. I who have taken pleasure in clasping a diamond bracelet round the wrist of a beautiful woman have been forced to accept a suit of clothes from a hag old enough to be my mother. Patience. Man is born to trouble as the sparks fly upward, but misfortune cannot last for ever. The time is ripe and soon we shall strike our blow."

He took up the greasy pack of cards and set them out in a number of little piles.

"Let us see what the cards say. They never lie. Ah, if I had only had greater faith in them I should have avoided the only action of my life that has weighed heavily on me. My conscience is at ease. I did what any man would do under the circumstances, but I regret that necessity forced upon me an action that I would willingly have avoided."

He looked through the cards, set some of them on one side on a system Ashenden did not understand, shuffled the remainder and once more put them in little piles.

"The cards warned me, I will never deny that, their warning was clear and definite. Love and a dark woman, danger, betrayal and death. It was as plain as the nose on your face. Any fool would have known what it meant and I have been using the cards all my life. There is hardly an action that I make without consulting them. There are no excuses. I was besotted. Ah, you of the Northern races do not know what love means, you do not know how it can prevent you from sleeping, how it can take your appetite for food away so that you dwindle as if from a fever, you do not understand what a frenzy it is so that you are like a madman and you will stick at nothing to satisfy your desire. A man like me is capable of every folly and every crime when he is in love, *si*, *Señor*, and of heroism. He can scale mountains higher than Everest and swim seas broader than the Atlantic. He is god, he is devil. Women have been my ruin."

Once more the Hairless Mexican glanced at the cards, took some out of the little piles and left others in. He shuffled them again.

"I have been loved by multitudes of women. I do not say it in vanity. I offer no explanation. It is mere matter of fact. Go to Mexico City and ask them what they know of Manuel Carmona and of his triumphs. Ask them how many women have resisted Manuel Carmona."

Ashenden, frowning a little, watched him reflectively. He wondered whether R., that shrewd fellow who chose his instruments with such a sure instinct, had not this time made a mistake, and he was uneasy. Did the Hairless Mexican really believe that he was irresistible or was he merely a blatant liar? In the course of his manipulations he had thrown out all the cards in the pack but four, and these now lay in front of him face downwards and side by side. He touched them one by one but did not turn them up.

"There is fate," he said, "and no power on earth can change it. I hesitate. This is a moment that ever fills me with apprehension and I have to steel myself to turn over the cards that may tell me that disaster awaits me. I am a brave man, but sometimes I have reached this stage and not had the courage to look at the four vital cards."

Indeed now he eyed the backs of them with an anxiety he did not try to hide.

"What was I saying to you?"

"You were telling me that women found your fascinations irresistible," replied Ashenden dryly.

"Once all the same I found a woman who resisted me. I saw her first in a house, a *casa de mujeres* in Mexico City, she was going down the stairs as I went up; she was not very beautiful, I had had a hundred more beautiful, but she had something that took my fancy and I told the old woman who kept the house to send her to me. You will know her when you go to Mexico City; they call her La Marqueza. She said that the girl was not an inmate, but came there only from time to time and had left. I told her to have her there next evening and not to let her go till I came. But I was delayed and when I arrived La Marqueza told me that the girl had said she was not used to being kept waiting and had gone. I am a good-natured fellow and I do not mind if women are capricious and teasing, that is part of their charm, so with a laugh I sent her a note of a hundred *duros* and promised that on the following day I would be punctual. But when I went, on the minute, La Marqueza handed me back my hundred *duros* and told me the girl did not fancy me. I laughed at her impertinence. I took off the diamond ring I was wearing and told the old woman to give her that and see whether it would induce her to change her mind. In the morning La Marqueza brought me in return for my ring—a red carnation. I did not know whether to be amused or angry. I am not used to being thwarted in my passions, I never hesitate to spend money (what is it for but to squander on pretty women?), and I told La Marqueza to go to the girl and say that I would give her a thousand *duros* to dine with me that night. Presently she came back with the answer that the girl would come on the condition that I allowed her to go home immediately after dinner. I accepted with a shrug of the shoulders. I did not think she was serious. I thought that she was saying that only to make herself more desired. She came to dinner at my house. Did I say she was not beautiful? She was the most beautiful, the most exquisite creature I had ever met. I was intoxicated. She had charm and she had wit. She had all the *gracia* of the Andalusian. In one word she was adorable. I asked her why she had treated me so casually and she laughed in my face. I laid myself out to be agreeable. I exercised all my skill. I surpassed myself. But when we finished dinner she rose from her seat and bade me good-night. I asked her where she was going. She said I had promised to let her go and she trusted me as a man of honour to keep my word. I expostulated, I reasoned, I raved, I stormed. She held me to my word. All I could induce her to do was to consent to dine with me the following night on the same terms.

"You will think I was a fool, I was the happiest man alive; for seven days I paid her a thousand silver *duros* to dine with me. Every evening I waited for her with my heart in my mouth, as nervous as a *novillero* at his first bull-fight, and every evening she played with me, laughed at me, coquetted with me and drove me frantic. I was madly in love with her. I have never loved anyone so much before or since. I could think of nothing else. I was distracted. I neglected everything. I am a patriot and I love my country. A small band of us had got together and made up our minds that we could no longer put up with the misrule from which we were suffering. All the lucrative posts were given to other people, we were being made to pay taxes as though we were tradesmen, and we were exposed to abominable affronts. We had money and men. Our plans were made and we were ready to strike. I had an infinity of things to do, meetings to go to, ammunition to get, orders to give, I was so besotted over the woman that I could attend to nothing.

"You would have thought that I should be angry with her for making such a fool of me, me who had never known what it was not to gratify my smallest whim; I did not believe that she refused me to inflame my desires, I believed that she told the plain truth when she said that she would not give herself to me until she loved me. She said it was for me to make her love me. I thought her an angel. I was ready to wait. My passion was so consuming that sooner or later, I felt, it must communicate itself to her; it was like a fire on the prairie that devours everything around it; and at last—at last she said she loved me. My emotion was so terrific that I thought I should fall down and die. Oh, what rapture! Oh, what madness! I would have given her everything I possessed in the world, I would have torn down the stars from heaven to deck her hair; I wanted to do something to prove to her the extravagance of my love, I wanted to do the impossible, the incredible, I wanted to give her myself, my soul, my honour, all, all I had and all I was; and that night when she lay in my arms I told her of our plot and who we were that were concerned in it. I felt her body stiffen with attention, I was conscious of a flicker of her eyelids, there was something, I hardly knew what, the hand that stroked my face was dry and cold; a sudden suspicion seized me and all at once I remembered what the cards had told me: love and a dark woman, danger, betrayal and death. Three times they'd said it and I wouldn't heed. I made no sign that I had noticed anything. She nestled up against my heart and told me that she was frightened to hear such things and asked me if So-and-so was concerned. I answered her. I wanted to make sure. One after the other, with infinite cunning, between her kisses she cajoled me into giving every detail of the plot, and now I was certain, as certain as I am that you sit before me, that she was a spy. She was a spy of the President's and she had been set to allure me with her devilish charm and now she had wormed out of me all our secrets. The lives of all of us were in her hands and I knew that if she left that room in twenty-four hours we should be dead men. And I loved her, I loved her; oh, words cannot tell you the agony of desire that burned my heart; love like that is no pleasure; it is pain, pain, but the exquisite pain that transcends all pleasure. It is that heavenly anguish that the saints speak of when they are seized with a divine ecstasy. I knew that she must not leave the room alive and I feared that if I delayed my courage would fail me.

" 'I think I shall sleep,' she said.

" 'Sleep, my dove,' I answered.

" '*Alma de mi corazon*,' she called me. 'Soul of my heart.' They were the last words she spoke. Those heavy lids of hers, dark like a grape and faintly humid, those heavy lids of hers closed over her eyes and in a little while I knew by the regular movement of her breast against mine that she slept. You see, I loved her, I could not bear that she should suffer; she was a spy, yes, but my heart bade me spare her the terror of knowing what must happen. It is strange, I felt no anger because she had betrayed me, I should have hated her because of her vileness; I could not, I only felt that my soul was enveloped in night. Poor thing, poor thing. I could have cried in pity for her. I drew my arm very gently from around her, my left arm that was, my right was free, and raised myself on my hand. But she was so beautiful, I turned my face away when I drew the knife with all my strength across her lovely throat. Without awaking she passed from sleep to death."

He stopped and stared frowning at the four cards that still lay, their backs upward, waiting to be turned up.

"It was in the cards. Why did I not take their warning? I will not look at them. Damn them. Take them away."

With a violent gesture he swept the whole pack on to the floor.

"Though I am a free-thinker I had masses said for her soul." He leaned back and rolled himself a cigarette. He inhaled a long breathful of smoke. He shrugged his shoulders. "The Colonel said you were a writer. What do you write?"

"Stories," replied Ashenden.

"Detective stories?"

"No."

"Why not? They are the only ones I read. If I were a writer I should write detective stories."

"They are very difficult. You need an incredible amount of invention. I devised a murder story once, but the murder was so ingenious that I could never find a way of bringing it home to the murderer, and, after all, one of the conventions of the detective story is that the mystery should in the end be solved and the criminal brought to justice."

"If your murder is as ingenious as you think the only means you have of proving the murderer's guilt is by the discovery of his motives. When once you have found a motive the chances are that you will hit upon evidence that till then had escaped you. If there is no motive the most damning evidence will be inconclusive. Imagine for instance that you went up to a man in a lonely street on a moonless night and stabbed him to the heart. Who would ever think of you? But if he was your wife's lover, or your brother, or had cheated or insulted you, then a scrap of paper, a bit of string or a chance remark would be enough to hang you. What were your movements at the time he was killed? Are there not a dozen people who saw you before and after? But if he was a total stranger you would never for a moment be suspected. It was inevitable that Jack the Ripper should escape unless he was caught in the act."

Ashenden had more than one reason to change the conversation. They were parting at Rome and he thought it necessary to come to an understanding with his companion about their respective movements. The Mexican was going to Brindisi and Ashenden to Naples. He meant to lodge at the Hotel de Belfast, which was a large second-rate hotel near the harbour frequented by commercial travellers and the thriftier kind of tripper. It would be as well to let the General have the number of his room so that he could come up if necessary without inquiring of the porter, and at the next stopping-place Ashenden got an envelope from the station-buffet and made him address it in his own writing to himself at the post-office in Brindisi. All Ashenden had to do then was to scribble a number on a sheet of paper and post it.

The Hairless Mexican shrugged his shoulders.

"To my mind all these precautions are rather childish. There is absolutely no risk. But whatever happens you may be quite sure that I will not compromise you."

"This is not the sort of job which I'm very familiar with," said Ashenden. "I'm content to follow the Colonel's instructions and know no more about it than it's essential I should."

"Quite so. Should the exigencies of the situation force me to take a drastic step and I get into trouble I shall of course be treated as a political prisoner. Sooner or later Italy is bound to come into the war on the side of the Allies and I shall be released. I have considered everything. But I beg you very seriously to have no more anxiety about the outcome of our mission than if you were going for a picnic on the Thames."

But when at last they separated and Ashenden found himself alone in a carriage on the way to Naples he heaved a great sigh of relief. He was glad to be rid of that chattering, hideous and fantastic creature. He was gone to meet Constantine Andreadi at Brindisi and if half of what he had told Ashenden was true, Ashenden could not but congratulate himself that he did not stand in the Greek spy's shoes. He wondered what sort of a man he was. There was a grimness in the notion of his coming across the blue Ionian, with his confidential papers and his dangerous secrets, all unconscious of the noose into which he was putting his head. Well, that was war, and only fools thought it could be waged with kid gloves on.

Ashenden arrived in Naples and, having taken a room at the hotel, wrote its number on a sheet of paper in block letters and posted it to the Hairless Mexican. He went to the British Consulate, where R. had arranged to send any instructions he might have for him, and found that they knew about him and everything was in order. Then he put aside these matters and made up his mind to amuse himself. Here in the South the spring was well advanced and in the busy streets the sun was hot. Ashenden knew Naples pretty well. The Piazza di San Ferdinando, with its bustle, the Piazza del Plebiscito, with its handsome church, stirred in his heart pleasant recollections. The Strada di Chiara was as noisy as ever. He stood at

corners and looked up the narrow alleys that climbed the hill pre-
cipitously, those alleys of high houses with the washing set out to dry
on lines across the street like pennants flying to mark a feast-day:
and he sauntered along the shore, looking at the burnished sea with
Capri faintly outlined against the bay, till he came to Posilippo,
where there was an old, rambling and bedraggled *palazzo* in which in
his youth he had spent many a romantic hour. He observed the
curious little pain with which the memories of the past wrung his
heart-strings. Then he took a fly drawn by a small and scraggy pony
and rattled back over the stones to the *Galleria*, where he sat in the
cool and drank an *americano* and looked at the people who loitered
there, talking, for ever talking with vivacious gestures, and,
exercising his fancy, sought from their appearance to divine their
reality.

For three days Ashenden led the idle life that fitted so well the
fantastical, untidy and genial city. He did nothing from morning
till night but wander at random, looking, not with the eye of the
tourist who seeks for what ought to be seen, nor with the eye of the
writer who looks for his own (seeing in a sunset a melodious phrase or
in a face the inkling of a character) but with that of the tramp to
whom whatever happens is absolute. He went to the museum to
look at the statue of Agrippina the Younger, which he had particular
reasons for remembering with affection, and took the opportunity
to see once more the Titian and the Brueghel in the picture gallery.
But he always came back to the church of Santa Chiara. Its grace,
its gaiety, the airy persiflage with which it seemed to treat religion
and at the back of this its sensual emotion; its extravagance, its elegance of line; to Ashenden it seemed to express, as it were in one
absurd and grandiloquent metaphor, the sunny, dusty, lovely city
and its bustling inhabitants. It said that life was charming and sad;
it's a pity one hadn't any money, but money wasn't everything, and
anyway why bother when we are here to-day and gone to-morrow,
and it was all very exciting and amusing, and after all we must make
the best of things: *facciamo una piccola combinazione.*

But on the fourth morning, when Ashenden, having just stepped
out of his bath, was trying to dry himself on a towel that absorbed
no moisture, his door was quickly opened and a man slipped into
his room.

"What d'you want?" cried Ashenden.

"It's all right. Don't you know me?"

"Good Lord, it's the Mexican. What have you done to yourself?"

He had changed his wig and wore now a black one, close-cropped,
that fitted on his head like a cap. It entirely altered the look of him

and though this was still odd enough, it was quite different from that which he had borne before. He wore a shabby grey suit.

"I can only stop a minute. He's getting shaved."

Ashenden felt his cheeks suddenly redden.

"You found him then?"

"That wasn't difficult. He was the only Greek passenger on the ship. I went on board when she got in and asked for a friend who had sailed from the Piræus. I said I had come to meet a Mr. George Diogenidis. I pretended to be much puzzled at his not coming, and I got into conversation with Andreadi. He's travelling under a false name. He calls himself Lombardos. I followed him when he landed and do you know the first thing he did? He went into a barber's and had his beard shaved. What do you think of that?"

"Nothing. Anyone might have his beard shaved."

"That is not what I think. He wanted to change his appearance. Oh, he's cunning. I admire the Germans, they leave nothing to chance, he's got his whole story pat, but I'll tell you that in a minute."

"By the way, you've changed your appearance too."

"Ah, yes, this is a wig I'm wearing; it makes a difference, doesn't it?"

"I should never have known you."

"One has to take precautions. We are bosom friends. We had to spend the day in Brindisi and he cannot speak Italian. He was glad to have me help him and we travelled up together. I have brought him to this hotel. He says he is going to Rome to-morrow, but I shall not let him out of my sight; I do not want him to give me the slip. He says that he wants to see Naples and I have offered to show him everything there is to see."

"Why isn't he going to Rome to-day?"

"That is part of the story. He pretends he is a Greek business man who has made money during the war. He says he was the owner of two coasting steamers and has just sold them. Now he means to go to Paris and have his fling. He says he has wanted to go to Paris all his life and at last has the chance. He is close. I tried to get him to talk. I told him I was a Spaniard and had been to Brindisi to arrange communications with Turkey about war material. He listened to me and I saw he was interested, but he told me nothing and of course I did not think it wise to press him. He has the papers on his person."

"How do you know?"

"He is not anxious about his grip, but he feels every now and then round his middle, they're either in a belt or in the lining of his vest."

"Why the devil did you bring him to this hotel?"

"I thought it would be more convenient. We may want to search his luggage."

"Are you staying here too?"

"No, I am not such a fool as that. I told him I was going to Rome by the night train and would not take a room. But I must go, I promised to meet him outside the barber's in fifteen minutes."

"All right."

"Where shall I find you to-night if I want you?"

Ashenden for an instant eyed the Hairless Mexican, then with a slight frown looked away.

"I shall spend the evening in my room."

"Very well. Will you just see that there's nobody in the passage?"

Ashenden opened the door and looked out. He saw no one. The hotel in point of fact at that season was nearly empty. There were few foreigners in Naples and trade was bad.

"It's all right," said Ashenden.

The Hairless Mexican walked boldly out. Ashenden closed the door behind him. He shaved and slowly dressed. The sun was shining as brightly as usual on the square and the people who passed, the shabby little carriages with their scrawny horses, had the same air as before, but they did not any longer fill Ashenden with gaiety. He was not comfortable. He went out and called as was his habit at the Consulate to ask if there was a telegram for him. Nothing. Then he went to Cook's and looked out the trains to Rome: there was one soon after midnight and another at five in the morning. He wished he could catch the first. He did not know what were the Mexican's plans; if he really wanted to get to Cuba he would do well to make his way to Spain, and, glancing at the notices in the office, Ashenden saw that next day there was a ship sailing from Naples to Barcelona.

Ashenden was bored with Naples. The glare in the streets tired his eyes, the dust was intolerable, the noise was deafening. He went to the *Galleria* and had a drink. In the afternoon he went to a cinema. Then, going back to his hotel, he told the clerk that since he was starting so early in the morning he preferred to pay his bill at once, and he took his luggage to the station, leaving in his room only a despatch-case in which were the printed part of his code and a book or two. He dined. Then returning to the hotel he sat down to wait for the Hairless Mexican. He could not conceal from himself the fact that he was exceedingly nervous. He began to read, but the book was tiresome, and he tried another; his attention wandered and he glanced at his watch. It was desperately early; he took up his

book again, making up his mind that he would not look at his watch
till he had read thirty pages, but though he ran his eyes conscientiously down one page after another he could not tell more than
vaguely what it was he read. He looked at the time again. Good God,
it was only half-past ten. He wondered where the Hairless Mexican
was, and what he was doing; he was afraid he would make a mess of
things. It was a horrible business. Then it struck him that he had
better shut the window and draw the curtains. He smoked innumerable cigarettes. He looked at his watch and it was a quarter past
eleven. A thought struck him and his heart began to beat against
his chest; out of curiosity he counted his pulse and was surprised to
find that it was normal. Though it was a warm night and the room
was stuffy his hands and feet were icy. What a nuisance it was, he
reflected irritably, to have an imagination that conjured up pictures
of things that you didn't in the least want to see! From his standpoint as a writer he had often considered murder and his mind went
to that fearful description of one in *Crime and Punishment*. He did
not want to think of this topic, but it forced itself upon him; his
book dropped to his knees and staring at the wall in front of him (it
had a brown wall-paper with a pattern of dingy roses) he asked himself how, if one had to, one would commit a murder in Naples. Of
course there was the Villa, the great leafy garden facing the bay in
which stood the aquarium; that was deserted at night and very
dark; things happened there that did not bear the light of day and
prudent persons after dusk avoided its sinister paths. Beyond Posilippo the road was very solitary and there were byways that led up
the hill in which by night you would never meet a soul, but how
would you induce a man who had any nerves to go there? You
might suggest a row in the bay, but the boatman who hired the boat
would see you; it was doubtful indeed if he would let you go on the
water alone; there were disreputable hotels down by the harbour
where no questions were asked of persons who arrived late at night
without luggage; but here again the waiter who showed you your
room had the chance of a good look at you and you had on entering
to sign an elaborate questionnaire.

Ashenden looked once more at the time. He was very tired. He
sat now not even trying to read, his mind a blank.

Then the door opened softly and he sprang to his feet. His flesh
crept. The Hairless Mexican stood before him.

"Did I startle you?" he asked smiling. "I thought you would
prefer me not to knock."

"Did anyone see you come in?"

"I was let in by the night-watchman; he was asleep when I rang and didn't even look at me. I'm sorry I'm so late, but I had to change."

The Hairless Mexican wore now the clothes he had travelled down in and his fair wig. It was extraordinary how different he looked. He was bigger and more flamboyant; the very shape of his face was altered. His eyes were shining and he seemed in excellent spirits. He gave Ashenden a glance.

"How white you are, my friend! Surely you're not nervous?"

"Have you got the documents?"

"No. He hadn't got them on him. This is all he had!"

He put down on the table a bulky pocket-book and a passport.

"I don't want them" said Ashenden quickly. "Take them."

With a shrug of the shoulders the Hairless Mexican put the things back in his pocket.

"What was in his belt? You said he kept feeling round his middle."

"Only money. I've looked through the pocket-book. It contains nothing but private letters and photographs of women. He must have locked the documents in his grip before coming out with me this evening."

"Damn," said Ashenden.

"I've got the key of his room. We'd better go and look through his luggage."

Ashenden felt a sensation of sickness in the pit of his stomach. He hesitated. The Mexican smiled not unkindly.

"There's no risk, *amigo*," he said, as though he were reassuring a small boy, "but if you don't feel happy, I'll go alone."

"No, I'll come with you," said Ashenden.

"There's no one awake in the hotel and Mr. Andreadi won't disturb us. Take off your shoes if you like."

Ashenden did not answer. He frowned because he noticed that his hands were slightly trembling. He unlaced his shoes and slipped them off. The Mexican did the same.

"You'd better go first," he said. "Turn to the left and go straight along the corridor. It's number thirty-eight."

Ashenden opened the door and stepped out. The passage was dimly lit. It exasperated him to feel so nervous when he could not but be aware that his companion was perfectly at ease. When they reached the door the Hairless Mexican inserted the key, turned the lock and went in. He switched on the light. Ashenden followed him and closed the door. He noticed that the shutters were shut.

"Now we're all right. We can take our time."

He took a bunch of keys out of his pocket, tried one or two and at last hit upon the right one. The suitcase was filled with clothes.

U

"Cheap clothes," said the Mexican contemptuously as he took them out. "My own principle is that it's always cheaper in the end to buy the best. After all one is a gentleman or one isn't a gentleman."

"Are you obliged to talk?" asked Ashenden.

"A spice of danger affects people in different ways. It only excites me, but it puts you in a bad temper, *amigo*."

"You see, I'm scared and you're not," replied Ashenden with candour.

"It's merely a matter of nerves."

Meanwhile he felt the clothes, rapidly but with care, as he took them out. There were no papers of any sort in the suitcase. Then he took out his knife and slit the lining. It was a cheap piece and the lining was gummed to the material of which the suitcase was made. There was no possibility of anything being concealed in it.

"They're not here. They must be hidden in the room."

"Are you sure he didn't deposit them in some office? At one of the consulates, for example?"

"He was never out of my sight for a moment except when he was getting shaved."

The Hairless Mexican opened the drawers and the cupboard. There was no carpet on the floor. He looked under the bed, in it, and under the mattress. His dark eyes shot up and down the room, looking for a hiding-place, and Ashenden felt that nothing escaped him.

"Perhaps he left them in charge of the clerk downstairs?"

"I should have known it. And he wouldn't dare. They're not here. I can't understand it."

He looked about the room irresolutely. He frowned in the attempt to guess at a solution of the mystery.

"Let's get out of here," said Ashenden.

"In a minute."

The Mexican went down on his knees, quickly and neatly folded the clothes, and packed them up again. He locked the bag and stood up. Then, putting out the light, he slowly opened the door and looked out. He beckoned to Ashenden and slipped into the passage. When Ashenden had followed him he stopped and locked the door, put the key in his pocket and walked with Ashenden to his room. When they were inside it and the bolt drawn Ashenden wiped his clammy hands and his forehead.

"Thank God, we're out of that!"

"There wasn't really the smallest danger. But what are we to do now? The Colonel will be angry that the papers haven't been found."

"I'm taking the five o'clock train to Rome. I shall wire for instructions there."

"Very well, I will come with you."

"I should have thought it would suit you better to get out of the country more quickly. There's a boat to-morrow that goes to Barcelona. Why don't you take that and if necessary I can come to see you there?"

The Hairless Mexican gave a little smile.

"I see that you are anxious to be rid of me. Well, I won't thwart a wish that your inexperience in these matters excuses. I will go to Barcelona. I have a visa for Spain."

Ashenden looked at his watch. It was a little after two. He had nearly three hours to wait. His companion comfortably rolled himself a cigarette.

"What do you say to a little supper?" he asked. "I'm as hungry as a wolf."

The thought of food sickened Ashenden, but he was terribly thirsty. He did not want to go out with the Hairless Mexican, but neither did he want to stay in that hotel by himself.

"Where could one go at this hour?"

"Come along with me. I'll find you a place."

Ashenden put on his hat and took his despatch-case in his hand. They went downstairs. In the hall the porter was sleeping soundly on a mattress on the floor. As they passed the desk, walking softly in order not to wake him, Ashenden noticed in the pigeon-hole belonging to his room a letter. He took it out and saw that it was addressed to him. They tiptoed out of the hotel and shut the door behind them. Then they walked quickly away. Stopping after a hundred yards or so under a lamp-post Ashenden took the letter out of his pocket and read it; it came from the Consulate and said: *The enclosed telegram arrived to-night and in case it is urgent I am sending it round to your hotel by messenger.* It had apparently been left some time before midnight while Ashenden was sitting in his room. He opened the telegram and saw that it was in code.

"Well, it'll have to wait," he said, putting it back in his pocket.

The Hairless Mexican walked as though he knew his way through the deserted streets and Ashenden walked by his side. At last they came to a tavern in a blind alley, noisome and evil, and this the Mexican entered.

"It's not the Ritz," he said, "but at this hour of the night it's only in a place like this that we stand a chance of getting something to eat."

Ashenden found himself in a long sordid room at one end of which a wizened young man sat at a piano; there were tables standing out from the wall on each side and against them benches. A number of persons, men and women, were sitting about. They were drinking beer and wine. The women were old, painted, and hideous; and their harsh gaiety was at once noisy and lifeless. When Ashenden and the Hairless Mexican came in they all stared and when they sat down at one of the tables Ashenden looked away in order not to meet the leering eyes, just ready to break into a smile, that sought his insinuatingly. The wizened pianist strummed a tune and several couples got up and began to dance. Since there were not enough men to go round some of the women danced together. The General ordered two plates of spaghetti and a bottle of Capri wine. When the wine was brought he drank a glassful greedily and then waiting for the *pasta* eyed the women who were sitting at the other tables.

"Do you dance?" he asked Ashenden. "I'm going to ask one of these girls to have a turn with me."

He got up and Ashenden watched him go up to one who had at least flashing eyes and white teeth to recommend her; she rose and he put his arm round her. He danced well. Ashenden saw him begin talking; the woman laughed and presently the look of indifference with which she had accepted his offer changed to one of interest. Soon they were chatting gaily. The dance came to an end and putting her back at her table he returned to Ashenden and drank another glass of wine.

"What do you think of my girl?" he asked. "Not bad, is she? It does one good to dance. Why don't you ask one of them? This is a nice place, is it not? You can always trust me to find anything like this. I have an instinct."

The pianist started again. The woman looked at the Hairless Mexican and when with his thumb he pointed to the floor she jumped up with alacrity. He buttoned up his coat, arched his back and standing up by the side of the table waited for her to come to him. He swung her off, talking, smiling, and already he was on familiar terms with everyone in the room. In fluent Italian, with his Spanish accent, he exchanged badinage with one and the other. They laughed at his sallies. Then the waiter brought two heaped platefuls of macaroni and when the Mexican saw them he stopped dancing without ceremony and, allowing his partner to get back to her table as she chose, hurried to his meal.

"I'm ravenous," he said. "And yet I ate a good dinner. Where did you dine? You're going to eat some macaroni, aren't you?"

"I have no appetite," said Ashenden.

But he began to eat and to his surprise found that he was hungry.

The Hairless Mexican ate with huge mouthfuls, enjoying himself vastly; his eyes shone and he was loquacious. The woman he had danced with had in that short time told him all about herself and he repeated now to Ashenden what she had said. He stuffed huge pieces of bread into his mouth. He ordered another bottle of wine.

"Wine?" he cried scornfully. "Wine is not a drink, only champagne; it does not even quench your thirst. Well, *amigo*, are you feeling better?"

"I'm bound to say I am," smiled Ashenden.

"Practice, that is all you want, practice."

He stretched out his hand to pat Ashenden on the arm.

"What's that?" cried Ashenden with a start. "What's that stain on your cuff?"

The Hairless Mexican gave his sleeve a glance.

"That? Nothing. It's only blood. I had a little accident and cut myself."

Ashenden was silent. His eyes sought the clock that hung over the door.

"Are you anxious about your train? Let me have one more dance and then I'll accompany you to the station."

The Mexican got up and with his sublime self-assurance seized in his arms the woman who sat nearest to him and danced away with her. Ashenden watched him moodily. He was a monstrous, terrible figure with that blond wig and his hairless face, but he moved with a matchless grace; his feet were small and seemed to hold the ground like the pads of a cat or a tiger; his rhythm was wonderful and you could not but see that the bedizened creature he danced with was intoxicated by his gestures. There was music in his toes and in the long arms that held her so firmly, and there was music in those long legs that seemed to move strangely from the hips. Sinister and grotesque though he was, there was in him now a feline elegance, even something of beauty, and you felt a secret, shameful fascination. To Ashenden he suggested one of those sculptures of the pre-Aztec hewers of stone, in which there is barbarism and vitality, something terrible and cruel, and yet withal a brooding and significant loveliness. All the same he would gladly have left him to finish the night by himself in that sordid dance-hall, but he knew that he must have a business conversation with him. He did not look forward to it without misgiving. He had been instructed to give Manuel Carmona certain sums in return for certain documents. Well, the documents were not forthcoming, and as for the rest—Ashenden knew nothing about that; it was no business of his. The Hairless Mexican waved gaily as he passed him.

"I will come the moment the music stops. Pay the bill and then I shall be ready."

Ashenden wished he could have seen into his mind. He could not even make a guess at its workings. Then the Mexican, with his scented handkerchief wiping the sweat from his brow, came back.

"Have you had a good time, General?" Ashenden asked him.

"I always have a good time. Poor white trash, but what do I care? I like to feel the body of a woman in my arms and see her eyes grow languid and her lips part as her desire for me melts the marrow in her bones like butter in the sun. Poor white trash, but women."

They sallied forth. The Mexican proposed that they should walk and in that quarter, at that hour, there would have been little chance of finding a cab; but the sky was starry. It was a summer night and the air was still. The silence walked beside them like the ghost of a dead man. When they neared the station the houses seemed on a sudden to take on a greyer, more rigid line, and you felt that the dawn was at hand. A little shiver trembled through the night. It was a moment of apprehension and the soul for an instant was anxious; it was as though, inherited down the years in their countless millions, it felt a witless fear that perhaps another day would not break. But they entered the station and the night once more enwrapped them. One or two porters lolled about like stage-hands after the curtain has rung down and the scene is struck. Two soldiers in dim uniforms stood motionless.

The waiting-room was empty, but Ashenden and the Hairless Mexican went to sit in the most retired part of it.

"I still have an hour before my train goes. I'll just see what this cable's about."

He took it out of his pocket and from the despatch-case got his code. He was not then using a very elaborate one. It was in two parts, one contained in a slim book and the other, given him on a sheet of paper and destroyed by him before he left allied territory, committed to memory. Ashenden put on his spectacles and set to work. The Hairless Mexican sat in a corner of the seat, rolling himself cigarettes and smoking; he sat there placidly, taking no notice of what Ashenden did, and enjoyed his well-earned repose. Ashenden deciphered the groups of numbers one by one and as he got it out jotted down each word on a piece of paper. His method was to abstract his mind from the sense till he had finished, since he had discovered that if you took notice of the words as they came along you often jumped to a conclusion and sometimes were led into error. So he translated quite mechanically, without paying attention to the words as he wrote them one after the other. When at last he had done he read the complete message. It ran as follows:

Constantine Andreadi has been detained by illness at Piræus. He will be unable to sail. Return Geneva and await instructions.

At first Ashenden could not understand. He read it again. He shook from head to foot. Then, for once robbed of his self-possession, he blurted out, in a hoarse, agitated and furious whisper:
"You bloody fool, you've killed the wrong man."

Giulia Lazzari

ASHENDEN was in the habit of asserting that he was never bored. It was one of his notions that only such persons were as had no resources in themselves and it was but the stupid that depended on the outside world for their amusement. Ashenden had no illusions about himself and such success in current letters as had come to him had left his head unturned. He distinguished acutely between fame and the notoriety that rewards the author of a successful novel or a popular play; and he was indifferent to this except in so far as it was attended with tangible benefits. He was perfectly ready to take advantage of his familiar name to get a better state-room in a ship than he had paid for, and if a Customs-house officer passed his luggage unopened because he had read his short stories Ashenden was pleased to admit that the pursuit of literature had its compensations. He sighed when eager young students of the drama sought to discuss its technique with him, and when gushing ladies tremulously whispered in his ear their admiration of his books he often wished he was dead. But he thought himself intelligent and so it was absurd that he should be bored. It was a fact that he could talk with interest to persons commonly thought so excruciatingly dull that their fellows fled from them as though they owed them money. It may be that here he was but indulging the professional instinct that was seldom dormant in him; they, his raw material, did not bore him any more than fossils bore the geologist. And now he had everything that a reasonable man could want for his entertainment. He had pleasant rooms in a good hotel and Geneva is one of the most agreeable cities in Europe to live in. He hired a boat and rowed on the lake or hired a horse and trotted sedately, for in that neat and orderly canton it it difficult to find a stretch of turf where you can have a good gallop, along the macadamised roads in the environs of the town. He wandered on foot about its old streets, trying among those grey stone houses, so quiet and dignified, to recapture the spirit of a past age. He read again with delight Rousseau's *Confessions*, and for the second or third time tried in vain to get on with *La Nouvelle Héloïse*. He wrote. He knew few people, for it was his business to keep in the background, but he had picked up a chatting acquaintance with several persons living in his hotel and he was not lonely. His life was sufficiently filled, it was varied, and when he had nothing else to do he could enjoy his own reflections; it was absurd to think that under these circumstances he could possibly be bored, and yet, like a little lonely cloud in the sky, he did see in the offing the possibility of boredom. There is a story that Louis XIV, having summoned a courtier to attend him on a ceremonial occasion, found himself ready to go as the courtier appeared; he turned to him and with icy majesty said, *J'ai failli attendre*, of which the only translation I can give, but a poor one, is, I have but just escaped waiting: so Ashenden might have admitted that he now but just escaped being bored.

It might be, he mused, as he rode along the lake on a dappled horse with a great rump and a short neck, like one of those prancing steeds that you see in old pictures, but this horse never pranced and he needed a firm jab with the spur to break even into a smart trot—it might be, he mused, that the great chiefs of the secret service in their London offices, their hands on the throttle of this great machine, led a life full of excitement; they moved their pieces here and here, they saw the pattern woven by the multitudinous threads (Ashenden was lavish with his metaphors), they made a picture out of the various pieces of the jigsaw puzzle; but it must be confessed that for the small fry like himself to be a member of the secret service was not as adventurous an affair as the public thought. Ashenden's official existence was as orderly and monotonous as a city clerk's. He saw his spies at stated intervals and paid them their wages; when he could get hold of a new one he engaged him, gave him his instructions and sent him off to Germany; he waited for the information that came through and despatched it; he went into France once a week to confer with his colleague over the frontier and to receive his orders from London; he visited the market-place on market-day to get any message the old butter-woman had brought him from the other side of the lake; he kept his eyes and ears open; and he wrote long reports which he was convinced no one read, till having inadvertently slipped a jest into one of them he received a sharp reproof for his levity. The work he was doing was evidently necessary, but it could not be called anything but monotonous. At one moment for something better to do he had considered the possibility of a flirtation with the Baroness von Higgins. He was confident now that she was an agent in the service of the Austrian Government and he looked forward to a certain entertainment in the duel he foresaw. It would be amusing to set his wits against hers. He was quite aware that she would lay snares for him and to avoid them would give him something to keep his mind from rusting. He found her not unwilling to play the game. She wrote him gushing little notes when he sent her flowers. She went for a row with him on the lake and letting her long white hand drag through the water talked of Love and hinted

at a Broken Heart. They dined together and went to see a performance, in French and in prose, of *Romeo and Juliet*. Ashenden had
not made up his mind how far he was prepared to go when he
received a sharp note from R. to ask him what he was playing at:
information "had come to hand" that he (Ashenden) was much in
the society of a woman calling herself the Baroness de Higgins, who
was known to be an agent of the Central Powers and it was most
undesirable that he should be on any terms with her but those of
frigid courtesy. Ashenden shrugged his shoulders. R. did not think
him as clever as he thought himself. But he was interested to discover,
what he had not known before, that there was someone in Geneva
part of whose duties at all events was to keep an eye on him. There
was evidently someone who had orders to see that he did not neglect
his work or get into mischief. Ashenden was not a little amused.
What a shrewd, unscrupulous old thing was R.! He took no risks;
he trusted nobody; he made use of his instruments, but, high or low,
had no opinion of them. Ashenden looked about to see whether he
could spot the person who had told R. what he was doing. He
wondered if it was one of the waiters in the hotel. He knew that R.
had a great belief in waiters; they had the chance of seeing so much
and could so easily get into places where information was lying about
to be picked up. He even wondered whether R. had got his news
from the Baroness herself; it would not be so strange if after all she
was employed by the secret service of one of the Allied nations.
Ashenden continued to be polite to the Baroness, but ceased to be
attentive.

He turned his horse and trotted gently back to Geneva. An ostler
from the riding-stables was waiting at the hotel door and slipping
out of the saddle Ashenden went into the hotel. At the desk the
porter handed him a telegram. It was to the following effect:

*Aunt Maggie not at all well. Staying at Hôtel Lotti, Paris. If possible
please go and see her. Raymond.*

Raymond was one of R.'s facetious *noms de guerre*, and since
Ashenden was not so fortunate as to possess an Aunt Maggie he
concluded that this was an order to go to Paris. It had always
seemed to Ashenden that R. had spent much of his spare time in
reading detective fiction and especially when he was in a good
humour he found a fantastic pleasure in aping the style of the shilling
shocker. If R. was in a good humour it meant that he was about to
bring off a coup, for when he had brought one off he was filled with
depression and then vented his spleen on his subordinates.

Ashenden, leaving his telegram with deliberate carelessness on the

desk, asked at what time the express left for Paris. He glanced at
the clock to see whether he had time to get to the Consulate before it
closed and secure his visa. When he went upstairs to fetch his passport the porter, just as the lift doors were closed, called him.

"*Monsieur* has forgotten his telegram," he said.

"How stupid of me," said Ashenden.

Now Ashenden knew that if an Austrian baroness by any chance
wondered why he had so suddenly gone to Paris she would discover
that it was owing to the indisposition of a female relative. In those
troublous times of war it was just as well that everything should be
clear and above board. He was known at the French Consulate
and so lost little time there. He had told the porter to get him a
ticket and on his return to the hotel bathed and changed. He was
not a little excited at the prospect of this unexpected jaunt. He
liked the journey. He slept well in a sleeping-car and was not disturbed if a sudden jolt waked him; it was pleasant to lie a while
smoking a cigarette and to feel oneself in one's little cabin so en-
chantingly alone; the rhythmical sound as the wheels rattled over
the points was an agreeable background to the pattern of one's
reflections, and to speed through the open country and the night
made one feel like a star speeding through space. And at the end
of the journey was the unknown.

When Ashenden arrived in Paris it was chilly and a light rain
was falling; he felt unshaved and he wanted a bath and clean linen;
but he was in excellent spirits. He telephoned from the station to
R. and asked how Aunt Maggie was.

"I'm glad to see that your affection for her was great enough to
allow you to waste no time in getting here," answered R., with the
ghost of a chuckle in his voice. "She's very low, but I'm sure it'll
do her good to see you."

Ashenden reflected that this was the mistake the amateur humorist, as opposed to the professional, so often made; when he made a
joke he harped on it. The relations of the joker to his joke should be
as quick and desultory as those of a bee to its flower. He should
make his joke and pass on. There is of course no harm if, like the
bee approaching the flower, he buzzes a little; for it is just as well to
announce to a thick-headed world that a joke is intended. But
Ashenden, unlike most professional humorists, had a kindly tolerance
for other people's humour and now he answered R. on his own lines.

"When would she like to see me, do you think?" he asked. "Give
her my love, won't you?"

Now R. quite distinctly chuckled. Ashenden sighed.

"She'll want to titivate a little before you come, I expect. You

know what she is, she likes to make the best of herself. Shall we say
half-past ten, and then when you've had a talk to her we might go
out and lunch together somewhere."

"All right," said Ashenden. "I'll come to the Lotti at ten-thirty."

When Ashenden, clean and refreshed, reached the hotel an orderly
whom he recognised met him in the hall and took him up to R.'s
apartment. He opened the door and showed Ashenden in. R. was
standing with his back to a bright log fire dictating to his secretary.

"Sit down," said R. and went on with his dictation.

It was a nicely furnished sitting-room and a bunch of roses in a
bowl gave the impression of a woman's hand. On a large table
was a litter of papers. R. looked older than when last Ashenden
had seen him. His thin yellow face was more lined and his hair was
greyer. The work was telling on him. He did not spare himself.
He was up at seven every morning and he worked late into the night.
His uniform was spick and span, but he wore it shabbily.

"That'll do," he said. "Take all this stuff away and get on with
the typing. I'll sign before I go out to lunch." Then he turned to
the orderly. "I don't want to be disturbed."

The secretary, a second-lieutenant in the thirties, obviously a
civilian with a temporary commission, gathered up a mass of papers
and left the room. As the orderly was following, R. said:

"Wait outside. If I want you I'll call."

"Very good, sir."

When they were alone R. turned to Ashenden with what for him
was cordiality.

"Have a nice journey up?"

"Yes, sir."

"What do you think of this?" he asked, looking round the room.
"Not bad, is it? I never see why one shouldn't do what one can to
mitigate the hardships of war."

While he was idly chatting R. gazed at Ashenden with a singular
fixity. The stare of those pale eyes of his, too closely set together,
gave you the impression that he looked at your naked brain and had
a very poor opinion of what he saw there. R. in rare moments of
expansion made no secret of the fact that he looked upon his fellow-
men as fools or knaves. That was one of the obstacles he had to
contend with in his calling. On the whole he preferred them
knaves; you knew then what you were up against and could take
steps accordingly. He was a professional soldier and had spent his
career in India and the Colonies. At the outbreak of the war he was
stationed in Jamaica and someone in the War Office who had had
dealings with him, remembering him, brought him over and put

him in the Intelligence Department. His astuteness was so great that he very soon occupied an important post. He had an immense energy and a gift for organisation, no scruples, but resource, courage and determination. He had perhaps but one weakness. Throughout his life he had never come in contact with persons, especially women, of any social consequence; the only women he had ever known were the wives of his brother officers, the wives of government officials and of business men; and when, coming to London at the beginning of the war, his work brought him into contact with brilliant, beautiful and distinguished women he was unduly dazzled. They made him feel shy, but he cultivated their society; he became quite a lady's man, and to Ashenden, who knew more about him than R. suspected, that bowl of roses told a story.

Ashenden knew that R. had not sent for him to talk about the weather and the crops, and wondered when he was coming to the point. He did not wonder long.

"You've been doing pretty well in Geneva," he said.

"I'm glad you think that, sir," replied Ashenden.

Suddenly R. looked very cold and stern. He had done with idle talk.

"I've got a job for you," he said.

Ashenden made no reply, but he felt a happy little flutter somewhere about the pit of his stomach.

"Have you ever heard of Chandra Lal?"

"No, sir."

A frown of impatience for an instant darkened the Colonel's brow. He expected his subordinates to know everything he wished them to know.

"Where have you been living all these years?"

"At 36, Chesterfield Street, Mayfair," returned Ashenden.

The shadow of a smile crossed R.'s yellow face. The somewhat impertinent reply was after his own sardonic heart. He went over to the big table, and opened a despatch-case that lay upon it. He took out a photograph and handed it to Ashenden.

"That's him."

To Ashenden, unused to Oriental faces, it looked like any of a hundred Indians that he had seen. It might have been the photograph of one or other of the rajahs who come periodically to England and are portrayed in the illustrated papers. It showed a fat-faced, swarthy man, with full lips and a fleshy nose; his hair was black, thick and straight, and his very large eyes even in the photograph were liquid and cow-like. He looked ill-at-ease in European clothes.

"Here he is in native dress," said R., giving Ashenden another photograph.

This was full-length, whereas the first had shown only the head and shoulders, and it had evidently been taken some years earlier. He was thinner and his great, serious eyes seemed to devour his face. It was done by a native photographer in Calcutta and the surroundings were naïvely grotesque. Chandra Lal stood against a background on which had been painted a pensive palm tree and a view of the sea. One hand rested on a heavily carved table on which was a rubber-plant in a flower-pot. But in his turban and long pale tunic he was not without dignity.

"What d'you think of him?" asked R.

"I should have said he was a man not without personality. There is a certain force there."

"Here's his dossier. Read it, will you?"

R. gave Ashenden a couple of typewritten pages and Ashenden sat down. R. put on his spectacles and began to read the letters that awaited his signature. Ashenden skimmed the report and then read it a second time more attentively. It appeared that Chandra Lal was a dangerous agitator. He was a lawyer by profession, but had taken up politics and was bitterly hostile to the British rule in India. He was a partisan of armed force and had been on more than one occasion responsible for riots in which life had been lost. He was once arrested, tried and sentenced to two years' imprisonment; but he was at liberty at the beginning of the war and seizing his opportunity began to foment active rebellion. He was at the heart of plots to embarrass the British in India and so prevent them from transferring troops to the seat of war and with the help of immense sums given to him by German agents he was able to cause a great deal of trouble. He was concerned in two or three bomb outrages which, though beyond killing a few innocent bystanders they did little harm, yet shook the nerves of the public and so damaged its morale. He evaded all attempts to arrest him, his activity was formidable, he was here and there; but the police could never lay hands on him, and they only learned that he had been in some city when, having done his work, he had left it. At last a high reward was offered for his arrest on a charge of murder, but he escaped the country, got to America, from there went to Sweden and eventually reached Berlin. Here he busied himself with schemes to create disaffection among the native troops that had been brought to Europe. All this was narrated dryly, without comment or explanation, but from the very frigidity of the narrative you got a sense of mystery and adventure, of hairbreadth escapes and dangers dangerously encountered. The report ended as follows:

"C. has a wife in India and two children. He is not known to have anything to do with women. He neither drinks nor smokes. He is said to be honest. Considerable sums of money have passed through his hands and there has never been any question as to his not having made a proper (!) use of them. He has undoubted courage and is a hard worker. He is said to pride himself on keeping his word."

Ashenden returned the document to R.

"Well?"

"A fanatic." Ashenden thought there was about the man something rather romantic and attractive, but he knew that R. did not want any nonsense of that sort from him. "He looks like a very dangerous fellow."

"He is the most dangerous conspirator in or out of India. He's done more harm than all the rest of them put together. You know that there's a gang of these Indians in Berlin; well, he's the brains of it. If he could be got out of the way I could afford to ignore the others; he's the only one who has any guts. I've been trying to catch him for a year, I thought there wasn't a hope; but now at last I've got a chance and, by God, I'm going to take it."

"And what'll you do then?"

R. chuckled grimly.

"Shoot him and shoot him damn quick."

Ashenden did not answer. R. walked once or twice across the small room and then, again with his back to the fire, faced Ashenden. His thin mouth was twisted by a sarcastic smile.

"Did you notice at the end of that report I gave you it said he wasn't known to have anything to do with women? Well, that *was* true, but it isn't any longer. The damned fool has fallen in love."

R. stepped over to his despatch-case and took out a bundle tied up with pale blue ribbon.

"Look, here are his love-letters. You're a novelist, it might amuse you to read them. In fact you should read them, it will help you to deal with the situation. Take them away with you."

R. flung the neat little bundle back into the despatch-case.

"One wonders how an able man like that can allow himself to get besotted over a woman. It was the last thing I ever expected of him."

Ashenden's eyes travelled to the bowl of beautiful roses that stood on the table, but he said nothing. R. who missed little, saw the glance and his look suddenly darkened. Ashenden knew that he felt like asking him what the devil he was staring at. At that moment R. had no friendly feelings towards his subordinate, but he made no remark. He went back to the subject in hand.

"Anyhow that's neither here nor there. Chandra has fallen madly in love with a woman called Giulia Lazzari. He's crazy about her."

"Do you know how he picked her up?"

"Of course I do. She's a dancer, and she does Spanish dances, but she happens to be an Italian. For stage purposes she calls herself La Malagueña. You know the kind of thing. Popular Spanish music and a mantilla, a fan and a high comb. She's been dancing all over Europe for the last ten years."

"Is she any good?"

"No, rotten. She's been in the provinces in England and she's had a few engagements in London. She never got more than ten pounds a week. Chandra met her in Berlin in a Tingel-tangel, you know what that is, a cheap sort of music-hall. I take it that on the Continent she looked upon her dancing chiefly as a means to enhance her value as a prostitute."

"How did she get to Berlin during the war?"

"She's been married to a Spaniard at one time; I think she still is though they don't live together, and she travelled on a Spanish passport. It appears Chandra made a dead set for her." R. took up the Indian's photograph again and looked at it thoughtfully. "You wouldn't have thought there was anything very attractive in that greasy little nigger. God, how they run to fat! The fact remains that she fell very nearly as much in love with him as he did with her. I've got her letters too, only copies, of course, he's got the originals and I dare say he keeps them tied up in pink ribbon. She's mad about him. I'm not a literary man, but I think I know when a thing rings true; anyhow you'll be reading them, and you can tell me what you think. And then people say there's no such thing as love at first sight."

R. smiled with faint irony. He was certainly in a good humour this morning.

"But how did you get hold of all these letters?"

"How did I get hold of them? How do you imagine? Owing to her Italian nationality Giulia Lazzari was eventually expelled from Germany. She was put over the Dutch frontier. Having an engagement to dance in England she was granted a visa and"—R. looked up a date among the papers—"and on the twenty-fourth of October last sailed from Rotterdam to Harwich. Since then she has danced in London, Birmingham, Portsmouth and other places. She was arrested a fortnight ago at Hull."

"What for?"

"Espionage. She was transferred to London and I went to see her myself at Holloway."

Ashenden and R. looked at one another for a moment without speaking and it may be that each was trying his hardest to read the other's thoughts. Ashenden was wondering where the truth in all this lay and R. wondered how much of it he could advantageously tell him.

"How did you get on to her?"

"I thought it odd that the Germans should allow her to dance quite quietly in Berlin for weeks and then for no particular reason decide to put her out of the country. It would be a good introduction for espionage. And a dancer who was not too careful of her virtue might make opportunities of learning things that it would be worth somebody's while in Berlin to pay a good price for. I thought it might be as well to let her come to England and see what she was up to. I kept track of her. I discovered that she was sending letters to an address in Holland two or three times a week and two or three times a week was receiving answers from Holland. Hers were written in a queer mixture of French, German and English; she speaks English a little and French quite well, but the answers were written entirely in English; it was good English, but not an Englishman's English, flowery and rather grandiloquent; I wondered who was writing them. They seemed to be just ordinary love-letters, but they were by way of being rather hot stuff. It was plain enough that they were coming from Germany and the writer was neither English, French nor German. Why did he write in English? The only foreigners who know English better than any continental language are Orientals, and not Turks or Egyptians either; they know French. A Jap would write English and so would an Indian. I came to the conclusion that Giulia's lover was one of that gang of Indians that were making trouble for us in Berlin. I had no idea it was Chandra Lal till I found the photograph."

"How did you get that?"

"She carried it about with her. It was a pretty good bit of work, that. She kept it locked up in her trunk, with a lot of theatrical photographs, of comic singers and clowns and acrobats; it might easily have passed for the picture of some music-hall artiste in his stage dress. In fact, later, when she was arrested and asked who the photograph represented she said she didn't know, it was an Indian conjuror who had given it her and she had no idea what his name was. Anyhow I put a very smart lad on the job and he thought it queer that it should be the only photograph in the lot that came from Calcutta. He noticed that there was a number on the back, and he took it, the number, I mean; of course the photograph was replaced in the box."

"By the way, just as a matter of interest how did your very smart lad get at the photograph at all?"

R.'s eyes twinkled.

"That's none of your business. But I don't mind telling you that he was a good-looking boy. Anyhow it's of no consequence. When we got the number of the photograph we cabled to Calcutta and in a little while I received the grateful news that the object of Giulia's affections was no less a person than the incorruptible Chandra Lal. Then I thought it my duty to have Giulia watched a little more carefully. She seemed to have a sneaking fondness for naval officers. I couldn't exactly blame her for that; they are attractive, but it is unwise for ladies of easy virtue and doubtful nationality to cultivate their society in war-time. Presently I got a very pretty little body of evidence against her."

"How was she getting her stuff through?"

"She wasn't getting it through. She wasn't trying to. The Germans had turned her out quite genuinely; she wasn't working for them, she was working for Chandra. After her engagement was through in England she was planning to go to Holland again and meet him. She wasn't very clever at the work; she was nervous, but it looked easy; no one seemed to bother about her, it grew rather exciting; she was getting all sorts of interesting information without any risk. In one of her letters she said: 'I have so much to tell you, *mon petit chou* darling, and what you will be *extrêmement intéressé* to know," and she underlined the French words."

R. paused and rubbed his hands together. His tired face bore a look of devilish enjoyment of his own cunning.

"It was espionage made easy. Of course, I didn't care a damn about her, it was him I was after. Well, as soon as I'd got the goods on her I arrested her. I had enough evidence to convict a regiment of spies."

R. put his hands in his pockets and his pale lips twisted to a smile that was almost a grimace.

"Holloway's not a very cheerful place, you know."

"I imagine no prison is," remarked Ashenden.

"I left her to stew in her own juice for a week before I went to see her. She was in a very pretty state of nerves by then. The wardress told me she'd been in violent hysterics most of the time. I must say she looked like the devil."

"Is she handsome?"

"You'll see for yourself. She's not my type. I dare say she's better when she's made up and that kind of thing. I talked to her like a Dutch uncle. I put the fear of God into her. I told her she'd get ten years. I think I scared her, I know I tried to. Of course she denied everything, but the proofs were there, I assured her she hadn't got a chance. I spent three hours with her. She went all to pieces and at last she confessed everything. Then I told her that I'd let her go scot-free if she'd get Chandra to come to France. She absolutely refused, she said she'd rather die; she was very hysterical and tiresome, but I let her rave. I told her to think it over and said I'd see her in a day or two and we'd have another talk about it. In point of fact I left her for a week. She'd evidently had time to reflect, because when I came again she asked me quite calmly what it was exactly that I proposed. She'd been in gaol a fortnight then and I expect she'd had about enough of it. I put it to her as plainly as I could and she accepted."

"I don't think I quite understand," said Ashenden.

"Don't you? I should have thought it was clear to the meanest intelligence. If she can get Chandra to cross the Swiss frontier and come into France she's to go free, either to Spain or to South America, with her passage paid."

"And how the devil is she to get Chandra to do that?"

"He's madly in love with her. He's longing to see her. His letters are almost crazy. She's written to him to say that she can't get a visa to Holland (I told you she was to join him there when her tour was over), but she can get one for Switzerland. That's a neutral country and he's safe there. He jumped at the chance. They've arranged to meet at Lausanne."

"Yes."

"When he reaches Lausanne he'll get a letter from her to say that the French authorities won't let her cross the frontier and that she's going to Thonon, which is just on the other side of the lake from Lausanne, in France, and she's going to ask him to come there."

"What makes you think he will?"

R. paused for an instant. He looked at Ashenden with a pleasant expression.

"She must make him if she doesn't want to go to penal servitude for ten years."

"I see."

"She's arriving from England this evening in custody and I should like you to take her down to Thonon by the night train."

"Me?" said Ashenden.

"Yes, I thought it the sort of job you could manage very well. Presumably you know more about human nature than most people. It'll be a pleasant change for you to spend a week or two at Thonon. I believe it's a pretty little place, fashionable too—in peace-time. You might take the baths there."

"And what do you expect me to do when I get the lady down to Thonon?"

"I leave you a free hand. I've made a few notes that may be useful to you. I'll read them to you, shall I?"

Ashenden listened attentively. R.'s plan was simple and explicit. Ashenden could not but feel unwilling admiration for the brain that had so neatly devised it.

Presently R. suggested that they should have luncheon and he asked Ashenden to take him to some place where they could see smart people. It amused Ashenden to see R., so sharp, sure of himself and alert in his office, seized as he walked into the restaurant with shyness. He talked a little too loud in order to show that he was at his ease and made himself somewhat unnecessarily at home. You saw in his manner the shabby and commonplace life he had led till the hazards of war raised him to a position of consequence. He was glad to be in that fashionable restaurant cheek by jowl with persons who bore great or distinguished names, but he felt like a schoolboy in his first top-hat, and he quailed before the steely eye of the *maître d'hôtel*. His quick glance darted here and there and his sallow face beamed with a self-satisfaction of which he was slightly ashamed. Ashenden drew his attention to an ugly woman in black, with a lovely figure, wearing a long row of pearls.

"That is Madame de Brides. She is the mistress of the Grand Duke Theodore. She's probably one of the most influential women in Europe, she's certainly one of the cleverest."

R.'s clever eyes rested on her and he flushed a little.

"By George, this is life," he said.

Ashenden watched him curiously. Luxury is dangerous to people who have never known it and to whom its temptations are held out too suddenly. R., that shrewd, cynical man, was captivated by the vulgar glamour and the shoddy brilliance of the scene before him. Just as the advantage of culture is that it enables you to talk nonsense with distinction, so the habit of luxury allows you to regard its frills and furbelows with a proper contumely.

But when they had eaten their luncheon and were drinking their coffee Ashenden, seeing that R. was mellowed by the good meal and his surroundings, went back to the subject that was in his thoughts.

"That Indian fellow must be a rather remarkable chap," he said.

"He's got brains, of course."

"One can't help being impressed by a man who had the courage to take on almost single-handed the whole British power in India."

"I wouldn't get sentimental about him if I were you. He's nothing but a dangerous criminal."

"I don't suppose he'd use bombs if he could command a few batteries and half a dozen battalions. He uses what weapons he can. You can hardly blame him for that. After all, he's aiming at nothing for himself, is he? He's aiming at freedom for his country. On the face of it it looks as though he were justified in his actions."

But R. had no notion of what Ashenden was talking.

"That's very far-fetched and morbid," he said. "We can't go into all that. Our job is to get him and when we've got him to shoot him."

"Of course. He's declared war and he must take his chance. I shall carry out your instructions, that's what I'm here for, but I see no harm in realising that there's something to be admired and respected in him."

R. was once more the cool and astute judge of his fellows.

"I've not yet made up my mind whether the best men for this kind of job are those who do it with passion or those who keep their heads. Some of them are filled with hatred for the people we're up against and when we down them it gives them a sort of satisfaction like satisfying a personal grudge. Of course they're very keen on their work. You're different, aren't you? You look at it like a game of chess and you don't seem to have any feeling one way or the other. I can't quite make it out. Of course for some sort of jobs it's just what one wants."

Ashenden did not answer. He called for the bill and walked back with R. to the hotel.

The train started at eight. When he had disposed of his bag Ashenden walked along the platform. He found the carriage in which Giulia Lazzari was, but she sat in a corner, looking away from the light, so that he could not see her face. She was in charge of two detectives who had taken her over from English police at Boulogne. One of them worked with Ashenden on the French side of the Lake Geneva and as Ashdenen came up he nodded to him.

"I've asked the lady if she will dine in the restaurant-car, but she prefers to have dinner in the carriage, so I've ordered a basket. Is that quite correct?"

"Quite," said Ashenden.

"My companion and I will go into the diner in turn so that she will not remain alone."

"That is very considerate of you. I will come along when we've started and have a chat with her."

"She's not disposed to be very talkative," said the detective.

"One could hardly expect it," replied Ashenden.

He walked on to get his ticket for the second service and then returned to his own carriage. Giulia Lazzari was just finishing her meal when he went back to her. From a glance at the basket he judged that she had not eaten with too poor an appetite. The detective who was guarding her opened the door when Ashenden appeared and at Ashenden's suggestion left them alone.

Giulia Lazzari gave him a sullen look.

"I hope you've had what you wanted for dinner," he said as he sat down in front of her.

She bowed slightly, but did not speak. He took out his case.

"Will you have a cigarette?"

She gave him a glance, seemed to hesitate, and then, still without a word, took one. He struck a match and, lighting it, looked at her. He was surprised. For some reason he had expected her to be fair, perhaps from some notion that an Oriental would be more likely to fall for a blonde; but she was almost swarthy. Her hair was hidden by a close-fitting hat, but her eyes were coal-black. She was far from young, she might have been thirty-five, and her skin was lined and sallow. She had at the moment no make-up on and she looked haggard. There was nothing beautiful about her but her magnificent eyes. She was big, and Ashenden thought she must be too big to dance gracefully; it might be that in Spanish costume she was a bold and flaunting figure, but there in the train, shabbily dressed, there was nothing to explain the Indian's infatuation. She gave Ashenden a long, appraising stare. She wondered evidently what sort of man he was. She blew a cloud of smoke through her nostrils and gave it a glance, then looked back at Ashenden. He could see that her sullenness was only a mask, she was nervous and frightened. She spoke in French with an Italian accent.

"Who are you?"

"My name would mean nothing to you, *madame*. I am going to Thonon. I have taken a room for you at the Hotel de la Place. It is the only one open now. I think you will find it quite comfortable."

"Ah, it is you the Colonel spoke to me of. You are my gaoler."

"Only as a matter of form. I shall not intrude upon you."

"All the same you are my gaoler."

"I hope not for very long. I have in my pocket your passport with all the formalities completed to permit you to go to Spain."

She threw herself back into the corner of the carriage. White with those great black eyes, in the poor light, her face was suddenly a mask of despair.

"It's infamous. Oh, I think I could die happy if I could only kill that old Colonel. He has no heart. I'm so unhappy."

"I am afraid you have got yourself into a very unfortunate situation. Did you not know that espionage was a dangerous game?"

"I never sold any of the secrets. I did no harm."

"Surely only because you had no opportunity. I understand that you signed a full confession."

Ashenden spoke to her as amiably as he could, a little as though he were talking to a sick person, and there was no harshness in his voice.

"Oh, yes, I made a fool of myself. I wrote the letter the Colonel said I was to write. Why isn't that enough? What is to happen to me if he does not answer? I cannot force him to come if he does not want to."

"He has answered," said Ashenden. "I have the answer with me."

She gave a gasp and her voice broke.

"Oh, show it to me, I beseech you to let me see it."

"I have no objection to doing that. But you must return it to me."

He took Chandra's letter from his pocket and gave it to her. She snatched it from his hand. She devoured it with her eyes, there were eight pages of it, and as she read the tears streamed down her cheeks. Between her sobs she gave little exclamations of love, calling the writer by pet names French and Italian. This was the letter that Chandra had written in reply to hers telling him, on R.'s instructions, that she would meet him in Switzerland. He was mad with joy at the prospect. He told her in passionate phrases how long the time had seemed to him since they were parted, and how he had yearned for her, and now that he was to see her again so soon he did not know how he was going to bear his impatience. She finished it and let it drop to the floor.

"You can see he loves me, can't you? There's no doubt about that. I know something about it, believe me."

"Do you really love him?" asked Ashenden.

"He's the only man who's ever been kind to me. It's not very gay, the life one leads in these music-halls, all over Europe, never resting, and men—they are not much, the men who haunt those places. At first I thought he was just like the rest of them."

Ashenden picked up the letter and replaced it in his pocket-book.

"A telegram was sent in your name to the address in Holland to say that you would be at the Hotel Gibbons at Lausanne on the fourteenth."

"That is to-morrow."

"Yes."

She threw up her head and her eyes flashed.

"Oh, it is an infamous thing that you are forcing me to do. It is shameful."

"You are not obliged to do it," said Ashenden.

"And if I don't?"

"I'm afraid you must take the consequences."

"I can't go to prison," she cried out suddenly, "I can't, I can't; I have such a short time before me; he said ten years. Is it possible I could be sentenced to ten years?"

"If the Colonel told you so it is very possible."

"Oh, I know him. That cruel face. He would have no mercy. And what should I be in ten years? Oh, no no."

At that moment the train stopped at a station and the detective waiting in the corridor tapped on the window. Ashenden opened the door and the man gave him a picture-postcard. It was a dull little view of Pontarlier, the frontier station between France and Switzerland, and showed a dusty *place* with a statue in the middle and a few plane-trees. Ashenden handed her a pencil.

"Will you write this postcard to your lover? It will be posted at Pontarlier. Address it to the hotel at Lausanne."

She gave him a glance, but without answering took it and wrote as he directed.

"Now on the other side write: 'Delayed at frontier but everything all right. Wait at Lausanne.' Then add whatever you like, *tendresses*, if you like."

He took the postcard from her, read it to see that she had done as he directed and then reached for his hat.

"Well, I shall leave you now; I hope you will have a sleep. I will fetch you in the morning when we arrive at Thonon."

The second detective had now returned from his dinner and as Ashenden came out of the carriage the two men went in. Giulia Lazzari huddled back into her corner. Ashenden gave the postcard to an agent who was waiting to take it to Pontarlier and then made his way along the crowded train to his sleeping-car.

It was bright and sunny, though cold, next morning when they reached their destination. Ashenden, having given his bags to a porter, walked along the platform to where Giulia Lazzari and the two detectives were standing. Ashenden nodded to them.

"Well, good-morning. You need not trouble to wait."

They touched their hats, gave a word of farewell to the woman, and walked away.

"Where are they going?" she asked.

"Off. You will not be bothered with them any more."

"Am I in your custody, then?"

"You're in nobody's custody. I'm going to permit myself to take you to your hotel and then I shall leave you. You must try to get a good rest."

Ashenden's porter took her hand-luggage and she gave him the ticket for her trunk. They walked out of the station. A cab was waiting for them and Ashenden begged her to get in. It was a longish drive to the hotel and now and then Ashenden felt that she gave him a sidelong glance. She was perplexed. He sat without a word. When they reached the hotel the proprietor—it was a small hotel, prettily situated at the corner of a little promenade, and it had a charming view—showed them the room that had been prepared for Madame Lazzari. Ashenden turned to him.

"That'll do very nicely, I think. I shall come down in a minute."

The proprietor bowed and withdrew.

"I shall do my best to see that you are comfortable, *madame*," said Ashenden. "You are here absolutely your own mistress and you may order pretty well anything you like. To the proprietor you are just a guest of the hotel like any other. You are absolutely free."

"Free to go out?" she asked quickly.

"Of course."

"With a policeman on either side of me, I suppose."

"Not at all. You are as free in the hotel as though you were in your own house and you are free to go out and come in when you choose. I should like an assurance from you that you will not write letters without my knowledge or attempt to leave Thonon without my permission."

She gave Ashenden a long stare. She could not make it out at all. She looked as though she thought it a dream.

"I am in a position that forces me to give you any assurance you ask. I give you my word of honour that I will not write a letter without showing it to you or attempt to leave this place."

"Thank you. Now I will leave you. I will do myself the pleasure of coming to see you to-morrow morning."

Ashenden nodded and went out. He stopped for five minutes at the police-station to see that everything was in order and then took the cab up the hill to a little secluded house on the outskirts of the town at which on his periodical visits to this place he stayed. It was pleasant to have a bath and a shave and get into slippers. He felt lazy and spent the rest of the morning reading a novel.

Soon after dark, for even at Thonon, though it was in France, it was thought desirable to attract attention to Ashenden as little as possible, an agent from the police-station came to see him. His name was Felix. He was a little dark Frenchman with sharp eyes and an unshaven chin, dressed in a shabby grey suit and rather down at heel, so that he looked like a lawyer's clerk out of work. Ashenden offered him a glass of wine and they sat down by the fire.

"Well, your lady lost no time," he said. "Within a quarter of an hour of her arrival she was out of the hotel with a bundle of clothes and trinkets that she sold in a shop near the market. When the afternoon boat came in she went down to the quay and bought a ticket to Evian."

Evian, it should be explained, was the next place along the lake in France and from there, crossing over, the boat went to Switzerland.

"Of course she hadn't a passport, so permission to embark was denied her."

"How did she explain that she had no passport?"

"She said she'd forgotten it. She said she had an appointment to see friends in Evian and tried to persuade the official in charge to let her go. She attempted to slip a hundred francs into his hand."

"She must be a stupider woman than I thought," said Ashenden.

But when next day he went about eleven in the morning to see her he made no reference to her attempt to escape. She had had time to arrange herself, and now, her hair elaborately done, her lips and cheeks painted, she looked less haggard than when he had first seen her.

"I've brought you some books," said Ashenden. "I'm afraid the time hangs heavy on your hands."

"What does that matter to you?"

"I have no wish that you should suffer anything that can be avoided. Anyhow, I will leave them and you can read them or not as you choose."

"If you only knew how I hated you."

"It would doubtless make me very uncomfortable. But I really don't know why you should. I am only doing what I have been ordered to do."

"What do you want of me now? I do not suppose you have come only to ask after my health."

Ashenden smiled.

"I want you to write a letter to your lover telling him that owing to some irregularity in your passport the Swiss authorities would not let you cross the frontier, so you have come here where it is very nice and quiet, so quiet that one can hardly realise there is a war, and you propose that Chandra should join you."

"Do you think he is a fool? He will refuse."

"Then you must do your best to persuade him."

She looked at Ashenden a long time before she answered. He suspected that she was debating within herself whether by writing the letter and so seeming docile she could not gain time.

"Well, dictate and I will write what you say."

"I should prefer you to put it in your own words."

"Give me half an hour and the letter shall be ready."

"I will wait here," said Ashenden.

"Why?"

"Because I prefer to."

Her eyes flashed angrily, but controlling herself she said nothing. On the chest of drawers were writing materials. She sat down at the dressing-table and began to write. When she handed Ashenden the letter he saw that even through her rouge she was very pale. It was the letter of a person not much used to expressing herself by means of pen and ink, but it was well enough, and when towards the end, starting to say how much she loved the man, she had been carried away and wrote with all her heart, it had really a certain passion.

"Now add: The man who is bringing this is Swiss, you can trust him absolutely. I didn't want the censor to see it."

She hesitated an instant, but then wrote as he directed.

"How do you spell, absolutely?"

"As you like. Now address an envelope and I will relieve you of my unwelcome presence."

He gave the letter to the agent who was waiting to take it across the lake. Ashenden brought her the reply the same evening. She snatched it from his hands and for a moment pressed it to her heart. When she read it she uttered a little cry of relief.

"He won't come."

The letter, in the Indian's flowery, stilted English, expressed his bitter disappointment. He told her how intensely he had looked forward to seeing her and implored her to do everything in the world to smooth the difficulties that prevented her from crossing the frontier. He said that it was impossible for him to come, impossible, there was a price on his head, and it would be madness for him to think of risking it. He attempted to be jocular, she did not want her little fat lover to be shot, did she?

"He won't come," she repeated, "he won't come."

"You must write and tell him that there is no risk. You must say that if there were you would not dream of asking him. You must say that if he loves you he will not hesitate."

"I won't. I won't."

"Don't be a fool. You can't help yourself."

She burst into a sudden flood of tears. She flung herself on the floor and seizing Ashenden's knees implored him to have mercy on her.

"I will do anything in the world for you if you will let me go."

"Don't be absurd," said Ashenden. "Do you think I want to become your lover? Come, come, you must be serious. You know the alternative."

She raised herself to her feet and changing on a sudden to fury flung at Ashenden one foul name after another.

"I like you much better like that," he said. "Now will you write or shall I send for the police?"

"He will not come. It is useless."

"It is very much to your interest to make him come."

"What do you mean by that? Do you mean that if I do everything in my power and fail, that . . ."

She looked at Ashenden with wild eyes.

"Yes, it means either you or him."

She staggered. She put her hand to her heart. Then without a word she reached for pen and paper. But the letter was not to Ashenden's liking and he made her write it again. When she had finished she flung herself on the bed and burst once more into passionate weeping. Her grief was real, but there was something theatrical in the expression of it that prevented it from being peculiarly moving to Ashenden. He felt his relation to her as impersonal as a doctor's in the presence of a pain that he cannot alleviate. He saw now why R. had given him this peculiar task; it needed a cool head and an emotion well under control.

He did not see her next day. The answer to the letter was not delivered to him till after dinner, when it was brought to Ashenden's little house by Felix.

"Well, what news have you?"

"Our friend is getting desperate," smiled the Frenchman. "This afternoon she walked up to the station just as a train was about to start for Lyons. She was looking up and down uncertainly so I went to her and asked if there was anything I could do. I introduced myself as an agent of the Sûreté. If looks could kill I should not be standing here now."

"Sit down, *mon ami*," said Ashenden.

"*Merci*. She walked away, she evidently thought it was no use to try to get on the train, but I have something more interesting to tell you. She has offered a boatman on the lake a thousand francs to take her across to Lausanne."

"What did he say to her?"

"He said he couldn't risk it."

"Yes?"

The little agent gave his shoulders a slight shrug and smiled.

"She's asked him to meet her on the road that leads to Evian at ten o'clock to-night so that they can talk of it again, and she's given him to understand that she will not repulse too fiercely the advances of a lover. I have told him to do what he likes so long as he comes and tells me everything that is of importance."

"Are you sure you can trust him?" asked Ashenden.

"Oh, quite. He knows nothing, of course, but that she is under surveillance. You need have no fear about him. He is a good boy. I have known him all his life."

Ashenden read Chandra's letter. It was eager and passionate. It throbbed strangely with the painful yearning of his heart. Love? Yes, if Ashenden knew anything of it there was the real thing. He told her how he spent the long hours walking by the lakeside and looking towards the coast of France. How near they were and yet so desperately parted! He repeated again and again that he could not come, and begged her not to ask him, he would do everything in the world for her, but that he dared not do, and yet if she insisted how could he resist her? He besought her to have mercy on him. And then he broke into a long wail at the thought that he must go away without seeing her, he asked her if there were not some means by which she could slip over, he swore that if he could ever hold her in his arms again he would never let her go. Even the forced and elaborate language in which it was written could not dim the hot fire that burned the pages; it was the letter of a madman.

"When will you hear the result of her interview with the boatman?" asked Ashenden.

"I have arranged to meet him at the landing-stage between eleven and twelve."

Ashenden looked at his watch.

"I will come with you."

They walked down the hill and reaching the quay for shelter from the cold wind stood in the lee of the custom-house. At last they saw a man approaching and Felix stepped out of the shadow that hid them.

"Antoine."

"*Monsieur Félix?* I have a letter for you; I promised to take it to Lausanne by the first boat to-morrow."

Ashenden gave the man a brief glance, but did not ask what had passed between him and Giulia Lazzari. He took the letter and by the light of Felix's electric torch read it. It was in faulty German.

"*On no account come. Pay no attention to my letters. Danger. I love you. Sweetheart. Don't come.*"

He put it in his pocket, gave the boatman fifty francs, and went home to bed. But the next day when he went to see Giulia Lazzari he found her door locked. He knocked for some time, there was no answer. He called her.

"Madame Lazzari, you must open the door. I want to speak to you."

"I am in bed. I am ill and can see no one."

"I am sorry, but you must open the door. If you are ill I will send for a doctor."

"No, go away. I will see no one."

"If you do not open the door I shall send for a locksmith and have it broken open."

There was a silence and then he heard the key turned in the lock. He went in. She was in a dressing-gown and her hair was dishevelled. She had evidently just got out of bed.

"I am at the end of my strength. I can do nothing more. You have only to look at me to see that I am ill. I have been sick all night."

"I shall not keep you long. Would you like to see a doctor?"

"What good can a doctor do me?"

He took out of his pocket the letter she had given the boatman and handed it to her.

"What is the meaning of this?" he asked.

She gave a gasp at the sight of it and her sallow face went green.

"You gave me your word that you would neither attempt to escape nor write a letter without my knowledge."

"Did you think I would keep my word?" she cried, her voice ringing with scorn.

"No. To tell you the truth it was not entirely for your convenience that you were placed in a comfortable hotel rather than in the local gaol, but I think I should tell you that though you have your freedom to go in and out as you like you have no more chance of getting away from Thonon than if you were chained by the leg in a prison cell. It is silly to waste your time writing letters that will never be delivered."

"*Cochon.*"

She flung the opprobrious word at him with all the violence that was in her.

"But you must sit down and write a letter that *will* be delivered."

"Never. I will do nothing more. I will not write another word."

"You came here on the understanding that you would do certain things."

"I will not do them. It is finished."

"You had better reflect a little."

"Reflect! I have reflected. You can do what you like; I don't care."

"Very well, I will give you five minutes to change your mind."

Ashenden took out his watch and looked at it. He sat down on the edge of the unmade bed.

"Oh, it has got on my nerves, this hotel. Why did you not put me in the prison? Why, why? Everywhere I went I felt that spies were on my heels. It is infamous what you are making me do. Infamous! What is my crime? I ask you, what have I done? Am I not a woman? It is infamous what you are asking me to do. Infamous."

She spoke in a high shrill voice. She went on and on. At last the five minutes were up. Ashenden had not said a word. He rose.

"Yes, go, go," she shrieked at him.

She flung foul names at him.

"I shall come back," said Ashenden.

He took the key out of the door as he went out of the room and locked it behind him. Going downstairs he hurriedly scribbled a note, called the boots and despatched him with it to the police-station. Then he went up again. Giulia Lazzari had thrown herself on her bed and turned her face to the wall. Her body was shaken with hysterical sobs. She gave no sign that she heard him come in. Ashenden sat down on the chair in front of the dressing-table and looked idly at the odds and ends that littered it. The toilet things were cheap and tawdry and none too clean. There were little shabby pots of rouge and cold-cream and little bottles of black for the eye-brows and eyelashes. The hairpins were horrid and greasy. The room was untidy and the air was heavy with the smell of cheap scent. Ashenden thought of the hundreds of rooms she must have occupied in third-rate hotels in the course of her wandering life from provincial town to provincial town in one country after another. He wondered what had been her origins. She was a coarse and vulgar woman, but what had she been when young? She was not the type he would have expected to adopt that career, for she seemed to have no advantages that could help her, and he asked himself whether she came of a family of entertainers (there are all over the world families in which for generations the members have become dancers or acrobats or comic singers) or whether she had fallen into the life accidentally through some lover in the business who had for a time made her his partner. And what men must she have known in all these years, the comrades of the shows she was in, the agents and managers who looked upon it as a perquisite of their position that they should enjoy her favours, the merchants or well-to-do tradesmen, the young sparks of the various towns she played in, who were attracted for the moment by the glamour of the dancer or the blatant sensuality of the woman! To her they were the paying customers and she accepted them indifferently as the recognised and admitted supplement to her miserable salary, but to them perhaps she was romance. In her bought arms they caught sight for a moment of the brilliant world of the capitals, and ever so distantly and however shoddily of the adventure and the glamour of a more spacious life.

There was a sudden knock at the door and Ashenden immediately cried out:

"*Entrez.*"

Giulia Lazzari sprang up in bed to a sitting posture.

"Who is it?" she called.

She gave a gasp as she saw the two detectives who had brought her from Boulogne and handed her over to Ashenden at Thonon.

"You! What do you want?" she shrieked.

"*Allons, levez vous,*" said one of them, and his voice had a sharp abruptness that suggested that he would put up with no nonsense.

"I'm afraid you must get up, Madame Lazzari," said Ashenden. "I am delivering you once more to the care of these gentlemen."

"How can I get up! I'm ill, I tell you. I cannot stand. Do you want to kill me?"

"If you won't dress yourself, we shall have to dress you, and I'm afraid we shouldn't do it very cleverly. Come, come, it's no good making a scene."

"Where are you going to take me?"

"They're going to take you back to England."

One of the detectives took hold of her arm.

"Don't touch me, don't come near me," she screamed furiously.

"Let her be," said Ashenden. "I'm sure she'll see the necessity of making as little trouble as possible."

"I'll dress myself."

Ashenden watched her as she took off her dressing-gown and slipped a dress over her head. She forced her feet into shoes obviously too small for her. She arranged her hair. Every now and then she gave the detectives a hurried, sullen glance. Ashenden wondered if she would have the nerve to go through with it. R. would call him a damned fool, but he almost wished she would. She went up to the dressing-table and Ashenden stood up in order to let her sit down. She greased her face quickly and then rubbed off the grease with a dirty towel, she powdered herself and made up her eyes. But her hand shook. The three men watched her in silence. She rubbed the rouge on her cheeks and painted her mouth. Then she crammed a hat down on her head. Ashenden made a gesture to the first detective and he took a pair of handcuffs out of his pocket and advanced towards her.

At the sight of them she started back violently and flung her arms wide.

"*Non, non, non. Je ne veux pas.* No, not them. No. No."

"Come, *ma fille,* don't be silly," said the detective roughly.

As though for protection (very much to his surprise) she flung her arms round Ashenden.

"Don't let them take me, have mercy on me; I can't, I can't."

Ashenden extricated himself as best he could.

"I can do nothing more for you."

The detective seized her wrists and was about to affix the handcuffs when with a great cry she threw herself down on the floor.

"I will do what you wish. I will do everything."

On a sign from Ashenden the detectives left the room. He waited for a little till she had regained a certain calm. She was lying on the floor, sobbing passionately. He raised her to her feet and made her sit down.

"What do you want me to do?" she gasped.

"I want you to write another letter to Chandra."

"My head is in a whirl. I could not put two phrases together. You must give me time."

But Ashenden felt that it was better to get her to write a letter while she was under the effect of her terror. He did not want to give her time to collect herself.

"I will dictate the letter to you. All you have to do is to write exactly what I tell you."

She gave a deep sigh, but took the pen and the paper and sat down before them at the dressing-table.

"If I do this and . . . and you succeed, how do I know that I shall be allowed to go free?"

"The Colonel promised that you should. You must take my word for it that I shall carry out his instructions."

"I *should* look a fool if I betrayed my friend and then went to prison for ten years."

"I'll tell you your best guarantee of our good faith. Except by reason of Chandra you are not of the smallest importance to us. Why should we put ourselves to the bother and expense of keeping you in prison when you can do us no harm?"

x

She reflected for an instant. She was composed now. It was as though, having exhausted her emotion, she had become on a sudden a sensible and practical woman.

"Tell me what you want me to write."

Ashenden hesitated. He thought he could put the letter more or less in the way she would naturally have put it, but he had to give it consideration. It must be neither fluent nor literary. He knew that in moments of emotion people are inclined to be melodramatic and stilted. In a book or on the stage this always rings false and the author has to make his people speak more simply and with less emphasis than in fact they do. It was a serious moment, but Ashenden felt that there were in it elements of the comic.

"I didn't know I loved a coward," he started. "If you loved me you couldn't hesitate when I ask you to come. . . . Underline *couldn't* twice." He went on: "When I promise you there is no danger. If you don't love me, you are right not to come. Don't come. Go back to Berlin where you are in safety. I am sick of it. I am alone here. I have made myself ill by waiting for you and every day I have said he is coming. If you loved me you would not hesitate so much. It is quite clear to me that you do not love me. I am sick and tired of you. I have no money. This hotel is impossible. There is nothing for me to stay for. I can get an engagement in Paris. I have a friend there who has made me serious propositions. I have wasted long enough over you and look what I have got from it. It is finished. Good-bye. You will never find a woman who will love you as I have loved you. I cannot afford to refuse the proposition of my friend, so I have telegraphed to him and as soon as I shall receive his answer I go to Paris. I do not blame you because you do not love me, that is not your fault, but you must see that I should be a stupid to go on wasting my life. One is not young for ever. Good-bye. Giulia."

When Ashenden read over the letter he was not altogether satisfied. But it was the best he could do. It had an air of verisimilitude which the words lacked because, knowing little English, she had written phonetically, the spelling was atrocious and the handwriting like a child's; she had crossed out words and written them over again. Some of the phrases he had put in French. Once or twice tears had fallen on the pages and blurred the ink.

"I leave you now," said Ashenden. "It may be that when next you see me I shall be able to tell you that you are free to go where you choose. Where do you want to go?"

"Spain."

"Very well, I will have everything prepared."

She shrugged her shoulders. He left her.

There was nothing now for Ashenden to do but wait. He sent a messenger to Lausanne in the afternoon, and next morning went down to the quay to meet the boat. There was a waiting-room next to the ticket-office and here he told the detectives to hold themselves in readiness. When a boat arrived the passengers advanced along the pier in line and their passports were examined before they were allowed to go ashore. If Chandra came and showed his passport, and it was very likely that he was travelling with a false one, issued probably by a neutral nation, he was to be asked to wait and Ashenden was to identify him. Then he would be arrested. It was with some excitement that Ashenden watched the boat come in and the little group of people gathered at the gangway. He scanned them closely but saw no one who looked in the least like an Indian. Chandra had not come. Ashenden did not know what to do. He had played his last card. There were not more than half a dozen passengers for Thonon, and when they had been examined and gone their way he strolled along the pier.

"Well, it's no go," he said to Felix, who had been examining the passports. "The gentleman I expected hasn't turned up."

"I have a letter for you."

He handed Ashenden an envelope addressed to Madame Lazzari on which he immediately recognised the spidery handwriting of Chandra Lal. At that moment the steamer from Geneva which was going to Lausanne and the end of the lake hove in sight. It arrived at Thonon every morning twenty minutes after the steamer going in the opposite direction had left. Ashenden had an inspiration.

"Where is the man who brought it?"

"He's in the ticket-office."

"Give him the letter and tell him to return to the person who gave it to him. He is to say that he took it to the lady and she sent it back. If the person asks him to take another letter he is to say that it is not much good as she is packing her trunk and leaving Thonon."

He saw the letter handed over and the instructions given and then walked back to his little house in the country.

The next boat on which Chandra could possibly come arrived about five and having at that hour an important engagement with an agent working in Germany he warned Felix that he might be a few minutes late. But if Chandra came he could easily be detained; there was no great hurry since the train in which he was to be taken to Paris did not start till shortly after eight. When Ashenden had finished his business he strolled leisurely down to the lake. It was light still and from the top of the hill he saw the steamer pulling out.

It was an anxious moment and instinctively he quickened his steps. Suddenly he saw someone running towards him and recognised the man who had taken the letter.

"Quick, quick," he cried. "He's there."

Ashenden's heart gave a great thud against his chest.

"At last."

He began to run too and as they ran the man, panting, told him how he had taken back the unopened letter. When he put it in the Indian's hand he turned frightfully pale ("I should never have thought an Indian could turn that colour," he said), and turned it over and over in his hand as though he could not understand what his own letter was doing there. Tears sprang to his eyes and rolled down his cheeks. ("It was grotesque; he's fat, you know.") He said something in a language the man did not understand and then in French asked him when the boat went to Thonon. When he got on board he looked about, but did not see him, then he caught sight of him, huddled up in an ulster with his hat drawn down over his eyes, standing alone in the bows. During the crossing he kept his eyes fixed on Thonon.

"Where is he now?" asked Ashenden.

"I got off first and Monsieur Felix told me to come for you."

"I suppose they're holding him in the waiting-room."

Ashenden was out of breath when they reached the pier. He burst into the waiting-room. A group of men, talking at the top of their voices and gesticulating wildly, were clustered round a man lying on the ground.

"What's happened?" he cried.

"Look," said Monsieur Felix.

Chandra Lal lay there, his eyes wide open and a thin line of foam on his lips, dead. His body was horribly contorted.

"He's killed himself. We've sent for the doctor. He was too quick for us."

A sudden thrill of horror passed through Ashenden.

When the Indian landed Felix recognised from the description that he was the man they wanted. There were only four passengers. He was the last. Felix took an exaggerated time to examine the passports of the first three, and then took the Indian's. It was a Spanish one and it was all in order. Felix asked the regulation questions and noted them on the official sheet. Then he looked at him pleasantly and said:

"Just come into the waiting-room for a moment. There are one or two formalities to fulfil."

"Is my passport not in order?" the Indian asked.

"Perfectly."

Chandra hesitated, but then followed the official to the door of the waiting-room. Felix opened it and stood aside.

"*Entrez.*"

Chandra went in and the two detectives stood up. He must have suspected at once that they were police-officers and realised that he had fallen into a trap.

"Sit down," said Felix. "I have one or two questions to put to you."

"It is hot in here," he said, and in point of fact they had a little stove there that kept the place like an oven. "I will take off my coat if you permit."

"Certainly," said Felix graciously.

He took off his coat, apparently with some effort, and he turned to put it on a chair, and then before they realised what had happened they were startled to see him stagger and fall heavily to the ground. While taking off his coat Chandra had managed to swallow the contents of a bottle that was still clasped in his hand. Ashenden put his nose to it. There was a very distinct odour of almonds.

For a little while they looked at the man who lay on the floor. Felix was apologetic.

"Will they be very angry?" he asked nervously.

"I don't see that it was your fault," said Ashenden. "Anyhow, he can do no more harm. For my part I am just as glad he killed himself. The notion of his being executed did not make me very comfortable."

In a few minutes the doctor arrived and pronounced life extinct.

"Prussic acid," he said to Ashenden.

Ashenden nodded.

"I will go and see Madame Lazzari," he said. "If she wants to stay a day or two longer I shall let her. But if she wants to go to-night of course she can. Will you give the agents at the station instructions to let her pass?"

"I shall be at the station myself," said Felix.

Ashenden once more climbed the hill. It was night now, a cold, bright night with an unclouded sky, and the sight of the new moon, a white shining thread, made him turn three times the money in his pocket. When he entered the hotel he was seized on a sudden with distaste for its cold banality. It smelt of cabbage and boiled mutton. On the walls of the hall were coloured posters of railway companies advertising Grenoble, Carcassonne and the bathing places of Normandy. He went upstairs and after a brief knock opened the door of Giulia Lazzari's room. She was sitting in front of her dressing-table, looking at herself in the glass, just idly, despairingly, apparently doing nothing, and it was in this that she saw Ashenden as he came in. Her face changed suddenly as she caught sight of his and she sprang up so vehemently that the chair fell over.

"What is it? Why are you so white?" she cried.

She turned round and stared at him and her features were gradually twisted to a look of horror.

"*Il est pris*," she gasped.

"*Il est mort*," said Ashenden.

"Dead! He took the poison. He had the time for that. He's escaped you after all."

"What do you mean? How did you know about the poison?"

"He always carried it with him. He said that the English should never take him alive."

Ashenden reflected for an instant. She had kept that secret well. He supposed the possibility of such a thing should have occurred to him. How was he to anticipate these melodramatic devices?

"Well, now you are free. You can go wherever you like and no obstacle shall be put in your way. Here are your ticket and your passport and here is the money that was in your possession when you were arrested. Do you wish to see Chandra?"

She started.

"No, no."

"There is no need. I thought you might care to."

She did not weep. Ashenden supposed that she had exhausted all her emotion. She seemed apathetic.

"A telegram will be sent to-night to the Spanish frontier to instruct the authorities to put no difficulties in your way. If you will take my advice you will get out of France as soon as you can."

She said nothing, and since Ashenden had no more to say he made ready to go.

"I am sorry that I have had to show myself so hard to you. I am glad to think that now the worst of your troubles are over and I hope that time will assuage the grief that I know you must feel for the death of your friend."

Ashenden gave her a little bow and turned to the door. But she stopped him.

"One little moment," she said. "There is one thing I should like to ask. I think you have some heart."

"Whatever I can do for you, you may be sure I will."

"What are they going to do with his things?"

"I don't know. Why?"

Then she said something that confounded Ashenden. It was the last thing he expected.

"He had a wrist-watch that I gave him last Christmas. It cost twelve pounds. Can I have it back?"

The Traitor

WHEN Ashenden, given charge of a number of spies working from Switzerland, was first sent there, R., wishing him to see the sort of reports that he would be required to obtain, handed him the communications, a sheaf of typewritten documents, of a man known in the secret service as Gustav.

"He's the best fellow we've got," said R. "His information is always very full and circumstantial. I want you to give his reports your very best attention. Of course Gustav is a clever little chap, but there's no reason why we shouldn't get just as good reports from the other agents. It's merely a question of explaining exactly what we want."

Gustav, who lived at Basle, represented a Swiss firm with branches at Frankfort, Mannheim, and Cologne, and by virtue of his business was able to go in and out of Germany without risk. He travelled up and down the Rhine, and gathered material about the movement of troops, the manufacture of munitions, the state of mind of the country (a point on which R. laid stress) and other matters upon which the Allies desired information. His frequent letters to his wife hid an ingenious code and the moment she received them in Basle she sent them to Ashenden in Geneva, who extracted from them the important facts and communicated these in the proper quarter. Every two months Gustav came home and prepared one of the reports that served as models to the other spies in this particular section of the secret service.

His employers were pleased with Gustav and Gustav had reason to be pleased with his employers. His services were so useful that he was not only paid more highly than the others, but for particular scoops had received from time to time a handsome bonus.

This went on for more than a year. Then something aroused R.'s quick suspicions; he was a man of an amazing alertness, not so much of mind, as of instinct, and he had suddenly a feeling that some hanky-panky was going on. He said nothing definite to Ashenden (whatever R. surmised he was disposed to keep to himself), but told him to go to Basle, Gustav being then in Germany, and have a talk with Gustav's wife. He left it to Ashenden to decide the tenor of the conversation.

Having arrived at Basle, and leaving his bag at the station, for he did not yet know whether he would have to stay or not, he took a tram to the corner of the street in which Gustav lived and, with a quick look to see that he was not followed, walked along to the house he sought. It was a block of flats that gave you the impression of decent poverty and Ashenden conjectured that they were inhabited by clerks and small tradespeople. Just inside the door was a cobbler's shop and Ashenden stopped.

"Does Herr Grabow live here?" he asked in his none too fluent German.

"Yes, I saw him go up a few minutes ago. You'll find him in."

Ashenden was startled, for he had but the day before received through Gustav's wife a letter addressed from Mannheim in which Gustav by means of his code gave the numbers of certain regiments that had just crossed the Rhine. Ashenden thought it unwise to ask the cobbler the question that rose to his lips, so thanked him and went up to the third floor, on which he knew already that Gustav lived. He rang the bell and heard it tinkle within. In a moment the door was opened by a dapper little man with a close-shaven round head and spectacles. He wore carpet slippers.

"Herr Grabow?" asked Ashenden.

"At your service," said Gustav.

"May I come in?"

Gustav was standing with his back to the light and Ashenden could not see the look on his face. He felt a momentary hesitation and gave the name under which he received Gustav's letters from Germany.

"Come in, come in. I am very glad to see you."

Gustav led the way into a stuffy little room, heavy with carved oak furniture, and on the large table covered with a table-cloth of green velveteen was a typewriter. Gustav was apparently engaged in composing one of his invaluable reports. A woman was sitting at the open window, darning socks, but at a word from Gustav rose, gathered up her things and left. Ashenden had disturbed a pretty picture of connubial bliss.

"Sit down, please. How very fortunate that I was in Basle! I have long wanted to make your acquaintance. I have only just this minute returned from Germany." He pointed to the sheets of paper by the typewriter. "I think you will be pleased with the news I bring. I have some very valuable information." He chuckled. "One is never sorry to earn a bonus."

He was very cordial, but to Ashenden his cordiality rang false. Gustav kept his eyes, smiling behind the glasses, fixed watchfully on Ashenden, and it was possible that they held a trace of nervousness.

"You must have travelled quickly to get here only a few hours after your letter, sent here and then sent on by your wife, reached me in Geneva."

"That is very probable. One of the things I had to tell you is that the Germans suspect that information is getting through by means of commercial letters and so they have decided to hold up all mail at the frontier for eight-and-forty hours."

"I see," said Ashenden amiably. "And was it on that account that you took the precaution of dating your letter forty-eight hours after you sent it?"

"Did I do that? That was very stupid of me. I must have mistaken the day of the month."

Ashenden looked at Gustav with a smile. That was very thin; Gustav, a business man, knew too well how important in his particular job was the exactness of a date. The circuitous routes by which it was necessary to get information from Germany made it difficult to transmit news quickly and it was essential to know precisely on what days certain events had taken place.

"Let me look at your passport a minute," said Ashenden.

"What do you want with my passport?"

"I want to see when you went into Germany and when you came out."

"But you do not imagine that my comings and goings are marked on my passport? I have methods of crossing the frontier."

Ashenden knew a good deal of this matter. He knew that both the Germans and the Swiss guarded the fontier with severity.

"Oh? Why should you not cross in the ordinary way? You were engaged because your connection with a Swiss firm supplying necessary goods to Germany made it easy for you to travel backwards and forwards without suspicion. I can understand that you might get past the German sentries with the connivance of the Germans, but what about the Swiss?"

Gustav assumed a look of indignation.

"I do not understand you. Do you mean to suggest that I am in the service of the Germans? I give you my word of honour . . . I will not allow my integrity to be impugned."

"You would not be the only one to take money from both sides and provide information of value to neither."

"Do you pretend that my information is of no value? Why then have you given me more bonuses than any other agent has received? The Colonel has repeatedly expressed the highest satisfaction with my services."

It was Ashenden's turn now to be cordial.

"Come, come, my dear fellow, do not try to ride the high horse.

You do not wish to show me your passport and I will not insist. You are not under the impression that we leave the statements of our agents without corroboration or that we are so foolish as not to keep track of their movements? Even the best of jokes cannot bear an indefinite repetition. I am in peace-time a humorist by profession and I tell you that from bitter experience." Now Ashenden thought the moment had arrived to attempt his bluff; he knew something of the excellent but difficult game of poker. "We have information that you have not been to Germany now, nor since you were engaged by us, but have sat here quietly in Basle, and all your reports are merely due to your fertile imagination."

Gustav looked at Ashenden and saw a face expressive of nothing but tolerance and good-humour. A smile slowly broke on his lips and he gave his shoulders a little shrug.

"Did you think I was such a fool as to risk my life for fifty pounds a month? I love my wife."

Ashenden laughed outright.

"I congratulate you. It is not everyone who can flatter himself that he has made a fool of our secret service for a year."

"I had the chance of earning money without any difficulty. My firm stopped sending me into Germany at the beginning of the war, but I learned what I could from the other travellers. I kept my ears open in restaurants and beer-cellars, and I read the German papers. I got a lot of amusement out of sending you reports and letters."

"I don't wonder," said Ashenden.

"What are you going to do?"

"Nothing. What can we do? You are not under the impression that we shall continue to pay you a salary?"

"No, I cannot expect that."

"By the way, if it is not indiscreet, may I ask if you have been playing the same game with the Germans?"

"Oh, no," Gustav cried vehemently. "How can you think it? My sympathies are absolutely pro-Ally. My heart is entirely with you."

"Well, why not?" asked Ashenden. "The Germans have all the money in the world and there is no reason why you should not get some of it. We could give you information from time to time that the Germans would be prepared to pay for."

Gustav drummed his fingers on the table. He took up a sheet of the now useless report.

"The Germans are dangerous people to meddle with."

"You are a very intelligent man. And after all, even if your salary is stopped, you can always earn a bonus by bringing us news that can be useful to us. But it will have to be substantiated; in future we pay only by results."

"I will think of it."

For a moment or two Ashenden left Gustav to his reflections. He lit a cigarette and watched the smoke he had inhaled fade into the air. He thought too.

"Is there anything particular you want to know?" asked Gustav suddenly.

Ashenden smiled.

"It would be worth a couple of thousand Swiss francs to you if you could tell me what the Germans are doing with a spy of theirs in Lucerne. He is an Englishman and his name is Grantley Caypor."

"I have heard the name," said Gustav. He paused a moment. "How long are you staying here?"

"As long as necessary. I will take a room at the hotel and let you know the number. If you have anything to say to me you can be sure of finding me in my room at nine every morning and at seven every night."

"I should not risk coming to the hotel. But I can write."

"Very well."

Ashenden rose to go and Gustav accompanied him to the door.

"We part without ill-feeling then?" he asked.

"Of course. Your reports will remain in our archives as models of what a report should be."

Ashenden spent two or three days visiting Basle. It did not much amuse him. He passed a good deal of time in the book-shops turning over the pages of books that would have been worth reading if life were a thousand years long. Once he saw Gustav in the street. On the fourth morning a letter was brought up with his coffee. The envelope was that of a commercial firm unknown to him and inside it was a typewritten sheet. There was no address and no signature. Ashenden wondered if Gustav was aware that a typewriter could betray its owner as certainly as a handwriting. Having twice carefully read the letter, he held the paper up to the light to see the watermark (he had no reason for doing this except that the sleuths of detective novels always did it), then struck a match and watched it burn. He scrunched up the charred fragments in his hand.

He got up, for he had taken advantage of his situation to breakfast in bed, packed his bag and took the next train to Berne. From there he was able to send a code telegram to R. His instructions were given to him verbally two days later, in the bedroom of his hotel at an hour when no one was likely to be seen walking along a corridor, and within twenty-four hours, though by a circuitous route, he arrived at Lucerne.

Having taken a room at the hotel at which he had been instructed to stay, Ashenden went out; it was a lovely day, early in August, and the sun shone in an unclouded sky. He had not been to Lucerne since he was a boy and but vaguely remembered a covered bridge, a great stone lion and a church in which he had sat, bored yet impressed, while they played an organ; and now, wandering along a shady quay (and the lake looked just as tawdry and unreal as it looked on the picture-postcards), he tried not so much to find his way about a half-forgotten scene as to reform in his mind some recollection of the shy and eager lad, so impatient for life (which he saw not in the present of his adolescence but only in the future of his manhood), who so long ago had wandered there. But it seemed to him that the most vivid of his memories was not of himself, but of the crowd; he seemed to remember sun and heat and people; the train was crowded and so was the hotel, the lake steamers were packed and on the quays and in the streets you threaded your way among the throng of holiday-makers. They were fat and old and ugly and odd, and they stank. Now, in war-time, Lucerne was as deserted as it must have been before the world at large discovered that Switzerland was the playground of Europe. Most of the hotels were closed, the streets were empty, the rowing boats for hire rocked idly at the water's edge and there was none to take them, and in the avenues by the lake the only persons to be seen were serious Swiss taking their neutrality, like a dachshund, for a walk with them. Ashenden felt exhilarated by the solitude and, sitting down on a bench that faced the water, surrendered himself deliberately to the sensation. It was true that the lake was absurd, the water was too blue, the mountains too snowy, and its beauty, hitting you in the face, exasperated rather than thrilled; but all the same there was something pleasing in the prospect, an artless candour, like one of Mendelssohn's *Songs Without Words*, that made Ashenden smile with complacency. Lucerne reminded him of wax flowers under glass cases and cuckoo clocks and fancy-work in Berlin wool. So long at all events as the fine weather lasted he was prepared to enjoy himself. He did not see why he should not at least try to combine pleasure to himself with profit to his country. He was travelling with a brand-new passport in his pocket, under a borrowed name, and this gave him an agreeable sense of owning a new personality. He was often slightly tired of himself and it diverted him for a while to be merely a creature of R.'s facile invention. The experience he had just enjoyed appealed to his acute sense of the absurd. R., it is true, had not seen the fun of it: what humour R. possessed was of a sardonic turn and he had no facility for taking in good part a joke at his own expense. To do that you must be able to look at yourself from the outside and be at the same time spectator and actor in the pleasant comedy of life. R. was a soldier and regarded introspection as unhealthy, un-English and unpatriotic.

Ashenden got up and strolled slowly to his hotel. It was a small German hotel, of the second class, spotlessly clean, and his bedroom had a nice view; it was furnished with brightly varnished pitch-pine, and though on a cold wet day it would have been wretched, in that warm and sunny weather it was gay and pleasing. There were tables in the hall and he sat down at one of these and ordered a bottle of beer. The landlady was curious to know why in that dead season he had come to stay and he was glad to satisfy her curiosity. He told her that he had recently recovered from an attack of typhoid and had come to Lucerne to get back his strength. He was employed in the Censorship Department and was taking the opportunity to brush up his rusty German. He asked her if she could recommend to him a German teacher. The landlady was a blond and blowsy Swiss, good-humoured and talkative, so that Ashenden felt pretty sure that she would repeat in the proper quarter the information he gave her. It was his turn now to ask a few questions. She was voluble on the subject of the war on account of which the hotel, in that month so full that rooms had to be found for visitors in neighbouring houses, was nearly empty. A few people came in from outside to eat their meals *en pension* but she had only two lots of resident guests. One was an old Irish couple who lived in Vevey and passed their summers in Lucerne and the other was an Englishman and his wife. She was a German and they were obliged on that account to live in a neutral country. Ashenden took care to show little curiosity about them— he recognised in the description Grantley Caypor—but of her own accord she told him that they spent most of the day walking about the mountains. Herr Caypor was a botanist and much interested in the flora of the country. His lady was a very nice woman and she felt her position keenly. Ah, well, the war could not last for ever. The landlady bustled away and Ashenden went upstairs.

Dinner was at seven, and, wishing to be in the dining-room before anyone else so that he could take stock of his fellow-guests as they entered, he went down as soon as he heard the bell. It was a very plain, stiff, white-washed room, with chairs of the same shiny pitch-pine as in his bedroom, and on the walls were oleographs of Swiss lakes. On each little table was a bunch of flowers. It was all neat and clean and presaged a bad dinner. Ashenden would have liked to make up for it by ordering a bottle of the best Rhine wine to be found in the hotel, but did not venture to draw attention to himself by extravagance (he saw on two or three tables half-empty bottles of table hock, which made him surmise that his fellow-guests drank thriftily), and so contented himself with ordering a pint of lager. Presently one or two persons came in, single men with some occupation in Lucerne and obviously Swiss, and sat down each at his own little table and untied the napkins that at the end of luncheon they had neatly tied up. They propped newspapers against their water-jugs and read while they somewhat noisily ate their soup. Then entered a very old tall bent man, with white hair and a drooping white moustache, accompanied by a little old white-haired lady in black. These were certainly the Irish colonel and his wife of whom the landlady had spoken. They took their seats and the colonel poured out a thimbleful of wine for his wife and a thimbleful for himself. They waited in silence for their dinner to be served to them by the buxom, hearty maid.

At last the persons arrived for whom Ashenden had been waiting. He was doing his best to read a German book and it was only by an exercise of self-control that he allowed himself only for one instant to raise his eyes as they came in. His glance showed him a man of about forty-five with short dark hair, somewhat grizzled, of middle height, but corpulent, with a broad red clean-shaven face. He wore a shirt open at the neck, with a wide collar, and a grey suit. He walked ahead of his wife, and of her Ashenden only caught the impression of a German woman self-effaced and dusty. Grantley Caypor sat down and began in a loud voice explaining to the waitress that they had taken an immense walk. They had been up some mountain the name of which meant nothing to Ashenden, but which excited in the maid expressions of astonishment and enthusiasm. Then Caypor, still in fluent German but with a marked English accent, said that they were so late they had not even gone up to wash, but had just rinsed their hands outside. He had a resonant voice and a jovial manner.

"Serve me quick, we're starving with hunger, and bring beer, bring three bottles. *Lieber Gott*, what a thirst I have!"

He seemed to be a man of exuberant vitality. He brought into that dull, overclean dining-room the breath of life and everyone in it appeared on a sudden more alert. He began to talk to his wife, in English, and everything he said could be heard by all; but presently she interrupted him with a remark made in an undertone. Caypor stopped and Ashenden felt that his eyes were turned in his

direction. Mrs. Caypor had noticed the arrival of a stranger and
had drawn her husband's attention to it. Ashenden turned the page
of the book he was pretending to read, but he felt that Caypor's gaze
was fixed intently upon him. When he addressed his wife again it
was in so low a tone that Ashenden could not even tell what language
he used, but when the maid brought them their soup Caypor, his
voice still low, asked her a question. It was plain that he was inquiring who Ashenden was. Ashenden could catch of the maid's reply
but the one word *länder*.

One or two people finished their dinner and went out picking their
teeth. The old Irish colonel and his old wife rose from their table
and he stood aside to let her pass. They had eaten their meal without exchanging a word. She walked slowly to the door; but the
colonel stopped to say a word to a Swiss who might have been a local
attorney, and when she reached it she stood there, bowed and with
a sheep-like look, patiently waiting for her husband to come and
open it for her. Ashenden realised that she had never opened a door
for herself. She did not know how to. In a minute the colonel with
his old, old gait came to the door and opened it; she passed out and
he followed. The little incident offered a key to their whole lives,
and from it Ashenden began to reconstruct their histories, circumstances and characters; but he pulled himself up; he could not allow
himself the luxury of creation. He finished his dinner.

When he went into the hall he saw tied to the leg of a table a bull-
terrier and in passing mechanically put down his hand to fondle the
dog's drooping soft ears. The landlady was standing at the foot of
the stairs.

"Whose is this lovely beast?" asked Ashenden.

"He belongs to Herr Caypor. Fritzi, he is called. Herr Caypor
says he has a longer pedigree than the King of England."

Fritzi rubbed himself against Ashenden's leg and with his nose
sought the palm of his hand. Ashenden went upstairs to fetch his hat,
and when he came down saw Caypor standing at the entrance of
the hotel talking with the landlady. From the sudden silence and
their constrained manner he guessed that Caypor had been making
inquiries about him. When he passed between them, into the street,
out of the corner of his eye he saw Caypor give a suspicious stare.
That frank, jovial red face bore then a look of shifty cunning.

Ashenden strolled along till he found a tavern where he could have
his coffee in the open and to compensate himself for the bottle of
beer that his sense of duty had urged him to drink at dinner ordered
the best brandy the house provided. He was pleased at last to have
come face to face with the man of whom he had heard so much and

in a day or two hoped to become acquainted with him. It is never very difficult to get to know anyone who has a dog. But he was in no hurry; he would let things take their course: with the object he had in view he could not afford to be hasty.

Ashenden reviewed the circumstances. Grantley Caypor was an Englishman, born according to his passport in Birmingham, and he was forty-two years of age. His wife, to whom he had been married for eleven years, was of German birth and parentage. That was public knowledge. Information about his antecedents was contained in a private document. He had started life, according to this, in a lawyer's office in Birmingham and then had drifted into journalism. He had been connected with an English paper in Cairo and with another in Shanghai. There he got into trouble for attempting to get money on false pretences and was sentenced to a short term of imprisonment. All trace of him was lost for two years after his release, when he reappeared in a shipping office in Marseilles. From there, still in the shipping business, he went to Hamburg, where he married, and to London. In London he set up for himself in the export business, but after some time failed and was made a bankrupt. He returned to journalism. At the outbreak of war he was once more in the shipping business, and in August, 1914, was living quietly with his German wife at Southampton. In the beginning of the following year he told his employers that owing to the nationality of his wife his position was intolerable; they had no fault to find with him and, recognising that he was in an awkward fix, granted his request that he should be transferred to Genoa. Here he remained till Italy entered the war, but then gave notice and with his papers in perfect order crossed the border and took up his residence in Switzerland.

All this indicated a man of doubtful honesty and unsettled disposition, with no background and of no financial standing; but the facts were of no importance to anyone till it was discovered that Caypor, certainly from the beginning of the war and perhaps sooner, was in the service of the German Intelligence Department. He had a salary of forty pounds a month. But though dangerous and wily no steps would have been taken to deal with him if he had contented himself with transmitting such news as he was able to get in Switzerland. He could do no great harm there and it might even be possible to make use of him to convey information that it was desirable to let the enemy have. He had no notion that anything was known of him. His letters, and he received a good many, were closely censored; there were few codes that the people who dealt with such matters could not in the end decipher and it might be that

sooner or later through him it would be possible to lay hands on the
organisation that still flourished in England. But then he did
something that drew R.'s attention to him. Had he known it none
could have blamed him for shaking in his shoes: R. was not a very
nice man to get on the wrong side of. Caypor scraped acquaintance
in Zurich with a young Spaniard, Gomez by name, who had lately
entered the British secret service, by his nationality inspired him
with confidence, and managed to worm out of him the fact that he
was engaged in espionage. Probably the Spaniard, with a very
human desire to seem important, had done no more than talk mysteriously; but on Caypor's information he was watched when he went
to Germany and one day caught just as he was posting a letter in a
code that was eventually deciphered. He was tried, convicted and
shot. It was bad enough to lose a useful and disinterested agent, but
it entailed besides the changing of a safe and simple code. R. was
not pleased. But R. was not the man to let any desire of revenge
stand in the way of his main object, and it occurred to him that if
Caypor was merely betraying his country for money it might be
possible to get him to take more money to betray his employers.
The fact that he had succeeded in delivering into their hands an
agent of the Allies must seem to them an earnest of his good faith.
He might be very useful. But R. had no notion what kind of man
Caypor was, he had lived his shabby, furtive life obscurely, and the
only photograph that existed of him was one taken for a passport.
Ashenden's instructions were to get acquainted with Caypor and
see whether there was any chance that he would work honestly for
the British: if he thought there was, he was entitled to sound him
and if his suggestions were met with favour to make certain
propositions. It was a task that needed tact and a knowledge of men.
If on the other hand Ashenden came to the conclusion that Caypor
could not be bought, he was to watch and report his movements.
The information he had obtained from Gustav was vague, but
important; there was only one point in it that was interesting, and
this was that the head of the German Intelligence Department in
Berne was growing restive at Caypor's lack of activity. Caypor was
asking for a higher salary and Major von P. had told him that he
must earn it. It might be that he was urging him to go to England.
If he could be induced to cross the frontier Ashenden's work was
done.

"How the devil do you expect me to persuade him to put his head
in a noose?" asked Ashenden.

"It won't be a noose, it'll be a firing squad," said R.

"Caypor's clever."

"Well, be cleverer, damn your eyes."

Ashenden made up his mind that he would take no steps to make Caypor's acquaintance, but allow the first advances to be made by him. If he was being pressed for results it must surely occur to him that it would be worth while to get into conversation with an Englishman who was employed in the Censorship Department. Ashenden was prepared with a supply of information that it could not in the least benefit the Central Powers to possess. With a false name and a false passport he had little to fear that Caypor would guess that he was a British agent.

Ashenden did not have to wait long. Next day he was sitting in the doorway of the hotel, drinking a cup of coffee and already half asleep after a substantial *mittagessen*, when the Caypors came out of the dining-room. Mrs. Caypor went upstairs and Caypor released his dog. The dog bounded along and in a friendly fashion leaped up against Ashenden.

"Come here, Fritzi," cried Caypor, and then to Ashenden: "I'm so sorry. But he's quite gentle."

"Oh, that's all right. He won't hurt me."

Caypor stopped at the doorway.

"He's a bull-terrier. You don't often see them on the Continent." He seemed while he spoke to be taking Ashenden's measure; he called to the maid: "A coffee, please, *fräulein*. You've just arrived, haven't you?"

"Yes, I came yesterday."

"Really? I didn't see you in the dining-room last night. Are you making a stay?"

"I don't know. I've been ill and I've come here to recuperate."

The maid came with the coffee and seeing Caypor talking to Ashenden put the tray on the table at which he was sitting. Caypor gave a laugh of faint embarrassment.

"I don't want to force myself upon you. I don't know why the maid put my coffee on your table."

"Please sit down," said Ashenden.

"It's very good of you. I've lived so long on the Continent that I'm always forgetting that my countrymen are apt to look upon it as confounded cheek if you talk to them. Are you English, by the way, or American?"

"English," said Ashenden.

Ashenden was by nature a very shy person, and he had in vain tried to cure himself of a failing that at his age was unseemly, but on occasion he knew how to make effective use of it. He explained now in a hesitating and awkward manner the facts that he had the day before told the landlady and that he was convinced she had already passed on to Caypor.

"You couldn't have come to a better place than Lucerne. It's an oasis of peace in this war-weary world. When you're here you might almost forget that there is such a thing as a war going on. That is why I've come here. I'm a journalist by profession."

"I couldn't help wondering if you wrote," said Ashenden, with an eagerly timid smile.

It was clear that he had not learnt that 'oasis of peace in a war-weary world' at the shipping-office.

"You see, I married a German lady," said Caypor gravely.

"Oh, really?"

"I don't think anyone could be more patriotic than I am. I'm English through and through and I don't mind telling you that in my opinion the British Empire is the greatest instrument for good that the world has ever seen, but having a German wife I naturally see a good deal of the reverse of the medal. You don't have to tell me that the Germans have faults, but frankly I'm not prepared to admit that they're devils incarnate. At the beginning of the war my poor wife had a very rough time in England and I for one couldn't have blamed her if she'd felt rather bitter about it. Everyone thought she was a spy. It'll make you laugh when you know her. She's the typical German *hausfrau* who cares for nothing but her house and her husband and our only child Fritzi." Caypor fondled his dog and gave a little laugh. "Yes, Fritzi, you are our child, aren't you? Naturally it made my position very awkward. I was connected with some very important papers, and my editors weren't quite comfortable about it. Well, to cut a long story short I thought the most dignified course was to resign and come to a neutral country till the storm blew over. My wife and I never discuss the war, though I'm bound to tell you that it's more on my account than hers, she's much more tolerant than I am and she's more willing to look upon this terrible business from my point of view than I am from hers."

"That is strange," said Ashenden. "As a rule women are so much more rabid than men."

"My wife is a very remarkable person. I should like to introduce you to her. By the way, I don't know if you know my name. Grantley Caypor."

"My name is Somerville," said Ashenden.

He told him then of the work he had been doing in the Censorship Department, and he fancied that into Caypor's eyes came a certain intentness. Presently he told him that he was looking for someone to give him conversation-lessons in German so that he might rub up his rusty knowledge of the language; and as he spoke a notion flashed across his mind: he gave Caypor a look and saw that the same notion had come to him. It had occurred to them at the same instant that it would be a very good plan for Ashenden's teacher to be Mrs. Caypor.

"I asked our landlady if she could find me someone and she said she thought she could. I must ask her again. It ought not to be very hard to find a man who is prepared to come and talk German to me for an hour a day."

"I wouldn't take anyone on the landlady's recommendation," said Caypor. "After all you want someone with a good North-German accent and she only talks Swiss. I'll ask my wife if she knows anyone. My wife's a very highly educated woman and you could trust her recommendation."

"That's very kind of you."

Ashenden observed Grantley Caypor at his ease. He noticed how the small, grey-green eyes, which last night he had not been able to see, contradicted the red good-humoured frankness of the face. They were quick and shifty, but when the mind behind them was seized by an unexpected notion they were suddenly still. It gave one a peculiar feeling of the working of the brain. They were not eyes that inspired confidence; Caypor did that with his jolly, good-natured smile, the openness of his broad, weather-beaten face, his comfortable obesity and the cheeriness of his loud, deep voice. He was doing his best now to be agreeable. While Ashenden talked to him, a little shyly still but gaining confidence from that breezy, cordial manner, capable of putting anyone at his ease, it intrigued him to remember that the man was a common spy. It gave a tang to his conversation to reflect that he had been ready to sell his country for no more than forty pounds a month. Ashenden had known Gomez, the young Spaniard whom Caypor had betrayed. He was a high-spirited youth, with a love of adventure, and he had undertaken his dangerous mission not for the money he earned by it, but from a passion for romance. It amused him to outwit the clumsy German and it appealed to his sense of the absurd to play a part in a shilling shocker. It was not very nice to think of him now six feet underground in a prison yard. He was young and he had a certain grace of gesture. Ashenden wondered whether Caypor had felt a qualm when he delivered him up to destruction.

"I suppose you know a little German?" asked Caypor, interested in the stranger.

"Oh, yes, I was a student in Germany, and I used to talk it fluently, but that is long ago and I have forgotten. I can still read it very comfortably."

"Oh, yes, I noticed you were reading a German book last night."

Fool! It was only a little while since he had told Ashenden that he had not seen him at dinner. He wondered whether Caypor had observed the slip. How difficult it was never to make one! Ashenden must be on his guard; the thing that made him most nervous was the thought that he might not answer readily enough to his assumed name of Somerville. Of course there was always the chance that Caypor had made the slip on purpose to see by Ashenden's face whether he noticed anything. Caypor got up.

"There is my wife. We go for a walk up one of the mountains every afternoon. I can tell you some charming walks. The flowers even now are lovely."

"I'm afraid I must wait till I'm a bit stronger," said Ashenden, with a little sigh.

He had naturally a pale face and never looked as robust as he was. Mrs. Caypor came downstairs and her husband joined her. They walked down the road, Fritzi bounding round them, and Ashenden saw that Caypor immediately began to speak with volubility. He was evidently telling his wife the results of his interview with Ashenden. Ashenden looked at the sun shining so gaily on the lake; the shadow of a breeze fluttered the green leaves of the trees; everything invited to a stroll: he got up, went to his room and throwing himself on his bed had a very pleasant sleep.

He went into dinner that evening as the Caypors were finishing, for he had wandered melancholy about Lucerne in the hope of finding a cocktail that would enable him to face the potato salad that he foresaw, and on their way out of the dining-room Caypor stopped and asked him if he would drink coffee with them. When Ashenden joined them in the hall Caypor got up and introduced him to his wife. She bowed stiffly and no answering smile came to her face to respond to Ashenden's civil greeting. It was not hard to see that her attitude was definitely hostile. It put Ashenden at his ease. She was a plainish woman, nearing forty, with a muddy skin and vague features; her drab hair was arranged in a plait round her head like that of Napoleon's Queen of Prussia; and she was squarely built, plump rather than fat, and solid. But she did not look stupid; she looked, on the contrary, a woman of character, and Ashenden, who had lived enough in Germany to recognise the type, was ready to believe that though capable of doing the housework, cooking the dinner and climbing a mountain, she might be also prodigiously well-informed. She wore a white blouse that showed a sunburned neck, a black skirt and heavy walking boots. Caypor addressing her in English told her in his jovial way, as though she did not know it already, what Ashenden had told him about himself. She listened grimly.

"I think you told me you understand German," said Caypor, his big red face wreathed in polite smiles but his little eyes darting about restlessly.

"Yes, I was for some time a student in Heidelberg."

"Really?" said Mrs. Caypor in English, an expression of faint interest for a moment chasing away the sullenness from her face. "I know Heidelberg very well. I was at school there for one year."

Her English was correct, but throaty, and the mouthing emphasis she gave her words was disagreeable. Ashenden was diffuse in praise of the old university town and the beauty of the neighbourhood. She heard him, from the standpoint of her Teutonic superiority, with toleration rather than with enthusiasm.

"It is well known that the valley of the Neckar is one of the beauty places of the whole world," she said.

"I have not told you, my dear," said Caypor then, "that Mr. Somerville is looking for someone to give him conversation lessons while he is here. I told him that perhaps you could suggest a teacher."

"No, I know no one whom I could conscientiously recommend," she answered. "The Swiss accent is hateful beyond words. It could do Mr. Somerville only harm to converse with a Swiss."

"If I were in your place, Mr. Somerville, I would try and persuade my wife to give you lessons. She is, if I may say so, a very cultivated and highly educated woman."

"*Ach*, Grantley, I have not the time. I have my own work to do."

Ashenden saw that he was being given his opportunity. The trap was prepared and all he had to do was fall in. He turned to Mrs. Caypor with a manner that he tried to make shy, deprecating and modest.

"Of course it would be too wonderful if you would give me lessons. I should look upon it as a real privilege. Naturally I wouldn't want to interfere with your work. I am just here to get well, with nothing in the world to do, and I would suit my time entirely to your convenience."

He felt a flash of satisfaction pass from one to the other and in Mrs. Caypor's blue eyes he fancied that he saw a dark glow.

"Of course it would be a purely business arrangement," said Caypor. "There's no reason that my good wife shouldn't earn a little pin-money. Would you think ten francs an hour too much?"

"No," said Ashenden, "I should think myself lucky to get a first-rate teacher for that."

"What do you say, my dear? Surely you can spare an hour, and you would be doing this gentleman a kindness. He would learn that all Germans are not the devilish fiends that they think them in England."

On Mrs. Caypor's brow was an uneasy frown and Ashenden could not but think with apprehension of that hour's conversation a day that he was going to exchange with her. Heaven only knew how he would have to rack his brain for subjects of discourse with that heavy and morose woman. Now she made a visible effort.

"I shall be very pleased to give Mr. Somerville conversation lessons."

"I congratulate you, Mr. Somerville," said Caypor noisily. "You're in for a treat. When will you start, to-morrow at eleven?"

"That would suit me very well if it suits Mrs. Caypor."

"Yes, that is as good an hour as another," she answered.

Ashenden left them to discuss the happy outcome of their diplomacy. But when, punctually at eleven next morning, he heard a knock at his door (for it had been arranged that Mrs. Caypor should give him his lesson in his room) it was not without trepidation that he opened it. It behoved him to be frank, a trifle indiscreet, but obviously wary of a German woman, sufficiently intelligent, and impulsive. Mrs. Caypor's face was dark and sulky. She plainly hated having anything to do with him. But they sat down and she began, somewhat peremptorily, to ask him questions about his knowledge of German literature. She corrected his mistakes with exactness and when he put before her some difficulty in German construction explained it with clearness and precision. It was obvious that though she hated giving him a lesson she meant to give it conscientiously. She seemed to have not only an aptitude for teaching, but a love of it, and as the hour went on she began to speak with greater earnestness. It was already only by an effort that she remembered that he was a brutal Englishman. Ashenden, noticing the unconscious struggle within her, found himself not a little entertained; and it was with truth that, when later in the day Caypor asked him how the lesson had gone, he answered that it was highly satisfactory; Mrs. Caypor was an excellent teacher and a most interesting person.

"I told you so. She's the most remarkable woman I know."

And Ashenden had a feeling that when in his hearty, laughing way Caypor said this he was for the first time entirely sincere.

In a day or two Ashenden guessed that Mrs. Caypor was giving him lessons only in order to enable Caypor to arrive at a closer intimacy with him, for she confined herself strictly to matters of literature, music and painting; and when Ashenden, by way of experiment, brought the conversation round to the war, she cut him short.

"I think that is a topic that we had better avoid, Herr Somerville," she said.

She continued to give her lessons with the greatest thoroughness, and he had his money's worth, but every day she came with the same sullen face and it was only in the interest of teaching that she lost for a moment her instinctive dislike of him. Ashenden exercised in turn, but in vain, all his wiles. He was ingratiating, ingenuous, humble, grateful, flattering, simple and timid. She remained coldly hostile. She was a fanatic. Her patriotism was aggressive, but disinterested, and obsessed with the notion of the superiority of all things German she loathed England with a virulent hatred because in that country she saw the chief obstacle to their diffusion. Her ideal was a German world in which the rest of the nations under a hegemony greater than that of Rome should enjoy the benefits of German science and German art and German culture. There was in the conception a magnificent impudence that appealed to Ashenden's sense of humour. She was no fool. She had read much, in several languages, and she could talk of the books she had read with good sense. She had a knowledge of modern painting and modern music that not a little impressed Ashenden. It was amusing once to hear her before luncheon play one of those silvery little pieces of Debussy; she played it disdainfully because it was French and so light, but with an angry appreciation of its grace and gaiety. When Ashenden congratulated her she shrugged her shoulders.

"The decadent music of a decadent nation," she said. Then with powerful hands she struck the first resounding chords of a sonata by Beethoven; but she stopped. "I cannot play, I am out of practice, and you English, what do you know of music? You have not produced a composer since Purcell!"

"What do you think of that statement?" Ashenden, smiling, asked Caypor, who was standing near.

"I confess its truth. The little I know of music my wife taught me. I wish you could hear her play when she is in practice." He put his fat hand, with its square, stumpy fingers, on her shoulder. "She can wring your heartstrings with pure beauty."

"*Dummer Kerl*," she said, in a soft voice. "Stupid fellow," and Ashenden saw her mouth for a moment quiver, but she quickly recovered. "You English, you cannot paint, you cannot model, you cannot write music."

"Some of us can at times write pleasing verses," said Ashenden, with good-humour, for it was not his business to be put out, and, he did not know why, two lines occurring to him he said them:

"*Whither, O splendid ship, thy white sails crowding,*
Leaning across the bosom of the urgent West."

"Yes," said Mrs. Caypor, with a strange gesture, "you can write poetry. I wonder why."

And to Ashenden's surprise she went on, in her guttural English, to recite the next two lines of the poem he had quoted.

"Come, Grantley, *mittagessen* is ready, let us go into the dining-room."

They left Ashenden reflective.

Ashenden admired goodness, but was not outraged by wickedness. People sometimes thought him heartless because he was more often interested in others than attached to them, and even in the few to whom he was attached his eyes saw with equal clearness the merits and the defects. When he liked people it was not because he was blind to their faults, he did not mind their faults but accepted them with a tolerant shrug of the shoulders, or because he ascribed to them excellencies that they did not possess; and since he judged his friends with candour they never disappointed him and so he seldom lost one. He asked from none more than he could give. He was able to pursue his study of the Caypors without prejudice and without passion. Mrs. Caypor seemed to him more of a piece and therefore the easier of the two to understand; she obviously detested him; though it was necessary for her to be civil to him her antipathy was strong enough to wring from her now and then an expression of rudeness; and had she been safely able to do so she would have killed him without a qualm. But in the pressure of Caypor's chubby hand on his wife's shoulder and in the fugitive trembling of her lips Ashenden had divined that this unprepossessing woman and that mean fat man were joined together by a deep and sincere love. It was touching. Ashenden assembled the observations that he had been making for the past few days and little things that he had noticed but to which he had attached no significance returned to him. It seemed to him that Mrs. Caypor loved her husband because she was of a stronger character than he and because she felt his dependence on her; she loved him for his admiration of her, and you might guess that till she met him this dumpy, plain woman with her dullness, good sense and want of humour could not have much enjoyed the admiration of men; she enjoyed his heartiness and his noisy jokes, and his high spirits stirred her sluggish blood; he was a great big bouncing boy and he would never be anything else and she felt like a mother towards him; she had made him what he was, and he was her man and she was his woman, and she loved him, notwithstanding his weakness (for with her clear head she must always have been conscious of that), she loved him, *ach*, *was*, as Isolde loved Tristan. But then there was the espionage. Even Ashenden with all his tolerance for human frailty could not but feel that to betray your country for money is not a very pretty proceeding. Of course she knew of it, indeed it was probably through her that Caypor had first been approached; he would never have undertaken such work if she had not urged him to it. She loved him and she was an honest and an upright woman. By what devious means had she persuaded herself to force her husband to adopt so base and dishonourable a calling? Ashenden lost himself in a labyrinth of conjecture as he tried to piece together the actions of her mind.

Grantley Caypor was another story. There was little to admire in him, but at that moment Ashenden was not looking for an object of admiration; but there was much that was singular and much that was unexpected in that gross and vulgar fellow. Ashenden watched with entertainment the suave manner in which the spy tried to inveigle him in his toils. It was a couple of days after his first lesson that Caypor after dinner, his wife having gone upstairs, threw himself heavily into a chair by Ashenden's side. His faithful Fritzi came up to him and put his long muzzle with its black nose on his knee.

"He has no brain," said Caypor, "but a heart of gold. Look at those little pink eyes. Did you ever see anything so stupid? And what an ugly face, but what incredible charm!"

"Have you had him long?" asked Ashenden.

"I got him in 1914 just before the outbreak of war. By the way, what do you think of the news to-day? Of course my wife and I never discuss the war. You can't think what a relief to me it is to find a fellow-countryman to whom I can open my heart."

He handed Ashenden a cheap Swiss cigar and Ashenden, making a rueful sacrifice to duty, accepted it.

"Of course, they haven't got a chance, the Germans," said Caypor, "not a dog's chance. I knew they were beaten the moment we came in."

His manner was earnest, sincere and confidential. Ashenden made a commonplace rejoinder.

"It's the greatest grief of my life that owing to my wife's nationality I was unable to do any war work. I tried to enlist the day war broke out, but they wouldn't have me on account of my age, but I don't mind telling you, if the war goes on much longer, wife or no wife, I'm going to do something. With my knowledge of languages I ought to be of some service in the Censorship Department. That's where you were, wasn't it?"

That was the mark at which he had been aiming and in answer now to his well-directed questions Ashenden gave him the information that he had already prepared. Caypor drew his chair a little nearer and dropped his voice.

"I'm sure you wouldn't tell me anything that anyone shouldn't know, but after all these Swiss are absolutely pro-German and we don't want to give anyone the chance of overhearing."

Then he went on another tack. He told Ashenden a number of things that were of a certain secrecy.

"I wouldn't tell this to anybody else, you know, but I have one or two friends who are in pretty influential positions, and they know they can trust me."

Thus encouraged, Ashenden was a little more deliberately indiscreet and when they parted both had reason to be satisfied. Ashenden guessed that Caypor's typewriter would be kept busy next morning and that extremely energetic Major in Berne would shortly receive a most interesting report.

One evening, going upstairs after dinner, Ashenden passed an open bathroom. He caught sight of the Caypors.

"Come in," cried Caypor in his cordial way. "We're washing our Fritzi."

The bull-terrier was constantly getting himself very dirty, and it was Caypor's pride to see him clean and white. Ashenden went in. Mrs. Caypor with her sleeves turned up and a large white apron was standing at one end of the bath, while Caypor, in a pair of trousers and a singlet, his fat, freckled arms bare, was soaping the wretched hound.

"We have to do it at night," he said, "because the Fitzgeralds use this bath and they'd have a fit if they knew we washed the dog in it. We wait till they go to bed. Come along, Fritzi, show the gentleman how beautifully you behave when you have your face scrubbed."

The poor brute, woebegone but faintly wagging his tail to show that however foul was this operation performed on him he bore no malice to the god who did it, was standing in the middle of the bath in six inches of water. He was soaped all over and Caypor, talking the while, shampooed him with his great fat hands.

"Oh, what a beautiful dog he's going to be when he's as white as the driven snow. His master will be as proud as Punch to walk out with him, and all the little lady-dogs will say: Good gracious, who's that beautiful aristocratic looking bull-terrier walking as though he owned the whole of Switzerland? Now stand still while you have your ears washed. You couldn't bear to go out into the street with dirty ears, could you? like a nasty little Swiss schoolboy. *Noblesse oblige*. Now the black nose. Oh, and all the soap is going into his little pink eyes and they'll smart."

Mrs. Caypor listened to this nonsense with a good-humoured

sluggish smile on her broad, plain face, and presently gravely took a towel.

"Now he's going to have a ducking. Upsie-daisy."

Caypor seized the dog by the fore-legs and ducked him once and ducked him twice. There was a struggle, a flurry and a splashing. Caypor lifted him out of the bath.

"Now go to mother and she'll dry you."

Mrs. Caypor sat down and taking the dog between her strong legs rubbed him till the sweat poured off her forehead. And Fritzi, a little shaken and breathless, but happy it was all over, stood, with his sweet stupid face, white and shining.

"Blood will tell," cried Caypor exultantly. "He knows the names of no less than sixty-four of his ancestors, and they were all nobly born."

Ashenden was faintly troubled. He shivered a little as he walked upstairs.

Then, one Sunday, Caypor told him that he and his wife were going on an excursion and would eat their luncheon at some little mountain restaurant; and he suggested that Ashenden, each paying his share, should come with them. After three weeks at Lucerne Ashenden thought that his strength would permit him to venture the exertion. They started early, Mrs. Caypor business-like in her walking boots and Tyrolese hat and alpenstock, and Caypor in stockings and plus-fours looking very British. The situation amused Ashenden and he was prepared to enjoy his day; but he meant to keep his eyes open; it was not inconceivable that the Caypors had discovered what he was and it would not do to go too near a precipice; Mrs. Caypor would not hesitate to give him a push and Caypor for all his jolliness was an ugly customer. But on the face of it there was nothing to mar Ashenden's pleasure in the golden morning. The air was fragrant. Caypor was full of conversation. He told funny stories. He was gay and jovial. The sweat rolled off his great red face and he laughed at himself because he was so fat. To Ashenden's astonishment he showed a peculiar knowledge of the mountain flowers. Once he went out of the way to pick one he saw a little distance from the path and brought it back to his wife. He looked at it tenderly.

"Isn't it lovely?" he cried, and his shifty grey-green eyes for a moment were as candid as a child's. "It's like a poem by Walter Savage Landor."

"Botany is my husband's favourite science," said Mrs. Caypor. "I laugh at him sometimes. He is devoted to flowers. Often when we have hardly had enough money to pay the butcher he has spent everything in his pocket to bring me a bunch of roses."

"*Qui fleurit sa maison fleurit son cœur*," said Grantley Caypor.

Ashenden had once or twice seen Caypor, coming in from a walk, offer Mrs. Fitzgerald a nosegay of mountain flowers with an elephantine courtesy that was not entirely displeasing; and what he had just learned added a certain significance to the pretty little action. His passion for flowers was genuine and when he gave them to the old Irish lady he gave her something he valued. It showed a real kindness of heart. Ashenden had always thought botany a tedious science, but Caypor, talking exuberantly as they walked along, was able to impart to it life and interest. He must have given it a good deal of study.

"I've never written a book," he said. "There are too many books already and any desire to write I have is satisfied by the more immediately profitable and quite ephemeral composition of an article for a daily paper. But if I stay here much longer I have half a mind to write a book about the wild flowers of Switzerland. Oh, I wish you'd been here a little earlier. They were marvellous. But one wants to be a poet for that, and I'm only a poor newspaper-man."

It was curious to observe how he was able to combine real emotion with false fact.

When they reached the inn, with its view of the mountains and the lake, it was good to see the sensual pleasure with which he poured down his throat a bottle of ice-cold beer. You could not but feel sympathy for a man who took so much delight in simple things. They lunched deliciously off scrambled eggs and mountain trout. Even Mrs. Caypor was moved to an unwonted gentleness by her surroundings; the inn was in an agreeably rural spot, it looked like a picture of a Swiss chalet in a book of early nineteenth-century travels; and she treated Ashenden with something less than her usual hostility. When they arrived she had burst into loud German exclamations on the beauty of the scene, and now, softened perhaps too by food and drink, her eyes, dwelling on the grandeur before her, filled with tears. She stretched out her hand.

"It is dreadful and I am ashamed, notwithstanding this horrible and unjust war I can feel in my heart at the moment nothing but happiness and gratitude."

Caypor took her hand and pressed it and, an unusual thing with him, addressing her in German, called her little pet-names. It was absurd, but touching. Ashenden, leaving them to their emotions, strolled through the garden and sat down on a bench that had been prepared for the comfort of the tourist. The view was of course spectacular, but it captured you; it was like a piece of music that was obvious and meretricious, but for the moment shattered your self-control.

And as Ashenden lingered idly in that spot he pondered over the mystery of Grantley Caypor's treachery. If he liked strange people he had found in him one who was strange beyond belief. It would be foolish to deny that he had amiable traits. His joviality was not assumed, he was without pretence a hearty fellow, and he had real good nature. He was always ready to do a kindness. Ashenden had often watched him with the old Irish colonel and his wife who were the only other residents of the hotel; he would listen good-humouredly to the old man's tedious stories of the Egyptian war, and he was charming with her. Now that Ashenden had arrived at terms of some familiarity with Caypor he found that he regarded him less with repulsion than with curiosity. He did not think that he had become a spy merely for the money; he was a man of modest tastes and what he had earned in a shipping-office must have sufficed to so good a manager as Mrs. Caypor; and after war was declared there was no lack of remunerative work for men over the military age. It might be that he was one of those men who prefer devious ways to straight for some intricate pleasure they get in fooling their fellows; and that he had turned spy, not from hatred of the country that had imprisoned him, nor even from love of his wife, but from a desire to score off the big-wigs who never even knew of his existence. It might be that it was vanity that impelled him, a feeling that his talents had not received the recognition they merited, or just a puckish, impish desire to do mischief. He was a crook. It is true that only two cases of dishonesty had been brought home to him, but if he had been caught twice it might be surmised that he had often been dishonest without being caught. What did Mrs. Caypor think of this? They were so united that she must be aware of it. Did it make her ashamed, for her own uprightness surely none could doubt, or did she accept it as an inevitable kink in the man she loved? Did she do all she could to prevent it, or did she close her eyes to something she could not help?

How much easier life would be if people were all black or all white, and how much simpler it would be to act in regard to them! Was Caypor a good man who loved evil or a bad man who loved good? And how could such unreconcilable elements exist side by side and in harmony within the same heart? For one thing was clear, Caypor was disturbed by no gnawing of conscience; he did his mean and despicable work with gusto. He was a traitor who enjoyed his treachery. Though Ashenden had been studying human nature more or less consciously all his life, it seemed to him that he knew as little about it now in middle age as he had done when he was a child. Of course R. would have said to him: Why the devil do you waste your time with such nonsense? The man's a dangerous spy and your business is to lay him by the heels.

That was true enough. Ashenden had decided that it would be useless to attempt to make any arrangement with Caypor. Though doubtless he would have no feeling about betraying his employers he could certainly not be trusted. His wife's influence was too strong. Besides, notwithstanding what he had from time to time told Ashenden, he was in his heart convinced that the Central Powers must win the war, and he meant to be on the winning side. Well, then Caypor must be laid by the heels, but how he was to effect that Ashenden had no notion. Suddenly he heard a voice.

"There you are. We've been wondering where you had hidden yourself."

He looked round and saw the Caypors strolling towards him. They were walking hand in hand.

"So this is what has kept you so quiet," said Caypor as his eyes fell on the view. "What a spot!"

Mrs. Caypor clasped her hands.

"*Ach Gott, wie schön!*" she cried. "*Wie schön.* When I look at that blue lake and those snowy mountains I feel inclined, like Goethe's Faust, to cry to the passing moment: Tarry."

"This is better than being in England with the excursions and alarums of war, isn't it?" said Caypor.

"Much," said Ashenden.

"By the way, did you have any difficulty in getting out?"

"No, not the smallest."

"I'm told they make rather a nuisance of themselves at the frontier nowadays."

"I came through without the smallest difficulty. I don't fancy they bother much about the English. I thought the examination of passports was quite perfunctory."

A fleeting glance passed between Caypor and his wife. Ashenden wondered what it meant. It would be strange if Caypor's thoughts were occupied with the chances of a journey to England at the very moment when he was himself reflecting on its possibility. In a little while Mrs. Caypor suggested that they had better be starting back and they wandered together in the shade of trees down the mountain paths.

Ashenden was watchful. He could do nothing (and his inactivity irked him) but wait with his eyes open to seize the opportunity that might present itself. A couple of days later an incident occurred that made him certain something was in the wind. In the course of his morning lesson Mrs. Caypor remarked:

"My husband has gone to Geneva to-day. He had some business to do there."

"Oh," said Ashenden, "will he be gone long?"

"No, only two days."

It is not everyone who can tell a lie, and Ashenden had the feeling, he hardly knew why, that Mrs. Caypor was telling one then. Her manner perhaps was not quite as indifferent as you would have expected when she was mentioning a fact that could be of no interest to Ashenden. It flashed across his mind that Caypor had been summoned to Berne to see the redoubtable head of the German secret service. When he had the chance he said casually to the waitress:

"A little less work for you to do, *fräulein*. I hear that Herr Caypor has gone to Berne."

"Yes. But he'll be back to-morrow."

That proved nothing, but it was something to go upon. Ashenden knew in Lucerne a Swiss who was willing on emergency to do odd jobs and, looking him up, asked him to take a letter to Berne. It might be possible to pick up Caypor and trace his movements. Next day Caypor appeared once more with his wife at the dinner-table, but merely nodded to Ashenden and afterwards both went straight upstairs. They looked troubled. Caypor, as a rule so animated, walked with bowed shoulders and looked neither to the right nor to the left. Next morning Ashenden received a reply to his letter: Caypor had seen Major von P. It was possible to guess what the Major had said to him. Ashenden well knew how rough he could be; he was a hard man and a brutal, clever and unscrupulous, and he was not accustomed to mince his words. They were tired of paying Caypor a salary to sit still in Lucerne and do nothing; the time was come for him to go to England. Guess-work? Of course it was guess-work, but in that trade it mostly was; you had to deduce the animal from its jaw-bone. Ashenden knew from Gustav that the Germans wanted to send someone to England. He drew a long breath; if Caypor went he would have to get busy.

When Mrs. Caypor came in to give him his lesson she was dull and listless. She looked tired and her mouth was set obstinately. It occurred to Ashenden that the Caypors had spent most of the night talking. He wished he knew what they had said. Did she urge him to go or did she try to dissuade him? Ashenden watched them again at luncheon. Something was the matter, for they hardly spoke to one another and as a rule they found plenty to talk about. They left

Y

the room early, but when Ashenden went out he saw Caypor sitting in the hall by himself.

"Hulloa," he cried jovially, but surely the effort was patent, "how are you getting on? I've been to Geneva."

"So I heard," said Ashenden.

"Come and have your coffee with me. My poor wife's got a head-ache. I told her she'd better go and lie down." In his shifty green eyes was an expression that Ashenden could not read. "The fact is, she's rather worried, poor dear; I'm thinking of going to England."

Ashenden's heart gave a sudden leap against his ribs, but his face remained impassive:

"Oh, are you going for long? We shall miss you."

"To tell you the truth, I'm fed up with doing nothing. The war looks as though it were going on for years and I can't sit here inde-finitely. Besides, I can't afford it, I've got to earn my living. I may have a German wife, but I am an Englishman, hang it all, and I want to do my bit. I could never face my friends again if I just stayed here in ease and comfort till the end of the war and never attempted to do a thing to help the country. My wife takes her German point of view and I don't mind telling you that she's a bit upset. You know what women are."

Now Ashenden knew what it was that he saw in Caypor's eyes. Fear. It gave him a nasty turn. Caypor didn't want to go to Eng-land, he wanted to stay safely in Switzlerand; Ashenden knew now what the major had said to him when he went to see him in Berne. He had got to go or lose his salary. What was it that his wife had said when he told her what had happened? He had wanted her to press him to stay, but, it was plain, she hadn't done that; perhaps he had not dared tell her how frightened he was; to her he had always been gay, bold, adventurous and devil-may-care; and now, the prisoner of his own lies, he had not found it in him to confess himself the mean and sneaking coward he was.

"Are you going to take your wife with you?" asked Ashenden.

"No, she'll stay here."

It had been arranged very neatly. Mrs. Caypor would receive his letters and forward the information they contained to Berne.

"I've been out of England so long that I don't quite know how to set about getting war-work. What would you do in my place?"

"I don't know; what sort of work are you thinking of?"

"Well, you know, I imagine I could do the same thing as you did. I wonder if there's anyone in the Censorship Department that you could give me a letter of introduction to."

It was only by a miracle that Ashenden saved himself from showing by a smothered cry or by a broken gesture how startled he was; but not by Caypor's request, by what had just dawned upon him. What an idiot he had been! He had been disturbed by the thought that he was wasting his time at Lucerne, he was doing nothing, and though in fact, as it turned out, Caypor was going to England it was due to no cleverness of his. He could take to himself no credit for the result. And now he saw that he had been put in Lucerne, told how to describe himself and given the proper information, so that what actually had occurred should occur. It would be a wonderful thing for the German secret service to get an agent into the Censorship Department; and by a happy accident there was Grantley Caypor, the very man for the job, on friendly terms with someone who had worked there. What a bit of luck! Major von P. was a man of culture and, rubbing his hands, he must surely have murmured: *stultum facit fortuna quem vult perdere*. It was a trap of that devilish R. and the grim major at Berne had fallen into it. Ashenden had done his work just by sitting still and doing nothing. He almost laughed as he thought what a fool R. had made of him.

"I was on very good terms with the chief of my department, I could give you a note to him if you liked."

"That would be just the thing."

"But of course I must give the facts. I must say I've met you here and only known you a fortnight."

"Of course. But you'll say what else you can for me, won't you?"

"Oh, certainly."

"I don't know yet if I can get a visa. I'm told they're rather fussy."

"I don't see why. I shall be very sick if they refuse me one when I want to go back."

"I'll go and see how my wife is getting on," said Caypor suddenly, getting up. "When will you let me have that letter?"

"Whenever you like. Are you going at once?"

"As soon as possible."

Caypor left him. Ashenden waited in the hall for a quarter of an hour so that there should appear in him no sign of hurry. Then he went upstairs and prepared various communications. In one he informed R. that Caypor was going to England; in another he made arrangements through Berne that wherever Caypor applied for a visa it should be granted to him without question; and these he despatched forthwith. When he went down to dinner he handed Caypor a cordial letter of introduction.

Next day but one Caypor left Lucerne.

Ashenden waited. He continued to have his hour's lesson with Mrs. Caypor and under her conscientious tuition began now to speak

German with ease. They talked of Goethe and Winckelmann, of art and life and travel. Fritzi sat quietly by her chair.

"He misses his master," she said, pulling his ears. "He only really cares for him, he suffers me only as belonging to him."

After his lesson Ashenden went every morning to Cook's to ask for his letters. It was here that all communications were addressed to him. He could not move till he received instructions, but R. could be trusted not to leave him idle long; and meanwhile there was nothing for him to do but have patience. Presently he received a letter from the consul in Geneva to say that Caypor had there applied for his visa and had set out for France. Having read this, Ashenden went on for a little stroll by the lake and on his way back happened to see Mrs. Caypor coming out of Cook's office. He guessed that she was having her letters addressed there too. He went up to her.

"Have you had news of Herr Caypor?" he asked her.

"No," she said. "I suppose I could hardly expect to yet."

He walked along by her side. She was disappointed, but not yet anxious; she knew how irregular at that time was the post. But next day during the lesson he could not but see that she was impatient to have done with it. The post was delivered at noon and at five minutes to she looked at her watch and him. Though Ashenden knew very well that no letter would ever come for her he had not the heart to keep her on tenter-hooks.

"Don't you think that's enough for the day? I'm sure you want to go down to Cook's," he said.

"Thank you. That is very amiable of you."

When a little later he went there himself he found her standing in the middle of the office. Her face was distraught. She addressed him wildly.

"My husband promised to write from Paris. I am sure there is a letter for me, but these stupid people say there's nothing. They're so careless, it's a scandal."

Ashenden did not know what to say. While the clerk was looking through the bundle to see if there was anything for him she came up to the desk again.

"When does the next post come in from France?" she asked.

"Sometimes there are letters about five."

"I'll come then."

She turned and walked rapidly away. Fritzi followed her with his tail between his legs. There was no doubt of it, already the fear had seized her that something was wrong. Next morning she looked dreadful; she could not have closed her eyes all night; and in the middle of the lesson she started up from her chair.

"You must excuse me, Herr Somerville, I cannot give you a lesson to-day. I am not feeling well."

Before Ashenden could say anything she had flung nervously from the room, and in the evening he got a note from her to say that she regretted that she must discontinue giving him conversation lessons. She gave no reason. Then Ashenden saw no more of her; she ceased coming in to meals; except to go morning and afternoon to Cook's she spent apparently the whole day in her room. Ashenden thought of her sitting there hour after hour with that hideous fear gnawing at her heart. Who could help feeling sorry for her? The time hung heavy on his hands too. He read a good deal and wrote a little, he hired a canoe and went for long leisurely paddles on the lake; and at last one morning the clerk at Cook's handed him a letter. It was from R. It had all the appearance of a business communication, but between the lines he read a good deal.

Dear Sir, it began, *The goods, with accompanying letter, despatched by you from Lucerne have been duly delivered. We are obliged to you for executing our instructions with such promptness.*

It went on in this strain. R. was exultant. Ashenden guessed that Caypor had been arrested and by now had paid the penalty of his crime. He shuddered. He remembered a dreadful scene. Dawn. A cold, grey dawn, with a drizzling rain falling. A man, blindfolded, standing against a wall, an officer very pale giving an order, a volley, and then a young soldier, one of the firing-party, turning round and holding on to his gun for support, vomiting. The officer turning paler still, and he, Ashenden, feeling dreadfully faint. How terrified Caypor must have been! It was awful when the tears ran down their faces. Ashenden shook himself. He went to the ticket-office and obedient to his orders bought himself a ticket for Geneva.

As he was waiting for his change Mrs. Caypor came in. He was shocked at the sight of her. She was blowsy and dishevelled and there were heavy rings round her eyes. She was deathly pale. She staggered up to the desk and asked for a letter. The clerk shook his head.

"I'm sorry, madam, there's nothing yet."

"But look, look. Are you sure? Please look again."

The misery in her voice was heartrending. The clerk with a shrug of the shoulders took out the letters from a pigeon-hole and sorted them once more.

"No, there's nothing, madam."

She gave a hoarse cry of despair and her face was distorted with anguish.

"Oh, God, oh, God," she moaned.

She turned away, the tears streaming from her weary eyes, and for a moment she stood there like a blind man groping and not knowing which way to go. Then a fearful thing happened, Fritzi, the bull-terrier, sat down on his haunches and threw back his head and gave a long, long melancholy howl. Mrs. Caypor looked at him with terror; her eyes seemed really to start from her head. The doubt, the gnawing doubt that had tortured her during those dreadful days of suspense, was a doubt no longer. She knew. She staggered blindly into the street.

His Excellency

WHEN Ashenden was sent to X and looked about him he could not but see that his situation was equivocal. X was the capital of an important belligerent state; but a state divided against itself; there was a large party antagonistic to the war and revolution was possible if not imminent. Ashenden was instructed to see what under the circumstances could best be done; he was to suggest a policy and, if it was approved by the exalted personages who had sent him, to carry it out. A vast amount of money was put at his disposal. The Ambassadors of Great Britain and the United States had been directed to afford him such facilities as were at their command, but Ashenden had been told privately to keep himself to himself; he was not to make difficulties for the official representatives of the two powers by divulging to them facts that it might be inconvenient for them to know; and since it might be necessary for him to give support under cover to a party that was at daggers drawn with that in office and with which the relations of the United States and Great Britain were extremely cordial it was just as well that Ashenden should keep his own counsel. The exalted personages did not wish the ambassadors to suffer the affront of discovering that an obscure agent had been sent to work at cross-purposes with them. On the other hand it was thought just as well to have a representative in the opposite camp, who in the event of a sudden upheaval would be at hand with adequate funds and in the confidence of the new leaders of the country.

But ambassadors are sticklers for their dignity and they have a keen nose to scent any encroachment on their authority. When Ashenden on his arrival at X paid an official call on Sir Herbert Witherspoon, the British Ambassador, he was received with a politeness to which no exception could be taken, but with a frigidity that would have sent a little shiver down the spine of a polar bear. Sir Herbert was a diplomat *de carrière* and he cultivated the manner of his profession to a degree that filled the observer with admiration. He did not ask Ashenden anything about his mission because he knew that Ashenden would reply evasively, but he allowed him to see that it was a perfectly foolish one. He talked with acidulous tolerance of the exalted personages who had sent Ashenden to X. He told Ashenden that he had instructions to meet any demands for help that he made and stated that if Ashenden at any time desired to see him he had only to say so.

"I have received the somewhat singular request to despatch telegrams for you in a private code which I understand has been given to you and to hand over to you telegrams in code as they arrive."

"I hope they will be few and far between, sir," answered Ashenden. "I know nothing so tedious as coding and decoding."

Sir Herbert paused for an instant. Perhaps that was not quite the answer he expected. He rose.

"If you will come into the Chancellery I will introduce you to the Counsellor and to the Secretary to whom you can take your telegrams."

Ashenden followed him out of the room, and after handing him over to the Counsellor the ambassador gave him a limp hand to shake.

"I hope I shall have the pleasure of seeing you again one of these days," he said, and with a curt nod left him.

Ashenden bore his reception with composure. It was his business to remain in obscurity and he did not wish any official attentions to attract notice to him. But when on the afternoon of the same day he made his call at the American Embassy he discovered why Sir Herbert Witherspoon had shown him so much coldness. The American ambassador was Mr. Wilbur Schäfer; he came from Kansas City and had been given his post when few suspected that a war was on the point of breaking out, as a reward for political services. He was a big stout man, no longer young for his hair was white, but well-preserved and exceedingly robust. He had a square, red face, clean-shaven, with a little snub nose and a determined chin. His face was very mobile and he twisted it continually into odd and amusing grimaces. It looked as though it were made out of the red india-rubber from which they made hot-water bottles. He greeted Ashenden with cordiality. He was a hearty fellow.

"I suppose you've seen Sir Herbert. I reckon you've got his dander up. What do they mean in Washington and London by telling us to despatch your code telegrams without knowing what they're all about? You know, they've got no right to do that."

"Oh, Your Excellency, I think it was only done to save time and trouble," said Ashenden.

"Well, what is this mission anyway?"

This of course was a question that Ashenden was not prepared to answer, but not thinking it politic to say so, he determined to give a reply from which the ambassador could learn little. He had already made up his mind from the look of him that Mr. Schäfer, though doubtless possessed of the gifts that enable a man to swing a presidential election this way or that, had not, at least nakedly for all men to see, the acuteness that his position perhaps demanded. He gave you the impression of a bluff, good-humoured creature who liked good cheer. Ashenden would have been wary when playing poker with him, but where the matter in hand was concerned felt himself fairly safe. He began to talk in a loose, vague way of the world at large and before he had gone far managed to ask the ambassador his opinion of the general situation. It was as the sound of the trumpet to the war-horse: Mr. Schäfer made him a speech that lasted without a break for twenty-five minutes, and when at last he stopped in exhaustion, Ashenden with warm thanks for his friendly reception was able to take his leave.

Making up his mind to give both the ambassadors a wide berth, he set about his work and presently devised a plan of campaign. But by chance he was able to do Sir Herbert Witherspoon a good turn and so was thrown again into contact with him. It has been suggested that Mr. Schäfer was more of a politician than a diplomat, and it was his position rather than his personality that gave weight to his opinions. He looked upon the eminence to which he had risen as an opportunity to enjoy the good things of life and his enthusiasm led him to lengths that his constitution could ill support. His ignorance of foreign affairs would in any case have made his judgment of doubtful value, but his state at meetings of the Allied ambassadors so often approached the comatose that he seemed hardly capable of forming a judgment at all. He was known to have succumbed to the fascination of a Swedish lady of undoubted beauty, but of antecedents that from the point of view of a secret service agent were suspect. Her relations with Germany were such as to make her sympathy with the Allies dubious. Mr. Schäfer saw her every day and was certainly much under her influence. Now it was noticed that there was from time to time a leakage of very secret information and the question arose whether Mr. Schäfer did not in these daily interviews inadvertently say things that were promptly passed on to the headquarters of the enemy. No one could have doubted Mr. Schäfer's honesty and patriotism, but it was permissible to be uncertain of his discretion. It was an awkward matter to deal with, but the concern was as great in Washington as in London and Paris, and Ashenden was instructed to deal with it. He had of course not been sent to X without help to do the work he was expected to do, and among his assistants was an astute, powerful and determined man, a Galician Pole, named Herbartus. After consultation with him it happened by one of those fortunate coincidences that occasionally come about in the secret service that a maid in the service of the Swedish lady fell ill and in her place the countess (for such she was) was very luckily able to engage an extremely respectable person from the neighbourhood of Cracow. The fact that before the war she had been secretary to an eminent scientist made her doubtless no less competent a housemaid.

The result of this was that Ashenden received every two or three days a neat report upon the goings-on at this charming lady's apartment, and though he learned nothing that could confirm the vague suspicions that had arisen he learned something else of no little importance. From conversations held at the cosy little *tête-à-tête* dinners that the countess gave the ambassador it appeared that His Excellency was harbouring a bitter grievance against his English colleague. He complained that the relations between himself and Sir Herbert were deliberately maintained on a purely official level. In his blunt way he said he was sick of the frills that damned Britisher put on. He was a he-man and a hundred-per-cent American and he had no more use for protocol and etiquette than for a snowball in hell. Why didn't they get together, like a couple of regular fellows, and have a good old crack? Blood was thicker than water, he'd say, and they'd do more towards winning the war by siting down in their shirt-sleeves and talking things out over a bottle of rye than by all their diplomacy and white spats. Now it was obviously very undesirable that there should not exist between the two ambassadors a perfect cordiality, so Ashenden thought it well to ask Sir Herbert whether he might see him.

He was ushered into Sir Herbert's library.

"Well, Mr. Ashenden, what can I do for you? I hope you're quite satisfied with everything. I understand that you've been keeping the telegraph lines busy."

Ashenden, as he sat down, gave the ambassador a glance. He was beautifully dressed in a perfectly cut tail-coat that fitted his slim figure like a glove, in his black silk tie was a handsome pearl, there was a perfect line in his grey trousers, with their quiet and distinguished stripe, and his neat, pointed shoes looked as though he had never worn them before. You could hardly imagine him sitting in his shirt-sleeves over a whisky high-ball. He was a tall, thin man, with exactly the figure to show off modern clothes, and he sat in his chair, rather upright, as though he were sitting for an official portrait. In his cold and uninteresting way he was really a very handsome fellow. His neat grey hair was parted on one side, his pale face was clean-shaven, he had a delicate, straight nose and grey eyes under grey eyebrows, his mouth in youth might have been sensual and well-shaped, but now it was set to an expression of sarcastic determination and the lips were pallid. It was the kind of face that suggested centuries of good breeding, but you could not believe it capable of expressing emotion. You would never expect to see it break into the hearty distortion of laughter, but at the most be for a moment frigidly kindled by an ironic smile.

Ashenden was uncommonly nervous.

"I'm afraid you'll think I'm meddling in what doesn't concern me, sir. I'm quite prepared to be told to mind my own business."

"We'll see. Pray go on."

Ashenden told his story and the ambassador listened attentively. He did not turn his cold, grey eyes from Ashenden's face, and Ashenden knew that his embarrassment was obvious.

"How did you find out all this?"

"I have means of getting hold of little bits of information that are sometimes useful," said Ashenden.

"I see."

Sir Herbert maintained his steady gaze, but Ashenden was surprised to see on a sudden in the steely eyes a little smile. The bleak, supercilious face became for an instant quite attractive.

"There is another little bit of information that perhaps you'd be good enough to give me. What does one do to be a regular fellow?"

"I am afraid one can do nothing, Your Excellency," replied Ashenden gravely. "I think it is a gift of God."

The light vanished from Sir Herbert's eyes, but his manner was slightly more urbane than when Ashenden was brought into the room. He rose and held out his hand.

"You did quite right to come and tell me this, Mr. Ashenden. I have been very remiss. It is inexcusable on my part to offend that inoffensive old gentleman. But I will do my best to repair my error. I will call at the American Embassy this afternoon."

"But not in too great state, sir, if I may venture a suggestion."

The ambassador's eyes twinkled. Ashenden began to think him almost human.

"I can do nothing but in state, Mr. Ashenden. That is one of the misfortunes of my temperament." Then as Ashenden was leaving he added: "Oh, by the way, I wonder if you'd care to come to dinner with me tomorrow night. Black tie. At eight-fifteen."

He did not wait for Ashenden's assent, but took it for granted, and with a nod of dismissal sat down once more at his great writing-table.

Ashenden looked forward with misgiving to the dinner to which Sir Herbert Witherspoon had invited him. The black tie suggested a small party, perhaps only Lady Anne, the ambassador's wife, whom Ashenden did not know, or one or two young secretaries. It did not presage a hilarious evening. It was possible that they might play bridge after dinner, but Ashenden knew that professional diplomats do not play bridge with skill: it may be supposed that they find it difficult to bend their great minds to the triviality of a parlour game. On the other hand he was interested to see a little more of the ambassador in circumstances of less formality. For it was evident that Sir Herbert Witherspoon was not an ordinary person. He was in appearance and manner a perfect specimen of his class and it is always entertaining to come upon good examples of a well-known type. He was exactly what you expected an ambassador to be. If any of his characteristics had been ever so slightly exaggerated he would have been a caricature. He escaped being ridiculous only by a hair's breadth and you watched him with a kind of breathlessness as you might watch a tight-rope dancer doing perilous feats at a dizzy height. He was certainly a man of character. His rise in the diplomatic service had been rapid and though doubtless it helped him to be connected by marriage with powerful families his rise had been due chiefly to his merit. He knew how to be determined when determination was necessary and conciliatory when conciliation was opportune. His manners were perfect; he could speak half a dozen languages with ease and accuracy; he had a clear and logical brain. He was never afraid to think out his thoughts to the end, but was wise enough to suit his actions to the exigencies of the situation. He had reached his post at X at the early age of fifty-three and had borne himself in the exceedingly difficult conditions created by the war and contending parties within the state with tact, confidence and once at least with courage. For on one occasion, a riot having arisen, a band of revolutionaries forced their way into the British Embassy and Sir Herbert from the head of his stairs had harangued them and notwithstanding revolvers flourished at him had persuaded them to go to their homes. He would end his career in Paris. That was evident. He was a man whom you could not but admire but whom it was not easy to like. He was a diplomat of the school of those Victorian ambassadors to whom could confidently be entrusted great affairs and whose self-reliance, sometimes it must be admitted tinctured with arrogance, was justified by its results.

When Ashenden drove up to the doors of the Embassy they were flung open and he was received by a stout and dignified English butler and three footmen. He was ushered up that magnificent flight of stairs on which had taken place the dramatic incident just related and shown into an immense room, dimly lit with shaded lamps, in which at the first glance he caught sight of large pieces of stately furniture and over the chimney-piece an immense portrait in coronation robes of King George IV. But there was a bright fire blazing on the hearth and from a deep sofa by the side of it his host, as his name was announced, slowly rose. Sir Herbert looked very elegant as he came towards him. He wore his dinner jacket, the most difficult costume for a man to look well in, with notable distinction.

"My wife has gone to a concert, but she'll come in later. She wants to make your acquaintance. I haven't asked anybody else. I thought I would give myself the pleasure of enjoying your company *en tête-à-tête.*"

Ashenden murmured a civil rejoinder, but his heart sank. He wondered how he was going to pass at least a couple of hours alone with this man who made him, he was bound to confess, feel extremely shy.

The door was opened again and the butler and a footman entered bearing very heavy silver salvers.

"I always have a glass of sherry before my dinner," said the ambassador, "but in case you have acquired the barbarous custom of drinking cocktails I can offer you what I believe is called a dry Martini."

Shy though he might be, Ashenden was not going to give in to this sort of thing with complete tameness.

"I move with the times," he replied. "To drink a glass of sherry when you can get a dry Martini is like taking a stage-coach when you can travel by the Orient Express."

A little desultory conversation after this fashion was interrupted by the throwing open of two great doors and the announcement that His Excellency's dinner was served. They went into the dining-room. This was a vast apartment in which sixty people might have comfortably dined, but there was now only a small round table in it, so that Sir Herbert and Ashenden sat intimately. There was an immense mahogany sideboard on which were massive pieces of gold plate, and above it, facing Ashenden, was a fine picture by Cana-letto. Over the chimney-piece was a three-quarter-length portrait of Queen Victoria as a girl with a little gold crown on her small, prim head. Dinner was served by the corpulent butler and the three very tall English footmen. Ashenden had the impression that the ambassador enjoyed in his well-bred way the sensation of ignoring the pomp in which he lived. They might have been dining in one of the great country houses of England; it was a ceremony they performed, sumptuous without ostentation, and it was saved from a trifling absurdity only because it was in a tradition; but the experience gained for Ashenden a kind of savour from the thought that dwelt with him that on the other side of the wall was a restless, turbulent population that might at any moment break into bloody revolution, while not two hundred miles away men in the trenches were sheltering in their dug-outs from the bitter cold and the pitiless bombardment.

Ashenden need not have feared that the conversation would proceed with difficulty and the notion he had had that Sir Herbert had asked him in order to question him about his secret mission was quickly dispelled. The ambassador behaved to him as though he were a travelling Englishman who had presented a letter of introduction and to whom he desired to show civility. You would hardly have thought that a war was raging, for he made to it only such references as showed that he was not deliberately avoiding a distressing subject. He spoke of art and literature, proving himself to be a diligent reader of catholic taste, and when Ashenden talked to him, from personal acquaintance, of the writers whom Sir Herbert knew only through their works, he listened with the friendly condescension which the great ones of the earth affect towards the artist. (Sometimes, however, they paint a picture or write a book, and then the artist gets a little of his own back.) He mentioned in passing a character in one of Ashenden's novels, but did not make any other reference to the fact that his guest was a writer. Ashenden admired his urbanity. He disliked people to talk to him of his books, in which indeed, once written, he took small interest, and it made him self-conscious to be praised or blamed to his face. Sir Herbert Witherspoon flattered his self-esteem by showing that he had read him, but spared his delicacy by withholding his opinion of what he had read. He spoke too of the various countries in which during his career he had been stationed and of various persons, in London and elsewhere, that he and Ashenden knew in common. He talked well, not without a pleasant irony that might very well have passed for humour, and intelligently. Ashenden did not find his dinner dull, but neither did he find it exhilarating. He would have been more interested if the ambassador had not so invariably said the right, wise and sensible thing upon every topic that was introduced. Ashenden was finding it something of an effort to keep up with this distinction of mind and he would have liked the conversation to get into its shirt-sleeves, so to speak, and put its feet on the table. But of this there was no chance and Ashenden once or twice caught himself wondering how soon after dinner he could decently take his leave. At eleven he had an appointment with Herbartus at the Hôtel de Paris.

The dinner came to an end and coffee was brought in. Sir Herbert knew good food and good wine and Ashenden was obliged to admit that he had fared excellently. Liqueurs were served with the coffee, and Ashenden took a glass of brandy.

"I have some very old Benedictine," said the ambassador. "Won't you try it?"

"To tell you the honest truth I think brandy is the only liqueur worth drinking."

"I'm not sure that I don't agree with you. But in that case I must give you something better than that."

He gave an order to the butler, who presently brought in a cob-webbed bottle and two enormous glasses.

"I don't really want to boast," said the ambassador as he watched the butler pour the golden liquid into Ashenden's glass, "but I venture to think that if you like brandy you'll like this. I got it when I was counsellor for a short time in Paris."

"I've had a good deal to do lately with one of your successors then."

"Byring?"

"Yes."

"What do you think of the brandy?"

"I think it's marvellous."

"And of Byring?"

The question came so oddly on the top of the other that it sounded faintly comic.

"Oh, I think he's a damned fool."

Sir Herbert leaned back in his chair, holding the huge glass with both hands in order to bring out the aroma, and looked slowly round the stately and spacious room. The table had been cleared of superfluous things. There was a bowl of roses between Ashenden and his host. The servants switched off the electric light as they finally left the room and it was lit now only by the candles that were on the table and by the fire. Notwithstanding its size it had an air of sober comfort. The ambassador's eyes rested on the really distinguished portrait of Queen Victoria that hung over the chimney-piece.

"I wonder," he said at last.

"He'll have to leave the diplomatic service."

"I'm afraid so."

Ashenden gave him a quick glance of inquiry. He was the last man from whom he would have expected sympathy for Byring.

"Yes, in the circumstances," he proceeded, "I suppose it's inevitable that he should leave the service. I'm sorry. He's an able fellow and he'll be missed. I think he had a career before him."

"Yes, that is what I've heard. I'm told that at the F.O. they thought very highly of him."

"He has many of the gifts that are useful in this rather dreary trade," said the ambassador, with a slight smile, in his cold and judicial manner. "He's handsome, he's a gentleman, he has nice manners, he speaks excellent French and he has a good head on his shoulders. He'd have done well."

"It seems a pity that he should waste such golden opportunities."

"I understand he's going into the wine business at the end of the war. Oddly enough he's going to represent the very firm from whom I got this brandy."

Sir Herbert raised the glass to his nose and inhaled the fragrance. Then he looked at Ashenden. He had a way of looking at people, when he was thinking of something else perhaps, that suggested that he thought them somewhat peculiar but rather disgusting insects.

"Have you ever seen the woman?" he asked.

"I dined with her and Byring at Larue's."

"How very interesting. What is she like?"

"Charming."

Ashenden tried to describe her to his host, but meanwhile with another part of his mind he recollected the impression she had made on him at the restaurant when Byring had introduced him to her. He had been not a little interested to meet a woman of whom for some years he had heard so much. She called herself Rose Auburn, but what her real name was few knew. She had gone to Paris originally as one of the troupe of dancers, called the Glad Girls, who performed at the Moulin Rouge, but her astonishing beauty had soon caused her to be noticed and a wealthy French manufacturer fell in love with her. He gave her a house and loaded her with jewels, but could not long meet the demands she made upon him, and she passed in rapid succession from lover to lover. She became in a short time the best-known courtesan in France. Her expenditure was prodigal and she ruined her admirers with cynical unconcern. The richest men found themselves unable to cope with her extravagance. Ashenden, before the war, had seen her once at Monte Carlo lose a hundred and eighty thousand francs at a sitting and that then was an important sum. She sat at the big table, surrounded by curious onlookers, throwing down packets of thousand-franc notes with a self-possession that would

have been admirable if it had been her own money that she was
losing.

When Ashenden met her she had been leading this riotous life,
dancing and gambling all night, racing most afternoons a week,
for twelve or thirteen years and she was no longer very young;
but there was hardly a line on that lovely brow, scarcely a crows-
foot round those liquid eyes, to betray the fact. The most astonishing thing about her was that notwithstanding this feverish and un-
ending round of senseless debauchery she had preserved an air of
virginity. Of course she cultivated the type. She had an exquisitely
graceful and slender figure, and her innumerable frocks were always
made with a perfect simplicity. Her brown hair was very plainly
done. With her oval face, charming little nose and large blue eyes
she had all the air of one or other of Anthony Trollope's charming
heroines. It was the keepsake style raised to such rareness that it
made you catch your breath. She had a lovely skin, very white
and red, and if she painted it was not from necessity but from
wantonness. She irradiated a sort of dewy innocence that was as
attractive as it was unexpected.

Ashenden had heard of course that Byring for a year or more
had been her lover. Her notoriety was such that a hard light of
publicity was shed on everyone with whom she had any affair,
but in this instance the gossips had more to say than usual because
Byring had no money to speak of and Rose Auburn had never
been known to grant her favours for anything that did not in some
way represent hard cash. Was it possible that she loved him? It
seemed incredible and yet what other explanation was there?
Byring was a young man with whom any woman might have fallen
in love. He was somewhere in the thirties, very tall and good-
looking with a singular charm of manner and of an appearance so
debonair that people turned round in the street to look at him;
but unlike most handsome men he seemed entirely unaware of the
impression he created. When it became known that Byring was the
amant de cœur (a prettier phrase than our English fancy man) of this
famous harlot he became an object of admiration to many women
and of envy to many men; but when a rumour spread abroad that
he was going to marry her consternation seized his friends and
ribald laughter everyone else. It became known that Byring's chief
had asked him if it was true and he had admitted it. Pressure was
put upon him to relinquish a plan that could only end in disaster.
It was pointed out to him that the wife of a diplomat has social
obligations that Rose Auburn could not fulfil. Byring replied that
he was prepared to resign his post whenever by so doing he would

not cause inconvenience. He brushed aside every expostulation and every argument; he was determined to marry.

When first Ashenden met Byring he did not very much take to him. He found him slightly aloof. But as the hazards of his work brought him from time to time into contact with him he discerned that the distant manner was due merely to shyness and as he came to know him better he was charmed by the uncommon sweetness of his disposition. Their relations, however, remained purely official so that it was a trifle unexpected when Byring one day asked him to dinner to meet Miss Auburn, and he could not but wonder whether it was because already people were beginning to turn the cold shoulder on him. When he went he discovered that the invitation was due to the lady's curiosity. But the surprise he got on learning that she had found time to read (with admiration, it appeared) two or three of his novels was not the only surprise he got that evening. Leading on the whole a quiet and studious life he had never had occasion to penetrate into the world of the higher prostitution and the great courtesans of the period were known to him only by name. It was somewhat astonishing to Ashenden to discover that Rose Auburn differed so little in air and manner from the smart women of Mayfair with whom through his books he had become more or less intimately acquainted. She was perhaps a little more anxious to please (indeed one of her agreeable traits was the interest she took in whomever she was talking to), but she was certainly no more made-up and her conversation was as intelligent. It lacked only the coarseness that society has lately affected. Perhaps she felt instinctively that those lovely lips should never disfigure themselves with foul words; perhaps only she was at heart still a trifle suburban. It was evident that she and Byring were madly in love with one another. It was really moving to see their mutual passion. When Ashenden took his leave of them, as he shook hands with her (and she held his hand a moment and with her blue, starry eyes looked into his) she said to him:

"You will come and see us when we're settled in London, won't you? You know we're going to be married."

"I heartily congratulate you," said Ashenden.

"And him?" she smiled, and her smile was like an angel's; it had the freshness of dawn and the tender rapture of a southern spring.

"Have you ever looked at yourself in the glass?"

Sir Herbert Witherspoon watched him intently while Ashenden (he thought not without a trace of humour) was describing the dinner-party. No flicker of a smile brightened his cold eyes.

"Do you think it'll be a success?" he asked now.

"No."

"Why not?"

The question took Ashenden aback.

"A man not only marries his wife, he marries her friends. Do you realise the sort of people Byring will have to mix with, painted women of tarnished reputation and men who've gone down in the social scale, parasites and adventurers? Of course they'll have money, her pearls must be worth a hundred thousand pounds, and they'll be able to cut a dash in the smart Bohemia of London. Do you know the gold fringe of society? When a woman of bad character marries she earns the admiration of her set, she has worked the trick, she's caught a man and become respectable, but he, the man, only earns its ridicule. Even her own friends, the old hags with their gigolos and the abject men who earn a shabby living by introducing the unwary to tradesmen on a ten per cent commission, even they despise him. He is the mug. Believe me, to conduct yourself gracefully in such a position you need either great dignity of character or an unparalleled effrontery. Besides, do you think there's a chance of its lasting? Can a woman who's led that wild career settle down to domestic life? In a little while she'll grow bored and restless. And how long does love last? Don't you think Byring's reflections will be bitter when, caring for her no longer, he compares what he is with what he might have been?"

Witherspoon helped himself to another drop of his old brandy. Then he looked up at Ashenden with a curious expression.

"I'm not sure if a man isn't wiser to do what he wants very much to do and let the consequences take care of themselves."

"It must be very pleasant to be an ambassador," said Ashenden.

Sir Herbert smiled thinly.

"Byring rather reminds me of a fellow I knew when I was a very junior clerk at the F.O. I won't tell you his name because he's by way of being very well known now and highly respected. He's made a great success of his career. There is always something a little absurd in success."

Ashenden slightly raised his eyebrows at this statement, somewhat unexpected in the mouth of Sir Herbert Witherspoon, but did not say anything.

"He was one of my fellow-clerks. He was a brilliant creature, I don't think anyone ever denied that, and everyone prophesied from the beginning that he would go far. I venture to say that he had pretty well all the qualifications necessary for a diplomatic career. He was of a family of soldiers and sailors, nothing very grand, but eminently respectable, and he knew how to behave in the great world without bumptiousness or timidity. He was well-read. He took an interest in painting. I dare say he made himself a trifle ridiculous; he wanted to be in the movement, but he was very anxious to be modern, and at a time when little was known of Gauguin and Cézanne he raved over their pictures. There was perhaps a certain snobbishness in his attitude, a desire to shock and astonish the conventional, but at heart his admiration of the arts was genuine and sincere. He adored Paris and whenever he had the chance ran over and put up at a little hotel in the Latin Quarter, where he could rub shoulders with painters and writers. As is the habit with gentry of that sort they patronised him a little because he was nothing but a diplomat and laughed at him a little because he was evidently a gentleman. But they liked him because he was always ready to listen to their speeches, and when he praised their works they were even willing to admit that, though a philistine, he had a certain instinct for the Right Stuff."

Ashenden noted the sarcasm and smiled at the fling at his own profession. He wondered what this long description was leading to. The ambassador seemed to linger over it partly because he liked it, but also because for some reason he hesitated to come to the point.

"But my friend was modest. He enjoyed himself enormously and he listened open-mouthed when these young painters and unknown scribblers tore to pieces established reputations and talked with enthusiasm of persons of whom the sober but cultured secretaries in Downing Street had never even heard. At the back of his mind he knew that they were rather a common, second-rate lot, and when he went back to his work in London it was with no regret, but with the feeling that he had been witnessing an odd and diverting play; now the curtain had fallen he was quite ready to go home. I haven't told you that he was ambitious. He knew that his friends expected him to do considerable things and he had no notion of disappointing them. He was perfectly conscious of his abilities. He meant to succeed. Unfortunately he was not rich, he had only a few hundreds a year, but his father and mother were dead and he had neither brother nor sister. He was aware that this freedom from close ties was an asset. His opportunity to make connections that would be of use to him was unrestricted. Do you think he sounds a very disagreeable young man?"

"No," said Ashenden in answer to the sudden question. "Most clever young men are aware of their cleverness, and there is generally a certain cynicism in their calculations with regard to the future. Surely young men should be ambitious."

"Well, on one of these little trips to Paris my friend became acquainted with a talented young Irish painter called O'Malley. He's an R.A. now and paints highly paid portraits of Lord Chancellors and Cabinet Ministers. I wonder if you remember one he did of my wife, which was exhibited a couple of years ago."

"No, I don't. But I know his name."

"My wife was delighted with it. His art always seems to me very refined and agreeable. He's able to put on canvas the distinction of his sitters in a very remarkable way. When he paints a woman of breeding, you know that it is a woman of breeding and not a trollop."

"It is a charming gift," said Ashenden. "Can he also paint a slut and make her look like one?"

"He could. Now doubtless he would scarcely wish to. He was living then in a small and dirty studio in the rue du Cherche Midi with a little Frenchwoman of the character you describe and he painted several portraits of her which were extremely like."

It seemed to Ashenden that Sir Herbert was going into somewhat excessive detail, and he asked himself whether the friend of whom he was telling a story that till now seemed to lead nowhither was in point of fact himself. He began to give it more of his attention.

"My friend liked O'Malley. He was good company, the type of the agreeable rattle, and he had a truly Irish gift of the gab. He talked incessantly and in my friend's opinion brilliantly. He found it very amusing to go and sit in the studio while O'Malley was painting and listen to him chattering away about the technique of his art. O'Malley was always saying that he would paint a portrait of him and his vanity was tickled. O'Malley thought him far from plain and said it would do him good to exhibit the portrait of someone who at least looked like a gentleman."

"By the way, when was all this?" asked Ashenden.

"Oh, thirty years ago. . . . They used to talk of their future and when O'Malley said the portrait he was going to paint of my friend would look very well in the National Portrait Gallery, my friend had small doubt in the back of his mind, whatever he modestly said, that it would eventually find its way there. One evening when my friend—shall we call him Brown?—was sitting in the studio and O'Malley, desperately taking advantage of the last light of day, was trying to get finished for the Salon that portrait of his mistress which is now in the Tate Gallery, O'Malley asked him if he would like to come and dine with them. He was expecting a friend of hers, she was called Yvonne by the way, and he would be glad if Brown would make a fourth. This friend of Yvonne's was an acrobat and O'Malley was anxious to get her to pose for him in the nude. Yvonne said she had a marvellous figure. She had seen O'Malley's work and was willing enough to sit and dinner was to be devoted to settling the matter. She was not performing then, but was about to open at the Gaîtés Montparnasses and with her days free was not disinclined to oblige a friend and earn a little money. The notion amused Brown, who had never met an acrobat, and he accepted. Yvonne suggested that he might find her to his taste and if he did she could promise him that he would not find her very difficult to persuade. With his grand air and English clothes she would take him for a *milord anglais*. My friend laughed. He did not take the suggestion very seriously. '*On ne sait jamais*,' he said. Yvonne looked at him with mischievous eyes. He sat on. It was Easter time and cold, but the studio was comfortably warm, and though it was small and everything was higgledy-piggledy and the dust lay heavy on the rim of the window, it was most friendly and cosy. Brown had a tiny flat in Waverton Street, in London, with very good mezzotints on the walls and several pieces of early Chinese pottery here and there, and he wondered to himself why his tasteful sitting-room had none of the comforts of home nor the romance that he found in that disorderly studio.

"Presently there was a ring at the door and Yvonne ushered in her friend. Her name, it appeared, was Alix, and she shook hands with Brown, uttering a stereotyped phrase, with the mincing politeness of a fat woman in a *bureau de tabac*. She wore a long cloak in imitation mink and an enormous scarlet hat. She looked incredibly vulgar. She was not even pretty. She had a broad flat face, a wide mouth and an upturned nose. She had a great deal of hair, golden, but obviously dyed, and large china-blue eyes. She was heavily made-up."

Ashenden began to have no doubt that Witherspoon was narrating an experience of his own, for otherwise he could never have remembered after thirty years what hat the young woman wore and what coat, and he was amused at the ambassador's simplicity in thinking that so thin a subterfuge could disguise the truth. Ashenden could not but guess how the story would end and it tickled him to think that this cold, distinguished and exquisite person should ever have had anything like an adventure.

"She began to talk away to Yvonne, and my friend noticed that she had one feature that oddly enough he found very attractive: she had a deep and husky voice as though she were just recovering from a bad cold and, he didn't know why, it seemed to him exceedingly pleasant to listen to. He asked O'Malley if that was her natural voice and O'Malley said she had had it as long as ever he had known her. He called it a whisky voice. He told her what Brown said about it and she gave him a smile of her wide mouth and said it wasn't due to drink, it was due to standing so much on her head. That was one of the inconveniences of her profession. Then the four of them went to a beastly little restaurant off the boulevard St. Michel where for two francs fifty including wine my friend ate a dinner that seemed to him more delicious than any he had ever eaten at the Savoy or Claridge's. Alix was a very chatty young person and Brown listened with amusement, with amazement even, while in her rich, throaty voice she talked of the varied incidents of the day. She had a great command of slang and though he could not understand half of it, he was immensely tickled with its picturesque vulgarity. It was pungent of the heated asphalt, the zinc bars of cheap taverns and racy of the crowded squares in the poorer districts of Paris. There was an energy in those apt and vivid metaphors that went like champagne to his anæmic head. She was a guttersnipe, yes, that's what she was, but she had a vitality that warmed you like a blazing fire. He was conscious that Yvonne had told her that he was an unattached Englishman, with plenty of money; he saw the appraising glance she gave him and then, pretending that he had noticed nothing, he caught the phrase, *il n'est pas mal*. It faintly amused him: he had a notion himself that he was not so bad. There were places, indeed, where they went further than that. She did not pay much attention to him, in point of fact they were talking of things of which he was ignorant and he could do little more than show an intelligent interest, but now and again she gave him a long look, passing her tongue quickly round her lips, that suggested that he only had to ask for her to give. He shrugged a mental shoulder. She looked healthy and young, she had an agreeable vivacity, but beyond her husky voice there was nothing particularly attractive in her. But the notion of having a little affair in Paris did not displease him, it was life, and the thought that she was a music-hall artiste was mildly diverting: in middle age it would doubtless amuse him to remember that he had enjoyed the favours of an acrobat. Was it la Rochefoucauld or Oscar Wilde who said that you should commit errors in youth in order to have something to regret in old age? At the end of dinner (and they sat over their coffee and brandy till late), they went out into the street and Yvonne proposed that he should take Alix home. He said he would be delighted. Alix said it was not far and they walked. She told him that she had a little apartment, of course mostly she was on tour, but she liked to have a place of her own, a woman, you know, had to be in her furniture, without that she received no consideration; and presently they reached a shabby house in a bedraggled street. She rang the bell for the *concierge* to open the door. She did not press him to enter. He did not know if she looked upon it as a matter of course. He was seized with timidity. He racked his brains, but could not think of a single thing to say. Silence fell upon them. It was absurd. With a little click the door opened; she looked at him expectantly; she was puzzled; a wave of shyness swept over him. Then she held out her hand, thanked him for bringing her to the door, and bade him good-night. His heart beat nervously. If she had asked him to come in he would have gone. He wanted some sign that she would like him to. He shook her hand, said goodnight, raised his hat and walked away. He felt a perfect fool. He could not sleep; he tossed from side to side of his bed, thinking for what a noodle she must take him, and he could hardly wait for the day that would permit him to take steps to efface the contemptible impression he must have made on her. His pride was lacerated. Wanting to lose no time he went round to her house at eleven to ask her to lunch with him, but she was out; he sent round some flowers and later in the day called again. She had been in, but was gone out once more. He went to see O'Malley on the chance of finding her, but she was not there, and O'Malley facetiously asked him how he had fared. To save his face he told him that he had come to the conclusion that she did not mean very much to him and so like a perfect gentleman he had left her. But he had an uneasy feeling that O'Malley saw through his story. He sent her a *pneumatique* asking her to dine with him next day. She did not answer. He could not understand it, he asked the porter of his hotel a dozen times if there was nothing for him, and at last, almost in desperation, just before dinner went to her house. The *concierge* told him she was in and he went up. He was very nervous, inclined to be angry because she had treated his invitation so cavalierly, but at the same time anxious to appear at his ease. He climbed the four flights of stairs, dark and smelly, and rang at the door to which he had been directed. There was a pause, he heard sounds within and rang again. Presently she opened. He had an absolute certitude that she did not in the least know who he was. He was taken aback, it was a blow to his vanity; but he assumed a cheerful smile.

" 'I came to find out if you were going to dine with me to-night. I sent you a *pneumatique*.'

"Then she recognised him. But she stood at the door and did not ask him in.

" 'Oh, no, I can't dine with you to-night. I have terrible megrim and I am going to bed. I couldn't answer your *pneumatique*, I mislaid it, and I'd forgotten your name. Thank you for the flowers. It was nice of you to send them.'

" ' Then you won't come and dine with me to-morrow night?'

" '*Justement*, I have an engagement to-morrow night. I'm sorry.'

"There was nothing more to say. He had not the nerve to ask her anything else and so bade her good-night and went. He had the impression that she was not vexed with him, but that she had entirely forgotten him. It was humiliating. When he went back to London without having seen her again, it was with a curious sense of dissatisfaction. He was not in the least in love with her, he was annoyed with her, but he could not get her quite out of his mind. He was honest enough to realise that he was suffering from nothing more than wounded vanity.

"During that dinner at the little restaurant off the Boul' Mich' she had mentioned that her troupe was going to London in the spring and in one of his letters to O'Malley he slipped in casually a phrase to the effect that if his young friend Alix happened to be coming to town he (O'Malley) might let him know and he would look her up. He would like to hear from her own ingenuous lips what she thought of the nude O'Malley had painted of her. When the painter some time afterwards wrote and told him that she was appearing a week later at the Metropolitan in the Edgware Road, he felt a sudden rush of blood to his head. He went to see her play. If he had not taken the precaution to go earlier in the day and look at the programme he would have missed her, for her turn was the first on the list. There were two men, a stout one and a thin one, with large black moustaches, and Alix. They were dressed in ill-fitting pink tights with green satin trunks. The men did various exercises on twin trapezes while Alix tripped about the stage, giving them handkerchiefs to wipe their hands on, and occasionally turned a somersault. When the fat man raised the thin one on his shoulders she climbed up and stood on the shoulders of the second, kissing her hand to the audience. They did tricks with safety bicycles. There is often grace, and even beauty, in the performance of clever acrobats, but this one was so crude, so vulgar that my friend felt positively embarrassed. There is something shameful in seeing grown men publicly make fools of themselves. Poor Alix, with a fixed and artificial smile on her lips, in her pink tights and green satin trunks, was so grotesque that he wondered how he could have let himself feel a moment's annoyance because when he went to her apartment she had not recognised

him. It was with a shrug of the shoulders, condescendingly, that
he went round to the stage door afterwards and gave the door-
keeper a shilling to take her his card. In a few minutes she came out.
She seemed delighted to see him.

" 'Oh, how good it is to see the face of someone you know in
this sad city,' she said. 'Ah, now you can give me that dinner you
asked me to in Paris. I'm dying of hunger. I never eat before the
show. Imagine that they should have given us such a bad place
on the programme. It's an insult. But we shall see the agent to-
morrow. If they think they can put upon us like that they are mistaken. *Ah, non, non et non!* And what an audience! No enthusiasm,
no applause, nothing.'

"My friend was staggered. Was it possible that she took her performance seriously? He almost burst out laughing. But she still
spoke with that throaty voice that had such a queer effect on his
nerves. She was dressed all in red and wore the same red hat in
which he had first seen her. She looked so flashy that he did not
fancy the notion of asking her to a place where he might be seen
and so suggested Soho. There were hansoms still in those days, and
the hansom was more conductive to love-making, I imagine, than
is the taxi of the present time. My friend put his arm round Alix's
waist and kissed her. It left her calm, but on the other hand did
not wildly excite him. While they ate a late dinner he made himself
very gallant and she played up to him agreeably; but when they got
up to go and he proposed that she should come round to his rooms
in Waverton Street she told him that a friend had come over from
Paris with her and that she had to meet him at eleven: she had
only been able to dine with Brown because her companion had a
business engagement. Brown was exasperated, but did not want to
show it, and when, as they walked down Wardour Street (for she
said she wanted to go to the Café Monico), pausing in front of a
pawnbroker's to look at the jewellery in the window, she went into
ecstasies over a bracelet of sapphires and diamonds that Brown
thought incredibly vulgar, he asked her if she would like it.

" ' But it's marked fifteen pounds,' she said.

"He went in and bought it for her. She was delighted. She made
him leave her just before they came to Piccadilly Circus.

" 'Now listen, *mon petit*,' she said, 'I cannot see you in London
because of my friend, he is jealous as a wolf, that is why I think it
is more prudent for you to go now, but I am playing at Boulogne
next week, why do you not come over? I shall be alone there. My
friend has to go back to Holland, where he lives.'

" 'All right,' said Brown, 'I'll come.'

"When he went to Boulogne—he had two days' leave—it was with the one idea of salving the wound to his pride. It was odd that he should care. I daresay to you it seems inexplicable. He could not bear the notion that Alix looked upon him as a fool and he felt that when once he had removed that impression from her he would never bother about her again. He thought of O'Malley too, and of Yvonne. She must have told them and it galled him to think that people whom in his heart he despised should laugh at him behind his back. Do you think he was very contemptible?"

"Good gracious, no," said Ashenden. "All sensible people know that vanity is the most devastating, the most universal and the most ineradicable of the passions that afflict the soul of man, and it is only vanity that makes him deny its power. It is more consuming than love. With advancing years, mercifully, you can snap your fingers at the terror and the servitude of love, but age cannot free you from the thraldom of vanity. Time can assuage the pangs of love, but only death can still the anguish of wounded vanity. Love is simple and seeks no subterfuge, but vanity cozens you with a hundred disguises. It is part and parcel of every virtue: it is the mainspring of courage and the strength of ambition; it gives constancy to the lover and endurance to the stoic; it adds fuel to the fire of the artist's desire for fame and is at once the support and the compensation of the honest man's integrity; it leers even cynically in the humility of the saint. You cannot escape it, and should you take pains to guard against it, it will make use of those very pains to trip you up. You are defenceless against its onslaught because you know not on what unprotected side it will attack you. Sincerity cannot protect you from its snare nor humour from its mockery."

Ashenden stopped, not because he had said all he had to say, but because he was out of breath. He noticed also that the ambassador, desiring to talk rather than to listen, heard him with a politeness that was strained. But he had made this speech not so much for his host's edification as for his own entertainment.

"It is vanity finally that makes man support his abominable lot."

For a minute Sir Herbert was silent. He looked straight in front of him as though his thoughts lingered distressfully on some far horizon of memory.

"When my friend came back from Boulogne he knew that he was madly in love with Alix and he had arranged to meet her again in a fortnight's time when she would be performing at Dunkirk. He thought of nothing else in the interval and the night before he was to start, he only had thirty-six hours this time, he could not sleep, so devouring was the passion that consumed him. Then he went over for a night to Paris to see her and once when she was disengaged for a week he persuaded her to come to London. He knew that she did not love him. He was just a man among a hundred others and she made no secret of the fact that he was not her only lover. He suffered agonies of jealousy but knew that it would only excite her ridicule or her anger if he showed it. She had not even a fancy for him. She liked him because he was a gentleman and well dressed. She was quite willing to be his mistress so long as the claims he made on her were not irksome. But that was all. His means were not large enough to enable him to make her any serious offers, but even if they had been, liking her freedom, she would have refused."

"But what about the Dutchman?" asked Ashenden.

"The Dutchman? He was a pure invention. She made him up on the spur of the moment because for one reason or another she did not just then want to be bothered with Brown. What should one lie more or less matter to her? Don't think he didn't struggle against his passion. He knew it was madness, he knew that a permanent connection between them could only lead to disaster for him. He had no illusions about her: she was common, coarse and vulgar. She could talk of none of the things that interested him, nor did she try, she took it for granted that he was concerned with her affairs and told him interminable stories of her quarrels with fellow-performers, her disputes with managers and her wrangles with hotel-keepers. What she said bored him to death, but the sound of her throaty voice made his heart beat so that sometimes he thought he would suffocate."

Ashenden sat uneasily in his chair. It was a Sheraton chair very good to look at, but hard and straight; and he wished that Sir Herbert had had the notion of going back to the other room where there was a comfortable sofa. It was quite plain now that the story he was telling was about himself and Ashenden felt a certain indelicacy in the man's stripping his soul before him so nakedly. He did not desire this confidence to be forced upon him. Sir Herbert Witherspoon meant nothing to him. By the light of the shaded candles Ashenden saw that he was deathly pale and there was a wildness in his eyes that in that cold and composed man was strangely disconcerting. He poured himself out a glass of water; his throat was dry so that he could hardly speak. But he went on pitilessly.

"At last my friend managed to pull himself together. He was disgusted by the sordidness of his intrigue; there was no beauty in it, nothing but shame; and it was leading to nothing. His passion was as vulgar as the woman for whom he felt it. Now it happened that Alix was going to spend six months in the North of Africa with her troupe and for that time at least it would be impossible for him to see her. He made up his mind that he must seize the opportunity and make a definite break. He knew bitterly that it would mean nothing to her. In three weeks she would have forgotten him.

"And then there was something else. He had come to know very well some people, a man and his wife, whose social and political connections were extremely important. They had an only daughter and, I don't know why, she fell in love with him. She was everything that Alix was not, pretty in the real English way, with blue eyes and pink and white cheeks, tall and fair; she might have stepped out of one of du Maurier's pictures in *Punch*. She was clever and well-read, and since she had lived all her life in political circles she could talk intelligently of the sort of things that interested him. He had reason to believe that if he asked her to marry him she would accept. I have told you that he was ambitious. He knew that he had great abilities and he wanted the chance to use them. She was related to some of the greatest families in England and he would have been a fool not to realise that a marriage of this kind must make his path infinitely easier. The opportunity was golden. And what a relief to think that he could put behind him definitely that ugly little episode, and what a happiness, instead of that wall of cheerful indifference and matter-of-fact good nature against which in his passion for Alix he had vainly battered his head, what a happiness to feel that to someone else he really meant something! How could he help being flattered and touched when he saw her face light up as he came into the room? He wasn't in love with her, but he thought her charming, and he wanted to forget Alix and the vulgar life into which she had led him. At last he made up his mind. He asked her to marry him and was accepted. Her family was delighted. The marriage was to take place in the autumn, since her father had to go on some political errand to South America and was taking his wife and daughter with him. They were to be gone the whole summer. My friend Brown was transferring from the F.O. to the diplomatic service and had been promised a post at Lisbon. He was to go there immediately.

"He saw his fiancée off. Then it happened that owing to some hitch the man whom Brown was going to replace was kept at Lisbon three months longer and so for that period my friend found himself at a loose end. And just when he was making up his mind what to do with himself he received a letter from Alix. She was coming back to France and had a tour booked; she gave him a long list of the places she was going to, and in her casual, friendly way said that they would have fun if he could manage to run over for a day or two. An insane, a criminal notion seized him. If she had shown any eagerness for him to come he might have resisted, it was her airy, matter-of-fact indifference that took him. On a sudden he longed for her. He did not care if she was gross and vulgar, he had got her in his bones, and it was his last chance. In a little while he was going to be married. It was now or never. He went down to Marseilles and met her as she stepped off the boat that had brought her from Tunis. His heart leaped at the pleasure she showed on seeing him. He knew he loved her madly. He told her that he was going to be married in three months and asked her to spend the last of his freedom with her. She refused to abandon her tour. How could she leave her companions in the lurch? He offered to compensate them, but she would not hear of it; they could not find someone to take her place at a moment's notice, nor could they afford to throw over a good engagement that might lead to others in the future; they were honest people, and they kept their word, they had their duty to their managers and their duty to their public. He was exasperated; it seemed absurd that his whole happiness should be sacrificed to that wretched tour. And at the end of the three months? What was to happen to her then? Oh, no, he was asking something that wasn't reasonable. He told her that he adored her. He did not know till then how insanely he loved her. Well, then, she said, why did he not come with her and make the tour with them? She would be glad of his company; they could have a good time together and at the end of three months he could go and marry his heiress and neither of them would be any the worse. For a moment he hesitated, but now that he saw her again he could not bear the thought of being parted from her so soon. He accepted. And then she said:

" 'But listen, my little one, you mustn't be silly, you know. The managers won't be too pleased with me if I make a lot of *chichi*, I have to think of my future, and they won't be so anxious to have me back if I refuse to please old customers of the house. It won't be very often, but it must be understood that you are not to make me scenes if now and then I give myself to someone whose fancy I take. It will mean nothing, that is business, you will be my *amant de cœur*.'

"He felt a strange, excruciating pain in his heart, and I think he went so pale that she thought he was going to faint. She looked at him curiously.

" 'Those are the terms,' she said. 'You can either take them or leave them.'

"He accepted."

Sir Herbert Witherspoon leaned forward in his chair and he was so white that Ashenden thought too that he was going to faint. His skin was drawn over his skull so that his face looked like a death's head, but the veins on his forehead stood out like knotted cords. He had lost all reticence. And Ashenden once more wished that he would stop, it made him shy and nervous to see the man's naked soul: no one has the right to show himself to another in that destitute state. He was inclined to cry:

"Stop, stop. You mustn't tell me any more. You'll be so ashamed." But the man had lost all shame.

"For three months they travelled together from one dull provincial town to another, sharing a filthy little bedroom in frowsy hotels; Alix would not let him take her to good hotels, she said she had not the clothes for them and she was more comfortable in the sort of hotel she was used to; she did not want her companions in the business to say that she was putting on side. He sat interminable hours in shabby cafés. He was treated as a brother by members of the troupe, they called him by his Christian name and chaffed him coarsely and slapped him on the back. He ran errands for them when they were busy with their work. He saw the good-humoured contempt in the eyes of managers and was obliged to put up with the familiarity of stage-hands. They travelled third-class from place to place and he helped to carry the luggage. He with whom reading was a passion never opened a book because Alix was bored by reading and thought that anyone who did was just giving himself airs. Every night he went to the music-hall and watched her go through that grotesque and ignoble performance. He had to fall in with her pathetic fancy that it was artistic. He had to congratulate her when it had gone well and condole with her when some feat of agility had gone amiss. When she had finished he went to a café and waited for her while she changed, and sometimes she would come in rather hurriedly and say:

" 'Don't wait for me to-night, mon chou, I'm busy.'

"And then he would undergo agonies of jealousy. He would suffer as he never knew a man could suffer. She would come back to the hotel at three or four in the morning. She wondered why he was not asleep. Sleep! How could he sleep with that misery gnawing at his heart? He had promised he would not interfere with her. He did not keep his promise. He made her terrific scenes. Sometimes he beat her. Then she would lose her patience and tell him she was sick of him, she would pack her things to go, and then he would go grovelling to her, promising anything, any submission, vowing to swallow any humiliation, if she would not leave him. It was horrible and degrading. He was miserable. Miserable? No, he was happier than he'd ever been in his life. It was the gutter that he wallowed in, but he wallowed in it with delight. Oh, he was so bored with the life he'd led hitherto, and this one seemed to him amazing and romantic. This was reality. And that frowsy, ugly woman with the whisky voice, she had such a splendid vitality, such a zest for life that she seemed to raise his own to some more vivid level. It really did seem to him to burn with a pure, gem-like flame. Do people still read Pater?"

"I don't know," said Ashenden. "I don't."

"There was only three months of it. Oh, how short the time seemed and how quickly the weeks sped by! Sometimes he had wild dreams of abandoning everything and throwing in his lot with the acrobats. They had come to have quite a liking for him and they said he could easily train himself to take a part in the turn. He knew they said it more in jest than in earnest, but the notion vaguely tickled him. But these were only dreams and he knew that nothing would come of them. He never really chaffered with the thought that when the three months came to an end he would not return to his own life with its obligations. With his mind, that cold, logical mind of his, he knew it would be absurd to sacrifice everything for a woman like Alix; he was ambitious, he wanted power; and besides, he could not break the heart of that poor child who loved and trusted him. She wrote to him once a week. She was longing to get back, the time seemed endless to her and he, he had a secret wish that something would happen to delay her arrival. If he could only have a little more time! Perhaps if he had six months he would have got over his infatuation. Already sometimes he hated Alix.

"The last day came. They seemed to have little to say to one another. They were both sad; but he knew that Alix only regretted the breaking of an agreeable habit, in twenty-four hours she would be as gay and full of spirits with her stray companion as though he had never crossed her path; he could only think that next day he was going to Paris to meet his fiancée and her family. They spent their last night in one another's arms weeping. If she'd asked him then not to leave her it may be that he would have stayed; but she didn't, it never occurred to her, she accepted his going as a settled thing, and she wept not because she loved him, she wept because he was unhappy.

"In the morning she was sleeping so soundly that he had not the heart to wake her to say good-bye. He slipped out very quietly, with his bag in his hand, and took the train to Paris."

Ashenden turned away his head, for he saw two tears form themselves in Witherspoon's eyes and roll down his cheeks. He did not even try to hide them. Ashenden lit another cigar.

"In Paris they cried out when they saw him. They said he looked like a ghost. He told them he'd been ill and hadn't said anything about it in order not to worry them. They were very kind. A month later he was married. He did very well for himself. He was given opportunities to distinguish himself and he distinguished himself. His rise was spectacular. He had the well-ordered and distinguished establishment that he had wanted. He had the power for which he had craved. He was loaded with honours. Oh, he made a success of life and there were hundreds who envied him. It was all ashes. He was bored, bored to distraction, bored by that distinguished, beautiful lady he had married, bored by the people his life forced him to live with; it was a comedy he was playing and sometimes it seemed intolerable to live for ever and ever behind a mask, sometimes he felt he couldn't bear it. But he bore it. Sometimes he longed for Alix so fiercely that he felt it would be better to shoot himself than to suffer such anguish. He never saw her again. Never. He heard from O'Malley that she had married and left her troupe. She must be a fat old woman now and it doesn't matter any more. But he had wasted his life. And he never even made that poor creature whom he married happy. How could he go on hiding from her year after year that he had nothing to give her but pity? Once in his agony he told her about Alix and she tortured him ever after with her jealousy. He knew that he should never have married her; in six months she would have got over her grief if he had told her he could not bear to, and in the end would have happily married somebody else. So far as she was concerned his sacrifice was vain. He was terribly conscious that he had only one life and it seemed so sad to think that he had wasted it. He could never surmount his immeasurable regret. He laughed when people spoke of him as a strong man: he was as weak and unstable as water. And that's why I tell you that Byring is right. Even though it only lasts five years, even though he ruins his career, even though this marriage of his ends in disaster, it will have been worth while. He will have been satisfied. He will have fulfilled himself."

At that moment the door opened and a lady came in. The ambassador glanced at her and for an instant a look of cold hatred crossed his face, but it was only for an instant; then, rising from the table, he composed his ravaged features to an expression of courteous suavity. He gave the incomer a haggard smile.

"Here is my wife. This is Mr. Ashenden."

"I couldn't imagine where you were. Why didn't you go and sit in your study? I'm sure Mr. Ashenden's been dreadfully uncomfortable."

She was a tall, thin woman of fifty, rather drawn and faded, but she looked as though she had once been pretty. It was obvious that she was very well-bred. She vaguely reminded you of an exotic plant, reared in a hot-house, that had begun to lose its bloom. She was dressed in black.

"What was the concert like?" asked Sir Herbert.

"Oh, not bad at all. They gave a Brahms Concerto and the Fire-music from the *Walküre*, and some Hungarian dances of Dvoràk. I thought them rather showy." She turned to Ashenden. "I hope you haven't been bored all alone with my husband. What have you been talking about? Art and Literature?"

"No, its raw material," said Ashenden.

He took his leave.

Mr. Harrington's Washing

WHEN Ashenden went on deck and saw before him a low-lying coast and a white town he felt a pleasant flutter of excitement. It was early and the sun had not long risen, but the sea was glassy and the sky was blue; it was warm already and one knew that the day would be sweltering. Vladivostok. It really gave one the sensation of being at the end of the world. It was a long journey that Ashenden had made from New York to San Francisco, across the Pacific in a Japanese boat to Yokohama, then from Tsuruki in a Russian boat, he the only Englishman on board, up the Sea of Japan. From Vladivostok he was to take the Trans-Siberian to Petrograd. It was the most important mission that he had ever had and he was pleased with the sense of responsibility that it gave him. He had no one to give him orders, unlimited funds (he carried in a belt next to his skin bills of exchange for a sum so enormous that he was staggered when he thought of them), and though he had been set to do something that was beyond human possibility he did not know this and was prepared to set about his task with confidence. He believed in his own astuteness. Though he had both esteem and admiration for the sensibility of the human race, he had little respect for their intelligence: man has always found it easier to sacrifice his life than to learn the multiplication table.

Ashenden did not much look forward to ten days on a Russian train, and in Yokohama he had heard rumours that in one or two places bridges had been blown up and the line cut. He was told that the soldiers, completely out of hand, would rob him of everything he possessed and turn him out on the steppe to shift for himself. It was a cheerful prospect. But the train was certainly starting and whatever happened later (and Ashenden had always a feeling that things never turned out as badly as you expected) he was determined to get a place on it. His intention on landing was to go at once to the British Consulate and find out what arrangements had been made for him; but as they neared the shore and he was able to discern the untidy and bedraggled town he felt not a little forlorn. He knew but a few words of Russian. The only man on the ship who spoke English was the purser and though he promised Ashenden to do anything he could to help him, Ashenden had the impression that he must not too greatly count upon him. It was a relief then, when they docked, to have a young man, small and with a mop of untidy hair, obviously a Jew, come up to him and ask if his name was Ashenden.

"Mine is Benedict. I'm the interpreter at the British Consulate. I've been told to look after you. We've got you a place on the train to-night."

Ashenden's spirits went up. They landed. The little Jew looked after his luggage and had his passport examined and then, getting into a car that waited for them, they drove off to the Consulate.

"I've had instructions to offer you every facility," said the Consul, "and you've only got to tell me what you want. I've fixed you up all right on the train, but God knows if you'll ever get to Petrograd. Oh, by the way, I've got a travelling companion for you. He's a man called Harrington, an American, and he's going to Petrograd for a firm in Philadelphia. He's trying to fix up some deal with the Provisional Government."

"What's he like?" asked Ashenden.

"Oh, he's all right. I wanted him to come with the American Consul to luncheon, but they've gone for an excursion in the country. You must get to the station a couple of hours before the train starts. There's always an awful scrimmage and if you're not there in good time someone will pinch your seat."

The train started at midnight and Ashenden dined with Benedict at the station restaurant, which was, it appeared, the only place in that slatternly town where you could get a decent meal. It was crowded. The service was intolerably slow. Then they went on to the platform, where, though they had still two hours to spare, there was already a seething mob. Whole families, sitting on piles of luggage, seemed to be camped there. People rushed to and fro, or stood in little groups violently arguing. Women screamed. Others were silently weeping. Here two men were engaged in a fierce quarrel. It was a scene of indescribable confusion. The light in the station was wan and cold and the white faces of all those people were like the white faces of the dead waiting, patient or anxious, distraught or penitent, for the judgment of the last day. The train was made up and most of the carriages were already filled to overflowing. When at last Benedict found that in which Ashenden had his place a man sprang out of it excitedly.

"Come in and sit down," he said. "I've had the greatest difficulty in keeping your seat. A fellow wanted to come in here with a wife and two children. My Consul has just gone off with him to see the stationmaster."

"This is Mr. Harrington," said Benedict.

Ashenden stepped into the carriage. It had two berths in it. The porter stowed his luggage away. He shook hands with his travelling companion.

Mr. John Quincy Harrington was a very thin man of somewhat less than middle height, he had a yellow, bony face, with large, pale-blue eyes and when he took off his hat to wipe his brow wet from the perturbation he had endured he showed a large, bald skull; it was very bony and the ridges and protuberances stood out disconcertingly. He wore a bowler-hat, a black coat and waistcoat, and a pair of striped trousers; a very high white collar and a neat, unobtrusive tie. Ashenden did not know precisely how you should dress in order to take a ten days' journey across Siberia, but he could not but think that Mr. Harrington's costume was eccentric. He spoke with precision in a high-pitched voice and in an accent that Ashenden recognised as that of New England.

In a minute the stationmaster came accompanied by a bearded Russian, suffering evidently from profound emotion, and followed by a lady holding two children by the hand. The Russian, tears running down his face, was talking with quivering lips to the stationmaster, and his wife between her sobs was apparently telling him the story of her life. When they arrived at the carriage the altercation became more violent and Benedict joined in with his fluent Russian. Mr. Harrington did not know a word of the language, but being obviously of an excitable turn broke in and explained in voluble English that these seats had been booked by the Consuls of Great Britain and the United States, respectively and though he didn't know about the King of England, he could tell them straight and they could take it from him that the President of the United States would never permit an American citizen to be done out of a seat on the train that he had duly paid for. He would yield to force, but to nothing else, and if they touched him he would register a complaint with the Consul at once. He said all this and a great deal more to the stationmaster, who of course had no notion what he was talking about, but with much emphasis and a good deal of gesticulation made him in reply a passionate speech. This roused Mr. Harrington to the utmost pitch of indignation, for shaking his fist in the stationmaster's face, his own pale with fury, he cried out:

"Tell him I don't understand a word he says and I don't want to understand. If the Russians want us to look upon them as a civilised people, why don't they talk a civilised language? Tell him that I am Mr. John Quincy Harrington and I'm travelling on behalf of Messrs. Crewe and Adams of Philadelphia with a special letter of introduction to Mr. Kerensky and if I'm not left in peaceful possession of this carriage Mr. Crewe will take the matter up with the Administration in Washington."

Mr. Harrington's manner was so truculent and his gestures so

z

menacing that the stationmaster, throwing up the sponge, turned on his heel without another word and walked moodily away. He was followed by the bearded Russian and his wife arguing heatedly with him and the two apathetic children. Mr. Harrington jumped back into the carriage.

"I'm terribly sorry to have to refuse to give up my seat to a lady with two children," he said. "No one knows better than I the respect due to a woman and a mother, but I've got to get to Petrograd by this train if I don't want to lose a very important order and I'm not going to spend ten days in a corridor for all the mothers in Russia."

"I don't blame you," said Ashenden.

"I am a married man and I have two children myself. I know that travelling with your family is a difficult matter, but there's nothing that I know to prevent you from staying at home."

When you are shut up with a man for ten days in a railway carriage you can hardly fail to learn most of what there is to know about him, and for ten days (for eleven to be exact) Ashenden spent twenty-four hours a day with Mr. Harrington. It is true that they went into the dining-room three times a day for their meals, but they sat opposite to one another; it is true that the train stopped for an hour morning and afternoon so that they were able to have a tramp up and down the platform, but they walked side by side. Ashenden made acquaintance with some of his fellow-travellers and sometimes they came into the compartment to have a chat, but if they only spoke French or German Mr. Harrington would watch them with acidulous disapproval and if they spoke English he would never let them get a word in. For Mr. Harrington was a talker. He talked as though it were a natural function of the human being, automatically, as men breathe or digest their food; he talked not because he had something to say, but because he could not help himself, in a high-pitched, nasal voice, without inflection, at one dead level of tone. He talked with precision, using a copious vocabulary and forming his sentences with deliberation; he never used a short word when a longer one would do; he never paused. He went on and on. It was not a torrent, for there was nothing impetuous about it, it was like a stream of lava pouring irresistibly down the side of a volcano. It flowed with a quiet and steady force that overwhelmed everything that was in its path.

Ashenden thought he had never known as much about anyone as he knew about Mr. Harrington, and not only about him, with all his opinions, habits and circumstances, but about his wife and his wife's family, his children and their schoolfellows, his employers and the alliances they had made for three or four generations with the best families of Philadelphia. His own family had come from Devonshire early in the eighteenth century and Mr. Harrington had been to the village where the graves of his forebears were still to be seen in the churchyard. He was proud of his English ancestry, but proud too of his American birth, though to him America was a little strip of land along the Atlantic coast and Americans were a small number of persons of English or Dutch origin whose blood had never been sullied by foreign admixture. He looked upon the Germans, Swedes, Irish and the inhabitants of Central and Eastern Europe who for the last hundred years have descended upon the United States as interlopers. He turned his attention away from them as a maiden lady who lived in a secluded manor might avert her eyes from the factory chimneys that had trespassed upon her retirement.

When Ashenden mentioned a man of vast wealth who owned some of the finest pictures in America Mr. Harrington said:

"I've never met him. My great-aunt Maria Penn Warmington always said his grandmother was a very good cook. My great-aunt Maria was terribly sorry when she left her to get married. She said she never knew anyone who could make an apple pancake as she could."

Mr. Harrington was devoted to his wife and he told Ashenden at unbelievable length how cultivated and what a perfect mother she was. She had delicate health and had undergone a great number of operations all of which he described in detail. He had had two operations himself, one on his tonsils and one to remove his appendix, and he took Ashenden day by day through his experiences. All his friends had had operations and his knowledge of surgery was encyclopædic. He had two sons, both at school, and he was seriously considering whether he would not be well-advised to have them operated on. It was curious that one of them should have enlarged tonsils, and he was not at all happy about the appendix of the other. They were more devoted to one another than he had ever seen two brothers be and a very good friend of his, the brightest surgeon in Philadelphia, had offered to operate on them both together so that they should not be separated. He showed Ashenden photographs of the boys and their mother. This journey of his to Russia was the first time in their lives that he had been separated from them and every morning he wrote a long letter to his wife telling her everything that had happened and a good deal of what he had said during the day. Ashenden watched him cover sheet after sheet of paper with his neat, legible and precise handwriting.

Mr. Harrington had read all the books on conversation and knew its technique to the last detail. He had a little book in which he noted down the stories he heard and he told Ashenden that when he was going out to dinner he always looked up half a dozen so that he should not be at a loss. They were marked with a G if they could be told in general society and with an M (for men) if they were more fit for rough masculine ears. He was a specialist in that peculiar form of anecdote that consists in narrating a long serious incident, piling detail upon detail, till a comic end is reached. He spared you nothing and Ashenden foreseeing the point long before it arrived would clench his hands and knit his brows in the strenuous effort not to betray his impatience and at last force from his unwilling mouth a grim and hollow laugh. If someone came into the compartment in the middle Mr. Harrington would greet him with cordiality.

"Come right in and sit down. I was just telling my friend a story. You must listen to it, it's one of the funniest things you ever heard."

Then he would begin again from the very beginning and repeat it word for word, without altering a single apt epithet, till he reached the humorous end. Ashenden suggested once that they should see whether they could find two people on the train who played cards so that they might while away the time with a game of bridge, but Mr. Harrington said he never touched cards and when Ashenden in desperation began to play patience he pulled a wry face.

"It beats me how an intelligent man can waste his time card-playing, and of all the unintellectual pursuits I have ever seen it seems to me that solitaire is the worst. It kills conversation. Man is a social animal and he exercises the highest part of his nature when he takes part in social intercourse."

"There is a certain elegance in wasting time," said Ashenden. "Any fool can waste money, but when you waste time you waste what is priceless. Besides," he added with bitterness, "you can still talk."

"How can I talk when your attention is taken up by whether you are going to get a black seven to put on a red eight? Conversation calls forth the highest powers of the intellect and if you have made a study of it you have the right to expect that the person you're talking to will give you the fullest attention he is capable of."

He did not say this acrimoniously, but with the good-humoured patience of a man who has been much tried. He was just stating a plain fact and Ashenden could take it or leave it. It was the claim of the artist to have his work taken seriously.

Mr. Harrington was a diligent reader. He read pencil in hand, underlining passages that attracted his attention and on the margin making in his neat writing comments on what he read. This he was

fond of discussing and when Ashenden himself was reading and
felt on a sudden that Mr. Harrington, book in one hand and pencil
in the other, was looking at him with his large pale eyes he began to
have violent palpitations of the heart. He dared not look up, he
dared not even turn the page, for he knew that Mr. Harrington
would regard this as ample excuse to break into a discourse, but
remained with his eyes fixed desperately on a single word, like a
chicken with its beak to a chalk line, and only ventured to breathe
when he realised that Mr. Harrington, having given up the attempt,
had resumed his reading. He was then engaged on a History of the
American Constitution in two volumes and for recreation was
perusing a stout volume that purported to contain all the great
speeches of the world. For Mr. Harrington was an after-dinner
speaker and had read all the best books on speaking in public. He
knew exactly how to get on good terms with his audience, just where
to put in the serious words that touched their hearts, how to catch
their attention by a few apt stories and finally with what degree of
eloquence, suiting the occasion, to deliver his peroration

Mr. Harrington was very fond of reading aloud. Ashenden had
had frequent occasion to observe the distressing propensity of Americans for this pastime. In hotel drawing-rooms at night after dinner
he had often seen the father of a family seated in a retired corner and
surrounded by his wife, his two sons and his daughter, reading to
them. On ships crossing the Atlantic he had sometimes watched
with awe the tall, spare gentleman of commanding aspect who sat in
the centre of fifteen ladies no longer in their first youth and in a
resonant voice read to them the history of Art. Walking up and
down the promenade deck he had passed honeymooning couples
lying on deck-chairs and caught the unhurried tones of the bride
as she read to her young husband the pages of a popular novel.
It had always seemed to him a curious way of showing affection.
He had had friends who had offered to read to him and he had
known women who had said they loved being read to, but he had
always politely refused the invitation and firmly ignored the hint.
He liked neither reading aloud nor being read aloud to. In his
heart he thought the national predilection for this form of entertainment the only flaw in the perfection of the American character.
But the immortal gods love a good laugh at the expense of human
beings and now delivered him, bound and helpless, to the knife of the
high priest. Mr. Harrington flattered himself that he was a very good
reader and he explained to Ashenden the theory and practice of the
art. Ashenden learned that there were two schools, the dramatic and
the natural: in the first you imitated the voices of those who spoke (if

you were reading a novel), and when the heroine wailed you wailed and when emotion choked her you choked too; but in the other you read as impassively as though you were reading the price-list of a mail-order house in Chicago. This was the school Mr. Harrington belonged to. In the seventeen years of his married life he had read aloud to his wife, and to his sons as soon as they were old enough to appreciate them, the novels of Sir Walter Scott, Jane Austen, Dickens and Brönte Sisters, Thackeray, George Eliot, Nathaniel Hawthorne and W. D. Howells. Ashenden came to the conclusion that it was second nature with Mr. Harrington to read aloud and to prevent him from doing so made him as uneasy as cutting off his tobacco made the confirmed smoker. He would take you unawares.

"Listen to this," he would say, "you must listen to this," as though he were suddenly struck by the excellence of a maxim or the neatness of a phrase. "Now just tell me if you don't think this is remarkably well put. It's only three lines."

He read them and Ashenden was willing to give him a moment's attention, but having finished them, without pausing for a moment to take breath, he went on. He went right on. On and on. In his measured high-pitched voice, without emphasis or expression, he read page after page. Ashenden fidgeted, crossed and uncrossed his legs, lit cigarettes and smoked them, sat first in one position, then in another. Mr. Harrington went on and on. The train went leisurely through the interminable steppes of Siberia. They passed villages and crossed rivers. Mr. Harrington went on and on. When he finished a great speech by Edmund Burke he put down the book in triumph.

"Now that in my opinion is one of the finest orations in the English language. It is certainly a part of our common heritage that we can look upon with genuine pride."

"Doesn't it seem to you a little ominous that the people to whom Edmund Burke made that speech are all dead?" asked Ashenden gloomily.

Mr. Harrington was about to reply that this was hardly to be wondered at since the speech was made in the eighteenth century, when it dawned upon him that Ashenden (bearing up wonderfully under affliction as any unprejudiced person could not fail to admit) was making a joke. He slapped his knee and laughed heartily.

"Gee, that's a good one," he said. "I'll write that down in my little book. I see exactly how I can bring it in one time when I have to speak at our luncheon club."

Mr. Harrington was a highbrow; but that appellation, invented by the vulgar as a term of abuse, he had accepted like the instrument

of a saint's martyrdom, the gridiron of Saint Laurence for instance
or the wheel of Saint Catherine, as an honorific title. He gloried in
it.
    "Emerson was a highbrow," he said. "Longfellow was a high-
brow. Oliver Wendell Holmes was a highbrow. James Russell
Lowell was a highbrow."
    Mr. Harrington's study of American literature had taken him no
further down the years than the period during which those eminent,
but not precisely thrilling, authors flourished.
    Mr. Harrington was a bore. He exasperated Ashenden, and
enraged him; he got on his nerves, and drove him to frenzy. But
Ashenden did not dislike him. His self-satisfaction was enormous
but so ingenuous that you could not resent it; his conceit was so
childlike that you could only smile at it. He was so well-meaning,
so thoughtful, so deferential, so polite that though Ashenden would
willingly have killed him he could not but own that in that short
while he had conceived for Mr. Harrington something very like
affection. His manners were perfect, formal, a trifle elaborate
perhaps (there is no harm in that, for good manners are the product
of an artificial state of society and so can bear a touch of the
powdered wig and the lace ruffle), but though natural to his good
breeding they gained a pleasant significance from his good heart.
He was ready to do anyone a kindness and seemed to find nothing
too much trouble if he could thereby oblige his fellow-man. He was
eminently *serviable*. And it may be that this is a word for which there
is no exact translation because the charming quality it denotes is not
very common among our practical people. When Ashenden was ill
for a couple of days Mr. Harrington nursed him with devotion.
Ashenden was embarrassed by the care he took of him and though
racked with pain could not help laughing at the fussy attention with
which Mr. Harrington took his temperature, from his neatly packed
valise extracted a whole regiment of tabloids and firmly doctored
him; and he was touched by the trouble he gave himself to get from
the dining-car the things that he thought Ashenden could eat. He
did everything in the world for him but stop talking.
    It was only when he was dressing that Mr. Harrington was silent,
for then his maidenly mind was singly occupied with the problem
of changing his clothes before Ashenden without indelicacy. He
was extremely modest. He changed his linen every day, neatly
taking it out of his suitcase and neatly putting back what was soiled;
but he performed miracles of dexterity in order during the process
not to show an inch of bare skin. After a day or two Ashenden gave
up the struggle to keep neat and clean in that dirty train, with one

lavatory for the whole carriage, and soon was as grubby as the rest of the passengers; but Mr. Harrington refused to yield to the difficulties. He performed his toilet with deliberation notwithstanding the impatient persons who rattled the door-handle, and returned from the lavatory every morning washed, shining and smelling of soap. Once dressed, in his black coat, striped trousers and well-polished shoes, he looked as spruce as though he had just stepped out of his tidy little red-brick house in Philadelphia and was about to board the street-car that would take him downtown to his office. At one point of the journey it was announced that an attempt had been made to blow up a bridge and that there were disturbances at the next station over the river; it might be that the train would be stopped and the passengers turned adrift or taken prisoner. Ashenden, thinking he might be separated from his luggage, took the precaution to change into his thickest clothes so that if he had to pass the winter in Siberia he need suffer as little as necessary from the cold; but Mr. Harrington would not listen to reason; he made no preparations for the possible experience and Ashenden had the conviction that if he spent three months in a Russian prison he would still preserve that smart and natty appearance. A troop of Cossacks boarded the train and stood on the platform of each carriage with their guns loaded, and the train rattled gingerly over the damaged bridge; then they came to the station at which they had been warned of danger, put on steam and dashed straight through it. Mr. Harrington was mildly satirical when Ashenden changed back into a light summer suit.

Mr. Harrington was a keen business man. It was obvious that it would need someone very astute to overreach him and Ashenden was sure that his employers had been well-advised to send him on this errand. He would safeguard their interests with all his might and if he succeeded in driving a bargain with the Russians it would be a hard one. His loyalty to his firm demanded that. He spoke of the partners with affectionate reverence. He loved them and was proud of them; but he did not envy them because their wealth was great. He was quite content to work on a salary and thought himself adequately paid; so long as he could educate his boys and leave his widow enough to live on, what was money to him? He thought it a trifle vulgar to be rich. He looked upon culture as more important than money. He was careful of it and after every meal put down in his note-book exactly what it had cost him. His firm might be certain that he would not charge a penny more for his expenses than he had spent. But having discovered that poor people came to the station at the stopping places of the train to beg and seeing that the war had really brought them to destitution he took care before each halt to supply himself with ample small change and in a shame-faced way, mocking himself for being taken in by such impostors, distributed everything in his pocket.

"Of course I know they don't deserve it," he said, "and I don't do it for them. I do it entirely for my own peace of mind. I should feel so terribly badly if I thought some man really was hungry and I'd refused to give him the price of a meal."

Mr. Harrington was absurd, but lovable. It was inconceivable that anyone should be rude to him, it would have seemed as dreadful as hitting a child; and Ashenden, chafing inwardly but with a pretence of amiability, suffered meekly and with a truly Christian spirit the affliction of the gentle, ruthless creature's society. It took eleven days at that time to get from Vladivostok to Petrograd and Ashenden felt that he could not have borne another day. If it had been twelve he would have killed Mr. Harrington.

When at last (Ashenden tired and dirty, Mr. Harrington neat, sprightly and sententious) they reached the outskirts of Petrograd and stood at the window looking at the crowded houses of the city, Mr. Harrington turned to Ashenden and said:

"Well, I never would have thought that eleven days in the train would pass so quickly. We've had a wonderful time. I've enjoyed your company and I know you've enjoyed mine. I'm not going to pretend I don't know that I'm a pretty good conversationalist. But now we've come together like this we must take care to stay together. We must see as much of one another as we can while I'm in Petrograd."

"I shall have a great deal to do," said Ashenden. "I'm afraid my time won't be altogether my own."

"I know," answered Mr. Harrington cordially. "I expect to be pretty busy myself, but we can have breakfast together anyway and we'll meet in the evening and compare notes. It would be too bad if we drifted apart now."

"Too bad," sighed Ashenden.

When Ashenden found himself alone in his bedroom for the first time, he sat down and looked about him. It had seemed an age. He had not the energy to start immediately to unpack. How many of these hotel bedrooms had he known since the beginning of the war, grand or shabby, in one place and one land after another! It seemed to him that he had been living in his luggage for as long as he could remember. He was weary. He asked himself how he was going to set about the work that he had been sent to do. He felt lost in the immensity of Russia and very solitary. He had protested when he was chosen for this mission, it looked too large an order, but his protests were ignored. He was chosen not because those in authority thought him particularly suited for the job, but because there was no one to be found who was more suited. There was a knock at the door and Ashenden, pleased to make use of the few words of the language he knew, called out in Russian. The door was opened. He sprang to his feet.

"Come in, come in," he cried. "I'm awfully glad to see you."

Three men entered. He knew them by sight, since they had travelled in the same ship with him from San Francisco to Yokohama, but following their instructions no communications had passed between them and Ashenden. They were Czechs, exiled from their country for their revolutionary activity and long settled in America, who had been sent over to Russia to help Ashenden in his mission and put him in touch with Professor Z., whose authority over the Czechs in Russia was absolute. Their chief was a certain Dr. Egon Orth, a tall thin man, with a little grey head; he was minister to some church in the Middle West and a doctor of divinity; but had abandoned his cure to work for the liberation of his country, and Ashenden had the impression that he was an intelligent fellow who would not put too fine a point on matters of conscience. A parson with a fixed idea has this advantage over common men, that he can persuade himself of the Almighty's approval for almost any goings-on. Dr. Orth had a merry twinkle in his eye and a dry humour.

Ashenden had had two secret interviews with him in Yokohama and had learnt that Professor Z., though eager to free his country from the Austrian rule and, since he knew that this could only come about by the downfall of the Central Powers, with the Allies body and soul, yet had scruples; he would not do things that outraged his conscience, all must be straightforward and above board, and so some things that it was necessary to do had to be done without his knowledge. His influence was so great that his wishes could not be disregarded, but on occasion it was felt better not to let him know too much of what was going on.

Dr. Orth had arrived in Petrograd a week before Ashenden and now put before him what he had learned of the situation. It seemed to Ashenden that it was critical and if anything was to be done it must be done quickly. The army was dissatisfied and mutinous, the Government under the weak Kerensky was tottering and held power only because no one else had the courage to seize it, famine was staring the country in the face and already the possibility had to be considered that the Germans would march on Petrograd. The Ambassadors of Great Britain and the United States had been apprised of Ashenden's coming, but his mission was secret even from them, and there were particular reasons why he could demand no assistance from them. He arranged with Dr. Orth to make an appointment with Professor Z. so that he could learn his views and explain to him that he had the financial means to support any scheme that seemed likely to prevent the catastrophe that the Allied governments foresaw of Russia's making a separate peace. But he had to get in touch with influential persons in all classes. Mr. Harrington with his business proposition and his letters to Ministers of State would be thrown in contact with members of the Government and Mr. Harrington wanted an interpreter. Dr. Orth spoke Russian almost as well as his own language and it struck Ashenden that he would be admirably suited to the post. He explained the circumstances to him and it was arranged that while Ashenden and Mr. Harrington were at luncheon Dr. Orth should come in, greeting Ashenden as though he had not seen him before, and be introduced to Mr. Harrington; then Ashenden, guiding the conversation, would suggest to Mr. Harrington that the heavens had sent in Dr. Orth the ideal man for his purpose.

But there was another person on whom Ashenden had fixed as possibly useful to him and now he said:

"Have you ever heard of a woman called Anastasia Alexandrovna Leonidov? She's the daughter of Alexander Denisiev."

"I know all about him of course."

"I have reason to believe she's in Petrograd. Will you find out where she lives and what she's doing?"

"Certainly."

Dr. Orth spoke in Czech to one of the two men who accompanied him. They were sharp-looking fellows, both of them, one was tall and fair and the other was short and dark, but they were younger than Dr. Orth and Ashenden understood that they were there to do as he bade them. The man nodded, got up, shook hands with Ashenden and went out.

"You shall have all the information possible this afternoon."

"Well, I think there's nothing more we can do for the present," said Ashenden. "To tell you the truth I haven't had a bath for eleven days and I badly want one."

Ashenden had never quite made up his mind whether the pleasure of reflection was better pursued in a railway carriage or in a bath. So far as the act of invention was concerned he was inclined to prefer a train that went smoothly and not too fast, and many of his best

ideas had come to him when he was thus traversing the plains of
France; but for the delight of reminiscence or the entertainment of
embroidery upon a theme already in his head he had no doubt that
nothing could compare with a hot bath. He considered now,
wallowing in soapy water like a water-buffalo in a muddy pond, the
grim pleasantry of his relations with Anastasia Alexandrovna
Leonidov.

In these stories no more than the barest suggestion has been
made that Ashenden was capable on occasions of the passion
ironically called tender. The specialists in this matter, those charming creatures who make a business of what philosophers know is but
a diversion, assert that writers, painters and musicians, all in short
who are connected with the arts, in the relation of love cut no very
conspicuous figure. There is much cry but little wool. They rave or
sigh, make phrases and strike many a romantic attitude, but in the
end, loving art or themselves (which with them is one and the same
thing) better than the object of their emotion, offer a shadow when
the said object, with the practical common-sense of the sex, demands
a substance. It may be so and this may be the reason (never before
suggested) why women in their souls look upon art with such a
virulent hatred. Be this as it may Ashenden in the last twenty years
had felt his heart go pit-a-pat because of one charming person after
another. He had had a good deal of fun and had paid for it with a
great deal of misery, but even when suffering most acutely from the
pangs of unrequited love he had been able to say to himself, albeit
with a wry face, after all, it's grist to the mill.

Anastasia Alexandrovna Leonidov was the daughter of a revolutionary who had escaped from Siberia after being sentenced to penal
servitude for life and had settled in England. He was an able man
and had supported himself for thirty years by the activity of a restless
pen and had even made himself a distinguished position in English
letters. When Anastasia Alexandrovna reached a suitable age she
married Vladimir Semenovich Leonidov, also an exile from his
native country, and it was after she had been married to him for
some years that Ashenden made her acquaintance. It was at the
time when Europe discovered Russia. Everyone was reading the
Russian novelists, the Russian dancers captivated the civilised world,
and the Russian composers set shivering the sensibility of persons
who were beginning to want a change from Wagner. Russian art
seized upon Europe with the virulence of an epidemic of influenza.
New phrases became the fashion, new colours, new emotions, and
the highbrows described themselves without a moment's hesitation
as members of the intelligentsia. It was a difficult word to spell but

an easy one to say. Ashenden fell like the rest, changed the cushions of his sitting-room, hung an eikon on the wall, read Chekoff and went to the ballet.

Anastasia Alexandrovna was by birth, circumstances and education very much a member of the intelligentsia. She lived with her husband in a tiny house near Regent's Park and here all the literary folk in London might gaze with humble reverence at pale-faced bearded giants who leaned against the wall like caryatids taking a day off; they were revolutionaries to a man and it was a miracle that they were not in the mines of Siberia. Women of letters tremulously put their lips to a glass of vodka. If you were lucky and greatly favoured you might shake hands there with Diaghileff, and now and again, like a peach-blossom wafted by the breeze, Pavlova herself hovered in and out. At this time Ashenden's success had not been so great as to affront the highbrows, he had very distinctly been one of them in his youth, and though some already looked askance, others (optimistic creatures with a faith in human nature) still had hopes of him. Anastasia Alexandrovna told him to his face that he was a member of the intelligentsia. Ashenden was quite ready to believe it. He was in a state when he was ready to believe anything. He was thrilled and excited. It seemed to him that at last he was about to capture that illusive spirit of romance that he had so long been chasing. Anastasia Alexandrovna had fine eyes and a good, though for these days too voluptuous, figure, high cheek-bones and a snub nose (this was very Tartar), a wide mouth full of large square teeth and a pale skin. She dressed somewhat flamboyantly. In her dark melancholy eyes Ashenden saw the boundless steppes of Russia, and the Kremlin with its pealing bells, and the solemn ceremonies of Easter at St. Isaac's, and forests of silver beeches and the Nevsky Prospekt; it was astonishing how much he saw in her eyes. They were round and shining and slightly protuberant like those of a Pekinese. They talked together of Alyosha in the *Brothers Karamazov*, of Natasha in *War and Peace*, of Anna Karenina and of *Fathers and Sons*.

Ashenden soon discovered that her husband was quite unworthy of her and presently learned that she shared his opinion. Vladimir Semenovich was a little man with a large, long head that looked as though it had been pulled like a piece of liquorice, and he had a great shock of unruly Russian hair. He was a gentle, unobtrusive creature and it was hard to believe that the Czarist government had really feared his revolutionary activities. He taught Russian and wrote for papers in Moscow. He was amiable and obliging. He needed these qualities, for Anastasia Alexandrovna was a woman of character: when she had a toothache Vladimir Semenovich suffered the agonies of the damned and when her heart was wrung by the suffering of her unhappy country Vladimir Semenovich might well have wished he had never been born. Ashenden could not help admitting that he was a poor thing, but he was so harmless that he conceived quite a liking for him, and when in due course he had disclosed his passion to Anastasia Alexandrovna and to his joy found it was returned he was puzzled to know what to do about Vladimir Semenovich. Neither Anastasia Alexandrovna nor he felt that they could live another minute out of one another's pockets, and Ashenden feared that, with her revolutionary views and all that, she would never consent to marry him; but somewhat to his surprise, and very much to his relief, she accepted the suggestion with alacrity.

"Would Vladimir Semenovich let himself be divorced, do you think?" he asked, as he sat on the sofa, leaning against cushions the colour of which reminded him of raw meat just gone bad, and held her hand.

"Vladimir adores me," she answered. "It'll break his heart."

"He's a nice fellow, I shouldn't like him to be very unhappy. I hope he'll get over it."

"He'll never get over it. That is the Russian spirit. I know that when I leave him he'll feel that he has lost everything that made life worth living for him. I've never known anyone so wrapped up in a woman as he is in me. But of course he wouldn't want to stand in the way of my happiness. He's far too great for that. He'll see that when it's a question of my own self-development I haven't the right to hesitate. Vladimir will give me my freedom without question."

At that time the divorce law in England was even more complicated and absurd than it is now and in case she was not acquainted with its peculiarities Ashenden explained to Anastasia Alexandrovna the difficulties of the case. She put her hand gently on his.

"Vladimir would never expose me to the vulgar notoriety of the divorce court. When I tell him that I have decided to marry you he will commit suicide."

"That would be terrible," said Ashenden.

He was startled, but thrilled. It was really very much like a Russian novel and he saw the moving and terrible pages, pages and pages, in which Dostoievsky would have described the situation. He knew the lacerations his characters would have suffered, the broken bottles of champagne, the visits to the gipsies, the vodka, the swoonings, the catalepsy and the long, long speeches everyone would have made. It was all very dreadful and wonderful and shattering.

"It would make us horribly unhappy," said Anastasia Alexandrovna, "but I don't know what else he could do. I couldn't ask him to live without me. He would be like a ship without a rudder or a car without a carburettor. I know Vladimir so well. He will commit suicide."

"How?" asked Ashenden, who had the realist's passion for the exact detail.

"He will blow his brains out."

Ashenden remembered *Rosmersholm*. In his day he had been an ardent Ibsenite and had even flirted with the notion of learning Norwegian so that he might, by reading the master in the original, get at the secret essence of his thought. He had once seen Ibsen in the flesh drink a glass of Munich beer.

"But do you think we could ever pass another easy hour if we had the death of that man on our conscience?" he asked. "I have a feeling that he would always be between us."

"I know we shall suffer, we shall suffer dreadfully," said Anastasia Alexandrovna, "but how can we help it? Life is like that. We must think of Vladimir. There is his happiness to be considered too. He will prefer to commit suicide."

She turned her face away and Ashenden saw that the heavy tears were coursing down her cheeks. He was much moved. For he had a soft heart and it was dreadful to think of poor Vladimir lying there with a bullet in his brain.

These Russians, what fun they have!

But when Anastasia Alexandrovna had mastered her emotion she turned to him gravely. She looked at him with her humid, round and slightly protuberant eyes.

"We must be quite sure that we're doing the right thing," she said. "I should never forgive myself if I'd allowed Vladimir to commit suicide and then found I'd made a mistake. I think we ought to make sure that we really love one another."

"But don't you know?" exclaimed Ashenden in a low, tense voice. "I know."

"Let's go over to Paris for a week and see how we get on. Then we shall know."

Ashenden was a trifle conventional and the suggestion took him by surprise. But only for a moment. Anastasia was wonderful. She was very quick and she saw the hesitation that for an instant troubled him.

"Surely you have no bourgeois prejudices?" she said.

"Of course not," he assured her hurriedly, for he would much sooner have been thought knavish than bourgeois, "I think it's a splendid idea."

"Why should a woman hazard her whole life on a throw? It's

impossible to know what a man is really like till you've lived with him. It's only fair to give her the opportunity to change her mind before it's too late."

"Quite so," said Ashenden.

Anastasia Alexandrovna was not a woman to let the grass grow under her feet and so having made their arrangements forthwith on the following Saturday they started for Paris.

"I shall not tell Vladimir that I am going with you," she said. "It would only distress him."

"It would be a pity to do that," said Ashenden.

"And if at the end of the week I come to the conclusion that we've made a mistake he need never know anything about it."

"Quite so," said Ashenden.

They met at Victoria Station.

"What class have you got?" she asked him.

"First."

"I'm glad of that. Father and Vladimir travel third on account of their principles, but I always feel sick on a train and I like to be able to lean my head on somebody's shoulder. It's easier in a first-class carriage."

When the train started Anastasia Alexandrovna said she felt dizzy, so she took off her hat and leaned her head on Ashenden's shoulder. He put his arm round her waist.

"Keep quite still, won't you?" she said.

When they got on to the boat she went down to the ladies' cabin and at Calais was able to eat a very hearty meal, but when they got into the train she took off her hat again and rested her head on Ashenden's shoulder. He thought he would like to read and took up a book.

"Do you mind not reading?" she said. "I have to be held and when you turn the pages it makes me feel all funny."

Finally they reached Paris and went to a little hotel on the Left Bank that Anastasia Alexandrovna knew of. She said it had atmosphere. She could not bear those great big grand hotels on the other side; they were hopelessly vulgar and bourgeois.

"I'll go anywhere you like," said Ashenden, "as long as there's a bathroom."

She smiled and pinched his cheek.

"How adorably English you are. Can't you do without a bathroom for a week? My dear, my dear, you have so much to learn."

They talked far into the night about Maxim Gorki and Karl Marx, human destiny, love and the brotherhood of man; and drank innumerable cups of Russian tea, so that in the morning Ashenden would willingly have breakfasted in bed and got up for luncheon; but Anastasia Alexandrovna was an early riser. When life was so short and there was so much to do it was a sinful thing to have breakfast a minute after half-past eight. They sat down in a dingy little dining-room the windows of which showed no signs of having been opened for a month. It was full of atmosphere. Ashenden asked Anastasia Alexandrovna what she would have for breakfast.

"Scrambled eggs," she said.

She ate heartily. Ashenden had already noticed that she had a healthy appetite. He supposed it was a Russian trait: you could not picture Anna Karenina making her midday meal off a bath-bun and a cup of coffee, could you?

After breakfast they went to the Louvre and in the afternoon they went to the Luxembourg. They dined early in order to go to the Comédie Française; then they went to a Russian cabaret where they danced. When next morning at eight-thirty they took their places in the dining-room and Ashenden asked Anastasia Alexandrovna what she fancied, her reply was:

"Scrambled eggs."

"But we had scrambled eggs yesterday," he expostulated.

"Let's have them again to-day," she smiled.

"All right."

They spent the day in the same manner except that they went to the Carnavalet instead of the Louvre and the Musée Guimet instead of the Luxembourg. But when the morning after in answer to Ashenden's inquiry Anastasia Alexandrovna again asked for scrambled eggs, his heart sank.

"But we had scrambled eggs yesterday and the day before," he said.

"Don't you think that's a very good reason to have them again to-day?"

"No, I don't."

"Is it possible that your sense of humour is a little deficient this morning?" she asked. "I eat scrambled eggs every day. It's the only way I like them."

"Oh, very well. In that case of course we'll have scrambled eggs."

But the following morning he could not face them.

"Will you have scrambled eggs as usual?" he asked her.

"Of course," she smiled affectionately, showing him two rows of large square teeth.

"All right, I'll order them for you; I shall have mine fried."

The smile vanished from her lips.

"Oh?" She paused a moment. "Don't you think that's rather

inconsiderate? Do you think it's fair to give the cook unnecessary work? You English, you're all the same, you look upon servants as machines. Does it occur to you that they have hearts like yours, the same feelings and the same emotions? How can you be surprised that the proletariat are seething with discontent when the bourgeoisie like you are so monstrously selfish?"

"Do you really think that there'll be a revolution in England if I have my eggs in Paris fried rather than scrambled?"

She tossed her pretty head in indignation.

"You don't understand. It's the principle of the thing. You think it's a jest, of course I know you're being funny, I can laugh at a joke as well as anyone, Chekoff was well-known in Russia as a humorist; but don't you see what is involved? Your whole attitude is wrong. It's a lack of feeling. You wouldn't talk like that if you had been through the events of 1905 in Petersburg. When I think of the crowds in front of the Winter Palace kneeling in the snow while the Cossacks charged them, women and children! No, no, no."

Her eyes filled with tears and her face was all twisted with pain. She took Ashenden's hand.

"I know you have a good heart. It was just thoughtless on your part and we won't say anything more about it. You have imagination. You're very sensitive. I know. You'll have your eggs done in the same way as mine, won't you?"

"Of course," said Ashenden.

He ate scrambled eggs for breakfast every morning after that. The waiter said: *"Monsieur aime les œufs brouillés."* At the end of the week they returned to London. He held Anastasia Alexandrovna in his arms, her head resting on his shoulder, from Paris to Calais and again from Dover to London. He reflected that the journey from New York to San Francisco took five days. When they arrived at Victoria and stood on the platform waiting for a cab she looked at him with her round, shining and slightly protuberant eyes.

"We've had a wonderful time, haven't we?" she said.

"Wonderful."

"I've quite made up my mind. The experiment has justified itself. I'm willing to marry you whenever you like."

But Ashenden saw himself eating scrambled eggs every morning for the rest of his life. When he had put her in a cab, he called another for himself, went to the Cunard office and took a berth on the first ship that was going to America. No immigrant, eager for freedom and a new life, ever looked upon the statue of Liberty with more heartfelt thankfulness than did Ashenden, when on that bright and sunny morning his ship steamed into the harbour of New York.

Some years had passed since then and Ashenden had not seen Anastasia Alexandrovna again. He knew that on the outbreak of the revolution in March she and Vladimir Semenovich had gone to Russia. It might be that they would be able to help him, in a way Vladimir Semenovich owed him his life, and he made up his mind to write to Anastasia Alexandrovna to ask if he might come to see her.

When Ashenden went down to lunch he felt somewhat rested. Mr. Harrington was waiting for him and they sat down. They ate what was put before them.

"Ask the waiter to bring us some bread," said Mr. Harrington.

"Bread?" replied Ashenden. "There's no bread."

"I can't eat without bread," said Mr. Harrington.

"I'm afraid you'll have to. There's no bread, no butter, no sugar, no eggs, no potatoes. There's fish and meat and green vegetables, and that's all."

Mr. Harrington's jaw dropped.

"But this is war," he said.

"It looks very much like it."

Mr. Harrington was for a moment speechless; then he said: "I'll tell you what I'm going to do, I'm going to get through with my business as quick as I can and then I'm going to get out of this country. I'm sure Mrs. Harrington wouldn't like me to go without sugar or butter. I've got a very delicate stomach. The firm would never have sent me here if they'd thought I wasn't going to have the best of everything."

In a little while Dr. Egon Orth came in and gave Ashenden an envelope. On it was written Anastasia Alexandrovna's address. He introduced him to Mr. Harrington. It was soon clear that he was pleased with Dr. Egon Orth and so without further to-do he suggested that here was the perfect interpreter for him.

"He talks Russian like a Russian. But he's an American citizen so that he won't do you down. I've known him a considerable time and I can assure you that he's absolutely trustworthy."

Mr. Harrington was pleased with the notion and after luncheon Ashenden left them to settle the matter by themselves. He wrote a note to Anastasia Alexandrovna and presently received an answer to say that she was going to a meeting, but would look in at his hotel about seven. He awaited her with apprehension. Of course he knew now that he had not loved her, but Tolstoi and Dostoievsky, Rimsky-Korsakoff, Stravinsky and Bakst; but he was not quite sure if the point had occurred to her. When between eight and half-past she arrived he suggested that she should join Mr. Harrington and him at dinner. The presence of a third party, he thought, would prevent any awkwardness their meeting might have; but he need not have had any anxiety, for five minutes after they had sat down to a plate of soup it was borne in upon him that the feelings of Anastasia Alexandrovna towards him were as cool as were his towards her. It gave him a momentary shock. It is very hard for a man, however modest, to grasp the possibility that a woman who has once loved him may love him no longer, and though of course he did not imagine that Anastasia Alexandrovna had languished for five years with a hopeless passion for him, he did think that by a heightening of colour, a flutter of the eyelashes, or a quiver of the lips she would betray the fact that she had still a soft place in her heart for him. Not at all. She talked to him as though he were a friend she was very glad to see again after an absence of a few days, but whose intimacy with her was purely social. He asked after Vladimir Semenovich.

"He has been a disappointment to me," she said. "I never thought he was a clever man, but I thought he was an honest one. He's going to have a baby."

Mr. Harrington, who was about to put a piece of fish into his mouth, stopped, his fork in the air, and stared at Anastasia Alexandrovna with astonishment. In extenuation it must be explained that he had never read a Russian novel in his life. Ashenden, slightly perplexed too, gave her a questioning look.

"I'm not the mother," she said with a laugh. "I am not interested in that sort of thing. The mother is a friend of mine and a well-known writer on Political Economy. I do not think her views are sound, but I should be the last to deny that they deserve consideration. She has a good brain, quite a good brain." She turned to Mr. Harrington. "Are you interested in Political Economy?"

For once in his life Mr. Harrington was speechless. Anastasia Alexandrovna gave them her views on the subject and they began to speak on the situation in Russia. She seemed to be on intimate terms with the leaders of the various political parties and Ashenden made up his mind to sound her on the possibility of her working with him. His infatuation had not blinded him to the fact that she was an extremely intelligent woman. After dinner he told Mr. Harrington that he wished to talk business with Anastasia Alexandrovna and took her to a retired corner of the lounge. He told her all he thought necessary and found her interested and anxious to help. She had a passion for intrigue and a desire for power. When he hinted that he had command of large sums of money she saw at once that through him she might acquire an influence in the affairs of Russia. It tickled her vanity. She was immensely patriotic, but like many patriots she had an impression that her own aggrandisement tended to the good of her country. When they parted they had come to a working agreement.

"That was a very remarkable woman," said Mr. Harrington next morning when they met at breakfast.

"Don't fall in love with her," smiled Ashenden.

This, however, was not a matter on which Mr. Harrington was prepared to jest.

"I have never looked at a woman since I married Mrs. Harrington," he said. "That husband of hers must be a bad man."

"I could do with a plate of scrambled eggs," said Ashenden, irrelevantly, for their breakfast consisted of a cup of tea without milk and a little jam instead of sugar.

With Anastasia Alexandrovna to help him and Dr. Orth in the background, Ashenden set to work. Things in Russia were going from bad to worse. Kerensky, the head of the Provisional Government, was devoured by vanity and dismissed any minister who gave evidence of a capacity that might endanger his own position. He made speeches. He made endless speeches. At one moment there was a possibility that the Germans would make a dash for Petrograd. Kerensky made speeches. The food shortage grew more serious, the winter was approaching and there was no fuel. Kerensky made speeches. In the background the Bolsheviks were active, Lenin was hiding in Petrograd, it was said that Kerensky knew where he was, but dared not arrest him. He made speeches.

It amused Ashenden to see the unconcern with which Mr. Harrington wandered through this turmoil. History was in the making and Mr. Harrington minded his own business. It was uphill work. He was made to pay bribes to secretaries and underlings under the pretence that the ear of great men would be granted to him. He was kept waiting for hours in antechambers and then sent away without ceremony. When at last he saw the great men he found they had nothing to give him but idle words. They made him promises and in a day or two he discovered that the promises meant nothing. Ashenden advised him to throw in his hand and return to America; but Mr. Harrington would not hear of it; his firm had sent him to do a particular job, and by gum, he was going to do it or perish in the attempt. Then Anastasia Alexandrovna took him in hand. A singular friendship had arisen between the pair. Mr. Harrington thought her a very remarkable and deeply wronged woman; he told her all about his wife and his two sons, he told her all about the Constitution of the United States; she on her side told him all about Vladimir Semenovich, and she told him about Tolstoi, Turgenev and

Dostoievsky. They had great times together. He said he couldn't manage to call her Anastasia Alexandrovna, it was too much of a mouthful; so he called her Delilah. And now she placed her inexhaustible energy at his service and they went together to the persons who might be useful to him. But things were coming to a head. Riots broke out and the streets were growing dangerous. Now and then armoured cars filled with discontented reservists careered wildly along the Nevsky Prospekt and in order to show that they were not happy took pot-shots at the passers-by. On one occasion when Mr. Harrington and Anastasia Alexandrovna were in a tram together shots peppered the windows and they had to lie down on the floor for safety. Mr. Harrington was highly indignant.

"An old fat woman was lying right on top of me and when I wriggled to get out Delilah caught me a clip on the side of the head and said: Stop still, you fool. I don't like your Russian ways, Delilah."

"Anyhow you stopped still," she giggled.

"What you want in this country is a little less art and a little more civilisation."

"You are bourgeoisie, Mr. Harrington, you are not a member of the intelligentsia."

"You are the first person who's ever said that, Delilah. If I'm not a member of the intelligentsia I don't know who is," retorted Mr. Harrington with dignity.

Then one day when Ashenden was working in his room there was a knock at the door and Anastasia Alexandrovna stalked in followed somewhat sheepishly by Mr. Harrington. Ashenden saw that she was excited.

"What's the matter?" he asked.

"Unless this man goes back to America he'll get killed. You really must talk to him. If I hadn't been there something very unpleasant might have happened to him."

"Not at all, Delilah," said Mr. Harrington, with asperity. "I'm perfectly capable of taking care of myself and I wasn't in the smallest danger."

"What is it all about?" asked Ashenden.

"I'd taken Mr. Harrington to the Lavra of Alexander Nevsky to see Dostoievsky's grave," said Anastasia Alexandrovna, "and on our way back we saw a soldier being rather rough with an old woman."

"Rather rough!" cried Mr. Harrington. "There was an old woman walking along the pavement with a basket of provisions on her arm. Two soldiers came up behind her and one of them snatched the basket from her and walked off with it. She burst out screaming and crying, I don't know what she was saying, but I can guess, and the other soldier took his gun and with the butt-end of it hit her over the head. Isn't that right, Delilah?"

"Yes," she answered, unable to help smiling. "And before I could prevent it Mr. Harrington jumped out of the cab and ran up to the soldier who had the basket, wrenched it from him and began to abuse the pair of them like pickpockets. At first they were so taken aback they didn't know what to do and then they got in a rage. I ran after Mr. Harrington and explained to them that he was a foreigner and drunk."

"Drunk?" cried Mr. Harrington.

"Yes, drunk. Of course a crowd collected. It looked as though it wasn't going to be very nice."

Mr. Harrington smiled with those large, pale-blue eyes of his.

"It sounded to me as though you were giving them a piece of your mind, Delilah. It was as good as a play to watch you."

"Don't be stupid, Mr. Harrington," cried Anastasia, in a sudden fury, stamping her foot. "Don't you know that those soldiers might very easily have killed you and me too, and not one of the bystanders would have raised a finger to help us?"

"Me? I'm an American citizen, Delilah. They wouldn't dare touch a hair of my head."

"They'd have difficulty in finding one," said Anastasia Alexandrovna, who when she was in a temper had no manners. "But if you think Russian soldiers are going to hesitate to kill you because you're an American citizen you'll get a big surprise one of these days."

"Well, what happened to the old woman?" asked Ashenden.

"The soldiers went off after a little and we went back to her."

"Still with the basket?"

"Yes. Mr. Harrington clung on to that like grim death. She was lying on the ground with the blood pouring from her head. We got her into the cab and when she could speak enough to tell us where she lived we drove her home. She was bleeding dreadfully and we had some difficulty in staunching the blood."

Anastasia Alexandrovna gave Mr. Harrington an odd look and to his surprise Ashenden saw him turn scarlet.

"What's the matter now?"

"You see, we had nothing to bind her up with. Mr. Harrington's handkerchief was soaked. There was only one thing about me that I could get off quickly and so I took off my . . ."

But before she could finish Mr. Harrington interrupted her.

"You need not tell Mr. Ashenden what you took off. I'm a

married man and I know ladies wear them, but I see no need to refer to them in general society."

Anastasia Alexandrovna giggled.

"Then you must kiss me, Mr. Harrington. If you don't I shall say."

Mr. Harrington hesitated a moment, considering evidently the pros and cons of the matter, but he saw that Anastasia Alexandrovna was determined.

"Go on then, you may kiss me, Delilah, though I'm bound to say I don't see what pleasure it can be to you."

She put her arms round his neck and kissed him on both cheeks, then without a word of warning burst into a flood of tears.

"You're a brave little man, Mr. Harrington. You're absurd but magnificent," she sobbed.

Mr. Harrington was less surprised than Ashenden would have expected him to be. He looked at Anastasia with a thin, quizzical smile and gently patted her.

"Come, come, Delilah, pull yourself together. It gave you a nasty turn, didn't it? You're quite upset. I shall have terrible rheumatism in my shoulder if you go on weeping all over it."

The scene was ridiculous and touching. Ashenden laughed, but he had the beginnings of a lump in his throat.

When Anastasia Alexandrovna had left them Mr. Harrington sat in a brown study.

"They're very queer, these Russians. Do you know what Delilah did?" he said, suddenly. "She stood up in the cab, in the middle of the street, with people passing on both sides, and took her pants off. She tore them in two and gave me one to hold while she made a bandage of the other. I was never so embarrassed in my life."

"Tell me what gave you the idea of calling her Delilah?" smiled Ashenden.

Mr. Harrington reddened a little.

"She's a very fascinating woman, Mr. Ashenden. She's been deeply wronged by her husband and I naturally felt a great deal of sympathy for her. These Russians are very emotional people and I did not want her to mistake my sympathy for anything else. I told her I was very much attached to Mrs. Harrington."

"You're not under the impression that Delilah was Potiphar's wife?" asked Ashenden.

"I don't know what you mean by that, Mr. Ashenden," replied Mr. Harrington. "Mrs. Harrington has always given me to understand that I'm very fascinating to women, and I thought if I called our little friend Delilah it would make my position quite clear."

"I don't think Russia's any place for you, Mr. Harrington," said Ashenden smiling. "If I were you I'd get out of it as quick as I could."

"I can't go now. I've got them to agree to my terms at last and we're going to sign next week. Then I shall pack my grip and go."

"I wonder if your signatures will be worth the paper they're written on," said Ashenden.

He had at length devised a plan of campaign. It took him twenty-four hours' hard work to code a telegram in which he put his scheme before the persons who had sent him to Petrograd. It was accepted and he was promised all the money he needed. Ashenden knew he could do nothing unless the Provisional Government remained in power for another three months; but winter was at hand and food was getting scarcer every day. The army was mutinous. The people clamoured for peace. Every evening at the Europe Ashenden drank a cup of chocolate with Professor Z. and discussed with him how best to make use of his devoted Czechs. Anastasia Alexandrovna had a flat in a retired spot and here he had meetings with all manner of persons. Plans were drawn up. Measures were taken. Ashenden argued, persuaded, promised. He had to overcome the vacillation of one and wrestle with the fatalism of another. He had to judge who was resolute and who was self-sufficient, who was honest and who was infirm of purpose. He had to curb his impatience with the Russian verbosity; he had to be good-tempered with people who were willing to talk of everything but the matter in hand; he had to listen sympathetically to ranting and rhodomontade. He had to beware of treachery. He had to humour the vanity of fools and elude the greed of the ambitious. Time was pressing. The rumours grew hot and many of the activities of the Bolsheviks. Kerensky ran hither and thither like a frightened hen.

Then the blow fell. On the night of November 7th, 1917, the Bolsheviks rose, Kerensky's ministers were arrested and the Winter Palace was sacked by the mob; the reins of power were seized by Lenin and Trotsky.

Anastasia Alexandrovna came to Ashenden's room at the hotel early in the morning. Ashenden was coding a telegram. He had been up all night, first at the Smolny, and then at the Winter Palace. He was tired out. Her face was white and her shining brown eyes were tragic.

"Have you heard?" she asked Ashenden.

He nodded.

"It's all over then. They say Kerensky has fled. They never even showed fight." Rage seized her. "The buffoon!" she screamed.

At that moment there was a knock at the door and Anastasia Alexandrovna looked at it with sudden apprehension.

"You know the Bolsheviks have got a list of people they've decided to execute. My name is on it, and it may be that yours is too."

"If it's they and they want to come in they only have to turn the handle," said Ashenden, smiling, but with ever so slightly odd a feeling at the pit of his stomach. "Come in."

The door was opened and Mr. Harrington stepped into the room. He was as dapper as ever, in his short black coat and striped trousers, his shoes neatly polished and a derby on his bald head. He took it off when he saw Anastasia Alexandrovna.

"Oh, fancy finding you here so early. I looked in on my way out, I wanted to tell you my news. I tried to find you yesterday evening, but couldn't. You didn't come in to dinner."

"No, I was at a meeting," said Ashenden.

"You must both congratulate me, I got my signatures yesterday, and my business is done."

Mr. Harrington beamed on them, the picture of self-satisfaction, and he arched himself like a bantam-cock who has chased away all rivals. Anastasia Alexandrovna burst into a sudden shriek of hysterical laughter. He stared at her in perplexity.

"Why, Delilah, what is the matter?" he said.

Anastasia laughed till the tears ran from her eyes and then began to sob in earnest. Ashenden explained.

"The Bolsheviks have overthrown the Government. Kerensky's ministers are in prison. The Bolsheviks are out to kill. Delilah says her name is on the list. Your minister signed your documents yesterday because he knew it did not matter what he did then. Your contracts are worth nothing. The Bolsheviks are going to make peace with Germany as soon as they can."

Anastasia Alexandrovna had recovered her self-control as quickly as she had lost it.

"You had better get out of Russia as soon as you can, Mr. Harrington. It's no place for a foreigner now and it may be that in a few days you won't be able to."

Mr. Harrington looked from one to the other.

"O my," he said. "O my!" It seemed inadequate. "Are you going to tell me that that Russian minister was just making a fool of me?"

Ashenden shrugged his shoulders.

"How can one tell what he was thinking of? He may have a keen sense of humour and perhaps he thought it funny to sign a fifty-million-dollar contract yesterday when there was every chance of his being stood against the wall and shot to-day. Anastasia Alexandrovna's right, Mr. Harrington, you'd better take the first train that'll get you to Sweden."

"And what about you?"

"There's nothing for me to do here any more. I'm cabling for instructions and I shall go as soon as I get leave. The Bolsheviks have got ahead of us and the people I was working with will have their work cut out to save their lives."

"Boris Petrovich was shot this morning," said Anastasia Alexandrovna with a frown.

They both looked at Mr. Harrington and he stared at the floor. His pride in this achievement of his was shattered and he sagged like a pricked balloon. But in a minute he looked up. He gave Anastasia Alexandrovna a little smile and for the first time Ashenden noticed how attractive and kindly his smile was. There was something peculiarly disarming about it.

"If the Bolsheviks are after you, Delilah, don't you think you'd better come with me? I'll take care of you and if you like to come to America I'm sure Mrs. Harrington would be glad to do anything she could for you."

"I can see Mrs. Harrington's face if you arrived in Philadelphia with a Russian refugee," laughed Anastasia Alexandrovna. "I'm afraid it would need more explaining than you could ever manage. No, I shall stay here."

"But if you're in danger?"

"I'm a Russian. My place is here. I will not leave my country when most my country needs me."

"That is bunk, Delilah," said Mr. Harrington very quietly.

Anastasia Alexandrovna had spoken with deep emotion, but now with a little start she shot a sudden quizzical look at him.

"I know it is, Samson," she answered. "To tell you the truth I think we're all going to have a hell of a time, God knows what's going to happen, but I want to see; I wouldn't miss a minute of it for the world."

Mr. Harrington shook his head.

"Curiosity is the bane of your sex, Delilah," he said.

"Go along and do your packing, Mr. Harrington," said Ashenden, smiling, "and then we'll take you to the station. The train will be besieged."

"Very well, I'll go. And I shan't be sorry either. I haven't had a decent meal since I came here and I've done a thing I never thought I should have to do in my life, I've drunk my coffee without sugar and when I've been lucky enough to get a little piece of black bread I've had to eat it without butter. Mrs. Harrington will never believe me when I tell her what I've gone through. What this country wants is organisation."

When he left them Ashenden and Anastasia Alexandrovna talked over the situation. Ashenden was depressed because all his careful schemes had come to nothing, but Anastasia Alexandrovna was excited and she hazarded every sort of guess about the outcome of this new revolution. She pretended to be very serious, but in her heart she looked upon it all very much as a thrilling play. She wanted more and more things to happen. Then there was another knock at the door and before Ashenden could answer Mr. Harrington burst in.

"Really the service at this hotel is a scandal," he cried heatedly, "I've been ringing my bell for fifteen minutes and I can't get anyone to pay the smallest attention to me."

"Service?" exclaimed Anastasia Alexandrovna. "There is not a servant left in the hotel."

"But I want my laundry. They promised to let me have it back last night."

"I'm afraid you haven't got much chance of getting it now," said Ashenden.

"I'm not going to leave without my laundry. Four shirts, two union suits, a pair of pyjamas, and four collars. I wash my handkerchiefs and socks in my room. I want my laundry and I'm not going to leave this hotel without it."

"Don't be a fool," cried Ashenden. "What you've got to do is to get out of here while the going's good. If there are no servants to get it you'll just have to leave your washing behind you."

"Pardon me, sir, I shall do nothing of the kind. I'll go and fetch it myself. I've suffered enough at the hands of this country and I'm not going to leave four perfectly good shirts to be worn by a lot of dirty Bolsheviks. No, sir. I do not leave Russia till I have my laundry."

Anastasia Alexandrovna stared at the floor for a moment; then with a little smile looked up. It seemed to Ashenden that there was something in her that responded to Mr. Harrington's futile obstinacy. In her Russian way she understood that Mr. Harrington could not leave Petrograd without his washing. His insistence had given it the value of a symbol.

"I'll go downstairs and see if I can find anybody about who knows where the laundry is, and if I can I'll go with you and you can bring your washing away with you."

Mr. Harrington unbent. He answered with that sweet and disarming smile of his.

"That's terribly kind of you, Delilah. I don't mind if it's ready or not, I'll take it just as it is."

Anastasia Alexandrovna left them.

"Well, what do you think of Russia and the Russians now?" Mr. Harrington asked Ashenden.

"I'm fed up with them. I'm fed up with Tolstoi, I'm fed up with Turgenev and Dostoievsky, I'm fed up with Chekoff. I'm fed up with the Intelligentsia. I hanker after people who know their mind from one minute to another, who mean what they say an hour after they've said it, whose word you can rely on; I'm sick of fine phrases, and oratory and attitudinising."

Ashenden, bitten by the prevailing ill, was about to make a speech when he was interrupted by a rattle as of peas on a drum. In the city, so strangely silent, it sounded abrupt and odd.

"What's that?" asked Mr. Harrington.

"Rifle-firing. On the other side of the river, I should think."

Mr. Harrington gave a funny little look. He laughed, but his face was a trifle pale; he did not like it, and Ashenden did not blame him.

"I think it's high time I got out. I shouldn't so much mind for myself, but I've got a wife and children to think of. I haven't had a letter from Mrs. Harrington for so long I'm a bit worried." He paused an instant. "I'd like you to know Mrs. Harrington, she's a very wonderful woman. She's the best wife a man ever had. Until I came here I'd not been separated from her for more than three days since we were married."

Anastasia Alexandrovna came back and told them that she had found the address.

"It's about forty minutes' walk from here and if you'll come now I'll go with you," she said.

"I'm ready."

"You'd better look out," said Ashenden. "I don't believe the streets are very healthy to-day."

Anastasia Alexandrovna looked at Mr. Harrington.

"I must have my laundry, Delilah," he said. " I should never rest in peace if I left it behind me and Mrs. Harrington would never let me hear the last of it."

"Come on then."

They set out and Ashenden went on with the dreary business of translating into a very complicated code the shattering news he had to give. It was a long message, and then he had to ask for instructions upon his own movements. It was a mechanical job and yet it was one in which you could not allow your attention to wander. The mistake of a single figure might make a whole sentence incomprehensible.

Suddenly his door was burst open and Anastasia Alexandrovna flung into the room. She had lost her hat and was dishevelled. She was panting. Her eyes were starting out of her head and she was obviously in a state of great excitement.

"Where's Mr. Harrington?" she cried. "Isn't he here?"

"No."

"Is he in his bedroom?"

"I don't know. Why, what's the matter? We'll go and look if you like. Why didn't you bring him along with you?"

They walked down the passage and knocked at Mr. Harrington's door; there was no answer; they tried the handle; the door was locked.

"He's not there."

They went back to Ashenden's room. Anastasia Alexandrovna sank into a chair.

"Give me a glass of water, will you? I'm out of breath. I've been running."

She drank the water Ashenden poured out for her. She gave a sudden sob.

"I hope he's all right. I should never forgive myself if he was hurt. I was hoping he would have got here before me. He got his washing all right. We found the place. There was only an old woman there and they didn't want to let us take it, but we insisted. Mr. Harrington was furious because it hadn't been touched. It was exactly as he had sent it. They'd promised it last night and it was still in the bundle that Mr. Harrington had made himself. I said that was Russia and Mr. Harrington said he preferred coloured people. I'd led him by side streets because I thought it was better, and we started to come back again. We passed at the top of a street and at the bottom of it I saw a little crowd. There was a man addressing them.

" 'Let's go and hear what he's saying,' I said.

"I could see they were arguing. It looked exciting. I wanted to know what was happening.

" 'Come along, Delilah,' he said. 'Let us mind our own business.'

" 'You go back to the hotel and do your packing. I'm going to see the fun,' I said.

"I ran down the street and he followed me. There were about two or three hundred people there and a student was addressing them. There were some working-men and they were shouting at him. I love a row and I edged my way into the crowd. Suddenly we heard the sound of shots and before you could realise what was happening two armoured cars came dashing down the street. There were soldiers in them and they were firing as they went. I don't know why. For fun, I suppose, or because they were drunk. We all scattered like a lot of rabbits. We just ran for our lives. I lost Mr. Harrington. I can't make out why he isn't here. Do you think something has happened to him?"

Ashenden was silent for a while.

"We'd better go out and look for him," he said. "I don't know why the devil he couldn't leave his washing."

"I understand, I understand so well."

"That's a comfort," said Ashenden irritably. "Let's go."

He put on his hat and coat, and they walked downstairs. The hotel seemed strangely empty. They went out into the street. There was hardly anyone to be seen. They walked along. The trams were not running and the silence in the great city was uncanny. The shops were closed. It was quite startling when a motor-car dashed by at breakneck speed. The people they passed looked frightened and downcast. When they had to go through a main thoroughfare they hastened their steps. A lot of people were there and they stood about irresolutely as though they did not know what to do next. Reservists in their shabby grey were walking down the middle of the roadway in little bunches. They did not speak. They looked like sheep looking for their shepherd. Then they came to the street down which Anastasia Alexandrovna had run, but they entered it from the opposite end. A number of windows had been broken by the wild shooting. It was quite empty. You could see where the people had scattered, for strewn about were articles they had dropped in their haste, books, a man's hat, a lady's bag and a basket. Anastasia Alexandrovna touched Ashenden's arm to draw his attention: sitting on the pavement, her head bent right down to her lap, was a woman and she was dead. A little way on two men had fallen together. They were dead too. The wounded, one supposed, had managed to drag themselves away or their friends had carried them. Then they found Mr. Harrington. His derby had rolled in the gutter. He lay on his face, in a pool of blood, his bald head, with its prominent bones, very white; his neat black coat smeared and muddy. But his hand was clenched tight on the parcel that contained four shirts, two union suits, a pair of pyjamas and four collars. Mr. Harrington had not let his washing go.